THE THREE MUSKETEERS

ALEXANDRE DUMAS
1802–1870

THE THREE MUSKETEERS

ALEXANDRE DUMAS

With an Introduction by
SIDNEY DARK

COLLINS
LONDON AND GLASGOW

*This edition is set from the first English translation
by William Barrow*

*First published 1844
This edition 1952
Latest reprint 1985*

ISBN 0 00 424501 6

*Printed and bound in Great Britain by
William Clowes Limited,
Beccles and London*

CONTENTS

CONTENTS

CONTENTS

ALEXANDRE DUMAS

ALEXANDRE DUMAS

ALEXANDRE DUMAS (known as Dumas Père) was born on July 24, 1802 at Villers-Cotterets, a small town about forty-five miles north-east of Paris. His father, General Dumas, was a mulatto; the natural son of Alexandre Antoine Davy de la Pailleterie, a nobleman who had settled in St. Domingo, and of a black slave girl, named Louise-Cézette Dumas. General Dumas had a distinguished career during the wars of the French Republic and under Bonaparte. At the time of his son's birth, General Dumas was living in retirement at Villers-Cotterets where in the year 1792 he had married Marie Louise Labouret. He died in 1806, leaving his widow and small son in straitened circumstances.

However for Alexandre Dumas, the years of childhood and adolescence were carefree enough; his education was scanty. At sixteen he became a clerk with a local solicitor, and in 1823, determined to make his way in life, he went to Paris. He succeeded in obtaining a post on the secretarial staff of the Duc d'Orléans (the future King Louis-Philippe) at a yearly salary of 1200 francs.

Soon Dumas established contact with young men of the literary world. He read avidly—especially history and the works of great writers—frequented the theatre and soon he himself began to write for the stage.

After a number of false starts and two minor successes his romantic play *Henry III et sa Cour* was accepted by the Théâtre-Français and given its first performance in 1829. It established his fame, literally, over night and brought him the friendship of Victor Hugo, Vigny and other writers and poets. The Duc d'Orléans gave him the sinecure of a librarian at 1200 francs a year.

Already, then, Dumas found himself up against a problem which was to trouble him all his life and was later to assume gigantic proportions—he could not adapt expenditure to revenue. It was a problem deeply rooted in traits of his character *e.g.* in his extravagant tastes, his vanity, his lack of common sense, his generosity. Another inexhaustible source of trouble throughout his life was his unending amorous entanglements. During the first weeks in Paris (1823) he formed a liaison with a young woman, Marie Lebay, by whom he had a son in 1824 whom he fully acknowledged in 1831. In 1831 also he had another child —a daughter—by another mistress. His marriage (1840) to the actress Ida Ferrier, was of short duration.

After *Henry III* Dumas wrote further plays in rapid succession, among them *Antony*, a modern romantic drama the success of which even surpassed the success of *Henry III*. In 1830 he participated in a somewhat comic opera fashion in the July revolution, and again in 1832, having only just recovered from the cholera, took part in a rising against Louis-Philippe his former protector. In 1844 appeared *The Three Musketeers*, the first and perhaps the most famous of Dumas historical romances which, in three distinct cycles, cover almost three centuries of French history. In 1844 also he produced *The Count of Monte Cristo*, the romantic adventure story of the prisoner of *Chateau d'If*. Dumas' industry was prodigious. For nearly forty years, during which he lived as full a life as any man could ever wish to live, he poured out books, plays and articles in an uninterrupted stream. He was frequently accused during his life-time of having employed (and exploited) others to write the books which brought him fame and fortune. The truth is that he employed collaborators who supplied and arranged material and submitted ideas for plots.

At the height of his success, Dumas' prosperity and extravagance of living knew no bounds. He built himself a fantastic castle which he called 'Monte Cristo,' (it was later sold piecemeal by order of his creditors), financed theatres and lavished hospitality on friends and strangers alike. In 1851 he went to live in Brussels where he worked on his *Mémoires*. Back in Paris he launched into some newspaper ventures which kept him in the public limelight but ultimately failed. Years of wandering followed. He went to Russia (1858), travelling in the style of a potentate, and soon after his return he set out for Sicily where he joined Garibaldi in whose cause he worked enthusiastically for four years.

The last years of his life Dumas spent in an atmosphere of ever increasing financial chaos, of loneliness, domestic difficulties and failing health. He died at his son's house in Dieppe on December 5th 1870.. H. D. R.

INTRODUCTION

INTRODUCTION

ALEXANDRE DUMAS the elder, the author of *The Three Musketeers*, was born in 1802. His father was born in the island of Saint Domingo and was the natural son of a French marquis and a negress mother. He gained considerable military distinction during the Napoleonic wars, and was at one time Commander-in-Chief of the army of the Pyrenees. The appearance of Alexandre Dumas betrayed his descent from a negress grandmother. His histrionic vivacity had in it, too, something that was curiously un-European, and he has been vividly described by Stevenson as 'that ventripotent mulatto.' In his early twenties Dumas began to write for the theatre and, with Victor Hugo, was one of the two outstanding figures of the beginning of the romantic period of French drama. While it was said that for his dramas Victor Hugo needed 'the cast-off clothes of history,' Alexandre Dumas required 'no more than a room in an inn, where people met in riding cloaks, to move the soul to the last degree of terror and of pity.'

The Three Musketeers, the first of the Dumas novels, was published in 1844. Dumas once boasted to Napoleon III that he had written twelve hundred volumes. Whether or not this is true it is certain that no great writer has ever written so much, and of his output of fiction it may be quite safely said that his finest achievements are *The Three Musketeers* and its sequels *Twenty Years After* and *The Vicomte de Bragelonne*. This triology was written in collaboration with Auguste Maquet. As a matter of fact, a large proportion of the Dumas fiction was created in collaboration. It is possible that much of the less worthy work was entirely written by the collaborator, Dumas being content merely to put his name on the title-page. The proof, however, that it was the genius of Dumas and that alone that has given immortality to his great books is the fact that without him his collaborators were nothing but second-rate hacks whose work has long ago been forgotten. Addressing Dumas in his *Letters to Dead Authors*, Andrew Lang says: 'These ghosts, when uninspired by you were faint and impotent as "the strengthless tribes of the dead" in Homer's Hades, before Odysseus had poured forth the blood that gave them a momentary valour. It was from you and your inexhaustible vitality that these collaborating spectres drew what life they possessed; and when they parted from you they shuddered back into their nothingness.'

The historical material for *The Three Musketeers* was found in the *Mémoires de Monsieur D'Artagnan*, published at the beginning of the eighteenth century, but Dumas added to the dry bones of history the pulsing flesh and blood of his own imagination. In a sense the characters in Dumas are types rather than individuals. In *The Three Musketeers*, D'Artagnan is the typical Gascon adventurer, Athos is the typical gentleman of the period despite his happily unusual melancholy, Aramis is the typical worldly priest. Porthos, the thick-headed gallant giant, alone has definite individuality. But types though they may be, the Dumas characters are infinitely attractive, and all the world will agree with Stevenson when he says: 'Perhaps my dearest and best friend outside of Shakespeare is D'Artagnan . . . . I know not a more human soul, nor, in his way, a finer; I shall be very sorry for the man who is so much of a pedant in morals that he cannot learn from the Captain of Musketeers.'

The Three Musketeers and its sequels are really a series of dramatic incidents bound together so far as the first of them is concerned by the plots and intrigues of Milady. In this, his first success as a novelist, Dumas owed a great deal to his experience as a writer of drama, for each incident is carried to its proper climax and finishes with an effective 'curtain.' It has often been pointed out that one of the charms of Dumas is that though his romances deal with hard-living soldiers and generally anything but prudish ladies, they are extraordinarily free from any real offence. This is certainly true of *The Three Musketeers*, with the exception of D'Artangan's indefensible relations with Milady.

Thanks again to the fact that he began his literary life as a dramatist, Alexandre Dumas is a master of dialogue. In this respect he is the superior of Walter Scott. He continually makes his characters tell their own story. A notable example of this in *The Three Musketeers* is the famous scene at the Bastion Saint-Gervais. Dumas is the master storyteller. He never intrudes his own personality into his narratives, and he is far more interested in incidents than in character. Incident is piled on incident with unfailing invention, a wealth of colour and never-flagging vivacity. The novelist catches hold of his reader at the beginning and never lets him go until the last chapter is finished. As a creator of character there is no question that Dumas is Scott's inferior. As a story-teller he has few equals in literary history, and though he is magnificently indifferent to accuracy of detail, his novels reflect the atmosphere of the period with which they deal and afford more important information concerning past ages than can possibly be obtained from the dry-as-dust historian. The Richelieu, the Louis XIII, the Anne of Austria, the Buckingham of *The Three Musketeers*, are in essentials the personages as they lived in the world and played their parts in the European drama, though it must be admitted that from the novel alone one would learn little of the greatness of Richelieu or of his essentially constructive statesmanship.

Few historical characters, indeed, have been more maligned and misrepresented in romance than Cardinal Richelieu, and it is one of the qualities of *The Three Musketeers* that although it tells only a little of the real man, what it does tell—his courage, his persistence, his ruthlessness in achieving his purpose—is certainly true. The capture of La Rochelle, which supplies some of the most thrilling events in the novel, was a necessary part of Richelieu's political policy. At the beginning of his period of power he declared his intention 'to ruin the Huguenot party, lower the pride of the nobles, lead all subjects to their duty, and restore the country's name among foreign nations.' The Huguenots had set up a state within a state and their power had to be destroyed, but after the fall of La Rochelle, Richelieu persuaded the king to re-affirm the privileges granted to the Protestants by Henry IV, and thanks to him they had fifty years' prosperity before the era of persecution that began with the Revocation of the Edict of Nantes by Louis XIV. It is, of course, suggested by Dumas, and it has been often repeated, that Richelieu was in love with Anne of Austria, and that her preference for the Duke of Buckingham was the reason for his hatred of the queen and her lover. As a matter of fact, Richelieu was jealous of Anne's influence with the king and regarded her, not without reason, as a political enemy. As for Buckingham, his intrigues in Spain and his futile patronage of the Huguenots marked him as the enemy of France. There is no reason to believe that

Richelieu had, as Dumas relates, anything to do with the Puritan fanatic who assassinated Buckingham at Portsmouth. But if such a plan for removing his enemy had seemed to him feasible he certainly would have adopted it.

Alexandre Dumas himself was an amazing person. He earned large sums of money and spent prodigally. He built himself a huge house at Saint Germain-en-Laye, called Monte Cristo, which was filled all the year round by a crowd of men and women who lived on his bounty. He founded a theatre, particularly for the performance of his own plays. He started a daily paper. He travelled in Africa and in Russia. In 1860 he fought with Garibaldi in Sicily and afterwards lived for four years in Naples. Finally, worn out and weary, he died at his son's house near Dieppe in 1870. No two men were ever more unlike than the hearty, reckless Alexandre Dumas, the father, and the rather priggish and precise Alexandre Dumas, the son. 'Alexandre loves preaching overmuch,' Dumas once said of his son, and no man had less patience with moralists and moralising. There is a striking description of Dumas in 1865 in the famous *Journal of the de Goncourts*.

'He is a sort of giant with a negro's hair now turned pepper and salt, with a little hippopotamus-like eye, clear and sharp, and which watches even when it seems covered over, and an enormous face with features resembling the vaguely hemispherical outlines which caricaturists introduce into their versions of the moon. There is, I cannot say how, something about him of a showman, or of a traveller from *The Thousand and One Nights*. He talks a great deal without much brilliancy, without much biting quality, and without much colour; he only gives us facts, curious facts, paradoxical facts, stunning facts which he draws with a hoarse voice from an immense store of memories. And he talks always of himself, but with a childlike vanity in which there is nothing irritating.'

Edmond de Goncourt was a venomous old gentleman whose descriptions of his contemporaries never suffered from excessive good nature, but this is probably a very accurate picture of the author of *The Three Musketeers* in the later years of his life.

SIDNEY DARK

THE THREE MUSKETEERS

AUTHOR'S PREFACE

IT is about a year ago, that in making researches in the Bibliotheque Nationale for my History of Louis the Fourteenth, I by chance met with the Memoirs of Monsieur d'Artagnan, printed by Peter the Red at Amsterdam—as the principal works of that period, when authors could not adhere to the truth without running the risk of the Bastile, generally were. The title attracted my notice; I took the Memoirs home, with the permission of the librarian, and actually devoured them.

It is not my intention here to make analysis of this curious work, but to satisfy myself by referring such of my readers to the work itself as appreciate the pictures of those times. They will there discover portraits traced by the hand of a master; and although these sketches are mostly drawn on the doors of a barrack, or the walls of an inn, they will not find them less true than those likenesses of Louis XIII, of Anne of Austria, of Richelieu, Mazarin, and the majority of the courtiers of that age, drawn by M. Anguetil.

But, as every one knows, that which strikes the eccentric mind of the poet, does not always make an impression on the great mass of readers. So, whilst admiring (as all others doubtless will do) the details which we have described, the thing which strikes us most, is one which certainly had not attracted the attention of any other person. D'Artagnan relates, that on his first visit to M. de Treville, Captain of the Royal Musketeers, he met three young men in the ante-chamber, serving in the illustrious corps into which he solicited the honour of being admitted, and bearing the names of Athos, Porthos, and Aramis.

We confess that these foreign names struck us much, and we suspected that they were feigned appellations, by which d'Artagnan had perhaps concealed the names of illustrious persons; if, perchance, the bearers of them had not themselves chosen them, when, through caprice, discontent, or lack of fortune, they had donned the simple coat of a Musketeer. Therefore we could not rest satisfied till we had found in contemporary literature some trace of the extra-ordinary titles which had so forcibly excited our curiosity. The mere catalogue of the books we read to gain this end would fill a whole chapter, which would perhaps be very instructive, but certainly far from amusing, to our readers. We will, therefore, content ourselves with saying, that at the very moment when, discouraged by such fruitless investigations, we were about to abandon our researches, we at last, guided by the counsels of our illustrious and learned friend, Paulin Pâris, discovered a manuscript folio, numbered 4772, or 4773, we forget which, having for its title—

THE MEMOIRS OF M. LE COMTE DE LA FERE;
Relating to some of the Events which passed in France
about the End of the Reign of Louis XIII,
and the Beginning of the Reign
of Louis XIV

Our pleasure may be guessed, when, in turning over this manuscript, our last hope, we found at the twentieth page the name of Athos; at the twenty-first, the name of Aramis; at the twenty-seventh, the name of Porthos.

The discovery of a manuscript entirely unknown, at a period when historical knowledge was raised to such a high pitch, appeared to be almost a miracle. We therefore quickly requested permission to print it, that we might one day introduce ourselves to the Academy of Inscriptions and Belles Lettres with the goods of others, if we do not happen (as is very probable) to enter the French Academy on our own merits.

This permission was most graciously accorded; which we here declare, to give a public contradiction to those malevolent persons who pretend that government is not inclined to indulge authors.

We offer to-day the first part of this valuable manuscript to our readers, restoring to it the title which suits it, and promising, if (as we doubt not) this should meet with the success it merits, to publish immediately the second.

In the meantime, as the godfather is a second father, we invite our readers to look to *us*, and not to the Comte de la Fere, for his amusement or his ennui.

I

The Three Presents of M. D'Artagnan, the Father

On the first Monday of the month of April, 1625, the small town of Meung, the birthplace of the author of the 'Romance of the Rose,' appeared to be in a state of revolution, as complete as if the Huguenots were come to make a second siege of La Rochelle. Many of the townsmen, observing the flight along the high street, of women who left their children to squall at the doorsteps, hastened to don their armour, and, fortifying their courage, which was inclined to fail, with a musket or a partisan, proceeded towards the inn of the Jolly Miller, to which a vast and accumulating mob was hastening with intense curiosity.

At that period alarms were frequent, and few days passed without some bourg or other registering in its archives an event of this description. There were the nobles, who made war on each other; there was the king, who made war on the cardinal; there was the Spaniard, who made war on the king; then, besides these wars, concealed or overt, secret or public, there were bandits, mendicants, Huguenots, wolves and lacqueys, who made war on the whole world. The townsmen always armed themselves against the bandits, the wolves, and the lacqueys; frequently against the nobles and the Huguenots; sometimes against the king; but never against the cardinal or the Spaniard. From this custom, therefore, it arose, that on the aforesaid first Monday in the month of April, 1625, the burghers, hearing a noise, and seeing neither the yellow and red flag, nor the livery of the Duke of Richelieu, rushed towards the inn of the Jolly Miller. Having reached it, every one could see and understand the cause of this alarm. A young man—

But let us trace his portrait with one stroke of the pen. Fancy to yourself Don Quixote at eighteen—Don Quixote peeled, without his coat of mail or greaves—Don Quixote clothed in a woollen doublet, whose blue colour was changed to an *undyable* shade, a shade between the lees of wine and a cerulean blue. The countenance long and brown; the cheek-bones high, denoting acuteness; the muscles of the jaw enormously developed—an infallible mark by which a Gascon may be recognised, even without the cap, and our youth wore a cap, adorned with a sort of feather; the eye full and intelligent; the nose hooked, but finely formed; the whole figure too large for a youth, yet too small for an adult; an inexperienced eye would have taken him for the son of a farmer on a journey, had it not been for the long sword, which, hanging from a leathern belt, banged against the heels of its owner whilst he was walking, and against the rough coat of his steed when he was mounted;—for our youth had a steed, and this steed was at the same time so remarkable as to attract observation. It was a Beaunese sheltie, of about twelve or fourteen years of age, yellow as an orange, without any hair on its tail, but abundance of galls on its legs, and which, whilst carrying its head lower than its knees, making the application of a martingale unnecessary, yet managed gallantly its eight leagues a day. Unfortunately, these useful qualities of the steed were so well concealed under its strange coat and eccentric gait, that at a time when every one knew something of horses, the apparition of the aforesaid sheltie at Meung, which it had entered about a quarter of an hour before, by the gate of Beaugency, produced a somewhat unfavourable sensation or impression, which extended even to its master. And this impression was the more painful to young d'Artagnan (for that was the name of the Don Quixote of this second Rozinante), that he could not conceal from himself the ridiculous light in which he, albeit so good a horseman, was placed by such a steed. He had, therefore, sighed deeply when he accepted the gift from M. d'Artagnan, his father: he knew that such a beast was worth about twenty francs. It is true that the words which accompanied the present were above price.

'My son,' said the Gascon gentleman, in that pure Beaunese patois or dialect, which Henry IV. could never entirely shake off—'my son, this horse was born in the paternal homestead about thirteen years ago, and has remained in it ever since, which ought to make you regard it with affection. Never sell it; let it die honourably of old age, and in tranquillity; and should you make a campaign with it, take as much care of it as you would of an old servant. At the court, if you should ever have the honour to be presented—an honour, however, to which your long line of noble ancestors entitles you—support with dignity the name of gentleman, which has been honourably borne by your ancestors, for the sake of you and yours, for more than 500 years. Never submit quietly to the slightest indignity, except it proceed from the cardinal or the king. It is by his courage —mark this well—it is by his courage alone, that a gentleman makes his way nowadays. Whoever hesitates one moment, lets perhaps that chance escape him, which fortune, for that moment alone, has offered him. You are young, and ought to be brave, for two reasons: the first, because you are a Gascon; the second, because you are my son. Have no fear of many imbroglios, and look about for adventures. You have been taught to handle the sword; you have muscles of iron, a wrist like steel; fight whenever you can, the more so because duels are forbidden, and consequently it requires twice as much courage to fight. I have to give you but fifteen crowns, my son, besides the horse, and the advice which you have heard. Your mother will add to them the recipe for a certain balsam, which she received from a Bohemian woman, and which has the miraculous power of curing every wound which has fallen short of the heart. Take advantage of all, and live long and happily. I have only one word more to add, and it is the offer of an example: not my own, for I have never been at court; I have only served in the religious wars as a volunteer. I wish to speak to you of M. de Treville, once my neighbour, who has had the honour of playing, whilst a boy, with our king, Louis XIII, whom God preserve. Sometimes their play turned to battles, and in these battles the king did not always conquer; yet his conquests by M. de Treville imbued him with a great deal of esteem and friendship for him. Afterwards, M. de Treville fought other battles; indeed, merely during his journey to Paris, he fought five times; from the death of the late monarch, to the majority of the young king, he has fought seven times, without reckoning campaigns and sieges; and since that majority till now, perhaps a hundred times! And yet, in spite of edicts, ordinances, and writs, behold him now captain of the Musketeers; that is, chief of a legion of Cæsars, upon whom the king mainly depends, and who are feared by the cardinal, who, as every one knows, is not easily alarmed. Moreover, M. de Treville gains ten thousand crowns a year, and therefore is a man of consequence. He began the world as you do. Go to him with this letter, and let your conduct be regulated by him, that you may meet with the same results.'

Hereupon M. d'Artagnan, the father, girded his own sword upon his son, tenderly kissed him on either cheek, and gave him his blessing. Leaving the paternal chamber, the young man found his mother waiting with the famous recipe, which, from the advice he had just received, it seemed very probable that he would require to use pretty often. The adieus were longer and more tender on this side than on the other; not but that M. d'Artagnan loved his son, who was his only child, but that M. d'Artagnan was a man who would have considered it unworthy of himself to give way to any sentiment; whilst Madame d'Artagnan was a woman, and, what is more, a mother. She wept much; and, to the credit of M. d'Artagnan the younger, we may as well say that, whatever efforts he made to remain firm, as became the future Musketeer, nature gained the day, and he shed many tears, some of which he had great difficulty in concealing.

Our youth took his way the same day, furnished with the three paternal gifts, which were, as we have said, the fifteen crowns, the steed, and the letter to M. de Treville. As may be well imagined, the advice was thrown into the bargain. With such a *vade mecum*, d'Artagnan found himself, morally and physically, the counterpart of the hero of Cervantes, to whom we so happily compared him, when our duty as his historian obliged us to draw his portrait. Don Quixote took windmills for giants, and sheep for armies; d'Artagnan considered every smile an insult, and even a look a provocation. Therefore, his fist was doubled from Tarbes to Meung; and, from one cause or another, his hand was on the pommel of his sword ten times a day. However, the fist did not descend upon any jaw, nor did the sword leave its scabbard. It was not that the unlucky yellow sheltie did not excite many a smile on the countenances of passers-by; but as beside the said yellow sheltie clashed a sword of respectable length, and above the sword glistened an eye rather stern than fierce, the wayfarers repressed their mirth, or, if their mirth surpassed their prudence, they took care only to laugh on one side of their faces, like the ancient masques. D'Artagnan, therefore, remained dignified and uninterrupted in his susceptibility, even to this fatal town of Meung. But there, when he dismounted at the door of the Jolly Miller, without any one, either landlord, waiter, or hostler, coming to hold the stirrup of his horse, d'Artagnan perceived at the open window of a room, on the ground-floor, a gentleman of distinguished air and handsome figure, although with a countenance slightly grim, conversing with two persons who appeared to listen to him with deference.

D'Artagnan naturally thought, according to his usual custom, that they were talking about him, and listened accordingly. This time, however, he was partly correct: *he* was not the subject of conversation, but his horse was. The gentleman appeared to be enumerating to his hearers all his qualities; and since, as I have said, his hearers appeared to pay him great deference, they every moment laughed heartily.

Now, since even the slightest smile was sufficient to rouse the anger of our youth, we may well imagine what effect such unbounded mirth was likely to produce upon him. Nevertheless, d'Artagnan wished first to examine the countenance of the impertinent fellow who thus laughed at him. He therefore fixed his stern look upon the stranger, and saw a man from forty to forty-five years of age, with eyes black and piercing, complexion pale, nose strongly-marked, and moustache black and carefully trimmed. He was attired in a violet-coloured doublet and breeches, with points of the same colour, with no other ornament than the sleeves through which the shirt passed. This doublet and these breeches, though new, displayed divers wrinkles and creases, as if they had been for some time packed up in a portmanteau. D'Artagnan made these observations with the rapidity of a most minute observer, and doubtless with an instinct which told him that this unknown was to have a vast influence on his future life.

At the very moment that d'Artagnan fixed his eyes upon the gentleman with the violet doublet, that individual made one of his wisest and most profound remarks upon the Beaunese sheltie. His two auditors roared with laughter, and he himself, contrary to his usual custom, permitted a sort of sickly smile to wander over his countenance. This time there was no room for doubt. D'Artagnan was really insulted. Being convinced of this, he pulled his cap over his eyes, and trying to imitate the courtly airs which he had seen among some chance Gascon nobility in their provincial visits, he placed one hand on the guard of his sword, and the other on his hip. Unfortunately, the nearer he advanced, the more angry he grew, so that instead of the high and dignified language which he had prepared as the prelude to his challenge, he found nothing at the tip of his tongue but a rough personality, which he accompanied with a furious gesture.

'Hollo, sir!' he cried; 'you, sir, who hide yourself behind

the shutter—yes, you! tell me what you are laughing at, and we will laugh together.'

The gentleman slowly turned his eyes from the steed to his rider, as if it required some time to comprehend that these strange reproaches were addressed to himself; then, when he could no longer doubt it, he slightly knit his brows, and, after a pretty long pause, with an accent of irony and insolence impossible to describe, answered d'Artagnan, 'I am not speaking to you, sir.'

'But *I* am speaking to you,' cried the young man, exasperated by this mixture of insolence and good manners—this polite contempt.

The unknown regarded him yet a moment with a slight smile, and then leaving the window, slowly sauntered out of the inn, and stationed himself opposite the horse, at two paces from d'Artagnan. His calm face and jeering aspect redoubled the mirth of his companions, who still remained at the window. D'Artagnan, seeing him come out, drew his sword a foot out of its scabbard.

'This horse decidedly *is*, or rather *has* been, a buttercup,' continued the unknown, pursuing his remarks, and addressing his auditors at the window, without appearing to notice the exasperation of d'Artagnan, who, nevertheless, swelled and strutted between them; 'it is of a colour,' he continued, 'well known in botany, but as yet very rare amongst horses.'

'A man may laugh at a horse, who would not dare to laugh at its master,' cried the disciple of Treville with fury.

'I do not often laugh, sir,' answered the unknown, 'as you may yourself discover by the expression of my countenance; but yet I mean to preserve the right of laughing when I please.'

'And I,' roared out d'Artagnan, 'do not permit any one to laugh when I do *not* please.'

'Really, sir!' continued the unknown, more quietly than ever; 'well, that is sound sense;' and turning on his heel, he essayed to re-enter the inn by the front door, opposite which d'Artagnan, on arriving, had observed a horse ready saddled.

But d'Artagnan was not the man to let any one who had had the insolence to mock him thus escape; he therefore drew his sword and pursued him, exclaiming, 'Turn, turn, Master Jester, that I may not strike you behind!'

'Strike me!' said the other, quickly turning round, and regarding the youth with as much astonishment as contempt; 'go along with you, my dear boy; you are mad.' Then, in a low voice, as if he were speaking to himself, he added, 'It is annoying: what a prize for his majesty, who is everywhere seeking fire-eaters to recruit his guards.'

He had scarcely finished, when d'Artagnan made such a furious thrust at him, that, had he not jumped back briskly, it is probable the jest would have been his last. Perceiving now, however, that the affair was *beyond* a joke, the unknown drew his sword, saluted his adversary, and gravely put himself on guard; but at the same moment his two auditors, accompanied by the host, fell pell-mell upon d'Artagnan, with sticks, shovels, and tongs. This caused such a complete diversion of the attack, that, whilst d'Artagnan himself turned to face this shower of blows, his opponent put up his sword with the same calm as before, and, from an actor, became a spectator of the combat—a character which he supported with the same imperturbability, yet all the time muttering, 'Plague upon these Gascons! Put him on his orange-coloured horse, and let him go.'

'Not before I have slain you, you coward!' cried d'Artagnan, all the time making the best resistance he could, and not yielding one step to his three opponents, who showered their blows upon him.

'Yet another gasconade!' murmured the gentleman; 'upon my word these Gascons are incorrigible; keep up the dance, since he actually wishes it; when he is tired he will say that he has had enough.'

But the stranger did not yet know with what a stubborn personage he had to deal. D'Artagnan was not the man ever to sue for quarter. The contest therefore continued for some moments longer, until at last, completely worn out, d'Artagnan dropped his sword, which was broken in two by a blow from a stick, while at the same instant another blow, which cut open his forehead, stretched him on the ground almost senseless.

It was now that all the burghers hastened to the scene of action. Fearing a disturbance, the landlord, assisted by his servants, carried the wounded man into the kitchen, where some care was given him. As for the stranger, he returned to the window, and viewed the crowd with evident marks of impatience, seeming rather annoyed at their refusal to go away.

'Well, how is that madman now?' said he, turning, and addressing the host, who came to inquire in what state his guest was.

'Is your excellency safe and well?' demanded the host.

'Yes, perfectly so, mine host; but I wish to know what is become of this youth.'

'He is better,' replied the host; 'but he was quite senseless.'

'Indeed!' said the gentleman.

'But before he quite lost his senses, he rallied all his strength to challenge and defy you,' added the landlord.

'Well, this young fellow is the very devil himself,' said the gentleman.

'Oh, no, your excellency, oh, no,' replied the host, with a contemptuous grin, 'he is not the devil, for while he was senseless we rummaged his outfit, and in his bundle we found but one shirt, and in his pocket only twelve crowns, which fact, however, did not prevent his saying, just before he fainted, that, had this happened in Paris, you should quickly have repented it, but as it has taken place here you will not have to repent it until later.'

'Therefore,' coolly observed the stranger, 'he doubtless is a prince of the blood in disguise.'

'I give you this information, sir,' said the host, 'that you may keep yourself on your guard.'

'And did he not name any one in his anger?'

'Yes, he slapped his pocket, and said, 'We shall see what M. de Treville will say to this insult offered to his *protégé*.'

'M. de Treville?' said the unknown, becoming more attentive; 'he slapped his pocket, and mentioned the name of M. de Treville?—Let us see, my good host: whilst this young man was senseless, you did not fail, I am sure, to examine that pocket: what did it contain?'

'A letter, adressed to M. de Treville, captain of the Musketeers.'

'Really?'

'Just as I have the honour to tell your excellency," said the host.

The latter, who had no great penetration, did not remark the expression which these words brought upon the countenance of the stranger, who now left the windowsill, on which his elbow had rested, and frowned like a man disturbed all of a sudden.

'The devil!' muttered he between his teeth; 'could Treville have sent this Gascon? He is very young; but a thrust of a sword is a thrust of a sword, whatever may be the age of him that gives it, and one distrusts a boy less than an oldster; a slight obstacle is sufficient to thwart a project.' And the stranger fell into a reverie which lasted some minutes. 'Come, mine host,' at length he said, 'will you not rid me of this madman? I cannot conscientiously kill him, and yet,' he added with a menacing air, 'he much annoys me. Where is he?'

'In my wife's chamber, on the first storey, where they are dressing his wounds.'

'Are his clothes and his bag with him? Has he taken off his doublet?'

'On the contrary, they are below in the kitchen,' said the host; 'but since this young madman annoys you—'

'Doubtless; he causes a disturbance in your inn, which no respectable people can bear. Go to your room, make out my bill, and give orders to my servants.'

'What, sir, must you be off?'

'Yes. I ordered you to saddle my horse; have I not been obeyed?'

'Yes; and your excellency may see your horse standing under the grand entrance, quite ready for the road.'

'Very well; then do as I have ordered.'

'Heyday!' said the host to himself; 'can he be afraid of this young boy?' But a commanding look from the stranger cut him short; he humbly bowed, and left the apartment.

'My lady must not see this strange fellow,' said the stranger; 'as she is already late, she must soon pass. I had better mount my horse and go to meet her. If I could only just learn the contents of that letter addressed to Treville.' And thus muttering, the unknown descended to the kitchen.

In the meantime, the landlord, who doubted not that this youth's presence drove the stranger from his inn, had gone to his wife's chamber, and found that d'Artagnan had regained consciousness. Then, whilst he made him comprehend that the police might be severe on him for having attacked a great lord (for, according to the host's idea, the stranger could be nothing less than a great lord), he persuaded him, in spite of his weakness, to resume his journey.

D'Artagnan, half stunned, without doublet, his head completely bandaged, arose, and, pushed out by the host, began to descend the stairs; but, on reaching the kitchen, the first object he saw was his opponent, who was quietly talking at the door of a heavy carriage, drawn by two large Norman horses. The person with whom he conversed was a woman of from twenty to twenty-two years of age, whose head appeared, through the window of the carriage, like a picture in a frame. We have already said how rapidly d'Artagnan caught the expression of a countenance; he saw, therefore, at the first glance, that the lady was young and attractive. Now, this beauty was the more striking to him, as it was completely different from that of his own southern country. She was a pale, fair person, with long curling hair falling on her shoulders, large blue languishing eyes, rosy lips, and alabaster hands. She conversed with the unknown with great vivacity.

'So, his eminence commands me——' said she.

'To return immediately to England, and apprise him, with all speed, whether the duke has left London,' said the unknown.

'And as to my other instructions?' demanded the fair traveller.

'They are enclosed in this box, which you will not open until you are on the other side of the Channel.'

'Good; and you? What are you going to do?'

'I return to Paris.'

'Without chastising this insolent boy?' demanded the lady.

The unknown was about to reply, but ere he could do so, d'Artagnan, who had heard every word, rushed to the door-way. 'It is that insolent boy,' he cried, 'who chastises others, and I hope that this time he who deserves chastisement will not escape him.'

'Will not escape him?' echoed the unknown, knitting his brows.

'No, in the presence of a woman you would hesitate to fly, I presume.'

'Consider,' said the lady, seeing the gentleman place his hand to his sword, 'consider that the slightest delay might ruin all.'

'You are right,' said the gentleman; 'you go your way, and I will go mine;' and, saluting the lady with a bow, he got into the saddle, whilst the coachman whipped his horses. The lady and gentleman therefore went off at a gallop towards the opposite ends of the street.

'Hollo! your bill!' shouted mine host, whose affection for the traveller was changed to the most profound contempt when he saw him departing without paying.

'Pay, rascal,' cried the traveller, as he galloped off, to his valet, who threw three or four pieces of silver at the feet of the landlord, and set off at full speed the way his master went.

'Oh, coward! wretch! false-hearted gentleman!' cried d'Artagnan, rushing after the valet. But he was still too feeble from his wounds to bear such an effort. Scarcely had he gone ten paces, before his ears tingled, a vertigo seized him, a cloud passed before his eyes, and he fell down in the street, with a final cry of 'Coward! coward! coward!'

'He is a sad coward verily,' murmured the host, who now, approaching d'Artagnan, endeavoured to soothe him by this flattery, as the heron in the fable her friend the snail.

'Yes, a sad coward,' murmured d'Artagnan; but *she is* beautiful.'

'Who is she?' said the landlord.

'My lady!' murmured d'Artagnan, and again fainted away.

'Never mind,' said the host; 'although I have lost two, at any rate I have secured this one, whom I am sure of keeping for some days; at all events, I shall gain eleven crowns.'

It must be borne in mind that eleven crowns was the exact sum which remained in d'Artagnan's purse; and the host had reckoned upon eleven days' illness, at a crown a day. On this point, however, he reckoned without his guest. The following day d'Artagnan left his couch, went down to the kitchen, and, besides certain ingredients, the names of which have not descended to posterity, demanded some wine, oil, and rosemary, which, with his mother's recipe in his hand, he compounded into a salve, wherewith he anointed his numerous wounds, renewing his plasters himself, and not allowing the interposition of any leech.

Thanks, no doubt, to the Bohemian salve, and perhaps also to the absence of the leech, d'Artagnan found himself on foot in the evening, and almost cured by the next day. But at the moment he was paying for this wine, oil and rosemary, the sole expense he had incurred (for he had been completely abstinent, whilst, on the contrary, if one believed the hostler, the yellow horse had eaten three times as many oats as one would have supposed possible from his size), d'Artagnan found nothing in his pocket but his little purse, with its eleven crowns. As for the letter to M. de Treville, that was gone. The young man began by looking very patiently for this letter, turning out and rummaging his pockets and fobs twenty times, rummaging his valise again and again, and opening and shutting his purse; but when he was quite convinced that the letter was not to be found, he gave full vent to another fit of rage in a manner which was like to make necessary a second decoction of wine and spiced oil. For, upon beholding this young scatter-brain raging, and threatening to destroy everything in his establishment, if the letter were not found, the host had already seized upon a spit, his wife upon the handle of a broom, and the servants upon the same weapons they had wielded the evening before.

'My letter of introduction!' cried d'Artagnan, 'my letter of introduction! or, by St. Denis, I will spit you all like so many ortolans.'

One circumstance prevented the youth from accomplishing his threat, which was, that his sword, as we have said, had unfortunately been broken in two in the first struggle—a mischance he had entirely forgotten; consequently, when d'Artagnan went to draw it in earnest, he found himself armed only with the stump, about eight or ten inches long, which the host had carefully thrust into the scabbard. As for the rest of the blade, the cook had adroitly set it aside for a larding-pin. And yet it is probable that this deception would not have stopped our fiery youth, had not the host reflected that the demand which his guest made was perfectly just.

'But after all,' said he, lowering his spit, 'where is this letter?'

'Yes, where is this letter?' roared d'Artagnan; 'and let me tell you that this letter is for M. de Treville, and that it must be found, otherwise M. de Treville will know to have it found—I'll answer for it!'

This threat completely frightened mine host. Next to the king and the cardinal, M. de Treville was the man whose name was most frequently in the mouths of the military, and indeed of the citizens. There was, certainly, Father Joseph; but *his* name was never mentioned except in an undertone; so great was the terror which his gray eminence, as the familiar of the cardinal was called, inspired. Therefore, throwing away his spit, and ordering his wife to do the same with her broom-handle, and the servants with their weapons, he himself set the example by commencing a diligent search for the letter.

'Did this letter contain anything valuable?' said he, after some moments of fruitless search.

'I should rather think it did,' cried the Gascon, who calculated on the letter to make his way at court; 'it contained my fortune.'

'Were they bills on the Bank of Spain?' demanded the host, much disturbed.

'Bills on the private treasury of his majesty!' replied d'Artagnan, who, calculating on entering the king's service through this letter of introduction, thought he might, without lying, make this somewhat rash reply.

'The devil!' exclaimed the host, at his wit's end.

'But it is of no consequence,' continued d'Artagnan, with his native assurance; 'the money is nothing, the letter is all I want. I had rather have lost a thousand pistoles than that!' He might as well have made it twenty thousand, but a certain youthful modest restrained him. A sudden flash of light illumined the mind of the host, who was uttering maledictions at finding nothing.

'This letter is not lost!' he cried.

'Isn't it?' said d'Artagnan.

'No it has been taken from you.'

'Taken! and by whom?'

'By the stranger, yesterday; he went into the kitchen, where your doublet was lying; he was there for a time entirely alone; and I will lay a wager it was he who stole it from you.'

'You really think so?' said d'Artagnan, only half convinced, for he knew better than anybody the strictly personal value of the letter, and saw nothing in it to excite cupidity. The fact is, that none of the servants or travellers who were there could have gained anything by the theft.

'You say, then,' continued d'Artagnan, 'that you suspect this impertinent gentleman?'

'I tell you that I am quite certain of it,' said the host; 'when I informed him that your worship was the *protégé* of M. de Treville, and that you had a letter for that illustrious noble, he appeared much disturbed, demanded where the letter was, and immediately went into the kitchen, where your doublet was lying.'

'Then he is the robber,' said d'Artagnan; 'I will complain to M. de Treville, and he will lay my complaint before his majesty.'

And he majestically drew from his pocket two crowns, which he handed to the host, who followed him cap in hand, to the archway, where he remounted his yellow horse, which carried him without further accident to the gate of St. Antoine, at Paris. There its owner sold the animal for three crowns; which was a good price, considering that d'Artagnan had over-ridden him in the last part of the journey. The dealer to whom he sold the sheltie for these nine francs, did not conceal from the young man that he paid this exorbitant sum merely on account of the originality of his colour.

D'Artagnan therefore entered Paris on foot, carrying his small valise under his arm, and proceeded until he found a lodging suitable to his slender resources. This chamber was a sort of garret, situated in the Rue des Fossoyeurs, near the Luxembourg. Having paid the luck-penny, he took possession of his lodging, and passed the remainder of the day in sewing on his doublet and breeches sundry laces which his mother had secretly taken from a nearly new doublet of the elder M. d'Artagnan. He then repaired to the Quai de la Feraille, to procure a new blade for his sword; after which he returned to the Louvre, and learned from the first musketeer he met where M. de Treville's hotel was situated. This he ascertained to be in the Rue de Vieux Colombier; that is, in the very neighbourhood where he had himself taken up his abode; a circumstance which he construed into a happy omen of the success of his expedition.

These matters disposed of, and satisfied with the manner in which he had behaved at Meung, without remorse for the present, confident in the present, and full of hope for the future, he went to bed and slept the sleep of the brave. This sleep, still that of a rustic, lasted till nine o'clock in the morning, the hour at which he rose to repair to the hotel of this famed M. de Treville, who, according to d'Artagnan's father, was the third personage in the realm.

2

The Antechamber of M. de Treville

M. DE TROISVILLE, as his family was yet called in Gascony, or M. de Treville, as he called himself in Paris, had actually begun life like d'Artagnan; that is to say, without being worth a sou, but with that fund of audacity, esprit, and resolution, which makes the poorest Gascon gentleman often inherit more in imagination than the richest nobleman of Perigord or Berri receives in reality. His daring and haughty courage—still more haughty in success—at the time when blows fell thick as hail, had raised him to the top of that difficult ladder which is called court favour, and which he had climbed four rungs at a time. He was the confidential friend of the king, who, as every one knows, greatly honoured the memory of his father, Henry IV. The father of M. de Treville had served the latter so faithfully in his wars against the League, that, for want of ready money—(a commodity which, during his life, was very scarce with the Bearnese, who constantly paid his debts with what he never had occasion to borrow, that is to say, with his genius)—for want of ready money, as we have said, he had authorised him, after the reduction of Paris, to take for his arms—'Un lion d'or passant, sur gueules,' with the motto, *'fidelis et fortis.'* It was a great deal of honour, but not much profit; therefore, when the illustrious companion of Henri the Great died, the sole inheritance he left his son was his sword, with the arms and motto. Thanks, however, to this double legacy, and to the name without tarnish which accompanied it, M. de Treville was admitted into the household of the young prince, where he made such good use of his sword, and was so true to his motto, that Louis XIII., one of the best hands with the rapier in his own kingdom, used to say, that if he had a friend who was going to fight, he would advise him to take for a second, first himself, and then Treville, or even perhaps Treville before himself. On this account Louis had a real affection for Treville; a *royal* affection, an *egotistical* affection, it must be allowed, but an affection nevertheless. In those unhappy days it was an important consideration to surround oneself with men of Treville's stamp. Many could take for their device the epithet of *'fortis,'* which formed the second part of the motto, but very few men could claim the epithet *'fidelis,'* which formed the first part of it. Treville was one of the few: his was one of those rare organisations with the intelligence and obedience of the mastiff, and a blind courage, and a ready hand, one to whom the eye had been given only to see whether the king was dissatisfied with any one, and the hand only to strike the offending person—a Besme, a Maurevers, a Poltrot de Méré, a Vitry; in short, Treville only wanted an opportunity; but he watched for it, and was resolved to seize it by its three hairs if ever it came within reach of his grasp. Louis XIII. therefore appointed Treville captain of the musketeers, who, by their devotion, or rather fanaticism, became what his ordinary troops were to Henry III., and his Scottish guard to Louis XI. In this respect the cardinal was not behind the king; for when he saw the formidable picked guard with which Louis surrounded himself, this second, or rather this first, king of France, wished also to have his own guard; he therefore, as well as the king, had his musketeers; and these two potent rivals were seen selecting for their service, from all the provinces of France, and even from all foreign countries, men famous for their skill as swordsmen. It was not rare for Richelieu and the king, over their game of chess in the evening, to dispute concerning the merits of their respective followers. Each boasted of the deportment and the courage of his own; and whilst openly inveighing against duels and imbroglios, they secretly excited their respective partisans to fight, and experienced immoderate delight, or intense chagrin, at their respective victories or defeats. Thus at least says the memoir of one who was concerned in some of these defeats, and many of these victories.

Treville had seized on the weak point in his master's character; and to this knowledge he owed the long and constant favour of a king who has not left behind him the reputation of having been constant in his friendships. He paraded his musketeers before the cardinal Armand Duplessis with an air of insolence which made the gray moustache of his eminence curl with anger. Treville also thoroughly understood the war of that period, when, if you lived not at the expense of the enemy, you lived at that of your countrymen. His soldiers formed a legion of very devils, under no discipline but his own. Swaggering bullies, given to wine, the king's musketeers, or rather M. de Treville's, spread themselves through the taverns, the public walks, and the theatres, talking loud, curling their moustaches, jingling their swords, hustling the guards of the cardinal when they met them, indulging, in the open street, in a thousand jokes; sometimes killed, but then certain of being lamented and avenged; sometimes killing, but then quite certain not to languish in prison, since M. de Treville was always at hand to procure their pardon and release. Therefore M. de Treville was lauded in every tone, sung of in every key, by these men, who adored him; yet, hang-dogs as they were, they trembled before him as scholars before their master, obedient to a word, and ready to meet death to wipe away any reproach. M. de Treville had used this powerful lever, first, for the king and his friends, and next, for himself and his own friends. The captain of the musketeers was, therefore, admired, feared, and loved, which state constitutes the apogee of human affairs.

Louis XIV. absorbed all the lesser stars of his court, by his vast brilliancy; but his father, '*Sol pluribus impar*,' imparted his personal splendour to many of his favourites —his individual valour to each of his courtiers. Besides the king's levee, and that of the cardinal, there were then at Paris at least two hundred smaller ones, fairly exclusive; and amongst these two hundred smaller levees, that of M. de Treville was one of those most frequented. From six o'clock in the morning during summer, and eight in the winter, the courtyard of his hotel, in the Rue du Vieux Colombier, resembled a camp. From fifty to sixty musketeers, who appeared to relieve each other, and to present a number always imposing, were stalking about incessantly, armed to the teeth, and ready for anything. From one end to the other of one of those long staircases, on whose space our modern civilisation would build an entire mansion, ascended and descended those petitioners who sought favours; with provincial gentlemen, eager to be enrolled; and liveried lacqueys of every colour, in the act of delivering messages from their masters to M. de Treville. In the antechamber, on long circular benches, reclined the *élite*, that is, such of them as had assembled; a continual buzzing prevailed from morning till night; whilst M. de Treville, in his cabinet adjoining the antechamber, received visits, listened to complaints, gave his orders, and, like the king in his balcony at the Louvre, had only to place himself at his window to review his men and their arms.

On the day when d'Artagnan presented himself, the assembly was very imposing, especially to a provincial just arrived in Paris. It is true, this provincial was a Gascon, and at this period more especially, d'Artagnan's countrymen had the reputation of not being easily intimidated. In fact, as soon as any one had passed the threshold of the massive door, studded with long square nails, he found himself in the midst of a troop of swordsmen, who were cruising about the court, talking, quarrelling, and jesting with each other. To clear a path through these eddies, it was necessary to be an officer, a man of rank, or a pretty woman. It was, therefore, in the midst of this crowd and disorder that our youth, holding his long rapier against his slender legs, and the rim of his beaver in his hand, advanced with palpitating heart, yet with that sort of half smile of provincial embarrassment which wishes to create a good impression. When he had passed one group, he breathed more freely; but he perceived that they turned to look at him, and d'Artagnan, who to that day had invariably entertained a pretty good opinion of himself, for the first time in his life thought himself ridiculous. When he had reached the staircase it was still worse; on the first step were four musketeers, who amused themselves in the following manner, whilst ten or a dozen of their companions waited on the landing-place till it was their turn to have a share in the game. One of them on a higher step, with a naked sword in his hand, prevented, or endeavoured to prevent, the other three from mounting the stairs; whilst these three skirmished with him very actively with their swords. D'Artagnan at first took these swords for foils, and thought they were *buttoned;* but he soon found, by certain scratches, that each weapon was as sharp as possible, and at each of these scratches, not only the spectators, but the actors themselves, laughed most heartily. The one who held the higher step at that time, kept his opponents at bay in a dexterous manner. A circle was formed round him, the condition of the game being, that at every hit, he who was struck should relinquish the pastime, and surrender his turn of reception by M. de Treville to the one who had touched him. In five minutes three were grazed, one on the hand, one on the chin, and another on the ear, by this defender of the staircase, who was himself untouched—a proof of his skill which, according to the rules of the game, entitled him to three turns of favour. This sport surprised our young traveller, although he did not wish it to appear that he was astonished. He had seen in his own province (that province where, moreover, the fiery passions are so promptly roused) a good many provocatives to duels, and yet the gasconade of these four players appeared much stronger than any he had heard of even in Gascony. He fancied he was transported into that famous country of giants where Gulliver afterwards went, and was so much frightened. And yet he had not reached the end: the landing-place and antechamber still remained. On the landing-place they did not fight, but recounted histories of the fair sex; and in the antechamber, tales of the court. On the landing-place d'Artagnan blushed; in the antechamber he shuddered. But if his good manners were shocked on the landing-place, his respect for the cardinal was scandalised in the antechamber. There, to his great astonishment, he heard the policy which made all Europe tremble, openly criticised, as well as the private life of the cardinal, which so many powerful men had been punished for attempting to scrutinise. That great man, whom d'Artagnan's father had so deeply reverenced, M. de Treville and his men made their butt, deriding his bandy legs and crooked back. Some sang carols on Madame d'Aiguillon, his mistress, and Madame de Combalet, his niece; whilst others planned adventures against the pages and guards of the cardinal duke himself. All these things appeared to d'Artagnan monstrous impossibilities. Nevertheless, when the name of the king accidentally slipped out in the midst of these jokes on the cardinal, a sort of momentary gag stopped all their jeering mouths; they looked around with hesitation, and seemed to doubt the discretion of the wall of M. de Treville's cabinet. But some allusion soon brought back the conversation to his eminence. The wit was of the most brilliant kind, and none of his actions was uncommented upon. 'Verily,' thought d'Artagnan with terror, 'these gentry will soon be put into the Bastile and hanged. Doubtless, I shall accompany them, for having heard all they have said. I shall, without doubt, be taken for an accomplice. What would my father say—he who enjoined me so strongly to respect the cardinal—if he knew that I was in the company of such reprobates?'

Of course, while d'Artagnan dared not join in the conversation, he kept his eyes and ears wide open, and every sense on the alert, that he might lose nothing; and in spite of the paternal advice, he found himself drawn by his tastes and instinct, rather to praise than blame the incredible things he heard around him. Nevertheless, as he was absolutely a stranger to the crowd of M. de Treville's courtiers, and it was the first time he had been seen there, some one came to inquire what he wanted. At this question he humbly gave his name, relying on his being a countryman, and requested the servant to solicit a moment's audience of M. de Treville —a request which the inquirer, in the tone of a protector, promised to make at the proper time.

D'Artagnan, a little recovered from his first surprise, had now time to study the dresses and countenances of those around him. In the midst of the most animated group was a musketeer of great height, of a haughty countenance, and so fantastical a costume as to attract general attention. He did not wear his uniform tunic, which was not absolutely indispensable at that period of less liberty, yet greater independence, but a close coat of celestial blue, slightly faded and worn, and on this coat a magnificent border of gold embroidery, which glittered like scales upon a sunlit stream; a long mantle or cloak of crimson velvet hung gracefully from his shoulders, discovering the front alone of his splendid belt, from which depended his enormous rapier. This musketeer, who had just come from guard, complained of having caught cold, and coughed occasionally with great affectation. Therefore, as he averred, he had taken his cloak; and whilst he was talking loudly over the group, and proudly curling his moustache, every one much admired the embroidered belt, and d'Artagnan more than any one else.

'What would you have?' said the musketeer. 'It is the fashion; I know very well that it is foolish, but it is the fashion; besides, one must spend one's hereditary property on something or other.'

'Ah, Porthos!' cried one of the bystanders, 'do not try to make us believe that this lace comes from the paternal generosity: it was given you by the veiled lady with whom I met you the other Sunday, near the gate of St. Honore.'

'No, upon my honour, and by the faith of a gentleman, I bought it with my own money,' said he whom they called Porthos.

'Yes, as I bought this new purse with what my mistress put in the old,' cried another musketeer.

'But it is true,' said Porthos, 'and the proof is, that I paid twelve pistoles for it.'

The wonder and admiration were redoubled, though the doubt still existed.

'Is it not so, Aramis?' inquired Porthos, turning to another musketeer.

The person thus appealed to formed a perfect contrast to the one who thus questioned him, and who designated him by the name of Aramis. He was a young man, not more than twenty-two or twenty-three years of age, with a soft and ingenuous countenance, a black and mild eye, and cheeks rosy and damask as an autumnal peach; his slender moustache marked a perfect straight line along his upper lip; his hands appeared to dread hanging down, for fear of making their veins swell; and he was continually pinching the tips of his ears, to make them preserve a delicate and transparent carnation hue. Habitually he talked little and slowly, often bowed, laughed quietly, merely showing his teeth, which were good, and of which, as of the rest of his person, he appeared to take the greatest care. He replied to his friend's question by affirmative inclination of the head, and this affirmation appeared to settle all doubt concerning the embroidery. They therefore continued to admire it, but said no more about it; and by a sudden change of thought, the conversation at once passed to another subject.

'What do you think of this story of Chalais's squire?' inquired another musketeer, not addressing any one in particular, but the company in general.

'And what does he say?' demanded Porthos in a conceited tone.

'He says that he found Rochefort, the tool of the cardinal, at Brussels, disguised as a Capuchin friar; and that this cursed Rochefort, thanks to his disguise, had deceived M. de Laignes, simpleton as he is.'

'He *is* a simpleton,' said Porthos; 'but is it a fact?'

'I heard it from Aramis,' answered the musketeer.

'Really!'

'Ah, you know it well enough, Porthos,' said Aramis. 'I told it you myself yesterday evening; do not let us talk any more about it.'

'Not talk any more about it! that's your view of the matter,' said Porthos; 'not talk any more about it! Egad, you would make short work of it. What! the cardinal sets a spy upon a gentleman, robs him of his correspondence through a traitor, a robber, a gallowsbird; cut Chalais's throat through this spy, and by means of this correspondence, under the flimsy pretext that he desired to kill the king, and marry monsieur to the queen! No one knew one word of this enigma; you told us of it yesterday evening, to the great astonishment of every one; and whilst we are still all amazed at the news, you come to-day and say to us, 'Let us talk no more about it!' '

'Well, then, since it better suits your humour, let us talk about it,' calmly replied Aramis.

'Were I poor Chalais's squire,' cried Porthos, 'this Rochefort would pass a bad minute with me!'

'And the red duke would make but short work with you,' replied Aramis.

'Ah, the red duke! bravo, bravo, the red duke!' exclaimed Porthos, with an approving nod, and clapping his hands; 'the *red* duke is charming! Rest assured, my dear fellow, that I will disseminate the title. What a genius he has, this Aramis! what a pity that you could not follow your vocation, my dear fellow; what an exquisite abbé you would have made!'

47

'Oh, it is a mere transitory delay,' replied Aramis; 'one day or other *I shall* be one; for you well know, Porthos, that I continue to study theology with that intention.'

'He will actually do as he says,' replied Porthos; 'he will do it, sooner or later.'

'Very soon,' said Aramis.

'He only waits for one thing to decide what he will do, and to resume his cassock, which is hung up behind his uniform,' replied another musketeer.

'And what event does he wait for?' inquired another.

'He waits till the queen has given an heir to the crown of France.'

'Let us not jest on this subject, gentlemen,' said Porthos; 'thank God, the queen is yet of an age to give it one.'

'It is said that the Duke of Buckingham is in France,' observed Aramis with a mocking laugh, which gave to his remark, simple as it was in appearance, a meaning sufficiently scandalous.

'Aramis, my friend, this time you are wrong,' rejoined Porthos, 'and your wit always leads you too far. It would be the worse for you if M. de Treville heard you talking in this manner.'

'Do not lecture me, Porthos,' cried Aramis, in whose soft eye something like the lightning's flash now passed.

'My dear fellow, be either musketeer or abbé; be one or the other; but not one and the other,' exclaimed Porthos. 'You may remember that Athos told you the other day, that you eat at every rack. But let us not dispute, I beseech you; it would be perfectly useless. You know what is settled between you and me and Athos: you go to Madame d'Aiguillon's, and you pay *her* attentions; you then repair to Madame de Bois Tracy, the cousin of Madame de Chevreuse, and a woman in whose good graces you are thought to stand highly. Nay, my dear fellow, confess not your good fortune: no one demands your secret; every one knows your discretion; but since you possess this virtue yourself, surely you will not grudge some portion of it to the queen. Let who will talk about the king and the cardinal, but the queen is sacred; and if you discuss her at all, let it be respectfully.'

'Porthos, you are as presumptuous as Narcissus!' said Aramis; 'you know that I detest moralising, except from Athos. As to you, my dear fellow, you have rather too splendid a belt to be powerful on that subject. I will be an abbé if it suits me; in the meantime I am a musketeer, in which character I say what I choose, and at this moment I choose to tell you that you irritate me.'

'Aramis!'

'Porthos!'

'That will do! gentlemen! gentlemen!' cried out all around them.

'M. de Treville awaits M. d'Artagnan,' interrupted the lackey, opening the door of the cabinet.

At this declaration, during which the door remained open, every one was silent; and in the midst of this general silence the young Gascon, passing through part of the antechamber, entered the cabinet of the captain of the musketeers, felicitating himself with all his heart upon just escaping the conclusion of this singular quarrel.

3

The Audience

M. DE TREVILLE was at this moment in a very bad humour; nevertheless, as the young man bowed to the ground, he politely saluted him, and smiled on receiving his compliments, which in their accent, recalled both his youth and his country at the same time—a double recollection, which makes a man smile at every period of his life. But going towards the antechamber, and making a sign with his hand to d'Artagnan, as if requesting permission to finish with others before he began with him, he called three times, raising his voice each time so as to run through the intermediate scale between the tone of command and that of anger—'Athos!' —'*Porthos*'—'ARAMIS!' The two musketeers, whose acquaintance we have already made, and who answered to the two last of these three names, immediately quitted the group of which they formed a portion, and advanced towards the cabinet, the door of which was closed immediately they had passed its threshold. Their bearing, although not quite calm, was at the same time full of dignity and submission, and their apparent indifference excited the admiration of d'Artagnan, who saw in these men a species of demi-gods, and in their chief an Olympian Jupiter, armed with all his thunders.

When the two musketeers had entered, and the door was

closed behind them—when the murmuring buzz of the antechamber, to which the summons that had been given had doubtless furnished a new topic, had recommenced— when, lastly, M. de Treville had paced the whole length of his cabinet three or four times in silence, but with a frowning brow, passing each time before Porthos and Aramis, upright and mute as on parade, he suddenly stopped directly in front of them, and measuring them from top to toe with an angry look, exclaimed, 'Do you know what the king said to me, and that not later than last evening? Do you know, gentlemen?'

'No,' answered the two musketeers, after a moment's silence; 'no, sir, we do not.'

'But we hope you will do us the honour of informing us,' added Aramis in his most polished tone, and with the most graceful bow.

'He told me that, for the future, he should recruit his musketeers from those of the cardinal.'

'From those of the cardinal! And why?' demanded Porthos with heat.

'Because he saw very well that his thin dregs required to be enlivened by some good and generous wine!'

The two musketeers blushed up to the very eyes. D'Artagnan knew not where he was, and wished himself a hundred feet below the earth.

'Yes, yes,' continued M. de Treville, becoming more warm, 'yes, his majesty was right; for, upon my honour, the musketeers cut but a sorry figure at court. Yesterday, whilst playing with the king, the cardinal recounted, with an air of condolence which much annoyed me, that on the previous day these cursed musketeers, these devils incarnate—and he dwelt on these words with an ironical accent, which annoyed me the more—these cutters and slashers—(looking at me with the eye of a tiger)—had loitered beyond closing time in a tavern in the Rue Ferou, and that a picquet of his guards (I thought he would laugh in my face) had been obliged to arrest the disturbers. 'Od's-life! you ought to know something about this. Arrest the musketeers! You were amongst them—you, sirs! do not deny it; you were recognised, and the cardinal named you. But it is all my own fault; yes, *my* fault; for I choose my own men. Look ye, Aramis! why did you ask me for a tunic, when a cassock suited you so well? Hark ye, Porthos! have you got such a splendid belt, only to hang to it a sword of straw? And Athos—I do not see Athos; where is *he*?'

'Sir,' answered Aramis, in a melancholy tone, 'he is ill, very ill.'

'Ill! very ill, say you? and of what disorder?'

'We fear it is the small-pox,' answered Porthos, anxious to put in a word; 'and this would be very distressing, since it would certainly spoil his face.'

'The small-pox! This is a marvellous story you are telling me, Porthos! Ill of small-pox at his age! No, no; but doubtless he is wounded, perhaps killed. Ah! if I were certain of this! Zounds, gentlemen, I do not understand why you haunt such loose places, why you quarrel in the streets, and play with the sword in the crossways; and I do not wish you to afford mirth for the cardinal's guards, who are brave men, quiet, and skilful, who never throw themselves open to an arrest, and who, moreover, would not allow themselves to be arrested, not they! I am sure they would rather die than be arrested or escape! It is you who fly! who scamper away! A fine thing for the royal musketeers, indeed!'

Porthos and Aramis shook with rage. They could have strangled M. de Treville, had they not perceived that his great affection for them was the foundation of all he said.

As it was, they stamped on the carpet, bit their lips till the blood ran, and grasped the hilts of their swords with all their might.

M. de Treville's summons for Athos, Porthos, and Aramis had, as we have said, been heard outside the room; and those who remained in the antechamber had concluded, from the sound of his voice, that he was in a towering rage. Ten curious heads, therefore, rested against the tapestry, and grew pale with anger, for their ears, glued to the door, lost not one word of what was said, whilst they rapidly repeated the taunting language of their captain to all who were in the antechamber. In an instant the whole hotel, from the door of the cabinet to the outer gate, was in a state of commotion.

'So! the musketeers of the king allow themselves to be arrested by the guards of the cardinal!' continued M. de Treville, not less excited within than were his soldiers without, but jerking out and mincing his words, and plunging them, as one may say, one by one, like poniards, into the bosoms of his auditors. 'So, six of his excellency's guards arrest six of his majesty's musketeers! Sangdieu! I have taken my resolve, I will go hence to the Louvre, where I shall tender to the king my resignation as captain of the musketeers, and demand a lieutenancy in the cardinal's guards; and if I fail in this, mortdieu, I will turn abbé!'

At these words the murmurs without broke into a regular explosion; nothing but oaths and curses were everywhere heard. 'Morbleu!' 'Sangdieu!' and 'Death to all the devils!' resounded through the hotel. D'Artagnan hastily glanced around the cabinet in search of some tapestry behind which he might hide himself, and failing in this, felt an almost uncontrollable desire to get under the table.

'Well, captain,' said Porthos, almost beside himself, 'the truth is, we were six against six, but were unawares set upon, and before we had time to draw our swords, two of our party fell dead, and Athos was so grievously wounded as to be scarcely in better plight. You know him well, captain; twice he endeavoured to rise, and twice he fell back; and yet we did not yield ourselves up. No, we were dragged away by force; but escaped on the road. As for Athos, they believed him dead, so quietly left him on the field of battle, not thinking he was worth carrying away. That is the truth. Zounds! captain, one cannot gain every battle; even the great Pompey lost that of Pharsalia; and Francis, who, I have heard, was as brave as most men, lost the battle of Pavia.'

'And I can assure you that I killed one fellow with his own sword,' said Aramis, 'for mine broke at the first parry. Killed or poniarded him, as you please!'

'I did not know these circumstances,' said M. de Treville, in a somewhat milder tone; 'from what I now learn, the cardinal must have exaggerated.'

'But I beseech you, sir—' said Aramis, who seeing his captain more calm, ventured to hazard a request—'I beseech you, sir, do not say that Athos is wounded; he would be in despair if it came to the king's ears; as the wound is very severe, having, after passing through the shoulder, penetrated the chest, it is not impossible——'

At this moment the door opened, and a noble and beautiful face, but frightfully pale, appeared.

'Athos!' exclaimed both the gentlemen.

'Athos!' repeated M. de Treville himself.

'You inquired for me,' said Athos, to M. de Treville, in a perfectly calm but feeble voice. 'My comrades informed me that you commanded my presence, and I hastened to obey you; here I am, sir; what do you require me for?' And with these words the musketeer, perfectly arrayed, and girded as usual, entered the cabinet with a firm step.

M. de Treville, touched to the heart by this proof of endurance, rushed towards him. 'I was just going to tell these gentlemen,' added he, 'that I forbid my musketeers to expose their lives unnecessarily; for brave men are dear to the king, and his majesty knows that his musketeers are the bravest on the earth. Your hand, Athos!' And without waiting till he responded to this proof of affection, M. de Treville seized his hand, and pressed it with much warmth, and without observing that Athos, notwithstanding his command over himself, uttered a cry of pain, and became even more pale than before, if it were possible.

In spite of the secrecy which had been observed respecting it, the severe wound which Athos had received was well known to his comrades, and his unlooked-for arrival had produced a great sensation amongst them. The door of the cabinet had, since his entrance, remained ajar; and, as two or three heads were, in the warmth of the general feeling, thrust through the opening of the tapestry, a simultaneous burst of applause followed the last words of their captain. M. de Treville would, doubtless, have sternly and instantly checked this infraction of the laws of propriety; but at the moment he suddenly felt the hand of Athos grasp his own, and, on looking at him, perceived that he was fainting. He had rallied all his powers to struggle against his pain during the interview; but he could now no longer sustain it, and fell senseless upon the carpet.

'A surgeon!' cried M. de Treville; 'mine—or, rather, the king's—a surgeon! or my brave Athos will die!' At these exclamations of M. de Treville, every one rushed into the cabinet, and before he could stop them, pressed round the wounded man. But this eagerness would have been useless, had not the surgeon been found in the hotel. Forcing his way through the spectators, he approached Athos, who was still insensible; and as the pressure of the crowd occasioned him much inconvenience, he directed as the first step of all, that the guardsman should be instantly conveyed into an adjoining apartment. M. de Treville immediately opened a door, and pointed out the way to Porthos and Aramis, who bore off their comrade in their arms.

The cabinet of M. de Treville, that place usually deemed sacred, became for the moment an adjunct to the antechamber, and one in which every one discoursed, talked loud, swore, and consigned the cardinal and all his guards to the infernal regions. In a few moments Porthos and Aramis re-entered, having left M. de Treville and the surgeon with the wounded man. At length M. de Treville himself followed, and announced that Athos had recovered his senses; whilst the surgeon declared that there was nothing in his situation to alarm his friends, his weakness being occasioned entirely by the loss of blood.

Upon a signal from M. de Treville, every one now retired except d'Artagnan, who did not abandon his audience, but, with true Gascon tenacity, held his ground. When all the intruders had left the room, and the door was again closed, M. de Treville turned round, and found himself alone with the young man. The event which had just taken place had in some measure disarranged the previous train of his ideas; and he therefore now inquired what this persevering visitor required. D'Artagnan repeated his name; and M. de Treville recalling the past and present, instantly became aware of his situation.

'Pardon,' said he smiling, 'pardon, my dear countryman, but I had entirely forgotten you. What do you want? A captain is merely the father of a family, but burdened with a heavier responsibility than an ordinary parent; for soldiers are great children; but, as I maintain, it is my duty to see that the orders of the king, and more especially those of the cardinal, are carefully executed.'

D'Artagnan could not repress a smile; and this smile satisfied M. de Treville that he was not dealing with a fool. Therefore he came at once to the point, and, at the same time, changed the subject.

'I have loved your father,' said he; 'what can I do for his son? Tell me quickly, for my time is not my own.'

'Sir,' said d'Artagnan, 'in quitting Tarbes, and coming here, I wished to ask from you, as a memorial of the friendship which you have not forgotten, the uniform of a musketeer; but from what I have seen during these last two hours, I more fully comprehend the extreme importance of the favour, and tremble lest I may not be deemed a fit recipient.'

'It is truly a great favour, young man,' said M. de Treville; 'but it cannot be so far above you as you believe, or, at least, seem to believe. However, a decision his majesty has provided for this case; and I regret to inform you, that no one is received among the musketeers who has not passed the ordeal of some campaigns, performed certain brilliant actions, or served for two years in some less favoured regiment than our own.'

54

D'Artagnan bowed in silence, but at the same time feeling more eager to don the uniform of the musketeers, since that object could only be obtained with great difficulty.

'But,' continued M. de Treville, fixing his piercing look upon his countryman, as if he wished to penetrate the inmost recesses of his heart, 'but for the sake of my ancient friend, your father, I wish to do something for you. Young man, we cadets of Bearn are not in general overburdened with wealth, and I fear that matters are not much improved in this respect since I left the province. Your purse, therefore, can scarce be as full as it was.'

D'Artagnan drew himself up with a proud air, which seemed to say, 'I ask charity of none.'

'It is well, young man, it is very well; I understand your feelings. I came to Paris myself with only four crowns in my pocket, and I would have fought any one who had dared to dispute my ability to purchase the Louvre.'

D'Artagnan assumed a still prouder air. Thanks to the sale of his horse, he began the world with four crowns more than M. de Treville.

'I should say, therefore, that however large may be the sum you really possess, you ought to preserve it. In the meantime you must perfect yourself in all those accomplishments which become a gentleman, and I will this day write a letter to the director of the Royal Academy, who will receive you to-morrow without any fee. Do not refuse this trifling favour. Gentlemen of the highest rank and wealth often solicit without being able to obtain it, the same gift. You will there learn to ride, to fence, and to dance; you will form a circle in good society; and from time to time you must personally apprise me of your progress, and let me know if I can do anything for you.'

D'Artagnan, ignorant as he was of the manners of high society, felt the coldness of this reception.

'Alas, sir,' said he, 'I now deeply feel the want of the letter of introduction which my father gave me for you.'

'I am, in truth, somewhat surprised,' replied M. de Treville, 'that you should have undertaken so long a journey without that viaticum, so essential to every Bearnese.'

'I had one, sir and a good one—thank God!' cried d'Artagnan, 'but was perfidiously robbed of it;' and with a degree of warmth and an air of truth which charmed M. de Treville, he recounted his adventure at Meung, accurately describing his unknown adversary.

'It was very strange,' said M. de Treville musingly. 'You spoke of me openly, did you?'

'Yes, sir, I certainly committed that imprudence; but such a name as yours served me as a shield on my journey; therefore you can guess if I frequently covered myself with it or no!'

It was an age of flattery, and M. de Treville loved the incense as well as a king or a cardinal. He could not help smiling, therefore, with evident satisfaction; but this smile soon passed away, and returning to the adventure at Meung, he continued—

'Tell me, had not this gentleman a slight scar on the cheek?'

'Yes, as if left by a pistol-ball.'

'Was he not a man of commanding air?'

'Yes.'

'Of a tall figure?'

'Yes.'

'With an olivine complexion?'

'Yes, yes, that is he: but do you know this man, sir? Ah! if I ever meet him—and I will find him, I swear to you, even were he in hell——'

'He attended a woman did he not?' continued M. de Treville.

'At least he departed after he had conversed a moment with the one he had attended.'

'Do you know the subject of their conversation?'

'He gave her a box, which he said contained her instructions, and desired her not to open it until she arrived in London.'

'Was this woman an Englishwoman?'

'He called her "my lady." '

'It is he,' murmured Treville: 'it must be; I thought he was at Brussels.'

'Oh, sir,' exclaimed d'Artagnan, 'if you know this man, tell me who and whence he is, and I will hold you absolved even of your promise to admit me amongst the musketeers; for before and above everything else, I long to avenge myself.'

'Beware, young man,' said M. de Treville. 'Should you perceive this man walking on the one side of the street, instead of seeking your revenge, proceed yourself on the opposite side; precipitate not yourself against such a rock, upon which you will assuredly be shattered like glass.'

'That fear will not deter me, should I ever meet him,' said d'Artagnan.

'In the meantime, do not seek him,' replied Treville. 'If you take my advice——'

But all at once M. de Treville paused, as if struck by a sudden suspicion: the deadly hatred which the young traveller so openly avowed for this man who had deprived him of his father's letter—which was in itself a very improbable circumstance—might not this apparent enmity conceal some perfidy? Was not this young man sent by his eminence? Did not he come to lay a trap for him? Was not this pretended d'Artagnan an emissary of the cardinal, whom the latter sought to introduce into his house, and whom he wished to place near him to worm himself into his confidence, and afterwards to betray him, as was often done in similar cases? He looked more earnestly at d'Artagnan than at first, and was but slightly reassured by the appearance of that countenance, beaming with acute talent and affected humility. 'I know very well that he is a Gascon,' thought he; 'but he is just as likely to be one for the cardinal as for me. Yet I will try him further.'

'Young man,' said he slowly, 'as the son of mine ancient friend—for I consider the history of this lost letter as true—I wish, in order to compensate for the coolness which you perceived in my first reception, to reveal to you the secrets of our politics. The king and the cardinal are the best of friends; their apparent disputes are merely to deceive fools; and I do not wish that my countryman, a handsome cavalier, a brave youth, formed to rise in the world, should be the dupe of all these pretences, and, like a simpleton, rush headlong into the snare which has made awful examples of so many others. Rest assured, that I am entirely devoted to these two all-powerful masters, and that all my serious proceedings can never have any other object in view than the service of the king, and of the cardinal, who is one of the most illustrious geniuses that France has ever produced. Now, young man, regulate your conduct by this; and should you, through your family or connections, or even your instincts, bear the slightest hostility towards the cardinal, such as you may have seen burst forth occasionally amongst our nobility, take your leave, and quit me. I can assist you in a thousand ways, without attaching you to my own person. At all events, I hope my frankness will make you my friend, for you are the first young man to whom I have as yet spoken in this manner.'

Treville ceased speaking, but he thought to himself,

'If the cardinal has really sent me this young fox. he would not surely fail—he knows how much I loathe him—to tell his spy that the best way of paying court to me, is to rail at himself. Therefore, in spite of my protestations, the cunning fellow will doubtless say that he holds his eminence in detestation.'

The result, however, was far different from M. de Treville's anticipations. D'Artagnan replied, with the utmost simplicity, 'Sir, I am come to Paris with sentiments and intentions exactly similar to those you have just expressed. My father charged me to obey no one but the king, the cardinal, and yourself, whom he considers the three greatest men in France.' D'Artagnan, it will be perceived, added M. de Treville to the others, but he considered that this addition would do no harm. 'Hence,' he continued, 'I have the greatest veneration for the cardinal, and the most profound respect for his actions. It is, therefore, so much the better for me, sir, if, as you say, you speak frankly to me, since you will then do me the honour to esteem this similarity of opinions; but if, on the contrary, as may be very natural, you entertain any feelings of distrust respecting me, so much the worse, as I shall then feel that I am ruined by speaking the truth. But in any case, you will at least honour me with your esteem, which I value more than anything else.'

M. de Treville was astonished. So much penetration, and yet so much candour, excited his admiration, although they failed in wholly removing his doubts. The more superior this youth was to other young men, the more formidable a traitor would he make. Nevertheless, he grasped d'Artagnan's hand, and said to him, 'You are an honest fellow; but at present I can only do for you what I have promised. In the meantime, my hotel shall always be open to you; so that, having access to me at all times, and being ready to take advantage of every opportunity, you will probably hereafter obtain what you desire.'

'That is to say,' replied d'Artagnan, 'that you will wait till I have become worthy of it. Very well,' he added, with Gascon familiarity; 'rest assured that you will not have to wait long;' and he bowed to retire, as if the future lay with himself.

'But wait a moment,' said M. de Treville, stopping him; 'I promised you a letter to the director of the Academy. Are you too proud to accept it, my little gentleman?'

'No, sir,' replied d'Artagnan; 'and I will answer for it that the same fate that overtook my father's letter shall not occur to this, which I will take good care shall reach its destination; and woe be to him who shall attempt to deprive me of it.'

M. de Treville smiled at this gasconade, and leaving his young countryman in the embrasure of the window, where they had been talking, sat down to write the promised letter of introduction. In the meantime, d'Artagnan, who had nothing better to do, beat a march on the window, looking at the musketeers, who had followed each other, and watching them rounding the corner of the street. M. de Treville, having written the letter and sealed it, approached the young man to give it to him; but at the very moment when d'Artagnan held out his hand to receive it, M. de Treville was astonished to perceive his *protégé* spring up, redden with anger, and rush out of the cabinet, exclaiming—

' 'Od's blood! he shall not escape me this time!'

'And who is he?' demanded M. de Treville.

'It is *he*—the robber!' replied d'Artagnan. 'Oh, what a traitor!'—and he vanished.

'Deuce take the madman!' murmured M. de Treville, 'unless it is, after all, a clever mode of giving me the slip, seeing that he has failed in his attempts.'

4

*The Shoulder of Athos, the Belt of Porthos, and the
Handkerchief of Aramis*

D'ARTAGNAN, quite furious, had passed through the ante-chamber in three bounds, and reached the staircase, which he was about to descend by four steps at a time, when he suddenly ran full butt against a musketeer, who was leaving M. de Treville's suite of rooms by a private door, and butting his shoulder, made him utter a cry, or rather a howl. 'Excuse me,' said d'Artagnan, trying to continue his course; 'excuse me; I am in a great hurry.'

But he had hardly descended the first step, before a hand of iron seized him by the scarf and stopped him. 'You are in a hurry!' exclaimed the musketeer, as pale as a sheet, 'and under this pretext you dash against me. You say, 'Excuse me,' and think that is sufficient. But it is not so, my young man. Do you imagine, because you heard M. de Treville address us somewhat bluntly to-day that any one may speak to us as *he* speaks? Undeceive yourself, comrade: you are not M. de Treville?'

'Upon my word—' said d'Artagnan, seeing that it was Athos, who, after the treatment of the surgeon, was now returning to his apartments—'upon my word, I did not run against you on purpose; and not having done it on purpose, I said, 'Excuse me.' It appears to me, therefore, quite sufficient. Nevertheless, I repeat—and this time perhaps it *is* an excess of courtesy—that, upon my honour, I am in a hurry, a confounded hurry: loose me therefore, I beseech you, and permit me to go about my business.'

'Sir,' said Athos, releasing him, 'you are by no means polite; it is evident that you come from a distance.'

D'Artagnan had already descended three or four steps, but at the remark of Athos, he stopped short. 'Sir,' said he, 'from whatever distance I may come, I assure you that you are not the individual to give me a lesson in good manners.'

'Perhaps I am,' replied Athos.

'Ah! would that I were not in such a hurry,' exclaimed d'Artagnan, 'and that I were not running after some one!'

'Monsieur in a hurry! you will find me without running; do you understand?'

'Near the Carmes-Deschaux.'

'At what hour?'

'About twelve o'clock.'

'Very well, I will be there.'

'Take care that you do not make me wait too long,' said Athos, 'for I tell you plainly, at a quarter past twelve, it is I that will run after you, and cut off your ears as you go!'

'Good!' exclaimed d'Artagnan; 'but I will take special care to be there at ten minutes before twelve.'

And he commenced running again as if possessed by devils, hoping still to catch the unknown, whose slow pace could not yet have carried him beyond his reach. But at the corner of the street Porthos was talking with one of the soldiers on guard, and between these two there was just space enough for a man to pass. D'Artagnan fancied that this space was sufficient for him, and he shot forward to rush like an arrow between the two. He had not, however, made allowance for the wind, which, whilst he was passing, actually bellied out the enormous cloak of Porthos, into which he fairly plunged. Doubtless Porthos had cogent reasons for not abandoning this most essential portion of his dress; and therefore, instead of letting go the corner which he held, he drew it more closely towards him, so that d'Artagnan found himself rolled up in the velvet, by a rotatory motion which is clearly explained by the obstinate resistance of Porthos.

D'Artagnan, hearing the musketeer swear, wished to escape from under the cloak, which completely blinded him, and sought for an outlet from the folds. Above all things he feared that he had injured the freshness of the magnificent belt, of which we have heard so much; but on recovering his powers of vision he found his nose jammed between the shoulders of Porthos; that is, exactly on the belt. Alas! like the majority of the fine things of this world, which are only made for outward show, the belt was of gold in front, and of simple leather behind. In fact, Porthos, proud as he was, being unable to afford a belt entirely of gold, had procured one of which the half at least was of that metal. And this may perhaps account for the cold under which Porthos had avowed himself as suffering, and the consequent need of the cloak.

' 'Od's-boddikins!' cried Porthos, making every effort to free himself from d'Artagnan, who kept poking his nose into his back; 'you are mad to throw yourself in this manner upon people.'

'Excuse me,' said d'Artagnan, reappearing from beneath the shoulder of the giant, 'but I was in a hurry; I am running after some one——'

'Do you shut your eyes when you run?' demanded Porthos.

'No,' answered d'Artagnan, somewhat piqued, 'no; and, thanks to my eyes, I can see what others do not see.'

Whether Porthos understood him or not, he yet gave way to his anger. 'Sir,' said he, 'you will get yourself chastised, if you thus rub against the musketeers.'

'Chastised, sir!' said d'Artagnan; 'your expression is harsh.'

'It is such as becomes a man who is accustomed to face his enemies.'

'Ah, by St. Denis,' replied d'Artagnan, 'I know well that you would not turn your back upon yours!' and the young man, delighted with his joke, marched off, laughing outrageously.

Porthos foamed with anger, and was hastening after him; but d'Artagnan turned and said—

'By and by, by and by, when you are without your cloak.'

'At one o'clock, then, behind the Luxembourg,' shouted Porthos.

'Very well, at one o'clock,' answered d'Artagnan, as he turned into the street adjoining.

But neither in the street which he had just traversed, nor in that down which he looked, did he see any one. Slowly as the stranger had walked, he had disappeared. Perhaps he had entered some house. D'Artagnan inquired after him of every one he met; he even went down to the ferry, returned by the Rue de Seine and La Croix Rouge, but no one, actually no one, was to be seen. This pursuit, however, was so far serviceable to him, that, as the perspiration bathed his forehead, his heart grew cool, and he then began to reflect on the events which had just transpired. They were numerous and inauspicious. It was scarcely eleven o'clock and already the morning had brought with it the loss of M. de Treville's favour, since he must have deemed the mode in which d'Artagnan left him extremely abrupt; beside this, he had picked up good duels, with two men, each of them capable of slaying three d'Artagnans; and, lastly, these duels were with musketeers, with two of those very men whom he esteemed so highly as to rank them in his mind and heart above all the world. The Fates were against him; sure of being killed by Athos, it is clear our youth did not care much about Porthos. However, as hope is the last thing which is extinguished in man's heart, he began to hope he might survive—it might be, to be sure, with some terrible wounds; and under the impression that he should survive, he gave himself the following rebukes as a guard for the future:—'What a hare-brained fellow I am! What a booby! This brave and unlucky Athos was wounded on the shoulder, against which I must therefore run full butt like a ram. The only thing which surprises me is, that he did not kill me at once. He would have been justified in doing so, for the pain I caused him must have been excruciating. As for Porthos— oh! as for Porthos, upon my word, it is even more droll.' And in spite of all his efforts to restrain himself, the youth began to laugh, at the same time looking round lest this solitary merriment, which to those who might see him must appear without cause, should offend any one passing. 'As to Porthos,' he continued, 'it is more droll; but I am not the less a miserable giddy-pate, to throw myself thus upon people, without saying 'take care.' And, besides, does any

one look under a person's cloak to search for what no one sup-
poses to be there? He would doubtless have pardoned me,
had I not spoken to him of that cursed belt. It was, it is true,
only by insinuation—yes, but a neat insinuation. I'faith a
pretty business! Foolish Gascon that I am—a pretty kettle
of fish I shall make. Come, my friend, d'Artagnan,' he
continued, addressing himself with all the amenity to which
he thought himself entitled; 'should you escape, which is
not very probable, you must practise courtesy for the future;
hereafter every one must admire you, and must quote you
as a model. To be obliging and polite is not to be cowardly.
Observe Aramis: he is softness and grace personified. And
yet did any one ever pretend to say that Aramis was a
coward? No; and for the future I will in all points make him
my model. Ah! singular enough, here he is.'

D'Artagnan, thus walking and soliloquising, had arrived
within a few paces of the hotel d'Aiguillon, and before this
hotel he perceived Aramis talking gaily with three gentlemen
of the king's guards. On the other hand, although Aramis
perceived d'Artagnan, he had not forgotten that it was
before this young man that M. de Treville had given way
to passion, and a witness of the reproaches that the musketeers had received was by no means agreeable to him. He
therefore pretended not to see him; but d'Artagnan, full of
his new-formed plans of conciliation and courtesy,
approached the four young men, making them a profound
obeisance, accompanied by a gracious smile. Aramis bowed
slightly, but did not smile. Silence fell upon the group.
D'Artagnan had acuteness enough to perceive that he was
an intruder; but he was not sufficiently skilled in the ways
of polite society to withdraw himself dexterously from a
false position, such as is generally that of a man who joins
those he scarcely knows, and intrudes himself into a conversation in which he has no interest. He therefore sought
within himself for some means of retreat which might be
the least awkward, when he suddenly perceived that Aramis
had dropped his handkerchief, and, inadvertently no
doubt had put his foot upon it. The moment appeared to be
favourable for repairing his ill-timed intrusion; he therefore stooped down with the most graceful air imaginable,
drew the handkerchief from under the musketeer's foot,
notwithstanding the efforts he made to retain it there, saying,
as he presented it to Aramis, 'I believe, sir, this is a handkerchief which you would be sorry to lose.'

The handkerchief was, in fact, richly embroidered, and had a coronet and arms in one of its corners. Aramis blushed excessively, and snatched, rather than took, the handkerchief from the hands of the Gascon.

'Ah! ah!' said one of the guards, 'will you still insist, most discreet Aramis, that you are on bad terms with Madame de Bois Tracy, when that gracious lady condescends to lend you her handkerchief?'

Aramis threw such a glance at d'Artagnan, as makes a man understand that he has gained a mortal enemy. Then, resuming his soft air, 'You guess wrong, comrades,' said he; 'this handkerchief is not mine, and I know not why this gentleman has had the fancy to give it to me, rather than to one of you; and as a proof of what I say, here is my own in my pocket.' So saying, he drew from his pocket his own handkerchief, a very handsome one, of fine cambric, although cambric at that time was very dear; but it was without embroidery, without arms, and adorned with a simple cipher, that of its owner.

This time d'Artagnan was silent. He had discovered his mistake. But the friends of Aramis would not allow themselves to be convinced by his denial; and one of them, addressing the young musketeer with an affected air of solemnity, said—

'If the fact is as you assert, my dear Aramis, I shall be compelled to demand possession of the handkerchief, de Bois Tracy being, as you are aware, one of my most intimate friends, and I should not wish any one to display his wife's property by way of a trophy.'

'You make this demand with a bad grace,' replied Aramis; 'and on this ground alone, even were I to admit its justice fundamentally, I should still refuse compliance with your request.'

'The fact is,' modestly observed d'Artagnan, 'I did not see the handkerchief fall from the pocket of M. Aramis; he had his foot upon it, however, and hence my reason for supposing that it belonged to him.'

'And you were mistaken, sir,' coldly replied Aramis, not very grateful for the apology. Then, turning to the guardsman who had avowed himself the friend of de Bois Tracy, he added, 'Besides, on reflection my worthy comrade, I am the friend of de Bois Tracy as well as yourself, and this handkerchief, strictly speaking, might have come from your pocket as well as from mine.'

'No, upon my honour,' said the musketeer.

'You swear by your honour, and I pledge my word; therefore one of us must evidently lie. But come, Monterau, let us do something better than indulge in counter assertions and denials: let each of us take half.'

'Of the handkerchief?'

'Yes.'

'Perfectly fair,' cried the other two guardsmen; 'decidedly the judgement of Solomon. Aramis, you are certainly cram-ful of wisdom!' exclaimed the young men, indulging in hearty laughter; and the affair, as may be imagined, was thus deprived of further importance. Immediately afterwards the conversation ceased, and the friends separated, with a cordial shaking of hands, the three guardsmen going one way, and Aramis another.

'Now is my opportunity for making my peace with this gentleman,' mentally ejaculated d'Artagnan, who had kept somewhat aloof during the latter part of the conversation, and who now, impelled by this good feeling, approached Aramis, who was departing without taking any further notice of him.

'I hope, sir, that you will excuse me,' said he, addressing Aramis.

'Sir,' rejoined the latter, 'you must permit me to remark, that you have not acted in this affair as a man of good breeding ought to have done.'

'What inference, sir, am I to draw from your remark?'

'Why, sir, I take it for granted that you are not a fool; and that, although coming from Gascony, you must be well aware that no one walks upon pocket-handkerchiefs without sufficient reason for so doing. Zounds, sir, Paris is not paved with cambric!'

'You do me injustice, sir, in thus endeavouring to mortify me,' said d'Artagnan, in whom the inherent love of quarrelling began to operate much more forcibly than his previous pacific intentions. 'I am a Gascon, it is true; and, as you do not require to be informed, the Gascons are not very long-suffering; therefore, when they have once apologised, even should it be for some imprudence, they consider that they have done one half more than they ought to do.'

'What I have said to you, sir,' retorted Aramis, 'is not for the purpose of seeking a quarrel with you. Thank God! I am no bully; and being a musketeer only temporarily, I never fight except when I am compelled, and then with the utmost reluctance. This, however, is a serious affair, for a lady here is compromised by you.'

'Say rather by us,' cried d'Artagnan.

'Why did you perpetrate such a stupid blunder as to give me this handkerchief?'

'Why were you so stupid as to let it fall?'

'I have declared, and I repeat, sir, that this handkerchief did not come from my pocket.'

'Well, then, you have twice lied; for I myself saw it fall from your pocket.'

'Ah, is this the tone you choose to assume, Sir Gascon? Well, I must teach you how to behave better.'

'And I will send you back to your missal, M. Abbé; so draw, if you please, this instant?'

'No, I thank you, my fine fellow; not here, at any rate. Do you not perceive that we are opposite the hotel d'Aiguillon, which is full of the cardinal's creatures. In fact, who can say that it is not his eminence who has commissioned you to procure my head for him Now, as it happens that I entertain what may appear to you a ridiculous affection for my head, provided it remains tolerably firm on my shoulders, I wish, before parting with it, to kill you. But keep yourself quite easy on that score; I will kill you at leisure, in a retired and secret spot, where you may not be able to boast of your death to any one.'

'I am quite agreeable,' replied d'Artagnan; 'but do not be puffed up; and here, take away your handkerchief, whether it belongs to you or not; probably you may have tears to dry.'

'Spoken like a true Gascon, sir,' said Aramis.

'Yes; but that is no reason why you should delay our little affair, unless, indeed, you are influenced by more prudential motives.'

'I know well that prudence, although indispensable to churchmen, is a virtue unknown to the musketeers,' replied Aramis, 'and being, as I have informed you, only a soldier temporarily, I am resolved to remain prudent. At two o'clock I shall have the honour of awaiting you at the hotel of M. de Treville, whence I will conduct you to a more convenient spot.'

The two young men then bowed to each other, and parted. Aramis proceeded towards the Luxembourg; whilst d'Artagnan, finding that the time approached, took the road to the Carmes Deschaux, all the while inwardly ejaculating—'Positively, I cannot escape! but at all events, if I am killed, it will be by a musketeer.'

5

The King's Musketeers and the Cardinal's Guards

D'ARTAGNAN was friendless in Paris. He therefore went to
meet Athos without being provided with a second, having
made up his mind to be satisfied with those which accompanied his adversary. Besides, he fully intended to offer the
brave musketeer all suitable apologies, but, at the same time,
to betray nothing having the slightest appearance of timidity
or weakness. He also feared such a result from this duel as
may be naturally anticipated in an affair of the kind, where
a young and vigorous man fights with an opponent who is
wounded and enfeebled; and in which, should the former be
vanquished, the triumph of his opponent is doubled; whilst,
should the former prove the conqueror, he is not only
accused of being brave at small risk, but even his courage
is regarded as extremely doubtful. Moreover, unless we have
been unsuccessful in our attempt to portray the true
character of our adventurer, the reader must have already
remarked, that d'Artagnan was no common type. Therefore,
although he could not divest himself of the idea that his
death was inevitable, he had by no means resolved quietly to
resign himself to his fate with that patience which another
less courageous than himself might perhaps have displayed
in such a case. He pondered upon the different characters
of those with whom he was about to engage, and at length
began to obtain a clearer view of his situation. By means of
the sincere apology which he contemplated, he hoped to
conciliate Athos, whose aristocratic air and austere manner
quite delighted him. Then he flattered himself that he might
intimidate Porthos by the adventure of the belt, whose story,
if he were not instantaneously killed, he might relate to
every one, so as to overwhelm him with ridicule. Lastly, as
regarded the quiet Aramis, he entertained very slight
apprehensions; for, supposing that he should survive to fight
him, he entertained no doubt of his ability to make short work
of him, or, at all events, by wounding him in the face (as
Cæsar recommended his men to do with Pompey's soldiers),
to spoil for ever that beauty of which he was so vain. In fine,

67

d'Artagnan now brought into action those principles of unconquerable and steady resolve which the counsels of his father had implanted in his heart—counsels which, as we know, had instructed him to submit to nothing like indignity unless it proceeded from the king, the cardinal, or M. de Treville.

Full of these ideas, he sped as if on wings towards the convent des Carmes Deschaux—a building without windows, adjoining a chapel of ease of the Pré-aux-Clercs, and surrounded by dry meadows, which generally served as a rendezvous for those combatants who had no time to lose. As d'Artagnan came in sight of the small open space in front of the convent, it struck the hour of noon, and Athos had already been about five minutes on the ground He was therefore as punctual as the Samaritan woman, and the most rigorous casuist in the laws of duelling could have found nothing to censure.

Athos, who continued to suffer severely from his wound, although it had again been dressed by M. de Treville's surgeon, had seated himself on a large stone, where he awaited his adversary with that air of calmness and dignity which never forsook him. As d'Artagnan approached, he arose, and politely advanced some steps to meet him; whilst d'Artagnan, on his part, went towards his antagonist bowing until his plume touched the ground.

'Sir,' said Athos, 'I expected two of my friends who are to act as my seconds, but they are not yet arrived. I am surprised that they should be so late, as they are generally punctual!'

'I have no second, sir,' said d'Artagnan; 'I only arrived in Paris yesterday; consequently I am unknown to any one here except M. de Treville, to whom I was introduced by my father, who has the honour to claim his friendship.'

Athos mused for an instant, and then said: 'So M. de Treville is your only acquaintance?'

'Yes, sir, I know no one but him.'

'Oh, then,' continued Athos *sotto voce,* 'if I should kill you, I shall acquire the reputation of a child-eater.'

'Not entirely so, sir,' answered d'Artagnan, with a bow which was not devoid of dignity, 'not quite so; since you do me the honour to draw your sword against me whilst suffering from a wound which must occasion you great inconvenience.'

'Inconvenience! Upon my honour I assure you that you

hurt me confoundedly. But I will use my left hand, as I usually do under such circumstances. Yet do not imagine that by this means I do you a favour, as I fight equally well with either hand. Indeed, it will rather be a disadvantage to you, a left-handed man being a very trying opponent to one who is not used to it. I regret, therefore, that I did not apprise you sooner of this circumstance.'

'Really, sir,' said d'Artagnan, again bowing, 'you are so very courteous that I cannot be sufficiently grateful.'

'You overwhelm me,' replied Athos, with the air of a well-bred man; 'if it be not disagreeable to you, pray let us converse upon some other subject. Ah! how you did hurt me! how my shoulder still burns!'

'Would you permit me——?' said d'Artagnan, some-what timidly.

'To do what, sir?' inquired Athos.

'I have a salve which is quite a panacea for wounds— a salve which my mother gave me, and which I have tried upon myself with success.'

'And what of it?' continued Athos.

'Why, sir, I am certain that in less than three days this salve would cure you; and at the end of that time, when your cure is completed, it would be a great honour for me to cross swords with you.'

D'Artagnan uttered these words with a simplicity which did honour to his courtesy, without in the slightest degree detracting from his courage.

'By my faith!' exclaimed Athos, 'this is a proposition which much pleases me; not that I should think of accepting it; but it savours of the perfect knight, and it was thus that, in the days of Charlemagne, those brave men, whom every man of honour should make his model, spoke. Unfortunately, however, we do not live in the times of the great emperor, but in those of the cardinal; and three days hence, however well we might preserve our secret, it would be known that we were going to fight, and we should be prevented. But,' he added, with some impatience, 'these seconds are laggards.'

'If you are in haste, sir,' said d'Artagnan, with the same simplicity that had the moment before characterised his proposition to put off the duel for three days—'if you are in haste, and should wish to dispose of me at once, dispense with the seconds, I beseech you.'

'This speech of yours pleases me still more,' said Athos,

gracefully bowing to d'Artagnan, 'it does not seem that of a man who lacks either head or heart. I admire men of your stamp, and, if we are spared, I shall hereafter have sincere pleasure in your acquaintance. Meantime, let us wait for these gentlemen, I pray you. I have plenty of time, and it will be more according to rule. Ah! see, here comes one of them.'

And as he spoke, the gigantic form of Porthos was seen at the end of the Rue de Vaugirard.

'What!' exclaimed d'Artagnan, 'is M. Porthos one of your seconds!'

'Yes, have you any objection to him?'

'Oh, certainly not!'

'And here is the other.'

D'Artagnan looked in the direction indicated by Athos, and beheld Aramis.

'What!' cried he, in a tone of yet greater astonishment. 'is M. Aramis the other of your seconds?'

'Certainly; are you not aware that one is rarely seen without the other, and that amongst the musketeers and guards, at court and in the town, we are known as Athos, Porthos, and Aramis, or the three inseparables? But as you come from Dax or Pau——'

'From Tarbes,' said d'Artagnan.

'You may very naturally be ignorant of all this.'

'Really, gentlemen,' said d'Artagnan, 'you are well named; and should my adventure become known, it will at least prove that like draws to like.'

In the meantime Porthos approached, shook hands with Athos, and turning towards d'Artagnan, seemed lost in astonishment. We may mention, in passing, that he had changed his belt, and laid aside his cloak.

'It is with this gentleman that I am about to fight,' said Athos, pointing towards d'Artagnan, and at the same time saluting him.

'And I also am going to fight him,' replied Porthos.

'But not till one o'clock' interrupted d'Artagnan.

'And I also—it is with him that *I* am to fight,' said Aramis, who had arrived on the ground, just after Porthos.

'Our appointment, however is for two o'clock,' replied d'Artagnan, with the same coolness.

'But what are you going to fight about, Athos?' demanded Aramis.

'Upon my faith, I do not well know, except that he hurt my shoulder.'

'And you, Porthos?'

'I fight because I fight,' replied Porthos colouring.

Athos, whom nothing escaped, perceived a slight smile curling the lips of the Gascon.

'We had a dispute about dress,' said d'Artagnan.

'And you, Aramis?' demanded Athos.

'Me? I fight on account of a theological dispute,' answered Aramis, making a sign to d'Artagnan that he wished him to conceal the true cause of their duel.

'Really!' said Athos, who observed d'Artagnan smile again.

'Yes, a point of St. Augustine, on which we could not agree,' said the Gascon.

'Decidedly he is a man of spirit,' murmured Athos.

'And now that you are all arrived, gentlemen,' said d'Artagnan, 'permit me to offer my apologies.'

A frown passed over the brow of Athos, a haughty smile glided over the lips of Porthos, and a negative sign was the reply of Aramis.

'You do not rightly understand me, gentlemen,' said d'Artagnan, elevating his head, on which a sunbeam played, gilding its fine and manly lines. 'I wish to apologise because it is improbable that I shall be able to pay my debt to all three; for M. Athos has the right to kill me first, which greatly decreases the value of your bill, M. Porthos, whilst it renders yours, M. Aramis, of scarcely the slightest value. Therefore, gentlemen, on that account alone, I again repeat my offer of apology. And now upon your guard!'

And with the most gallant and fearless mien he drew his sword.

His blood was fairly roused, and at that moment he would have drawn his sword against all the musketeers in the kingdom with as little hesitation as he then did against Athos, Porthos, and Aramis.

It was a quarter past twelve, the sun was at its meridian, and the situation chosen for the encounter was exposed to its fierce heat.

'It is very hot,' said Athos, drawing his sword, 'and yet I cannot take off my doublet, for just now I perceived that my wound bled, and I fear to distress this gentleman by showing him blood which he has not drawn from me himself.'

'True, sir,' replied d'Artagnan, 'but I assure you that, whether drawn by myself or by any other person, I shall always see with regret the blood of so brave a gentleman; I will therefore follow your example, and fight in my doublet.'

'Come,' said Porthos, 'a truce to these compliments. Remember that we also await our turn.'

'Speak for yourself only, Porthos, when you choose to be so rude,' interposed Aramis. 'As for me, I consider the courtesies which have passed between these gentlemen as worthy of men of the highest honour.'

'When you please, sir,' said Athos, placing himself on his guard.

'I was at your service,' said d'Artagnan, crossing his sword.

But the two rapiers had scarcely met, when a party of the cardinal's guards, commanded by M. de Jussac, appeared at the corner of the convent.

'The cardinal's guards!' exclaimed Porthos and Aramis at the same ~~ ~. 'Sheathe swords—gentlemen—sheathe swo⌐

But it wa⌐ too late. The combatants had been seen in a position which left no doubt of their intentions.

'Hollo!' cried Jussac, advancing towards them, and giving a signal to his men to do the same. 'Hollo, musketeers! What, fighting here? And the edicts—are they forgotten, eh?'

'You are extremely generous, gentlemen of the guards,' said Athos, in a tone of the most bitter animosity, for Jussac had been one of the aggressors on the night before last. 'If we saw you fighting, I promise you that we should not prevent it; therefore let us alone, and you will enjoy the spectacle without any of the pain.'

'Gentlemen,' answered Jussac, 'it is with regret I declare that what you request is impossible. Duty must take precedence of everything else. Sheathe, therefore, if you please, and follow us.'

'Sir,' said Aramis, parodying Jussac's manner, 'if it depended upon ourselves, we should accept your polite invitation with the utmost pleasure; but unfortunately the thing is impossible. M. de Treville has forbidden it. Move on, therefore; it is the best thing you can do.'

This mockery exasperated Jussac. 'We will charge you,' said he, 'if you disobey.'

'They are five,' said Athos in a low voice, 'and we are only three; we shall be beaten again, and we must die here; for I positively swear that I will not again appear before the captain a vanquished man.'

Athos, Porthos, and Aramis closed up to each other, whilst Jussac drew up his men. This moment of delay sufficed for d'Artagnan to form his resolution. It was one of those moments weighed with a man's whole destiny; it was a choice, once made, must be adhered to. To fight was to disobey the law, to risk his head, and, by one blow, to make an enemy of a minister more powerful than the king himself. All this the young man plainly perceived, and we must do him the justice to declare that he did not hesitate a single instant.

'Gentlemen,' said he, 'you must allow me to correct one thing which you have said. You affirmed that you were but three; but it appears to me that there are four of us.'

'You are not one of us,' said Porthos.

'True,' replied d'Artagnan, 'I have not the dress, but I have the heart and soul of a musketeer; I feel it, sir, and it impels me along, as it were, by force.'

'Hark ye, young man!' cried Jussac, who doubtless, from d'Artagnan's gestures and the expression of his countenance, had divined his intentions; 'you may retire; we permit you; save your skin, and that quickly.'

But d'Artagnan moved not a step.

'You are unquestionably a man of spirit,' said Athos, pressing the young man's hand.

'Come, come; decide, decide!' exclaimed Jussac.

'We must make up our minds,' said Porthos and Aramis.

'You are truly generous,' said Athos to d'Artagnan.

But all three thought of d'Artagnan's youth, and feared his inexperience.

'We are but three, and one of us wounded, exclusive of this boy,' remarked Athos; 'and yet it will be said that we were four men.'

'Ay, but to retreat!' said Porthos.

'It is difficult,' said Athos.

'Quite impossible!' said Aramis.

D'Artagnan comprehended the cause of their irresolution. 'Gentlemen,' said he, 'only try me, and I pledge you my honour that I will not leave this spot except as a conqueror.'

'What is your name, my fine fellow?' said Athos.

'D'Artagnan, sir.'

'Well, then, Athos, Porthos, Aramis, and d'Artagnan, forward!' exclaimed Athos.

'So, you have made up your minds, gentlemen?' cried Jussac for the third time.

'Quite so,' replied Athos.

'And what is your resolve?' demanded Jussac.

'We are about to have the honour of charging you,' replied Aramis, raising his hat with one hand, and drawing his sword with the other.

'Ah! you resist!' cried Jussac.

'Mortdieu! Does that surprise you?'

And the nine combatants rushed upon each other with a fury which did not, however, exclude a kind of method. Athos took Cahusac, one of the cardinal's favourites; Porthos selected Biscarrat; and Aramis found himself opposed to two adversaries. As for d'Artagnan, he sprang towards Jussac himself.

The heart of the young Gascon throbbed violently, not with fear, but with eagerness. He fought with the fury of an enraged tiger, turning round his adversary, and every moment changing his guard and position. Jussac, as we have before said, was a most skilful and experienced swordsman; nevertheless, he found the utmost difficulty in defending himself against his adversary, who, active and nimble, perpetually deviated from all the received rules of fencing, attacking on all sides at once, and yet at the same time guarding himself like one who had the greatest respect in the world for his own person. At length the struggle was brought to a conclusion by Jussac's rashness. Furious at being thus held at bay by one whom he regarded as a mere boy, he became less cautious, and committed various indiscretions; whilst d'Artagnan, who, although deficient in practice, had a profound knowledge of the theory of the art, redoubled his agility. Jussac, eager to dispatch him, made a tremendous lunge, at the same time breaking ground; but d'Artagnan parried the thrust, and whilst Jussac recovered himself, he glided like a serpent under his weapon, and passed his sword through his body; Jussac fell heavily on the ground.

D'Artagnan now cast a rapid and anxious glance over the field of battle. Aramis had already killed one of his adversaries, but the other pressed him sharply. He was, however, in very good trim, and could well defend himself. Biscarrat and Porthos had both received wounds, Porthos in the arm, and his adversary in the thigh; but as neither of these wounds was severe, they only fought the more fiercely. Athos, wounded afresh by Cahusac, looked more and more pale, but did not yield an inch; he had merely changed hands, and fought with his left. According to the laws of duelling at that period, d'Artagnan was at liberty to assist any one of his companions; and whilst he sought to ascertain which of them most required his aid, he caught a glance from Athos, which served instead of speech. Athos would have died sooner than call for assistance; but his look plainly denoted how much he required support. D'Artagnan at once comprehended his meaning, and with a single bound he fell on Cahusac's flank, exclaiming, 'Turn, sir guardsman, or I kill you!'

Cahusac did turn, just as Athos, whom his extreme courage had alone sustained, sunk upon one knee. 'Hollo, young man!' exclaimed Athos, 'do not kill him, I beseech you; I have an old affair to settle with him when I am cured. Disarm him only; deprive him of his sword—that's it—good, very good!'

This exclamation escaped Athos on perceiving the sword of Cahusac flying from his hand a distance of twenty paces. D'Artagnan and Cahusac both rushed forward to secure the weapon; but d'Artagnan being the most active, reached it first, and placed his foot upon it. Cahusac then went to the guardsman killed by Aramis, seized his rapier, and was returning to d'Artagnan; but on his way he encountered Athos, who during this momentary pause had recovered his breath, and fearing that d'Artagnan might kill his opponent, wished to renew the contest. D'Artagnan perceived that he would offend Athos if he did not permit him to have his own way; and in a few minutes Cahusac fell pierced in the throat. At the same moment Aramis placed the point of his sword at the breast of his fallen adversary, and compelled him to sue for mercy.

Porthos and Biscarrat alone remained fighting. Porthos, whilst fighting, indulged himself in a thousand fantastic jests and humours, asking Biscarrat what time of day it was, and congratulating him on the company his brother had just obtained in the regiment of Navarre. This jesting, however, gained him no advantage; for Biscarrat was one of those indomitable spirits who die, but do not surrender. It was time, however, to stop the fight, as the guard might arrive, and arrest all the combatants, whether wounded or not, whether royalists or cardinalists. Athos, Aramis, and d'Artagnan, therefore, surrounded Biscarrat, and summoned him to surrender. Although alone against all four, and with a wound which had passed through his thigh, Biscarrat refused to yield: but Jussac, raising himself on his elbow, requested him to desist. Biscarrat, however, like d'Artagnan, was a Gascon: he therefore only laughed, and pretended not to hear; and finding time, between the parries, to point with his sword to the ground at his feet—

'Here,' said he, 'will Biscarrat die, the sole survivor of those that were with him.'

'But they are four—four against one!' cried Jussac; 'yield, I command you!'

'Ah, if you command me, it is another thing,' said Biscarrat 'you are my commander, and I must obey.'

And suddenly springing backwards, he broke his sword across his knee, in order that he might not give it up, threw the pieces over the wall of the convent; and then, crossing his arms, he whistled a cardinalist air.

Bravery is always respected, even in an enemy. The musketeers saluted Biscarrat with their swords, and returned them to their scabbards. D'Artagnan did the same; and then, assisted by Biscarrat, the only one who remained on his legs, he carried Jussac, Cahusac, and that one of the adversaries of Aramis who was only wounded, under the porch of the convent. The fourth, as we have said, was dead. They then rang the bell, and confiscating four out of the five swords, they set off, intoxicated with joy, towards M. de Treville's hotel. They proceeded arm in arm, occupying the whole breadth of the street; and as they detained every musketeer they met, the march soon became like a triumphal procession. D'Artagnan's heart was in a delirium of exultation, as he marched between Athos and Porthos.

'If I am not yet a musketeer,' said he to his new friends, whilst passing the threshold of M. de Treville's hotel, 'I am at least next door to one. Is it not so?'

6

His Majesty King Louis the Thirteenth

THE affair made a great noise. M. de Treville strongly censured his musketeers in public; but privately they heard only his congratulations. As, however, it was essential that no time should be lost in gaining the king, M. de Treville hastened to the Louvre. But he was too late; the king was closeted with the cardinal, and M. de Treville was informed that his majesty was engaged, and could not then see any one. In the evening, M. de Treville returned. The king was at play, and was winning; and his majesty, being very covetous, was in an excellent humour. Therefore, as soon as he saw M. de Treville, he exclaimed—

'Come here, my captain, that I may chide you. Are you aware that his eminence came to complain to me of your musketeers, and with so much emotion as to be indisposed? Well, really, these musketeers of yours are perfect devils—thorough hang-dogs!'

'No, sire,' replied M. de Treville, who at the first glance saw the turn the affair was likely to take. 'No, on the contrary, they are good creatures, gentle as lambs, and who, I am confident, have only one wish, that their swords should never leave their scabbards except in time of war. But what are they to do? the guards of the cardinal are continually seeking opportunities of quarrelling with them; and, for the honour of the regiment, the poor young men are obliged to defend themselves."

'Hark ye, M. de Treville,' said the king; 'hark ye! Is this a religious fraternity—these men of yours—that you are speaking of? Truly, my dear captain, I am half inclined to deprive you of your command, and bestow it upon Mademoiselle de Chemerault, to whom I have promised an abbey. Do not suppose, however, that I give implicit credence to this simple story of yours. I am called Louis the Just; M. de Treville; and soon, very soon, we shall see——'

'And it is because I confide in that justice, sire, that I shall calmly and patiently await your majesty's good pleasure.'

'Wait then, sir, wait then,' said the king,' and it will not be long.'

In fact, at that moment the chances of the game turned against the king, who began to lose what he had before gained. Therefore he was not sorry to find an excuse (to use an expression of the gaming table, of which we confess we know not the origin) for making Charlemagne. The king therefore rose, and putting into his pocket the money which was before him, and most of which he had won—

'La Vieuville,' said he, 'take my place. I must talk with M. de Treville on an affair of importance. Ah! I had eighty louis before me: lay down the same sum, that those who have lost may not want their revenge. Justice above all things!'

Then turning towards M. de Treville, and walking with him towards a recess in one of the windows—

Well, sir,' continued he, 'you affirm that it is the guards of his eminence who seek quarrels with your musketeers?'

'Yes, sire; invariably.'

'Well, and how did this affair happen? Relate the facts; for you know, my dear captain, a judge must hear both parties.'

'Oh! by my faith, in the most simple and natural manner: three of my best soldiers, whom your majesty knows by name, and whose services you have often appreciated, and who, I can assure your majesty, are wholly devoted to your service—three of my best soldiers, Athos, Porthos, and Aramis, had made a party of pleasure with a young Gascon, a volunteer, whom I had introduced to them the same morning. The party was to be held at St. Germain's, I believe; and the rendezvous was fixed at Carmes-Deschaux, when it was interrupted by de Jussac, Cahusac, Biscarrat, and two other musketeers of the cardinal who doubtless did not assemble there in such force without some intention in opposition to the edicts.'

'Ah! you give me ground for a conjecture,' said the king; 'doubtless they came there to have an affair of honour.'

'I do not accuse them, sire, but I leave your majesty to judge what five armed men could be doing in a spot so retired as is the neighbourhood of the convent.'

'Very true, Treville; yes, you are right.'

'But, when they saw my musketeers, they changed their intentions, and forgot their individual and personal hatred, to indulge their enmity towards our corps; for your majesty well knows that the musketeers, who are wholly for the king, and nothing but the king, are the natural enemies of the guards, who are for the cardinal alone.'

'Yes, Treville,' said the king sorrowfully; 'and it is a sad thing, believe me, thus to see two parties in France—two royal heads, as it were, under one crown. But this must be brought to an end. You say, then, that the guards sought a difference with the musketeers?'

'I say it is probable that this was the case, but I do not swear to it, sire. Your majesty well knows how difficult it is to discover the truth, unless, indeed, one were gifted with that admirable penetration which has caused Louis XIII. to be named *the Just*.'

'There again you are right, Treville. But your musketeers were not alone; there was a boy with them.'

'Yes, sire, and a wounded man; so that three of the king's

musketeers, of whom one was wounded, and this boy, not only made head against five of the most formidable of the cardinal's guards, but even bore four of them to the earth.'

'Why, it is a complete victory!' exclaimed the king, radiant with joy—'a most complete victory!'

'Yes, sire, as complete as that of the bridge of Cé.'

'Four men—of whom one was wounded, and another a boy—do you say?'

'A stripling; but who behaved so nobly on this occasion, that I shall take the liberty of recommending him to your majesty.'

'What is his name?'

'D'Artagnan, sire; he is the son of one of my oldest friends—the son of a man who was engaged in the Partizan war on the side of the king your father, of glorious memory.'

'And you say this youth acquitted himself bravely? Tell me all about it, Treville, for you know how I love to hear of war and combats.'

And the king placed himself in an attentive posture, at the same time twirling his moustache in a military manner.

'Sire,' replied M. de Treville, 'as I have already told you, M. d'Artagnan is almost a child; and as he has not the honour of being a musketeer, he was in plain clothes. The cardinal's guards, perceiving his youth and also that he was a civilian, invited him to retire before they commenced their assault.'

'Thus we may clearly perceive, Treville,' interrupted the king, 'that it was the guards who began the attack.'

'Most assuredly, sire, there cannot be a doubt on the subject. They therefore warned him to retire; but he replied that as he was at heart a musketeer, and wholly devoted to his majesty, he should remain with the musketeers.'

'Brave youth!' murmured the king

'And he did remain with them; and in him your majesty has the resolute and valiant champion who gave Jussac that terrific sword thrust which has so much enraged the cardinal.'

'He who wounded Jussac?' exclaimed the king. 'He—a boy! Treville, it is impossible!'

'It is as I have the honour to inform your majesty.'

'Jussac! one of the best duellists in the realm!'

'Yes, sire; but he has now found his master.'

'Treville, I must see this young man,' said Louis; 'I must see him; and if I can do anything—— However, we will think about that.'

'When will your majesty condescend to receive him?'

'To-morrow, at twelve, Treville.'

'Shall I bring him alone?'

'No, bring the other three. I wish to thank them all at the same time. Men so brave are rare, Treville, and such devotion ought to be rewarded.'

'At twelve, sire, we will be at the Louvre.'

'By the private staircase, Treville—by the private staircase; it is unnecessary to let the cardinal know it.'

'Yes, sire.'

'You understand, Treville; an edict is always an edict; at all events, fighting is forbidden by the law.'

'But this combat,' said Treville, 'is altogether different from the common duels; it was a sudden brawl; and the proof of it is, that there were five of the cardinal's guards against three of the musketeers and M. d'Artagnan.'

'It is quite true,' said the king; 'yet, nevertheless, Treville, come by the private staircase.'

Treville smiled; but conceiving that he had already secured an important advantage, by thus inducing the pupil to rebel against his master, he respectfully saluted the king, and, with his permission, made his retiral.

The same evening the three musketeers were apprised of the honour intended for them. As they had long known the king, they were not much enchanted by the news; but d'Artagnan, with his Gascon imagination, saw in it his future fortunes, and passed the night amid golden dreams. By eight in the morning he was with Athos, whom he found dressed, and ready to go out.

As they were not to see the king until twelve o'clock, and Athos had engaged to meet Porthos and Aramis at a tennis-court, near the Luxembourg stables, to play a match of tennis, he invited d'Artagnan to join them. Although ignorant of the game, which he had never played, d'Artagnan accepted the invitation, not knowing how otherwise to dispose of his time in the interval. Porthos and Aramis were already there, knocking the balls about. Athos, who was very skilful in all athletic games, went to one side with d'Artagnan, and challenged them. But at the first movement which he made, although he played with his left hand, he found that his wound was too fresh to permit such an exertion. D'Artagnan, therefore, remained alone; and as he declared that he was too unskilful to play a regular game, they only sent the balls about, without counting the points. One of these balls, however, driven by the Herculean hand of Porthos, passed so near d'Artagnan as to satisfy him that, had it hit him full in the face, instead of going on one side, his royal audience would have been lost, as, in all probability, he would thereby have been rendered unfit to be presented to the king. Now, since, in his Gascon imagination, all his fortune depended upon this audience, he politely saluted Porthos and Aramis, declaring that he would not renew the game until he was up to their standard, and then took his station near the ropes and the gallery.

Unfortunately for d'Artagnan, amongst the spectators there was one of the cardinal's guards, who was irritated by the previous night's defeat of his companions, and had resolved to take the first opportunity of avenging it. He now believed that this opportunity had arrived, and addressing a bystander—

'It is no wonder,' said he, 'that this young man is afraid of the ball; he is, doubtless, a musketeer recruit.'

D'Artagnan turned as if bitten by a serpent, and looked fiercely at the guardsman who had uttered this insolent remark.

'I'faith,' continued the latter, proudly curling his moustache, 'you may look at me as much as you please, my little gentleman. What I have said, I mean.'

'And since what you have said explains itself,' replied d'Artagnan, in a low voice, 'I will thank you to follow me.'

'Ah! indeed! and when, pray?' said the guardsman, with the same air of mockery.

'Immediately, if you please.'

'Doubtless you know who I am?'

'I have not the slightest idea; and, what is more, I do not care.'

'And yet you are wrong; for if you knew my name, perhaps you would be less courageous.'

'Indeed! and pray what is your name?' said d'Artagnan.

'Bernajoux, at your service.'

'Well, M. Bernajoux,' replied d'Artagnan with the utmost tranquillity, 'I shall await you at the gate.'

'Proceed, sir; I will follow you.'

'But do not be in too great haste, sir,' said d'Artagnan, 'lest it should be perceived that we go out together; for, considering how we are about to be engaged, you must be aware that too many witnesses might prove inconvenient.'

'There is some sense in that,' replied the guardsman, much surprised that his name had not produced a greater effect on the young man.

The name of Bernajoux was indeed known to every one, except d'Artagnan; for he was one of those who constantly figured in the daily brawls which all the edicts of the king and the cardinal could not suppress.

Porthos and Aramis were so much occupied by their game, and Athos was watching them so attentively, that they did not even perceive the departure of their young companion, who, as he had promised, waited a moment at the door for his opponent. In fact, d'Artagnan had no time to lose, considering the expected audience, which was fixed for twelve o'clock. He therefore cast his eyes around, and seeing that there was no one in the street—

'Faith, sir,' said he to his adversary, 'although your name is Bernajoux, it is very fortunate for you that you have to deal with a musketeer recruit only. However, be content: I will do my best. On your guard, sir!'

'But,' said he whom d'Artagnan thus addressed, 'it appears to me this place is badly chosen, and that we should be better behind the abbey of St. Germain, or in the Pré-aux-Clercs.'

'True enough,' replied d'Artagnan, 'but, unfortunately, my time is precious, as I have an important engagement precisely at twelve; therefore draw, sir, draw!'

Bernajoux was not the man to wait the repetition of such a compliment. In an instant, therefore, his sword glittered in his hand, and he rushed upon his adversary, whom, on account of his extreme youth, he hoped to intimidate.

But d'Artagnan had served his apprenticeship the evening before, and now fresh, and elated with his victory, as well as inflamed with hopes of future favour, he was fully resolved not to recede an inch. The two swords were therefore engaged even to the guard; and as d'Artagnan kept his ground firmly, his adversary was obliged to retreat a single step. By this movement Bernajoux's sword deviated from 'opposition,' and d'Artagnan, seizing the opportunity, made a lunge which wounded his adversary in the shoulder. He immediately stepped back one pace, and raised his sword; but Bernajoux, declaring that it was nothing, made a blind thrust at d'Artagnan, and impaled himself upon his sword. Nevertheless, as Bernajoux neither fell, nor declared himself vanquished, but merely retreated towards the hotel of M. de la Tremouille, in whose service he had a relative, d'Artagnan, ignorant of the severity of his adversary's wound, pressed him closely, and doubtless would have despatched him by a third thrust, had not the clash of the rapiers reached the tennis-court, from which now rushed, sword in hand, two of the guardsman's friends (who had heard him exchange words with d'Artagnan), and fell upon the conqueror. But Athos, Porthos, and Aramis, now also joined the fray; and at the moment when the two guardsmen attacked their young comrade, forced them to turn. At that instant Bernajoux fell; and as the guards were then only two against four, they began to cry out—'To our aid! hotel de la Tremouille!' At this cry, all the inmates of the hotel rushed out, and fell upon the four friends; who, on their side, exclaimed 'Help, musketeers!'

The latter cry was very common; for it was known that the musketeers hated the cardinal, and they were beloved for the very hatred they bore towards his eminence. Hence, in those quarrels, the guards of all the other regiments, excepting those actually belonging to the Red Duke, as Aramis had designated the cardinal, generally sided with the king's musketeers. Of three guardsmen, who were passing, of the company of M. des Essarts, two came to the assistance of the four friends, whilst the third ran to the hotel of M. de Treville, crying, 'Help! musketeers, help!' As usual, M. de Treville's hotel was full of soldiers, who ran to the assistance of their comrades, and the battle became general. But the superiority of force was with the musketeers; and the cardinal's guards, with M. de la Tremouille's people, retired into the hotel, the doors of which they secured in time to exclude their opponents. As for the wounded man, he had been carried away at first, and, as we have said, in very bad plight.

Excitement amongst the musketeers and their allies was at its height, and they deliberated whether they should not set fire to the hotel, to punish the insolence of M. de la Tremouille's retainers, who had presumed to charge the king's musketeers. The proposition had been made and received with enthusiasm, when fortunately it struck eleven o'clock; and d'Artagnan and his companions, remembering their audience, and not wishing a feat so daring to be performed without their aid, succeeded in quelling the commotion; they therefore contented themselves with throwing some stones at the door, and then left the place. Besides, those whom they regarded as their leaders had just left them to proceed towards the hotel of M. de Treville, who, already aware of this fresh insult, awaited their arrival.

'Quick, to the Louvre!' said he; 'to the Louvre, without losing one moment; and let us endeavour to see the king before the cardinal prejudices him. We will narrate the affair as a consequence of that of yesterday, and the two will be disposed of together.'

M. de Treville, accompanied by the four young men, hastened towards the Louvre; but, to the great surprise of the captain of the musketeers, he was informed that the king had gone to the chase in the forest of St. Germain. M. de Treville caused this intelligence to be twice repeated, and each time his companions observed his countenance become darker.

'Had his majesty formed the intention of hunting, yesterday?' demanded he.

'No, your excellency,' replied the valet. 'The master of the hounds came this morning to announce that he had roused a stag; at first the king said he would not go, but subsequently he could not resist the pleasure which the chase promised him, and he set out after dinner.'

'And has the king seen the cardinal?' demanded M. de Treville.

'In all probability,' replied the valet, 'for this morning I saw the horses harnessed to the cardinal's carriage; I inquired where it was going, and was told to St. Germain.'

'We are anticipated,' said M. de Treville. 'I shall see the king this evening; but, as for you, I would not counsel you at present to attempt it.'

The advice was too reasonable; especially as that of a man who knew the king too well, to be opposed by the young men. M. de Treville therefore requested them to return to their respective homes, and await his orders.

On reaching his hotel, it occurred to M. de Treville that it would be prudent to be in advance with his complaint. He therefore despatched a letter to M. de la Tremouille, requesting him to dismiss from his house the cardinal's guards; and, further, to reprimand his own people for charging the musketeers. M. de la Tremouille, however, being already prejudiced by his equerry, whose relative Bernajoux was, replied that neither M. de Treville nor his musketeers had a right to complain, but, on the contrary, he himself; the musketeers having not only attacked and wounded his people, but also threatened to burn his mansion. Now, as a dispute between two such great men might last a long time, each being likely to adhere obstinately to his opinion, M. de Treville thought of an expedient to bring it to a close; and this was to go himself to M. de la Tremouille. He therefore repaired to his hotel, and caused himself to be announced.

The two noblemen saluted each other politely, for, although they were not friends, they yet esteemed each other. They were both brave and honourable men; and as M. de la Tremouille was a protestant, and therefore rarely saw the king, he intrigued on no side, and had contracted few prejudices in his social relations. On the present occasion, however, his reception of his visitor, though polite, was colder than usual.

'Sir,' said M. de Treville, 'we each believe that we have cause of complaint against the other, and I am now here to see if we cannot together clear up the matter.'

'Most willingly,' replied M. de la Tremouille, 'but I tell you beforehand that I have full information, and am satisfied all the blame rests with your musketeers.'

'You are too just a man, sir, and too reasonable,' observed M. de Treville, 'not to accept the proposition I shall now make to you.'

'Proceed, sir; I will hear it.'

'How is M. Bernajoux, the relative of your equerry?'

'Why, sir,' replied Tremouille, 'he is very ill indeed. Besides the wound which he received in the arm, and which is not dangerous, he has also received another, which has passed through his lungs; so that the physician gives but a poor account of him.'

'But does the wounded man retain his senses?' inquired Treville.

'Perfectly.'

'Can he speak?'

'With difficulty; but still he *can* speak.'

'Well, then, sir, let us interview him. Let us adjure him in the name of that God before whom, perhaps, he is about to appear, to tell the truth. I will acknowledge him as the judge, even in his own cause; and I will abide by his explanation.'

M. de la Tremouille reflected for a moment, and as it would have been difficult to conceive a more reasonable proposition, he agreed to it.

They therefore proceeded together to the chamber of the wounded man, who, when he saw them enter his apartment, endeavoured to raise himself in bed; but being too feeble, and, exhausted by the effort, he fell back, almost insensible.

M. de la Tremouille approached his bed, and by the application of some smelling-salts, restored him to consciousness. Then, in order to avoid any future imputation of having influenced the guardsman, M. de la Tremouille invited M. de Treville to question him himself.

The result was as M. de Treville had foreseen. Lingering as he was between life and death, Bernajoux had not the slightest idea of concealing the truth, and therefore gave a true narration of the occurrence. This was all that M. de Treville required; so wishing Bernajoux a speedy recovery, he took leave of M. de la Tremouille; and having regained his own hotel, he immediately summoned the four friends to dine with him.

M. de Treville received the best company; but, of course, all were anti-cardinalists. It may be readily imagined, therefore, that the conversation turned upon the two defeats which the cardinal's guards had sustained; and as d'Artagnan had been the hero of the last two days, he received all the congratulations; which Athos, Porthos and Aramis yielded to him with pleasure, not only as true comrades, but as men who had had their turn too often not to let him have his.

About six o'clock, M. de Treville announced his intention of proceeding to the Louvre; but, as the original hour of audience was past, instead of obtaining admission by the private staircase, he placed himself in the antechamber, with the four young men. The king was not yet returned from the chase; but our friends had scarcely waited half an hour amongst the crowd of courtiers, before the doors were opened and his majesty was announced.

This announcement caused d'Artagnan to shudder with emotion. The important moment was arrived upon which, in all probability, his future fate depended. His eyes, therefore, were fixed with intense anxiety on the door through which the king was about to enter.

Louis XIII. appeared, followed by his attendants. He was attired in his hunting-dress, still covered with dust; he was heavily booted; and in his hand he held his riding-whip. At the first glance, d'Artagnan perceived that the king was in a violent rage. This humour, though distinctly visible in his majesty's features, did not prevent the courtiers from ranging themselves along the sides of the room; and as, in the royal antechamber, it is better to be seen by an irritable and angry eye, than not to be seen at all, the three musketeers did not hesitate to step forward, although d'Artagnan, on his part, concealed himself behind them as much as possible. Yet though Athos, Porthos, and Aramis were personally known to the king, he passed on as if he had never seen them before, without either looking at or addressing them. But when his eyes rested for a moment upon M. de Treville, the latter met them with so much firmness, that the king turned aside his gaze, and, muttering to himself, entered his apartment.

'The aspects are unfavourable,' said Athos smiling; 'we shall not be knighted this time.'

'Wait here ten minutes,' said M. de Treville, 'and if I do not return to you in that time, proceed to my hotel as it will be useless for you to wait longer for me.'

The young men waited ten minutes, a quarter of an hour, even twenty minutes; and then, finding that M. de Treville did not return, they departed, very uneasy with the turn things were taking.

M. de Treville, who had boldly entered the royal cabinet, found his majesty in a very bad humour; he was seated in an arm-chair, venting his irritation by striking his boots with the handle of his whip. This, however, M. de Treville did not appear to notice, but with the utmost composure he inquired after his majesty's health.

'Bad, very bad,' replied the king. 'I am dull and dispirited.'

This was, in fact, the worst malady of Louis XIII., who often withdrew to a window with one of his courtiers, saying to him, 'Come, sir, let us be bored together.'

'I regret to find your majesty thus,' said M. de Treville. 'Have you not, then, enjoyed the pleasure of the chase?'

'A fine pleasure, truly! By my faith, all goes to ruin, and I know not whether it is the game that is no longer so swift a-foot, or the dogs that have no noses. We roused a stag of ten tines; we ran him for six hours; and when we were on the point of taking him, and just as Saint Simon was about to place his horn to his mouth, to sound the 'mort'—*crac*, all the pack went off on the wrong scent, in pursuit of a brocket. You will thus see that I must now renounce the chase with hounds, as I have already relinquished it with falcons. Ah! I am a most unhappy king, M. de Treville; I had only one ger-falcon remaining, and he died yesterday.'

'Truly, sire, I can estimate your misfortune; it is, indeed, very great; but there are yet, I believe, a goodly number of falcons, hawks, and tercels, remaining.'

'But who is to train them? The falconers are all gone; and I alone now preserve the true art of venery. With me, all will be lost, and the game will hereafter be taken by snares, pitfalls, and traps. Oh! had I only leisure to instruct scholars! But then there is the cardinal, who never leaves me any leisure, and who is ever talking to me of Spain, of Austria, and of England! But apropos of the cardinal, I am very angry with you, M. de Treville.'

The latter had anticipated this turn of the conversation. From his long and intimate knowledge of the king, he was well aware that complaints of this nature were only a sort of prelude, as it were, to arouse his majesty's courage to the proper pitch, which he had on this occasion attained.

'In what have I had the misfortune to offend your majesty?' inquired M. de Treville feigning the utmost astonishment.

'Is it thus that you discharge your office, sir?' continued the king, answering one question by another; 'was it for this that I created you captain of my musketeers—that they should assassinate a man, excite a whole neighbourhood, and threaten to burn all Paris, without your saying a word to me on the subject? However,' added the king, 'without doubt you have come here to accuse yourself, and, having committed all the rioters to safe custody, inform me that justice has been satisfied.'

'Sire,' said M. de Treville, with the utmost composure, 'I am, on the contrary, come to demand justice.'

'And against whom?' exclaimed the king.

'Against calumniators!' replied M. de Treville.

'Ah! this is something quite new,' rejoined the king. 'Do you pretend to say that your three confounded musketeers, and your Bearnese recruit, did not rush like madmen on poor Bernajoux, and so ill-treat him, that he is probably now dying? Do you also pretend to say, that they did not lay siege to the hotel of the Duke de la Tremouille, and that they did not propose to burn it—which, during a period of war, would have been of little consequence, seeing it is merely a nest of Huguenots, but which, nevertheless, in time of peace, is a bad example. Say, are you about to deny these matters?'

'And who has related to your majesty all this fine story?' quietly demanded M. de Treville.

'Who has related to me this fine story, sir? Who should it be, pray, but he who watches whilst I sleep; who labours whilst I amuse myself; who manages everything within and without the realm; in Europe, as well as in France?'

'Your majesty no doubt means God,' said M. de Treville, 'for I know no other being who can be so far above your majesty.'

'No, sir; I speak of the pillar of the state; of my only servant—of my only friend—of the cardinal.'

'His eminence is not his holiness, sir!'

'What do you mean by that, sir?'

'That it is only the pope who is infallible; the infallibility which he possesses does not extend to cardinals.'

'You would say, then,' said the king, 'that he deceives me; you would say that he betrays me?'

'No, sire,' said M. de Treville, 'but I say that he deceives himself; I say, that he has been deceived; I say, that he has hastily accused his majesty's musketeers, towards whom he is unjust; and that he has not drawn his information from authentic sources.'

'The accusation comes from M. de la Tremouille—from the duke himself. What say you to that?' asked the king.

'I might say that he is too deeply interested in the question, to be an impartial witness; but, far from doing that, sire, I, knowing the duke for a loyal gentleman, willingly refer to him, but on one condition.'

'What is that?' said the king.

'It is that your majesty will send for him; will question him, but by yourself, face to face, without witnesses; and that I may see your majesty as soon as you have parted from the duke.'

'Ay, marry, indeed!' said the king; 'and you will be judged by what the duke may say?'

'Yes, sire.'

'You will accept his judgment?'

'Without hesitation!' replied Treville.

'And you will submit to the reparations he may require?'

'Entirely!'

'La Chesnaye!' exclaimed the king, 'La Chesnaye, let some one go immediately to inquire for M. de la Tremouille. I wish to speak with him this evening.'

'Your majesty gives me your word that you will not speak with any one between M. de la Tremouille and myself?' asked Treville.

'With no one, on the word of a gentleman!' replied the king.

'To-morrow, then, sire?'

'To-morrow, sir.'

'At what hour will it please your majesty?'

'At any hour you desire!'

'But in coming too early in the morning, I fear I may wake your majesty!'

'Wake me! Do I sleep? I never sleep now, sir! I may dream sometimes; nothing more. So come as early as you like, at seven o'clock if you choose; but I will not spare you, if your musketeers are in fault!'

'If my musketeers are guilty, sire, the guilty shall be delivered up to your majesty to await your pleasure. Does your majesty require anything else? You have but to speak and you shall be obeyed!'

'No, sir, no! It is not without reason that I have been named Louis the Just. Farewell, then, till to-morrow, sir! Farewell!'

'May God preserve your majesty till then!'

However little the king might sleep. M. de Treville slept even less. He had told the three musketeers and their comrade, to be with him at half-past six in the morning; and he took them with him without telling them anything, or making them any promise; confessing to them that their favour, as well as his own, was not worth more than the chances of a cast of dice.

He left them at the foot of the staircase. If the king remained angry with them, they were to go away unnoticed; but, if his majesty consented to receive them, they would be ready at a call.

On entering the king's antechamber, M. de Treville found Chesnaye there, who informed him that M. de la Tremouille could not be found the evening before, and returned too late to be presented at the Louvre; that he had, in fact, but just arrived, and was now with the king.

This circumstance much pleased M. de Treville, who was certain that nothing could come between M. de la Tremouille's deposition, and his own audience. Scarcely, indeed, had ten minutes elapsed before the door of the king's cabinet opened, and de Treville saw M. de la Tremouille come out. The duke immediately said to him,

'M. de Treville, his majesty sent for me; to inquire into the affair that happened yesterday morning at my hotel. I have told him the truth, that the fault lay with my people, and that I was ready to make you my excuses. As I have met you will you now receive them, and do me the favour always to consider me as one of your friends!'

'Sir,' said M. de Treville, 'I was so convinced of your loyalty, that I did not wish for any other defender with his majesty than yourself. I see that I did not deceive myself; and I thank you that there is still one man in France, of whom I may say what I have said of you, without danger, deception, or mistake.'

'It is well! it is well!' said the king, who had heard all these compliments. 'Only tell him, Treville, since he wishes for your friendship, that I also wish for his, but that he neglects me; that it is just three years since I have seen him; and that he only comes to a levee when invited. Tell him this for me; for those are the kind of things which a king cannot say for himself!'

'Thanks, sire! thanks!' exclaimed the duke. 'But let me assure your majesty that it is not those whom you see every day (I do not refer to M. de Treville) who are the most devoted to you.'

'Ah! you heard what I said! So much the better, duke! so much the better!' said the king, advancing to the door. 'Ah! it is you, Treville! where are your musketeers? I commanded you the day before yesterday to bring them! Why are they not here?'

'They are below, sire, and with your permission, Chesnaye will call them up.'

'Yes, yes! let them come directly; it will soon be eight o' clock, and at nine I have an appointment. Go, duke! and, above all things, forgot not to return Come in, Treville!'

The Duke bowed and departed. The moment that he opened the door, the three musketeers and d'Artagnan conducted by Chesnaye, appeared at the top of the stairs.

'Come, my brave fellows!' said the king, 'I must scold you!'

The musketeers approached, with obeisances, d'Artagnan following behind.

'What! the devil!' continued the king, 'seven of his eminence's guards regularly doubled up by you four in two days! It is too many, gentlemen; it is too many: at this rate, his eminence will have to renew his regiment in three weeks, and I shall have to enforce the edicts in their full rigour. I say nothing of one by chance; but seven in two days, I repeat it, are too many, a great deal too many!'

'But your majesty perceives that they have come in sorrow and repentance, to excuse themselves.'

'In sorrow and repentance! hum!' said the king. 'I do not put much trust in their hypocritical faces. There is, above all, a Gascon face in the background there! Come here, you, sir!'

D'Artagnan, who comprehended that the compliment was addressed to him, approached his majesty with a desperately desponding look.

'What! you told me it was a young man! But this is a mere boy, M. de Treville, quite a boy. Did he give that terrible wound to Jussac?'

'Yes! And those two beautiful sword thrusts to Bernajoux,' said M. de Treville.

'Really!'

'Without reckoning,' said Athos, 'that if he had not rescued me from the hands of Biscarrat, I should certainly not have had the honour of paying my very humble reverence to your majesty.'

'Why, M. de Treville, this Bearnese must be the very devil. Ventre saint-gris, as the king, my sire, would have said, at this rate many doublets must be riddled, and lots of swords broken. Now, the Gascons are always poor, are they not?'

'Sire, I must say that they have found no mines of gold in their mountains, though the Almighty owed them that recompense for the manner in which they supported the cause of your father.'

'Which is to say, is it not, Treville, that it was the Gascons who made me king, as I am my father's son? Well, let it be so; I will not contradict it. La Chesnaye, go and see if, by rummaging my pockets, you can find forty pistoles; and if you find them, bring them to me. And now let me hear, young man, with your hand on your heart, how this affair happened?'

D'Artagnan told all the circumstances of the adventure; how, not being able to sleep, from the expectation of seeing his majesty, he went to his friend's house three hours before the time of the audience; how they went together to the tennis-court! and how, on account of the fear he betrayed of being struck upon his face by the ball, he had been rallied by Bernajoux, who had narrowly escaped paying for his raillery with his life; and M. de Tremouille, who was innocent, with the loss of his hotel.

'It is exactly so,' murmured the king; 'yes, it is exactly as the duke recounted the affair. Poor cardinal! Seven men in two days, and seven of his most valued soldiers, too! But this is sufficient, gentlemen; do you understand? You have taken your revenge for the Rue Ferou, and more than enough. You ought now to be satisfied.'

'So we are, if your majesty is,' said Treville.

'Yes! I am,' replied the king; and taking a handful of gold from the hand of Chesnaye, and putting it into d' Artagnan's, he added, 'there is a proof of my satisfaction.'

At this period, the independent notions which are now current were not yet in fashion. A gentleman received money from the king's hand, without being humiliated. D'Artagnan, therefore, put the forty pistoles into his pocket, without any other ceremony than that of warmly thanking his majesty for the gift.

'There,' said the king, examining his watch, 'now that it is half-past eight, retire. I have told you that I have an appointment at nine. Thanks for your devotion, gentlemen! I may rely upon it, may I not?'

'Oh! sire!' replied the four at once, 'we will allow ourselves to be cut in pieces in your defence!'

'Well! well! But it will be much better to remain whole, and you will be far more useful to me in that state. Treville,' added the king, in a low voice, as the others retired, 'as you have no commission vacant in the musketeers, and as we have decided that it should be necessary to pass a certain probation before entering that corps, place this young man in your brother-in-law, M. des Essarts', company of guards. Ah! I quite enjoy the thought of the grimace that the cardinal will make: he will be furious; but I do not care, I am quite right this time.'

The king bowed to Treville, and the latter joined his musketeers, whom he found sharing the forty pistoles which his majesty had given d'Artagnan

The cardinal was in reality as furious as his master had anticipated—so furious, in fact, that for eight days he took no hand at the king's card-table. But this did not prevent the king from putting on the most charming face, and asking, every time he met him, in a most insinuating tone—

'Well! M. le Cardinal! how is your poor Bernajoux? and your poor Jussac?'

7

The Domestic Manners of the Musketeers

WHEN d'Artagnan had left the Louvre, and had consulted his friends what he ought to do with his portion of the forty pistoles, Athos advised him to order a good dinner, and Porthos and Aramis to hire a lackey.

The dinner was accomplished on the same day; and the lackey waited at table. The dinner had been ordered by Athos; and the lackey, who had been provided by Porthos, was a Picard, whom the glorious musketeer had enlisted, on that very day, for that occasion, whilst he was sauntering about on the bridge of Latournelle, spitting into the stream. Porthos pretended that this occupation was a proof of a meditative organization, and had hired him without any other testimonial. The magnificent appearance of the gentleman, on whose account he had been hired, seduced Planchet, for that was the name of the Picard. He had, indeed, been slightly disappointed when he found, on his arrival, that the situation he expected was already held by a brother lackey of the name of Mousqueton; and when Porthos told him that his *ménage*, though on a large scale, did not admit of two servants, and that he must therefore wait on d'Artagnan. But when he attended at the dinner which his master gave, and saw him, when paying, draw from his pocket a handful of gold, he believed his fortune made, and thanked Heaven that he had fallen into the possession of such a Crœsus. In that opinion he remained until the feast was ended, and he had made up for his long abstinence by an attack upon the remnants. But, on making his master's bed. the visions of Planchet all vanished. There was only that one bed in the chambers, which consisted merely of an anteroom and bedroom. Planchet slept upon a coverlet, with which d'Artagnan from that time forward dispensed, taken from d'Artagnan's bed.

Athos, on his part, had a valet, whom he had drilled to his service in a manner peculiar to himself, and whom he called Grimaud. He was very taciturn, this worthy signor— we mean Athos, not his man. For the four or five years that he had lived in the closest intimacy with his companions, Porthos and Aramis, these two had often seen him smile, but never remembered to have heard him laugh. His words were brief and expressive; saying what he wished them to express, but no more; he employed no ornaments or embellishments whatever. Although Athos was scarcely thirty, and was possessed of great personal and mental attractions, no one ever knew him to have had a mistress. He never spoke of the female sex; and although he did not prevent such conversation from others, it was evident, from bitter and misogynous remarks, that it was disagreeable to him His reserve, austerity, and silence, made him almost an old man, and he had therefore accustomed Grimaud, that he might not interrupt his habits, to obey a simple gesture, or even a motion of his lips. He never addressed him orally but in extreme cases. Sometimes Grimaud. who feared his master like fire, but at the same time was greatly attached to him believed he understood him perfectly, rushed forward to execute his orders, and did something directly contrary to what was wanted. Then Athos shrugged his shoulders, and, in cold blood, belaboured him soundly. On such days he spoke a little.

Porthos, as is easy to see, had a character diametrically opposed to that of Athos: he not only spoke a great deal, but in a loud voice. It must be owned, to do him justice, that it was of little consequence to him, whether any one attended to him or not; he talked for the mere pleasure of speaking, or of hearing himself talk; and talked, too, of everything but the sciences, which he never alluded to but to express the inveterate hatred he had from his infancy entertained towards savants. He had not such an aristocratic air as Athos, and the sense of his inferiority on that point had, at the commencement of their connection, made him often unjust towards that gentleman, whom he endeavoured to surpass by the splendour of his dress. But, in his simple uniform coat, merely, and by the manner in which he carried himself, Athos took at once the rank to which he was entitled, and sent the foppish Porthos back to the second place. Porthos consoled himself by making M. de Treville's antechamber, and the guardroom of the Louvre, ring with the account of his conquests—a subject upon which Athos never spoke—and boasted of none lower than a foreign princess, who was deeply enamoured of him.

An old proverb says, 'Like master like man.' Let us then

pass from the valet of Athos, to the valet of Porthos, from Grimaud to Mousqueton. Mousqueton was a Norman, whose pacific name of Boniface, his master had changed to the much more sonorous and warlike one of Mousqueton. He had entered Porthos' service on the sole payment of dress, board, and lodging, but in a sumptuous manner; and he only demanded two hours a day to provide for his other wants. Porthos had accepted the bargain, and things went on wonderfully well. He had old doublets and cloaks cut up and turned in a manner that made Mousqueton cut a very good figure.

As to Aramis, whose character we believe we have sufficiently explained, and which, as well as those of his comrades, we shall more fully develop hereafter, his lackey was named Bazin. Thanks to the hopes which his master entertained of some day taking orders, he was always dressed in black as became a churchman's servant. He was of the province of Berri; thirty-five or forty years of age; mild, peaceable, and fat; and passed his leisure in reading devotional treatises. He was dexterous in preparing a dinner for two; of excellent quality, though of few dishes. In all else he was dumb, blind, deaf, and of approved fidelity.

Now that we know, at least superficially, the masters and the men, let us turn to their habitations.

Athos dwelt in the Rue Ferou, at two paces from the Luxembourg. His habitation, or lodging, consisted of two small rooms in a very neatly-furnished house, whose mistress was still young and pretty, but ogled him in vain. Some few fragments of long-departed splendour adorned the walls of this modest lodging; such as a richly-mounted sword, which looked of the age of Francis I., and of which the handle alone, encrusted with precious stones, might be worth about two hundred pistoles. Nevertheless, Athos, even in moments of the greatest distress, could never be persuaded to dispose of or to pawn it. This sword had long excited the envy of Porthos, who would willingly have given ten years of his life for the possession of it.

One day when, as he said, he had an appointment with a duchess, he endeavoured to borrow it of Athos. But his friend, without saying a word, emptied his pockets of all his money and trinkets, purses, points, and gold chains, and offered them all to Porthos; but as for the sword, he said, it was fixed to its place, and must only leave it when its master quitted the lodging. Besides this sword, he had the portrait of a nobleman, of the time of Henry III., dressed with great elegance, and adorned with the order of the Saint-Esprit; and this portrait had some slight resemblance to Athos, a certain family likeness, which denoted that this great noble, a royal knight, was his ancestor. Lastly, a box of splendid jewellery-work, with the same arms as the sword and portrait, completed a mantel decoration, which clashed fearfully with the furniture. Athos always carried the key of this box; but one day he opened it before Porthos, and Porthos could bear witness that it contained only letters and papers; love-letters, and family records, no doubt.

Porthos inhabited a lodging of vast size, and of most sumptuous appearance, in the Rue du Vieux Colombier. Every time Porthos passed the windows of this house, at one of which Mousqueton always appeared in splendid livery, he raised his head and hand, saying, 'Behold my habitation!' But no one ever found him at home, nor did he ever ask any one in; and it was therefore impossible to form an idea of the reality of those riches which this sumptuous appearance promised.

As for Aramis, he dwelt in a small apartment, comprising a drawing-room, a dining-room, and a sleeping chamber, which were situate on the ground-floor, and had access to a small garden, fresh, green, shady, and quite impenetrable to the eyes of the surrounding neighbourhood.

We have already had occasion to know how d'Artagnan was lodged, and have already formed an acquaintance with his lackey, Master Planchet.

D'Artagnan, who was naturally very curious, as men of talent generally are, made every effort to find out who Athos, Porthos, and Aramis really were; for, under one of those assumed appellations, each of these young men concealed his real name.

It was evident they were of good origin, too, particularly Athos, who might be known as a nobleman at a league's distance. He therefore tried from Porthos to get some information concerning Athos and Aramis; and assailed Aramis, to find out something concerning Porthos.

Unfortunately, Porthos knew no more of the life of his silent comrade than that which has been told. It was said that he had met with great misfortunes of the heart, and that a terrible treachery had for ever poisoned the happiness of this gallant man. What this treachery was, no one knew.

As for Porthos, except his real name, with which M. de

Treville alone was acquainted, as well as with those of his two comrades also, his life was easily discovered. Vain and indiscreet, he was as easily seen through as crystal. The only thing which could mislead the investigator would have been a belief in all the good which he announced of himself.

As for Aramis, with the appearance of entire openness he was enveloped in mystery. He replied but little to the questions put to him about others, and entirely eluded those which related to himself. One day d'Artagnan, having questioned him a long time about Porthos, and having learned the report of his love affair with a princess, wished to ascertain something of a similar nature as regarded himself.

'And you, my dear companion,' said he, 'I have an opinion that you are familiar with coats of arms: witness a certain handkerchief.'

Aramis was not angry this time, but he put on a most modest air, and said, affectedly: 'My dear fellow, do not forget that I wish to enter the church, and that I fly from all worldly things. That handkerchief was not a love-token for me, but was left by mistake at my house by one of my friends. I was obliged to take it for fear of compromising him, and his mistress. As for myself, I am, like Athos, indifferent to these affairs.'

'But what the devil! you are not an abbé, but a musketeer!' exclaimed d'Artagnan.

'A musketeer, my dear fellow, for a time, as the cardinal says; a musketeer by accident, but a churchman at heart, believe me. Athos and Porthos have foisted me in, to occupy my time. I had, at the moment I was going to be ordained, a slight difficulty with—— But that does not much interest you, and I take up your valuable time.'

'On the contrary,' said d'Artagnan; 'it interests me much, and I have at present actually nothing to do.'

'Yes, but I have my breviary to say,' replied Aramis, 'then some verses to compose, which Madame d'Aiguillon has requested of me; then I must go into the Rue St. Honoré, to buy some rouge for Madame de Chevreuse; so you see, my dear friend, that though you are not in a hurry, I am;' and Aramis, tenderly pressing his young companion's hand, took leave of him.

D'Artagnan could not, with all his pains, learn any more of his three new friends; he therefore determined to believe all that was at present said of their past life, and hope for better and more full information from the future. In the meantime, he considered Athos an Achilles, Porthos an Ajax, and Aramis a Joseph!

The days of the four young men passed happily on. Athos played, and always with ill-luck; yet he never borrowed a sou of his friends, although he lent to them when he could. And, when he played on credit, he always awoke his creditor at six in the morning to pay him the debt of the evening before. Porthos had his humours: one day, if he gained, he was insolent and splendid; and when he lost, he disappeared entirely for a time, and then came back, wan and thin, but with his pockets stored with coin. As for Aramis, he never played; he was the worst musketeer, and the most unpleasant guest possible. He always wanted to study; even in the middle of dinner, when all expected him to spend two or three hours in the midst of the wine and company, out came his watch, and he would say—rising with a graceful smile, and taking leave of the company—that he must consult a casuist with whom he had an appointment.

Planchet, d'Artagnan's valet, nobly supported his good fortune. He received thirty sous a day; and, during a month, entered the lodgings gay as a chaffinch, and affable to his master. When the wind of adversity began to blow on the household of the Rue des Fossoyeurs—that is to say, when Louis XIII.'s forty pistoles were eaten up, or nearly so—he began to utter complaints which d'Artagnan found very nauseous, Porthos indelicate, and Aramis ridiculous. On this account, Athos advised d'Artagnan to dismiss the rascal; Porthos wished him to thrash him first; and Aramis declared that a master should never listen to anything but his servant's compliments.

'It is very easy for you to talk,' replied d'Artagnan; 'for you, Athos, who live mutely with Grimaud, and forbid him to speak; and, consequently, can never hear anything unpleasant from him; for you Porthos, who live magnificently, and are a sort of demigod to your valet, Mousqueton; for you, in fine, Aramis, who, being always engaged in thought, make your servant Bazin, who is a mild, religious man, respect you; but I—who am without stability or resources—I, who am neither musketeer nor guardsman—what can I do to inspire Planchet with affection, terror, or respect?'

'The thing is weighty,' answered the three friends; 'the

discipline of your establishment is in the balance. With valets, as with women, it is necessary to prove master at once, if you wish to keep them with you; let us therefore reflect!'

D'Artagnan reflected, and resolved to thrash Planchet provisionally, which was executed as conscientiously as he acted in all other affairs. Then, after having drubbed him soundly, he forbade him to quit his service without permission. 'For,' said he, 'the future cannot be unfavourable to me; I have an infallible expectation of better times, and your fortune is therefore made if you remain with me. Yes! I am too good a master to let your prospects be sacrificed, by giving you the notice you demand.'

This manner of proceeding gave the musketeers great respect for d'Artagnan's policy: and Planchet was seized with equal admiration, and spoke no more of leaving him.

The lives of the four young men were now passed alike. D'Artagnan, who had formed no habits whatever, as he had but just arrived from the provinces and fallen into the midst of a world entirely new to him, immediately assumed those of his friends.

They rose at eight in the winter, and at six in the summer; and went to take the countersign and see what was doing at M. de Treville's. D'Artagnan, though he was not a musketeer, performed the duties of one with great punctuality. He was always on guard, as he always accompanied that one of his friends whose turn it chanced to be. Every one at the hotel knew him, and regarded him as a comrade. M. de Treville, who, at the first glance took his measure, and had a sincere affection for him, did not cease to recommend him to the king.

The three musketeers had, on their parts, a great affection for their young companion. The friendship which united these four men, and the necessity of seeing each other three or four times a day, whether the affair were one of honour or of pleasure, made them run after each other like shadows; and they were always to be seen seeking each other, from the Luxembourg to the Place de Saint Sulpice, or from the Rue du Vieux Colombier to the Luxembourg.

In the meantime, the promises of M. de Treville were fulfilled. One fine day, the king commanded M. de Chevalier des Essarts to take d'Artagnan, as a recruit, into his company of guards. It was not without a sigh that d'Artagnan put on the uniform, which he would have exchanged for that of the musketeers at the cost of ten years of his existence. But M. de Treville promised him that favour after a cadetship of two years; a cadetship which, however, might be abridged. if he should find an opportunity of distinguishing himself by some brilliant action. D'Artagnan retired with this promise, and entered on his service the next day.

Then it was that Athos. Porthos, and Aramis, mounted guard, in turn. with d'Artagnan. when the duty came to him. The company of M. des Essarts. therefore, on the day that it received the youthful Gascon, received four men, in the place of one!

8

The Court Intrigue

NEVERTHELESS, the forty pistoles of Louis XIII., like everything else in this world, after having had a beginning, had also an end; and, after the end, our four companions fell into difficulties. Athos, at first, supported the association from his own private funds; to him succeeded Porthos, and, thanks to one of his occasional disappearances, he supplied the necessities of his friends for about fifteen days. Lastly, came the turn of Aramis. who performed his part with a good grace, on the strength of a few pistoles. procured. as he asserted, by the sale of some of his theological books. After all these resources were exhausted. they had recourse to M. de Treville, who made some advances of pay; but these could not go very far with our musketeers, who had had advances already; while the young guardsman had as yet no pay due. When they were at last almost destitute, they mustered, as a last resource, about eight or ten pistoles, which Porthos staked at play; but. being in ill-luck, he lost not only them, but twenty-five more, for which he gave his word of honour. Their difficulties thus became transformed to actual bankruptcy; and the four half-starved soldiers, followed by their lackeys, were seen running about the promenades and guard-rooms, picking up dinners wherever they could find them; for whilst in prosperity they had, by Aramis's advice, sown repasts right and left, in order that they might reap some in the season of adversity. Athos received four invitations, and every time took his three friends and their lackeys with him; Porthos had six chances, of which, also. they all took advantage; but Aramis had eight, for he, as may be seen, was a man who made but little noise over a good deal of work. As for d'Artagnan, who scarcely knew any one in the capital, he only found a breakfast on chocolate at the house of a Gascon priest. and one dinner with a cornet of the guards. He took his little army with him to the priest—whose two months' stock of provisions it mercilessly consumed—and to the cornet's. who gave them quite a banquet; but, as Planchet observed. however much we may devour. it still makes only a single meal.

D'Artagnan, therefore, was somewhat humbled at returning only one meal and a half for the feasts which Athos, Porthos, and Aramis had procured him. He thought himself a burden to the clique; forgetting, in his youthful sincerity, that he had supported that clique throughout a whole month. It was, by this reflection that his ardent mind was set to work. He conceived that this coalition of four brave. enterprising, and active young men, ought to have some nobler aim than idle walks, fencing lessons, and more or less amusing jests. In fact, four such men as they—so devoted to each other with their purses or their lives; so ready to support each other without surrendering an inch; executing, either singly or together, the common resolutions; menacing the four cardinal points at one time, or concentrating their united efforts on some single focus—ought inevitably. either secretly or openly, either by mine or trench, by stratagem or force, to find a way to what they had in view, however well defended or however distant that object might be. The only thing that surprised d'Artagnan was, that this capacity had never yet occurred to his companions. He himself now thought of it seriously, racking his brain to find a direction for his individual power four times multiplied. with which he felt assured that he migh., as with the lever which Archimedes sought, succeed in moving the world.—But his meditations were disturbed by a gentle knock at the door.

D'Artagnan roused Planchet, and told him to see who was there. But from this phrase of *rousing Planchet*, it must not be supposed that it was night. No! it was four in the afternoon; but two hours had elapsed since Planchet, on coming to ask his master for some dinner, had been answered—

'He who sleeps, dines!'

And Planchet was having dinner on this economical fare.

A man of plain and simple appearance, who had a bourgeois air, was introduced.

Planchet would have liked, by way of dessert, to hear the conversation; but the man declared to d'Artagnan that what he had to say being urgent and confidential, he would wish to be alone with him. D'Artagnan therefore dismissed Planchet, and begged his visitor to be seated.

There was a momentary silence, during which the two men regarded one another inquisitively, after which d'Artagnan bowed as a signal of attention.

'I have heard M. d'Artagnan mentioned as a very brave young man,' said the citizen, 'and this it is that has determined me to confide a secret to him.'

'Speak, sir, speak!' exclaimed d'Artagnan, who instinctively suspected something profitable.

The citizen paused; and then continued—'I have a wife, who is seamstress to the queen, and who is not without wit or beauty. I was induced to marry her, three years ago, though she had but a small dowry, because M. de la Porte, the queen's cloak-bearer, is her godfather and patron.'

'Well, sir?' demanded d'Artagnan.

'Well, sir,' replied the citizen, 'she was abducted yesterday morning, as she left her workroom.'

'And by whom has she been abducted?' inquired d'Artagnan.

'I do not know positively, sir,' said the other; 'but I suspect a certain person.'

'And who is this person whom you suspect?'

'One who has for a long time pursued her.'

'The deuce he has!'

'But, allow me to tell you, sir, that there is less of love than of policy in all this.'

'Less of love than of policy!' exclaimed d'Artagnan, with an air of profound reflection; 'and whom do you suspect?'

'I scarcely know whether I ought to mention names.'

'Sir,' said d'Artagnan, 'permit me to observe, that I have absolutely demanded nothing from you; it is *you* who have come to *me;* it is you who told me that you had a secret to confide to me; do then as you please; there is yet time to draw back.'

'No, sir, you have the air of an honourable man, and I can trust you. I believe it is in consequence of no love affair of her own that my wife has been entrapped, but be-

cause of an amour of a lady of far more exalted station than
her own!'

'Ah, ah! can it be on account of some amour of Madame
de Bois Tracy?' asked d'Artagnan; who wished to appear
familiar with Court circles.

'Higher, sir, higher!'

'Of Madame d'Aiguillon?'

'Higher yet!' said the citizen.

'Of Madame de Chevreuse?'

'Higher still! much higher!'

'Of the——'

And here d'Artagnan paused.

'Yes!' answered the frightened citizen. in such a low
voice as scarcely to be audible.

'And who is the other party?' said d'Artagnan.

'Who can it be, if not the Duke of——?' replied the
mercer.

'With the Duke of——?'

'Yes, sir,' replied the citizen, in a still lower tone.

'But how do you know all this?'

'How do I know it!' said the mercer.

'Yes! How do you know it? You must tell me all or
nothing, you understand,' said d'Artagnan.

'I know it from my wife, sir—from my wife herself.'

'And from whom does she know it?'

'From M. de la Porte. Did I not tell you that she is his
god-daughter? Well! M. de la Porte, who is the confidential
agent of the queen, had placed her near her majesty, that
the poor thing—abandoned as she is by the king, watched
as she is by the cardinal, and betrayed as she is by all—
might at any rate have some one in whom she could confide.'

'Ah, ah! I begin to understand,' said d'Artagnan.

'Now, sir, my wife came home four days ago. One of the
conditions of our marriage was, that she should come and
see me twice a week; for, as I have the honour to inform
you, she is my love as well as my wife. Well, sir, she came
to inform me, in confidence, that the queen is at the present
time in great alarm.'

'Really?' said d'Artagnan.

'Yes! the cardinal, as it appears, spies upon her and
prosecutes her more than ever; he cannot pardon her the
episode of the Sarabande—you know the story of the
Sarabande, sir?'

'Egad! I should think I do!' replied d'Artagnan; who

knew nothing at all about it, but would not for the world appear ignorant.

'So that it is no longer hatred now, but revenge!' said the citizen.

'Really!' replied d'Artagnan.

'And the queen believes——'

'Well! what does the queen believe?'

'She believes that they have forged a letter in her name to the Duke of Buckingham.'

'In her majesty's name?'

'Yes, to entice him to Paris; and when they have got him here, to lead him into some snare."

'The deuce! But your wife, my dear sir—what is her part in all this?'

'They know her devotion to the queen, and want to separate her from her mistress; and either to intimidate her into betraying her majesty's secrets, or seduce her into serving as a spy upon her.'

'It seems probable!' said d'Artagnan; 'but, do you know her abductor?'

'I have told you that I believe I know him!'

'His name?'

'I have not an idea what it is; all I know is that he is a creature of the cardinal—the minister's tool.'

'But you know him by sight?'

'Yes; my wife pointed him out one day.'

'Has he any mark by which he may be recognised?'

'Yes, certainly; he is a man of aristocratic appearance, and has a dark skin, a tawny complexion, piercing eyes, white teeth, and a scar on his forehead.'

'A scar on his forehead!' cried d'Artagnan; 'and with white teeth, piercing eyes, dark complexion, and proud air—it is my man of Meung!'

'Your man, do you say?'

'Yes, yes!' said d'Artagnan; 'but that has nothing to do with this affair. Yet I mistake! It has, on the contrary, a great deal to do with it; for if your man is mine also, I shall at one blow perform two acts of revenge.—But where can I meet with him?'

'I have not the slightest idea.'

'Have you no clue to his abode?'

'None whatever. One day, when I accompanied my wife to the Louvre, he came out as she entered, and she pointed him out to me.'

'Plague on it!' murmured d'Artagnan; 'this is all very vague. But how did you hear of the abduction of your wife?'

'From M. de la Porte.'

'Did he tell you the details?'

'He knew none.'

'You have got no information from other quarters?'

'Yes, I have received——'

'What?'

'But I know not whether I should inform you.'

'You return to your hesitation; but permit me to observe, that you have now advanced too far to recede.'

'I do not draw back,' exclaimed the citizen, accompanying the assurance with an oath, to support his courage; besides, on the honour of Bonancieux——'

'Then your name is Bonancieux?' interrupted d'Artagnan.

'Yes, that is my name.'

'You say, on the honour of Bonancieux! Pardon this interruption, but the name appears not to be unknown to me.'

'It is very possible, sir, for I am your landlord.'

'Ah, ah!' said d'Artagnan, half rising, 'ah, you are my landlord?'

'Yes, sir, yes; and as for the three months that you have been in my house (diverted, no doubt, by your great and splendid occupations), you have forgotten to pay me my rent, and as, likewise, I have not once asked you for payment, I thought that you would have some regard on account of my delicacy in that respect.'

'Why, I have no alternative, my dear M. Bonancieux,' answered d'Artagnan, 'believe me, I am grateful for such a proceeding, and shall, as I have said, be most happy if I can be of use in any way.'

'I believe you, I believe you,' interrupted the citizen; 'and as I said, on the honour of Bonancieux, I have confidence in you.'

'Then go on with your account.'

The citizen drew a paper from his pocket, and gave it to d'Artagnan.

'A letter!' exclaimed the young man.

'Which I received this morning.'

D'Artagnan opened it, and, as the light commenced to wane, he approached the window, followed by Bonancieux.

'Do not seek for your wife,' read d'Artagnan: 'she will

be returned to you when she is no longer required. If you make a single attempt to discover her, you are lost!'

'Well, this is pretty positive!' continued d'Artagnan; 'but, after all, it is only a threat.'

'Yes, but this threat frightens me, sir: I am not at all warlike, and I fear the Bastile.'

'Humph!' said d'Artagnan, 'I do not like the Bastile any more than you do; if it was only a sword thrust, now, it would be of no consequence!'

'And yet I had depended much on your assistance.'

'Quite right!'

'Seeing you always surrounded by musketeers of haughty carriage, and perceiving that those musketeers belonged to M. de Treville, and, consequently, were the enemies of the cardinal, I thought that you and your friends, whilst gaining justice for our poor queen, would be enchanted at doing his eminence an ill turn.'

'Unquestionably!'

'And then I thought, that, owing me three months' rent, which I never demanded——'

'Yes, yes, you have already mentioned that reason, and I consider it excellent.'

'Reckoning, moreover, that as long as you will do me the honour of remaining in my house, I should make no reference to rent——'

'Good, again!' said d'Artagnan.

'And, added to that, calculating upon offering you fifty pistoles, should you be at all distressed at this time, which I dont' say for a moment——'

'Wonderfully good! You are rich, then, my dear M. Bonancieux!'

'Say, rather, in easy circumstances, sir. I have amassed something like two or three thousand crowns a year in the linen-drapery line; and more particularly, by investing something in the last voyage of the celebrated navigator, Jean Mocquet; so that you understand, sir—— Ah! but——' exclaimed the citizen.

'What?' demanded d'Artagnan.

'What do I see there?'

'Where?'

'In the street, opposite your windows; in the opening of that entry—a man wrapped in a cloak!'

'It is he!' cried d'Artagnan and the citizen in one breath; each having at the same moment recognised his man.

'Ah!' this time he shall not escape me!' exclaimed d'Artagnan, rushing out, sword in hand.

On the staircase he met Athos and Porthos, who were coming to see him. They stood apart, and he passed between them like a meteor.

'Ah, where are you running to?' cried the two musketeers.

'The man of Meung!' ejaculated d'Artagnan, as he disappeared.

D'Artagnan had more than once related to his friends his adventure with the stranger, and also the apparition of the fair traveller, to whom this man appeared to confide such an important missive. Athos was of opinion that d'Artagnan had lost the letter during the quarrel, since a gentleman, such as he had described the unknown to be, must have been incapable of theft: Porthos only saw in the affair an amorous appointment, which d'Artagnan and his yellow horse had disturbed; and Aramis had said. these kind of things being mysterious. had better not be searched into. From the few words which escaped d'Artagnan. they understood therefore. what was his object; and concluding that he would return. after he had found his man, they proceeded to his apartment.

When they entered the room which d'Artagnan had just quitted. they found it empty; for the landlord, fearing the consequences of the meeting and duel which he doubted not was about to take place between the young man and the stranger, had judged it most prudent to decamp.

9

D'Artagnan Begins to Show Himself

As Athos and Porthos had anticipated, d'Artagnan returned in half an hour. He had again missed his man, who had disappeared as if by enchantment. The young Gascon had run through all the neighbouring streets, sword in hand, but found no one resembling him. Whilst d'Artagnan was engaged in this pursuit, Aramis had joined his companions, so that on his return he found the re-union complete.

'Well!' exclaimed they. when they saw him enter, covered with perspiration, and furious.

'Well!' said he, throwing his sword on the bed; 'this man

must be the devil himself: he disappeared like a phantom, a shadow, a spectre!'

'Do you believe in apparitions?' demanded Athos and Porthos.

'I only believe in what I see; and as I have never seen an apparition, I do not believe in them.'

'The Bible declares that one appeared to Saul!' said Aramis.

'Be it how it may,' said d'Artagnan, 'man or devil, body or shadow, illusion or reality, this man is born to be my bane; for his escape has caused us to lose a fine opportunity —one, gentlemen, by which a hundred pistoles, or more, were to be gained!'

'How is that?' asked Aramis and Porthos; but Athos, true to his principle of silence, merely interrogated d'Artagnan by a look.

'Planchet,' said d'Artagnan, 'go to my landlord, M. Bonancieux, and tell him to send me half a dozen bottles of Beaugency, which is my favourite wine.'

'Ah! then you have credit with your landlord?' demanded Porthos.

'Yes, from this day,' said d'Artagnan; 'and be assured that if the wine is bad, we will send to him for better.'

'You should use, and not abuse,' sententiously remarked Aramis.

'I always said that d'Artagnan had the best head of the four,' said Athos; who, having delivered himself of this opinion, which d'Artagnan acknowledged by a bow, relapsed into his usual silence.

'But now let us hear what is the scheme,' demanded Porthos.

'Yes,' said Aramis, 'confide in us, my dear friend; at least, if the honour of some lady be not compromised.'

'Be easy,' replied d'Artagnan, 'the honour of no one shall be in danger from what I have to tell you.' He then related, word for word, his intercourse with his landlord; and how the man who had carried off the worthy mercer's wife was the same with whom he had quarrelled at the Jolly Miller, at Meung.

'The thing looks well,' said Athos, after he had tasted the wine like a connoisseur, and testified by an approving nod of the head that it was good; and had calculated also whether it was worth while to risk four heads for sixty or seventy pistoles.

'But, observe,' said d'Artagnan, 'that there is a woman in the case; a woman who is carried off, and no doubt threatened, perhaps tortured, merely on account of her fidelity to her royal mistress.'

'Take care, d'Artagnan—take care,' said Aramis; 'in my opinion you are too interested in Madame Bonancieux. Woman was created for our destruction; and from her all our miseries arise.'

Athos frowned, and bit his lip, whilst he listened to this profound opinion.

'It is not for Madame Bonancieux that I distress myself,' said d'Artagnan, 'but for the queen, whom the king abandons, whom the cardinal persecutes, and who sees the execution of all her truest friends in succession.'

'But why will she love what we most detest—the English and the Spaniards?' asked Athos.

'Spain is her country,' replied d'Artagnan, 'and it is but natural that she should love the Spaniards, who are her compatriots. As to your first reproach, I never heard that she loved *the* English, but *an* Englishman.'

'And truly,' replied Athos, 'one must confess, that that Englishman is well worthy of being loved. I never saw a man of a more noble air.'

'Besides, you do not consider the perfect style in which he dresses,' said Porthos. 'I was at the Louvre the day he scattered his pearls, and I picked up two which I sold for twenty pistoles. Do you know him, Aramis?'

'As well as you do, gentlemen; for I was one of those who arrested him in the garden at Amiens, where the queen's equerry, M. de Putange, had introduced me. I was at the seminary at that time, and the adventure appeared to me to bear hard upon the king.'

'Which would not hinder me,' said d'Artagnan, 'from taking him by the hand, and conducting him to the queen; if it were only to enrage the cardinal. Our one eternal enemy is the cardinal; and if we could find the means of doing him some injury, I confess that I would willingly risk my life to employ them.'

'And the mercer told you, d'Artagnan,' said Athos, 'that the queen thought they had decoyed Buckingham into France by some false information?'

'She fears so! And I am convinced,' added d'Artagnan, 'that the abduction of this woman, one of the queen's suite, has some connection with the circumstances of which we are speaking, and perhaps with the presence of his grace the Duke of Buckingham in Paris.'

'The Gascon is full of imagination,' said Porthos.

'I like to hear him talk,' said Athos; 'his dialect amuses me.'

'Gentlemen,' said Aramis, 'listen!'

'Let us attend to Aramis!' exclaimed the three friends.

'Yesterday, I was at the house of a learned doctor of theology whom I sometimes consult on technical difficulties.'

Athos smiled.

'He lives in a retired spot, convenient to his tastes and his profession. Now, just as I was leaving his house——'

Here Aramis hesitated.

'Well!' said his auditors—'just, as you were leaving his house?'

Aramis appeared to make an effort, like a man who, in the full swing of making up a story, finds himself suddenly arrested by an unforeseen obstacle; but, as the eyes of his three friends were upon him, he could not by any means draw back.

'This doctor has a niece,' continued Aramis.

'Oh! he has a niece,' interrupted Porthos.

'Yes, a lady of the highest morality,' said Aramis.

The three friends began to laugh.

'Ah! if you either laugh or make insinuations, you shall hear no more,' said Aramis.

'We are credulous as the Mahometans, and dumb as catafalks!' said Athos.

'Then I will continue,' said Aramis. 'This niece comes sometimes to see her uncle, and as she was there by chance yesterday at the same time that I was, I was obliged to offer to conduct her to the carriage.'

'Ah! the niece of this doctor has a carriage,' interrupted Porthos, whose chief fault consisted in having too long a tongue. 'A desirable connection, my friend!'

'Porthos,' said Aramis, 'I have often intimated to you, that you are very indiscreet, and it does you no good in the eyes of gentlemen.'

'Gentlemen,' said d'Artagnan, who saw how the adventure arose, 'the thing is serious; let us endeavour to avoid joking. Go on, Aramis; go on.'

'All of a sudden a tall, dark man, with the manners of a gentleman—like your man, d'Artagnan——'

'The same, perhaps,' said the Gascon.

'It is possible!' said Aramis; 'however, he approached me, accompanied by six or seven men, who followed him at about ten paces' distance, and then, in the most polite tone, said, 'My lord duke, and you, madame,' addressing the lady——'

'What! the doctor's niece?' said Porthos.

'Silence, Porthos,' said Athos; 'you are insupportable.'

'"Please to enter that carriage, without resistance, and in silence."'

'He took you for Buckingham?' said d'Artagnan.

'Almost certainly,' said Aramis.

'But this lady?' said Porthos.

'He took her for the queen,' said d'Artagnan.

'Precisely!' said Aramis.

'The Gascon is the devil!' said Athos; 'nothing escapes him!'

'The fact is,' said Porthos, 'that Aramis is about the height, and has something of the figure, of the handsome duke; and yet one would think that the uniform of a musketeer——'

'I had on an enormous cloak.

'In the month of July! Excellent!' cried Porthos; 'was the doctor afraid that you might be recognised?'

'I can conceive,' said Athos, 'that the spy might be deceived by the figure; but the countenance?'

'I had a large hat,' replied Aramis.

'Good heavens!' exclaimed Porthos, 'what extraordinary precautions for studying theology?'

'Gentlemen,' said d'Artagnan, 'do not let us lose our time in badinage; let us rather make inquiries, and discover the mercer's wife, who might prove a key to the intrigue.'

'What! a woman of such an inferior condition! Do you think it likely, d'Artagnan?' asked Porthos, with a derisive pout.

'Have I not told you, gentlemen,' said d'Artagnan, 'that she is the god-daughter of la Porte, who is the confidential servant of the queen. Perhaps it is her majesty's policy to seek assistance from a source so humble. Lofty heads are visible at a distance, and the cardinal has a good eye.'

'Well, then,' said Porthos, 'come to terms with the mercer immediately, and good terms.'

'It is unnecessary,' said d'Artagnan; 'if he should not pay us, we shall be well enough paid from another quarter.'

At this moment a noise of hasty steps was heard upon the stairs; the door opened with a crash, and the unhappy mercer rushed into the room in which this council had taken place.

'Oh, gentlemen!' he exclaimed, 'save me, save me! In the name of heaven save me! There are four men come to arrest me!'

Porthos and Aramis arose.

'One moment,' cried d'Artagnan, making them a sign to sheath their swords, which they had half drawn—'wait one moment; it is not courage, but diplomacy, that is necessary here!'

'Nevertheless,' said Porthos, 'we will not permit—'

'Give d'Artagnan a free hand,' said Athos; 'he is the cleverest of the party, and, for my part, I declare that I will obey him. Do what you like, d'Artagnan.'

As this speech was uttered, the four guards appeared at the door of the ante-room, but seeing four musketeers standing there, with swords by their sides, they hesitated to advance any farther.

'Enter, gentlemen, enter,' said d'Artagnan; 'you are in my apartment, and we are all the loyal subjects of the king and cardinal.'

'Then, gentlemen, you will not oppose any obstacle to the execution of our orders?' demanded he who appeared to be the leader of the party.

'On the contrary, we would assist you were it necessary.'

'What is he saying?' inquired Porthos.

'You are stupid!' said Athos. 'Silence!'

'But you promised to assist me!' whispered the poor mercer.

'We cannot assist you in prison,' hastily replied d'Artagnan, in an undertone; 'and if we appear to defend you, we shall be arrested also.'

'It seems to me, however——' said the poor man.

'Come, gentlemen, come,' said d'Artagnan aloud. 'I have no motive for defending this person; I saw him to-day for the first time, and on what occasion he will himself tell you. He came to demand his rent—did you not, M. Bonancieux? —Answer!'

'It is the plain truth!' cried the mercer; 'but the gentleman does not add——'

'Silence about me! silence concerning my friends! silence, more especially, about the queen!' whispered d'Artagnan, 'or you will destroy us all, without saving yourself,—Go, go, gentlemen, take away this man!'

So saying, d'Artagnan pushed the poor bewildered mercer into the hands of the guard, at the same time exclaiming—

'You are a rascally niggard! You come to demand money

of *me*, a musketeer!—to prison with you! Gentlemen, I say again, take him to prison; and keep him under lock and key as long as possible; that will give me time to pay.'

The officers overwhelmed d'Artagnan with thanks, and carried off their prey.

As they were leaving, d'Artagnan detained the leader.

'Suppose we drank to each other's health? said he, filling two glasses with the Beaugency, for which he was indebted to the liberality of M. Bonancieux.

'It will be a great honour to me,' replied the leader of the guards; 'and I accept the offer with gratitude.'

'Here's to you, then, M. —— You have the advantage of me, sir.'

'Boisrenard.'

'M. Boisrenard!'

'I drink to you, sir, but, in return, you have the advantage of me.'

'D'Artagnan.'

'To your health, M. d'Artagnan!'

'And, above all,' said d'Artagnan, as if carried away by his enthusiasm, 'to the health of the king and the cardinal.'

The officer might have doubted d'Artagnan's sincerity had the wine been bad; but it was excellent, and he was satisfied.

'But what devil's own villainy have you done now?' exclaimed Porthos, when the officer had joined his companions, and the four friends found themselves alone. 'For shame! Four musketeers allow a miserable creature, who implored their assistance, to be arrested in the midst of them! and, more than that, a gentleman to tipple with a bailiff!'

'Porthos,' said Aramis, 'Athos has already told you that you are stupid; and I am of his opinion. D'Artagnan, you are a great man; and when you are in M. de Treville's situation, I beg your interest to procure me an abbey.'

'Ah! I am quite in the dark!' said Porthos. 'Do you also, Athos, approve of what d'Artagnan has done?'

'Most assuredly!' said Athos. 'I not only approve of it, but I congratulate him.'

'And now, gentlemen,' said d'Artagnan, not deigning to explain himself to Porthos—' 'All for one—one for all!' this is our motto, is it not?'

'Nevertheless——' said Porthos.

'Stretch out your hand and swear,' cried Athos and Aramis at the same time.

Conquered by the example, but muttering in a low tone, Porthos stretched out his hand, and the four friends repeated with one voice the formal motto dictated by d'Artagnan—

'All for one; and one for all!'

'That is right. Now, retire to your homes,' said d'Artagnan, as if he had never been accustomed to anything but to command others. 'But,' he added, 'be watchful; for remember, that from this moment we are at issue with the cardinal!'

10

A Mousetrap of the Seventeenth Century

THE mousetrap is not a modern invention. As soon as societies had, in establishing themselves, instituted some kind of police, that police in its turn invented mousetraps.

As our readers are perhaps not familiar with the slang of the Rue de Jerusalem, and as it is, although we have been engaged in authorship for fifteen years, the first time that we have used the word in this signification, let us explain to them what a mousetrap is.

When an individual has been arrested, in any house whatever, on suspicion of some crime, his arrest is kept secret; four or five men are placed in ambush in the front room of this house; all who knock are admitted, and also locked in and detained; and, in this manner, at the end of three or four days, they can lay their fingers on all the frequenters of the establishment.

This, reader, is a mousetrap! and into such a one was M. Bonancieux's apartment transformed. Whoever applied there, was seized and examined by the cardinal's people. But as there was a private court leading to the first floor, which d'Artagnan occupied, his visitors were all exempt from this detention. The three musketeers, however, were, in fact, the only visitors he had; and each of these had, by this time, commenced a separate search, but had discovered nothing. Athos had even gone so far as to question M. de Treville—a circumstance which, considering his habitual taciturnity, had greatly surprised his captain. But M. de Treville knew nothing about it; excepting that the last time he had seen either the king, the queen, and the cardinal, the cardinal was very morose, the king very uneasy, and the queen's eyes were red from watching or weeping. But this last circumstance had not attracted much of his notice, as the queen had, since her marriage, both watched and wept frequently.

Furthermore, M. de Treville strongly advised Athos to be active in the king's service, and more particularly in the queen's, and requested him to transmit the advice to his companions.

As to d'Artagnan, he did not stir out of his lodgings. He had converted his room into an observatory. From his own windows he saw everybody who came into the trap; and as he had taken up some squares from the floor, and dug up the deafening, so that nothing but a ceiling separated him from the room below, where the examinations were made, he heard all that passed between the inquisitors and the accused. The interrogatories, which were preceded by a strict search, were almost always in these terms—

'Has Madame Bonancieux entrusted you with anything for her husband or any other person?'

'Has M. Bonancieux entrusted you with anything for his wife, or any one else?'

'Has either of them made any verbal communication to you?'

'If they knew anything, they would not put such questions as these,' said d'Artagnan to himself. 'But what are they trying to find out? Whether the Duke of Buckingham is in Paris at present; and if he has not had, or is not about to have, an interview with the queen?'

D'Artagnan stopped at this idea, which, after all that he had heard, was not without its probability. In the meantime, however, both the mousetrap and the vigilance of d'Artagnan remained in operation.

Just as it was striking nine on the evening of the day after poor Bonancieux's arrest, and just as Athos had left d'Artagnan to go to M. de Treville's, whilst Planchet, who had not made the bed, was about to do so, there was a knocking at the street door, which was immediately opened, and shut again: it was some new prey caught in the trap.

D'Artagnan rushed towards the unpaved part of his room, and laid himself down to listen. In a short time cries were heard, and then groans, which someone endeavoured to stifle.

There was no thought of examination.

'The devil!' said d'Artagnan to himself; 'it seems to me

to be a woman; they are searching her, and she resists; the wretches are using violence!'

In spite of his prudence, d'Artagnan had some trouble to restrain himself from interfering in the scene which was being enacted underneath.

'I tell you, gentlemen, that I am the mistress of the house; I am Madame Bonancieux. I tell you that I am a servant of the queen's!' exclaimed the unfortunate woman.

'Madame Bonancieux!' murmured d'Artagnan; 'shall I be so fortunate as to have found her whom everybody searches for in vain?'

'You are the very person we were waiting for,' replied the officers.

The voice became more and more stifled. Violent struggling made the wainscot rattle. The victim was offering all the resistance that one woman could offer against four men.

'Forgive me, gentlemen, by——' murmured the voice, which then uttered only inarticulate sounds.

'They are gagging her! They are going to abduct her!' ejaculated d'Artagnan, raising himself up with a bound. 'My sword!—Right! it is by my side!—Planchet!'

'Sir.'

'Run, and seek Athos, Porthos, and Aramis; one of the three must be at home; perhaps all. Tell them to arm themselves, and hasten here. Ah, now I remember Athos is with M. de Treville.'

'But where are you going, sir?—Where *are* you going?'

'I shall get down through the window,' said d'Artagnan, 'that I may be there sooner. Replace the squares, sweep the floor, go out by the door, and hasten whither I have told you.'

'Oh! sir, you will be killed!' cried Planchet.

'Hold your tongue, idiot!' exclaimed d'Artagnan.

Then, grasping the window-sill, he dropped from the first storey, which was fortunately not high, without giving himself even a scratch. He then went immediately and knocked at the door, muttering—

'I in my turn am going to be caught in the mouse-trap; but woe betide the cats who shall deal with such a mouse!'

Scarcely had the knocker sounded beneath the young man's hand, ere the tumult ceased, and footsteps approached. The door was opened, and d'Artagnan, armed with his naked sword, sprang into the apartment of M. Bonancieux. The door, doubtless moved by a spring, closed automatically behind him.

Then might those who yet inhabited the unfortunate house of M. Bonancieux, as well as the nearest neighbours, hear loud outcries, stampings, and the clashing of swords and the continual crash of furniture. After a moment more, those who had looked from their windows to learn the cause of this surprising noise, might see the door open, and four men clothed in black, not merely go out, but fly like frightened crows, leaving on the ground, and at the corners of the house, their feathers and wings, that is to say, portions of their coats and fragments of their cloaks.

D'Artagnan had come off victorious, without much difficulty, it must be confessed; for only one of the officers was armed, and he had only gone through a form of defence. It is quite true that the other three had endeavoured to knock down the young man with chairs, stools, and crockery, but two or three scratches from the Gascon's sword had scared them. Ten minutes had sufficed for their defeat, and d'Artagnan had remained master of the field of battle.

The neighbours, who had opened their windows with the indifference habitual to the inhabitants of Paris at that season of perpetual disturbances and riots, closed them again when they saw the four men escape; their instinct told them no more was to be seen for the time. Besides, it was getting late; and then, as well as now, people went to bed early in the quarter of the Luxembourg.

When d'Artagnan was left alone with Madame Bonancieux, he turned towards her. The poor woman was reclining in an easy chair, almost senseless. D'Artagnan examined her with a rapid glance.

She was a charming woman, about twenty-two or twenty-three years of age; with blue eyes, a nose slightly turned up, beautiful teeth, and a complexion of intermingled rose and opal. Here, however, ended the charms which might have confounded her with a lady of high birth. Her hands were white, but not delicately formed; and her feet did not indicate a woman of quality. Fortunately, d'Artagnan was not of an age to be nice in these matters.

Whilst d'Artagnan was examining Madame Bonancieux, and had got, as we have said, to her feet, he saw on the ground a fine cambric handkerchief, which, naturally, he picked up; and, at the corner of it, he discovered the same cipher that he had seen on the handkerchief which had nearly caused him and Aramis to cut one another's throats. Since that time d'Artagnan had mistrusted all coronetted handkerchiefs; and he now put that which he had picked up into Madame Bonancieux's pocket, without saying a word. At that moment Madame Bonancieux recovered her senses. She opened her eyes, looked around her in affright, and saw that the room was empty, and that she was alone with her deliverer. She immediately held out her hands to him, with a smile—and Madame Bonancieux had the most charming smile in the world.

'Ah! sir.' said she, 'it is you who have saved me; allow me to thank you!'

'Madame,' replied d'Artagnan, 'I have only done what any gentleman would have done in my situation. You owe me no thanks.'

'Yes, yes, sir, I do; and I hope to prove to you that this service has not been for naught. But what did these men, whom I at first took for robbers, want with me? and why is not M. Bonancieux here?'

'Madame, these men were far more dangerous than any robbers would have been, for they are agents of the cardinal; and as for your husband, M. Bonancieux, he is not here, because he was taken yesterday to the Bastile.'

'My husband in the Bastile!' cried Madame Bonancieux. 'Oh, my God! what can he have done, poor, dear man! Why, he is innocence itself!'

And something like a smile glanced across the yet alarmed countenance of the young woman.

'As to what he has been doing, madame,' said d'Artagnan, 'I believe that his only crime consists in having at the same time the good fortune and the misfortune of being your husband.'

'Then, sir, you know?'

'I know that you were carried off, madame.'

'But by whom? do you know that? Oh, if you know, pray tell me!'

'By a man about forty or forty-five years of age, with dark hair, a brown complexion, and a scar on the left temple.'

'Just so, just so: but his name?'

'Ah! his name—I don't know it myself.'

'And did my husband know that I had been carried off?'

'He had been informed of it by a letter sent him by the ravisher himself.'

'And does he suspect,' demanded Madame Bonancieux, with some confusion, 'the cause of this abduction?'

'He attributes it, I believe, to some political cause.'

'At first I doubted whether it was so, but now, as I think, he does; and so my dear M. Bonancieux did not mistrust me for a single instant?'

'Ah! so far from that, madame, he was too proud of your prudence and your love.'

A second smile, almost imperceptible, glided over the rosy lips of the beautiful young woman.

'But,' continued d'Artagnan, 'how did you make your escape?'

'I profited by a moment in which I was left alone; and as I learned this morning the cause of my abduction, by the help of my sheets I got out of the window, and hurried here, where I expected to find my husband.'

'To place yourself under his protection?'

'Oh, no! poor dear man! I knew that he was incapable of protecting me; but, as he might be of some service to us, I wished to put him on his guard.'

'Against what?'

'Alas! that is not my secret; and I dare not tell it to you.'

'Besides,' said d'Artagnan—'(pardon me, madame, if, protector as I am, I remind you of prudence)—besides, I think that we are scarcely in a situation suitable for confidences. The men whom I have put to flight will return reinforced, and if they find us here, we shall be lost. I have sent to summon three of my friends, but it is uncertain whether they may be at home!'

'Yes! yes! you are right,' said Madame Bonancieux, in alarm; 'let us fly: let us escape!'

And seizing d'Artagnan by his arm, she eagerly drew him along.

'But whither shall we fly? where shall we escape to?' said d'Artagnan.

'Let us get away from this place first, and then, having got clear of it, we shall see.'

Without taking the trouble to shut the door, the two young people hastily passed down the Rue des Fossoyeurs, crossed the Rue des Fosses Monsieur le Prince, and did not stop until they reached the Place de St. Sulpice.

'And now, what next?' inquired d'Artagnan; 'and whither would you like me to conduct you?'

'I confess that I scarcely know whither,' said Madame Bonancieux. 'I had intended, through my husband, to intimate my escape to M. de la Porte, so that the latter might tell us exactly what has happened at the Louvre within the last three days, and whether there would be any danger in my presenting myself there.'

'But I,' said d'Artagnan, 'can go and inform M. de la Porte.'

'Undoubtedly; yet there is one difficulty. M. Bonancieux is known at the Louvre, and would be allowed to enter; whilst you, not being known, would not be admitted.'

'Nonsense!' said d'Artagnan: 'there is doubtless a porter at some wicket of the Louvre who is devoted to you, and who, thanks to some countersign——'

Madame Bonancieux looked earnestly at the young man. 'And if I trusted you with this countersign,' said she, 'would you undertake to forgot it as soon as you had made use of it?'

'On my word of honour! on the faith of a gentleman!' said d'Artagnan, with that accent of truth which never can mislead.

'Well, I believe you! You look like a man of honour, and your fortune perhaps may depend on your devotion.'

'I will perform, without any promises, and conscientiously, whatever I can to serve the king, and to be acceptable to the queen,' said d'Artagnan; 'use me, therefore, as a friend!'

'But what is to become of me in the meantime?'

'Have you no acquaintance, to whose house M. de la Porte can come for you?'

'No, I would rather not trust to any one!'

'Wait,' said d'Artagnan; 'we are now just by Athos's door; yes, this is the best way!'

'And who is Athos?'

'A friend of mine.'

'But, if he is at home, and sees me?'

'But he is not there, and I will take away the key when I have placed you in his apartment.'

'Suppose he should return?'

'He will not return; besides, if he should, he will be told that I have brought a woman here, and that she is now in his apartment.'

'But don't you see this will compromise me very much?'

'What need you care! no one knows you. Besides, we are not in a position to be particular.'

'Well, let us go to your friend's house, then; where does he live?'

'In the Rue Ferou—two steps from here.'

'Come, then.' And the two proceeded on their way. As d'Artagnan had foreseen, Athos was not at home; so taking the key, which they were in the habit of giving to him as a friend of the musketeer, he ascended the stairs, and introduced Madame Bonancieux into the little apartment which we have already described.

'You are now at home,' said he. 'Lock the door inside, and do not open it to any one, unless you hear three knocks—thus;' and he tapped three times—two taps together, pretty hard, and, after a short interval, a gentler tap.

'That will do,' said Madame Bonancieux; 'and now let me give you my instructions.'

'I am all attention.'

'Present yourself at the postern of the Louvre, on the side of the Rue de l'Echelle; and ask for Germain.'

'Very well; and what next?'

'He will ask you what you want; you must answer by these words—'Tours and Brussels'—and he will immediately listen to your commands.'

'And what shall I tell him to do?'

'To go and find M. de la Porte, the queen's valet-de-chambre.'

'And when M. de la Porte has come?'

'You will send him to me.'

'Very well. But where, and how, shall I see you again?'

'Do you feel particularly anxious to see me again?'

'Particularly.'

'Well, then, leave that to my care; and be at ease.'

'I rely upon your word.'

'And quite right.'

D'Artagnan took leave of Madame Bonancieux, with the most amorous glance that he could possibly concentrate upon her charming little person; and whilst he was descending the stairs, he heard the door behind him double locked. In two bounds he was at the Louvre; and, as he entered the small door in the Rue de l'Echelle, it struck ten; so that all the events we have just related had transpired within half an hour.

Everything happened just as Madame Bonancieux had predicted. Germain heard the watchword with a bow, and in ten minutes de la Porte was in the porter's lodge; and in two words d'Artagnan told him what had occurred, and where Madame Bonancieux was to be found. La Porte made himself certain of the address by having it twice repeated, and then hurried away. But he had scarcely taken ten steps, before he returned.

'Young man,' said he, 'let me give you some good counsel.'

'What is it?'

'You may possibly get into some trouble on account of this affair.'

'Do you think so?'

'I do! Have you any friend whose clock is slow?'

'Suppose I have?'

'Go and pay him a visit, that he may be able to bear witness that you were in his company at half-past nine. In law, that is what is called an *alibi*.'

D'Artagnan thought the advice prudent. He therefore took to his heels, and reached M. de Treville's; but, instead of entering the drawing-room, with the rest of the company, he asked to be admitted into the cabinet, and as he was one of the habitual frequenters of the hotel, no objection was made to this; and M. de Treville was soon informed that his young compatriot, having something of importance to communicate, solicited a private interview.

In five minutes M. de Treville was there, and asked d'Artagnan what he could do for him, and to what he was indebted for a visit at such a late hour?

'Forgive me, sir,' said d'Artagnan (who had taken advantage of the moment he was left alone, to put the clock back three quarters of an hour), 'but I thought, as it was only twenty-five minutes past nine, it was not yet too late to wait upon you.'

'Twenty-five minutes past nine!' exclaimed M. de Treville, looking at the clock, 'it is impossible!'

'Look for yourself, sir,' said d'Artagnan, 'the clock shows it.'

'You are right,' replied M. de Treville: 'I should have thought it was later. But what can I do for you?'

Then d'Artagnan entered into a long story about the queen; expressing all the fears that he entertained upon her majesty's account, and recounting all that he had heard about the cardinal's designs against Buckingham; and this with a degree of tranquillity and consistency by which M. de Treville was the more readily duped, inasmuch as he had himself, as we have already said, remarked that something fresh was stirring between the cardinal, the king, and the queen.

Just as the clock was striking ten, d'Artagnan arose, and took his leave of M. de Treville, who thanked him for his information, expressed on him an incessant earnestness in the service of the king and queen, and returned to his saloon.

But d'Artagnan remembered, at the bottom of the stairs, that he had forgotten his cane; he therefore hastened up again, re-entered the cabinet, and with one touch of his finger put the clock to its right time, so that it might not be seen the next day to have been wrong: then, satisfied that he had a witness there to prove his *alibi*, he again descended the stairs, and soon found himself in the street.

II

The Intrigue Becomes Confused

WHEN his visit to M. de Treville was ended, d'Artagnan took, in pensive mood, the longest road to return to his own home.

But what were the meditations which thus led him from his way; contemplating, with successive sighs and smiles, the stars that glittered in the sky.

Alas! he was intent on Madame Bonancieux. To an apprentice musketeer, the charms of that young person raised her almost into an ideal of love. Pretty, mysterious, and initiated into all the court secrets, which reflected so much charming seriousness over her seductive features, he supposed her, also, to be not wholly unimpassioned, which is an irresistible attraction to novices in these engagements of the heart. He felt, moreover, that he had delivered her from the hands of miscreants who wished to search and maltreat her; and this important service had prepossessed her with a sentiment of gratitude towards him, which might easily be made to take a character of greater tenderness.

So rapidly do our dreams travel on imagination's wings, that d'Artagnan already fancied himself accosted by some messenger from Madame Bonancieux, handing to him an appointment for an interview, or a diamond or a chain of gold. We have already intimated that the young cavaliers were not then ashamed of accepting presents from their king; and we may add, that, in those times of easy morality, they were not more scrupulous in respect of their mistresses, and that these latter almost always conferred upon them some precious and durable memorials, as though they were endeavouring to overcome the instability of their sentiments by the solidity of gifts.

Men did not then blush at owing their advancement to women; and we might refer to many amongst the heroes of that age of gallantry, who would neither have won their spurs at first, nor their battles afterwards, but for the better or worse furnished purse which some mistress had suspended at their saddle-bow.

Now, d'Artagnan possessed nothing. His provincial hesitation—that superficial varnish, and ephemeral bloom, that down on the peach—had evaporated in the storm of somewhat unorthodox advice which the three musketeers had given to their friend. According to the curious customs of the time, he had come to look upon himself as being just as much engaged in a campaign whilst he was at Paris, as though he had been in Flanders. Spaniard there, woman here: yet, in either case, there was an enemy to overcome, and contributions to raise.

But let us not disguise that the young Gascon was, at present, influenced by a nobler and more disinterested feeling. The mercer had confessed to him that he was rich; and it was easy to infer that, with a simpleton like Bonancieux, the wife would be the keeper of the purse. But nothing of this kind had contributed to that sentiment which the sight of Madame Bonancieux had inspired, and selfishness had been almost disregarded in the dawning love which had arisen from his interview. We say almost—for the assurance that a young, lovely, charming and witty woman is rich also, has a tendency, not to diminish, but rather to corroborate, this growth of sentiment. In easy circumstances, there are a crowd of aristocratic cares and caprices which accord well with beauty. A white and fine stocking, a silken dress, a lace kerchief, a pretty little shoe, a becoming ribband, do not make an ugly woman pretty, but they make a pretty woman irresistible; whilst her hands, moreover, are sure to be the gainers by her wealth; for the hands—in women, especially—must remain idle to be beautiful.

Now, as the reader very well knows—for we have made no secret of the state of his finances—d'Artagnan was not a man of large fortune. It is true that he quite expected to become so, at some future time; but the date which he had himself fixed on for that happy transformation, was as yet far distant. In the meantime, what sorrow would it be to see the woman whom one idolizes sighing for the thousand trifles in which so much of the happiness of womankind consists, and to be unable to procure them for her. But when the woman is rich, although the lover is poor, the gifts which he cannot present, she can provide for herself; and then, although it may most frequently be with the husband's money that these enjoyments are obtained, it is not commonly to this husband that the gratitude is shown.

Thus disposed to become the most passionate of admirers, d'Artagnan had not ceased to be a devoted friend. In the midst of his more tender feelings towards the mercer's wife, he was not forgetful of his companions. The pretty Madame Bonancieux was the very woman to take on an excursion to the plain of Saint Denis, or the fair at St. Germain, in company with Athos, Porthos, and Aramis, to whom he should be so proud to show his charming conquest. And then—as d'Artagnan had happened to remark of late—after a long walk one gets hungry; and they would have some of those pleasant little dinners, during which one touches on this side the hand of a friend, on that the foot of a mistress. Finally, in moments of emergency, in great extremities, might it not be his happiness to be the saviour of his friends?

But what of M. Bonancieux, whom d'Artagnan had given over to the keeping of the officers; disowning him aloud, whilst, in a whisper, he assured him of his care? We must confess to our readers, that d'Artagnan had never thought of him at all; or, if he did think of him, it was merely to congratulate himself, that he was very well where he was, wherever that might be. Love is the most selfish of all our passions.

Nevertheless, let our readers take comfort: though d'Artagnan forgets his landlord, or pretends to forget him, under the excuse of not knowing where he has been taken, we have not forgotten him, and do know where he is. But, for the present, let us act like the amorous Gascon. As for the worthy mercer, we will return to him by and by.

D'Artagnan, whilst meditating on his future love, and conversing with the night, and smiling on the stars, proceeded along the Rue de Cherche Midi, or Chasse Midi, as it was then called. Being in Aramis's neighbourhood, he thought he might as well pay him a visit, to explain why he had sent Planchet with the invitation to come immediately to the mousetrap.

If Planchet had found Aramis at home, the latter had probably hastened to the Rue des Fossoyeurs, and, finding nobody there but his other two friends, perhaps, they would all have been in ignorance of what the summons meant. This dilemma needed some explanation; or, at least, so said d'Artagnan aloud.

But, in his inner soul, he thought that this call would give him an opportunity of talking of the pretty Madame Bonancieux, with whom his mind, if not his heart, was already quite occupied. It is not in regard to a first love that we must look for discretion. The joy with which such a love is attended is so exuberant, that it must overflow, or it would suffocate us.

For the last two hours Paris had been dark and nearly deserted. Eleven o'clock was striking from all the clocks of the Faubourg St. Germain; the time was mild, and d'Artagnan was passing down a small street situated on the ground where the Rue d'Assas now stands, where the air was redolent of odours which were borne on the wind along the Rue de Vaugiraud, from gardens that the evening dews and the gentle gales refreshed. Afar off, though deadened by substantial shutters, was heard the revelry of the wine shops which were scattered over the flat quarters. Having reached the end of this street, d'Artagnan turned to the left. The house where Aramis lived was situated between the Rue Cassette and the Rue Servandoni.

D'Artagnan had already passed by the Rue Cassette, and could just perceive the door of his friend's house, embosomed amidst sycamores and clematis, when he saw something like a shadow which came out of the Rue Servandoni. This something was enveloped in a cloak, and d'Artagnan at first thought that it was a man; but from the smallness of its size, the irresolution of its manner, and its impeded step, he soon became convinced that it must be a woman. And, moreover, this woman, as though she was uncertain of the house she sought for, lifted up her eyes to examine, stopped, turned back, and then retraced her steps. D'Artagnan was at a loss.

'Suppose I should go and proffer my services!' thought

he. 'By her manner it is evident that she is young, and perhaps she is pretty. Oh, yes! But then a woman who runs about the streets at this hour, seldom goes out except to meet her lover. Plague! if I should interrupt an appointment, it would be but a bad kind of introduction.'

The young woman, however, still came forward, counting the windows and the houses. This was not indeed a long or difficult operation. There were but three hotels in that part of the street, and but two windows looking upon the thoroughfare; of which one was that of a pavilion, parallel to the pavilion of Aramis, and the other that of Aramis himself.

'By Jove!' said d'Artagnan to himself, as he suddenly remembered the theologian's niece—'by Jove! it would be droll if this wandering dove is looking for my friend's house. But, upon my soul, it seems very like it. Ah, my dear Aramis! I will be satisfied about it once and for all.'

Making himself as small as possible, d'Artagnan concealed himself in the most obscure part of the street, near a stone bench placed at the back of a niche.

The young woman continued to advance; for, besides the lightness of her step which had betrayed her, a slight, small cough had also denoted a gentle voice. D'Artagnan concluded that this cough was a signal.

Nevertheless, whether this cough had been answered by some corresponding signal which had ended the uncertainties of her nocturnal search, or whether, without any such external aid, she perceived herself to have found her journey's end, the lady advanced resolutely, and knocked three times, at equal intervals, and with a bent finger, on the shutter of Aramis's window.

'It is really at Aramis's house,' muttered d'Artagnan. 'Ah, Mr. Hypocrite, I catch you studying theology!'

Scarcely had the three taps been given, before the inner casement opened, and a light appeared.

'Ah, ah!' said the listener, 'not at the door, but the window! Ah! ah! the visit was expected. Come, the shutter will be opened presently, and the lady will get in by escalade. Good!'

But, to his great astonishment, the shutter continued closed; and, what was more, the light, which had flashed for an instant, disappeared, and all became dark again.

D'Artagnan thought that this could not last, and continued to watch with all his eyes and ears. He was right;

In a few seconds, two knocks were heard from the inside; and when the young woman of the street answered by one knock, the shutter opened.

It may be judged if d'Artagnan did not look and listen eagerly.

Unfortunately, the light had been removed into some other room; but the eyes of the young man were accustomed to the darkness Besides, it is said that the eyes of Gascons, like those of cats, have the faculty of seeing in the night.

D'Artagnan was able, therefore, to see the young woman take from her pocket something white, which she unfolded quickly, and which took the form of a pocket handkerchief, and she then drew the attention of the person she addressed to the corner of the object she unfolded.

This reminded d'Artagnan of the handkerchief he had found at the feet of Madame Bonancieux, which, also, had recalled to his recollection the one that he had drawn from under the foot of Aramis.

What the deuce, then, could this handkerchief mean?

Situated as he was, d'Artagnan could not see the countenance of Aramis—we say Aramis, because the young man had no doubt that it was his friend who was conversing from the inside with the lady on the outside. His curiosity, therefore, overcame his prudence; and, profiting by the earnest attention which the sight of the handkerchief excited in the two persons whom we have described, he left his place of concealment, and, quickly as lightning, yet with cautious step, placed himself near a corner of the wall, from which his eye could completely overlook the inside of Aramis's apartment.

On reaching this spot, he was scarcely able to restrain an exclamation of surprise. It was not Aramis who was conferring with the midnight visitor, but a woman. D'Artagnan could just discern enough to recognise the general aspect of her vesture, but not to distinguish her features. At that moment the woman in the room drew a handkerchief from her own pocket, and exchanged it for the one which had been shown to her. A few words were then pronounced by the two women, the shutter was closed, and the woman in the street returned, and, lowering the hood of her cloak passed within four paces of d'Artagnan. But her precaution had been taken too late; he had already recognised Madame Bonancieux.

Madame Bonancieux! The suspicion had already crossed

his mind when he saw her take the handkerchief from her pocket; but what probability was there that Madame Bonancieux, who had sent for M. de la Porte, in order that he might conduct her to the Louvre, should be coursing through the streets of Paris at half-past eleven at night, at the hazard of being carried off a second time? It must unquestionably be on some important affair; and what affair is of importance to a woman of twenty-five but love?

But was it on her own account, or that of some other person, that she exposed herself to this risk? This was the inward doubt of the young man, whom the demon of jealousy was now tormenting, as though he had been an acknowledged lover. To satisfy himself as to where Madame Bonancieux was going, there was, in fact, one very simple way, which was to follow her. So simple, indeed, did this course appear, that d'Artagnan adopted it naturally, and as it were by instinct.

But, at the sight of the young man who moved from the wall, like a statue escaping from its alcove, and at the sound of his steps behind her, Madame Bonancieux uttered a faint scream, and fled.

D'Artagnan ran after her. It was no great difficulty for him to catch a woman encumbered by a large cloak. He overtook her, in fact, before she had gone a third of the length of the street. The poor woman was exhausted, not by fatigue, but terror; and when d'Artagnan put his hand upon her shoulder, she sunk upon one knee, exclaiming in a suffocated voice—

'I will die before you learn anything.'

D'Artagnan raised her up, by placing his arm round her waist, but, perceiving by her weight that she was upon the point of fainting, he hastened to encourage her by protestations of devotion. These protestations were of no avail against Madame Bonancieux, for they may easily be made with the most mischievous intentions in the world; but the voice was everything. The young woman thought that she recognised that voice. She opened her eyes, threw one glance upon the man who had so frightened her, and, seeing that it was d'Artagnan, gave utterance to a cry of joy.

'Oh! it is you, it is you,' said she. 'God be thanked!'

'Yes, it is I,' said d'Artagnan, 'whom God has sent to guard you.'

'And was it with this intent that you followed me,' asked

the young woman, with a smile full of coquetry; for all her fears had vanished, and her love of badinage had resumed its ascendancy, on the instant that she recognised a friend in him whom she had dreaded as a foe.

'No,' replied d'Artagnan. 'No, I confess that it is chance which put me on your track. I saw a woman knocking at the window of one of my friends.'

'Of one of your friends!' interrupted Madame Bonancieux.

'Yes, certainly! Aramis is one of my intimates.'

'Aramis! who is he?'

'Come, now, do you pretend to tell me that you do not know Aramis?'

'It is the first time that I ever heard his name.'

'Then it is the first time that you have visited this house?'

'Yes, indeed!'

'And you did not know that a young man occupied it?'

'No.'

'A musketeer?'

'By no means.'

'Then it was not him that you came to look for?'

'Most assuredly not! Besides, you must have plainly seen that the person whom I talked to was a woman.'

'That is true; but then this woman is one of Aramis's friends!'

'I know nothing about that.'

'Why, she lodges at his house.'

'That is not my affair.'

'But who is she?'

'Oh! that is not my secret.'

'My dear Madame Bonancieux, you are very charming, but you are at the same time the most mysterious creature.'

'Is that to my loss?'

'No; on the contrary, it lends you enchantment!'

'As that is the case, give me your arm.'

'With great pleasure; what now?'

'Now take care of me.'

'Where to?'

'Where I am going.'

'But where may that be?'

'You will see, since you will leave me at the door.'

'May I wait for you there?'

'That would be useless.'

'Then you will return alone?'

'Possibly.'

'But the person who will accompany you afterwards—will it be a man or a woman?'

'I do not know yet.'

'But I will find out.'

'And how so?'

'I will wait to see you come out.'

'In that case, adieu!'

'But, why?'

'I do not want you!'

'But you claimed my protection.'

'I claimed the assistance of a gentleman. and not the vigilance of a spy.'

'You are severe.'

'How would you call those who follow people who don't want them?'

'Indiscreet!'

'The term is too mild!'

'Come, madame, I see that one must obey you.'

'Why deprive yourself of the merit of doing so at once?'

'Is there none in my repentance?'

'But do you sincerely repent?'

'I don't know that myself. But I do know that I promise to do just what you wish, if you will let me accompany you where you are going.'

'And you will leave me afterwards?'

'Yes.'

'Without awaiting my exit?'

'Certainly.'

'On your word of honour?'

'On the word of a gentleman!'

'Then take my arm, and let us get on.'

D'Artagnan offered his arm, which Madame Bonancieux, half laughing and half trembling, accepted, and they reached the top of the Rue de la Harpe; but the young woman appeared to hesitate there, as she had hesitated before at the Rue Vaugirard. Nevertheless, by certain marks, she appeared to recognise a door, which she approached.

'Now, sir,' said she, 'it is here that my business calls me. I return you a thousand thanks for your good company, which has saved me from all the dangers to which I should have been exposed alone; but the time is now come for you to keep your word. You must leave me here.'

'And will you be exposed to no danger in returning?'

'I shall only have to fear robbers.'

'Is that nothing?'

'What could they take from me? I have not a farthing in my possession!'

'You forget that beautiful embroidered handkerchief, with the arms on it.'

'Which?'

'That which I found at your feet, and replaced in your pocket.'

'Silence! Silence! you imprudent man! Would you ruin me?'

'You see now that there is still some danger, since one word makes you tremble, and you confess that if this word was heard you would be ruined. Come now, madame,' continued d'Artagnan, seizing her hand, 'be more generous; put some confidence in me; have you not read in my eyes that my heart is full of sympathy and devotion?'

'Yes,' said Madame Bonancieux; 'and do but ask me for my own secrets, and I will trust you with them all; but those of others are a different matter.'

'Very well!' replied d'Artagnan, 'then I will find them out. Since these secrets have an influence on your life, it is necessary that they should become mine also.'

'Have a care!' exclaimed the young woman, in a tone of seriousness which made d'Artagnan shudder involuntarily. 'Oh! do not interfere in anything that concerns me; do not seek to aid me in any of my undertakings;—avoid them, I beseech you, in the name of the interest that you feel for me, and in the name of that service which you rendered to me, and which I never shall forget whilst my life lasts! Let me advise you rather to think of me no more; let my existence be obliterated from your mind; let me be to you as though you had never chanced to see me.'

'Would you like Aramis to do the same, madame?' asked d'Artagnan, full of jealousy.

'This makes the second or third time that you have mentioned that name, sir, although I have already told you that I do not know the owner of it.'

'You do not know the man at whose window-shutters you went to knock? Come, madame, you must think me credulous indeed!'

'Confess that it is to keep me talking here, that you have invented this tale, and this person.'

'I invent nothing, madame—nothing. I am telling the exact truth!'

'And you say that one of your friends lives in that house?'

'I say it, and I repeat it for the third time—that house is inhabited by a friend of mine, and that friend is Aramis.'

'All this will be explained by and by,' murmured the young woman; 'and now, sir, be silent.'

'If you could see into my heart,' said d'Artagnan, 'you would discover so much curiosity, that you would have pity on me: and so much love, that you would directly satisfy my curiosity. You ought not to distrust those who love you!'

'You come quickly to love, sir,' said the young woman, shaking her head.

'It is because love has come quickly on me, and for the first time; and I am not yet twenty years of age.'

The young woman stole a glance at him.

'Listen,' continued d'Artagnan; 'I am already on the track: three months ago I was near fighting a duel with Aramis on account of a handkerchief like that which you showed the lady who was at his house; it was on account of a handkerchief marked in the same manner, I am positive.'

'Sir,' said the young woman, 'you really bore me, I declare, with these questions.'

'But you, madame, prudent as you are, suppose you were arrested with this handkerchief upon you, and the handkerchief was seized, would you not be compromised?'

'How so? Are not the initials my own—C. B.—Constance Bonancieux?'

'Or, Camille de Bois Tracy.'

'Silence, sir! Again I say, silence! Oh, since the dangers which I run do not deter you, think of those you may run yourself.'

'I?'

'Yes, you. There is the danger of imprisonment and death in knowing me.'

'Then I will never leave you!'

'Sir,' said the young woman, in a tone of supplication, clasping her hands as she spoke; 'in the name of heaven, by the honour of a soldier, by the courtesy of a gentleman, I implore you to leave me. See! it is now striking twelve, the very hour at which I am expected.'

'Madame,' said the young man, bowing, 'I can refuse nothing solicited in those terms. Be reassured; I leave you.'

'But you will not follow—will not watch me?'

'No, I shall return home immediately.'

'Ah! I was convinced that you were an honourable man!'

exclaimed Madame Bonancieux, offering one of her hands to him, as she placed the other on the knocker of a small door, which was well-nigh concealed in a recess.

D'Artagnan seized the hand which was offered to him, and kissed it eagerly.

'Alas!' exclaimed d'Artagnan, with that unpolished simplicity which women sometimes prefer to the delicacies of politeness, because it illuminates the depths of thought, and proves that feeling is more powerful than reason, 'I wish I had never seen you!'

'Well!' said Madame Bonancieux, in a tone almost affectionate, and pressing the hand which held hers, 'well! I will not say the same as you do; that which is lost to-day may not be lost for ever. Who knows whether, when I am freed from my present embarrassments, I may not satisfy your curiosity?'

'And do you make the same promise regarding my love?' asked the overjoyed d'Artagnan.

'Oh! I dare give no promises in that respect. It must depend upon the sentiments with which you may inspire me.'

'But, at present, madame?'

'At present, sir, I have not got beyond gratitude.'

'Alas! you are too charming; and only take advantage of my love.'

'No, I take advantage of your generosity, that's all. But, believe me, with some people, nothing can be wholly lost.'

'You make me the happiest of men. Oh! do not forget this evening, and this promise?'

'Be assured, I will remember everything at the right time and place. But now go; go, in heaven's name! I was expected at midnight, and am behind my time.'

'By five minutes.'

'But, under certain circumstances, five minutes are five ages.'

'Yes! when one loves.'

'Well, who has told you that this is not a love-affair?'

'It is a man who expects you!' cried d'Artagnan; 'a man!'

'There, now, the discussion is about to be renewed,' cried Madame Bonancieux, with a half smile, which was not altogether exempt from impatience.

'No! I am going. I trust you; I wish to have all the merit of my devotion, even if I am a fool for it! Adieu! madame, adieu.'

Then, as though he felt himself too weak to relinquish the fair hand he held but by a shock, he hastily ran off, whilst

Madame Bonancieux rapped three times at the door, slowly and regularly, as she had before done at the window-shutter.

At the corner of the street he turned, but the door had been opened and closed again, and the mercer's pretty wife had disappeared.

D'Artagnan proceeded on his way. He had promised Madame Bonancieux not to watch her; and, had his life depended on a knowledge of the place that she was going to, or the person who went with her, he would still have gone home, as he had promised to do. In five minutes he was in the Rue des Fossoyeurs.

'Poor Athos,' said he, 'he will not understand this. He will have fallen asleep waiting for me, or he will have returned home, and will have learned that there has been a woman there. A woman at *his* house! After all,' continued d'Artagnan, 'there certainly was one at Aramis's. All this is very strange, and I shall be extremely curious to know how it will end.'

'Badly, sir, badly,' replied a voice, which the young man recognised as that of Planchet, for in soliloquising aloud, in the manner of persons who are deeply occupied, he had entered the passage, at the bottom of which was his own staircase.

'How, badly! what are you saying, you fool?' said d'Artagnan, 'and what has happened?'

'All sorts of misfortunes.'

'What misfortunes?'

'In the first place, M. Athos is arrested.'

'Arrested! Athos arrested! and what for?'

'He was found in your lodgings, and they mistook him for you.'

'And by whom has he been arrested?'

'By the guard which was brought by the men in black whom you put to flight.'

'Why did he not give his name? Why not say that he was not concerned in this affair?'

'He was very careful not to do that, sir. On the contrary, he came near me and said—"Thy master wants his liberty just now, and I do not need mine; since he knows all, and I know nothing. They will believe him to be in custody, and that will give him time; in three days I will declare who I am, and they will be obliged to let me go."'

'Brave Athos! noble heart!' muttered d'Artagnan. 'I recognise him well in that! And what did the officers do?'

'Four of them took him either to the Bastile or to Fort

l'Eveque; and two remained with the men in black, rummaging everywhere, and carrying away all your papers. The other two mounted guard at the door whilst all this was doing; and at last they went away, leaving the house empty and the door open.'

'And Porthos and Aramis?'

'I could not find them; they have not been.'

'But they may come at any moment, for you left word that I was waiting for them.'

'Yes, sir.'

'Well, then, do not stir from here. If they should come, tell them what has happened, and that they must wait for me at the Pine-apple Tavern. There might be some danger here; the house may be watched. I will run to M. de Treville's, to tell him all this, and then will rejoin them there.'

'Very well, sir,' said Planchet.

'But you will remain? you will not be afraid,' said d'Artagnan, turning back a step to encourage his lackey.

'Be easy, sir,' said Planchet; 'you do not know me yet. I am brave when I please to set about it; the great thing is to get me in the right mind. Besides, I come from Picardy.'

'Then it is all settled,' said d'Artagnan; 'you will rather die than desert your post.'

'Yes, sir; and I will stick at nothing to prove my attachment to you.'

'Good,' said d'Artagnan to himself; 'it is plain that the method I have followed with this lad is decidedly a proper one. I will adopt it henceforth on every occasion.'

And as fast as his legs, which were already somewhat fatigued, could carry him, he ran towards the Rue de Colombier.

M. de Treville was not at home. His company was on guard at the Louvre; and he was at the Louvre with it.

It was necessary, however, to see M. de Treville. It was important that he should be informed of these events. D'Artagnan determined, therefore, to obtain an entrance at the Louvre. His uniform, as one of M. de Essarts's guards, ought to be a passport for admission.

He therefore went down the Rue des Petits-Augustins, and along the Quai to reach the Pont-Neuf. He had half a mind to cross the ferry; but on reaching the side of the river he mechanically put his hand into his pocket, and found that he had not enough to pay the ferryman.

When he reached the top of the Rue Guénégaud, he saw

two persons, whose appearance struck him, coming out of the Rue Dauphine. They were a man and a woman. The woman resembled in figure Madame Bonancieux; and the man had such a look of Aramis that he might be mistaken for him. Besides, the woman had on the black mantle which d'Artagnan still seemed to see delineated on the shutter in the Rue Vaugirard, and on the door in the Rue de la Harpe. Moreover, the man wore the uniform of the musketeers.

The hood of the woman was lowered, and the man held his handkerchief before his face. This double precaution showed that they were both anxious to escape recognition.

They went over the bridge, and this was also d'Artagnan's road, as he was going to the Louvre; he therefore followed them.

Scarcely, however, had he taken twenty steps, before he was convinced that the woman was Madame Bonancieux, and the man Aramis.

At the very instant he felt fermenting in his heart all the suspicious torments of jealousy.

He was doubly betrayed; betrayed both by his friend, and by her whom he had already loved as a mistress.

Madame Bonancieux had sworn to him that she did not know Aramis; and a quarter of an hour after she had made this oath he found her hanging on his arm.

D'Artagnan did not reflect that he had only known the mercer's pretty wife during the last three hours; that she only owed him a little gratitude for having delivered her from the men in black, who wished to carry her away; and that she had made him no promise. He looked upon himself as an outraged lover; as deceived, and laughed at; and the flush of anger passed over his face, as he resolved to ascertain the truth.

The young couple perceived that they were followed, and they increased their haste. D'Artagnan, however, had made his determination; he passed by them, and then returned towards them just as they were opposite the Samaritan, which was lighted by a lamp that threw its radiance over all that part of the bridge.

D'Artagnan stopped in front of them, and they stopped also.

'What do you want, sir?' asked the musketeer, recoiling a step, and in a foreign accent, which proved to d'Artagnan that he had at least deceived himself in one of his conjectures.

'It is not Aramis!' exclaimed d'Artagnan.

'No, sir, it is not Aramis; and as I find by your exclamation that you mistook me for another, I excuse you.'

'Excuse me indeed!' said d'Artagnan.

'Yes,' replied the unknown; 'now let me pass on, since it is not with me that you have anything to do.'

'You are right, sir,' said d'Artagnan; 'it is not with you that I have anything to settle, it is with the lady.'

'With the lady! You do not even know her,' exclaimed the stranger.

'You are mistaken, sir. I do know her.'

'Ah!' said Madame Bonancieux, in a reproachful tone; 'I had your word of honour as a soldier, your promise as a gentleman, and I hoped I might have trusted to them.'

'And I,' said D'Artagnan, in confusion, 'I had your promise.'

'Take my arm, madame,' said the stranger, 'and let us proceed.'

But d'Artagnan—stunned, overwhelmed, annihilated by all that had happened—remained standing, with his arms crossed, before the musketeer and Madame Bonancieux.

The former came forward two paces, and put d'Artagnan aside with his hand.

D'Artagnan made one bound backwards, and drew his sword.

At the same moment, and with the quickness of lightning, the stranger drew his.

'In God's name, my lord!' said Madame Bonancieux, throwing herself between the combatants, and seizing their swords with both her hands—

'My lord!' cried d'Artagnan, enlightened by a sudden idea; 'My lord! pardon me, sir, but can you be——'

'My Lord Duke of Buckingham!' said Madame Bonancieux, in a very low voice, 'and now you may destroy us all.'

'My lord—madame—pardon me; a thousand pardons; but, my lord, I loved her, and was jealous. *You* know, my lord, what it is to love! Pardon me, and tell me how I may die in your grace's cause.'

'You are a brave youth,' said Buckingham, offering him a hand, which d'Artagnan pressed respectfully. 'You offer me your services, and I accept them. Follow us, at the distance of twenty paces, to the Louvre, and if any one dogs our steps, kill him!'

D'Artagnan put his naked sword under his arm, let the duke and Madame Bonancieux go forward about twenty steps, and then followed them, ready to execute to the letter the instructions of the elegant and noble minister of Charles I.

But, unfortunately, the young volunteer had no opportunity of affording this proof of his devotion to the duke; and the young woman and the handsome musketeer entered the Louvre, by the wicket in the Rue de l'Echelle, without encountering any interruption.

As for d'Artagnan, he went immediately to the Pineapple, where he found Porthos and Aramis waiting for him.

But without giving them any further reason for the trouble he had caused them, he told them that he had concluded by himself the business for which he at first thought he should have wanted their assistance.

And now, carried on as we have been by our history, let us leave our three friends to return each to his own home, whilst we follow, amidst the tortuous corridors of the Louvre, the Duke of Buckingham and his guide.

12

George Villiers, Duke of Buckingham

MADAME BONANCIEUX and the duke entered the Louvre without any difficulty; Madame Bonancieux was known to be of the household of the queen; and the duke wore the uniform of the musketeers of M. de Treville, who, as we have said, were on guard that evening. Besides, Germain was devoted to the queen, and, if anything happened, Madame Bonancieux would be accused of having introduced her lover into the Louvre—that was all! She took the blame upon herself; her reputation would be lost, it is true; but of what value in the world was the reputation of a mercer's little wife?

When they were once inside the court, the duke and the young woman kept close to the wall for about twenty paces; at the end of which Madame Bonancieux tried a small private door, which was usually open during the day, but closed at night. The door opened, and they both entered, and found themselves in total darkness; but Madame Bonancieux was well acquainted with all the turnings and twistings of this part of the Louvre, which was appropriated to the persons of the royal suite. She shut all the doors behind her, took the duke by the hand and going some steps on tip-toe, seized hold of a banister, put a foot upon the staircase, and began to ascend it. The duke had already counted two flights, when she turned to the left, went through a long corridor, descended another stage, walked a few steps forward, introduced a key into a lock, opened a door, and pushed her companion into a room lighted only by a night-lamp, saying to him—'Remain here, my lord duke; some one will come immediately.' Then she went out by the same door, locking it after her, so that the duke found himself literally a prisoner.

Yet though thus deserted, as it were, the duke, it must be confessed, did not feel the slightest fear. One of the prominent features of his character was the love of adventure and romance. Brave, determined, and enterprising, it was not the first time he had risked his life in such adventures. He had learned that this pretended message of Anne of Austria, on the faith of which he had come to Paris, was a snare; and, instead of returning to England, he had taken advantage of his position, and assured the queen that he would not depart without seeing her. The queen had at first positively refused an interview; but, fearing lest the duke might be guilty of some folly in his rage, she had resolved to see him, and to entreat him to return directly; when, on the very evening on which Madame Bonancieux was charged to conduct him to the Louvre, that lady was herself carried off. During two days it was not known what had become of her, and everything continued in suspense. But Madame Bonancieux once free, and in communication with la Porte, affairs had resumed their course; and she had now accomplished the perilous enterprise, which, but for her abduction, she would have executed three days before. Buckingham being left alone, approached a looking-glass. The dress of a musketeer became him wondrously. At thirty-five years old, he was justly considered as the handsomest man, and the most complete gentleman, of France or England. The favourite of two kings, rich as Crœsus, all-powerful in a realm which he disturbed and tranquillised as he pleased, George Villiers, Duke of Buckingham, had engaged in one of those fabulous existences which remain, throughout the course of ages, an astonishment to posterity. Confident in himself, convinced of his power, and satisfied that the laws which restrain other people could not reach him, he went straight to the object he had fixed upon, even when that object was so elevated, and so dazzling, that it would have been madness in another to have even glanced towards it.

It was thus that he had managed to approach the beautiful and haughty Anne of Austria many times, and to make her love him for his brilliant qualities.

Placing himself before the glass, the duke arrayed his beautiful fair hair, of which the pressure of his hat had disarranged the curls, and put his moustache in order; and then, his heart swelling with joy; happy and elated at having reached the moment he had so long desired, he smiled to himself proudly and hopefully.

At that moment a door concealed in the tapestry opened, and a woman appeared. Buckingham saw the reflection in the glass; he uttered a cry; it was the queen!

Anne of Austria was at that time twenty-six or twenty-seven years of age; that is, she was in all the glory of her beauty. Her deportment was that of a queen, or a goddess. Her eyes, which shone like emeralds, were perfectly beautiful, but at the same time full of gentleness and majesty. Her mouth was small and rosy; and though her under lip, like that of the princes of the house of Austria, protruded slightly beyond the other, her smile was eminently gracious, but at the same time could be profoundly haughty in its scorn. Her skin was celebrated for its velvet softness, and her hand and arm were of such surpassing beauty as to be immortalised, as incomparable, by all the poets of the time. Admirably, too, did her hair, which in her youth had been fair, but had now become chestnut, and which she wore plainly dressed, and with a great deal of powder, shade a face, on which the most rigid critic could have desired only a little less rouge, and the most fastidious sculptor only a little more delicacy in the formation of the nose.

Buckingham remained an instant perfectly dazzled. Anne of Austria never had appeared to him so beautiful even in the midst of balls, and festivals, and entertainments, as she now appeared, in her simple robe of white satin, and accompanied by Donna Estefana, the only one of her Spanish ladies who had not been driven from her by the jealousy of the king and the persecutions of the cardinal.

Anne of Austria advanced two steps; the duke threw himself at her feet, and before the queen could prevent him, had kissed the hem of her robe.

'My lord, you already know that it was not I who sent for you from England?'

'Oh! yes! madame; yes, your majesty!' exclaimed Buckingham. 'I know that I have been a fool, a madman, to believe that the snow could have been animated, that the marble could grow warm; but what would you expect? The lover easily believes in love; nor has my journey been entirely in vain, since I behold you now.'

'Yes,' replied Anne, 'but you know why, and how, I see you, my lord. I see you because, insensible to all my distress, you persist in remaining in a city where, by remaining, you risk your own life, and my honour; I see you, to tell you that everything separates us—the depths of the sea, the enmity of nations, the sanctity of vows! It is sacrilege to struggle against such things, my lord! And, lastly, I see you to tell you, that I must never see you more.'

'Speak, madame—speak, queen.' said Buckingham; 'the softness of your voice repays the sternness of your words. You speak of sacrilege; but the sacrilege is in the separation of hearts, which God had formed for one another!'

'My lord,' cried the queen, 'you forget that I have never said I loved you.'

'But neither have you ever said that you did not love me; and indeed, to say so, would be a proof of the greatest ingratitude on the part of your majesty. For tell me, where would you find a love like mine— a love, which neither time, nor absence, nor despair can extinguish, and which is recompensed by a riband, by a glance, a word? It is now three years, madame, since I saw you for the first time, and for three years have I adored you thus. Will you allow me to describe to you your dress on that occasion, and to tell the detail of the ornaments you wore? Mark me! I seem to see you now, seated, in the Spanish manner, upon cushions, wearing a dress of green satin, embroidered in silver and in gold, with pendant sleeves, fastened around your beautiful arms by large diamonds: you wore, also, a close ruff; and a small hat, of the same colour as your dress and adorned with a heron's plume, upon your head. Oh! thus, thus, with closed eyes do I behold you as you then were; and I open my eyes again, only to see you now, a hundred times more lovely still!'

'What folly,' murmured Anne of Austria, who dared not be offended with the duke for preserving her portrait so faithfully in his heart: 'what folly to nourish so useless a passion on such memories as these!'

'Alas! what would your majesty exact? I have nothing but memories; they are my happiness, my treasure, and my hope. Each meeting with you is a new jewel that I enshrine within the casket of my heart. This is the fourth of them that you have let fall, and that I have eagerly secured. Yes, in three years, madame, I have seen you only four times: the first I have already recalled to you; the second was at Madame de Chevreuse's; the third was in the gardens of Amiens.'

'My Lord!' exclaimed the queen, blushing, 'do not refer to that evening!'

'Oh! rather let me dwell upon it, madame, for it is the one radiant, blissful night of my existence! Does your majesty remember how lovely a night it was? The air was laden with odoriferous sweetness, and the blue sky was studded with innumerable stars. Ah! madame, I was alone with you for an instant then, and you were about to make me the confidant of your griefs—of the isolation of your life, and the deep sorrows of your heart. You were leaning on my arm— on this one, madam—and, when I bent my head towards you, I felt my face gently touched by your beautiful hair; and every time that I so felt it, I trembled through every vein. Oh! queen! queen! you know not the heavenly bliss, the joys of paradise, comprised in such a moment. Goods, fortune, glory, life, gladly would I give them all for another interview like that on such a night; for, madame, I will swear that then, at least on that night, you loved me!'

'My lord, it is possible that the influence of the place, the charm of that enchanting evening, the fascination of your looks, and the thousand circumstances which sometimes concur in leading a woman onwards to her fall, may have grouped themselves around me on that fatal night; but you are not ignorant, my lord, that the queen gave succour to the weakness of the woman; and that at the first word that you presumed to say, at the first liberty that you dared to take, I summoned others to my presence there!'

'Alas! it is but too true, and any feebler love than mine would never have survived the test: but my love, madame, came out from it more ardent, and immortalised. You thought to escape from me by returning to Paris;— you believed that I should never dare to quit the treasure which my master had commanded me to guard;—but what cared I for all the treasures and all the kings upon the earth! In one week, madame, I was on my return. On that occasion, madame, you had nothing to complain of; I had risked favour, and life, to see you for a single second; I did not even touch your hand; and forgave me when you found I was submissive and repentant.'

'Yes, my lord, but you are well aware that calumny

fastened even upon those follies in which I had so small a share. Prompted by the cardinal, the king felt extreme resentment. Madame de Vernet was dismissed; Putange was banished; and Madame de Chevreuse was disgraced. And do you not remember, my lord, that when you wished to return as an ambassador to France, it was his majesty himself by whom you were opposed.'

'Yes! and France is about to pay with a war for that opposition. I cannot see you again, madame; well! I will take care that you shall continually hear of me. What do you suppose to have been the true aim of that expedition to Rhe, and that league which I am projecting with the Protestants? The delight of seeing you! I am well enough aware that I have no chance of reaching Paris at the head of an army; but then, this war must bring about a peace; peace will require negotiations; and those negotiations shall be made by none but me. They will no longer dare to reject me then; and I shall return to Paris, and behold you once again, and be, for an instant, happy. It is but too true that my enjoyment will have been bought by the blood of thousands of human beings; but what will their lives be to me, provided that my eyes are blessed once more by seeing you! This may be folly, madame—perhaps madness; but tell me, pray, had ever woman a more impassioned lover, had ever a queen a more enthusiastic servant?'

'My lord! my lord! the witnesses you call for your defence accuse you. These very proofs, that you would give me of your love, are themselves almost crimes!'

'But only because you do not love me, madame. Oh! if you loved me, how different would these circumstances seem, but the joy would be too great, and I should go mad. You spoke but now, madame, of Madame de Chevreuse; but, oh! how much less cruel was that lady than you are! Holland loved her, and she responded to his love.'

'Madame de Chevreuse was not a queen!' murmured Anne of Austria; subdued, in spite of herself, by the expression of a passion so profound.

'And would you then love me if you were not? Oh! tell me, madame! say, that you would love me? let me believe that it is but the dignity of your rank that has come between you and me! let me believe that if you had been but Madame de Chevreuse, there might have been hope for the unhappy Buckingham! Oh! charming queen! thanks for these sweet words—a thousand, thousand thanks!'

'Alas! my lord! you have misunderstood me; I did not mean to let you infer——'

'Hush! hush!' exclaimed the duke. 'Be not so cruel as to correct an error that is so full of happiness to me! You have yourself told me that I have been drawn into a snare; and I perhaps shall leave my life in it, for, strangely enough, for some time I have had presentiments of an approaching death.'—And the duke smiled, with a sad, yet winning smile.

'Oh, God !' exclaimed the queen, in a tone of terror, which manifested, more fully than she might have wished, her interest in the duke.

'But I did not tell you this to alarm you, madame. No, it is even ridiculous to speak of it; and, believe me, I do not give importance to such silly dreams. But the words which you have just uttered, the hope which you almost gave me, would be a recompense for everything, even for my life!'

'Oh! but I,' said Anne of Austria—'I also have had my presentiments. I dreamed that I saw you stretched upon the earth, all bloody from a wound.'

'On the left side, and inflicted by a knife, was it not?' said the duke.

'Yes, my lord! it was in the left side, and by a knife. But who could have told you of my dream? I have never spoken of it but in my prayers to God.'

'I ask for no more. You love me, madame! yes, you love me!'

'I love you?'

'Yes, you! Would God send to you the same dreams as to me, if you did not love me? Should we be visited by the same presentiments, if our two existences did not meet in our hearts? Yes, queen, you love me, and you weep for me!'

'Oh, my God! my God!' exclaimed the queen, 'this is more than I can bear. In the name of heaven, my lord, withdraw! I know not whether I love you or not; but this I know, that I will never break my vow at the altar. Have pity on me then, and leave this kingdom. Oh! if you should be wounded in France—if you should die in France—if I could imagine that your love for me had been the cause of your death, I should never be consoled. The thought would madden me! Depart then, depart, I beseech you.'

'Oh! how beautiful you are now! How devotedly I love you!' exclaimed Buckingham.

'Depart, I implore you, and return hereafter,' continued the queen. 'Come back as an ambassador, as a minister;

come back, surrounded by your guards who will defend you, and your servants who will watch over you, and then I shall have no fear for your life, and shall have some happiness in seeing you!'

'Oh! but is it really true what you now tell me?'

'Yes.'

'Give me, then, some pledge of your regard—some object which has once been yours—to satisfy me that I have not been indulging in a dream; something that you have once worn, and that I may wear now—a ring, a necklace, or a chain!'

'And will you go if I give you what you ask?'

'Yes!'

'Immediately?'

'Yes!'

'You will quit France, and will return to England?'

'Yes, I swear I will.'

'Wait, then; wait, sir.'

And Anne of Austria returned to her chamber, and came back almost in an instant, holding in her hand a small casket of rosewood, with her monogram encrusted in gold.

'Here my lord, here! keep this as a memorial of me!'

Buckingham took the casket, and again sank upon his knee.

'You promised me to go,' said the queen.

'And I will keep my word! Your hand, madame, and I leave you!'

Closing her eyes, and leaning on Donna Estefana—for she felt her strength was failing her—Anne of Austria extended her hand.

On that beautiful hand Buckingham pressed his lips passionately, and then arose.

'Before six months have passed,' said he, 'if I be not dead, I will see you again, if I must turn the world upside down to accomplish it.'

And true to his promise, he rushed out of the room.

In the corridor he found Madame Bonancieux awaiting him; and, with the same precaution, and the same good fortune, she led him forth out of the Louvre.

13

Monsieur Bonancieux

THERE was in all this affair, as might be remarked, a person of whom, in spite of his precarious situation, we have appeared to take very little notice. This person was M. Bonancieux, a respectable martyr to the political and amorous intrigues which so thoroughly entangled themselves together in that chivalrous and gallant age. Fortunately, as our readers may or may not remember, we have promised not to lose sight of him.

The officers who had arrested him, conducted him at once to the Bastile, where he had to pass, all trembling as he was before a company of soldiers, who were charging their muskets.

Taken from there into a partly subterraneous gallery, he had to endure the most brutal insults and ill-treatment. The attendants saw that he was not a nobleman, and they treated him therefore like a beggar.

In about half an hour, a registrar came to put an end to his tortures, but not to his anxiety, by ordering that he should be conducted to the question chamber. They generally questioned prisoners in their own cells, but they did not observe so much ceremony with M. Bonancieux.

Two guards laid hold of the mercer, and made him cross a court, and then, entering a corridor where there were three sentinels, they opened a door and pushed him into a low room, which only contained a table, a chair, and a commissary. The commissary was seated on the chair, and was engaged in writing at the table.

The two guards led the prisoner to the table, and at a signal from the commissary, went out of earshot. The commissary, who had till then kept his head bent down over his papers, raised it up to see who he had before him. This commissary was a man with a very crabbed look; a sharp nose; cheeks yellow and puffed out; small, but piercing eyes; and with a countenance reminding one, at the same time, of a polecat and a fox. His head, supported by a long and flexible neck, was thrust out of his full black robe, and balanced itself with a motion very much like that of a turtle putting its head out of its shell.

He began by asking M. Bonancieux his christian name and surname, his age, profession, and place of abode.

The accused replied that his name was Jacques Bonancieux, that his age was 51 years, that he was a retired mercer, and lived in the Rue des Fossoyeurs, No. 11.

Instead of continuing his questions, the commissary then made him a long speech on the danger of an obscure citizen interfering in public affairs. With this exordium he combined an exposition of the power and actions of the cardinal—that incomparable minister, the conqueror of all preceding ministers, and the example for all future ministers—whom no one could oppose or thwart with impunity.

After this second part of his discourse, he fixed his hawk's eye on poor Bonancieux, and exhorted him to reflect upon the seriousness of his situation.

This the mercer had already done: he wished M. de la Porte at the devil for having put it into his head to marry his god-daughter, and cursed the hour when that god-daughter had been received into the queen's service.

The foundation of M. Bonancieux's character was profound selfishness, mingled with sordid avarice, the whole being seasoned with excessive cowardice. The love which he entertained towards his young wife was quite a secondary sentiment, and could not stand against those primary feelings which we have just enumerated.

Bonancieux, in fact, reflected on what had been said to him.

'But, Mr. Commissary,' he timidly observed, 'believe me, that I know well and appreciate the incomparable merit of his eminence, by whom we have the honour of being governed.'

'Really!' said the commissary, with a doubtful look; 'but if this be true, how came you to be in the Bastile?'

'How I am there, or rather, why I am there,' replied Bonancieux, 'is what it is utterly impossible for me to tell you, seeing that I do not know myself; but most certainly it is not for having offended the cardinal, consciously at least.'

'It is certain, nervertheless, that you must have committed some crime, as you are here accused of high treason.'

'Of high treason!' cried Bonancieux, confounded; 'of high treason! And how can you believe that a poor mercer, who hates the Huguenots, and abhors the Spaniards, can be accused of high treason? Reflect, sir—the thing is a moral impossibility.'

'M. Bonancieux,' said the commissary, regarding the accused with his little eyes, as though he had the power of looking into the very depths of his heart, 'M. Bonancieux, you have a wife.'

'Yes, sir,' replied the trembling mercer, perceiving that it was on her account that he was now about to be inculpated; 'that is to say, I had one.'

'What? you had one! And what have you done with her, that you have her no longer?'

'Some one has carried her off, sir!'

'Some one has taken her from you?' said the commissary. 'Ah!'

Bonancieux perceived by this 'ah!' that matters were getting worse and worse.

'Some one has taken her from you,' resumed the commissary. 'And do you know who has been guilty of this abduction?'

'I think I know.'

'Who is it?'

'Remember that I affirm nothing, Mr. Commissary—I only suspect.'

'Whom do you suspect? Come, don't hesitate to speak.'

M. Bonancieux was in the greatest perplexity. Ought he to deny everything, or to confess? From a total denial, it might be inferred that he knew too much to admit; and, by a general confession, he might give evidence of his good faith.

He determined, therefore, to have no concealments.

'I suspect,' said he, 'a tall, dark man, of lofty air, who has all the appearance of a man of rank. He followed us, I think, many times, when I went to fetch my wife from the gate of the Louvre.'

The commissary appeared somewhat disturbed.

'And his name?' said he.

'Oh! as to his name, I do not know it; but if I should meet him, I could recognise him amongst a thousand persons.'

The brow of the commissary grew dark.

'You could recognise him amongst a thousand, you say?' continued he.

'That is to say,' replied Bonancieux, who saw that he had made a false step, 'that is to say——'

'You have said that you could recognise him,' said the commissary; 'very well, that is enough for to-day; it is necessary, before we proceed any further, that some one should be informed that you know the person who has carried off your wife.'

'But I did not tell you that I knew him!' cried M. Bonancieux, in despair. 'I told you, on the contrary——'

'Take away the prisoner!' exclaimed the commissary to the two guards.

'Where to?' asked the registrar.

'To a dungeon.'

'To which?'

'Oh! to the first that offers, provided it be secure,' answered the commissary, with an indifference which filled the breast of poor Bonancieux with horror and dismay.

'Alas! alas!' said he, 'I am undone. My wife must have committed some frightful crime; and I am supposed to be an accomplice, and shall be punished with her. She must have said something—have confessed that I was her confidant. A woman is such a weak creature! A dungeon! The first that offers! that's it. A night is soon passed; and then, to-morrow, to the wheel, to the gibbet! Oh! my God, my God, have pity on me!'

Without in the least attending to the lamentations of Master Bonancieux, that were of a kind to which they were tolerably well accustomed, the two guards took him by the arms, and led him away, while the commissary hastily wrote a letter, for which his officer waited.

Bonancieux did not close an eye; not because his dungeon was very uncomfortable, but because his anxiety was very great. He sat upon his stool the whole night, trembling at every noise; and when the first rays of light penetrated his chamber, Aurora herself appeared to him to be dressed in funereal array.

Suddenly he heard the bolts withdrawn, and gave a terrible start. He believed that they were coming to conduct him to the scaffold; and, therefore, when he saw that it was only the commissary and his attendant, he was almost ready to embrace them.

'Your affair has become sadly complicated since last evening, my fine fellow,' said the commissary. 'I advise you to tell the whole truth, for your repentance alone can mitigate the anger of the cardinal.'

'But I am ready to tell everything,' said Bonancieux;

'everything, at least, that I know; question me, I beseech you!'

'In the first place, where is your wife?'

'I have just told you that some one has carried her off.'

'Yes, but since five o'clock yesterday evening, thanks to you, she has escaped.'

'My wife escaped!' cried Bonancieux; 'oh! the wretch! Sir, if she has escaped, I assure you it is not my fault!'

'What were you doing, then, in the apartment of your neighbour, M. d'Artagnan, with whom you had a long conference in the course of the day?'

'Ah, yes, Mr. Commissary, yes, that is true; and I confess I was wrong in that; yes, I was in M. d'Artagnan's apartments.'

'And why?'

'To entreat him to assist me in finding my wife. I thought I had a right to reclaim her. I was mistaken, it appears, and I humbly beg your pardon.'

'And what answer did M. d'Artagnan give?'

'M. d'Artagnan promised me his assistance; but I soon perceived that he betrayed me.'

'You would mislead justice! M. d'Artagnan made an agreement with you; and in virtue of that agreement, he put to flight the officers who had arrested your wife, and has now secreted her from all our researches.'

'M. d'Artagnan has hidden away my wife? Alas! what do you tell me?'

'Fortunately, M. d'Artagnan is in our power, and you shall be confronted with him.'

'Ah, faith! I desire nothing better,' cried M. Bonancieux. 'I shall not be sorry to see the face of an acquaintance.'

'Bring in M. d'Artagnan,' said the commissary to the two guards.

The guards brought in Athos.

'M. d'Artagnan,' said the commissary, addressing Athos, 'declare what passed between you and that other gentleman.'

'But,' cried M. Bonancieux, 'that is not M. d'Artagnan that you show me there.'

'What! not M. d'Artagnan?' cried the commissary.

'By no means,' answered Bonancieux.

'What *is* the gentleman's name?' demanded the commissary.

'I cannot tell you; I don't know him!' replied Bonancieux.

'What! you do not know him?'

'No.'

'You have never set eyes on him?'

'Yes; but I do not know his name.'

'Your name?' demanded the commissary of Athos.

'Athos!' answered the musketeer.

'But that is not the name of a man; it is the name of a mountain!' cried the unfortunate commissary, who began to get confused.

'It is my name,' calmly replied Athos.

'But you said your name was d'Artagnan.'

'I said so?'

'Yes, you!'

'The fact is, that they said to me—you are M. d'Artagnan. I replied—do you think so? My guards said they were sure of it. I did not wish to contradict them; besides, I might be mistaken.'

'Sir! you mock the majesty of justice.'

'Not at all,' calmly replied Athos.

'You are M. d'Artagnan?'

'You see that you still tell me so.'

'But,' cried M. Bonancieux, 'I tell you, Mr. Commissary, 'that there is not the smallest doubt. M. d'Artagnan is my lodger, and, consequently, as he does not pay his rent, I know him only too well. M. d'Artagnan is a young man of nineteen or twenty years of age, at most, and this gentleman is at least thirty. M. d'Artagnan is in the guards of M. des Essarts, and this gentleman is in the company of M. de Treville's musketeers: observe the uniform.'

'By heavens! it is true!' muttered the commissary. 'It is true, by God!'

At this instant the door was quickly opened, and one of the turnkeys of the Bastile introduced a messenger, who gave the commissary a letter.

'Oh! the wretch!' exclaimed the commissary.

'What? of whom do you speak? It is not of my wife, I hope.'

'On the contrary, it is of her. Your affairs are in a nice state.'

'Do me the pleasure,' said the exasperated mercer, 'to tell me, sir, how my affairs can be made worse by what my wife does whilst I am in prison?'

'Because what she does is the consequence of an infernal plan arranged between you!'

'I swear to you, Mr. Commissary, that you are in the

most profound error; that I know nothing in the world of my wife's actions; that I am completely ignorant of what she has done; and that, if she has committed follies, I renounce her, I give her the lie, and I curse her.'

'And now,' said Athos, 'if you have no further business with me, dismiss me. Your M. Bonancieux is very tiresome.'

'Take the prisoners back to their dungeons,' said the commissary, pointing to Athos and Bonancieux, 'and guard them more strictly than ever.'

'Nevertheless,' said Athos, with his usual tranquillity, 'your business is with M. d'Artagnan; I do not well see how I can supply his place!'

'Do what I have ordered,' cried the commissary; 'and the most solitary confinement—do you hear?'

The two followed the guards, Athos shrugging his shoulders, and M. Bonancieux uttering lamentations which might have softened the heart of a tiger.

They took the mercer into the same dungeon where he had passed the night, and left him there throughout the whole day. Hour after hour did poor Bonancieux weep like a very mercer; he was not at all a man of warlike soul, as he himself told us.

About nine o'clock in the evening, just as he had made up his mind to go to bed, he heard steps in his corridor. These steps approached his dungeon, the door opened, and the guards appeared.

'Follow me,' said a sergeant who commanded the guards.

'Follow you!' cried Bonancieux, 'follow you at this time of night! And where? my God!'

'Where we have orders to conduct you.'

'But that is no answer.'

'It is, nevertheless, the only answer you will get.'

'O Lord! O Lord!' muttered the poor mercer, 'now I am lost!'

He followed, mechanically, and without resistance.

He went down the same corridor as before, crossed a first court, then a second floor; and then, at the entrance gate, he found a carriage surrounded by four horse guards. They made him enter this carriage; the sergeant placed himself at his side; the door was locked, and they both found themselves in a moving prison.

The carriage proceeded slowly, like a funeral coach. Through the padlocked bars the prisoner could only see the horses and the pavement. But, like a true Parisian as he was, Bonancieux recognised each street by its corners, its lamps, and its signs. At the moment they reached St. Paul, where the criminals of the Bastile were executed, he nearly fainted, and crossed himself twice. He thought the carriage would have stopped there; but it went on, nevertheless. Farther on, he was seized with great fear: it was in skirting the cemetery of St. Jean, where the state criminals were buried. One thing alone encouraged him, which was, that before burying them, one generally cut off their heads; and his head was yet upon his shoulders. But when the carriage took the road to La Grève, and he perceived the painted roof of the Hotel de Ville, and saw that the carriage went under its colonnade, he thought it was all over with him, and wished to confess himself to the sergeant; and, on the refusal of the latter, uttered such piteous cries, that the sergeant declared that if he continued to deafen him so, he would put a gag on him. This threat reassured him a little: if they meant to execute him at the Grève, it was scarcely worth while to gag him, as they had nearly reached the place of execution. In fact, the carriage crossed this fatal place without stopping. There was only the Croix du Trahoir, then, to fear; and the carriage took the exact road to it.

This time there was no further room for doubt. It was at the Croix du Trahoir that inferior criminals were executed. Bonancieux had flattered himself, by considering that he was worthy of St. Paul, or the place de Grève. It was at the Croix du Trahoir that his journey and his destiny would end. He could not yet see this unhappy cross, but he felt it, as it were, loom before him. When he was only about twenty paces from it, he heard a noise, and the carriage stopped. This was more than poor Bonancieux could bear: already crushed by the successive emotions he had experienced, he uttered a feeble cry, or rather groan, which might have been taken for the last sigh of a dying man, and fainted.

14

The Man of Meung

THE mob that stopped the way was produced, not by the expectation of seeing a man hanged, but by the contemplation of man who was already hanging. After a moment's hindrance, the carriage proceeded on its way, passed through the crowd, went along the Rue St. Honore, and turning at the Rue des Bons Enfants, stopped at a low doorway.

When the door opened, two guards, assisted by the sergeant, received Bonancïeux in their arms, and pushed him into a court; they then made him ascend a staircase, and placed him in an antechamber. All these operations were performed nearly mechanically, as far as he was concerned. He had walked as in a dream, he had seen things as through a mist; he had heard without understanding; and they might have executed him then without his making the slightest resistance, or uttering an appeal for mercy.

He remained passive on the bench, with his back resting against the wall, and his arms hanging down, on the very spot where his guards had placed him.

And yet, as, in looking around him, he saw nothing threatening, as no real danger was indicated, as the bench was comfortably stuffed, as the wall was covered with beautiful cordovan leather, and as long curtains of red damask, held by gilt brackets, hung before the windows, he became by degrees aware that his fears were exaggerated, and began to move his head from right to left, and vertically. At this motion, which no one opposed, he resumed a little courage, ventured to draw up one leg, and then the other; and, at last, supporting himself upon his hands, he raised himself on the bench, and found himself on his feet.

At this moment an officer of pleasant appearance opened a door, exchanged a few words with some person in the next room, and then, turning towards the prisoner, said—

'Is it you who are called Bonancieux?'

'Yes, sir,' stammered the mercer, more dead than alive, 'at your service.'

'Enter!'

The officer bade the mercer precede him; and the latter, obeying without reply, entered a room where he appeared to be expected.

It was a large cabinet, the walls of which were furnished with offensive and defensive weapons—a close and suffocating room, in which there was already a fire, although it was scarcely yet the end of September. A square table, loaded with books and papers, and on which there was unrolled an immense plan of the town of Rochelle, occupied the middle of the apartment. In front of the chimney-piece there stood a man of middle height, with a proud and haughty air, piercing eyes, a large forehead, and an emaciated countenance, which was yet further elongated by an imperial, surmounted by a pair of moustaches.

Although this man was scarcely thirty-six or thirty-seven years old, both imperial and moustaches were beginning to grow gray. His appearance, except that he wore no sword, was military; and his buff leather boots, which were yet slightly covered with dust, pointed out that he had been on horseback during the day.

This individual was Armand-Jean Duplesiss, Cardinal de Richelieu; not as he is represented—broken down like an old man, suffering like a martyr, his body shattered, his voice extinguished, buried in an enormous easy-chair, no longer living but by the power of his genius, and no longer supporting the struggle against Europe but by the eternal energy of his extraordinary mind—but such as he really was at this period; that is, a skilful and gallant cavalier, already feeble in body, but upheld by that moral force which made him one of the most unparalleled of mankind, and now preparing, after sustaining the Duc de Nevers in his duchy of Mantua, and taking Nismes, Castres, and Elzes, to drive the English from the Isle of Rhé, and to undertake the siege of La Rochelle.

At first sight, nothing denoted that it was the cardinal, and it was impossible for those who were unacquainted with his appearance to guess in whose presence they were.

The poor mercer remained standing at the door, whilst the eyes of the person we have been describing fixed themselves upon him as if they would penetrate his most secret thoughts.

'Is that this Bonancieux?' he demanded, after a moment's pause.

'Yes, my lord!' replied the officer.

'Very well; give me those papers, and leave us.'

The officer took the papers indicated, gave them to him who asked for them, bowed to the very ground, and left the room.

In these papers Bonancieux recognised his examinations at the Bastile. From time to time the man by the chimney-piece lifted his eyes from the papers, and plunged them, like two poniards, into the very heart of the poor mercer.

At the end of ten minutes' reading, and ten seconds' scrutiny of Bonancieux, he had made up his mind.

'That head has never conspired,' murmured the cardinal; 'but never mind, let us see.' Then he said slowly, 'You are accused of high treason.'

'That is what they have already told me, my lord!' said Bonancieux, giving his interrogator the same title that he had heard the officer give him; 'but I give you my oath, that I knew nothing about it.'

The cardinal suppressed a smile.

'You have conspired with your wife, with Madame de Chevreuse, and with my Lord Duke of Buckingham.'

'I admit, my lord,' replied the mercer, 'I have heard all those names mentioned by her.'

'And on what occasion?'

'She said that the Cardinal de Richelieu had enticed the Duke of Buckingham to Paris, to destroy him and the queen.'

'She said that, did she?' cried the cardinal, with great violence.

'Yes, my lord; but I told her that she was wrong in saying such a thing, and that his eminence was incapable——'

'Hold your tongue—you are a fool!' replied the cardinal.

'That is exactly what my wife said to me, my lord.'

'Do you know who carried off your wife?'

'No, my lord.'

'But you had some suspicions?'

'Yes, my lord; but as these suspicions appeared to displease the commissary, I have them no longer.'

'Your wife has escaped: did you know that?'

'Not at the time, my lord; I learned it, since I have been in prison, from the commissary, who is a most amiable man.'

The cardinal suppressed another smile.

'Then you do not know what has become of your wife since her escape?'

'Not positively, my lord; but she has probably returned to the Louvre.'

'At one o'clock this morning she had not yet returned there.'

'Ah! good God! but what can have become of her?'

'Have no fear—it will soon be known; nothing escapes the cardinal; the cardinal knows everything.'

'In that case, my lord, do you believe that the cardinal will tell me what has become of my wife?'

'Perhaps so; but it is necessary, first, that you should tell me all you know in relation to the connection of your wife with Madame de Chevreuse.'

'But, my lord, I know nothing about it; I never saw her.'

'When you went to fetch your wife from the Louvre, did she return directly to your house?'

'Scarcely ever. She had business to transact with the queen's drapers, to whom I convoyed her.'

'And how many linen-drapers were there?'

'Two, my lord.'

'Where do they live?'

'One in the Rue Vaugirard, and the other in the Rue de la Harpe.'

'Did you accompany your wife into these houses?'

'Never, my lord. I always waited for her at the door.'

'And what excuse did she make for entering alone?'

'None: she told me to wait, and I waited.'

'You are a most accommodating husband, my dear M. Bonancieux,' said the cardinal.

'He has called me 'my dear monsieur,'' said the mercer to himself. ''Pon my faith, things are taking a good turn.'

'Should you know those doors again?'

'Yes.'

'Do you know the numbers?'

'Yes.'

'What are they?'

'No. 25 in the Rue Vaugirard, and No. 75 in the Rue de la Harpe.'

'Good!' said the cardinal; and, taking a silver bell, he rang it.

'Go,' said he in a low voice, to the officer who entered— 'go and find Rochefort, and tell him to come here directly, if he is within.'

'The count is already here,' said the officer, 'and requests an immediate audience of your eminence.'

'Your eminence!' muttered Bonancieux, who knew that

such was the title ordinarily given to the cardinal; your eminence!'

'Let him come in, then, let him come in!' said Richelieu eagerly.

The officer hurried out of the room with that rapidity with which the cardinal was generally obeyed by his followers.

'Your eminence!' again muttered Bonancieux, rolling his eyes in astonishment.

Two seconds had scarcely elapsed after the officer left the room before the door opened again, and another person entered.

'It is he!' exclaimed Bonancieux.

'Who is he?' demanded the cardinal.

'He who ran away with my wife.'

The cardinal rang a second time, and the officer reappeared.

'Put this man into the hands of the two guards, and let him wait till I send for him.'

'No, my lord, no, it is not he!' exclaimed Bonancieux; 'no, I was mistaken; it is another person, not at all like him. The gentleman is an honest man.'

'Take away that simpleton!' said the cardinal.

The officer took him by the arm, and led him to the antechamber, where he was met by the two guards.

The person who had last entered impatiently followed Bonancieux with his eyes till he was gone, and, when the door was closed behind him—

'They have met,' he said, eagerly approaching the cardinal.

'Who?' demanded the cardinal.

'Those two.'

'The queen and the duke!' cried the cardinal.

'Yes.'

'And where?'

'At the Louvre!'

'Are you sure?'

'Perfectly sure!'

'Who told you of it?'

'Madame de Lannoy, who is entirely devoted to your eminence, as you well know!'

'Why did she not tell you sooner?'

'Either by chance, or by mistrust, the queen made Madame de Surgis sleep in her room, and kept it throughout the day.'

'Very well; we have been beaten; let us try to have our revenge.'

'Be assured that I will assist your eminence with all my soul.'

'How did this happen?'

'At half-past twelve the queen was with her women.'

'Where?'

'In her bed-chamber, where a pocket-handkerchief was brought her from her seamstress.'

'Well?'

'The queen immediately showed great emotion; and grew pale, under her rouge.'

'Well! what then?'

'Nevertheless, she arose; and, in an agitated voice said, "ladies, wait ten minutes for me; I will return." Then, opening the door of her alcove, she went out.'

'Why did not Madame de Lannoy come and tell you directly?'

'There was no certainty about the matter; besides, the queen had said, "ladies, wait for me." And Madame de Lannoy dared not disobey her majesty.'

'And how long did the queen remain absent from her room?'

'Three-quarters of an hour.'

'Did none of her women accompany her?'

'Only Donna Estefana.'

'And she returned?'

'Yes, but only to take a small rosewood casket, bearing her initials, with which she went out again directly.'

'And when she came back, finally, did she bring the casket with her?'

'No!'

'Does Madame de Lannoy know what the casket contained?'

'Yes! the diamond studs which his majesty presented to the queen.'

'And she came back without the casket?'

'Yes.'

'Then the opinion of Madame de Lannoy is, that she gave this casket to Buckingham?'

'She is sure of it.'

'How so?'

'During the day, Madame de Lannoy, in her office of tirewoman to the queen, looked for this casket, appeared uneasy at not finding it, and ended by inquiring for it of the queen.'

'And then the queen——'

'The queen blushed deeply, and answered that, having the evening before broken one of the studs, she had sent it to her jeweller's to be repaired.'

'You must go there. and ascertain whether that is true, or not.'

'I have been.'

'Well, and the goldsmith——?'

'The goldsmith has heard nothing about it.'

'Good! good! Rochefort, all is not lost, and perhaps -perhaps all is for the best!'

'The fact is, that I have no doubt but what the genius of your eminence——'

'May repair the errors of my agent! Is that what you mean?'

'It was just what I was about to say, if your eminence had permitted me to finish the sentence.'

'Now, do you know where the Duchess de Chevreuse and the Duke of Buckingham concealed themselves?'

'No, my lord; my agents have no positive information upon that point.'

'I know it myself, though.'

'You! my lord?'

'Yes, or at least I have no doubt of it. They lived, the one in the Rue Vaugirard, at No. 25, and the other in the Rue de la Harpe, No. 75.'

'Would your eminence wish me to arrest them both?'

'It is too late; they will be gone.'

'Never mind; there is no harm in trying!'

'Take ten of my guards, and ransack the two houses.'

'It shall be done, my lord!'

So saying, Rochefort rushed from the room.

When the cardinal was left alone, he remained a moment in thought, and then rang a third time.

The officer who had come before appeared again.

'Bring in the prisoner,' said the cardinal.

'Master Bonancieux was again brought in, and, at a sign from the cardinal, the officer withdrew.

'You have deceived me,' said the cardinal, with great severity.

'I!' cried Bonancieux; 'I deceive your eminence!'

'When your wife went to the Rue Vaugirard, and the Rue de la Harpe, she did not go to linen-drapers.'

'Good God! To whom did she go, then?'

'She went to see the Duchesse de Chevreuse, and the Duke of Buckingham.'

'Yes!' said Bonancieux, with a flash of recollection; 'yes, exactly so; your eminence is right. I often told my wife that it was astonishing that linen-drapers should live in such houses; in houses which had no signs; and every time I said so, my wife began to laugh. Ah! my lord!' he continued, throwing himself at the feet of his eminence, 'it is plain that you are the cardinal, the great cardinal—the man of genius, whom all the world reveres!'

The cardinal, small as was the triumph to be achieved over a being so vulgar as was Bonancieux, did not the less enjoy it for a moment. Then, as if a new idea struck him, he smiled, and, stretching out his hand to the mercer—

'Rise, my friend,' said he, 'you are a worthy fellow.'

'The cardinal has taken my hand! I have touched the hand of the great man!' exclaimed Bonancieux; 'the great man has called me his friend!'

'Yes, my friend, yes,' said the cardinal, in that paternal tone which he was sometimes able to assume, but which only deceived those who did not know him; 'and as you have been unjustly suspected, we must make you some amends. Here, take this bag of a hundred pistoles, and forgive me.'

'*I* forgive *you*, my lord!' said Bonancieux, hesitating to take the bag, from a fear that this supposed gift was only a jest. 'But you were quite at liberty to have me arrested; you are quite at liberty to send me to the torture; you are quite at liberty to hang me; you are the master, and I should not have the smallest word to say against it. Forgive you, my lord! But you cannot mean that!'

'Ah! my dear M. Bonancieux, you are very generous; I see it, and I thank you. But you must take this bag, and then you will go away not very discontented—will you?'

'I go away perfectly enchanted, my lord!'

'Adieu, then; or, rather, *au revoir;* for I hope that we shall see each other again.'

'As often as my lord may please; I am at your eminence's command.'

'It shall be often, depend upon it; for I have found your conversation quite charming.'

'Oh! my lord!'

'Farewell, till our next meeting, M. Bonancieux—till our next meeting.'

Bonancieux, at a sign from the cardinal's hand, bowed to the very ground, and then backed himself out of the room. When he was in the anteroom, the cardinal heard him, in his enthusiasm, crying out, at the top of his voice: 'Long live his eminence! long live the great cardinal!'

Richelieu listened with a smile to this noisy manifestation of the enthusiastic feelings of Master Bonancieux: and, when his shouts were lost in the distance: 'There,' he said, 'is a man who would henceforth die for me!'

The cardinal then set himself to examine with great attention the map of La Rochelle, which was spread out upon the table, and to mark with a pencil the position of the famous breakwater which, eighteen months afterwards, closed the port of the besieged city.

Whilst he was most deeply occupied with these strategic meditations, the door opened, and Rochefort reappeared.

'Well!' said the cardinal, with vivacity, which proved what consequence he attached to the intelligence that he expected from the count.

'Well!' said the latter, 'a young woman, between twenty-six and twenty-eight years old, and a man of about thirty-five or forty years of age, have really lodged in the houses indicated by your eminence; but the woman left last night, and the man this morning.'

'It was they!' exclaimed the duke, whose eyes were fixed upon the clock: 'but now,' he continued, 'it is too late to follow them. The duchess is at Tours, and the duke at Boulogne. It is in London that they must be overtaken.'

'What are your eminence's commands?'

'Let not one word be said of what has passed. Let the queen remain in perfect peace of mind; let her be ignorant that we know her secret; let her believe that we are hunting after some conspiracy. Send me Séguier, the keeper of the seals.'

'And this man? What has your eminence done with him?'

'What man?' demanded the cardinal.

'This Bonancieux.'

'I have done all that could be done with him. I have set him to spy upon his wife.'

The Count de Rochefort bowed low, like a man who felt the great superiority of his master, and withdrew.

As soon as the cardinal was again alone, he seated himself

once more, and wrote a letter, which he sealed with his private signet, and then rang his bell. The officer entered for the fourth time.

'Tell Vitry to come here,' said the cardinal, 'and order him to be ready for a journey.'

In another moment the man he had sent for was standing before him, booted and spurred.

'Vitry,' said he, 'you must go off at once, without an instant's delay, to London. You must not stop one moment on the road, and you will give this letter to my lady. There is a cheque for two hundred pistoles; go to my treasurer, and get the money. You shall have the same sum if you return in six days, having performed my commission with success!'

The messenger, without answering one word, bowed; took the letter, and the order for two hundred pistoles, and left the room.

These were the contents of the letter—

'MY LADY,

'Be present at the first ball where you can meet the Duke of Buckingham. He will have on his doublet twelve diamond studs; get close to him, and cut off two.

'As soon as these studs are in your possession, let me know it.'

15

Civilians and Soldiers

ON the day after these events had happened, as Athos had not returned to them, d'Artagnan and Porthos informed M. de Treville of his disappearance.

As for Aramis, he had requested leave of absence for five days, and it was said that he was at Rouen on some family affairs.

M. de Treville was the father of his soldiers. The humblest individual amongst them, from the time that he put on the uniform of the company, was as certain of his assistance and support, as M. de Treville's own brother could have been.

He went, therefore, at once to the criminal lieutenant.

The officer who commanded at La Croix Rouge was sent for, and from various inquiries it was ascertained that Athos was at that time lodged at Fort l'Eveque.

Athos had been subjected to the same trials as we have seen Bonancieux exposed to.

We have witnessed the confrontation of the two prisoners. Athos, who, till then, had said nothing, from fear that d'Artagnan had not had the time he needed, from that moment declared that his name was Athos, and not d'Artagnan. He added that he knew neither M. nor Madame Bonancieux; that he had never spoken either to the one or the other; and that he had gone at about ten at night to pay a visit to his friend, M. d'Artagnan, but until that hour he had been at M. de Treville's, where he had dined. Twenty witnesses, he added, could confirm this fact, and he named many distinguished gentlemen, amongst whom was the Duc de la Tremouille.

The second commissary was as much surprised as the first, at this simple but firm declaration of the musketeer, on whom he would gladly have taken that revenge which civilians so much love to take on soldiers; but the names of Treville and la Tremouille demanded consideration.

Athos was, therefore, sent to the cardinal; but his eminence was, unfortunately, at the Louvre with the king.

It was just at this time that M. de Treville, having in vain sought Athos from the lieutenant and the governor of Fort l'Eveque, came to make an application to his majesty; to whom he had, as captain of the musketeers, the right of immediate access upon all occasions.

The prejudices of the king against the queen are well known—prejudices which were skilfully fostered by the cardinal, who, in political intrigues, had much greater fear of women than of men. One of the chief causes of this prejudice was the friendship of the queen for Madame de Chevreuse. These two women gave his eminence more uneasiness than the Spanish war, the rupture with England, and the embarrassment of the finances, all combined. He was convinced that Madame de Chevreuse served the queen, not only in political intrigues, but—what was far more vexatious to him—in amorous intrigues as well.

At the first word which the cardinal had uttered, that Madame de Chevreuse, who was exiled to Tours, and had been supposed to be in that city, had come to Paris, and had stayed there five days, escaping the police, the king became furiously enraged. At once capricious, and a false husband, Louis still wished to be distinguished as *the just* and *the chaste*. Posterity will, with difficulty, understand this character, which history explains, not by reasoning, but by facts.

But when the cardinal added that not only had Madame de Chevreuse been to Paris, but that the queen had renewed her friendship with her by means of one of those mysterious correspondences which were then called *cabals*—when he affirmed that he, the cardinal, had all but unravelled the threads of this intrigue—when, at the moment that he was about to detect in the very fact, provided with the fullest proofs, an emissary of the queen, who was in communication with the exile, a musketeer, had dared violently to interrupt the course of justice, by falling, sword in hand, upon the honest officers of the law, who had been charged to examine the whole affair with impartiality, in order to lay it before the king—Louis was no longer able to restrain himself. He took a step towards the queen's apartments, with that pale and speechless indignation, which, when it burst out, led that prince to acts of the most unfeeling cruelty.

And yet, in all this, the cardinal had not said one word concerning the Duke of Buckingham.

It was at that moment that M. de Treville entered, cool, polite, and with a manner perfectly unobjectionable.

Warned of what had taken place by the presence of the cardinal, and by the change in the king's countenance, M. de Treville felt himself as strong as Samson in the presence of the Philistines.

The king had already placed his hand upon the handle of the door; but, at the noise of M. de Treville's entrance, he turned round.

'You come in good time, sir,' said his majesty; who, when his passions were thoroughly excited, never dissembled, 'for I hear fine things of your musketeers.'

'And I,' said Treville coolly, 'have fine things to tell you of your civilians.'

'What is that you say?' said the king haughtily.

'I have the honour to inform your majesty,' said Treville in the same tone, 'that a party of lawyers, commissaries, and police agents—people very respectable in their way, but very bitter, as it appears, against the military—have presumed to arrest in a house, to drag through the public streets, and to cast into Fort l'Eveque (and all this under an order which they refuse to show me), one of my musketeers or rather of yours, sir, of irreproachable conduct, of an almost illustrious reputation, and favourably known to your majesty—M. Athos!'

'Athos,' said the king mechanically; 'yes, I certainly do know that man!'

'Your majesty may remember,' said M. de Treville, 'M. Athos is the musketeer who, in the vexatious duel that you heard of, had the misfortune to wound M. de Cahusac severely;—by the bye, my lord,' continued Treville, addressing the cardinal, 'M. de Cahusac is entirely recovered, is he not?'

'Yes, thank you,' said the cardinal, biting his lips with anger.

'M. Athos,' continued Treville, 'had gone to visit one of his friends who was from home, a young Bearnese, a cadet in his majesty's guards, in the company of Essarts; but scarcely had he settled himself in his friend's room, and taken up a book whilst waiting, when a cloud of bailiffs and soldiers, mingled together, laid siege to the house, and broke open several doors.'

The cardinal here made the king a sign, which signified, 'It was on account of the business which I have been telling you.'

'We know all that,' said the king, 'for it was all done in our service.'

'And was it,' asked Treville, 'in your majesty's service, also, that one of my musketeers, who was perfectly innocent, has been seized, placed between two guards like a criminal, and marched through the midst of an insolent crowd, although he is a gallant man, who has shed his blood for your majesty ten times, and is yet ready to shed it again?'

'Bah,' said the king, somewhat shaken; 'and was that really the way of it?'

'M. de Treville does not say,' replied the cardinal with the greatest indifference, 'that this innocent musketeer, this gallant man, had, only one hour before, attacked, sword in hand, four commissaries delegated by me to collect information concerning an affair of the greatest importance.'

'I defy your eminence to prove it,' cried Treville, with true Gascon frankness, and true military bluntness 'for, an hour before, M. Athos, who, I can assure you, is a man of the noble origin, did me the honour, after having dined with me, of conversing in my drawing-room with the Count de Chalons and the Duc de la Tremouille.'

The king looked at the cardinal.

'It is proved by a deposition,' said the cardinal, in answer to the mute interrogation of the king; 'and the individuals who were ill-treated have prepared what I have now the honour to present to your majesty.'

'Is the affidavit of a civilian of equal value with the word of honour of a soldier?' demanded Treville fiercely.

'Come, come, Treville, be silent,' said the king.

'If his eminence has any suspicions against one of my musketeers,' replied Treville, 'the justice of the cardinal is so well known, that I should myself demand an inquiry.'

'In the house in which this attack on justice has been made,' said the immovable cardinal, 'there lodges, I believe, a Bearnese, a friend of the musketeer.'

'Your eminence probably alludes to M. d'Artagnan?'

'I allude to a *protégé* of yours, M. de Treville.'

'Yes, your eminence; precisely so.'

'Do you not suspect this young man of having led M. Athos astray?'

'M. Athos—a man nearly double his own age,' broke in M. de Treville. 'No, sir; besides, M. d'Artagnan passed the evening at my house!'

'Ah!' said the cardinal, 'everybody seems to have passed the evening at your house.'

'Does his eminence doubt my word?' exclaimed Treville, his face flushed with anger.

'No, God forbid!' said the cardinal; 'but, only, at what hour was he at your house?'

'Oh! as to that, I can speak with certainty to your eminence; for, as he entered, I remarked that it was half-past nine by the clock, although I had believed it to be later.'

'And at what hour did he leave your hotel?'

'At half-past ten—exactly one hour after this event happened.'

'But, at least, M. Athos was seized in that house, in the Rue des Fossoyeurs!' said the cardinal, who did not for a moment doubt the loyalty of M. de Treville, yet felt that victory was leaving him.

'Is it unlawful for a friend to visit a friend? or for a musketeer of my company to keep company with a guard of M. des Essarts?'

'Yes, when the house where he associates with his friend is suspected.'

'This house is suspected, Treville!' said the king: 'perhaps you did not know that.'

'Indeed, sire, I did not know it. But, although it might be suspected, I deny that it was in that part which M. d'Artagnan inhabits; for I can assure you, sir, if I may believe what he has said, that there does not exist a more devoted servant of your majesty, or a more profound admirer of the cardinal.'

'Is it not this d'Artagnan who wounded Jussac in that unfortunate encounter which took place one day near the convent des Carmes Dechaux?' demanded the king, looking at the cardinal, who coloured with spite. 'And wounded Bernajoux the next day.'

'Yes, sire, yes; it is the same. Your majesty has a good memory!'

'Come, what shall we decide upon?' said the king.

'That concerns your majesty more than me,' answered the cardinal. 'I assert his guilt.'

'And I deny it,' said Treville. 'But his majesty has judges—let them determine on the affair.'

'Exactly so,' said the king, let us refer the matter to the judges: it is their business to judge, and they shall judge it.'

'Only,' said Treville, 'it is a sad thing, in these unhappy times in which we live, that the purest life, the most indisputable virtue, cannot secure a man from disgrace and persecution. The army will be but little satisfied, I can answer for it, at being the object of such rigorous treatment at the hands of the police.'

'The expression was imprudent, but Treville had thrown it out purposely. He wished for an explosion; because the mine flames out as it explodes, and the flame enlightens us.

'The police!' cried the king, taking up Treville's words. 'Affairs of the police! And what do you know about them, sir? Busy yourself with your musketeers, and don't perplex my brain. It would seem, to hear you, that if a musketeer is arrested, France is imperilled. Ah! what a fuss about a musketeer! I will arrest ten, fifty, a hundred, ay, even the whole company, nor will any one utter a word!'

'The instant that they are suspected by your majesty,' said Treville, 'the musketeers become guilty. I am ready, therefore, to surrender my sword; for, after having accused my soldiers, I do not doubt that the cardinal will conclude by accusing me; and it is unquestionably better that I should deliver myself up as a prisoner with M. Athos, who is already arrested, and with M. d'Artagnan, who will doubtless before long be so too.'

'Gascon head! will you have done?' said the king.

'Sire,' said Treville, without in the least lowering his voice, 'give me up my musketeer, or let him be tried!'

'He shall be tried,' said the king.

'Well, so much the better: for then I shall demand your majesty's permission to plead his cause.'

The king dreaded an outbreak.

'If his eminence,' said he, 'had not any personal motives——.'

The cardinal saw which way the king was tending, and anticipated him.

'Pardon me,' said he, 'but the moment that the king sees in me a prejudiced judge, I retire.'

'Come,' said the king to M. de Treville, 'do you swear to me by my father, that M. Athos was at your house during this event, and that he had nothing to do with it?'

'By your glorious father, and by yourself, whom I love and venerate most in the world, I swear it!'

'You must reflect, sire,' said the cardinal, 'that if we thus release this prisoner, the truth cannot be discovered.'

'M. Athos shall always be forthcoming,' said Treville, 'when it may please the lawyers to interrogate him. He will not run away. I stand surety for him.'

'In reality he will not desert,' said the king; 'he can always be found, as Treville says. Besides,' added he, lowering his voice, and regarding the cardinal with a supplicating air, 'put them in security: it is politic.'

This policy of Louis XIII. made Richelieu smile.

'Give your order, sire,' said he, 'for you have the privilege of pardon.'

'The privilege of pardon applies only to the guilty,' said Treville, who wished to have the last word, 'and my musketeer is innocent .It is not a pardon, therefore, that your majesty is going to grant, but justice.'

'Is he at Fort l'Eveque?' asked the king.

'Yes, sire, and in a solitary dungeon, like the worst of criminals.'

' 'Od's blood!' said the king, 'what is to be done?'

'Sign the order for his release,' said the cardinal, 'and all will be ended. I believe, like your majesty, that M. de Treville's security is more than sufficient.'

Treville bowed respectfully, with a joy not unmingled with fear. He would have preferred an obstinate resistance on the part of the cardinal, to this sudden concession.

The king signed the order of release, and Treville carried it away immediately.

At the moment he was going out, the cardinal gave him a friendly smile, and said to the king—

'Great harmony exists between the officers and the soldiers of your musketeers, sire; it must be very beneficial to the service, and reflects honour on them all.'

'He will play me some scurvy trick presently,' thought Treville; 'one never has the last word with such a man. But let me hasten, for the king may change his mind soon; and, after all, it is more difficult to put a man back into the Bastille, or Fort l'Eveque, once he has got out of it, than to keep him prisoner there when they have already caught him.'

M. de Treville entered Fort l'Eveque triumphantly, and set at liberty his musketeer, who had not lost his calm indifference.

And the first time that he saw d'Artagnan, he said to him, 'You have escaped well: your sword-thrust to Jussac is now paid for; that to Bernajoux still remains; but you must not be too confident.'

M. de Treville had reason to distrust the cardinal, and to think that all was not ended; for scarcely had the captain of musketeers closed the door behind him before his eminence said to the king—

'Now that we are alone together, we must have some serious conversation, if it please your majesty. Sire, the Duke of Buckingham has been in Paris for five days, and left it only this morning.'

16

In which the Keeper of the Seals, Séguier, looked more than once after the bell, that he might ring it as he had been used to do

IT is impossible to form an idea of the impression which these few words produced on the king. He grew red and pale by turns, and the cardinal saw immediately that he had regained, by a single stroke, all the ground that he had previously lost.

'The Duke of Buckingham at Paris!' said the king; 'and what has he been doing there?'

'No doubt plotting with your enemies, the Huguenots and the Spaniards.'

'No, by God, no! Plotting, rather against my honour, with Madame de Chevreuse, Madame de Longueville, and the Conde.'

'Oh! sire, what an idea! The queen is too good, and, above all, loves your majesty too well.'

'Woman is feeble,' said the king: 'and as for her loving me too well, I have my own opinion about that!'

'Nevertheless, I maintain that the Duke of Buckingham came to Paris for an entirely political object.'

'And I am just as sure that he came for other purposes; but, if the queen is guilty, let her tremble!'

'After all,' said the cardinal, 'however unwilling I am to dwell upon a treason of this kind, your majesty, by your words, reminds me that Madame de Lannoy, whom, by your majesty's order, I have several times questioned, told me this morning that, the night before last, the queen was up very late, that this morning she was weeping very much, and that she had been writing throughout the whole day.'

'That confirms it!' said the king: 'writing to *him*, no doubt. Cardinal, I must have the queen's papers!'

'But how are we to get them, sire? It appears to me that neither I nor your majesty ought to undertake such an office.'

'How did they proceed towards the Maréchale d'Ancre,' said the king, in the most violent rage; 'they first ransacked her chests, and at last searched her person.'

'The Maréchale d'Ancre was only the Maréchale d'Ancre, a Florentine adventuress: but the august spouse of your majesty is Anne of Austria, Queen of France; that is, one of the greatest princesses in the world.'

'That only makes her the more criminal! The more she has forgotten the high position in which she is placed, the lower she has fallen. For a long time, now, I have been determined to put an end to all these petty intrigues of politics and love. There is, also, one La Porte in her service.'

'Whom I believe to be the master-spirit in all this.'

'Then you think as I do—that she is deceiving me,' said the king.

'I believe, and I repeat it to your majesty, that the queen plots against the king's power, but I have not said against his honour.'

'And I tell you, against both. I tell you that the queen

does not love me; I tell you that she loves another; I tell you that she loves this infamous Duke of Buckingham! Why did not you arrest him whilst he was in Paris?'

'Arrest the duke! arrest the prime minister of Charles I. Think, sire, what a commotion! And then, if the suspicions of your majesty had any foundation, which I much doubt, what a dreadful exposure—what horrible scandal.'

'But if he exposed himself to it, like a vagabond and a pilferer, he ought——'

Louis stopped, catching himself on the verge of a dreadful expression, whilst Richelieu, stretching out his neck, in vain expected the word which hung upon the king's lips.

'He ought——'

'Nothing,' said the king, 'nothing. But,' added he, 'during all the time that he was in Paris, you did not ever lose sight of him?'

'Never, sire!'

'Where did he reside?'

'In the Rue de la Harpe, at No. 75.'

'Where is that?'

'Near the Luxembourg.'

'And you are certain that the queen and he did not see each other?'

'I believe that the queen is too much attached to her duty, sire!'

'But they corresponded: it is to him that the queen was writing all day! Duke, I must have those letters.'

'Sire, and yet——'

'Duke, at whatever cost, I must have them!'

'I would observe to your majesty, however——'

'And would you also betray me, cardinal, since you thus oppose my wishes? Are you in league with the Spaniard, and the English; with Madame de Chevreuse, and with the queen?'

'Sire,' replied the cardinal, with a smile, 'I thought myself far removed from any such suspicion.'

'But cardinal, you hear what I say: I will have these letters!'

'There can be only one way.'

'What is that?'

'It is to charge M. de Séguier, the keeper of the seals, with this commission. The matter is wholly within his scope.'

'Let him be sent for immediately.'

'He must be at my house, sire. I sent for him there, and

when I came to the Louvre, I left word that he should wait for me!'

'Let him be sent for instantly!'

'Your majesty's orders shall be executed; but——'

'But what?'

'But the queen may perhaps refuse to obey.'

'What, my orders?'

'Yes, if she does not know that these orders come from the king.'

'Well, then, that she may have no doubt, I will convey the orders to her myself!'

'Your majesty will not forget that I have done all I could to prevent a rupture!'

'Yes, duke, yes; I know that you are very indulgent, perhaps too indulgent, to the queen; and I can tell you we must have some talk about that hereafter.'

'Whenever your majesty pleases; but I shall be always happy and proud to sacrifice myself for the harmony which I should wish to see between the king and queen of France.'

'Well and good, cardinal; but, in the meantime, send for the chancellor. And now I hasten to the queen.'

Then, opening the door of communication, Louis entered into the corridor which led from his own apartments to those of Anne of Austria.

The queen was surrounded by her ladies, Madame de Guitaut, Madame de Sablé, Madame de Monthazon, and Madame de Guéméné. In a corner was the Spanish lady of the bed-chamber, Donna Estafana, who had accompanied her majesty from Madrid. Madame Guéméné was reading aloud, and everybody was listening to her, except the queen, who had promoted this reading that she might, under the pretence of paying attention, indulge the train of her own thoughts.

These thoughts, all gilded as they were by a dying beam of love, were not therefore the less sad. Anne of Austria— deprived of the confidence of her husband, pursued by the hatred of the cardinal, who could never pardon her repulsion of a softer sentiment, and having constantly before her eyes the case of the queen-mother whom that hatred had tormented throughout her life, although, if the memoirs of the times are to be believed, Marie de Medici had begun by granting to the cardinal the sentiment which Anne of Austria had persisted in refusing him—Anne of Austria had seen her most devoted servants, her most confidential companions, her dearest favourites, fall around her. Like those unhappy beings who are endowed with a baleful nature, she brought misfortune upon everything she touched. Her friendship was a fatal gift, which attracted persecution. Madame de Chevreuse and Madame de Vernal were banished; and La Porte did not conceal from his mistress that he was in momentary expectation of an arrest.

It was at the very instant that she was profoundly indulging in these melancholy reflections that the door opened, and the king entered.

The reader became immediately silent; the ladies arose; and all was silence.

As for the king, he made no show of politeness; only stopping before the queen.

'Madame,' said he in a nervous voice, 'you are about to receive a visit from the chancellor, who will make known to you certain commands with which I have charged him.'

The unhappy queen, who was often threatened with divorce, with exile, and even with death, grew pale beneath her rouge, and could not restrain herself from saying—

'But why that visit, sire? What can the chancellor have to say, which your majesty could not tell me personally?'

The king turned on his heel without any answer; and almost at the same moment, the captain of the guards, M. de Guitaut, announced the presence of the chancellor.

Before the chancellor appeared, the king had already left the apartment by another door.

The chancellor entered, half smiling, and half blushing. As we shall probably fall into his company again in the course of this history, there will be no harm in our readers making acquaintance with him now.

This chancellor was a pleasant fellow. It was by des Roches le Masle, a canon of Notre-Dame, who had formerly been the cardinal's valet, that he had been recommended to his eminence, as one entirely devoted to his interests. The cardinal trusted him, and was always well served.

The following is one of the many stories which were circulated concerning him:

After a stormy youth, he had retired into a monastery to expiate, at least for a time, the follies of his juvenile years. But, in entering into this holy place, the poor penitent had been unable to close the door so quickly but that the passions which he flew from could enter with him. They worried him, in fact, unceasingly; and the superior—to whom he had confided this disgrace, and who wished to preserve him from it as far as he was able—advised him, in order to drive out the diabolical tempter, to have recourse to the bell-rope, and to pull it with his utmost might; since, on hearing this admonitory sound, the monks would understand that a brother was beset by temptation, and the whole community would instantly proceed to prayers.

The counsel seemed good to the future chancellor, who exorcised the evil spirit by a large volume of prayers, which were offered up by the monks. The devil, however, is not easily displaced, when he has once got into garrison; and in proportion as these exorcisms were multiplied, the temptations were increased; so that the unceasing clamour of the bell, by day and by night, perpetually announced the extreme need of mortification which the penitent experienced.

The monks no longer enjoyed a moment's rest. By day, they did nothing but go up and down the chapel stairs; and by night, besides complines and matins, they were obliged to jump out of their beds at least twenty times, to prostrate themselves upon the flooring of their cells.

It is not known whether the devil quitted his hold, or the monks got tired out; but at the end of three months the penitent reappeared in the world, with the reputation of being more terribly possessed by the evil spirit than any one who had ever lived.

On leaving the convent, he entered the magistracy, and became president in the place of his uncle. He then joined the cardinal's party, in doing which he evinced no small sagacity; became chancellor; served his eminence zealously against Anne of Austria; stimulated the judge in the business of Chalais; encouraged the efforts of the royal forest-master, M. de Laffemas; and, finally, invested with the fullest confidence of the cardinal, which he had so well won, he had just received that singular commission, in the execution of which he now presented himself before the queen.

The queen was standing when he entered, but as soon as she perceived him she seated herself in her easy-chair, and making a sign for her ladies to place themselves on their cushions and stools, said, in a tone of supreme haughtiness—

'What do you want, sir; and for what object do you come here?'

'To make, madame, in the king's name, and without

abating the respect which I entertain for your majesty, an exact examination of all your papers.'

'What, sir! an examination of my papers—of mine! Truly, it is a most disgraceful act!'

'Deign to pardon me, madame, but in this affair I am only an instrument of the royal will. Has not his majesty but just left the room; and did he not himself invite you to expect this visit?'

'Search, then, sir; I am, it seems, a criminal. Estafana, give up the keys of my tables and desks.'

The chancellor went through the formality of searching throughout the room, although he well knew that it was not there that the queen would hide the important letter which she had that day written.

But when he had, at least twenty times, opened all the drawers, and shut them again, it became necessary, in spite of any hesitation he might experience, to end the business by searching the queen herself. The chancellor advanced, therefore, towards her majesty, and, with a nervous tone and manner, said—

'And now I must make the principal search.'

'And what is that?' demanded the queen, who did not, or rather would not, understand him.

'His majesty is certain that a letter has been written by you during the day; and he knows that it has not yet been forwarded to its destination. This letter is not to be found either in your table, or your desk, and yet it must be somewhere.'

'Would you dare to lay your hand upon your queen?' asked Anne of Austria, assuming all her haughtiness, and fixing on the chancellor eyes which had become almost threatening.

'I am a faithful subject of the king, madame, and everything that his majesty may order, I shall execute.'

'Well, it is true!' exclaimed the queen, 'and the spies of the cardinal have served him faithfully. I *have* written a letter to-day, and that letter is not gone. It is here!' and her majesty placed her beautiful hand upon her bosom.

'Give me the letter, then, madame,' said the chancellor.

'I will only give it to the king, sir,' said the queen.

'If his majesty had wished the letter to be handed to him, madame, he would have demanded it himself. But I repeat, it is to me that he gave the order to obtain it, and, if you did not give it up——'

'Well! what then?'

'It is me that he has ordered to take it.'

'How? What can you mean?'

'That my orders go very far, madame, and that I am authorised to seek for this suspected paper, even on the person of your majesty.'

'Horrible!' exclaimed the queen.

'Be more compliant, then, madame.'

'This conduct is infamous in its violence! Cannot you see that, sir?'

'The king commands it! Therefore, madame, excuse me.'

'I will not endure it. No! no! I will die rather!' said the queen, in whom the imperial blood of Spain and Austria revolted at the outrage.

The chancellor made a most reverential bow, but it was evident that he did not mean to recede one step in the accomplishment of his commission. Just as an executioner's man might have done in the torture-chamber, he approached Anne of Austria, from whose eyes large tears of rage were gushing.

The queen was, as we have already said, of a singular beauty. The commission, therefore, was a delicate one; but the king had come, from very jealousy of Buckingham, to be no longer jealous of any other person.

At that moment the chancellor, Séguier, was no doubt looking out for the rope of the memorable bell; but, not finding it, he summoned up his resolution, and moved his hand towards the place where the queen had admitted that the paper was concealed.

Anne of Austria—blanched as though it had been by the approach of death—receded for a single step. Then, supporting herself by leaning with her left hand on a table which stood behind her, she drew with her right the paper from her bosom, and presented it to the keeper of the seals.

'Here, sir, take the letter,' cried the queen, in a trembling, sobbing voice; 'take it, and free me from your odious presence.'

The chancellor, who was also trembling from an emotion easy to conceive, took the letter, bowed to the very ground, and withdrew.

Scarcely was the door closed upon him, before the queen fell nearly senseless into the arms of her women.

The chancellor carried the letter to the king, without having read one syllable of its contents. His majesty took it with a trembling hand, and looked for the address but, finding none, he became very pale, and opened the paper slowly. Then, seeing by the first words that it was addressed to the King of Spain, he read it very rapidly.

It was a complete plan of attack against the cardinal. The queen invited her brother and the Emperor of Austria to make a show—offended as they were by the policy of Richelieu, whose constant aim it was to humble the house of Austria—of declaring war against France, and to lay down the dismissal of the cardinal as a condition of peace; but, of love, there was not one single word in all the letter.

The king, in great delight, inquired whether the cardinal was still at the Louvre. The answer was that his eminence was in the official cabinet, awaiting his majesty's commands.

The king immediately hastened to him.

'Here, duke,' said he, 'you were right, and I was wrong. The whole intrigue is political, and love was not the subject of this letter. But, on the other hand, there is a good deal about you.'

The cardinal took the letter, and read it with the greatest attention; and when he had reached the end, he read it a second time.

'Well, your majesty,' said he, 'you see how far my enemies go: they threaten you with two wars if you do not dismiss me. Truly, sire, in your place I would yield to such pressing inducements; and, on my part, I should be truly happy to retire from affairs of state.'

'What are you saying, duke?'

'I say, sire, that my health fails under these excessive struggles and eternal labours. I say, that in all probability I shall be unable to support the fatigues of the siege of La Rochelle; and that it would be better for you to appoint either M. de Condé, or M. de Bassompierre, or some valiant man whose profession is to conduct a war, instead of me, a churchman, continually turned aside from my vocation to engage in affairs for which I am entirely unfit. You will be more prosperous in the interior of the kingdom, sire; and I doubt not that you will also be more triumphant abroad.'

'Duke,' said the king, 'your irony does not deceive me. Depend upon it, that all those who are mentioned in this letter shall be punished as they deserve;—even the queen herself.'

'What can your majesty mean? God forbid that the queen

should be harassed upon my account! She has always believed me her enemy, sire, though your majesty can testify that I have ever taken her part warmly, even against yourself. Oh! if she betrayed your majesty's honour, it would be a very different thing, and I should be the first to say—no mercy, sire, no mercy on the guilty! Happily, there is nothing of the kind here; and your majesty has just obtained a new proof of her innocence!'

'It is true, cardinal, and you were right, as you always are; but yet the queen has none the less deserved all my anger.'

'It is you, sire, who have incurred hers; and when she seriously resents your conduct, I shall not blame her. Your majesty has treated her with great severity!'

'It is thus that I will always treat my enemies, and yours, duke, however lofty they may be, and whatever risk I may incur from being severe towards them.'

'The queen is my enemy, but not yours, sire; she is, on the contrary, a submissive, irreproachable, and devoted wife: permit me, then, to intercede for her with your majesty.'

'Let her humble herself, then, and make the first overtures.'

'On the contrary, sire, set her the example: you were wrong first, since you were suspicious of the queen.'

'Make the first overtures?' said the king. 'Never!'

'Sire, I beseech you!'

'Besides, how could I make overtures?'

'By doing something which you know will be agreeable to her.'

'What?'

'Give a ball. You know how much the queen loves dancing, and I will answer for it that her anger will not resist such an attention.'

'Cardinal, you know that I do not like these worldly pleasures.'

'Her majesty will be only the more grateful to you, as she knows your antipathy to this amusement. Besides, it will enable her to wear those beautiful diamond studs which you gave her on her birthday, and with which she has not yet had any opportunity to adorn herself.'

'We shall see, cardinal; we shall see,' said the king, who, in his delight at finding the queen merely guilty of a fault about which he did not much care, and innocent of a crime which he greatly dreaded, was quite ready to reconcile himself with her. 'We shall see; but, upon my honour, you are too indulgent.'

'Sire,' said the cardinal, 'leave severity to ministers: indulgence is a regal virtue: make use of it, and you will reap its benefits.'

Hearing the clock strike eleven, the cardinal made an obeisance, and begged permission to retire; beseeching his majesty to make his peace with the queen.

Anne of Austria, who, after the seizure of her letter, expected some reproaches, was much surprised the next day to see the king make some attempts at a reconciliation with her. The first emotion was repulsion: her pride as a woman, and her dignity as a queen, had both been so cruelly outraged, that she was unable to meet these first advances of the king. But, vanquished by the advice of her ladies, she at last appeared to be disposed to forgiveness. The king took advantage of this favourable moment to tell her that he thought of giving an immediate entertainment.

An entertainment was so rare a thing to the poor queen, that at this declaration, as the cardinal had foreseen, the last trace of her resentment vanished, if not from her heart, at any rate from her countenance. She asked on what day this entertainment was to be given; but the king answered that, on that point, he must consult the cardinal.

Not a day elapsed, in fact, but the king asked the cardinal when it was to be; and, day by day, his eminence deferred it upon some pretext or other. Thus did ten days pass away.

On the eighth day after the scene we have described, the cardinal received a letter with the London post-mark, and containing only these few lines—

'I have got them, but cannot leave London for want of money. Send me five hundred pistoles, and, four or five days after having received them, I shall be in Paris.'

On the very day that the cardinal received this letter, the king asked the usual question.

Richelieu counted on his fingers, and said to himself in a low voice—

'She will reach Paris,' she says, 'four or five days after the receipt of this money.' Four or five days will be required for the money to get there; four or five days for her to return; that makes ten days. Allow for contrary winds and accidents of fate, and the weakness of a woman, and let us fix it at twelve days.'

'Well, duke,' said the king, 'have you calculated?'

'Yes, sire: this is the 20th of September; the city magistrates will give an entertainment on the 3rd of October. That will

suit exactly, for you will not have the appearance of going
out of your way to please the queen.'

Then the cardinal added—

'By the way, sire, do not forget to tell her majesty, *the
evening before the fête*, that you wish to see how the diamond
studs become her.'

17

The Bonancieux Household

IT was the second time that the cardinal had recalled the
king's attention to these diamond studs. His majesty had
been struck by this circumstance, and supposed that the
recommendation concealed some mystery.

More than once had his majesty been annoyed that the
cardinal's police—which, without having attained the perfection of that of modern times, was nevertheless very good—
was better informed than he himself was of what was taking
place in his own royal household. He hoped, therefore, to
glean some information from a conversation with the queen,
and then to return to the cardinal, and tell him some secret
which his eminence might, or might not, be acquainted
with, but whose exposition, in either case, must raise him
very much in the eyes of his minister.

He went accordingly to the queen, and, in his habitual
way, accosted her with threats against those by whom she
was surrounded. The queen bowed her head, and allowed
the torrent to pass by without reply, hoping that it would
at last exhaust itself. But that was not his majesty's design.
He wished for a discussion, in which some light or other
might be struck out, being convinced that the cardinal had
kept something back, and was springing upon him one of
those terrible surprises which his eminence so well knew
how to contrive. He obtained his object by perseverance in
accusing.

'But,' said Anne of Austria, wearied of these vague attacks,
'but, sire, you do not tell me all that you have in your heart.
What have I done? What crime have I committed? It is
impossible that your majesty should make all this disturbance
about a letter written to my brother!'

The king, being attacked in such a direct manner himself,

did not know what to answer. He thought that this was the time to issue the injunction which he had been charged to make on the eve of the ball.

'Madame,' said he, with dignity, 'there will soon be a ball at the Hotel de Ville. I desire that, to honour our worthy magistrates, you will be present at it in state dress, and, above all, adorned by those diamond studs which I gave you on your birthday. There is my answer.'

And terrible that answer was. The queen believed that his majesty knew all her secret; and that the cardinal had persuaded him to that long dissimulation of seven or eight days, which, moreover, accorded well with his own character. She became excessively pale; rested her beautiful hand, which looked then as though it were of wax, upon a bracket; and, gazing at the king with terrified eyes, answered not a word.

'You hear me, madame,' said the king, who thoroughly enjoyed this embarrassment, but without guessing its cause; 'you hear me?'

'Yes, sire, I hear you,' stammered the queen.

'You will be present at this ball?'

'Yes.'

'With your diamond studs?'

'Yes.'

The paleness of the queen, if possible, increased; and the king perceived, and enjoyed it, with that cold-blooded cruelty which was one of the worst parts of his character.

'It is settled then,' said he, 'and that is all I had to say to you.'

'But on what day will this ball take place?' asked Anne of Austria.

The king instinctively felt that he ought not to reply to this question, which the queen had put to him in an almost dying voice.

'Almost immediately, madame,' said he; 'but I do not exactly remember the precise date. I will ask the cardinal about it.'

'It was the cardinal, then, who told you of this ball?' said the queen.

'Yes, madame,' said the astonished king; 'but what of that?'

'And was it he who told you to request me to appear in these studs?'

'That is to say, madame——'

'It was he, sire; it was he!'

'Well, what does it signify, whether it was the cardinal or me? Is there any crime in the request?'

'No, sire.'

'Then you will appear?'

'Yes, sire!'

'Very well,' said the king, retiring; 'very well; I shall depend upon it.'

The queen curtseyed, less from etiquette, than because her knees bent under her.

His majesty departed, enchanted.

'I am lost,' muttered the queen; 'lost, for the cardinal evidently knows all, and he it is who pushes forward the king, who, as yet, is in ignorance, but will soon be made acquainted with the whole. I am lost! My God! my God!'

She knelt down upon a cushion, and prayed, with her head buried between her palpitating arms. Her position, was, in fact, terrible. Buckingham had returned to London. Madame de Chevreuse was at Tours. More closely watched than ever, the queen felt painfully certain that one of her ladies had betrayed her, without knowing which. La Porte could not quit the Louvre. She had not a soul in the world in whom she could trust.

In the prospect of the ruin which was hanging over her, and the desolation which she experienced, the queen gave way to tears and sobs.

'Cannot I be of any service to your majesty?' said a voice, full of gentleness and pity.

The queen turned eagerly, for there could be no deception in the expression of that voice; it was the voice of a friend.

In fact, at one of those doors which opened into the queen's apartment, appeared the pretty Madame Bonancieux. She had been engaged arranging dresses and linen in a closet when the king entered, and, being unable to get out, had heard the whole of the conversation.

The queen uttered a cry on seeing herself surprised; for, in her agitation, she did not recognise the young woman who had been given to her by La Porte.

'Oh, do not be afraid,' said Madame Bonancieux, joining her hands, and crying herself, at the queen's agony. 'I am your majesty's slave, in body and in soul; and far as I am below you, inferior as my position may be, I believe that I have found a way of relieving your majesty from your difficulty!'

'You? oh, Heaven! you!' exclaimed the queen. 'But let me see you, let me look you in the face. I am betrayed on all sides: may I confide in you?'

'Oh! madame!' said the young woman, falling on her knees, 'oh! doubt me not. On my soul, I am ready to die for your majesty.'

This exclamation came from the very depths of the heart, and it was impossible to distrust it.

'Yes,' continued Madame Bonancieux, 'there are traitors here; but, by the blessed name of the Virgin, I swear to you that there is no one more devoted to your majesty than I am. Those diamond studs that the king has mentioned, you gave to the Duke of Buckingham, did you not? They were within the little rosewood casket which he carried under his arm. Am I mistaken? Is it not as I have said?'

'Oh! my God, my God!' muttered the queen, her teeth chattering with affright.

'Well, these studs,' said Madame Bonancieux, 'must be got back again.'

'Yes, without doubt,' said the queen; 'but how can it be done? How can we succeed?'

'Some one must be sent to the duke.'

'But who? who? None can be trusted.'

'Have confidence in me, madame; do me this honour, my queen, and I will find a messenger.'

'But it will be necessary to write!'

'Oh, yes, that is indispensable. But two words from your majesty's hand, and under your own private seal, will serve.'

'But those two words! They will be my condemnation —divorce! exile!'

'Yes, if they fall into the wrong hands. But I will undertake that these two words shall be delivered according to their address.'

'Oh! my God! must I then entrust my life, my honour, my reputation, to your hands?'

'Yes! yes, madame, you must, and I will preserve them all.'

'But how? Tell me that, at least.'

'My husband has been set at liberty these two or three days. I have not yet had time to see him. He is a worthy, honest man, incapable of hatred or love. He will do what I wish: he will set out at my request, without knowing what he carries; and he will deliver your majesty's letter, without even knowing it is your majesty's, to the address which it may bear.'

The queen seized the young woman's hands with a passionate impulse, looked at her as if to read the depths of her heart, and then, seeing nothing but sincerity in her beautiful eyes, kissed her tenderly.

'Do this,' exclaimed she, 'and you will have saved me my life and my honour!'

'Oh! do not exaggerate the service which I have the honour to render you. I have nothing to save for your majesty. You are only the victim of treacherous plots.'

'It is true, it is true, my child,' said the queen; 'you are right.'

'Give me this letter, then, madame, for time presses.'

The queen ran to a small table, on which there were pens, ink, and paper, and wrote two lines, which she sealed with her own seal, and handed to Madame Bonancieux.

'And now,' said the queen, 'we forget one thing, which is very necessary.'

'And what is that, madame?'

'Money.'

Madame Bonancieux blushed.

'Yes, it is true,' said she; 'and I will confess to your majesty that my husband——'

'Your husband has none. Is that what you would say?' said the queen.

'Yes, he has got it, but he is very avaricious: that is his chief fault. Nevertheless, let not your majesty be uneasy; we will find means.'

'And I have got none either;' (those who may read the memoirs of Madame de Motteville will not be astonished at this reply) 'but wait a minute!'

The queen ran to her jewel-box.

'Here,' said she; 'here is a ring of great value, as I am assured. It was given me by my brother, the King of Spain; it is mine, and I may dispose of it. Take this ring, convert it into money, and let your husband set out.'

'In one hour you shall be obeyed.'

'You see the address,' said the queen, speaking so low that she could scarcely be heard—'*To my Lord Duke of Buckingham, London.*'

'The letter shall be delivered to himself alone!'

'Generous child!' exclaimed Anne of Austria.

Madame Bonancieux kissed the queen's hand, concealed the letter in her bosom, and disappeared with the lightness of a bird.

In ten minutes she was at her own house. She had not seen her husband since his liberation, as she had told the queen, and was therefore ignorant of the change which had taken place in him regarding the cardinal—a change which his eminence's flattery and money had effected, and which had been strengthened by two or three visits from Rochefort, who had become Bonancieux's best friend, having persuaded him that the abduction of his wife had proceeded from no culpable sentiment, but was merely a political precaution.

She found M. Bonancieux alone. The poor man was with great difficulty restoring some order to his house, where he had found the furniture almost destroyed, and the chests mostly empty;—justice not being one of the three things which King Solomon points out as leaving no traces of their course. As for the servant-girl, she had fled on the arrest of her master. Terror had taken such hold of the poor thing, that she never ceased walking until she had reached Burgundy, her native province.

The worthy mercer had, as soon as he reached home, announced his happy return to his wife, and she had replied by congratulations, and an assurance that the first moment she could snatch from her duties should be altogether devoted to a visit to him.

The first moment had been five days in arriving, which, in other circumstances, might have appeared rather long to Master Bonancieux; but he had ample food for reflection in the visit he had paid the cardinal, and in those which he had received from Rochefort; and it is well known that nothing makes the time pass so well as reflection.

And the reflections of Bonancieux were, besides, all of a rosy tint. Rochefort called him his good friend, his dear Bonancieux, and did not cease to tell him that the cardinal thought very highly of him. The mercer already saw himself on the high road to honours and fortune.

On her part, Madame Bonancieux had reflected also; but, it must be confessed, on other things than ambition. In spite of all she could do, her thoughts would turn towards that handsome young man, who was so brave, and seemed to be so full of love. Married at eighteen, and having always lived in the midst of her husband's friends, who were but little calculated to excite the affections of one whose sentiments were more elevated than her station, Madame Bonancieux had remained insensible to all vulgar impressions.

But, at that period more particularly, the title of gentleman had great influence over the citizens; and d'Artagnan was a gentleman, and, besides, wore the uniform of the guards, which, except that of the musketeers, was the most highly appreciated by the fair sex. He was, moreover, young, handsome, and adventurous; and he talked of love like one who loved, and is eager to be loved in return. All this was more than enough to turn a heart of twenty-three years of age; and Madame Bonancieux had just arrived at that period of her life.

The happy married couple, although they had not met for more than eight days, and during that time some grave events had happened, addressed each other with a certain pre-occupation of mind. Nevertheless, M. Bonancieux manifested sincere joy, and advanced towards his wife with open arms.

Madame Bonancieux offered her forehead to be kissed.

'Let us have a little talk,' said she.

'What!' said the astonished Bonancieux.

'Yes, certainly. I have something of the greatest importance to tell you.'

'Really! and I have some questions of importance to put to you. Explain to me your abduction, I beg of you.'

'That is of no consequence just now,' said Madame Bonancieux.

'And what is this affair of consequence, then? Is it about my imprisonment?'

'I heard of that on the same day; but, as you were guilty of no crime, as you were connected with no intrigue, and as you knew nothing that could compromise you, I only attached to that event the importance which it merited.'

'You speak of it with little concern, madame,' replied Bonancieux, hurt at the slight interest which his wife manifested in him. 'Do you not know that I was incarcerated for one day and one night in a dungeon of the Bastile?'

'A night and a day are soon passed. But let us have done with your captivity, and return to the object of my return to you.'

'What! the object of your return to me! Then is it not the desire of seeing your husband, from whom you have been separated for eight days?' demanded the mercer, cut to the quick.

'It is that first, and something else afterwards.'

'Speak!'

'An affair of the very greatest importance; on which, perhaps, our future fortune may depend.'

'Our fortune has a very different look since I saw you last, Madame Bonancieux; and I should not wonder if, some months hence, it should excite the envy of many.'

'Yes, particularly if you will follow the instructions which I am going to give you.'

'Me?'

'Yes, you. There is a good and sacred action to be performed, sir, and much money to be gained at the same time.'

Madame Bonancieux knew that, in speaking to her husband of money, she attacked his weak side. But a man, even a mercer, when he has conversed ten minutes with a Cardinal Richelieu, is no longer the same man.

'Much money to be gained?' said Bonancieux, pouting.

'Yes, a great deal.'

'About how much?'

'A thousand pistoles, perhaps.'

'Then what you are going to ask of me is of serious consequence?'

'Yes.'

'What must I do?'

'Set out immediately. I will give you a paper, which you will not let out of your own possession under any pretence whatever, and which you will deliver to the proper person.'

'And where am I go to?'

'To London.'

'I go to London! Come, now, you are joking. I have no business at London.'

'But others have business for you there.'

'Who are these others? I tell you, beforehand, I will do nothing in the dark; and I wish to know, not only to what I expose myself, but also for whom I expose myself.'

'An illustrious person sends you, and an illustrious person will receive you: the recompense will surpass your desires, and this is all that I can concede you.'

'Intrigues again! nothing but intrigues! Thank you, I am now somewhat distrustful of them: the cardinal has rather enlightened me on that subject.'

'The cardinal,' cried Madame Bonancieux; 'have you seen the cardinal?'

'He sent for me,' proudly answered the mercer.

'And were you imprudent enough to accept his invitation?'

'I ought to say that I had not the choice whether I would accept it or not, for I was between two guards. It is true, also, that as I did not then know his eminence, I should have been greatly delighted if I could have avoided the visit.'

'And he treated you ill—he threatened you?'

'He gave me his hand and called me his friend,' said Bonancieux: 'his friend! do you hear, madame, I am the friend of the great cardinal?'

'Of the great cardinal!'

'But perhaps you will not allow him that title, madame?'

'I dispute nothing; but I tell you, that the favour of a minister is ephemeral; that he must be mad who attaches himself to one. There are powers above a minister's which do not rest on the caprice of one man, or the issue of one event; and it is to these powers that one ought to cleave.'

'I am very sorry, madame, but I know no other power than that of the great man whom I have the honour to serve.'

'You serve the cardinal?'

'Yes, madame; and, as his servant, I will not permit you to engage in plots which compromise the safety of the state, or to assist the intrigues of a woman who is not French, but Spanish, in her soul. Happily, the great cardinal is there: his vigilant eye watches and penetrates the very depths of the heart.'

Bonancieux was repeating, word for word, a sentence he had heard from the Count de Rochefort; but the poor woman, who had entirely relied upon her husband, and had, in this hope, stood surety for him to the queen, did not the less shudder, both at the danger from which she had just escaped, and the utter helplessness of her present state. And yet, knowing the weakness, and, above all, the avarice of her husband, she did not despair of leading him into her schemes.

'Ah! you are cardinalist, sir!' cried she; 'ah! you serve the party who ill-uses your wife, and insults your queen!'

'The interests of individuals are nothing in comparison to the interests of the public. I am for those who serve the state!' said Bonancieux emphatically.

This was another of Rochefort's phrases which he had retained, and now made use of at the first opportunity.

'And do you know what the state you speak of is?' asked

Madame Bonancieux, shrugging her shoulders. 'Be content at being a private citizen, and cling to that side which offers you the greatest advantages.'

'Ah! ah!' said Bonancieux, striking a bag whose goodly paunch gave out a silvery sound; 'what do you say to this, Mistress Preacher?'

'Where did this money come from?'

'Can't you guess?'

'From the cardinal?'

'From him, and from my friend the Count de Rochefort.'

'The Count de Rochefort! Why, that is the man who carried me off!'

'Possibly, madame!'

'And do you accept money from such a man?'

'Did you not tell me that this abduction was entirely political?'

'Yes: but then it was designed to make me betray my mistress—to drag from me, by tortures, confessions which might compromise the honour, and perhaps the life, of my august mistress.'

'Madame,' said Bonancieux, 'your august mistress is a perfidious Spaniard; and the cardinal does only what is quite right.'

'Sir,' said the young woman, 'I knew that you were cowardly, avaricious, and imbecile, but I did not know that you were infamous.'

'Madame,' said Bonancieux, who had never before seen his wife angry, and who recoiled before this conjugal rage; 'madame, what are you saying?'

'I say that you are a wretch!' continued Madame Bonancieux, who saw that she was recovering some influence over her husband. 'Ah! you are a politician! and, moreover, a cardinalist politician! Ah, you sell yourself, both body and soul, to the devil for gold!'

'No, but to the cardinal.'

'No difference,' cried the young woman. 'He who says Richelieu, says Satan.'

'Hold your tongue, madame; hold your tongue: you might be heard!'

'Yes, you are right, and I should be ashamed for any one to know your cowardice!'

'But what do you require of me, then? Let me hear!'

'I have told you that you should set off this instant for London, sir; and should loyally and truly perform the commission with which I condescend to entrust you. On this condition, I forget and forgive everything; and what is more,' she added, holding out her hand, 'I restore to you my affection!'

Bonancieux was a coward, and a miser; but he loved his wife and was therefore subdued.

A man of fifty cannot long be cross with a woman of three-and-twenty. Madame Bonancieux saw that he hesitated.

'Come,' said she; 'have you determined?'

'But, my dear woman, reflect a little on what you require of me. London is a long way from Paris—a very long way. And perhaps the business may involve some dangers.'

'What does that signify, if you escape then?'

'Well, then,' said the mercer, 'listen, Madame Bonancieux. I decidedly refuse. Intrigues frighten me. I have seen the Bastile. Oh! it is frightful, that Bastile! It makes my flesh creep, only to think of it. I was threatened with the torture. Do you know what the torture is? Wedges of wood, which they drive alongside your legs till the very bones split! No, most decidedly, I will not go. Why the deuce do you not go yourself? for, really, I begin to think I must have been mistaken about you until now. I suspect that you are a man, and a very violent one too!'

'And you! you are a very woman—a miserable, stupid, soulless woman. What! you are afraid! Well, then, if you do not set out this instant, I will have you arrested by order of the queen, and clapped into that Bastile which you dread so much.'

Bonancieux sunk into a deep consideration. He carefully balanced the two enmities in his brain—that of the cardinal against that of the queen: but the cardinal's preponderated enormously.

'Have me arrested by the queen!' said he; 'well, I will get myself liberated through his eminence.'

Madame Bonancieux saw that she had gone too far this time, and she trembled at her own rashness. She looked with terror for an instant at this stupid figure, as invincible in its obstinacy as all fools who are in fear.

'Well, then,' said she, 'so let it be. Perhaps, after all, you are right: a man sees further in politics than a woman does, and you more particularly, M. Bonancieux, who have chatted with the cardinal. And yet it is very hard,' continued she, 'that my husband, that a man on whose affection I thought I could rely, should treat me so unkindly, and not satisfy my request.'

'It is because your requests may lead too far,' said Bonancieux triumphantly, 'that I distrust them!'

'I renounce them, then,' said the young woman, with a sigh; 'let us talk no more about them.'

'If you would only tell me what I was to do in London,' resumed Bonancieux, who remembered, somewhat too late, that Rochefort had advised him to worm out all his wife's secrets.

'It is unnecessary that you should know it,' said the young woman, who was now restrained by an instinctive distrust; 'it was about a trifle such as women sigh for—about a purchase by which money might be gained.'

But the more the young woman defended it, the more important did Bonancieux esteem the secret which she refused to confide to him. He determined, therefore, to go immediately to the Count de Rochefort, and tell him that the queen was seeking for a messenger to send to London.

'Pardon me, if I leave you, my dear Madame Bonancieux,' said he, 'but not knowing that you were coming to see me, I had made an appointment with one of my friends. I will return directly. If you will only wait half a minute for me, as soon as I have done with this friend, I will return; and, as it begins to get late, I will accompany you to the Louvre.'

'Thanks, sir,' said Madame Bonancieux; 'you are not brave enough to be any protection whatever to me, and I will return alone to the Louvre.'

'As you please, Madame Bonancieux,' replied the ex-mercer. 'Shall I see you again soon?'

'Certainly. Next week I hope that I shall have a little liberty, and I will take advantage of it, to come and put our things in some order. They must be a good deal deranged.'

'Very well; I shall expect you. Have you any further commands for me?'

'Me? none in the world.'

'*Au revoir*, then.'

'*Au revoir*.'

Bonancieux kissed his wife's hand, and hastened away.

'So,' said Madame Bonancieux, when her husband had shut the street door, and she found herself alone—'so, nothing remained for that fool but to become a cardinalist!

And I, who answered for him to the queen—I who promised
my poor mistress—ah! my God! my God! she will take me
for one of those wretches who swarm the palace, and who
are placed about her as spies. Ah! M. Bonancieux, I never
loved you much, but it is worse than that now! I hate you;
and, upon my word, you shall pay for this!'

At the moment that she uttered these words, a knock on
the ceiling made her raise her head, and a voice, which
came through the floor, called out to her—

'Dear Madame Bonancieux, open the little door in the
alley, and I will come down to you.'

18

The Lover and the Husband

'Ah, madame,' said d'Artagnan, as he entered the door
which the young woman opened for him, 'allow me to tell
you that you have but a sorry husband.'

'What! have you heard our conversation?' eagerly
demanded Madame Bonancieux, looking anxiously at
d'Artagnan.

'Every word of it.'

'But, good God! how could you?'

'By a plan of my own, whereby I also heard the more
animated conversation which you had with the cardinal's
myrmidons.'

'And what did you understand from what we said?'

'A thousand things. First, that your husband is, happily,
a fool and a blockhead; I am heartily glad of this, since it
gives me an opportunity of engaging myself in your service;
and God knows I am willing to throw myself in the fire
for you. Then, that the queen wants some brave, intelligent,
and devoted man, to go to London for her. I have, at least,
two of the three qualifications which you require, and here
I am.'

Madame Bonancieux did not answer, but her heart beat
with joy, and a secret hope sparkled in her eyes.

'And what security will you give me,' she demanded, 'if
I consent to entrust you with this commission?'

'My love for you. Come, speak; command: what is there
to be done?'

'My God! my God!' uttered the young woman, 'ought I to confide such a secret to you, sir? You are almost a child!'

'Oh! I see, you want some one who will answer for me.'

'I confess that it would give me more confidence.'

'Do you know Athos?'

'No.'

'Porthos?'

'No.'

'Aramis?'

'No. Who are these gentlemen?'

'They belong to the king's musketeers. Do you know M. de Treville, their captain?'

'Yes, him I do know—not personally, but from having heard him mentioned to the queen as a brave and honourable gentleman.'

'You would not fear that he would betray you for the cardinal?'

'Certainly not.'

'Well, then, reveal to him your secret, and ask him whether, however important, however precious, however terrible it may be, you may not entrust it safely to me.'

'But this secret is not mine, and I must not thus disclose it.'

'You were going to confide it to M. Bonancieux,' said d'Artagnan, with some sharpness.

'As one would confide a letter to a hollow tree, to the wing of a pigeon, or the collar of a dog.'

'And yet you know that I love you.'

'You say so.'

'I am an honourable man.'

'I believe it.'

'I am brave.'

'Oh! of that I am sure.'

'Put me to the proof, then.'

Madame Bonancieux looked at the young man, restrained only by a last, lingering hesitation. But there was so much ardour in his eyes, and so much persuasiveness in his voice, that she felt constrained to trust him. Besides, she was in one of those positions in which it is necessary to run great risks for the sake of great results. The queen might be as certainly lost by too much caution, as by too much confidence. We must confess, also, that the involuntary sentiment which she experienced for this young protector determined her to speak.

'Listen,' said she; 'I yield to your protestations and

assurances; but I swear to you, before God, who hears us, that if you betray me, and my enemies let me escape, I will destroy myself, and accuse you of my death.'

'And I swear to you, before God, madame,' said d'Artagnan, 'that if I am seized whilst performing the orders you may give me, I will die sooner than do or say anything to compromise any one.'

Then the young woman confided to him the terrible secret, part of which had been by chance disclosed to him opposite the Samaritan.

This was their declaration of mutual love. D'Artagnan glowed with joy and pride. This secret which he possessed, this woman whom he loved—the confidence and the love made him a giant.

'I am off,' said he. 'I am off directly.'

'What! you are going? And what about your regiment? your captain?'

'Upon my life, you made me forget all about them, dear Constance. Yes, you are right; I must get leave of absence.'

'Another obstacle!' murmured Madame Bonancieux sorrowfully.

'Oh,' said d'Artagnan, after a moment's reflection, 'I shall easily manage that, never fear.'

'How so?'

'I will interview M. de Treville this evening, and will request him to ask this favour for me of his brother-in-law, M. des Essarts.'

'Now for another thing,' said Madame Bonancieux.

'And what is that?' inquired d'Artagnan, seeing that she hesitated.

'Perhaps you have got no money?'

'Take away the '*perhaps*',' said d'Artagnan, smiling.

'Then,' said Madame Bonancieux, opening a chest, and taking from it the bag which her husband had so lovingly caressed half an hour before, 'take this bag.'

'That which belonged to the cardinal!' exclaimed d'Artagnan, with a hearty laugh, as, thanks to the uplifted squares, he had not lost one syllable of the conversation between the mercer and his wife.

'Yes, the cardinal's,' replied Madame Bonancieux; 'you see that it makes a very imposing appearance.'

'Egad!' cried d'Artagnan, 'it will be doubly amusing to save the queen with his eminence's money.'

'You are an amiable and charming young man,' said

Madame Bonancieux; 'and depend upon it, her majesty will not prove ungrateful.'

'Oh! I am abundantly rewarded already,' said d'Artagnan 'I love you, and you allow me to tell you so; and even this is more happiness than I had dared to hope for.'

'Hush!' said Madame Bonancieux, starting.

'What is the matter?'

'Some one is speaking in the street.'

'It is the voice——'

'Of my husband. Yes, I recognise it.'

D'Artagnan ran and bolted the door.

'He shall not enter till I am gone,' said he; 'and when I have left, you will open the door.'

'But I ought to be gone too; and the disappearance of this money—how am I to explain it, if I am here?'

'You are right—we must both go.'

'Go? but how? He will see us if we go out.'

'Then we must go up to my room.'

'Ah!' exclaimed Madame Bonancieux, 'you say that in a tone that frightens me.'

Madame Bonancieux pronounced these words with tearful eyes. D'Artagnan perceived the tear, and threw himself upon his knees in deep emotion.

'On the word of a gentleman,' said he, 'in my room you shall be as sacred as in a temple.'

'Let us go, then, my friend,' said she; 'I trust in that word.'

D'Artagnan carefully unfastened the bolt, and both, light as shadows, glided through the inner door into the court, and, noiselessly ascending the stairs, entered, d'Artagnan's chamber.

Once in his own room, the young man, for greater security, barricaded the door; and then they both went to the window, and, through a chink of the shutter, saw M. Bonancieux talking to a man in a cloak.

At the sight of the man in the cloak, d'Artagnan made a spring, and, partly drawing his sword, rushed towards the door.

It was the man of Meung.

'What are you going to do?' cried Madame Bonancieux; 'you will ruin us all.'

'But I have sworn to kill that man!' said d'Artagnan.

'Your life is at present consecrated, and does not belong to you. In the queen's name, I forbid you to throw yourself into any danger beyond that of the journey.'

'And in your own name do you command nothing?'

'Yes, in my own name,' said Madame Bonancieux, with emotion; 'in my own name, I entreat you. But listen: I think they are talking about me.'

D'Artagnan approached the window, and listened.

M. Bonancieux had opened his door, and finding the room empty, had returned to the man in the cloak, whom he had left for an instant alone.

'She is gone,' said he; 'she must have returned to the Louvre.'

'You are quite sure,' replied the stranger, 'that she had no suspicion of your object in going out?'

'No,' said Bonancieux, with much self-complacence; 'she is a woman of too superficial an intellect.'

'And the young guardsman—is he at home?'

'I do not think he is. As you may perceive, his shutter is closed, and there is no light in his room.'

'Never mind; we had better make certain.'

'How so?'

'By rapping at his door. I will ask his servant.'

'Go!'

Bonancieux re-entered his room, passed through the same door which had just given egress to the two fugitives, ascended to d'Artagnan's landing-place, and knocked.

No one answered. Porthos, in order to make a display, had borrowed Planchet for that evening; and as for d'Artagnan, he was careful to give no sign of his presence.

At the moment that Bonancieux's knock resounded on the door, the young people felt their hearts bound.

'There is no one at home,' said Bonancieux.

'Let us go into your room, nevertheless; we shall be in greater privacy than at the door.'

'Ah! my God,' said Madame Bonancieux, 'we shall not hear any more.'

'On the contrary,' said d'Artagnan, 'we shall hear all the better.'

D'Artagnan lifted up the three or four squares which made another St. Denys's ear of his chamber, laid a piece of carpet on the floor, kneeled down upon it, and then made a sign to Madame Bonancieux to lean, as he was doing, over the aperture.

'You are sure that there is no one?' said the stranger.

'Quite,' said Bonancieux.

'And you think that your wife——'

'Is returned to the Louvre.'

'Without speaking to any other person than yourself?'

'I am sure of it.'

'It is a point of the greatest importance: do you understand?'

'Then the intelligence I have given you is of some value?'

'Very great, my dear Bonancieux; I would not disguise it to you.'

'Then the cardinal will be satisfied with me.'

'I do not doubt it.'

'The great cardinal!'

'You are quite sure that, in her conversation with you, your wife mentioned no names?'

'I am almost sure.'

'She did not mention either Madame de Chevreuse, or the Duke of Buckingham, or Madame de Vernel?'

'No; she merely said that she wished to send me to London, in the service of an illustrious person.'

'The traitor!' muttered Madame Bonancieux.

'Hush!' said d'Artagnan, taking her hand, which she gave up to him without a thought.

'Never mind,' said the man in the cloak; 'you are a block-head for not pretending to accept the commission; then you would have had the letter in your possession. The state, which is in danger, would have been saved, and you——'

'And I?'

'Well! and you—the cardinal would have given you letters of nobility.'

'Did he tell you so?'

'Yes, I know that he wished to surprise you with this present.'

'Be easy,' replied Bonancieux, 'my wife adores me, and there is plenty of time yet.'

'The ninny!' whispered Madame Bonancieux.

'Be quiet!' said d'Artagnan, pressing her hand more closely.

'What! is there yet time?' said the man in the cloak.

'I shall proceed to the Louvre, ask for Madame Bonancieux, say that I have considered the affair, obtain the letter, and hasten to the cardinal.'

'Well! go quickly. I will soon return, to know the result of your proceedings.'

The stranger then departed.

'The wretch!' said Madame Bonancieux, referring to her husband.

'Silence!' said d'Artagnan, again pressing her hand, and this time yet more warmly.

A terrible hullaballoo interrupted the reflections of d'Artagnan and Madame Bonancieux.

It was her husband, who had just discovered the loss of his bag, and was exclaiming against the robber.

'Oh, my God!' exclaimed Madame Bonancieux: 'he will awaken all the neighbourhood.'

Bonancieux cried out for a long time; but, as such cries were of common occurrence, they attracted no attention in the Rue des Fossoyeurs; and as the mercer's house was, moreover, in no very good repute, finding that nobody came to his help, he went out, still uttering his outcries, which they heard gradually dying away in the direction of the Rue du Bac.

'And, now that he is gone, it is your turn to depart.' said Madame Bonancieux. 'Be brave, but, above all, be prudent, and remember that you serve the queen.'

'The queen, and you!' exclaimed d'Artagnan. 'Be assured, beautiful Constance, that I shall return worthy of her gratitude; but shall I return worthy, also, of your love?'

The young woman only replied by the glowing blush that mantled on her cheek. After a few moments, d'Artagnan went out in his turn, enveloped in a long cloak, which was cavalierly thrust backward by the sheath of his enormous sword.

Madame Bonancieux followed him with that long look of affection which woman fixes on the man she loves; but, as soon as he had turned the corner of the street, she sank upon her knees, and, joining her hands, exclaimed—

'Oh, my God! preserve the queen, and preserve me!'

19

The Plan of Campaign

D'ARTAGNAN went straight to M. de Treville. He had reflected that the cardinal would, in a few minutes, be put upon his guard by that cursed stranger, who appeared to be his agent, and he very wisely thought that there was not a moment to lose.

The heart of the young man overflowed with joy. An

adventure was presented to him, by which both gold and glory might be won, and which, as a first encouragement, brought him into communication with the woman he adored. This chance had thus given to him, at once, more than he had even dared to solicit from Providence.

M. de Treville was in his saloon, surrounded by his usual circle of gentlemen. D'Artagnan, who was known as an intimate of the house, went directly to his cabinet, and asked to speak to him on business of importance.

He had scarcely been there five minutes before M. de Treville entered. At the first glance, and from the joy which sparkled in d'Artagnan's eyes, the worthy captain at once perceived that some new scheme was really in his mind.

On his way there, d'Artagnan had been considering whether he should confide in M. de Treville, or merely ask for a free leave of absence for a secret expedition. But M. de Treville had always been so kind to him, was so entirely devoted to the king and queen, and so cordially hated the cardinal, that the young man determined to tell him all the affair.

'You sent for me, my young friend?' said M. de Treville.

'Yes, sir,' said d'Artagnan, 'and you will pardon me, I hope, for having disturbed you, when you know the importance of the occasion.'

'Speak, then. I am all attention.'

'It is nothing less,' said d'Artagnan, speaking low, 'than that the honour—and perhaps the life—of the queen is at stake.'

'What are you saying,' said M. de Treville, looking round, to be certain that they were alone.

'I say, sir, that chance has made me master of a secret.'

'Which you will guard with your life, I hope, young man.'

'But which I ought to impart to you, sir; for you alone can assist me in the mission which has just been entrusted on behalf of her majesty.'

'Is this secret your own?'

'No, sir, it is the queen's.'

'Are you authorised by the queen to impart it to me?'

'No, sir; for, on the contrary, the most profound secrecy is recommended.'

'And why, then, are you about to betray it to me?'

'Because, as I tell you, without you I am powerless; and I fear that you will refuse me the favour which I come to solicit. unless you know the purpose for which it is solicited.'

'Keep your secret, young man, and tell me what you want.'

'I wish you to obtain for me, from M. des Essarts, a leave of absence for fifteen days.'

'When?'

'This very night.'

'Do you leave Paris?'

'I go on a mission.'

'Can you tell me where?'

'To London.'

'Has any one an interest in preventing the success of your design?'

'The cardinal, I believe, would give all the world to prevent that success,'

'And do you go alone?'

'Yes.'

'In that case, you will not get past Bondy. It is I who tell you so, on the word of Treville.'

'And why so?'

'You will be assassinated.'

'I shall be doing my duty.'

'But your mission will not be performed.'

'That is true,' said d'Artagnan.

'Believe me,' said M. de Treville, 'in every enterprise of this kind, there ought to be four at least, in order that one may succeed.'

'Ah! sir, you are right,' said d'Artagnan; 'but you know Athos, Porthos, and Aramis, and you can judge whether I may employ them.'

'Without imparting to them the secret, which I should rather not know?'

'We have sworn to one another, once for all, a blind confidence, and a devotion proof against all trials; besides, you can tell them that you have the fullest confidence in me, and they will not be more incredulous than yourself.'

'I can give each of them a leave of absence for fifteen days, and that is all:—to Athos, who still suffers from his wound, to go to the waters of Forges; and to Porthos and Aramis, to follow their friend, whom they do not wish to abandon in his melancholy condition. My sending their leave will be a proof that I authorise the expedition.'

'Thank you—a thousand thanks, sir, for your goodness!'

'Go, and find them, then, immediately; and let everything be settled this very night. But, first, write me your request to

M. des Essarts. Perhaps you had a spy at your heels, and your visit, which is in that case already known to the cardinal, will be thus accounted for.'

D'Artagnan wrote his request in due form; and M. de Treville, as he received it from him, assured him that before two in the morning the four furloughs should be at the respective homes of the travellers.

'Have the goodness to send mine to the lodgings of Athos,' said d'Artagnan. 'I should be afraid of some disagreeable encounter if I returned home again.'

'Don't be uneasy. Farewell, and a good journey to you,' said M. de Treville; 'but,' added he, recalling him, 'apropos——'

D'Artagnan returned.

'Have you got any money?'

D'Artagnan replied by shaking the bag which he had in his pocket.

'Have you enough?' said M. de Treville.

'Three hundred pistoles.'

'That will do: you might go to the end of the world with that.'

D'Artagnan bowed to M. de Treville, and pressed the hand which he offered him with respect, mingled with gratitude. From the time of his arrival in Paris, this excellent man had been uniformly entitled to his highest esteem: he had found him always consistent, honourable, and elevated.

His first visit was to Aramis. He had not been to his friend's lodgings since the evening when he had followed Madame Bonancieux; and, what is more, he had scarcely seen him since; but whenever he had met him he fancied that he saw a corroding sorrow stamped upon his countenance.

This evening, also, Aramis was sorrowful and dreamy. D'Artagnan put some questions to him concerning this continued melancholy; but Aramis ascribed it to a commentary on the eighteenth chapter of St. Augustin, which he was obliged to write in Latin by the following week, and which much occupied him.

When the two friends had been talking some time, a servant of M. de Treville brought a sealed packet.

'What is that?' demanded Aramis.

'The leave of absence which monsieur has demanded,' replied the servant.

'Me? I have not demanded a leave.'

'Hold your tongue, and take it,' said d'Artagnan. 'And here, my friend, here is a half pistole for your trouble; you will tell M. de Treville that M. Aramis very sincerely thanks him. Go.'

The servant bowed to the ground, and left the room.

'What does all this mean?' inquired Aramis.

'Pack what you may want for a fifteen days' journey, and follow me.'

'But I cannot leave Paris at present, without knowing——' Aramis stopped himself.

'What is become of *her*? is that not it?' continued d'Artagnan.

'Whom?' resumed Aramis.

'The lady who was here—the lady with the embroidered handkerchief.'

'Who told you there was a lady here?' said Aramis, becoming as pale as death.

'I saw her.'

'And do you know who she is?'

'I think I have a fair idea, at least.'

'Listen,' said Aramis: 'since you know so many things, do you know what has become of this lady?'

'I presume that she has returned to Tours.'

'To Tours? Yes! that may be; you evidently know her. But how is it that she returned to Tours, without saying anything to me about it?'

'Because she was in fear of being arrested.'

'Why did she not write to me?'

'Because she was afraid of compromising you.'

'D'Artagnan, you give me new life!' cried Aramis. 'I believed that I was despised; deceived. I was so happy to see her again! I could not believe that she had hazarded her liberty to see me; and yet for what other cause could she have returned to Paris?'

'For the same cause which this day obliges us to go to England.'

'And what is that cause?' demanded Aramis.

'You shall know it some day, Aramis; but, for the present, I will imitate the discretion of *the doctor's niece*.'

Aramis smiled, for he remembered the tale he had told his friends on a certain evening.

'Well, then, since she has left Paris—and you are sure of it, d'Artagnan—nothing more detains me here, and I am ready to follow you. You say we are going——'

'To Athos, at present; and, if you wish to come, I beg you will make haste, for we have already lost too much time. *Apropos*, tell Bazin.'

'Does Bazin accompany us?' inquired Aramis.

'Perhaps so. At any rate, it is better that he should follow us to Athos.'

Aramis called Bazin, and after having told him to come to them at Athos's—

'Let us go, then,' said he, taking his cloak, his sword, his pistols, and fruitlessly opening three or four drawers in hopes of finding a few stray pistoles. Then, when he was quite satisfied that this search was useless, he followed d'Artagnan, wondering how it was that the young guardsman knew, as well as he did, who the lady was to whom he had afforded hospitality, and knew better than he did where she was now gone.

Just as they were going out, he laid his hand on d'Artagnan's arm, and looking earnestly at him—

'You have not spoken to any one about this lady?' said he.

'To no one in the world.'

'Not even to Porthos and Athos?'

'I have not breathed a word to them about it.'

'That's right.'

Satisfied on that important point, Aramis went on his way with d'Artagnan, and they both soon reached Athos's lodgings.

'They found him holding his leave absence in one hand, and M. de Treville's letter in the other.

'Can you explain to me,' said he, 'what these mean that I have just received?'

'My dear Athos,—I very much wish, as your health absolutely requires it, that you should repose yourself for fifteen days. Go, therefore, and take the waters of Forges, or any others which may agree better with you, and get well quickly. Yours affectionately,   Treville.'

'Well,' said d'Artagnan, 'the leave and the letter mean that you must follow me.'

'To the waters of Forges?'

'There or elsewhere.'

'On the king's service?'

'The king's or the queen's. Are we not the servants of both?'

At this moment Porthos entered.

'Egad!' said he, 'here's a curious circumstance. Since when have they granted leave to the musketeers, without their asking for it?'

'Ever since they have had friends who ask it for them.' said d'Artagnan.

'Ah! ah!' said Porthos, 'it appears that there is something fresh in the wind.'

'Yes, we are off,' said Aramis.

'To what country?' demanded Porthos.

'Upon my word, I do not know exactly,' said Athos; 'ask d'Artagnan.'

'To London, gentlemen,' said d'Artagnan.

'To London,' said Porthos; 'and what are you going to do there?'

'And that is what I cannot tell you, gentlemen; you must trust to me.'

'But, to go to London money is necessary, and I have none,' said Porthos.

'Nor I,' said Aramis.

'Nor I,' said Athos.

'I have,' said d'Artagnan, lugging his treasure out of his pocket and laying it on the table. 'There are in that bag three hundred pistoles; let each of us take seventy-five, which is quite enough to go to London and to return. Besides, be easy; we shall not all reach London.'

'And why not?'

'Because, according to all probability, some of us will be left on the road.'

'Is it a campaign, then, that we are about to undertake?'

'Yes, and a most dangerous one, I forewarn you.'

'Ah! but, since we risk our lives, I, at least, would rather know the object,' said Porthos.

'That will do you a mighty deal of good,' replied Athos.

'Nevertheless,' said Aramis, 'I am of the same opinion as Porthos.'

'Pray,' said d'Artagnan, 'does the king usually give you his reasons? He tells you bluntly—gentlemen, they are fighting in Gascony, or in Flanders; go, and fight; and you go. As for any reasons—you do not trouble your heads about them.'

'D'Artagnan is right,' said Athos. 'Behold our three leaves of absence, which come from M. de Treville; and here are three hundred pistoles, which come from I know not where. Let us go and be killed where we are told to go. Is life worth so many questions? D'Artagnan, I am ready to follow you.'

'And I also,' said Porthos.

'And I also,' said Aramis. 'I shall not be sorry to leave Paris, after all. I need distractions.'

'Well, you will have quite enough of them, gentlemen, depend upon it!' said d'Artagnan.

'And now, when must we set off?' inquired Athos.

'Directly,' said d'Artagnan; 'not a minute must be lost.'

'Hollo, Grimaud, Planchet, Mousqueton, Bazin!' bawled out the four young men, calling their servants: 'polish our boots, and fetch our horses from the hotel.'

In fact, each musketeer left at the general hotel, as at a barrack, his own horse and that of his servant.

Planchet, Mousqueton, Grimaud, and Bazin, departed in the utmost haste.

'Now, let us arrange the plan of the campaign,' said Porthos. 'Where are we to go first?'

'To Calais,' said d'Artagnan; 'it is the most direct line to London.'

'Well,' said Porthos, 'my advice is as follows——'

'Speak! What is it?'

'Four men travelling together will be suspected. D'Artagnan must therefore give his instructions to each of us. I will go first, by way of Boulogne, to clear the road; Athos shall set out, two hours after, by that of Amiens; Aramis will follow us by that of Noyon; and as for d'Artagnan, he will travel by that which he likes best, in Planchet's clothes; whilst Planchet himself shall follow, in the uniform of the guards, to pass for d'Artagnan.'

'Gentlemen,' said Athos, 'my advice is not to include the servants in anything of this kind; a secret may, *perchance*, be betrayed by gentlemen; but is almost always sold by servants.

'The plan of Porthos appears to me to be impracticable,' said d'Artagnan, 'as I do not myself know what instructions I could give you. I am the bearer of a letter—that is all. I have not, and I cannot make, three copies of this letter, since it is sealed. We must, therefore, in my opinion, travel in company. This letter is here, in this pocket;' and he pointed out the pocket which contained the letter. 'If I am killed, one of you will take it, and will continue the journey; if he is killed, it will be another's turn; and so on. Provided only one should arrive, it is all that is necessary.'

'Bravo, d'Artagnan! Your advice is also mine,' said Athos. 'Nevertheless, we must be consistent. I am going to take the waters, and you will accompany me; but instead of going to Forges, I am going to the seaside: I may take my choice. If anybody wants to arrest us, I show M. de Treville's letter, and you will show your leaves of absence: if they attack us, we will defend ourselves; if they interrogate us, we must maintain sharply that we had no other intention than to dip ourselves a certain number of times in the sea. They would have too easy a conquest over four separate men; whilst four men united make a troop. We will arm our four servants with musquetoons and pistols; and if they send an army against us, we will give battle, and the survivor, as d'Artagnan has said, will deliver the letter.'

'Well done,' said Aramis; 'you do not speak often, Athos; but when you do speak, it is like St. John with the golden mouth. I adopt the plan of Athos.'

'And you, Porthos?'

'And I also,' said Porthos, 'if it suits d'Artagnan. As the bearer of the letter, he is naturally the leader of the enterprise. Let him decide, and we will execute.'

'Well, then,' said d'Artagnan. 'I decide that we adopt the plan of Athos, and that we set out in half an hour.'

'Agreed!' exclaimed the three musketeers, in chorus.

And each, plunging his hand into the bag, took from it seventy-five pistoles, and made his preparations to depart at the appointed time.

20

The Journey

At two o'clock in the morning our four adventurers left Paris, by the Porte St. Denis. Whilst the darkness lasted they continued silent. In spite of themselves, they felt the influence of the obscurity, and suspected an ambuscade at every step.

With the first streak of day, their tongues became unbound, and gaiety returned with the sun. It was as on the eve of battle: the heart beat, and the eyes sparkled; and they felt that the life which they were, perhaps, about to leave, was, after all, a pleasant and a precious thing.

The appearance of the cavalcade was of the most

formidable character: the black horses of the musketeers, their martial bearing, and that military custom which made these noble chargers march in rank, were all indications of their calling, which would have betrayed the strictest incognito. The valets followed, armed to the teeth.

All went on well as far as Chantilly, where they arrived at about eight in the morning, and where they were obliged to breakfast. They dismounted at a tavern, which was recommended by the sign of St. Martin, giving half his cloak to a beggar. They ordered their servants not to unsaddle their horses, and to be ready to depart at a moment's notice.

They entered the common room of the inn, and placed themselves at table. A gentleman, who had arrived by the Dampmartin road, was seated at the table, breakfasting. He entered into conversation, concerning the rain and the fine weather. The travellers replied: he drank to their healths, and they returned his politeness. But at the moment when Mousqueton came to announce that the horses were ready, and as they arose from table, the stranger proposed to Porthos, to drink the cardinal's health. Porthos replied, that he desired nothing better, provided the stranger would, in turn, drink the health of the king. The stranger exclaimed that he knew no other king than his eminence. On this, Porthos told him he must be drunk, and the stranger drew his sword.

'You have done a foolish thing,' said Athos; 'but never mind; you cannot draw back now: kill the fellow, and come after us as fast as you can.'

And all three mounted their horses and departed at full speed; whilst Porthos promised his adversary to perforate him in all the fashions known to the fencing school.

'There goes one of us,' said Athos, after they had travelled five hundred paces.

'But why did that man attack Porthos, rather than the others?' said Aramis.

'Because, from Porthos speaking louder than the rest of us, he took him for the leader of the party,' said d'Artagnan.

'I always said,' muttered Athos, 'that the Gascon youth was a well of wisdom.'

The travellers proceeded on their way.

At Beauvais they stopped two hours, as much to breathe their horses, as to wait for Porthos. At the end of that time, as neither Porthos nor any intelligence of him had arrived, they resumed their journey.

About a league from Beauvais, at a point where the way was narrowed between two banks, they met eight or ten men, who, taking advantage of the road being unpaved at this place, seemed to be engaged in digging holes, and making muddy ruts.

Aramis, fearing to dirty his boots in this artificial slough, apostrophised them rudely. Athos wished to restrain him, but it was too late. The workmen began to rail at the travellers; and, by their insolence, even ruffled the temper of the cool Athos, who urged his horse against one of them.

At this aggression, each of these men drew back to the ditch, and took from it a musket that was concealed there. The result was, that our seven travellers were literally riddled by shot. Aramis received a ball through the shoulder, and Mousqueton another in the fleshy part of the back, below the loins. But Mousqueton alone fell from his horse; not that he was seriously wounded, but that he could not see his wound, he no doubt thought it far more dangerous than it really was.

'This is an ambuscade,' said d'Artagnan: 'let us not burn priming, but away.'

Aramis, wounded as he was, seized the mane of his horse, which carried him off with the others. That of Mousqueton had rejoined them, and galloped riderless by their side.

'That will give us a spare horse,' said Athos.

'I should much prefer a hat,' said d'Artagnan, 'for mine has been carried off by a ball. It is very lucky, faith, that my letter was not within it.'

'Ah! but they will kill poor Porthos, when he comes up,' said Aramis.

'If Porthos were upon his legs, he would have rejoined us ere this,' said Athos. 'It is my opinion, that, in the combat, the drunkard grew sober.'

They galloped on for two more hours, although the horses were so fatigued, that it was to be feared they would break down on the way.

The travellers had made a detour by cross-roads, hoping thereby to be less molested; but, at Crevecœur, Aramis declared that he could go no farther. In fact, it had required all the courage which he concealed beneath his elegant form and polished manners, to proceed so far. At each movement he grew paler; and they were at last obliged to support him on his horse. Putting him down at the door of a wine-shop, and leaving with him Bazin, who was more hindrance than help in a skirmish, they set off again, in hopes of reaching Amiens, and passing the night there.

'Zounds!' said Athos, when they found themselves once more upon the way, reduced to two masters, with Grimaud and Planchet, 'Zounds! I will be their dupe no more. I promise you that they shall not make me open my mouth, or draw my sword, between here and Calais. I swear——'

'Don't swear,' said d'Artagnan, 'but gallop; that is, if our horses will consent to it.'

And the travellers dug their spurs into the flanks of their horses, which, thus urged, recovered some degree of strength. They reached Amiens at midnight, and dismounted at the sign of the Golden Lily.

The innkeeper had the look of the most honest fellow upon earth. He received the travellers with a candlestick in one hand, and his cotton nightcap in the other. He wished to lodge the two travellers, each in a charming chamber; but, unfortunately, these two chambers were at opposite extremities of the hotel. D'Artagnan and Athos declined them.

The host objected, that he had no others worthy of their excellencies; but they declared that they would rather sleep in the common room, on mattresses, upon the floor. The host insisted, but the travellers were obstinate, and carried their point.

They had just arranged their beds, and barricaded the door, when some one knocked at the shutters. They inquired who was there, and, on recognising the voices of their servants, opened the window. It was indeed Planchet and Grimaud.

'Grimaud will be quite able to guard the horses,' said Planchet, 'and, if the gentlemen like, I will sleep across their door, by which means they will be certain that no one can get at them.'

'And on what will you sleep?' asked d'Artagnan.

'This is my bed,' replied Planchet, strewing a bundle of straw.

'Come, then,' said d'Artagnan, 'you are quite right: the countenance of our host does not at all please me; it is far too polite.'

'Nor me, either,' said Athos.

Planchet got in at the window, and laid himself across the doorway; whilst Grimaud shut himself up in the stable, promising that at five in the morning he and the four horses should be ready.

The night passed quickly enough. Some one attempted, about two o'clock, to open the door; but, as Planchet awoke with a start, and cried out, 'Who is there?' he was answered that it was a mistake; and then the footsteps retreated.

At four in the morning a great noise was heard from the stables. Grimaud had endeavoured to awake the ostlers, and they had made an attack upon him. When the window was opened, they saw the poor fellow lying senseless, with his head split open by a blow from a broom handle.

Planchet went into the courtyard, and wanted to saddle the horses, but the horses were completely foundered. That of Grimaud, which had travelled for five or six hours with an empty saddle the evening before, might have continued its journey; but, by an inconceivable mistake, the veterinary surgeon, whom they had brought, as it appeared, to bleed the landlord's horse, had bled that of Grimaud instead.

This began to be vexatious. All these successive accidents were perhaps the result of chance; but they might also be the effect of design. Athos and d'Artagnan stepped out, whilst Planchet went to inquire whether there were three horses to be sold in the neighbourhood. At the door were two horses ready saddled, fresh, and vigorous. This was just the thing. He asked where their masters were; and was informed that they had passed the night there, and were now paying their bill.

Athos went down to settle their account, whilst d'Artagnan and Planchet remained at the door. The innkeeper was in a distant lower room, which Athos was requested to enter.

Athos went in confidently, and took out two pistoles to pay. The host was alone, and seated at his desk, one of the drawers of which was partly open. He took the money which Athos gave him, turned it over in his hands, and suddenly exclaiming that the pieces were bad, declared that he would have him and his companion arrested as passers of false coin.

'You rascal,' said Athos, as he went towards him, 'I will cut off your ears.'

But the host stooped down, and taking two pistols from the drawer, presented them at Athos, vociferating, at the same time, for help.

At that very moment, four men, armed to the teeth, rushed in through the side doors, and fell upon Athos.

'I am seized!' bawled Athos, with the utmost strength of his lungs; 'away with you, d'Artagnan; spur on! spur on!' and he fired off his two pistols.

D'Artagnan and Planchet did not wait to be twice warned. They unfastened the two horses which were standing at the door, jumped upon them, dug the spurs into their flanks, and went off at full gallop.

'Do you know what has become of Athos?' asked d'Artagnan, as they hurried on.

'Oh, sir,' said Planchet, 'I saw two men fall at his two shots, and it seemed to me, through the window, as if he were working away at the others with his sword.'

'Brave Athos!' ejaculated d'Artagnan. 'And then to know that I must abandon you! Well! the same thing awaits us, perhaps, at ten paces hence. Forward! Planchet, forward! You are a brave fellow.'

'I told you so, sir,' replied Planchet; 'the Picards are only known by being used. Besides, I am in my own country here, and that stimulates me.'

And both of them, spurring on as fast as possible, arrived at St. Omer without a moment's stay. At St. Omer they breathed their horses, with their bridles looped on their arms for fear of accident, and ate a morsel standing in the street; after which they again set off.

At a hundred paces from the gate of Calais, d'Artagnan's horse fell, and could by no means be got up again; the blood gushed from his eyes and nose. That of Planchet still remained; but he had chosen to halt, and nothing could induce him to continue his exertions.

Fortunately, as we have said, they were only a hundred paces from the town. They therefore left the two steeds upon the high road, and ran to the harbour. Planchet made his master remark a gentleman who had just arrived with his lackey, and was not above fifty yards before them.

They hastily drew near this gentleman, who appeared to be exceedingly busy. His boots were covered with dust, and he inquired whether he could not pass over to England instantaneously.

'Nothing easier,' replied the master of a vessel then ready for sailing, 'but an order arrived this morning to let no one leave without permission from the cardinal.'

'I have got that permission,' said the gentleman, drawing a paper from his pocket; 'there it is.'

'Get it countersigned by the governor of the port,' said the master of the vessel, 'and give me the preference.'

'Where shall I find the governor?'

'At his country house.'

'And where is his country house situated?'

'At a quarter of a league from the town: see, you may distinguish it from here—yonder slated roof, at the foot of the little hill.'

'Very well,' said the gentleman; and, followed by his servant, he took the road to the governor's country house.

D'Artagnan and Planchet followed him, at the distance of five hundred yards.

Once out of the town, d'Artagnan hurried forwards, and made up on the gentleman as he entered a small wood.

'Sir,' said d'Artagnan, 'you appear in particular haste?'

'No one can be more so, sir.'

'I am very sorry for it,' said d'Artagnan, 'for, as I am in a hurry also, I want you to render me a favour.'

'What is it?'

'To let me pass the Straits before you.'

'Impossible!' said the gentleman. 'I have done sixty leagues in forty-four hours, and I must be in London by noon to-morrow.'

'And I,' said d'Artagnan, 'have gone the same distance in forty hours, and must be in London by ten o'clock to-morrow.'

'Sorry to disappoint you, sir; but I have got here first, and will not go over second.'

'I am grieved also, sir,' said d'Artagnan, 'but I have got here second, and mean to go over first.'

'The king's service!' said the gentleman.

'My own service!' replied d'Artagnan.

'But, it seems to me, that this is a poor quarrel which you are seeking to make?'

'Zounds! what would you have it?'

'What do you want?'

'Do you want to know?'

'Certainly.'

'Very well! I want the order that you have in your pocket, as I have none, and must have one.'

'I presume you are joking.'

'I never joke!'

'Let me pass, sir.'

'You shall not pass.'

'My gallant, I will blow your brains out. Hollo! Lubin, my pistols.'

'Planchet,' said d'Artagnan, 'take care of the man—I will manage the master.'

Planchet, encouraged by what had already happened, rushed upon Lubin, and as he was strong and vigorous, laid him on his back, and put his knee upon his breast. 'Do your business, sir,' said Planchet to his master, 'I have settled mine.'

Seeing this, the gentleman drew his sword, and fell on d'Artagnan; but he had to do with rather a tough customer.

In three seconds d'Artagnan gave him three wounds, saying, at each thrust—

'One for Athos, one for Porthos, and one for Aramis.'

At the third stroke the gentleman fell like a log.

D'Artagnan thought he was dead, or at least that he had fainted, and approached him to seize the order; but, at the moment that he stretched out his hand to search for it, the wounded man, who had not dropped his sword, stabbed him with it on the chest, saying—

'One for you!'

'And one more for you! and the best last!' cried d'Artagnan, furiously pinning him to the earth with a fourth wound through the body.

This time the gentleman closed his eyes and fainted.

D'Artagnan felt in the pocket where he had seen him place the order for his passage, and took it. It was in the name of the Count de Wardes.

Then, throwing a last glance on the handsome young man, who was scarcely twenty-five years old, and whom he left lying there senseless, and perhaps dead, he breathed a sigh at the strange destiny which leads men to destroy each other for the interests of those they scarcely know, and who often are not even aware of their existence.

But he was soon disturbed in these reflections by Lubin, who was howling with all his might, and crying for aid.

Planchet put his hand upon his throat, and squeezed it as hard as he could.

'Sir,' said he, 'as long as I hold him so, he will not cry out; but the moment I leave go, he will begin again. I can see he is a Norman, and the Normans are monstrously obstinate.'

In fact, squeezed as he was, Lubin still endeavoured to sound his pipes.

'Stop!' said d'Artagnan; and, taking his handkerchief, he gagged him.

'Now,' said Planchet, 'let us bind him to a tree.'

The thing was properly done. They then placed the

Count de Wardes near his servant; and, as the night began to fall, and as both the bound man and the wounded one were some paces in the wood, it was clear that they must remain there till the next morning.

'And now,' said d'Artagnan, 'to the house of the governor.'

'You are wounded, I fear?' said Planchet.

'It is nothing: let us now think of what is of the most consequence; we can attend to my wound afterwards; besides, it does not appear to be very dangerous.'

And they both proceeded, with prodigious strides, towards the country house of the worthy functionary.

The Count de Wardes was announced.

D'Artagnan was introduced.

'Have you an order signed by the cardinal?' asked the governor.

'Yes, sir,' said d'Artagnan, 'here it is.'

'Ah! ah! it is regular and explicit,' said the governor.

'That is quite natural,' answered d'Artagnan; 'I am one of his most faithful servants.'

'It appears that his eminence wishes to hinder some one from reaching England.'

'Yes, a certain d'Artagnan, a Bearnese gentleman, who left Paris with three of his friends, intending to go to London.'

'Do you know him personally?' inquired the governor.

'Whom?'

'This d'Artagnan.'

'Perfectly well.'

'Give me some description of him, then.'

'Nothing is easier.'

And then d'Artagnan gave, feature for feature, the exact description of the Count de Wardes.

'Has he any attendant?' demanded the governor.

'Yes, a servant named Lubin.'

'We will watch for them, and, if we can lay hands upon them, his eminence may be assured that they shall be sent back to Paris, under a sufficient escort.'

'In so doing, sir,' said d'Artagnan, 'you will merit the gratitude of the cardinal.'

'Will you see him on your return, count?'

'Without doubt.'

'Tell him, I beseech you,' said the governor, 'that I am his most humble servant.'

'I will not fail to do so.'

Delighted by this assurance, the governor countersigned

the order, and returned it to d'Artagnan; who lost no time in useless compliments, but, having bowed to him and thanked him, took his leave.

Once out of the house, they took a circuitous path to avoid the wood, and entered the town by another gate.

The barque was still ready to sail, and the master waited on the quay.

'Well?' said he, seeing d'Artagnan.

'Here is my pass countersigned.'

'And the other gentleman.'

'He is not going over to-day,' said d'Artagnan; 'but make yourself easy, I will pay for the passage of both.'

'In that case, let us be off,' said the master.

'Away, then!' cried d'Artagnan; and he and Planchet springing into the boat, in five minutes they were on board the vessel.

It was full time, for when they were half a league out at sea, d'Artagnan saw a flash, and heard a detonation; it was the sound of the cannon that announced the closing of the port.

It was now time to think about his wound. Happily it was, as d'Artagnan had supposed, not at all dangerous; the point of the sword had struck against a rib, and glanced along the bone; and, as the shirt had stuck to the wound at once, scarcely a drop of blood had flowed.

D'Artagnan was overpowered with fatigue; and a mattress being spread for him on the deck, he threw himself upon it and slept.

The next morning, at break of day, he found himself at not less than three or four leagues from the shores of England. The wind had been gentle during the night, and they had made but little progress.

At two o'clock they cast anchor in the harbour of Dover, and at half past two d'Artagnan landed in England, exclaiming—

'Here I am, at last.'

But this was not enough; he must get to London. In England posting was pretty well regulated. D'Artagnan and Planchet took each a post-horse; a postillion galloped before them; and in a few hours they reached the gates of London.

The duke was hunting, at Windsor, with the king.

D'Artagnan knew nothing of London; he knew not one word of English; but he wrote the word *Buckingham* on a piece of paper, and every one could direct him to the mansion of the duke.

D'Artagnan inquired for the duke's confidential valet, who, having accompanied him in all his journeys, spoke French perfectly. He told him that he came from Paris on an affair of life and death, and that he must speak with his master without an instant's delay.

The confidence with which d'Artagnan spoke satisfied Patrick (for that was the name of the minister's minister). He ordered two horses to be saddled, and took upon himself the charge of guiding the young guardsman. As for poor Planchet, they had taken him off his horse as stiff as a stake. The poor fellow was quite exhausted; but d'Artagnan seemed to be made of iron.

They reached Windsor Castle, where they learned that the king and the duke were out hawking, in some marshes, two or three miles off.

In twenty minutes they reached the place. Patrick heard his master's voice, calling his hawk.

'Whom shall I announce to my lord?' said Patrick.

'The young man,' said d'Artagnan, 'who sought a quarrel with him one evening on the Pont Neuf, opposite the Samaritan.'

'A strange recommendation,' said Patrick.

'You will see that it is as good as any one could be.'

'Patrick gave his horse the rein, reached the duke, and told him, in the very words which we have just used, that a messenger awaited him.

Buckingham at once remembered d'Artagnan; and fearing that something had happened in France, of which information had been sent to him, he only gave himself time to ask where the messenger was; and having recognised the uniform of the guards at that distance, he rode at full speed straight up to d'Artagnan. Patrick judiciously kept himself in the background.

'No misfortune has befallen the queen?' cried Buckingham.

'I think not, sir; but I believe that she is in great danger, from which your grace alone can rescue her.'

'I,' said Buckingham; 'and how shall I be sufficiently happy to render her any service? Speak! speak!'

'Take this letter,' said d'Artagnan.

'This letter! and from whom comes this letter?'

'From her majesty, I believe.'

'From her majesty,' said Buckingham, growing so pale that d'Artagnan thought he was about to fall.

And he broke the seal.

'What is this rent?' asked he, showing d'Artagnan a place where it was pierced through.

'Ah!' said d'Artagnan, 'I did not perceive it before: the sword of the Count de Wardes must have done that, when it was boring a hole in my chest.'

'Are you wounded?' inquired Buckingham.

'Oh! a mere trifle,' said d'Artagnan—'a mere scratch.'

'Just Heaven! what have I read?' exclaimed Buckingham. 'Patrick, remain here—or, rather, find the king, wherever he may be, and tell his majesty that I humbly beseech him to excuse me, but that an affair of the very greatest importance calls me to London. Come, sir, come.'

And both took their way to the capital at full gallop.

21

The Countess de Winter

As they hurried on, the duke heard from d'Artagnan, not really all that had occurred, but all that d'Artagnan himself knew. By putting together what fell from the lips of the young man, and what was supplied by his own recollections, he was enabled to form a pretty exact idea of that position, of the seriousness of which the queen's letter, short as it was, afforded abundant proof. But what most astonished him was that the cardinal, interested as he was that this youth should not set foot in England, had not managed to stop him on his way. It was then, and on the expression of this astonishment, that d'Artagnan related to him the precautions which had been taken, and how, thanks to the devotion of his three friends, whom he had left bleeding here and there upon the road, he had managed to get off with merely the wound which had pierced the queen's letter, and which he had so terribly repaid to M. de Wardes. Whilst listening to this account, given with the greatest simplicity, the duke looked from time to time on the young man with astonishment, as if he could not comprehend how so much prudence, courage, and devotion, could be combined with a countenance which did not yet show the traces of twenty years.

The horses went like the wind, and they were soon at the gates of London. D'Artagnan had supposed that, on entering the town, the duke would slacken his pace; but he did not:

he continued his course at the same rate, caring little for upsetting those who were in his way. In fact, in passing through the city, two or three accidents of this kind happened but Buckingham did not even turn his head to see what had become of those he had knocked over. D'Artagnan followed him, in the midst of cries which sounded very much like maledictions.

On entering the courtyard of his mansion, Buckingham jumped off his horse, and, without caring what became of him, threw the bridle over his neck and rushed towards the staircase. D'Artagnan did the same, with somewhat more uneasiness, nevertheless, for these noble animals, whose merit he appreciated; but he had the satisfaction of seeing three or four servants hurrying from the kitchens and stables, and immediately laying hold of the horses. The duke walked so quickly, that d'Artagnan had some difficulty in following him. He passed through many saloons, magnificent to a degree which the most distinguished nobles of France could not even imagine, and came at last to a bed-chamber, which was at once a miracle of taste and splendour. In the alcove of this chamber, there was a door in the tapestry, which the duke opened by a small golden key, which he carried suspended at his neck by a chain of the same metal. Through politeness, d'Artagnan remained behind; but at the moment that Buckingham stepped over the threshold of this door, he turned, and perceiving the hesitation of the young man—

'Come,' said he, 'and if you have the happiness of being admitted into the presence of the queen of France, tell her what you have beheld.'

Encouraged by this invitation, d'Artagnan followed the duke, who closed the door behind him.

They found themselves in a small chapel, splendidly illuminated by a profusion of wax lights, and carpeted with Persian silk carpets, embroidered with gold. Above a kind of altar, and under a dais of blue velvet, surmounted by red and white plumes, there was a portrait, of the size of life, representing Anne of Austria, and so perfectly resembling her, that d'Artagnan uttered a cry of surprise on seeing it: one would have believed that the queen was just about to speak.

On the altar, and under the portrait, was the casket which contained the diamond studs.

The duke approached the altar, and, after kneeling as a priest might do before the cross, opened the casket.

'Here,' said he, drawing from the casket a large piece of

blue riband, all glittering with diamonds—'here are those precious studs, with which I had made an oath to be buried. The queen gave them to me: she now takes them away: her commands, like those of Heaven, shall be obeyed in everything.'

Then he began to kiss, one by one, the diamonds, from which he was about to part; but suddenly he uttered a terrible cry.

'What is the matter?' demanded d'Artagnan in alarm; 'what has befallen you, my lord?'

'All is lost!' said Buckingham, becoming as pale as death. 'Two of the studs are gone; there are but ten.'

'Has your grace lost them, or do you suppose that they have been stolen?'

'Some one has stolen them,' replied the duke; 'and it is the cardinal who has managed it. See, the ribands which held them have been cut with scissors.'

'Has your grace any suspicion as to who has committed the theft? Perhaps the person has still got them.'

'Stop, stop!' said the duke. 'The only time I have worn these studs was at a ball at Windsor, a week ago. The Countess de Winter, with whom I had been on cold terms, approached me during the ball. This appearance of reconciliation was really the vengeance of an offended woman. Since that day I have not seen her. That woman is an agent of the cardinal's.'

'What! has he got agents, then, all over the world?' asked d'Artagnan.

'Oh, yes,' replied Buckingham, grinding his teeth with rage; 'yes, he is a terrible adversary. But, yet, when will this ball take place?'

'Next Monday.'

'Next Monday! Five more days; it is more time than we shall need. Patrick!' exclaimed the duke, opening the door of the chapel, 'Patrick!'

His confidential valet appeared.

'My jeweller and my secretary!' The valet departed, with a silent promptitude, which proved the habit he had acquired of blind and dumb obedience.

But, although the jeweller had been the first sent for, it was the secretary who, as he resided in the mansion, came first. He found Buckingham seated before a table, and writing some orders with his own hand.

'Jackson,' said he, 'you will go to the Lord Chancellor,

and tell him that I charge him with the execution of these orders. I desire them to be made public immediately.'

'But, my lord duke, if the Lord Chancellor should question me about the motives which have induced your grace to adopt so extraordinary a measure, what am I to answer?'

'That such is my pleasure, and that I am not obliged to give to anybody an account of my motives.'

'Is that to be the reply which he is to transmit to the king,' replied the secretary, smiling, 'if by chance his majesty should have the curiosity to inquire why no vessel must weigh anchor in a British port?'

'You are right, sir,' answered Buckingham; 'he will, in that case, tell the king that I have decided on war, and that this measure is my first act of hostility against France.'

The secretary bowed and departed.

'There, we may be quite easy on that point,' said Buckingham, turning towards d'Artagnan. 'If the studs have not yet gone to France, they will not arrive till after you.'

'How so?'

'I have just laid an embargo on the ships at present in his majesty's ports, and, without express permission, not one will dare to raise its anchor.'

D'Artagnan looked with wonder at the man who thus employed, in the service of his love, the unlimited power with which he was entrusted by the king.

Buckingham saw, from the expression of his countenance, what was passing in the youth's mind, and smiled.

'Yes,' said he, 'yes, it is Anne of Austria who is my true queen: at her lightest word I would betray my country—my king—my God! She desired of me not to send to the Protestants of la Rochelle the aid that I had promised them, and she has been obeyed. I forfeited my word; but of what consequence was that, whilst her will was gratified? Say, was I not nobly recompensed for my obedience, since it was to that obedience that I owe her portrait?'

D'Artagnan marvelled at the fragile unseen threads on which the destinies of nations and the lives of men may sometimes be suspended.

He was immersed in these reflections, when the jeweller entered. He was an Irishman, but one who was most skilful in his calling, and who confessed that he gained a hundred thousand livres a year by the Duke of Buckingham.

'O'Reilly,' said the duke, conducting him to the chapel,

'look at these diamond studs, and tell me what they are worth a-piece.'

The goldsmith glanced at the elegant manner in which they were mounted, calculated one by one the value of the diamonds, and without hesitation replied—

'Fifteen hundred pistoles each, my lord.'

'How many days would be required to make two studs like those? You see that two are wanting.'

'A week, my lord.'

'I will pay three thousand pistoles each for them, but I must have them the day after to-morrow.'

'Your grace shall have them.'

'You are an invaluable man, O'Reilly, but this is not all: these studs must not be entrusted to any one; it is necessary that some one should make them in this house.'

'Impossible, my lord. I am the only person who can make them, so that no one could discover the difference between the new and the old studs.'

'Therefore, my dear O'Reilly, you are my prisoner, and even if you wished to leave my palace now, you could not. Tell me which of your workmen you want, and describe the tools which they must bring you.'

The jeweller knew the duke, and that all remonstrances would be useless. He therefore made up his mind at once.

'May I inform my wife?' said he.

'Oh! you may even see her, my dear O'Reilly,' said the duke: 'your captivity shall not be harsh, I assure you; and, as every inconvenience should have its recompense, here is a present of a thousand pistoles, beyond the price of the two studs, to make you forget the annoyance you may experience.'

D'Artagnan could not recover from the surprise which he felt at the minister, who made such a profuse use of men and millions.

As for the jeweller, he wrote to his wife, sending her the order for a thousand pistoles, and requesting her to send him in exchange his most skilful apprentice, and an assortment of diamonds, of which he sent her the weight and description, along with a list of the requisite tools.

Buckingham conducted the jeweller to the chamber prepared for him, which was, in half an hour, converted into a workshop. He then placed a sentinel at each door, with strict orders to allow no one to pass except his valet, Patrick. It need scarcely be added, that O'Reilly and his assistant were absolutely forbidden to go out, on any pretext whatever.

This being arranged, the duke turned to d'Artagnan.

'Now, my young friend,' said he, 'England belongs to us two. What do you desire?'

'A bed,' answered d'Artagnan. 'I confess that, at present, that is what I stand most in need of.'

Buckingham allotted d'Artagnan a room which adjoined his own. He wished to keep the young man at his side; not that he distrusted him, but that he might have some one to whom he could constantly talk about the queen.

An hour afterwards the order was posted throughout London, that no ship would be permitted to leave the ports for France—not even the packet-boat with letters. In everybody's opinion, this was a declaration of war between the two kingdoms.

At eleven o'clock on the second day, the diamond studs were finished, and so exactly imitated, such perfect facsimiles, that Buckingham himself could not distinguish the new one from the old. Even the most skilful in such matters would have been deceived as he was.

He immediately summoned d'Artagnan.

'Here,' said he, 'are the diamond studs which you have come to fetch; and witness for me that I have done everything which human powers could accomplish.'

'Rest assured, my lord, that I will truly represent what I have seen. But your grace gives me the studs without the casket.'

'The casket would only encumber you. Besides, the box is the more precious to me, now that I have nothing else. You will say that I preserve it.'

'I will perform your commission, my lord, to the letter.'

'And now,' said Buckingham, looking earnestly at the young man, 'how can I ever repay my debt to you?'

D'Artagnan blushed, even to the white of his eyes. He saw that the duke wanted to find some means of making him a present; and the idea that his own blood, and that of his companions, should be paid for in English gold, was strangely repugnant to him.

'Let us understand one another, my lord,' said d'Artagnan, 'and state the case fairly, that there may be no misconception. I am in the service of the king and queen of France, and belong to the guards of M. des Essarts, who, as well as M. de Treville, is more particularly attached to their majesties. Everything that I have done has therefore been for the queen, and not at all for your grace. And more than that, perhaps I should not have taken a single step in the affair, if it had not been to please some one, who is as dear to me as the queen is to you.'

'Yes,' said the duke, 'and I believe that I know who that person——'

'My lord, I have not named her,' said d'Artagnan quickly.

'It is true,' replied the duke. 'I must therefore be grateful to that person for your devotion.'

'Just so, my lord; for, now that we are about to go to war, I confess that I see nothing in your grace but an Englishman, and, consequently, an enemy, whom I should be still more delighted to meet on the field of battle, than in the park at Windsor, or in the galleries of the Louvre. This, however, will not prevent me from executing every particular of my mission, and welcoming death, if need be, in its accomplishment; but I repeat to your grace, that you have nothing more to thank me for, in this second interview, than for what I have already done for you in the first.'

'We say, in our country, 'proud as a Scotchman,' muttered Buckingham.

'And we,' answered d'Artagnan, 'say, 'proud as a Gascon.' The Gascons are the Scotchmen of France.'

D'Artagnan bowed to the duke, and was about to take his leave.

'Well!' said the duke, 'are you going in that manner! But what course will you take? How will you get off?'

'True.'

'Egad! you Frenchmen stick at nothing.'

'I had forgotten that England is an island, and that your grace is its king.'

'Go to the port, ask for the brig *Sund*, and give this letter to the captain. He will take you to a small harbour, where you will certainly not be expected, and where few but fishing-boats go.'

'And the name of this harbour is——'

'St. Valery. But listen:—when you are landed there, you will go to a wretched wine-shop, without either name or sign, a true sailor's boozing-ken; you cannot mistake it, for there is but one.'

'And then?'

'You will ask for the host, and you will say to him, '*Forward.*'

'What does that mean?'

'It is the watchword which commands him to assist you on your way. He will give you a horse ready saddled, and show you the road that you must take; and you will, in this manner, find four relays upon your road. If you please, at each of them, to give your address at Paris, the four horses will follow you there; you already know two of them, and appear to have estimated them as an amateur. They are those which we rode, and you may trust me that the others are not inferior. These four horses are equipped for the field. Proud as you are, you will not refuse to accept one, and to present the three others to your companions. Besides, they are to help you in fighting against us. The end justifies the means, as you French say—do you not?'

'Yes, my lord, I accept your presents,' said d'Artagnan; 'and, God willing, we shall make good use of them.'

'Now, give me your hand, young man. Perhaps we may soon meet on the field of battle; but, in the meantime, I hope we part good friends.'

'Yes, my lord, but with the hope of soon being enemies.'

'Be contented; I give you my promise that we shall.'

'I depend upon your grace's word.'

D'Artagnan bowed to the duke, and hastened towards the port.

Opposite the Tower of London he found the vessel to which he had been directed, and gave his letter to the captain, who got it countersigned by the governor of the port, and then prepared to sail immediately.

Fifty vessels were waiting, in readiness to sail. On passing one of them, side by side, d'Artagnan thought he saw the woman of Meung—the same whom the unknown gentleman had called *my lady,* and whom he himself had thought so beautiful; but, thanks to the current and the favourable breeze, his vessel glided on so swiftly, that in a few minutes it had left the others far behind. The next morning, about nine o'clock, he landed at St. Valery.

D'Artagnan immediately went to the appointed wine shop, which he recognised by the outcries from within. The war between France and England was spoken of as certain, and the joyous sailors were making merry.

D'Artagnan pushed through the crowd, approached the host, and pronounced the word *'forward.'* The host immediately made him a sign to follow him, went out by a door which led into the courtyard, conducted him to the stables, where there stood a horse, ready saddled, and then asked him whether he needed anything else.

'I want to know the road I am to take,' said d'Artagnan.

'Go from this place to Blangy, and from Blangy to Neufchatel. At Neufchatel go to the tavern of the Golden Harrow; give the password to the innkeeper, and you will find, as here, a horse ready saddled.'

'Have I anything to pay?' asked d'Artagnan.

'Everything is paid,' said the host, 'and most liberally. Go, then, and God protect you!'

'Amen!' said the young man, as he galloped off.

In four hours he was at Neufchatel.

Strictly following his instructions at Neufchatel, as at St. Valery, he found a saddled horse awaiting him; and when he was about to transfer the pistols from the one saddle to the other, he perceived that the holsters were already duly furnished.

'Your address at Paris?'

'D'Artagnan—Hotel des Gardes, company des Essarts.'

'Very good,' answered the innkeeper.

'What road am I to take?' demanded d'Artagnan.

'That of Rouen: but you will pass the town on your right. At the little village of Ecouis you will halt. There is but one tavern, the French Crown. Do not judge of it from its looks; for it will have in its stables a horse of equal value with this.'

'The same watchword?'

'Exactly.'

'Adieu, master.'

'A good journey, sir. Do you require anything else?'

D'Artagnan said no, by a shake of his head, and went off again at full speed. At Ecouis, the same scene was enacted. He found a host equally well prepared, a horse equally fresh and ready. He left his address as before, and departed in the same way for Pontoise. At Pontoise he changed his horse for the last time; and, at nine o'clock, he entered the courtyard of M. de Treville's hotel, at full gallop.

He had got over nearly sixty leagues in twelve hours.

M. de Treville received him just as though he had seen him the same morning, only pressing his hand a little more warmly than usual. He informed him that the company of M. des Essarts was on guard at the Louvre, and that he might repair to his post.

22

The Ballet of 'The Merlaison'

THE next morning nothing was talked of in Paris but the ball which the magistrates were to give to the king and queen, and in which their majesties were to dance the famous ballet of *The Merlaison*, which was the favourite ballet of the king.

For the last week every preparation had been in progress at the Hotel de Ville for this important entertainment. The city carpenter had erected scaffolding, on which the ladies who were invited were to be seated; the city chandler had furnished the rooms with two hundred wax lights, which was an unprecedented luxury at that time; and twenty violins had been engaged, at double the price usually paid, on the understanding that they were to play throughout the whole of the night.

At ten in the morning, the Sieur de la Coste, ensign of the king's guards, followed by two officers, and many archers of the guards, came to demand of Clement, the city-registrar, all the keys of the gates, chambers, and closets of the hotel. These keys were given to him immediately, each bearing a label indicating to what it belonged: and, from that moment, the Sieur de la Coste had the superintendence of all the doors and avenues.

Duhalier, the captain of the guards, came in his turn, at eleven o'clock, and brought with him fifty archers, who stationed themselves immediately at the respective doors which had been assigned to them in the Hotel de Ville.

At three o'clock, there arrived two companies of guards, one French, the other Swiss. The company of French guards was composed of equal numbers of the troops of M. Duhalier, and of M. des Essarts.

The company began to arrive at six o'clock, and were at once conducted to the places prepared for them in the grand saloon.

The lady of the first president arrived at nine o'clock. As she was, next to the queen, the most distinguished individual of the entertainment, she was received by the gentlemen of the city, and conducted to a box opposite to that of the queen.

At ten o'clock, a collation of sweetmeats was prepared for the king—in the small room on the side of the church of St. Jean—before the city's sideboard of silver, which was guarded by four archers.

At midnight, loud cries and multitudinous acclamations resounded through the streets. It was the king, who was proceeding from the Louvre to the Hotel de Ville, along thoroughfares illuminated throughout their length by coloured lamps.

The magistrates, clothed in their robes of cloth, and preceded by the sergeants, each holding a torch in his hand, hastened to receive the king, whom they met upon the steps, where the provost of the merchants complimented and welcomed him; to which his majesty replied by excuses for the lateness of his arrival, for which he blamed the cardinal, who had detained him till eleven o'clock, discoursing on affairs of state.

His majesty, in full dress, was accompanied by his royal highness the king's brother, the Count de Soissons, the Grand Prior, the Duke de Longueville, the Duke d'Elbeuf, the Count d'Harcourt, the Count de la Roche Guyon, M. de Liancourt, M. de Baradas, the Count de Cramail, and the Chevalier de Souveray.

Every one remarked that the king looked preoccupied and unhappy.

A closet had been prepared for the king, and a second one for his royal brother. In each of these closets were laid out masquerade dresses. A similar preparation had been made for the queen, and for the president's lady. The lords and ladies in their majesties' suite were to dress themselves, two by two, in apartments set aside for thàt purpose. Before he entered his closet, the king desired to be apprised of the cardinal's arrival as soon as it had taken place.

Half an hour after the arrival of the king, fresh acclamations resounded: these announced the arrival of the queen. The magistrates went through the same formalities as before, and, preceded by their sergeants, advanced to meet their illustrious guest.

The queen entered the room; and it was remarked that, like the king, she looked sad, and also weary.

The moment that she entered, the curtain of a small gallery, which had till then been closed, was opened, and the pale face of the cardinal appeared, clothed as a Spanish cavalier. His eyes fixed themselves on those of the queen, and a smile of terrible joy passed across his lips. The queen was there without her diamond studs.

Her majesty remained for a short time, receiving the compliments of the city gentlemen, and answering the salutations of the ladies.

Suddenly the king appeared, with the cardinal, at one of the doors of the saloon. The cardinal spoke to him in a low voice, and the king was very pale.

The king broke through the crowd, and without a mask, and with the ribands of his doublet scarcely tied, approached the queen, and, in an agitated voice, said—

'Madame, wherefore, I pray you, have you not on your diamond studs, when you knew that I wished to see them?'

The queen looked around her, and saw, behind the king, the cardinal, smiling with a satanic smile.

'Sire,' replied the queen, in an agitated voice, 'because, amidst this great crowd, I feared some accident might befall them.'

'There you were wrong, madame. I made you this present in order that you might adorn yourself with it. I tell you that you were wrong.'

The voice of the king trembled with anger. Every one looked, and listened with astonishment, not at all understanding this extraordinary scene.

'Sire,' said the queen, 'I can send for them from the Louvre, where they are; and thus the wishes of your majesty will be accomplished.'

'Do so, madame, and that immediately; for in one hour the ballet will begin.'

The queen bowed submissively, and followed the ladies who were to conduct her to her closet.

The king also retired to his.

There was a momentary excitement and confusion in the saloon. Every one could perceive that something had occurred between the king and queen; but both of them had spoken so low, that, as all had kept at a respectful distance, no one had heard anything. The violins played most strenuously, but no one attended to them.

The king left his closet first. He wore a most elegant hunting dress, and his brother and the other nobles were dressed in the same costume. This was the kind of dress most becoming to the king; and, thus habited, he truly seemed the first gentleman of his realm.

The cardinal approached the king, and gave him a box, in which his majesty found two diamond studs.

'What does this mean?' demanded the king.

'Nothing,' answered the cardinal; 'only, if the queen has the studs, which I must doubt, count them, sire, and if you only find ten, ask her majesty who can have robbed her of these two.'

The king looked at the cardinal as if to ask what this meant; but he had not time to put any further questions. An exclamation of admiration burst from every lip. If the king appeared to be the first gentleman of his realm, the queen was indisputably the most beautiful woman in France.

It must be allowed, of course, that her costume of a huntress fitted her most charmingly. She wore a beaver hat with blue feathers, a robe of pearl gray velvet, fastened with diamond clasps, and a skirt of blue satin, embroidered with silver. Over her left shoulder glittered the studs, suspended by a bow of the same colour as the feathers and the skirt.

The king trembled with joy, and the cardinal with anger. Yet, distant as they were from the queen, they could not count the studs; and although the queen had them, the question was, were there ten or twelve?

At this moment the violins sounded the announcement of the ballet. The king advanced with the president's lady, with whom he was to dance; and his royal highness with the queen. They took their places, and the ballet began.

The king figured opposite the queen; and, as often as he passed her, he looked devouringly at the studs, which he could not manage to count. A cold moisture hung upon the cardinal's brow.

The ballet lasted an hour; there were sixteen figures. At its conclusion, amidst the applause of the whole assemblage, every one conducted his partner to her place; but the king profited by his privilege to leave his partner where she was, and advanced quickly towards the queen.

'I thank you, madame,' said he, 'for the deference you have paid to my wishes: but I believe you have lost two studs, and I bring them to you.'

At these words, he offered her the two studs which he had received from the cardinal.

'What, sire,' cried the queen, affecting surprise, 'do you give me two more: why, that will make me have fourteen.'

In fact, the king counted them, and found the twelve studs upon her majesty's shoulder.

The king summoned the cardinal.

'Well, what does all this mean, cardinal?' demanded the king, in a severe tone.

'It means, sire,' answered the cardinal, 'that I wished her majesty to accept these two studs; but, not daring myself to make her the offer, I have adopted this method.'

'And I am the more grateful to your eminence,' replied the queen, with a smile that proved she was not the dupe of this ingenious gallantry, 'as I am certain that these two studs have cost you more than the other twelve cost his majesty.'

Then, having curtseyed to the king and the cardinal, the queen took her way to the chamber where she had dressed, and where she was now to remove her ball costume.

The attention which we have been obliged to bestow upon the illustrious personages introduced at the commencement of this chapter, has diverted us for a time from him to whom Anne of Austria was indebted for the unprecedented triumph which she had just gained over the cardinal, and who, obscure, unknown, and lost amidst the crowd at one of the doors, contemplated from that station a scene which was incomprehensible to all but four persons—the king, the queen, the cardinal, and himself.

The queen had returned to her apartment, and d'Artagnan was going to retire, when some one lightly touched his shoulder. He turned, and saw a young woman, who made a sign that he should follow her. This young woman wore a black velvet mask; but, in spite of that precaution, which, after all, was taken more against others than himself, he immediately recognised his ordinary guide, the gay and witty Madame Bonancieux.

They had met on the previous evening, but only for an instant, at the lodge of Germain, the Swiss, where d'Artagnan had inquired for her. The anxiety of the young woman to communicate the good news of her messenger's fortunate return to the queen, prevented the two lovers from exchanging more than a few words. On this account d'Artagnan followed Madame Bonancieux, influenced by the double sentiment of love and curiosity. During their progress, and as the corridors became more deserted, he endeavoured to stop the young woman, to touch her, and to gaze upon her, were it but for a moment; but, quick as a bird, she glided

between his hands; and, when he wished to speak, she placed
her finger on her lip, and, with a slight gesture of command
which was full of grace, reminded him that he was under
the dominion of a power which he must blindly obey, and
which interdicted even the least complaint. After a few turns,
Madame Bonancieux opened a door, and pushed the young
man into a closet, which was quite dark. There she again
enjoined silence, and opening a second door concealed in
the tapestry, through which a brilliant light emanated, she
disappeared.

D'Artagnan remained an instant motionless, and wondering where he was: but, shortly, a ray of light, which
penetrated into this chamber, a warm and perfumed air,
which reached him, and the conversation of two or three
women, in language at once respectful and elegant, in which
the word *majesty* was frequently repeated—clearly indicated
to him that he was in a closet adjacent to the queen's
apartment.

The young man kept himself in the shade, and listened.

The queen appeared gay and happy, which seemed greatly
to astonish the ladies who surrounded her, who were
accustomed to see her almost always full of care.

The queen attributed this joyous feeling to the beauty of
the fête, and to the pleasure which she had experienced in
the ballet; and as it is not allowable to contradict a queen,
whether she smiles or weeps, every one expiated on the
gallantry of these aldermen of the good city of Paris.

Although d'Artagnan did not know the queen, he soon
distinguished her voice from those of the others—first by a
slight foreign accent, and then by that tone of command
usually characteristic of the speech of sovereigns. He heard
her approach and retire from that open door, and once or
twice saw the shadow of her person intercept the light.
Suddenly, however, a hand and arm, of an adorable form
and colour, were passed through the tapestry. D'Artagnan
comprehended that this was his reward: he threw himself
upon his knees, seized this hand, respectfully pressed his
lips upon it, and then it was withdrawn, leaving in his what
he soon recognised to be a ring. The door was immediately
shut, and d'Artagnan was again left in complete darkness.

He put the ring upon his finger, and once more waited.
It was evident that all was not yet ended. After the recom-
pense of his loyalty, should come the recompense of his love.
Besides, although the ballet had been danced, the entertain-

ment was scarcely yet begun. The supper was to take place at three, and the clock of St. John had, a short time before, already struck a quarter to three.

By degrees, in fact, the sound of voices diminished in the neighbouring chamber, and the ladies were then heard to leave it; after which, the door of the cabinet was opened, and Madame Bonancieux entered quickly.

'You come at last,' cried d'Artagnan.

'Silence,' said the young woman, putting her hand upon his lips; 'get out again the same way you came.'

'But where and when shall I see you?' cried d'Artagnan.

'A note, which you will find at your lodgings, will tell you. Go! go!'

And, at these words, she opened the door of the corridor, and pushed d'Artagnan out of the cabinet.

He obeyed like a child, without resistance or even objection, which proves that he was very positively in love.

23

The Appointment

D'ARTAGNAN ran the whole of the way home; and, although it was three in the morning, and he had to pass through the worst parts of Paris, he met with no misadventure. There is known to be a particular deity for drunkards and lovers.

He found the door in the passage open, ascended his stairs, and knocked gently, in a way agreed upon between him and his servant. Planchet, whom he had sent back two hours before, from the Hotel de Ville, to wait for him, came and opened the door.'

'Has any one brought for me a letter?' eagerly inquired d'Artagnan.

'No one has brought a letter,' said Planchet, 'but there is one which came of itself.'

'What do you mean, stupid?'

'I mean, that when I came in, although I had the key of your apartment in my pocket, and although this key had never been out of my possession, I found a letter on the green cover of the table in your bed-chamber.'

'And where is that letter?'

'I left it where it was, sir. It is not natural for letters to enter gentlemen's rooms in this manner. If, indeed, the window had been found open, I should say nothing: but it was hermetically closed. Take care, sir, for there is certainly some magic in it.'

In the meantime, the young man had rushed into his chamber, and opened the letter. It was from Madame Bonancieux, and expressed in these terms:—

'Warm thanks are to be given and transmitted to you. You must be at St. Cloud this evening, at ten o'clock, opposite the pavilion, which stands at the angle of M. d'Estrées' house.

'C. B.'

On reading this letter, d'Artagnan felt his heart dilating and contracting in that delicious spasm which is the torture and delight of lovers.

It was the first note he had received—the first appointment that had been granted to him. His heart, expanding in the intoxication of his joy, felt as though it would faint at the portal of that terrestrial paradise which is denominated love.

'Well, sir,' said Planchet, who had seen his master's colour come and go, 'was I not right, and is not this some wicked transaction?'

'You are mistaken, Planchet; and the proof is, here is a crown for you to drink my health.'

'I thank you, sir, and will strictly follow your directions; but it is not the less true, that letters which thus enter closed houses——'

'Fall from heaven, my friend—fall from heaven!'

'Then you are happy, sir?'

'My dear Planchet, I am the happiest of men.'

'And I may take advantage of your happiness, and go to bed.'

'Yes, go.'

'May all Heaven's blessings fall upon you, sir; but it is not the less true, that this letter——'

And Planchet retired, shaking his head with an air of doubt, which all the liberality of d'Artagnan had not been able entirely to remove.

As soon as he was left alone, d'Artagnan read his note over and over again, and kissed, at least twenty times, these lines traced by the hand of his beautiful mistress. At length he retired to bed, and slept, and was visited by golden dreams.

At seven o'clock in the morning, d'Artagnan arose, and called Planchet, who at the second summons opened the door, his countenance yet bearing traces of his uneasiness on the previous evening.

'Planchet,' said he, 'I am going out, probably for the whole day; you are therefore free till seven o'clock in the evening; but you must be ready at that hour, with two horses.'

'Well!' said Planchet, 'I suppose we are going to have our skins pierced again in a few places.'

'You will take your carbine and pistols.'

'Well, then! did I not say so?' exclaimed Planchet. 'There, I was sure of it—that cursed letter!'

'But be easy now, simpleton: it is only a party of pleasure.'

'Yes, like that most delightful journey the other day, when it rained balls, and grew caltrops.'

'If you are afraid, Planchet, I will go without you. I like better to travel alone, than with a timid companion.'

'You insult me, sir,' said Planchet. 'I thought, however, that you had seen me at work.'

'Yes, but I suppose that you expended all your courage on that one occasion.'

'You shall see, at a fitting time, that some yet remains; only, I entreat you not to be too prodigal of it, if you wish it to last long.'

'Do you think that you have got still sufficient to spend some this evening?'

'I hope so.'

'Well, then, I depend upon you.'

'At the hour appointed I will be ready; but I thought there was only one horse in the guard stables.'

'Perhaps there may be only one there at present; but, in the evening, there will be four.'

'It seems as if our journey was an expedition to provide fresh horses for ourselves.'

'Exactly so,' said d'Artagnan; and, giving Planchet a last warning gesture, off he went.

Bonancieux was at his door, and d'Artagnan designed to pass by without speaking to the worthy mercer; but the latter accosted him so politely and kindly, that the tenant was obliged not only to bow in return, but also to enter into conversation with him.

How, indeed, was it possible not to display some slight complaisance towards the husband of a pretty woman who has just made an appointment with one at St. Cloud's, opposite the pavilion of M. d'Estrées, for that very evening? D'Artagnan approached him, therefore, with the most amiable manner that he was able to assume.

The conversation naturally turned on the poor man's imprisonment; and M. Bonancieux, not knowing that the young man had overheard his conversation with the man of Meung, related the persecutions of that monster. M. de Laffemas, whom he styled, throughout the whole of his narrative, the cardinal's executioner, and discoursed freely concerning the Bastile, the bolts, the dungeons, the air-holes, the grates, and instruments of torture.

D'Artagnan listened with the most exemplary attention: then, when he had ended—

'And Madame Bonancieux,' said he—'do you know who carried her off? for I do not forget that it is to that vexatious occurrence that I owe the happiness of your acquaintance.'

'Ah!' answered M. Bonancieux, 'they took good care not to tell me that; and my wife, on her part, has sworn by all that's sacred that she did not know. But you, yourself,' continued Bonancieux, in a tone of the most perfect goodfellowship, 'what has become of you for the last few days? I have never seen either you or your friends; and it was not on the pavement of Paris, I should suppose, that you picked up all the dust which Planchet brushed off your boots last night.'

'You are right, my dear M. Bonancieux: I and my friends have been making a little journey.'

'Was it far from here?'

'Oh, lord, no! merely about forty leagues. We went to conduct M. Athos to the waters of Forges, where my friends have remained.'

'And you have come back, have you?' resumed M. Bonancieux, with the most spiteful look possible. 'A handsome youth like you cannot get long leave of absence from his mistress. And you were impatiently expected at Paris, were you not? ha!'

'Faith,' said the young man, laughing, 'I confess it the more willingly, my dear M. Bonancieux, as I perceive that I can conceal nothing from you. Yes, I was expected, and most impatiently, I assure you.'

A slight shade passed over Bonancieux's countenance, but it was so slight, that d'Artagnan did not perceive it.

'And you are about to be rewarded for your diligence?' continued the mercer, with a slight alteration of voice, which d'Artagnan did not perceive, any more than the cloud which had passed a moment before, over the face of the worthy man.

'I hope you may prove a true prophet!' exclaimed d' Artagnan, laughing.

'My reason for accosting you,' continued Bonancieux, 'is merely to learn whether you will return late.'

'Why this question, my dear landlord?' asked d'Artagnan. 'Is it because you intend to wait for me?'

'No, it is because, ever since my imprisonment, and the robbery which was committed on me, I am frightened every time I hear a door opened, and particularly at night. By our lady! I cannot help it: I am no soldier, truly!'

'Well do not be frightened if I enter at one, two, or three o'clock in the morning, or even if I do not enter at all.'

Bonancieux became so pale at this that d'Artagnan could not but observe it, and asked him what was the matter.

'Nothing,' replied Bonancieux, 'nothing. Only, since my misfortunes, I am subject to these feelings, which seize me on a sudden, and make me shudder. Don't trouble yourself about that—you who have enough to occupy you in your approaching happiness.'

'Oh, I am occupied in my present happiness.'

'Not yet; wait a little: you said that it should be to-night.'

'Well! the night will come, thank God! and perhaps you also may expect it as impatiently as me. Perhaps, this evening Madame Bonancieux intends to visit the conjugal home.'

'Madame Bonancieux is not disengaged this evening.' gravely replied Bonancieux; 'she is detained at the Louvre, by her official duty.'

'So much the worse for you, my dear landlord; so much the worse. When I am happy myself, I should like all the world to be so too: but that appears to be impossible.'

And the young man went off, laughing loudly at the joke, which he alone, as he imagined, could comprehend.

'Laugh as you like,' said Bonancieux, in a sepulchral tone.

But d'Artagnan was already too far off to hear him; and, if he had heard him, in the disposition of mind in which he then was, he would not have heeded him.

He went towards the hotel of M. de Treville; his visit of the evening before having been, as it may be remembered, very short, and very little explanatory.

He found M. de Treville in the heartiest joy. The king

and queen had been most gracious to him at the ball. The cardinal, it is true, had been very ungracious. At one o'clock in the morning, he had retired, under the pretext of indisposition. As to their majesties, they had not returned to the Louvre till six in the morning.

'Now,' said M. de Treville, lowering his voice, and looking cautiously around the room to be sure that they were alone —'now, my young friend, let us talk of yourself; for it is evident that your safe return is connected with the king's joy, the queen's triumph, and his eminence's humiliation. You must take care of yourself.'

'What have I to fear,' answered d'Artagnan, 'so long as I have the good fortune to enjoy their majesties' favour?'

'Everything, believe me. The cardinal is not the man to forget being made a fool of, at least until he has settled accounts with the person who has made a fool of him; and that person seems to me to be a certain youth of my acquaintance.'

'Do you believe that the cardinal has got so far as you have, and knows that I am the individual who has been to London?'

'The devil! you have been to London! And is it from London you bring that beautiful diamond which glitters on your finger? Take care, my dear d'Artagnan; the present of an enemy is not a good thing. Is not there a certain Latin verse upon the subject? Stop a moment!'

'Yes, undoubtedly,' said d'Artagnan, who had never been able to knock the first rule of the rudiments into his head, and who had driven his preceptor to despair by his ignorance. 'Yes, undoubtedly, there must be one.'

'Yes,' said M. de Treville, who had a small amount of learning, 'there is one certainly, and M. Benserade was quoting it to me the other day: wait a moment. Ah! here it is:—

Timeo Danaos et dona ferentes,

which means, "Distrust the enemy with a present in his hand."'

'This diamond does not come from an enemy, sir,' replied d'Artagnan; 'it comes from the queen.'

'From the queen!' said M. de Treville. Oh! oh! Truly, it is a complete royal jewel, which is worth a thousand pistoles, as fully as it is a single farthing. By whom did the queen send it you to?'

'She handed it to me herself.'

'Where was that?'

'In the closet adjoining the apartment where she changed her dress,'

'How?'

'In giving me her hand to kiss.'

'And you have kissed the queen's hand,' said M. de Treville, looking at d'Artagnan.

'Her majesty did me the honour to grant me that favour.'

'And in the presence of witnesses? Imprudent! doubly imprudent!'

'No, sir; no one saw her,' replied d'Artagnan; and he related to M. de Treville how everything had occurred.

'Oh! women, women!' cried the old soldier, 'I recognise them well, by their romantic imaginations: everything which is at all mysterious charms them. Then you saw the arm, and that was all? You might meet the queen, and not recognise her? She might meet you, and not recognise you?'

'No; but thanks to this diamond——' replied the young man.

'Listen,' said M. de Treville. 'Will you allow me to give you some advice—some good advice—a friend's advice?'

'You will do me honour, sir,' replied d'Artagnan.

'Well, then, go to the first jeweller's you can find, and sell this diamond for what he will give you for it. However great a miser he may be, you will get at least eight hundred pistoles. The pistoles have no name, young man; but this ring has a terrible one, which might destroy him who wears it.'

'Sell this ring—a ring given me by my sovereign! Never!'

'Then turn the stone within, poor simpleton; for every one knows that a Gascon youth does not find such gems in his mother's jewel-case.'

'You suspect, then, that I have some cause for fear?' said d'Artagnan.

'I mean to say, young man, that he who sleeps over a mine, when the match is lighted, ought to think himself in safety in comparison with you.'

'The devil! 'said d'Artagnan, whom M. de Treville's serious tone began to disturb. 'The devil! And what am I to do?'

'Above all things, be always on your guard. The cardinal has a tenacious memory and a long arm: believe me, he will play you some trick.'

'But what?'

'Ah! has he not at his command all the wiles of Satan? The least that can happen to you will be an arrest?'

'What! Would they dare to arrest a man in his majesty's service?'

'Egad! they did not scruple much in the case of Athos? At any rate, young madcap, believe a man who has been thirty years at court: do not slumber in your security, or you are lost. On the contrary, I warn you to see enemies everywhere. If any one seeks to pick a quarrel with you, avoid it, even if it should be but a child of ten years of age: if you are attacked, by night or day, beat a retreat, without being ashamed of it: if you pass over a bridge, try the planks, for fear one should break beneath your feet: if you walk past a house which is being built, look up in the air, lest a stone should fall upon your head: if you come home late, let your servant follow you, and let him be armed, if, even, you can make sure of your servant. Distrust everybody—your friend, your brother, and your mistress—but your mistress most of all!'

'D'Artagnan blushed.

'My mistress!' he mechanically repeated: 'and why her, more, than any one else?'

'Because a mistress is one of the favourite agents of the cardinal: he has no one more expeditious. A woman sells you for ten pistoles—witness Delilah. You know the scriptures, eh?'

D'Artagnan thought of the appointment which Madame Bonancieux had made for that very evening; but we must say, to the praise of our hero, that the bad opinion which M. de Treville entertained of women in general, did not inspire him with the slightest suspicion of his pretty landlady.

'But, apropos, resumed M. de Treville, 'what has become of your three companions?'

'I was just going to inquire whether you had not received any tidings of them?'

'None whatever, sir.'

'Well, I left them behind me on my way—Porthos, at Chantilly, with a duel on his hands; Aramis, at Crevecœur, with a bullet in his shoulder; and Athos, at Amiens, under an accusation of passing bad money.'

'Look there, now!' said M. de Treville. 'And how did you escape yourself?'

'By a miracle, sir, I ought to confess: with a sword thrust

in the chest, and by pinning the Count de Wardes on his back, on the road to Calais, as one might pin a butterfly upon the tapestry.'

'There again! De Wardes—one of the cardinal's men, and a cousin of Rochefort's. Come, my dear friend, an idea has struck me.'

'Speak, sir.'

'In your shoes, there is one thing that I would do.'

'What is it?'

'Whilst his eminence was seeking for me at Paris, I would take, without sound of drum or trumpet, the road to Picardy, and would endeavour to find out what had become of my three companions. Surely, in any case, they merit this slight attention on your part.'

'The advice is good, sir, and to-morrow I will go.'

'To-morrow! and why not this evening?'

'This evening, sir, I am detained at Paris by an affair of importance.'

'Ah, young man! young man! some little love affair. Take care! I repeat it once more, it is woman who has always ruined us, even from the beginning, is ruining us, and will still ruin us to the end. Be advised by me, and depart this evening.'

'Impossible, sir.'

'Have you given your word?'

'Yes, sir.'

'That is another matter; but promise me, that, if you are not killed to-night, you will set out to-morrow.'

'I promise you.'

'Do you want money?'

'I have fifty pistoles remaining: it is as much as I shall require, I think.'

'But your companions?'

'I think that they can be in no want. We left Paris each with seventy-five pistoles in his pocket.'

'Shall I see you before your departure?'

'I think not, sir; unless anything new should occur.'

'Well, a good journey to you!'

'Thanks, sir.'

And d'Artagnan took his leave of M. de Treville, more than ever touched by his paternal solicitude for his musketeers.

He went successively to the homes of Athos, Porthos, and Aramis; but none of them had returned. Their servants were also absent, and nothing had been heard of either masters or lackeys.

He might possibly have gained some tidings of them from their mistresses, but he knew not those of Porthos and Aramis; and Athos had none.

In passing the hotel of the guards, he looked in at the stables. Three of the four horses were already there. Planchet, quite astounded, was busy currying them, and had already finished two out of the three.

'Ah, sir,' said Planchet, 'how glad I am to see you.'

'And why so, Planchet?' demanded the young man.

'Can you depend on M. Bonancieux, our landlord?'

'I? not in the slightest degree.'

'And you are quite right, too, sir.'

'But why do you ask the question?'

'Because, whilst you were talking to him, I looked, without listening, sir; and his countenance changed colour two or three times.'

'Bah!'

'You did not observe it, sir, preoccupied as you were by the letter you had just received; but I, on the contrary, who had been put on my guard by the strange manner in which this letter had got into the house, did not let one change of his countenance escape me.'

'And what did you discover?'

'That he is a traitor.'

'Really?'

'And, moreover, the moment you had turned the corner of the street, M. Bonancieux took his hat, shut his door, and began to run in an opposite direction.'

'Upon my word, you are quite right, Planchet: all this looks suspicious enough; but be contented—we will not pay him one farthing of rent till all this is satisfactorily explained.'

'You joke, sir, but you will see.'

'What would you have, Planchet? That which will happen is written.'

'Then, sir, you do not renounce your expedition this evening?'

'On the contrary, Planchet, the more I dislike M. Bonancieux, the more inclined am I to keep the appointment made in this letter, which disturbs you so much.'

'Then it is your determination?'

'Immovably so, my friend; therefore, at seven o'clock, be ready here at the hotel, and I will come and find you.'

Planchet, seeing there was no hope of making his master renounce his project, heaved a profound sigh, and set to work grooming the third horse.

As for d'Artagnan, who was fundamentally a young man of great economy, instead of going to his own home, he went and dined with the young Gascon priest, who, during the temporary distress of the four friends, had given them a breakfast of chocolate.

24

The Pavilion

AT nine o'clock, d'Artagnan was at the Hotel des Gardes. He found Planchet under arms, and the fourth horse arrived. Planchet was armed with his carbine and pistol. D'Artagnan had provided himself with his sword, and placed two pistols in his belt. They each bestrode a horse, and went off quietly. It was a dark night, and none saw them depart. Planchet followed his master at the distance of ten paces.

D'Artagnan passed over the quays, went out by the gate of La Conference, and proceeded along the charming road— far more beautiful then than now—which leads to St. Cloud.

As long as they continued in the town, Planchet kept the respectful distance that he had fixed for himself; but, when the road became more lonely and obscure, he gradually drew nearer, so that, when they entered the Bois de Boulogne, he found himself quite naturally riding side by side with his master. In fact, we must not deny that the waving of the trees, and the reflection of the moon amongst the sombre copses, caused him much uneasiness. D'Artagnan perceived that something extraordinary was incommoding his lackey.

'Well, Planchet,' demanded he, 'what ails you, now?'

'Do you not find, sir, that woods are like churches?'

'And why, Planchet?'

'Because one is as much afraid of speaking loudly in the one as in the other.'

'Why dare you not speak loudly, Planchet—because you are in fear?'

'Yes, sir; in fear of being heard.'

'Fear of being heard! Our conversation is very proper, my dear Planchet, and no one would find anything in it to censure.'

'Ah, sir,' replied Planchet, returning to the ruling idea in his mind, 'that M. Bonancieux has a sly gloom about the eyebrows, and something so unpleasant in the working of his lips!'

'What the plague makes you think so much of M. Bonancieux?'

'Sir, we think of what one must, and not of what one would.'

'Because you are a coward, Planchet.'

'Let us not confound prudence with cowardice, sir. Prudence is a virtue.'

'And you are very virtuous, are you not, Planchet?'

'Is not that the barrel of a musket, sir, shining below there? Suppose we were to stoop our heads?'

'Really,' muttered d'Artagnan, who remembered the advice of M. de Treville—'really, this animal will finish by making me afraid.' And he put his horse at a trot.

Planchet followed his master's movements, precisely as if he had been his shadow, and soon found himself trotting by his side.

'Must we travel in this manner all the night, sir?' demanded he.

'No, Planchet, for you are at your journey's end.'

'What! I am at my journey's end? And you, sir?'

'I shall go some little way farther.'

'And leave me here alone, sir?'

'Are you afraid, Planchet?'

'No; but I will merely observe to you, sir, that the night will be very cold; that cold causes rheumatism; and that a lackey who has the rheumatism makes but a sorry servant, especially to such an active master as yourself!'

'Well, then, if you are cold, you can enter one of those wine shops which you see down there; but you must be waiting for me before the door, at six o'clock to-morrow morning.'

'But, sir, I have most dutifully eaten and drunk the crown that you gave me this morning; so that I have not got even a stray sou remaining, in case I should feel cold.'

'There is a half-pistole. Good-bye till to-morrow morning.'

D'Artagnan got off his horse, threw the bridle to Planchet, and hurried away, closely enveloped in his cloak.

'Good God! how cold I am!' exclaimed Planchet, as soon as he had lost sight of his master; and, eager as he was to warm himself, he hastened to rap at the door of a house, which had all the appearance of a suburban dram-shop.

In the meantime, d'Artagnan, who had taken a narrow cross-road, reached St. Cloud; but, instead of proceeding along the main street, he turned behind the castle, went down a narrow, unfrequented lane, and soon found himself opposite the appointed pavilion. It was situated in a perfect desert of a place. A long wall, at the corner of which was the pavilion, ran along one side of this lane; and, on the other a hedge hid from the wayfarer a small garden, at the bottom of which there stood a miserable cottage.

He had now reached the place of appointment; and as he had not been told to announce his presence by any signal, he waited.

Not a sound was heard: he might have fancied himself a hundred leagues from the capital. D'Artagnan cast a glance behind him, and then leaned his back against the hedge. Beyond this hedge, and garden, and cottage, a heavy mist enveloped in its shade that vast immensity where Paris slept—an immensity, void and open in which some luminous points glittered like the funereal stars of that vast pandemonium of suffering and sin.

But to d'Artagnan, all aspects indicated beauteous forms; all images were wreathed in smiles; all darkness was transparent light. The appointed hour was on the eve of striking.

In fact, at the end of a few minutes, the belfry of St. Cloud slowly emitted ten strokes from its broad sonorous jaws.

There was something melancholy in that voice of bronze, which thus breathed its lamentations in the night. But each of those sounds, which told the hour he sighed for, vibrated harmoniously in the heart of the young man.

His eyes were fixed on the pavilion, which stood at the corner of the wall, and of which all the windows were closed with shutters, except one upon the first floor.

From this window there shone a soft light, which silvered over the trembling foliage of two or three linden trees, which formed a group outside the park. Doubtless, behind that little window, which was so kindly lighted up, the pretty Madame Bonancieux awaited him. A lingering sentiment of diffidence restrained her; but, now that the hour had struck, the window would be opened, and d'Artagnan would at last receive from the hands of Love, the meed of his devotion.

Flattered by this sweet belief, d'Artagnan waited a half-hour, without any impatience, keeping his eyes fixed upon that charming little abode; and distinguishing, through the upper part of the window, a part of those gilded cornices of the ceiling which gave evidence of the elegance of the remainder of the apartment.

The belfry of St. Cloud proclaimed half-past ten.

But, this time, without his knowing why, a shudder ran through the veins of d'Artagnan. Perhaps, also, the cold began to affect him, and he mistook for a moral impression what was in reality a sensation altogether physical.

Then the idea occurred to him, that he had mistaken the hour of appointment, and that it must have been at eleven, instead of ten.

He approached the window, placed himself under the ray of light, drew the letter from his pocket, and read it again. He was not mistaken: the appointment was really for ten o'clock.

He resumed his post, becoming uneasy at the silence and solitude.

It struck eleven.

D'Artagnan began to fear that something had really happened to Madame Bonancieux.

He clapped his hands three times—the usual signal of lovers—but nothing, not even echo, returned an answer. And then he thought, with some displeasure, that the young woman had perhaps fallen asleep whilst waiting for him.

He approached the wall, and attempted to climb it; but the wall was newly rough-cast, and he broke his nails to no purpose.

At this moment he thought of the trees, of which the leaves were still silvered over by the light; and, perceiving that one drooped over the road, he fancied that, from amidst its branches, he might be able to see into the pavilion.

The tree was easy to climb. Besides, d'Artagnan was scarcely twenty years of age, and, therefore, well remembered his school-boy habits. In an instant he was in the midst of its branches, and through the transparent windows, his eyes plunged into the interior of the pavilion.

Strange it was—and it made him shudder from the soles of his feet to the hair of his head—to find that that gentle flame, that quiet lamp, threw light upon a scene of frightful disarray: one of the panes of the window was demolished; the door of the room had been broken open, and hung, half-broken, on its hinges; a table, which must have been covered with an elegant supper, lay upon the ground; and glasses in fragments, and crushed fruits, were thickly spread upon the floor. Everything in the room indicated a violent and desperate struggle; and d'Artagnan believed that he could even detect, amidst this strange medley, some strips of clothes, and some stains of blood, congealed on the tablecloth and curtains.

With his heart beating horribly, he hastily descended to the ground, to examine if he could not find some further traces of violence.

The small and gentle light still shone amidst the calmness of the night. D'Artagnan then perceived—what had escaped him at first, when nothing prompted him to so close a scrutiny—that the ground was broken in one place, and dug up in another, and was marked by confused impressions of the footsteps of both men and horses. The wheels of a carriage, which seemed to have come from Paris, had, moreover, left upon the soft soil a deep rut, which proceeded no further than the pavilion, and then returned again towards Paris. And, last of all, in pursuing his researches, he found near the wall a woman's torn glove. But this glove, wherever it had not come in contact with the mud, was irreproachably fresh. It was one of those perfumed gloves which the lover likes to pull from a pretty hand.

As d'Artagnan pursued these investigations, at every fresh discovery, a more abundant and more icy moisture stood upon his brow; his heart was wrung with fearful anguish, and his respiration almost failed.

'And yet,' said he to encourage himself, 'perhaps this pavilion had nothing to do with Madame Bonancieux. Her appointment was *before* the pavilion, not *within* it. She has possibly been detained in Paris by her duties, or, probably, by her husband's jealousy.'

But all these reflections were beaten down, destroyed, driven to flight, by that internal sentiment of grief, which, on some occasions, takes exclusive possession of our entire being, and announces, in an unmistakable language, that some great suffering hovers over our heads.

And then d'Artagnan became almost frantic. He ran upon the highway, hastened along the road he had come by, and advanced as far as the ferry-boat, and questioned the ferryman.

About seven o'clock in the evening, the ferryman had ferried over a woman, enveloped in a dark cloak, who seemed to be exceedingly anxious to escape recognition; but, precisely on account of her precautions, he had been the more observant, and had discovered that she was young and pretty.

There were then, as now, crowds of young and pretty women, who came to St. Cloud, and who had reasons for desiring to remain unseen; yet d'Artagnan doubted not for an instant, that it was Madame Bonancieux whom the ferryman had brought across.

D'Artagnan took advantage of the lamp in the ferryman's cottage, to read the note of Madame Bonancieux once more, and to assure himself that he had made no mistake—that the appointment was really at St. Cloud, and not elsewhere, and before the pavilion of M. d'Estrées, and not in another street.

Everything concurred to prove to d'Artagnan that his presentiments were not groundless, and that some great misfortune had actually occurred.

He ran back towards the castle, fancying that, during his absence, something new might have taken place at the pavilion, and that some fresh instructions might be awaiting him there.

The lane was still deserted, and the same calm, soft light streamed from the window.

D'Artagnan then remembered that dark and wretched cottage, which doubtless had seen, and might perhaps also speak.

The gate of the enclosure was shut, but he jumped over the hedge, and, in spite of the barking of a chained dog, approached the cottage.

At his first summons, no one answered. A death-like silence prevailed here, as well as in the pavilion: yet, as this cottage was his last resource, he persisted.

Now he fancied he heard a slight noise within—a timid noise, which seemed itself to be afraid of being heard.

Then d'Artagnan ceased to knock, and made entreaties in such a piteous accent of fear, mingled with flattery, that his voice would have reassured the most timorous.

At length an old worm-eaten shutter was opened, or rather, half opened, and instantly shut again, as soon as the light of a miserable lamp, which was burning in a corner, had disclosed the belt, the hilt of the sword, and the pistols of d'Artagnan. And yet, quick as had been the movement, he had been able to see the head of an old man. 'In the name of Heaven!' said he, 'listen to me. I expected some one who is not come. I am dying from anxiety. Has any misfortune happened in your neighbourhood? Speak!'

The window was again slowly opened, and the same countenance reappeared, only it was paler than before.

D'Artagnan told his story simply, merely withholding names: he stated that he had an appointment with a young woman, before this pavilion; and that, not seeing her come, he had climbed the linden tree, and had, by the light of the lamp, perceived the disorder of the room.

The old man listened attentively, with many signs of assent; and when d'Artagnan had ended, shook his head in a manner which was not encouraging.

'What do you mean?' exclaimed d'Artagnan; 'in the name of Heaven, explain yourself!'

'Oh, sir!' said he, 'do not ask me anything; for, if I should tell you what I have seen, most assuredly no good will befall me.'

'You have seen something, then?' exclaimed d'Artagnan. 'In that case, in Heaven's name,' continued he, throwing him a pistole, 'tell me what you have seen, and, on the honour of a gentleman, not one of your words shall pass my lips.'

The old man read so much honesty and grief in d'Artagnan's countenance, that he made him a sign to listen, and said, in a low voice—

'It was about nine o'clock that I heard some noise in the street, and wishing to know what it was, I was going to my gate, when I saw some people trying to get in. As I am poor, and have no fear of being robbed, I went to open it, and saw three men a few paces from me. In the shade was a carriage, with horses harnessed to it, and also some led horses. These led horses evidently belonged to the three men, who were dressed for riding.

'Ah, my good sirs,' I cried, 'what do you want?'

'You ought to have a ladder,' said one, who appeared to be the leader of the party.

'Yes, sir, that with which I gather my fruit.'

'Give it to us, and go back into your house; and here is a crown for the trouble we give you. But, remember, if you say one word about what you see or hear—for, however we may threaten you, I am sure you will both hear and see all that we do—you are a lost man.'

'At these words he threw me a crown, which I picked up, and he took my ladder. In fact, having fastened the gate in the hedge after them, I pretended to enter my house, but I went out again by the back door, and, gliding in the shade, I came to those alder bushes, from the shelter of which I could see everything, without being seen myself.

'The three men had brought up the carriage without any noise: they pulled out of it a fat, short, gray little man, shabbily dressed in a sad-coloured doublet, who carefully mounted the ladder, looked sulkily into the window, came down with a wolf's steps, and muttered in a low voice— 'It is she!'

'He who had spoken to me immediately went to the door of the pavilion, which he opened with a key which he had about him, and then shut the door after him, and disappeared.

'The other two men mounted the ladder simultaneously. The little old man remained at the carriage door, the coachman took care of his horses, and a lackey of the led ones. Suddenly great outcries resounded from the pavilion, and a woman ran to the window, and opened it as if to throw herself out. But, as soon as she saw the two men, she threw herself back, and the two men rushed into the chamber after her.

'Then I saw nothing more; but I heard the noise of breaking furniture. The woman screamed, and cried for help: but her cries were soon stifled. The three men returned to the window, carrying the woman in their arms; and two of them came down the ladder, and bore her to the carriage, into which the little old man entered with her. He who had remained in the pavilion shut the window, came out at the door directly after, and satisfied himself that the woman was in the carriage: his two companions were already on their horses waiting for him; he sprang into his saddle, and the groom took his place beside the coachman: the carriage, escorted by the three horsemen, departed at a gallop, and all was over. From that moment until your arrival I have neither seen nor heard anything.'

D'Artagnan, overwhelmed by these terrible tidings, remained motionless and speechless, whilst the demons of jealousy and anger raged in his heart.

'But, my gentleman,' said the old man, on whom this mute despair had more effect than cries and tears would have produced, 'do not despond: they have not killed her; that is the great thing.'

'Do you know, at all,' said d'Artagnan, 'who is the man who conducted this infernal expedition?'

'I do not know him.'

'But, as he spoke to you, you could see him?'

'Ah! it is his appearance that you want to know?'

'Yes.'

'A tall, lean, brown man, with black moustaches, a dark eye, and the look of a gentleman.'

'That's it,' cried d'Artagnan; 'him again. The same man—always the same! It is my evil genius, apparently. And the other?'

'Which?'

'The little one.'

'Oh, he was not a gentleman, I answer for it. Besides, he did not carry a sword, and the others treated him with no sort of respect.'

'Some servant,' muttered d'Artagnan. 'Ah, poor woman! poor woman! what have they done with her?'

'You promised me to be secret,' said the old man.

'And I renew my promise. Be satisfied! I am a gentleman: a gentleman has only his word, and I have given you mine.'

D'Artagnan returned towards the ferry, almost heart-broken. Sometimes he could not believe that it was Madame Bonancieux, and hoped to find her the next day at the Louvre. Sometimes he fancied that she had an intrigue with another, and had been discovered and carried off by some third party who was jealous of him. He doubted, sorrowed, and despaired.

'Oh!' cried he, 'if I had but my friends here! I should at any rate have some hopes of finding her; but who knows what is become of them also?'

It was then nearly midnight, and he must at once find Planchet. D'Artagnan searched successively every wineshop where he perceived a little light, but nowhere could he find his servant.

At length, after examining half a dozen, he began to reflect that the search was rather fortuitous. He had himself said six o'clock in the morning: therefore, wherever Planchet was, he was fully justified.

Besides, it occurred to the young man, that, by remaining in the neighbourhood of the place where this event had happened, he might gather some information. At the sixth wine-shop, as we have said, he therefore remained, and asking for a bottle of their best wine, placed himself in the darkest corner, and determined there to await the return of day. But this time, too, his hope was disappointed; and, although he opened his ears to every sound, he heard nothing—amidst the oaths, and gestures, and abuse which were exchanged by the workmen, lackeys, and cab-drivers, who composed the honourable society of which he was a part—that could put him at all upon the track of the poor ill-used woman. He was obliged, therefore, after having emptied his bottle, and in order that he might avoid remark, to occupy himself in seeking for the easiest posture in which to sleep as best he could. It must be remembered that d'Artagnan was not twenty years old; and at that age sleep has undeniable rights, which must be submitted to, even by the most desolate hearts.

About six o'clock in the morning d'Artagnan awoke, with that feeling of discomfort which generally comes with the break of day after an uneasy night. His toilet did not occupy him long; and, having searched himself to see that no one had taken advantage of his sleep to rob him, and found his diamond on his finger, his purse in his pocket, and his pistols in his belt, he paid for his wine, and sallied forth to try whether he should be more fortunate in seeking for his servant in the morning than at night. And the first thing that he perceived, through the damp, gray fog, was honest Planchet who, with the two horses, was waiting for him at the door of a miserable little wine-shop, before which d'Artagnan had passed without even suspecting its existence.

25

Porthos

INSTEAD of returning directly home, d'Artagnan dismounted at M. de Treville's door, and rapidly ascended the staircase. He was determined to tell him, this time, all that had occurred. Doubtless the captain would give him good advice in this affair; and, as M. de Treville saw the queen almost daily, he might draw some information from her majesty concerning the poor woman, who was unquestionably being punished for her devotion to her mistress.

M. de Treville listened to the young man's recital with a gravity which proved that he saw something more in this adventure than an amour: and, when d'Artagnan had finished—

'Hum!' said he: 'this savours of his eminence a mile off.'

'But what am I to do?' said d'Artagnan.

'Nothing, absolutely nothing, just now; but leave Paris, as I have told you, as soon as possible. I will see the queen, and tell her the details of the disappearance of this poor woman, of which she is, doubtless, ignorant, and these details will guide her, on her side; and, on your return, I may possibly have some good news to give you. Trust to me.'

D'Artagnan knew, that, although a Gascon, M. de Treville was not accustomed to make promises, and that, when by chance he did make one, he always performed it to the full and more. He therefore took his leave, full of gratitude for the past and the future; and the worthy captain, who, on his side, felt a lively interest for this brave and resolute young man, affectionately pressed his hand as he wished him a good journey.

Determined instantaneously to put M. de Treville's advice into execution, d'Artagnan hastened towards the Rue des Fossoyeurs, to look to the packing of his portmanteau. On approaching No. 11, he perceived M. Bonancieux, in morning costume, standing at his door. Everything that the prudent Planchet had said the evening before, about the sinister character of his landlord, now recurred to his mind, and he looked at him more attentively than he had ever done before. In fact, besides that yellow sickly paleness, which indicates the infiltration of the bile into the blood, and which might be only accidental, d'Artagnan remarked something gruffly perfidious in the wrinkles of his face.

A rascal does not laugh in the same manner as an honest man; a hypocrite does not weep with the same kind of tears as a sincere man. All imposture is a mask; and, however well the mask may be made, it may always, with a little attention, be distinguished from the true face.

Now, it seemed to d'Artagnan that M. Bonancieux wore a mask, and that this mask was a most disagreeable one.

He was going, therefore, from his repugnance to the man, to pass by him without speaking; when M. Bonancieux, as on the previous day, addressed him.

'Well, young man,' said he, it seems that we are rather late of nights. Seven o'clock in the morning! Plague! It appears that you reverse customs, and return home when others emerge.'

'No one could throw that in your teeth, M. Bonancieux.' said the young man; 'you are the model of regularity. It is true, that when one has a young and pretty wife, one need not run after happiness; happiness comes home to seek us, does it not, M. Bonancieux?'

Bonancieux became pale as death, and grinned a horrible smile.

'Ah, ah! you are a pleasant fellow. But where the plague have you been running this night, my young master? It appears as if the by-lanes were rather dirty.'

D'Artagnan lowered his eyes to his own boots, which were covered with mud; but in doing this, he happened to look at the shoes and hose of the mercer: one would have said that they had been dipped in the same slough, for both were stained with spots of exactly the same appearance.

A sudden idea came across d'Artagnan's mind. That little, fat, gray, short man, like a lackey, clothed in a sad-coloured suit, and treated with no sort of respect by the swordsmen of the escort, was Bonancieux himself. The husband had assisted in the abduction of his wife.

A strong desire seized d'Artagnan to fly at the mercer's throat, and strangle him; but he was a prudent youth, as we have said, and he restrained himself.

Nevertheless, his change of countenance was so visible, that Bonancieux was frightened, and endeavoured to retreat a step or two; but he was exactly before the half of the door that was closed, and the material obstacle which he thus encountered compelled him to keep the same place.

'Ah!' said d'Artagnan, 'you who joke in this manner, my brave fellow—it appears to me, that if my boots need a rub of the sponge, your shoes also want a brush. And have you been rambling, too, Master Bonancieux? By my faith, it would be quite unpardonable in a man of your age, and who, moreover, has got a wife as pretty as yours is.'

'Oh! mon Dieu, no,' said Bonancieux; 'but yesterday I went to St. Maude, to gain some information concerning a servant, whom I cannot do without; and, as the roads were dirty, I have collected all this mud, which I have not yet had time to get rid of.'

The place which Bonancieux had mentioned, as the end of his journey, was a new proof in confirmation of the suspicions that d'Artagnan had formed. Bonancieux had said St. Maude, because St. Maude was in an exactly opposite direction to St. Cloud.

This probability was the first consolation he had found! If Bonancieux knew where his wife was, it would always be possible, by using extreme measures, to force the mercer to unclose his teeth and let out his secret. The great thing was, to change this probability into certainty.

'Pardon me, my dear M. Bonancieux,' said d'Artagnan, 'if I treat you without ceremony; but nothing makes me so thirsty as want of sleep: hence, I have a furious thirst. Allow me to beg a glass of water of you; you know you refuse such a thing to a neighbour.'

And without waiting for the permission of his landlord, d'Artagnan entered the house, and cast a hasty glance at the bed. The bed was undisturbed: Bonancieux had not slept in it. He had, therefore, only returned an hour or two before, having accompanied his wife to the place where they had conducted her, or, at any rate, for the first stage.

'Thank you, M. Bonancieux,' said d'Artagnan, emptying the glass; 'that is all I wanted of you. Now I will go home: I am going to make Planchet brush my boots, and when he has finished them, I will send him, if you like, to brush your shoes.'

He left the mercer quite stupified by this singular adieu, and wondering whether he had not run his own neck into a noose.

At the top of the stairs he found Planchet, frightened out of his wits.

'Ah, sir,' cried the lackey, as soon as he saw his master; 'here, indeed, is something new; and how long you seemed to me in returning.'

'What is the matter now?' demanded d'Artagnan.

'Ah! I will give you leave to guess a hundred, nay, a thousand times, before you find out the visitor I have received on your behalf during your absence.'

'When was that?'

'About half an hour ago, whilst you were with M. de Treville.'

'And who has been here? Come, speak!'

'M. de Cavois.'

'M. de Cavois?'

'Yes, no other.'

'The captain of his eminence's guards?'

'Yes, himself!'

'He came to arrest me?'

'I suspected so, sir, in spite of his wheedling way.'

'He had a wheedling way, do you say?'

'That is to say, he was all honey, sir.'

'Really!'

'He said he came from his eminence, who had the greatest goodwill towards you, to beg you to follow him to the Palais-Royal.'

'And you answered him?'

'That the thing was impossible, seeing that you were from home, as he might perceive.'

'And what did he say then?'

'That you must not fail to go there some time during the day, and then he added, in a whisper: 'Tell your master that his eminence is perfectly well-disposed towards him, and that his fortune probably depends upon this interview.'

'The snare is unskilful enough for the cardinal,' said the young man, smiling.

'And as I discovered the snare, I told him that you would be quite in despair on your return.'

'Where is he gone?' demanded M. de Cavois. 'To Troyes, in Champagne,' answered I. 'And when did he go?' says he. 'Yesterday evening!'

'Planchet, my friend,' interrupted d'Artagnan, 'you are truly a valuable man.'

'You understand, sir, I thought that there would be time enough, if you wished to see M. de Cavois, to give me the lie, by saying that you had not gone. It would then be me who had told the lie; and, as I am not a gentleman, I may tell lies, you know.'

'Be easy, Planchet, you shall preserve your reputation as a man of truth: in one quarter of an hour we will be off.'

'It was just the advice I was going to offer you, sir. And where are we going now, if it is not being too curious?'

'Egad! exactly the opposite way to that which you said I was gone. Besides, are you not in as much anxiety to know what has become of Grimaud, Mousqueton, and Bazin, as I to hear of Athos, Porthos, and Aramis?'

'Yes, indeed, sir,' said Planchet, 'and I will set off as soon as you please. The air of the country, I believe, will suit us both better than the air of Paris, just now. Therefore——'

'Therefore, prepare the baggage, Planchet, and let us be off. I will march off first, with my hands in my pockets, that there may be no suspicion. You will join me at the Hotel des Gardes. Apropos, Planchet, I believe that you are right regarding our landlord, and that he is decidedly a most horrible rascal.'

'Ah! believe me, sir, when I tell you anything in future: I am a physiognomist!'

D'Artagnan descended first, as was agreed; and, that he might have nothing to reproach himself with, he went again to the lodgings of his three friends, but no intelligence of them had been received—only a perfumed letter, most elegantly

addressed, had arrived for Aramis. D'Artagnan took charge
of it. Ten minutes afterwards, Planchet rejoined him at the
stables. D'Artagnan, that no time might be lost, had already
saddled his own horse.

'That will do,' said he to Planchet, when he had fastened
on his valise. 'Now saddle the other three, and let us be off.'

'Do you believe we shall travel faster with two horses
a-piece?' asked Planchet, with his sharp look.

'No, Mister Jester,' replied d'Artagnan, 'but, with our
four horses, we may bring our three friends back—that is,
if we can find them.'

'Which would be a great chance,' replied Planchet; 'but
we must not distrust the mercy of God.'

'Amen!' said d'Artagnan, bestriding his horse.

They left the Hotel des Gardes by the opposite ends of
the street, as the one was to quit Paris by the barrier of La
Vilette, the other by the barrier of Montmartre, to rejoin
each other at St. Denis—a stratagetic manœuvre, which,
being punctually executed, was crowned with the most
fortunate results. Thus, d'Artagnan and Planchet entered
Pierrefitte together.

Planchet, it must be confessed, was more courageous by
day than by night. But yet his natural prudence did not
forsake him for an instant: he had forgotten none of the incidents of the former journey, and took every one for an enemy
whom he met upon the road. On this account, he always had
his hat off, for which he was severely rebuked by d'Artagnan,
who feared that this excess of politeness might cause Planchet
to be taken for the valet of a man of little consequence.

Nevertheless, whether the passengers were really softened
by Planchet's extreme urbanity, or whether no enemies
were stationed on the young man's path, our two travellers
arrived, without any accident, at Chantilly, and dismounted
at the tavern of the Great St. Martin, the same at which
they had stopped upon their last journey.

The landlord, seeing a young man, followed by a servant
and two led horses, advanced respectfully to his door. Now,
as he had already travelled eleven leagues, d'Artagnan judged that he had better stop here, whether Porthos were at
the hotel or not. But it might not be prudent, at first, to make
any inquiries about the musketeer. The result of these
reflections was, that d'Artagnan, without asking any information from anybody, dismounted, recommended the horses
to his servant's care, and entering a small room, reserved for

those who wished to be alone, called for a bottle of the best wine, and as good a breakfast as the landlord could supply —a call which corroborated the high estimate that the innkeeper had already formed of his guest at first sight.

D'Artagnan was served with a celerity which was quite miraculous. The regiment of guards was composed of the first gentlemen in the realm; and d'Artagnan, travelling with a servant and four splendid horses, could not fail of creating a sensation, in spite of the simplicity of his uniform. The host wished to wait on him himself: seeing which, d'Artagnan made him bring two glasses, and began the following conversation:—

'By my faith, mine host,' said d'Artagnan, filling two glasses, 'I have asked for the best wine, and, if you have deceived me, your sin will bring its own punishment, since, as I hate to drink alone, you are going to drink with me. Take this glass, then, and let us drink. To what shall we drink, that we may wound no one's feelings? Let us drink to the prosperity of your establishment!'

'Your lordship does me great honour, and I sincerely thank you for your good wishes.'

'But don't deceive yourself,' said d'Artagnan; 'there is more selfishness in my toast than you think for. It is only in prosperous houses that one gets well treated: in struggling inns everything runs to disorder, and the traveller is a victim to the landlord's embarrassment. Therefore, as I travel a great deal, and particularly on this road, I should like to see all the innkeepers making a fortune.'

'In fact,' said the landlord, 'it appears to me that this is not the first time I have seen you, sir.'

'Bah! I have passed through Chantilly perhaps ten times, and have stopped at least three or four times at your house. Yes, I was here about ten or twelve days ago, conducting three of my friends, musketeers; and one of them, by the bye, quarrelled with a stranger here—a man who sought a quarrel with him.'

'Ah! yes, true!' said mine host; 'I recollect it perfectly. Is it not of M. Porthos that your lordship speaks?'

'That is the very name of my travelling companion. Mon Dieu! my dear landlord, tell me, has any misfortune befallen him?'

'But your lordship must have remarked for yourself that he was not able to continue his journey.'

'In fact, he promised to overtake us, but we saw no more of him.'

'He has done us the honour to remain here.'

'What! he has done you the honour to remain here?'

'Yes, sir, in this hotel; and we are somewhat uneasy over it.'

'Why?'

'On account of certain expenses that he has incurred.'

'Well, but the expenses he has incurred he will pay.'

'Ah, sir, your words are a positive balm to my heart. We have been at considerable expense on his account; and only this morning the surgeon declared that, if M. Porthos did not pay him, he should proceed against me, as it was I who sent for him.'

'But is Porthos wounded, then?'

'I cannot tell you, sir.'

'What! you cannot tell me? You ought at any rate to know better than anybody else.'

'Yes; but, in our trade we do not tell all we know, sir—particularly when we have been warned that our ears shall answer for our tongue.'

'Well! can I see Porthos?'

'Certainly, sir. Go to the first landing-place on the staircase, and knock at No 1. Only, advise him that it is you!'

'What! advise him that it is me?'

'Yes; some accident might happen else.'

'And what accident could happen to me?'

'M. Porthos might mistake you for somebody belonging to the house, and might, in a fit of passion, either run you through with his sword, or blow out your brains.'

'Why, what have you been doing to him, then?'

'Oh! we asked him for money.'

'Ah! I comprehend now. That is a kind of demand that Porthos always receives badly when he is not in cash: but I know that he ought to have plenty.'

'So we thought also, sir. And, as the house is very regular, and our accounts are made up every week, on the eighth day we presented our little bill: but we seem to have hit upon an unlucky time, for, at the first word we dropped upon the subject, he sent us all to the very devil. It is true, he had been playing cards the evening before.'

'What! playing the evening before? And with whom?'

'Oh! good Lord, who can tell that? With some nobleman who was travelling this way, and to whom he sent to propose a game at lansquenet.'

'Just so: and the unlucky dog lost his all.'

'Even to his horse, sir: for, when the stranger was about to leave, we perceived that his servant was saddling M. Porthos's horse, and we remarked it to him; but he told us that we had better mind our own business, and that the horse was his own. So, we went immediately to let M. Porthos know what was going on; but he only answered, that we were scoundrels for doubting the word of a gentleman, and that, as this one had said that the horse belonged to him, it necessarily must be true.'

'I recognise him there, exactly,' muttered d'Artagnan.

'Then,' continued the innkeeper, I sent a message to him, that, as we did not seem likely to come to any understanding with one another about payment, I hoped that he would at least have the kindness to transfer the favour of his custom to my brother-landlord at *The Golden Eagle*, but M. Porthos replied that, as my hotel was the best, he desired to remain here. This answer was too complimentary for me to insist upon his leaving. I contented myself with begging him to resign his apartment, which is the most beautiful in the house and to be satified with a pretty little room upon the third floor. But to this M. Porthos replied, that he was every moment expecting his mistress, who was one of the highest ladies at court: and that I ought to understand that the chamber which he did me the honour to occupy in my house, was scarcely good enough yet for such a visitor. Nevertheless, fully recognising the truth of what he said, I felt it my duty to insist; but, without condescending to enter into any discussion with me, he put a pistol on his night-table, and, declared that at the first word which might be said to him about any moving whatsoever, either out of the house or in it, he would blow out the brains of the person who had been imprudent enough to interfere in what did not concern him. So, since that time, sir, nobody has once entered his room but his own servant.'

'Oh! Mousqueton is here, is he?'

'Yes, sir. Five days after his departure, he came back in a very ill humour: it seems that he, also had met with some unpleasantry on his way. But he is, unfortunately, rather nimbler than his master, so that he turns everything topsyturvy, and, under the pretext that we might refuse him what he asks for, takes anything he wants without asking at all.'

'The fact is,' replied d'Artagnan, 'that I have always remarked in Mousqueton a very superior intelligence and zeal,'

'Possibly so, sir; but if I should only find myself, four times in a year in contact with a similar intelligence and zeal, I should be a bankrupt.'

'No! Porthos will pay you.'

'Hum!' exclaimed the innkeeper, in a tone of doubt.

'He is the favourite of a lady of rank, who will not allow him to remain in trouble on account of a trifle such as he owes you.'

'If I only dared to say what I think about that.'

'What you think?'

'I might say more—what I know.'

'What you know?'

'Or, even, what I am quite sure of!'

'And what are you sure of? Come, say!'

'I should say that I know about this lady of rank.'

'You?'

'Yes, me!'

'And how came you to know about her?'

'Oh! sir, if I thought I could depend on your discretion.'

'Speak; and, on the word of a gentleman, you shall have no occasion to regret your confidence.'

'Well! sir, you can understand that uneasiness makes one do many things.'

'What have you done?'

'Oh! nothing but what a creditor has a right to do.'

'Well?'

'M. Porthos had handed us a note for this duchess, giving us orders to put it in the post. It was before his own servant came; and, as he could not leave his room, he was obliged to employ us in his commissions.'

'What next?'

'Instead of putting this letter in the post, which is uncertain, we took advantage of the occasion of one of our waiters going to Paris, and instructed him to deliver the letter to this duchess herself. That was fulfilling the intentions of M. Porthos, who had particularly enjoined us to be careful of the letter, was it not?'

'Nearly so.'

'Well, sir, do you know what this lady of rank is?'

'No. I have heard Porthos speak of her: that is all.'

'Do you know what this pretended duchess is?'

'I tell you again, I don't know her.'

'She is an attorney's wife, sir; an elderly woman, called Madame Coquenard, who is at least fifty years of age, and yet takes it upon herself to be jealous. It seemed very strange to me, a princess living in the Rue aux Ours!'

'How do you know this?'

'Because she put herself in a great passion on receiving the letter, saying that M. Porthos was a fickle man, and that it was on account of some woman that he had received this sword wound.'

'Then he has received a sword wound? replied d'Artagnan.

'Ah, Mon Dieu! what have I said?' cried the innkeeper.

'You said that M. Porthos had received a wound from a sword.'

'Yes; but he strongly enjoined me to say nothing about it.'

'And why?'

'Plague, sir! because he boasted that he would perforate the stranger with whom you left him in a dispute; whilst, on the contrary, this stranger stretched him on the ground, in spite of his rhodomontades. Now, as M. Porthos is a very vain-glorious man, except toward his duchess, whom he thought to soften by an account of his misadventure, he is not disposed to admit to anybody that he is suffering from a wound.'

'It is a sword wound, then that keeps him in his bed?'

'And a masterly one, I assure you. Your friend's soul must be absolutely pinned to his body.'

'Were you there, then?'

'I followed them, sir, from curiosity, so that I saw the combat, myself invisible.'

'And how did it happen?'

'Oh, the thing did not take long, I assure you. They placed themselves on guard: the stranger made a feint, and lunged, and that so rapidly, that, when M. Porthos parried, he had already three inches of steel in his chest. He fell back. The stranger put his sword to his throat; and M. Porthos, seeing himself at the mercy of his adversary, confessed himself vanquished. The stranger then asked his name: and hearing that he was M. Porthos, and not M. d'Artagnan, offered him his arm, and led him back to the hotel, mounted on horseback, and disappeared.'

'Then it was M. d'Artagnan that the stranger wanted?'

'It appears so.'

'And do you know what has become of him?'

'No, I had never seen him before that moment, and we have not seen him since.'

'Very well; I know all I want. And you say that M. Porthos' chamber is on the first floor, No. 1?'

'Yes, sir, the handsomest in the house—a chamber which I might have let ten or a dozen times.'

'Bah! Cheer up!' said d'Artagnan, laughing: 'Porthos will pay you with the cash of the duchess Coquenard.'

'Oh! sir, attorney's wife or duchess would be no matter to me, if she would only unloosen her purse-strings; but she has positively said that she is tired out by the inconstancies and exigencies of M. Porthos; and that she will not send him even a sou.'

'And did you communicate this reply to your guest?'

'No; we were too careful for that. He would have found out the fashion in which we had executed our commission.'

'Then he is still in expectation of the money?'

'Mon Dieu! yes. He wrote again yesterday: but his own servant this time took the letter to the post.'

'You say the attorney's wife is old and ugly?'

'Fifty years old, at least, sir, and far from handsome, from what Pathand says.'

'Be comforted, then. Her heart will melt towards him; and, at anyrate, Porthos cannot owe you much.'

'What! not much? It is twenty pistoles already, without reckoning the surgeon. Oh! he denies himself nothing: it is plain that he has always been accustomed to live well!'

'Well, even if the duchess should fail him, he will find friends, I can assure you. So my dear landlord, do not disturb yourself, and continue to be most attentive to his comfort.'

'You have promised me, sir, not to say a word about the attorney's wife, or the wound.'

'That is agreed—you have my word.'

'Oh! he would kill me, do you see!'

'Do not be afraid; he is not half such a devil as he seems!'

Saying these words, d'Artagnan mounted the stairs, leaving the landlord a little more encouraged concerning two things, of which he appeared to think a good deal—his money and his life.

At the top of the stairs, d'Artagnan found, on the most conspicuous door of the corridor, a gigantic No. 1 marked, with black ink. At this door he knocked, and, being invited from within, entered the room.

Porthos was lying down, and playing at lansquenet, with

Mousqueton, to keep his hand in, whilst a spit burdened with partridges, was turning before the fire, and, at the two corners of an immense chimney, there were boiling, on two chafing-dishes, two saucepans, from which exhaled the double odour of a fricassee of fowls, and a hotch-potch of fish, which delighted the olfactory nerves. Besides, the top of a desk and the marble slab of a commode were covered with empty bottles.

At sight of his friend, Porthos uttered a loud and joyful cry; whilst Mousqueton, rising respectfully, gave up his place to him, and went to glance into the two saucepans, of which he appeared to have particular charge.

'Ah! egad! it is you!' said Porthos. 'Welcome, welcome! Excuse me for not rising to meet you; but,' added he, looking with some anxiety at d'Artagnan, 'you know what has happened to me?'

'No.'

'Has the innkeeper told you nothing?'

'I asked for you, and came up directly.'

'Porthos appeared to breathe more freely.

'And what has happened to you, then, my dear Porthos?' continued d'Artagnan.

'It happened that, in lunging at my adversary, to whom I had already given three sword wounds, and whom I wished to finish by a fourth, my foot caught against a stone, and I sprained my knee.'

'Indeed!'

'Yes, upon my honour! Lucky it was for the rascal too, for I should otherwise have left him dead upon the spot, I assure you.'

'And what became of him?'

'Oh, I know nothing about that; he had had quite enough of it, and went away without asking for the remainder. But you, my dear d'Artagnan, what happened to you?'

'So that,' continued d'Artagnan, 'it is this sprain that keeps you in bed, my dear Porthos?'

'Ah, Mon Dieu! yes; that is all; but in a few days I shall be on my legs again.'

'But why did not you get yourself removed to Paris? You must have been sadly dull here?'

'It was my intention; but, my dear friend, I must confess one thing to you.'

'And what is that?'

'It is, that as I became cruelly dull, as you say, and as I

had in my pocket the seventy-five pistoles with which you provided me, I invited up a passing traveller, and proposed to him a game of dice. He agreed; and, faith, my seventy-five pistoles passed from my pocket into his, without reckoning my horse, which he carried off into the bargain. But you, my dear d'Artagnan.'

'What would you have, my dear Porthos? You cannot be favoured in all your pursuits,' said d'Artagnan. 'You know the proverb—'lose at play, and win at love.' You are too fortunate in love, for play not to revenge itself. But what do these changes of fortune signify to you? Happy dog! have you not still got your duchess to assist you?'

'Nay! look, my dear d'Artagnan, how unlucky I am,' replied Porthos, in the most unconcerned tone in the world. I have written to her to send me some fifty louis, for which I have particular occasion in my present position.'

'Well?'

'Well! She must be gone to her estate, for she has sent me no answer!'

'Really?'

'No; so I sent a second letter yesterday, rather more urgent than the first. But, my dear fellow, let us chat about your own affairs. I confess, I was beginning to feel some uneasiness on your account.'

'But your host has behaved pretty well to you, apparently,' said d'Artagnan, pointing to the teeming stewpans, and the empty bottles.

'So-so!' replied Porthos; 'but it is only two or three days ago, now, since the impudent fellow brought me up his bill, and I showed them the door—both himself and his bill; so that I am now living here in something of the style of a conqueror. And, as you see, being somewhat afraid of being attacked in my redoubts, I am armed to the very teeth.'

'Nevertheless,' said d'Artagnan, laughing, 'it seems that you sometimes make sorties.'

And he pointed to the stewpans and the bottles.

'It is not me, unfortunately,' said Porthos. 'This miserable sprain keeps me in my bed; but Mousqueton, there, forages the country for supplies. Mousqueton, my friend,' continued Porthos, 'you see that a reinforcement has arrived: we shall want an addition to our rations.'

'Mousqueton,' said d'Artagnan, 'there is a service you must do me.'

'What is it, sir?'

'To give your recipe to Planchet! I may chance to be besieged myself hereafter, and I should not be at all sorry to enjoy all the advantages with which you gratify your master.'

'Oh, sir,' said Mousqueton modestly, 'nothing is more easy. One must be a little adroit—that is all. I was brought up in the provinces, and my father, in his leisure moments, was something of a poacher.'

'And how was he occupied in business hours?'

'He was engaged in a pursuit, sir, which I have always found a very happy one.'

'What was that?'

'As it was in the time of the wars between the Catholics and Huguenots; and as he saw Catholics exterminating Huguenots, and Huguenots exterminating Catholics, all in the name of religion, he had made for himself a sort of mixed belief, which permitted him to be at one time a Catholic, and at another a Huguenot. He had a habit of walking out behind the hedges on the road side, with his carbine at his shoulder, and, when he saw a solitary Catholic coming, the Protestant religion immediately predominated in his mind, he lowered his carbine in the direction of the traveller, and then, when he was at ten paces from him, opened a conversation which almost always ended by the traveller relinquishing his purse to redeem his life. Of course, when he saw a Huguenot coming, he was seized with such an ardent Catholic zeal, that he could not comprehend how it had been possible for him, only a quarter of an hour before, to doubt the superiority of our most holy faith. For myself, sir, I am a Catholic; my father having, in conformity to his principles, made my elder brother a Huguenot.'

'And what was the end of the worthy man?' asked d'Artagnan.

'Most unfortunate, sir. He found himself caught in a defile, between a Catholic and a Huguenot, with whom he had done some business previously, and they both recognised him; so they united against him, and hung him on a tree. And then they came and boasted of their foolish work in the very wine-shop, in the village, where my brother and I were drinking.'

'And what did you do?' asked d'Artagnan.

'We let them talk,' replied Mousqueton. 'Then, as they went opposite roads when they left the wine-shop, my brother posted himself in the path of the Catholic, and I lay in wait for the Protestant. It was all settled two hours after: we had done the business of both of them—admiring the forethought of our poor father, who had taken the precaution to educate us each in a different faith.'

'In fact—as you say, Mousqueton—your father seems to have been a very intelligent fellow. And you tell me, that the worthy man was, in his leisure moments, a poacher?'

'Yes, sir; and it was he who taught me to set a snare, and fix a night-line. The consequence was, that when I found our shabby landlord was feeding us on coarse meats, fit possibly for clowns, but not at all suitable to stomachs so delicate as ours, I had recourse again to my old trade. As I sauntered through the woods, I laid my snares in the paths; and, as I reclined beside the water, I slipped my lines into the ponds. In this way, thank God, we have experienced no scarcity, as you may be satisfied, sir, of partridges or rabbits, of carps or eels, and these are light and wholesome viands, highly suitable to sick persons.'

'But wine,' said d'Artagnan. 'Your landlord furnishes the wine?'

'That is to say,' answered Mousqueton, 'yes and no!'

'What! yes and no?'

'He furnishes it, it is true; but he is unconscious of honour.'

'Explain yourself, Mousqueton; your conversation is deep.'

'This is the way of it; it chanced, that in my wanderings, I met with a Spaniard, who had seen many countries, and, amongst others, the New World.'

'And what connexion can there be between the New World and those bottles on the desk and drawers?'

'Patience, sir, everything will come in its turn.'

'That is fair, Mousqueton, I trust to you, and listen.'

'This Spaniard had a servant, who had accompanied him on his voyage to Mexico. This servant was a compatriot of mine, and we became attached to one another the more quickly, as our characters were much alike. We were both particularly fond of hunting; and he related to me how, in the Pampas, the natives hunt tigers and bulls, simply with nooses of rope, which they throw over the necks of these terrible animals. At first, I would not believe that they could attain so great a degree of address, as to throw the end of a rope on what they wished, at the distance of twenty or thirty paces. But, with the proof before me, I was obliged to recognise the truth of his recital. My friend placed a bottle at thirty paces off, and, at each throw, caught it by the neck in a running noose. I practised this exercise; and, as nature has given me some capacity, I can now throw the lasso as well as any man in the world. Well! do you understand? Our landlord has a well-furnished cellar, of which he never loses sight of the key. But this cellar has an air-hole, and through that air-hole I throw the lasso; and as I now know the best corner, I always draw from thence. This is the connection, sir, between the New World and the bottles on the desk and drawers. And now will you taste our wine? and, without prejudice, you will tell us what you think of it.'

'Thanks, my friend, thanks! But I have already breakfasted.'

'Well!' said Porthos, 'make all ready, Mousqueton; and whilst we breakfast, d'Artagnan will tell us what has happened to him during the ten days that he has been absent from us.'

Whilst Porthos and Mousqueton breakfasted with all the appetite of convalescents, and that brotherly familiarity which draws men together in misfortune, d'Artagnan related that Aramis, being wounded, had been obliged to stop at Crevecœur; that he had left Athos fighting at Amiens, with four men, who accused him of being a coiner; and that he himself had been compelled to run the Count de Wardes through the body, in order to reach England.

But there the confidence of d'Artagnan ended: he merely announced that, on his return from England, he had brought four splendid horses with him, one for himself, and one for each of their companions; and he concluded by informing Porthos that the one destined for him was already in the stables of the hotel.

At this moment Planchet entered: he intimated to his master that the horses were sufficiently refreshed, and that it would be possible to go to Clermont in time to pass the night there.

As d'Artagnan was pretty well satisfied as to Porthos's state, and was anxious to gain some information concerning his two other friends, he gave his hand to the invalid, and told him that he should now proceed to continue his inquiries. And, as he expected to return by the same road, if Porthos, in seven or eight days, was still at the hotel of the Great Saint Martin, he would take him up upon his way.

Porthos answered, that in all probability his sprain would

confine him till that time; and, moreover, he must wait at Chantilly for a reply from the duchess.

D'Artagnan wished him a speedy and favourable one; and, after having again commended him to the care of Mousqueton, and paid the landlord his own expenses, he once more took the road with Planchet, who was already relieved of one of the led horses.

26

The Thesis of Aramis

D'ARTAGNAN had said nothing to Porthos, either about his wound, or about the attorney's wife. Young as he was, our Bearnese was very discreet. Consequently, he had pretended to believe everything that the boasting musketeer had told him, convinced that no friendship can support itself against a secret discovered, especially when that secret wounds the pride; since one always has a certain moral superiority over those with whose frailties we are acquainted. In his plans for the future, resolved as he was to make his three friends the instruments of his success, d'Artagnan was not sorry to collect in his hand those invisible threads by the aid of which he meant to lead them.

Nevertheless, throughout the whole of his journey, an overwhelming sadness hung upon his heart: he thought of that young and pretty Madame Bonancieux, who was to have bestowed upon him the reward of his devotion. Let us, however, at once declare, that the young man's melancholy was not so much a regret for his own lost enjoyment, as a dread that something unfortunate had befallen the missing woman. He had himself no doubt that she was a victim of the cardinal's vengeance; and it was well known that this eminence's revenge was always terrible. But how had he himself found pardon in the eyes of the minister? This was what he did not know, but what M. de Cavois, the captain of the guard, would undoubtedly have communicated to him, had he found him at home.

Nothing passes the time, or shortens the path, like a thought which engrosses all the faculties of an individual's organization. Our external existence is as a sleep, of which this thought is the dream; and, whilst we are subjected to its influence, time has no longer any measure, nor is there any distance in space: we leave one place, and arrive at another, and are conscious of nothing between. Of the intervening scenes, the only remembrance preserved, is somewhat akin to the idea of an indefinite mist, partially broken by obscure images of mountains, trees, and plains. It was under the dominion of this hallucination, that d'Artagnan at the pace that his horse pleased to take, passed over the six or eight leagues, which separated Chantilly from Crevecœur, without having, on his arrival at the latter village, any recollection of the things he had encountered on the road. But there memory returned to him: he shook his head, perceived the tavern where he had left Aramis, and, putting his horse into a trot, reined in at the door.

It was not a landlord this time, but a landlady, who received him. D'Artagnan, being somewhat of a physiognomist, examined, at a glance, the fat and good-humoured face of the mistress of the place; this glance satisfied him that dissimulation was not necessary with her, and that he had nothing to fear from such a happy-looking countenance.

'My good lady,' demanded d'Artagnan, 'can you tell me what has become of one of my friends, whom I was obliged to leave here about twelve days ago?'

'A handsome young man, of about twenty-three or twenty-four years of age, mild, amiable, and handsome?'

'Exactly so; and, moreover, wounded in the shoulder.'

'Just so. Well, he is still here.'

'Ah, my dear lady,' said d'Artagnan, springing from his horse, and throwing the bridle to Planchet, 'you give me life! Where is this dear Aramis? Let me embrace him, for I confess that I long to see him.'

'Pardon me, sir, but I question whether he can see you at present.'

'Why not? is there a lady with him?'

'Oh! dear me, sir, what a question! Poor youth! No, sir, there is not a woman with him.'

'Who then?'

'The curate of Montdidier, and the superior of the Jesuits of Amiens.'

'Good God!' exclaimed d'Artagnan, 'is the poor young man so very ill?'

'No, sir, quite the contrary. But towards the end of his illness, he has been touched by grace, and has determined on taking holy orders.'

'Ah, true!' said d'Artagnan; 'I had forgotten that he was only a musketeer temporarily.'

'Do you still insist on seeing him, sir?'

'Oh, yes, more than ever.'

'Well, then, you have only to take the left-hand staircase in the courtyard, to No. 5, on the second floor.'

D'Artagnan quickly followed this direction, and found one of those outside staircases which may still be sometimes seen in the courtyards of old-fashioned inns. But it was no such easy matter to get admission to the future abbé. The avenues of Aramis's chamber were as strictly guarded as the gardens of Armidus. Bazin was stationed in the corridor, and barred the passage against him with the more intrepidity, as, after many years of trial, he saw himself at length on the eve of acquiring that distinction, of which he had always been ambitious.

In fact, the dream of poor Bazin had ever been to serve a churchman, and he impatiently expected the so-long-anticipated moment, when Aramis would at last throw off his military uniform, and adopt the cassock. It had only been by the daily reiteration of this promise, that he had been included to continue in the service of the musketeer, in which, as he said, he could not fail to forfeit his salvation.

Bazin was therefore at the very summit of happiness. There was every probability that his master would keep to his determination this time. The union of physical and moral pain, had produced the effect so long desired. Aramis, suffering at once in mind and body, had at length fixed his thoughts and eyes upon religion; and he had regarded, as a warning from heaven, the double accident which had befallen him—that is to say, the sudden disappearance of his mistress, and the wound in his shoulder.

In such a mood, it may be easily imagined that nothing could have been more disagreeable to Bazin than the appearance of d'Artagnan, which might throw his master again into the whirlwind of those worldly ideas, of which he had been so long the sport.

He resolved, therefore, bravely to defend the door; and as, betrayed by the landlady, he could not say that Aramis was out, he attempted to prove to the newcomer, that it would be the height of impropriety to interrupt the pious conversation which his master had maintained since morning and which, as Bazin added, could not be concluded before night.

But d'Artagnan paid no attention to the eloquent discourse of Bazin; not wishing to enter into a polemical discussion with his friend's valet, he simply put him aside with one hand, and turned the handle of the door of No. 5 with the other.

The door opened, and d'Artagnan entered the apartment.

Aramis, in a long black coat, and with his head encased in a kind of round flat cap, which was no bad representation of a skull cap, was seated at a long table, covered with rolls of paper, and enormous folios; on his right sat the superior of the Jesuits; and on his left, the curate of Montdidier. The curtains were half closed, giving entrance only to a subdued, mysterious light, appropriate to holy meditation. All those wordly objects which are apt to greet the eye in the chamber of a young man, and particularly when that young man is a musketeer, had disappeared, as though by enchantment; and, doubtless from a fear that the sight of them might recall his master's mundane inclinations, Bazin had laid hands upon the sword, the pistols, the plumed hat, and the embroidery and lace of every sort and kind.

But instead of these, d'Artagnan fancied he saw, in an obscure corner, something like a cord of discipline, hanging by a nail to the wall.

At the noise which d'Artagnan made on entering, Aramis raised his head, and recognised his friend. But, to the great surprise of the latter, this sight did not seem to produce much impression on the musketeer, so much was his mind detached from all terrestrial affairs.

'How are you, my dear d'Artagnan?' said Aramis. 'Believe me, I am glad to see you.'

'And I, also,' said d'Artagnan; 'although I am not yet quite sure that it is Aramis I am speaking to.'

'The same, the same, my friend; but what could make you doubt it?'

'I thought I had mistaken the room, and entered the chamber of a churchman. And then another terror seized me, when I found you in the company of these gentlemen —I feared you were dangerously ill.'

The two men in black launched a glance almost of menace at d'Artagnan, whose intention they perceived; but he did not on that account disturb himself.

'Perhaps I inconvenience you, my dear Aramis,' continued d'Artagnan; 'for, from what I see, I am led to suppose that you are confessing to these gentlemen.'

Aramis coloured slightly.

'Oh, no, on the contrary, my dear friend; and, as a proof of it, permit me to protest to you, that I rejoice at seeing you safe and sound!'

'Ah! he is coming to himself again,' thought d'Artagnan; 'this is fortunate!'

'This gentleman, who is my friend, has just escaped a serious danger,' continued Aramis, addressing the two ecclesiastics, as he pointed to d'Artagnan with his hand.

'Praise God for it, sir,' replied they, bowing their heads in concert.

'I have not failed to do so, reverend fathers,' replied the young man, as he returned their salutation.

'You are come just in the nick of time, my dear d'Artagnan,' continued Aramis, 'and, by taking part in our discussion, you will enlighten it by your ability. M. the Principal of Amiens, M. the Curate of Montdidier, and myself, are arguing certain theological questions, which have long interested us, and on which I shall be delighted to have your opinion.'

'The opinion of a soldier has but little weight,' replied d'Artagnan, who began to be uneasy at the turn things were taking; 'you may rely upon the knowledge of these gentlemen.'

The men in black bowed.

'On the contrary,' replied Aramis, 'your opinion will be of great value. The question is this: the Principal thinks that my thesis should be, above all things, dogmatic and didactic.'

'Your thesis! Are you preparing a thesis?'

'Certainly,' replied the Jesuit: 'for the examination preceding ordination, a thesis is rigorously demanded.'

'Ordination!' exclaimed d'Artagnan, who could scarcely believe what the landlady and Bazin had successively told him. 'Ordination!' and his eyes wandered in astonishment over the three persons who were before him.

'Now,' continued Aramis, disposing himself on his chair, in the same graceful manner as he would have done in the stall of a cathedral, and complacently examining his hand, which was as white and plump as that of a lady, and which he held up to make the blood flow out of it; 'now, M. d'Artagnan, as you have heard, the Principal would have my thesis dogmatic, whilst, for my own part, I think it ought to be idealistic. It is on this account that the Principal has proposed to me the following subject, which has never yet been treated of, and in which I recognise matter susceptible of most magnificent developments:—

'*Utraque manus in benedicendo clericis inferioribus necessaria sit.*'

D'Artagnan, whose extent of erudition we are aware of, did not knit his brows at this citation, any more than at that which M. Treville had made to him on the occasion of the presents which he supposed d'Artagnan to have received from the Duke of Buckingham.

'Which means,' resumed Aramis, in order to furnish him with every facility, 'to the lower order of priests both hands are indispensable, when they give the benediction.'

'Admirable and dogmatic,' repeated the curate, whose knowledge of Latin was about equal to d'Artagnan's, and who carefully watched the Jesuit, in order to keep pace with him, and to reproduce his words like an echo.

As for our young Gascon, he was profoundly indifferent to the enthusiasm of the two men in black.

'Yes, admirable! *prorsus admirabile!*' continued Aramis; 'yet demanding a deep investigation of the writings of the fathers, and of the holy books. But I have owned to these learned ecclesiastics, and that in great humility, that the watches of the guards, and the service of the king, have made me to some extent negligent of study. I should therefore feel more at home, *facilius natans*, in some subject of my own selection, which would be, in relation to these difficult questions, what morals are to metaphysics in philosophy.'

'See what an exordium!' exclaimed the Jesuit.

D'Artagnan was thoroughly tired; so, also, was the curate.

'*Exordium,*' repeated the curate, for the sake of saying something. '*Quem ad modum inter cœlorum immensitatem.*'

Aramis glanced at d'Artagnan, and saw that his friend was gaping in a way to dislocate his jaws.

'Let us speak French, father,' said he to the Jesuit. 'M. d'Artagnan will more truly enjoy our discourse.'

'Yes,' said d'Artagnan, 'I am fatigued by my journey, and all this Latin is beyond me.'

'Agreed,' said the Jesuit, somewhat piqued; whilst the delighted curate gave d'Artagnan a look of earnest gratitude. 'Well! see the conclusion which might be drawn from this scholium.

'Moses, the servant of God—he is only the servant, do you observe?—Moses blessed with the hands: he had his two arms held forth, whilst the Hebrews battled with their foes; therefore, he blessed with the two hands. Besides, what says the Gospel? *Imposuite manus,* and not *manum* lay on the hands, and not the hand.'

'Lay on the hands,' repeated the curate, performing at the same time the gesture.

'To St. Peter, again, of whom the popes are the successors,' continued the Jesuit, *'porrige digitos*—stretch out the fingers: do you perceive now?'

'Certainly,' said Aramis, in great delight; 'but the point is subtle.'

'The fingers,' resumed the Jesuit—'Saint Peter blessed with the fingers. The pope, then, blesses also with the fingers. And with how many fingers does he bless? With three fingers: one for the Father, one for the Son, and one for the Holy Ghost.'

They all crossed themselves at these words, and d'Artagnan thought it a duty to imitate the example.

'The pope is the successor of Saint Peter, and he represents the three divine powers—the remainder, *ordines inferiores,* of the ecclesiastical hierarchy, bless by the names of saints, archangels, and angels. The very humblest priests, such as our deacons and sacristans, bless with sprinklers, which simulate an indefinite number of blessing fingers. The subject is now simplified: *argumentum omni denudatum ornamento.* I could expand it,' continued the Jesuit, 'into two volumes of the size of this.'

And, in his enthusiasm, he thumped the folio Saint Chrysostom, which made the table bend beneath its weight.

D'Artagnan trembled.

'Assuredly,' said Aramis, 'I render justice to the beauties of this thesis, but, at the same time, I feel that it would overwhelm me. I had chosen this text—tell me, dear d'Artagnan, if it is not to your taste:—*"non inutile est desiderium in oblatione;"* or, still better—"a small regret is not unbecoming in an offering to the Lord."'

'Stop there!' vociferated the Jesuit, 'for that thesis borders on heresy. There is a proposition almost identical in the *Augustinus* of the heresiarch Jansenius, for which, sooner or later, that book will be burned by the executioner's hands. Take care, my young friend: you incline towards false doctrines; you will go astray, my young friend.'

'You will go astray,' said the curate, shaking his head in great concern.

'You are close upon the famous point of free-will, which is a fatal stumbling-block: you approach nearly the insinuations of the Pelagians and the semi-Pelagians.'

'But, reverend sir——' resumed Aràmis, somewhat stunned by the storm of arguments which descended on his head.

'How will you prove,' continued the Jesuit, without allowing him time to speak, 'that we ought to regret the world, when we offer ourselves to God? Listen to this dilemma: God is God, and the world is the devil; hence, to regret the world is to regret the devil. There is my reduction.'

'It is mine also,' said the curate.

'But, pray——' resumed Aramis.

'*Desideras diabolum!* unhappy man,' exclaimed the Jesuit.

'He regrets the devil! Ah! my young friend,' resumed the curate, with a groan, 'do not regret the devil, I beseech you!'

D'Artagnan was beginning to lose his wits. He seemed to be in a company of madmen, and to be in danger himself of becoming as mad as those he was listening to. Only, he was necessitated to hold his tongue, from not understanding the language in which they talked.

'But, listen to me,' interrupted Aramis, with a degree of politeness under which some impatience began to be perceptible; 'I do not say that I regret. No; I never will pronounce that phrase, which would be unorthodox.'

The Jesuit raised his arms towards heaven, and the curate did the same.

'No; but admit at least that it would be unbecoming merely to offer to the Lord that with which we are entirely disgusted. Am I right, d'Artagnan?'

'Quite so, I think, mon Dieu!' exclaimed the latter.

The curate and the Jesuit started from their seats.

'Now here is what I lay down—it is a syllogism. The world is not wanting in attractions: I quit the world: therefore, I make a sacrifice. Now, Scripture says positively, "make a sacrifice unto the Lord."'

'That is true,' admitted the antagonists.

'Then,' continued Aramis, pinching his ear to make it red, as he had before waved his hands to make them white; 'then, I have made a stanza upon this subject, which I showed, last year, to M. Voiture, and on which that great man highly complimented me.'

'A stanza!' exclaimed the Jesuit scornfully.

'A stanza!' responded the curate mechanically.

'Recite it, recite it,' vociferated d'Artagnan; 'that will be a little change.'

'No change; for it is religious,' replied Aramis; 'it is theology in verse.'

'The devil!' exclaimed d'Artagnan.

'Here it is,' said Aramis, with a gentle air of modesty, which was not altogether exempt from hypocrisy:—

'All you who mourn past happiness now flown,
    And live through long and weary days of woe,
  Your sorrows all a certain end shall know,
When tears are offered to your God alone,
        By you who mourn below!'

D'Artagnan and the curate seemed pleased. The Jesuit persisted in his opinion.

'Be cautious of a profane taste in a theological style. What, in fact, does St. Augustine say? *"Serverus sit clericorum sermo."* '

'Yes, let the sermon be clear,' said the curate.

'But,' hastily interrupted the Jesuit, on seeing his attendant blundering: 'but, your thesis will please the ladies, and that is all: it will have the popularity of one of Maître Patru's pleadings.'

'God grant it!' exclaimed Aramis, overjoyed.

'You say,' resumed the Jesuit, 'the world still speaks within you, in a loud voice—*altissimâ voce.* You follow the world, my young friend, and I fear that grace will not prove efficacious.'

'Doubt me not, reverend father; I answer for myself.'

'Worldly presumption!'

'I know my own heart, father: my resolution is irrevocable.'

'Then, you persist in pursuing this thesis?'

'I feel myself called to treat that, and not any other one. I shall therefore continue it; and I trust that, to-morrow, you will be contented with the emendations which I shall have made in it, under your advice.'

'Work slowly,' said the curate; 'we leave you in excellent dispositions.'

'Yes, the ground is all sown,' said the Jesuit, 'and we have no reason to fear that some part of the seed has fallen in stony places, and some upon the highway, and that the birds of the air have eaten up the remainder: "*aves cœli comederunt illam.*"'

'May the plague choke you with your Latin!' exclaimed d'Artagnan, whose patience would hold out no longer.

'Farewell, my son,' said the curate: 'farewell, till to-morrow.'

'Adieu, till to-morrow, rash youth,' said the Jesuit. 'You promise to be one of the lights of the church: God grant that this light prove not a devouring flame!'

D'Artagnan, who had been gnawing his nails with impatience for an hour, was beginning to reach the flesh.

The two men in black bowed to Aramis and d'Artagnan, and proceeded towards the door. Bazin, who had kept standing, and had listened to this controversy with a pious jubilation, rushed towards them, seized the breviary of the curate, and the missal of the priest, and walked respectfully before them to clear their path.

Aramis himself conducted them to the bottom of the stairs, and came up again to d'Artagnan, who was still deep in meditation.

When they were left alone, the two friends at first maintained an embarrassed silence. Nevertheless, it was imperative that one of them should speak first, and d'Artagnan seemed determined to leave that honour to his friend.

'You see me,' said Aramis, 'return to my original ideas.'

'Yes, as the gentleman said just now—efficacious grace has touched you.'

'Oh, these plans of retirement have long been formed, and you, my friend, have often heard me speak of them, have you not?'

'Yes, certainly; but I confess that I always thought you were joking.'

'What! about such things as these? Oh, d'Artagnan!'

'Why, we joke even in the face of death.'

'And we are wrong to do so,' said Aramis, 'for death is the gate which leads to salvation or to condemnation'

'Agreed,' said d'Artagnan. 'But do not let *us* discuss theology: you must have had enough for the day; and, as for me, I confess I have almost forgotten the little Latin that I ever knew; and besides, to tell the truth, I have eaten nothing since ten o'clock this morning, and am as hungry as twenty devils.'

'We will dine presently, my dear friend; only, you will remember, that this is Wednesday, and on that day I can neither eat meat, nor see any eaten. If you will be contented with my dinner, it is composed of boiled tetragones and fruit.'

'What do you mean by tetragones!' anxiously inquired d'Artagnan.

'I mean spinach,' replied Aramis; 'but for you, I will add some eggs, although it is a grave infraction of rule, eggs being certainly meat, since they produce chickens.'

'This feast is not very nourishing; but never mind: to remain with you, I will submit to it.'

'I am grateful to you for the sacrifice,' replied Aramis; 'but, if it be not beneficial to your body, depend upon it, it will be so to your soul.'

'So, Aramis, you decidedly entered the church? What will your friends say? What will M. de Treville say? They will look upon you as a deserter, I forewarn you.'

'I do not enter the church—I re-enter it. It was the church that I deserted for the world; for you are aware that I did violence to my inclinations in taking the uniform of a musketeer.'

'I know nothing about it.'

'Are you ignorant, then, of my reasons for quitting the seminary?'

'Entirely so.'

'Then listen to my history. Besides, the Scriptures say, 'confess yourselves to one another; and I shall confess to you, d'Artagnan.'

'And I give you absolution beforehand; you know that I am a good-hearted fellow.'

'Do not jest with sacred things, my friend.'

'Go on, then: I am listening.'

'I had been at the seminary from the age of nine years until I was one-and-twenty: in three days more I was to be an abbé, and all would have been over. One evening, when I went, according to my custom, to a house which I frequented with pleasure—what can be expected from the young but weakness?—an officer, who was jealous because I often read the *Lives of the Saints* to the mistress of the house, suddenly came in unannounced. On that very evening I had been translating an episode of Judith into verse, and was communicating it to the lady, who was paying me all sorts of compliments, and was leaning on my shoulder to read the verses over with me. The attitude, which was, I confess, rather free, offended the officer: he said nothing at the time but when I went out, he followed me and overtook me. 'M.

l'Abbé,' said he, 'do you like canings?'—'I cannot tell sir,' said I, 'no one having ever dared to give me any'— 'Well, then, hear me, M. l'Abbé: if you enter that house again, where I met you this evening, I will dare to do so.'

'I believe I was afraid: I became very pale; I perceived that my legs failed me; I sought for some answer, but found none; so I kept silent. The officer waited for my answer; but finding that it did not come, he began to laugh, turned upon his heel, and re-entered the house.

'I returned to the seminary. I am a gentleman born, and have a high spirit, as you have remarked, my dear d'Artagnan. The insult was terrible; and, entirely unknown as it was to the rest of the world, I felt it living and moving at my very heart's core. I declared to my superior, that I did not think myself sufficiently prepared for ordination, and at my request the ceremony was put off for a year. I sought out the best fencing-master in Paris; I engaged him for one lesson every day; and every day, throughout a whole year, I took that lesson. Then, on the very anniversary of the day on which I had been insulted, I hung my cassock on a peg; I took the complete costume of a cavalier, and went to a ball given by a lady of my acquaintance, where I knew that I should find my man. It was in the Rue des Frances-Bourgeois, very near La Force.

'My officer was indeed there. I went up to him. as he was singing a love ditty, and looking tenderly at a lady, and I interrupted him in the very middle of the second verse. 'Sir,' said I, 'are you still unwilling that I should enter a certain house in the Rue Payenne, and will you still give me a caning if I should take it into my head to disobey you?'

'The officer looked at me with astonishment, and then said, 'What do you want, sir? I do not know you.'—'I am,' said I, 'the little abbé who was reading the lives of the saints, and who translated Judith into verse.'—'Ah, ah! I remember, said the officer, merrily; 'and what do you want?'—'I would wish you to find leisure to take a walk with me.'—'To-morrow, with great pleasure, if you really wish it.'—'No, not to-morrow if you please, but immediately.'— 'If you positively require it.'—'Yes, I do positively require it.' —'Come, then, let us go,' said he. 'Ladies, do not disturb yourselves; only give me time to kill this gentleman, and I will return and finish the second verse.'

'We went out. I led him to the Rue Payenne, to the exact spot where, a year before, and exactly at the same hour, he had complimented me as I have related to you. The moon-light was superb. We drew our swords; and, at the first pass I struck him dead.'

'The devil!' exclaimed d'Artagnan.

'Now, as the ladies did not perceive their singer return, and as he was found in the Rue Payenne, with a frightful sword wound right through his body, it was thought that it was I who had so accomodated him, and the affair caused some scandal. I was, therefore, obliged, for a time, to give up the cassock. Athos, with whom I made acquaintance about that period, and Porthos, who had taught me, in addition to my fencing lessons, some merry thrusts, deter-mined me on demanding the uniform of a musketeer. The king had loved my father, who was killed at the siege of Arras, and this uniform was granted to me. Now, you will understand, that the day is now arrived for my return into the bossom of the church.'

'And why to-day, more than yesterday or to-morrow? What has happened to you now, to give you such miserable ideas?'

'This wound, my dear d'Artagnan, has been to me a warning from Heaven.'

'This wound—bah! it is almost healed. I am quite certain it is not that which causes the worst of your suffering.'

'And what is it?' said Aramis, colouring.

'You have a deeper one in your heart, Aramis—one that bleeds more—a wound made by a woman.'

The eye of Aramis sparkled involuntarily.

'Ah,' said he, concealing his emotion under a feigned negligence; 'do not speak of such things! Such thoughts are not for me; nor such solicitudes of love! *Vanitas vanitatum!* What, do you suppose then that my brain is turned? And for whom? Some pretty wench, some canon's daughter, to whom I might have paid my court in garrison? For shame!'

'Pardon, my dear Aramis, but I thought that you carried your aim a little higher.'

'Higher? And what am I, that I should have so much ambition? A poor musketeer, unprovided for and obscure, who hates servitude, and feels himself an intruder in the turmoil of the world.'

'Aramis! Aramis!' exclaimed d'Artagnan, looking on his friend with a glance of doubt.

'Dust,' continued Aramis, 'I return to dust. Life is full of sorrow and humiliation,' continued he, in deep affliction:

'all the threads which bind the woof of happiness break in our hands by turns: fragile, above all, are the threads of gold. Oh! my dear d'Artagnan,' added Aramis, infusing into his tone a slight degree of bitterness, 'believe me, you must conceal carefully whatever wounds you have. Silence is the last enjoyment of the unfortunate; let none know your grief; the curious would call up our tears, as insects suck the life-blood of a wounded deer.'

'Alas! my dear Aramis,' said d'Artagnan, sighing deeply in his turn, 'it is my own history which you are unfolding.'

'What?'

'Yes, a woman whom I loved, whom I adored, has just been carried away by force. I know not where she is, where she has been taken to: perhaps she is in prison—perhaps dead!'

'But you at least have the consolation of knowing that she did not quit you voluntarily, and that if you do not hear from her, it is because communication is prevented: whilst——'

'Whilst what?'

'Nothing,' replied Aramis; 'nothing.'

'Then you renounce the world for ever? It is a settled choice—an irrevocable determination.'

'Yes, for ever! You are my friend to-day; to-morrow you will be only as a shadow, or rather you will no longer exist for me. As for the world, it is at best no better than a sepulchre.'

'The plague! This is all very lamentable.'

'What would you desire? My vocation summons me—it impels me onwards!'

D'Artagnan smiled, but made no reply. Aramis continued:—

'Nevertheless, whilst I am still belonging to the world, I would talk with you about yourself, and our friends.'

'And I,' said d'Artagnan, 'would gladly have conferred with you about yourself, did I not see you so dissevered from all earthly things: at love, you cry shame; friends are shadows; and the world itself is but a sepulchre.'

'Alas! you will, at last, yourself find it so!' exclaimed Aramis, with a sigh.

'Let us waste no more words about that,' said d'Artagnan, 'and let us burn this letter, which possibly announces to you some new infidelity of some pretty waiting-maid.'

'What letter?' eagerly cried Aramis.

'A letter which came to your lodgings during your absence, and which I have taken charge of!'

'But from whom comes this letter?'

'Perhaps from some disconsolate wench, some waiting-maid of Madame de Chevreuse possibly, who was obliged to return to Tours with her mistress; and who, to make herself gaudy, has provided perfumed paper, and sealed the letter with a duchess's coronet!'

'What are you telling me?'

'I cannot surely have lost it,' gravely remarked the young man, pretending to search for it. 'But, happily, the world is a sepulchre—the men, and consequently the women, are shadows—and love is a sentiment at which you cry shame!'

'Ah! d'Artagnan! d'Artagnan! you kill me!' ejaculated Aramis.

'At last, here it is,' said d'Artagnan, drawing the letter from his pocket.

Aramis made a bound, seized the letter, and read, or rather devoured it, whilst his countenance gleamed with joy.

'The waiting-maid seems to write in a good style,' said the messenger carelessly.

'Thanks, d'Artagnan!' exclaimed the almost delirious Aramis. 'She could not help it: she was compelled to return to Tours: she has not been unfaithful to me: she loves me still. Come, my friend, let me embrace you: my happiness suffocates me!'

And the two friends began dancing round the folios of the venerable St. Chrysostom, treading gallantly on the leaves of the thesis, which had fallen to the ground. At this moment Bazin entered with the spinach and the omelette.

'Fly, wretch!' cried Aramis, throwing his skull-cap at Bazin's head. 'Return whence you came; take away these horrible vegetables and those frightful eggs! Ask for a larded hare, a fat capon, a leg of mutton and garlic, and four bottles of old Burgundy!'

Bazin, who looked at his master, and could make nothing of this change, let the omelette fall, in his despair, upon the spinach, and the spinach upon the carpet.

'Now is the time,' said d'Artagnan, 'to consecrate your existence to the King of kings, if you desire to do Him homage: *non in utile desirum in oblatione.*"'

'Go to the devil, with your Latin, my dear d'Artagnan. Let us drink! Egad! let us drink, and tell me a little of what has been going on in the world.'

27

The Wife of Athos

'Now we must obtain some intelligence of Athos,' said d'Artagnan to the joyous Aramis, after he had told him everything that had happened since their departure from Paris, and after an excellent dinner had made the one forget his thesis, and the other his fatigue.

'Do you believe, then, that any misfortune has befallen him?' demanded Aramis. 'Athos is so cool, so brave, and wields his sword so skilfully!'

'Yes, doubtless, and no one knows better than I do the courage and address of Athos. But I like better the shock of lances on my sword, than the blows of sticks; and I fear that Athos may have been beaten by the rabble, who hit hard, and do not leave off quickly. It is, I confess, on this account that I should like to set out as soon as possible.'

'I will endeavour to accompany you,' said Aramis, although I am scarcely in a fit state to mount a horse. Yesterday, I used the discipline, which you see on the wall; but the pain made me give up that pious exercise.'

'My dear friend, none ever heard of endeavouring to cure the wounds of a carbine by the strokes of a cat-o'-nine-tails. But you were ill; and, as illness makes the head light, I excuse you.'

'And when shall you set out?'

'To-morrow, at break of day. Rest as well as you can to-night, and to-morrow, if you are able, we will go together.'

'Farewell, then, till to-morrow,' said Aramis; 'for, iron as you are, you must surely want some rest.'

When d'Artagnan entered Aramis's room, the next morning, he found him looking out of the window.

'What are you looking at?' said he.

'Faith, I am admiring those three magnificent horses which the stable-boys are holding: it is a princely pleasure to travel on such animals.'

'Well, then, my dear Aramis, you will give yourself that pleasure, for one of those horses belongs to you.'

'Nonsense! and which!'

'Whichever you like, for I have no preference.'

'And the rich caparison which covers him—is that, also, mine?'

'Certainly.'

'You are laughing at me, d'Artagnan.'

'I have left off laughing since you began to speak French again.'

'And are those gilded holsters, that velvet housing, and that saddle, studded with silver, mine?'

'Yours! Just as that horse which steps so proudly is mine; and that other one, which caracoles so bravely, is for Athos.'

'I'faith, they are superb animals.'

'I am glad that they suit your taste.'

'Is it the king, then, who has made you this present?'

'You may be quite sure that it was not the cardinal: but do not disturb yourself as to whence they came, only be satisfied that one of them is your own.'

'I choose the one that the red-haired valet is holding.'

'Well chosen.'

'Thank God!' cried Aramis, 'this drives away the last remnant of my pain. I would mount such a horse with thirty bullets in my body. Ah! upon my soul, what superb stirrups. Hallo! Bazin, come here this instant.'

Bazin appeared, silent and melancholy, at the door.

'Polish up my sword, smarten my hat, brush my cloak, and load my pistols!' said Aramis.

'The last order is unnecessary,' said d'Artagnan, 'for there are loaded pistols in your holsters.'

Bazin sighed deeply.

'Come, Master Bazin, console yourself,' said d'Artagnan; 'the kingdom of heaven may be gained in any condition of life.'

'But he was already such a good theologian,' said Bazin, almost in tears; 'he would have become a bishop—perhaps even a cardinal.'

'Well! my poor Bazin, let us see, and reflect a little. What is the use of being a churchman, pray? You do not by that means avoid going to war; for you see that the cardinal is about to make his first campaign with a head-piece on, and a halbert in his hand; and M. de Nogaret de la Valette, what do you say to him? He is a cardinal too, and ask his lackey how often he has made lint for him.'

'Alas!' sighed Bazin, 'I know it, sir. The whole world is turned topsy-turvy, nowadays.'

During this talk the two young men and the poor lackey had gone downstairs.

'Hold my stirrup for me, Bazin,' said Aramis.

Aramis sprang into his saddle with his accustomed grace and activity; but, after some curvets and capers of the noble animal, the rider felt his pains so utterly insupportable, that he grew pale, and wavered in his seat. D'Artagnan, who, foreseeing such a misfortune, had kept his eye upon him, rushed towards him, caught him in his arms, and led him back again to his room.

'Never mind, my dear Aramis,' said he; 'take care of yourself. I will go alone in search of Athos.'

'You are a man of steel,' said Aramis.

'No,' replied he, 'I am fortunate—that is all. But what will you do whilst I am absent? No more theses; no more arguments on hands; no benedictions—hey!'

Aramis smiled.

'No, I shall make verses,' said he.

'Yes! Verses with the same perfume as the note of Madame de Chevreuse's waiting-maid. Teach Bazin prosody: that will fill him with delight; and, as for the horse, ride him for a little while every day, and that will make you accustomed to the work.'

'Oh! as for that, be satisfied that you shall find me ready to follow you.'

They bade each other adieu; and in a few minutes d'Artagnan, having commended his friend to the care of Bazin and the landlady, was trotting onwards on his way towards Amiens.

And in what condition should he find Athos? Should he even find him at all?

The position in which he had left him was critical, and it was not improbable that Athos might have been destroyed.

This idea clouded the brow of d'Artagnan, and made him mutter many a vow of vengeance.

Of all his friends, Athos was the eldest, and apparently the least akin to him in sympathies and tastes. And yet he had a marked preference for this gentleman. The noble and distinguished air of Athos—those flashes of dignity, which, from time to time, shone forth from the cloud in which he had voluntarily enveloped himself—that unalterable equanimity of temper, which made him the best companion in the world—that forced yet ironic gaiety—that courage, which would have been denominated blind, had it not been the result of the rarest coolness;—so many excellent qualities attracted more than the esteem, more even than the friendship, of d'Artagnan: they attracted his admiration.

In fact, by the side even of the elegant and noble courtier, M. de Treville, Athos, in his bright days, might advantageously sustain comparison. He was of only medium height, but his figure was so admirably formed and proportioned, that, more than once, in his sportive contests with Porthos, he had subdued the giant, whose physical power had become proverbial amongst the musketeers. His countenance, with its piercing eyes, and aquiline nose, and a chin chiselled like that of Brutus, had an indescribable character of dignity and grace. His hands, of which he took no care, were the despair of Aramis, who cherished his at a great expense of almond paste and perfumed oil. The sound of his voice was penetrating and, at the same time, melodious. And then—a something altogether indefinable in Athos, who shrunk from all display—there was a delicate knowledge of the world, and of the customs of the most brilliant society, that was perceptible, apparently without his being conscious of it, in all his minutest actions.

If a banquet was to be prepared, Athos could preside better than anybody else, placing every guest in the precise rank and station to which his ancestry, or his own achievements, had entitled him. If heraldic science was required, Athos knew all the noble families in the kingdom, their genealogies, their alliances, their arms, and the origin of their arms. Etiquette had no minutiæ with which he was not well acquainted. He knew the various rights of the great landowners; and so thoroughly understood hunting and falconry, that one day, in talking of that art, he had astonished the king himself, who was a past-master of it. Like all the noblemen of the time, he rode and fenced to perfection. And, more than that, his education had been so well attended to, even on scholastic points, which were rarely introduced amongst gentlemen of that age, that he smiled at the scraps of Latin which Aramis let fall, and which Porthos pretended to understand; and two or three times even, to the great astonishment of his friends, when Aramis had made some mistake in the rudiments, Athos had put a verb into its proper tense, or a noun into its case. Besides all this, his probity was unimpeachable, at a time when military men made so light of their religion and conscience; lovers, of the rigorous delicacy of our own days; and the poor, of the seventh commandment of their God.

Athos was, therefore, a very extraordinary man. And yet, this nature so distinguished, this creature so beautiful, this essence so fine, was seen to turn insensibly towards a material life, as old men often tend to physical and moral imbecility. In his hours of privation—and these were frequent—Athos was extinguished as respected all his luminous nature, and all his brilliant qualities disappeared as in a dark night. Then, in place of the vanished demi-god, there remained scarcely a human being: his head drooped, his eye was dull, his voice heavy and languid; and he would look for hours at nothing but his bottle and his glass, or at Grimaud, who, accustomed to obey him by signs, read in his look the smallest wish, which he immediately gratified. If the four friends met by chance, during one of these intervals, a word, escaping as if by a violent effort, was all that Athos could contribute to the conversation; but, to compensate for this deficiency, Athos alone drank as much as all the rest, without any other apparent effect than a more manifest contraction of the eyebrows, and a more profound melancholy.

D'Artagnan, with whose inquisitive and penetrating mind we are already acquainted, whatever motive he might have for indulging his curiosity on the subject, had been unable hitherto to assign any cause for this melancholy, or for its frequent recurrence. Athos never received any letters, and never did anything which was not known to his three friends. It could not be said that this sadness was a result of wine; for, on the contrary, he only drank, in the hope of conquering that which this remedy did really increase. His despondency could not be attributed to play; for, unlike Porthos, who indicated, by songs and oaths, all the fluctuations of fortune, Athos maintained the same impassability, whether he had won or lost. In the circle of the musketeers, he had been seen to win three thousand pistoles in an evening, and to lose them again, as well as his horse, his arms, or even his gold-embroidered gala belt, and to win back the whole of these, and a hundred louis over, without his handsome black eyebrow having been depressed or raised by a hair's-breadth; without his hand having lost its pearly hue; and without his conversation, which was on that particular evening cheerful, having ceased for one instant to be agreeable and calm.

Nor was it, as in the case of our neighbours the English,

an atmospheric influence which clouded over his countenance; for this sadness became more intense in the most brilliant seasons of the year: June and July were the bad months of Athos.

It was not about the present that he grieved; and he shrugged his shoulders when any one spoke to him of the future. His secret sorrow, then, had reference to the past, as had been vaguely told to d'Artagnan.

The mysterious complexion which was thus spread over him, only rendered more interesting the man who, neither by his eyes nor tongue, had ever, even in the most complete intoxication, revealed anything to the most skilfully conducted investigation.

'Well,' mused d'Artagnan, 'poor Athos may perhaps be now dead, and dead through my fault, for it was I who drew him into this affair, of which he knew neither the origin nor aim, and from which he could expect no benefit.'

'Without reckoning, sir,' said Planchet, 'that we probably owe our lives to him. You remember how he cried out: 'Away, d'Artagnan! I am seized!' and, after having discharged his two pistols, what a terrible noise he made with his sword! One would have believed there were twenty men, or, rather, twenty mad devils!'

These words redoubled d'Artagnan's eagerness. He urged forward his horse, which, needing no urging, carried him on at a gallop.

Towards eleven in the morning they caught sight of Amiens; and at half-past eleven they were at the door of the fatal inn.

D'Artagnan had often meditated, against the treacherous host, one of those genuine acts of vengeance which give no satisfaction, except in the anticipation. He entered the hotel with his hat over his eyes, his left hand on the hilt of his sword, making his riding-whip whistle with his right.

'Do you know me?' said he to the landlord, who came forward to welcome him.

'I have not that honour, sir,' replied the latter, his eyes dazzled by the splendid equipage with which d'Artagnan presented himself.

'Ah! you do not recognise me?'

'No, sir.'

'Well, then, two words will restore your recollection. What have you done with that gentleman, against whom you had the audacity, about a fortnight ago, to bring an accusation of passing bad money.'

The host turned pale, for d'Artagnan had assumed a most threatening attitude, and Planchet closely followed his master's example.

'Ah, sir, do not mention that,' replied the host, in a most lamentable tone of voice; 'ah, sir, how dearly have I paid for that fault! Alas! unfortunate has been my fate!'

'This gentleman, I ask—what has become of him?'

'Only deign to hear me, sir, and be merciful. Be seated, I beseech you!'

D'Artagnan, dumb from anger and anxiety, sat down, stern as a judge, and Planchet finally established himself behind his chair.

'This is the statement, sir,' said the trembling landlord; 'for now I recognise you. It was you who went away when I had that unhappy dispute with the gentleman of whom you speak.'

'Yes, it was I; so you see that you have no mercy to expect, if you do not tell the whole truth.'

'Condescend to listen, sir, and you shall hear everything.'

'I hear you.'

'I had been informed by the authorities that a celebrated coiner would arrive at my hotel, with several of his companions, all disguised under the uniform of guards or musketeers. Your horses, your servants, your features, gentlemen, were all exactly described.'

'What next? what next?' cried d'Artagnan, who soon discerned the source of this precise description.

'Therefore, under the direction of the authorities, who sent me a reinforcement of six men, I took such measures as I considered indispensable to secure the persons of these alleged coiners.'

'Well!' said d'Artagnan, whose ears were terribly wounded by this term *coiners*.

'Forgive me, sir, for speaking of such things, but they are truly my excuse. The authorities had frightened me; and you know that an innkeeper must respect the authorities.'

'But, once more, where is this gentleman? What has become of him? Is he dead, or is he alive.'

'Patience, sir, we have just come to that. Well, sir, you know what happened; and your hasty departure,' added the innkeeper, with a cunning, which did not escape d'Artagnan, 'seemed to justify my proceedings. The gentleman, your friend, defended himself desperately. His servant had, unfortunately, sought an unexpected quarrel with the officers of justice, who were disguised as stableboys.'

'Ah! the wretches!' cried d'Artagnan. 'You were all in the plot, and I know not why I should not exterminate you all!'

'Alas! no, sir, we were not all agreed, as you will soon perceive. The gentleman, your friend—pardon me for not giving him the honourable name which no doubt he bears, but we do not know that name—the gentleman, your friend, after having disabled two men by his pistol-shots, beat a retreat, defending himself with his sword, with which he also maimed another of my men, and with the flat side of which he stunned me.'

'But, hang man! will you make an end? Athos! what has become of Athos?'

'In beating his retreat, as I have told you, sir, he found behind him the cellar stairs, and, as the door was open, he rushed into it. Once there, he locked the door, and barricaded himself within; and, as we were sure of finding him there, we let him alone.'

'Yes,' said d'Artagnan, 'it was not thought necessary to kill him, but only to imprison him.'

'Good God! to imprison *him*, sir! He imprisoned himself, I swear! For, first, he had made a pretty severe business of it:—one man was killed outright and two were grievously wounded. The dead man and the two wounded ones were carried off by their companions, and I have never since heard any more of either party. I myself, when I had recovered my senses, went to find the governor, to whom I related everything that had taken place, and of whom I inquired what I was to do with the prisoner. But the governor seemed as if he were entirely ignorant of the matter: he told me that he did not know what I was talking about; that the orders I had received did not come from him; and that, if I had the misfortune to tell any one whatever, that he had anything to do with this disturbance he would have me hung. It appeared that I had made an error, sir; that I had arrested the wrong person; and that he who was to have been arrested had escaped.'

'But Athos!' cried d'Artagnan, who became doubly bold when he found that the authorities disclaimed the affair: 'what has become of him?'

'As I was in haste to repair the injury I had inflicted on the prisoner,' replied the innkeeper, 'I hurried to the cellar, to liberate him. Ah! sir, he was no longer a man—he was a devil! On proposing his liberation, he declared that it was a snare which was laid for him, and that before he came out he must impose conditions. I told him, with great humility— for I did not conceal from myself the awkward position in which I had placed myself by laying hands on one of his majesty's musketeers—I told him that I was ready to submit to his conditions.'

'First,' said he, 'you must give me back my servant, completely armed.'

'We hastened to obey this order; for, you understand, sir, that we were disposed to do everything that your friend wished. M. Grimaud—for he told us his name, although he speaks but little—M. Grimaud was sent down into the cellar, all wounded as he was; and his master having received him, barricaded the door again, and sent us about our business.'

'But, after all,' cried d'Artagnan, 'where is he? Where is Athos?'

'In the cellar, sir.'

'What, you rascal! have you kept him in the cellar all this time?'

'Good heavens! no, sir. We keep him in the cellar? You do not know, then, what he has been at there? Ah! if you could only persuade him to come out, sir, I should be for ever grateful to you—I would adore you as my patron saint!'

'Then he is there? I shall find him there?'

'Certainly, sir; he has obstinately persisted in remaining there. Every day we put through the air-hole some bread on the point of a pitchfork, and some meat too, when he asks for it; but, alas! it is not of bread and meat that he makes the greatest consumption. I endeavoured once to go down, with two of my servants; but he went into a terrible fury. I heard the click of his pistols, and of his servant's carbine. Then, when we asked what their intentions were, the mastered answered, that they had between them forty shots to fire, and that they would fire them all, even to the last, sooner than permit any one of us to put a foot in the cellar. Then, sir, I went and complained to the governor, who told me that I had only got what I deserved, and that this would teach me to insult honourable gentlemen who put up at my house.'

'So that, since that time—' replied d'Artagnan, who was unable to refrain from laughing at the piteous face of the innkeeper.

'So that, from that time, sir,' continued he, 'we lead the saddest life that can be imagined; for, sir, you must know, that all our provisions are in the cellar. Our wine in bottles is there, and our wine in casks; beer, oil, spices, lard, and sausages; and, as we are forbidden to go down, we are obliged to refuse provisions and drink to the travellers who come here, so that we lose custom every day. Should your friend stop in my cellar one more week, we shall be utterly ruined.'

'And serve you right, too, you knave! Could you not plainly see, by our appearance, that we were men of quality, and not coiners?'

'Yes, sir, yes; you are right,' said mine host. 'But, hark! hark! he is getting into a passion now.'

'No doubt somebody has disturbed him,' said d'Artagnan.

'But he needs must be disturbed,' exclaimed the host. 'Two English gentlemen have just come in.'

'Well, what then?'

'Well, the English gentlemen love good wine, as you know, sir; and these gentlemen have called for the best. My wife has, no doubt, asked permission of M. Athos to enter, to satisfy these gentlemen, and he has refused, as usual. Ah, merciful goodness! listen how the row increases.'

D'Artagnan did, in fact, hear a great noise proceeding from the cellar. He therefore arose, and, preceded by the landlord, who wrung his hands, and followed by Planchet, who carried his carbine ready cocked, he approached the scene of action. The two gentlemen were highly exasperated; they had travelled a long way, and were fainting with hunger and thirst.

'But it is positive tyranny,' cried they, in very good French, although with a foreign accent, 'that this downright madman will not allow these good people the use of their own wine. We will break open the door, and, if he is too furious, we will kill him.'

'Hold there, gentlemen!' exclaimed d'Artagnan, drawing his pistols from his belt; 'you will not kill any one, if you please.'

'Very good, very good,' said the calm voice of Athos, from behind the door; 'let these child-eaters enter, and we shall soon see.'

Brave as they appeared to be, the two Englishmen looked at one another with some degree of hesitation. One would have said that the cellar contained one of those ravenous ogres—those gigantic heroes of popular legend—whose cavern none could enter with impunity.

There was a moment of silence; but, at last, the two Englishmen were ashamed to retire, and the most impatient of them went down five or six steps of the staircase, and gave the door a kick, sufficient to break through a wall.

'Planchet,' said d'Artagnan, cocking his pistols, 'I will take the one that is up here; you take charge of him who is below. Ah! gentlemen, you wish for a fight, do you? Well! we will give you one!'

'My God!' cried the hollow voice of Athos, 'I think I hear d'Artagnan's voice.'

'Yes,' said d'Artagnan, raising his voice in his turn; 'it it I myself, my friend.'

'Good!' said Athos, 'then we'll handle these door-breakers!'

The gentlemen had drawn their swords, but finding themselves caught between two fires, they hesitated again for a moment. As before, however, pride carried the day, and a second kick made the door crash from top to bottom.

'Step aside, d'Artagnan, step aside,' cried Athos, 'I am going to fire.'

'Gentlemen,' cried d'Artagnan, whose coolness never forsook him—'gentlemen, think better of it. Wait a moment, Athos. You are about to begin a bad business, gentlemen, and will be riddled with shot. Here are I and my servant, who will give you three shots; you will receive the same number from the cellar; and then we shall still have our swords, which I and my friend can handle pretty well, I assure you. Let me arrange the affair. You shall have something to drink directly, I give you my word.'

'If there is any left,' growled Athos, in a sneering tone.

The innkeeper felt a cold perspiration trickling down his spine.

'What! if there is any left!' muttered he.

'What the deuce!' replied d'Artagnan, 'there must be some left; surely these two cannot have drunk out the cellar. Gentlemen, return your swords to their scabbards.'

'Well! put your pistols back into your belts.'

'Willingly.'

D'Artagnan set the example. Then, turning to Planchet, he made him a sign to uncock his carbine.

The Englishmen were satisfied, yet grumbled as they sheathed their swords. D'Artagnan gave them an account of Athos's imprisonment, and, as they were men of honour, they blamed the innkeeper.

'Now, gentlemen,' continued he, 'return to your chamber, and I answer for it, that in ten minutes you shall have everything you want.'

The Englishmen bowed and departed.

'Now that I am alone, my dear Athos,' said d'Artagnan, 'open the door to me, I implore you.'

'Directly,' said Athos.

Then was heard the sound of clashing fagots and groaning beams; these were the counterscarps and bastions of Athos, which the besieged was himself demolishing.

In another instant the door moved, and there was seen the pale face of Athos, who, with a rapid glance, surveyed the outworks.

D'Artagnan threw himself upon his neck, and embraced him tenderly. But, when he wished to lead him out of this humid habitation, he perceived that Athos staggered.

'You are wounded?' exclaimed he.

'Me? Not the least in the world. I am dead drunk, that's all; and never did man do more to become so. Vive Dieu! landlord, I must have drunk, for my own share, at least one hundred and fifty bottles.'

'Gracious heavens!' exclaimed the landlord; 'if the servant has drunk only half as much as the master, I am ruined.'

'Grimaud is too well-behaved a servant,' said Athos, 'to allow himself to live in the same manner as his master: he has therefore only drunk out of the cask. Hark! I verily believe that he has forgotten to put the spigot in. Do you hear? It is running.'

D'Artagnan broke out into a roar of laughter, which changed the landlord's shivers into a raging fever.

At the same time Grimaud made his appearance, behind his master, with his carbine on his shoulder, and his head shaking, like the drunken Satyr in Rubens' pictures. He was soaked, both before and behind, with an unctuous liquid, which the landlord recognised as his best olive oil.

The little company crossed the large room, and installed itself in the best apartment of the inn, of which d'Artagnan took possession authoritatively.

In the meantime, the landlord and his wife hastened with lamps into the cellar, from which they had been so long excluded, and where a frightful spectacle awaited them.

Beyond the fortifications, in which Athos had made a

breach to get out, and which were composed of fagots, planks, and empty casks, arranged according to the rules of strategic art, they saw here and there, floating amidst pools of oil and wine, the bones of all the hams that had been eaten; whilst a heap of broken bottles covered all the left-hand corner of the cellar; and a barrel, of which the tap had been left open, was losing through that opening the last drops of its blood. The image of devastation and death, as the poet of antiquity says, reigned there as on a battle-field.

Of fifty sausages, which had hung on the beams, scarcely ten remained.

The howlings of the landlord and his wife pierced through the vaulted ceiling of the cellar: d'Artagnan himself was affected by them; yet Athos did not even turn his head.

But rage succeeded grief. The innkeeper armed himself with a spit, and rushed, in a paroxysm of despair, into the room where the two friends were sitting.

'Some wine!' cried Athos, on seeing the landlord.

'Some wine!' exclaimed the astonished host. 'Some wine! Why, you have drunk more than a hundred pistoles' worth; and I am a ruined man!—ruined! lost! annihilated!'

'Bah!' said Athos, 'we were constantly thirsty.'

'But, even if you had been contented with drinking—but you have broken all the bottles.'

'Why, you pushed me on a heap, which rolled over. It was all your fault.'

'All my oil is lost!'

'Oil is a sovereign balm for wounds, and it was necessary that pour Grimaud should bathe those you had inflicted.'

'All my sausages are chewed away!'

'There is an enormous number of rats in that cellar!'

'You shall pay me for all this!' cried the exasperated landlord.

'Thrice-doomed knave!' exclaimed Athos. But he fell back immediately: he had exhausted all his strength. D'Artagnan hastened to shield him, by raising his riding-whip.

The host recoiled a step, and burst into tears.

'That will teach you,' said d'Artagnan, 'to behave with a little more politeness to the guests whom God sends you.'

'God!—say the devil!'

'My dear friend,' said d'Artagnan, 'if you assail our ears in this way again, we will all four go and shut ourselves in your cellar, and see whether the destruction is as great as you pretend.'

'Well, then, gentlemen,' said the landlord, 'I am wrong, I confess; but mercy is due to every sinner; you are noblemen, and I am only a poor innkeeper: you will have mercy on me.'

'Ah, if you talk in that manner,' said Athos, 'you will pierce my heart, and the tears will flow from my eyes, as the wine ran from your casks. I am not so great a devil as I look. Come—come here—and let us talk it over.'

The host approached, with some hesitation.

'Come here, I tell you, and do not be afraid,' continued Athos. 'At the moment I was about to pay you, I laid my purse upon the table.'

'Yes, my lord.'

'And that purse contained sixty pistoles: where is it?'

'Lodged at the register-office, my lord. It was said to be false money.'

'Well, then! recover my purse, and keep the sixty pistoles.'

'But your lordship well knows that the register-office never gives up what it has once got. If it was bad money, there might be some hope; but, unfortunately, it is all good coin.'

'Let us see,' said d'Artagnan: 'where is Athos's old horse?'

'In the stables.'

'How much is he worth?'

'Fifty pistoles, at the most.'

'He is worth eighty: take him, and say no more about it.'

'What! do you mean to sell my horse,' said Athos—'my Bajazet! And on what shall I make the campaign?—on Grimaud's?'

'I have brought you another,' said d'Artagnan.

'And a magnificent one,' cried the landlord.

'Then,' said Athos, 'if there be another, younger and handsomer, take the old one. And now let us have something to drink.'

'Of what sort?' said mine host, completely pacified.

'Of that which is at the bottom, near the laths: there are twenty-five bottles of it remaining: the others were broken by my fall. Bring up six.'

'This man is a perfect tun!' said the landlord to himself. 'If he should only remain here a fortnight, and pay for what he drinks, I should re-establish my affairs.'

'Now,' said Athos, 'whilst we are waiting for the wine, tell me what has become of the others. Come, let me hear.'

D'Artagnan recounted how he had found Porthos in bed

with a sprain, and Aramis between two theologians. As he ended his narration, the landlord entered with the bottles which had been ordered, and a ham, which had been, fortunately, left outside the cellar.

'That's right,' said Athos, filling his own glass and that of d'Artagnan; 'here's to Porthos and Aramis. But, my friend, what is the matter with you? and what has happened to you yourself? I fancy that you are looking sad.'

'Alas!' replied d'Artagnan, 'I am the most unhappy of you all.'

'You unhappy, d'Artagnan!' said Athos. 'Let me hear how you can be unhappy? Tell me that.'

'By and by,' said d'Artagnan.

'By and by! And why by and by? Is it because you think that I am drunk, d'Artagnan? Just understand, then, that my ideas are never clearer than when I am in my cups. Speak, therefore; I am all attention.'

D'Artagnan related his adventure with Madame Bonancieux. Athos heard him without even moving his eyebrow. Then, when he had ended—

'Those are all trifles,' said Athos; 'trifles.'

This was the favourite word of Athos.

'You repeat the word *trifles*, my dear Athos,' said d'Artagnan; 'and it comes with a bad grace from you, who have never loved.'

The dull eye of Athos lighted up suddenly; though it was but a momentary flash, and then it again became dull and wandering as before.

'It is true,' he said quietly, 'I *have* never loved.'

'You see, then, stony heart,' said d'Artagnan, 'that you are wrong to be so hard on us who have more tender natures.'

'Tender natures! wounded hearts!' exclaimed Athos.

'What are you saying?'

'I say that love is a lottery, in which he who wins gains death! You are very fortunate to have lost, believe me, my dear d'Artagnan; and if I have any advice to give you, it is to lose always.'

'She seemed to love me so much!'

'Of course, she *seemed*.'

'Oh! She loved me!'

'Child! There is not a man who has not, like you, believed that his mistress loved him; and there is not a man who has not been deceived by his mistress!'

'Except you, Athos, who never had one.'

'It is true,' said Athos, after a moment's silence, 'I never had one. Let us drink.'

'But then,' said d'Artagnan, 'philosopher as you are, instruct and console me: I want instruction and consolation.'

'Consolation—about what?'

'About my misfortune.'

'Your misfortune makes me laugh,' said Athos, shrugging his shoulders. 'I should be curious to know what you would say if I were to tell you a love story.'

'About yourself?'

'Or one of my friends—what does it signify?'

'Tell it me,' Athos; tell it.'

'Let us drink: that will be far better.'

'Drink, and tell your story.'

'Yes, I can do that,' said Athos, emptying and again filling his glass; 'the two things accompany one another admirably well.'

'I am attentive,' said d'Artagnan.

Athos collected himself; and, as he did so, d'Artagnan saw him grow more pale. He was at that point of intoxication at which vulgar tipplers fall down and sleep. As for him, he actually dreamed aloud, without sleeping. There was something awful in this somnambulism of intoxication.

'You absolutely wish it?' said he.

'I even entreat you,' replied d'Artagnan.

'Well then, it shall be as you desire. One of my friends— one of my friends, you understand—not myself,' said Athos, interrupting himself with a sombre smile—'one of the counts of my province, that is to say, of Berri, as noble as a Dandolo or a Montmorency, became enamoured, at twenty-five years of age, of a young girl of sixteen, who was as beautiful as love. Through the simplicity of her age, an ardent soul was perceptible; the soul, not of a woman, but of a poet. She did not merely please—she intoxicated the mind. Her home was in a small village, where she lived with her brother, who was a curate. They were new-comers into that part of the country. No one knew whence they came; and, on seeing her so beautiful, and her brother so pious, no one thought of inquiring. They were, moreover, said to belong to a good family. My friend, who was the great man of that neighbourhood, might have seduced her, or even seized upon her by force, if he had chosen. He was the master; and who would have thought of defending two unknown strangers? Unfortunately, he was a man of honour, and he married her. The fool! the ass! the idiot!'

'But why so, since he loved her?' said d'Artagnan.

'Wait a little,' replied Athos. 'He took her to his castle, and made her the first lady of the province, and, to do her justice, she filled her position admirably.'

'Well?' said d'Artagnan.

'Well! one day, when she was out hunting with her husband,' continued Athos, in a low voice, and speaking very quickly, 'she fell from her horse, and fainted. The count hastened to her assistance, and, as she seemed half-suffocated by her clothes, cut them with his dagger, so that her shoulder was exposed. Guess what there was upon her shoulder, d'Artagnan?' said Athos, with a convulsive burst of laughter.

'How can I tell!' demanded d'Artagnan.

'A fleur-de-lis,' said Athos. 'She was branded!'—And at one draught he emptied the glass which was in his hand.

'Horrible! What are you telling me?' cried d'Artagnan.

'The truth, my dear fellow! The angel was a fiend—the simple young girl had been a thief!'

'And what did the count do?'

'The count was a powerful noble: he had the undisputed right of executing justice on his domain: he tore off the remainder of her clothes, tied her hands behind her back, and hung her on a tree!'

'Oh, heavens, Athos, a murder!' cried d'Artagnan.

'Yes, a murder—nothing else!' said Athos, pale as death. 'But they leave me without wine, it seems.'

And he seized the last bottle by its neck, put it to his mouth, and emptied it at a draught, as though it had been a glass.

His head then fell on his two hands; whilst d'Artagnan remained before him, overwhelmed with horror.

'That has cured me of women—beautiful, poetic, and fascinating women,' said Athos, raising himself, and forgetting to preserve the mystery of an intervening count. 'May God grant as much to you! Let us drink.'

'And so she is dead?' stammered d'Artagnan.

'Egad!' said Athos—'hold your glass. Will you have some ham, you rogue? We cannot drink any more!'

'But her brother?' timidly added d'Artagnan.

'Her brother?' replied Athos.

'Yes, the priest.'

'Ah! I sought him, to hang him also; but he was too quick for me—he had fled the evening before.'

'And did any one ever discover who the wretch was?'

'It was the first lover and accomplice of the girl: a fine fellow, who had pretended to be a curate, that he might get his mistress married and provided for. He must have got quartered, I trust.'

'Oh! my God! my God!' exclaimed d'Artagnan, astounded by this horrible adventure.

'Eat some of this ham, d'Artagnan; it is exquisite,' said Athos, cutting a slice, which he put upon the young man's plate. 'What a misfortune that there were not four such hams in the cellar. I should have drunk fifty bottles more.'

D'Artagnan could no longer bear this conversation: it would have driven him mad. He let his head fall upon his hands, and pretended to sleep.

'The young men nowadays do not know how to stand their drink,' said Athos, looking at him with pity; 'and yet that is one of the best of them!'

28

The Return

D'ARTAGNAN had not recovered from the consternation produced by the terrible communication of Athos. Many things yet appeared to him obscure in this semi-confession. In the first place, it had been made by a man who was quite drunk, to another man who was half drunk; and yet, in spite of that confusion of the brain which is produced by two or three bottles of Burgundy, d'Artagnan, on awaking the next morning, had each of Athos's words as thoroughly present in his mind, as though they had been stamped upon it as they fell from his companion's lips. His doubts made him only the more eager to arrive at certainty; and he went to his friend's room with a determination to renew the conversation. But he found Athos quite himself again; that is to say, the acutest and most impenetrable of men.

Moreover, the musketeer, after he had exchanged a smile, and shaken hands with him, anticipated his thought.

'I was very tipsy last night, my dear d'Artagnan,' said he. 'I perceived it this morning by my tongue, which was still heavy, and my pulse, which was still agitated. I would bet that I uttered a thousand extravagances.'

And, as he said this, he looked at his friend with an earnestness which embarrassed him.

'No,' said d'Artagnan; 'if I remember right, you said nothing out of the common.'

'Ah! you astonish me. I thought that I had related some most lamentable story.'

And he looked at the young man as if he would have read the very depths of his heart.

'Faith,' replied d'Artagnan, 'it appears that I was even more tipsy than you were, since I remember nothing.'

Athos was not satisfied with this, and continued—

'You cannot fail to have observed, my dear friend, that each one has his own kind of drunkenness—sad or gay. Mine is of a melancholy sort; and, when once I am tipsy, my mania is to narrate all the lugubrious tales with which my foolish nurse has filled my brain. It is my failing—a great fault, I confess; but, barring that, I am an excellent drinker.'

Athos said this in such a natural manner, that d'Artagnan was shaken in his conviction.

'Ah, then, that is it,' said the young man, as if en-deavouring to recall the truth; 'that is it. I remember, as one recollects a dream, that we talked of people being hung.'

'Ah! you see,' said Athos, growing pale, but attempting to smile; 'I was sure of it. People being hanged is quite my nightmare.'

'Yes, yes,' replied d'Artagnan; 'and this is what I can recall to mind: yes, it was so; listen, then—it was something about a woman.'

'See there,' replied Athos, becoming almost livid; 'it is my best story, the one of the woman with fair hair; and when I tell that, I am sure to be dead drunk.'

'Yes, that is it,' said d'Artagnan; 'a story about a fair woman, tall and beautiful, with blue eyes.'

'Yes, who was hanged.'

'By her husband, who was a nobleman of your acquaint-ance,' said d'Artagnan, looking earnestly at Athos.

'Well, now, see how a man might be compromised, when one no longer knows what he is saying,' replied Athos, shrugging his shoulders, as if he pitied himself. 'Positively, I will not get tipsy any more, d'Artagnan; it is a very bad habit.'

D'Artagnan continued silent; and then, suddenly changing the conversation, Athos said—

'Apropos, I thank you for the horse you have brought me.'

'Do you like him?'

'Yes; but he would not stand work.'

'You are mistaken. I went ten leagues with him in less than an hour and a half, and he appeared as if he had only gone round the Place St. Sulpice.'

'Ah, then, you make me regret him.'

'Regret him?'

'Yes, for I have parted with him.'

'How is that?'

'The fact is, this morning I got up at six. You were sleeping like a deaf man, and I did not know what to do, being still quite stupefied by last night's debauch. I therefore went down to the common room, and saw one of the Englishman, who was buying a horse of a couper, his own having died the day before. I approached him, and, as I saw he was offering a hundred pistoles for a sorrel horse—'Egad, sir,' said I, 'I have also a horse to sell.'—'And a very handsome one, too,' said he; 'I saw him yesterday; your friend's servant was holding him.'—'Do you think he is worth a hundred pistoles?'—'Yes, will you sell him to me at that price?'—'No; but I will play you for him.'—'At what?'—'At dice.''

'No sooner said than done; and I lost the horse. Ah! but, after all,' continued Athos, 'I won back his caparison.'

D'Artagnan made a wry face.

'Does that annoy you?' asked Athos.

'Yes, indeed, I confess it does,' replied d'Artagnan. 'That horse ought to have led to our recognition on a battle-field: it was a pledge—a souvenir. Athos, you have done wrong.'

'But, my dear fellow, put yourself in my place,' replied the musketeer. 'I was horribly tired of myself; and then, upon my honour, I do not like English horses. Besides, if it is of any consequence that we should be recognised by any one, the saddle will do well enough for that, for it is very remarkable. As for the horse, we will find some excuse, as a reason for its disappearance. What the plague! a horse is mortal. Let us say that mine has had the glanders, or the farcy.'

But d'Artagnan did not laugh.

'I am sorry for this,' continued Athos, 'since you seem to set such a value on these animals, for I have not yet finished my tale.'

'Why, what more have you done?'

'After having lost my horse—nine against ten, for that was the throw—the idea came into my head to stake yours.'

'But you confined yourself to the mere idea, I hope?'

'No, I put it into execution instantaneously.'

'Ah! was ever such a thing heard of?' exclaimed d'Artagnan anxiously.

'I staked him—and lost.'

'My horse?'

'Yes; your horse—seven against eight, for I lost only by one point. You know the old proverb.'

'Athos, you have lost your senses, I swear.'

'My dear fellow, it was yesterday, when I was telling you those foolish stories, that you should have said that, and not this morning. I lost him, however, with all his ornaments and caparison.'

'But this is quite frightful!'

'Listen, now; you have not heard the end of it yet. I should be a most excellent player if I did not get so infatuated; but I do get infatuated, just as I am when I drink. Well, accordingly, I obstinately persevered at the game.'

'But what more could you stake? You had nothing left.'

'Yes, yes, my friend; there remained that diamond, which now glitters on your finger, and which I had noticed yesterday.'

'This diamond!' exclaimed d'Artagnan, putting his hand quickly on the ring.

'And as I am a judge of these things, having had some few of my own, I valued it at a thousand pistoles.'

'I hope,' said d'Artagnan very seriously, whilst he was half dead with alarm, 'that you did not make any mention of my diamond?'

'On the contrary, my dear friend, do you not see that this diamond became our last resource. I might, with that, win back our horses and their accoutrements; and, perhaps, money enough for our journey.'

'Athos, you make me tremble,' cried d'Artagnan.

'So I mentioned your diamond to my adversary, who had also remarked it. What the plague, my dear fellow! would you carry a star of heaven on your finger, and wish no one to observe it? Impossible!'

'Go on, my dear fellow, go on,' said d'Artagnan; 'for, upon my honour, you horrify me with your calmness.'

'We divided the diamond into ten parts, of a hundred pistoles each.'

'Oh! you are joking, on purpose to try me,' said d'Artagnan, whom anger began to catch by the hair, as Minerva caught Achilles, in the *Iliad*.

'No, I am not joking, by Heaven! I should like to have seen you in the same situation. For a whole fortnight I had not looked upon a human face, and had been brutalising myself in there by parleying only with bottles!'

'That was no reason why you should stake my diamond!' said d'Artagnan, closing his hand with a nervous contraction.

'Listen, then, to the end. Ten parts, of a hundred pistoles each, would be ten throws, without revenge. In thirteen throws I lost all—in thirteen throws! The number 13 has always been fatal to me. It was the 13th of July when——'

'Zounds!' cried d'Artagnan, arising from the table the morning's narrative making him forget that of the night before.

'Patience,' cried Athos. 'I had formed a plan. The Englishman was an original. I had seen him in the morning talking to Grimaud; and Grimaud had informed me that he had made proposals to engage him in his service. I staked Grimaud—the silent Grimaud—divided into ten portions.'

'Ah, well! was ever such a thing heard of!' said d'Artagnan bursting out into a laugh.

'Grimaud himself—do you understand? And by these ten parts of Grimaud, who is not worth a ducat when entire, I won back the diamond. Tell me now if perseverance is not a virtue.'

'Faith, it is all very droll,' said the now comforted d'Artagnan, holding his sides with laughter.

'So, you understand, finding myself in the right vein, I began anew upon the diamond.'

'Ah! the deuce!' said d'Artagnan, becoming again over-clouded.

'I won back your trappings, then your horse, then my own trappings, then my own horse, and then lost them all again. In short, I ended by recovering your trappings and mine: and that is how we now stand. It was a superb throw, and therefore I left off.'

D'Artagnan sighed as if the weight of the hotel had been taken off his breast.

'After all, my diamond is safe,' he said timidly.

'Untouched, my dear friend—besides the trappings of your Bucephalus and mine.'

'But what shall we do with our saddles, without horses?'

'I have an idea as to them.'

'Athos, you make me tremble.'

'Listen, d'Artagnan. You have not played for a long time.'

'And I have no desire to play.'

'Well, don't make a vow about it: you have not played for a long time. I should say, therefore, that you ought to be in luck.'

'Well! and what then?'

'Well, the Englishman and his companion are still here. I observed that they regretted the trappings. You seem to value your horse; and, in your place, I would stake my trappings against my horse.'

'But he would not wish for one set of trappings.'

'Stake the two. Egad! I am not an egotist, like you.'

'You would, would you?' said d'Artagnan, hesitating; for the confidence of Athos began to influence him unconsciously.

'Upon my honour, I would! on one throw.'

'But, having lost the horses, I should very much like to keep the trappings at least.'

'Then stake your diamond.'

'Oh, that is quite another thing: never, never!'

'The devil! I would propose to you to stake Planchet: but as that game has been tried once, the Englishman would not perhaps wish to try it again.'

'Decidedly, my dear Athos,' said d'Artagnan, 'I would prefer risking nothing.

'It is a pity,' said Athos coldly; 'the Englishman is well lined with pistoles. Egad! do try one throw—a throw is soon made.'

'And if I lose?'

'You will gain.'

'But if I lose?'

'Well! then you will surrender the trappings.'

'Well, here goes for one throw,' said d'Artagnan.

Athos went to look for the Englishman, and found him in the stables, where he was looking wistfully at the saddles. The opportunity was good. He made his conditions: the two sets of trappings against one horse, or a hundred pistoles, at choice. The Englishman calculated quickly; the two sets of trappings were well worth three hundred pistoles; so he agreed.

D'Artagnan trembled as he threw the dice, and only turned up the number three. His paleness quite frightened Athos, who contented himself with saying—

'That's a bad throw, comrade; you will have the horses all caparisoned, sir.'

The triumphant Englishman did not give himself the trouble even to shake the dice; and, so sure was he of winning, that he threw the ivory on the table without looking. D'Artagnan turned away to hide his ill-humour.

'Well, well, well!' said Athos, in his usual calm voice, 'this is a most extraordinary throw, and I have only seen it four times in my life:—two aces.'

The Englishman looked, and was seized with astonishment. D'Artagnan looked, and coloured with joy.

'Yes,' continued Athos, 'only four times: once, at M. de Crequis's; once, at my own house in the country, in my castle of —— when I had a castle; a third time, at M. de Treville's, where it astonished us all; and a fourth time at a wine-shop, where it fell to me, and I lost by it a hundred louis, and a supper.'

'Will the gentleman take back his horse?' said the Englishman.

'Certainly!' said d'Artagnan.

'Then, there is no revenge.'

'Our conditions were: 'no revenge.' Do you remember?'

'True. The horse shall be delivered to your servant, sir.'

'One moment,' said Athos. 'With your permission, sir, I desire to speak a private word with my friend.'

'Speak.'

Athos led d'Artagnan apart.

'Well!' said d'Artagnan, 'what do you want with me now, tempter? You want me to play, do you not?'

'No, I want you to reflect.'

'On what?'

'You are going to take back the horse?'

'Certainly.'

'You are wrong. I would take the hundred pistoles. You know that you staked the trappings against the horse, or a hundred pistoles, at your choice.'

'Yes!'

'I would take the hundred pistoles.'

'Would you? But I shall take the horse.'

'And you are wrong, I say again. What shall we do with one horse between us two? I cannot get up behind you: we shall have the appearance of the two sons of Aymon, who lost their brothers. And you would not mortify me by prancing about on this magnificent steed, close by my side. I would take the hundred pistoles without a moment's hesitation. We want money to return to Paris.'

'I really have such a fancy for this horse, Athos.'

'And you are wrong, my friend: a horse shies; a horse

stumbles and breaks his knees; a horse eats at a rack where a glandered horse has eaten just before; and thus you lose a horse, or rather a hundred pistoles. Then, it is necessary for the master to feed his horse; when, on the contrary, a hundred pistoles feed the master.'

'But how shall we return?'

'On our servants' horses, to be sure. It will be evident enough, from our appearance, that we are people of consequence.'

'A nice figure we shall cut on those hacks, whilst Aramis and Porthos are dashing about on their chargers.'

'Aramis! Porthos!' exclaimed Athos, and he began to laugh heartily.

'What now?' demanded d'Artagnan, who did not understand the cause of his friend's merriment.

'Nothing, nothing. Go on,' said Athos.

'And your advice is——'

'To take the hundred pistoles, d'Artagnan: with them we can feast till the end of the month. We have suffered much from fatigue, you know, and it will be well for us to repose ourselves for a time.'

'I repose myself? Oh, no! Athos; immediately on my return to Paris, I shall set out in search of that poor woman.'

'Well, do you think your horse will be as useful to you for that purpose as the gold? Take the hundred pistoles, my friend—take the hundred pistoles.'

D'Artagnan only wanted a good reason for giving up; and this appeared to him an excellent one. Besides, by resisting any longer, he feared that he should appear selfish. He therefore chose the hundred pistoles, which the Englishman immediately paid him.

Their only thought then was to set out. The peace, which they had finally sealed with the landlord, cost six pistoles, in addition to Athos's old horse. D'Artagnan and Athos took the horses of Planchet and Grimaud; and the two valets took to the road on foot, carrying the saddles on their heads.

Badly mounted as the two friends were, they soon left their servants behind them, and arrived at Crevecœr. At a distance they saw Aramis, leaning sorrowfully from the window, and, like Sister Anne, looking at the dust on the horizon.

'Hollo! hey! Aramis,' shouted out the two friends, 'what the plague are you doing there?'

'Ah, is it you, Athos? is it you, d'Artagnan?' said the young man. 'I was just thinking how rapidly the things of this world disappear. My English horse, which was getting more and more distant, and has just disappeared amidst a cloud of dust, was to me a living image of the mutability of terrestrial things. Life itself may be resolved into three words—'Erat, est, fuit.''

'And all this really means——' inquired d'Artagnan, who began to suspect the truth.

'It means that I have just been taken in in a bargain, and sold, for sixty louis, a horse, which, by the manner in which he moves, should be able to trot five leagues an hour.'

D'Artagnan and Athos burst out into a laugh.

'My dear d'Artagnan,' said Aramis, 'do not be too much displeased with me, I entreat you: necessity knows no law. Besides, I am the person punished, since this infamous horse-dealer has cheated me out of fifty louis at least. Ah! you are thrifty managers; you come on your servants' horses, and make them lead your chargers slowly and by short stages.'

At this moment a waggon, which for some minutes had been seen coming along the Amiens road, stopped, and out got Planchet and Grimaud, with their saddles on their heads. The waggon was going empty to Paris, and the two servants had engaged, as the price of their places, to keep the waggoner in drink throughout the journey.

'What does this mean?' said Aramis, as he saw them. 'Nothing but the saddles?'

'Do you understand now?' said Athos.

'My friends, it is exactly like me. I too have kept the trappings by instinct. Hallo, Bazin! lay my trappings alongside of those belonging to these gentlemen.'

'And what have you done with your doctors?' demanded d'Artagnan.

'I invited them to dinner the next day, my dear fellow,' said Aramis. 'There is some exquisite wine here, by the bye, and I made them both as drunk as I could. Then, the curate forbade me to abandon the coat, and the Jesuit entreated me to get him enrolled as a musketeer.'

'Without any thesis,' cried d'Artagnan—'without thesis! I demand, for my part, the suppression of the thesis!'

'Since that time I have lived very agreeably. I have begun a poem in one-syllable verse: it is rather difficult, but merit of every kind consists in conquering difficulty. It is gallant in character; and I will read to you the first canto. There are four hundred lines, and they only occupy a minute.'

'Faith,' said d'Artagnan, who detested verses almost as

much as he did Latin, 'add to the merit of the difficulty that of brevity, and you are, at least, sure that your poem will have two merits.'

'Besides,' continued Aramis, 'it is pervaded by a virtuous passion. Well, my friends,' added he, 'and so we return to Paris? Bravo! I am ready. And we shall fall in with the simple Porthos, once more? So much the better: you could not believe how I have missed that great ninny. I like to see him, so self complacent: it reconciles me to myself. Catch him selling his horse, even for a kingdom. I would I could see him on his horse, and in his saddle. He will have, I am sure, the look of the Great Mogul.'

After they had halted an hour to rest their horses, Aramis paid his bill, placed Bazin in the waggon with his companions, and they then set out to rejoin Porthos.

They found him almost entirely cured, and, consequently, less pale than when d'Artagnan saw him at his first visit. He was seated at a table, on which, although he was alone, there was displayed a dinner for four persons. This dinner consisted of viands admirably dressed, of choice wines, and splendid fruit.

'Mon Dieu!' said he, rising, 'you have come in the nick of time; I was just at the soup, and you will dine with me.'

'Oh, oh!' said d'Artagnan, 'it is not Mousqueton who has lassoed such bottles as these. Besides, here is a larded fricandeau, and a fillet of beef.'

'I am recruiting my strength,' said Porthos; 'I am recruiting my strength. Nothing weakens one so much as these devilish sprains. Have you ever had any sprains, Athos?'

'Never,' said Athos; 'only I remember that in our skirmish in the Rue de Ferou, I received a sword-thrust, which, at the end of fifteen or twenty days, produced exactly the same consequences as a sprain.'

'But this dinner was not for yourself alone, my dear Porthos?' said Aramis.

'No,' said Porthos; 'I expected some gentlemen from the neighbourhood, who have just sent word that they cannot come; but as you will take their places, I shall lose nothing by the exchange. Hollo, Mousequeton! bring chairs, and let the bottles be doubled!'

'Do you know what we are eating here?' asked Athos, after ten minutes had elapsed.

'Egad,' replied d'Artagnan, 'I am eating veal, larded with marrow.'

'And I, veal cutlets,' said Porthos.

'And I, capon,' said Aramis.

'You are all mistaken, gentlemen,' gravely replied Athos; 'you are eating horse.'

'Come, come!' said d'Artagnan.

'The horse?' cried Aramis, making a horrible face.

Porthos alone was silent.

'Yes, the horse. Is it not so, Porthos? Are we not eating the horse, and perhaps the saddle with it?'

'No, gentlemen, I have kept the caparison.'

'Faith, we are all bad alike,' said Aramis. 'One would say that we had done it by agreement.'

'What would you have?' said Porthos; 'the horse shamed my visitors, and I did not wish to humiliate them.'

'Then your duchess is still at the baths, is she not?' inquired d'Artagnan.

'Yes,' replied Porthos. 'Then the governor of the province, one of the gentlemen I expected here to-day, appeared to wish so much for him, that I gave him to him.'

'Gave him!' exclaimed d'Artagnan.

'Oh, yes—zounds, yes—that is the expression,' said Porthos, 'for he was certainly worth a hundred and fifty louis, and the rascal would only pay me eighty.'

'Without the saddle,' said Aramis.

'Yes, without the saddle.'

'You observe, gentlemen,' said Athos, 'that, after all, Porthos has made the best bargain of any of us.'

There was then a perfect shout of laughter, at which poor Porthos was altogether astonished; but they soon explained to him the reason of this mirth, in which, as usual, he participated noisily.

'So we are all in cash now,' said d'Artagnan.

'Not I for one,' said Athos. 'I found Aramis's Spanish wine so good, that I sent sixty bottles in the waggon with the servants, which has very much impoverished me.'

'And I,' said Aramis, 'had given almost my last sou to the church of Montdidier, and the Jesuits of Amiens; and I had, besides, made engagements which I was compelled to keep—masses ordered for myself, and for you, gentlemen, which will surely be said, and by which I do not doubt we shall be greatly benefited.'

'And do you believe that my sprain has cost me nothing?' said Porthos; 'not to mention Mousqueton's wound, for which I was obliged to have a surgeon in attendance upon him twice a day.'

'Well, well, I see,' said Athos, exchanging a smile with Aramis and d'Artagnan, 'that you have behaved nobly towards the poor lad. It is like a good master.'

'In short,' said Porthos, 'when my bill is paid, I shall have about thirty crowns remaining.'

'And I, about ten pistoles,' said Aramis.

'It appears,' said Athos, 'that we are the Crœsuses of the party. How much remains of your hundred pistoles, d'Artagnan?'

'Of my hundred pistoles? In the first place, I gave you fifty.'

'Did you really?'

'Most assuredly.'

'Ah! it is true; I recollect it.'

'Then I paid the landlord six!'

'What an animal that landlord was! Why did you give him six pistoles?'

'It was you who told me to give them to him.'

'It is true; in fact, I am too generous!—and the balance?'

'Twenty-five louis,' said d'Artagnan.

'And I,' said Athos, pulling out a few small coins from his pocket—'see what I've got.'

'You, nothing!'

'Faith! just so; or, at any rate, so little as to be not worth adding to the general store.'

'Now, let us reckon up how much we have got:— Porthos?'

'Thirty crowns!'

'Aramis?'

'Ten pistoles.'

'And you, d'Artagnan?'

'Twenty-five.'

'That makes in all——' said Athos.

'Four hundred and seventy-five livres,' said d'Artagnan, who calculated like Archimedes.

'When we reach Paris, we shall have four hundred,' said Porthos, 'besides the horse-trappings.'

'But our regimental mounts?' said Aramis.

'Well! the four horses of our servants will procure two fit for their masters, which we must draw lots for. With the four hundred livres we can get half a horse for one of the dismounted ones; and then we will give the dregs of our pockets to d'Artagnan, who is in luck, and he shall go and stake them at the first tennis-court we come to. There, now!'

'Let us dine,' said Porthos, 'for the second course is getting cold.'

And the four friends, now more at ease concerning the future, did honour to the repast, of which the remnants were abandoned to Mousqueton, Bazin, Planchet, and Grimaud.

On arriving in Paris, d'Artagnan found a note from M. des Essarts, announcing that, as his majesty had determined on opening the campaign on the first of May, he must immediately make ready his equipments.

He ran at once to his friends, whom he had only quitted half an hour before, and whom he found very melancholy, or, rather, very anxious. They were in grand consultation at Athos's, which always indicated a concern of some importance.

They had, in fact, each received a similar note from M. de Treville.

The four philosophers looked at one another in great amazement; M. de Treville never jested on a matter of discipline.

'And at what sum do you estimate these equipments?' asked d'Artagnan.

'Oh, one cannot say,' replied Aramis; 'we have just made our calculations with a Spartan economy, and fifteen hundred livres will be absolutely necessary for each.'

'Four times fifteen make sixty; that is six thousand livres,' said Athos.

'For my part,' said d'Artagnan, 'I think that a thousand livres would be sufficient for each. It is true that I speak, not as a Spartan, but as an attorney,'

This word *attorney* awoke Porthos.

'Stop! I have an idea!' said he.

'That is something, however; as for myself,' coolly observed Athos, 'I have not even the shadow of one; but, as for d'Artagnan, he is mad, gentlemen. A thousand livres! why, for my part alone, I am certain that I shall require two thousand.'

'Four times two make eight,' said d'Artagnan; 'so we shall want eight thousand livres for our accoutrements. It is true that we have already got the saddles.'

'But besides that,' said Athos, waiting till d'Artagnan, who was going to thank M. de Treville, had shut the door before he brought to light his idea, so full of promise for the future—'more than that, there is the beautiful diamond

which shines on the finger of our friend. By all the saints!
d'Artagnan is too good a comrade to leave his brothers in
difficulty, when he carries a king's ransom on his middle
finger.'

29

The Hunt after Equipments

THE most prudent of the four friends was certainly d'Artagnan, although in his capacity of guardsman, it was much
more easy to equip him than the musketeers, who were men
of rank. But our Gascon youth was, as may have been seen,
of a character not only economical, but almost parsimonious; yet, at the same time (explain the contradiction), almost
as vain-glorious as Porthos. To the thoughtfulness origin-
ating in his vanity, was now added a less selfish anxiety.
Whatever inquiries he had made concerning Madame
Bonancieux, he could obtain no tidings of her. M. de
Treville had spoken of her to the queen; but the queen did
not know what had become of her, and promised to have
some investigations set on foot. This promise, however, was
vague, and afforded little satisfaction to the troubled
d'Artagnan.

Athos never quitted his own apartment: he was determined not to take a single step to equip himself.

'There are fifteen days remaining yet,' said he to his
friends. 'Well, if at the end of those fifteen days I have found
nothing, or, rather, if nothing has come to find me, as I am
too good a Catholic to blow out my brains with a pistol, I
will seek a good quarrel with four of his eminence's guards, or
with eight Englishmen, and I will fight till one of them kills
me; which, calculating the number, cannot fail to come to
pass. It will then be said that I died in the king's service;
so that I shall have served him, without needing to furnish
myself with equipments.'

Porthos continued to walk with his hands behind his back,
saying, 'I will pursue my idea.'

Aramis, thoughtful and unadorned, said nothing.

It may be seen, from these disastrous details, that desolation reigned throughout the little community.

The servants, on their side, like the coursers of Hippolytus, partook of their masters' bitter grief. Mousqueton made a store of crusts; Bazin, who had always leaned towards devotion, haunted the churches; Planchet watched the flies buzzing about; and Grimaud, whom the general distress could not induce to break the silence which his master had imposed, sighed in a way to melt even the hearts of stones.

The three friends—for, as we have already said, Athos had sworn not to stir an inch in search of equipments— went out early, and came in late. They wandered through the streets, looking on every pavement to see if any passenger might not have dropped a purse. They might have been supposed to be pursuing a trail, so watchful were they at every step. And when they met, their desponding looks seemed to ask of one another—'Have you found anything?'

Nevertheless, as Porthos had been the first to find an idea, and as he had steadily pursued it, he was the first to act. He was a man of action, this worthy Porthos. D'Artagnan saw him one day going towards the church of St. Leun, and instinctively followed him. He entered the sacred edifice, after having raised his moustache, and pulled out his imperial, which operations always portended, on his part, the most irresistible intentions. As d'Artagnan took some precautions to conceal himself, Porthos fancied that he had not been perceived. D'Artagnan entered after him. Porthos went and ensconced himself on one side of a pillar, and d'Artagnan, still unseen, leaned himself against the other.

There was a sermon, and the church was therefore full. Porthos took advantage of this circumstance to ogle the ladies. Thanks to Mousqueton's good offices, the external appearance was far from announcing the internal distress. His hat was, indeed, rather napless, and his feather rather drooping; his embroidery was somewhat tarnished, and his lace a little frayed; but, in the subdued light, these trifles disappeared, and Porthos still looked the handsome Porthos.

D'Artagnan perceived on a pew, near the pillar against which Porthos and he were leaning, a sort of mature beauty, a little yellow, and slightly withered, but yet upright and haughty, under her black head-dress. The eyes of Porthos were furtively directed on this lady, and then fluttered vaguely over the other parts of the church.

On her part, the lady, from time to time, blushed, and, with the rapidity of lightning, cast a glance at the inconstant

Porthos, whose eyes immediately fluttered away with greater activity than before. It was quite clear that this was a game which much piqued the lady in the dark hood; for she bit her lips till they bled, scratched her nose, and shifted desperately on her seat.

As soon as Porthos saw this, he once more curled his moustache, again elongated his imperial, and then began to make signals to a fair lady who was near the choir, and who was not only a fair lady, but undoubtedly a lady of some consequence; for she had behind her a little negro boy, who had carried the cushion on which she knelt, and a waiting-woman, who carried the coroneted bag in which she brought her mass-book.

The lady in the black hood slily observed all these glances of Porthos, and remarked that they were fixed upon the lady with the velvet cushion, the little negro boy and the waiting-woman.

In the meantime, Porthos was playing hard—winking his eyes, pressing a finger on his lips, and calling up little killing smiles, which really were assassinating the susceptible dame he scorned.

Thus it was, that, by way of *meâ culpâ*, and whilst beating her hand against her breast, she sent forth such a sonorous sigh, that everybody—even the lady with the red cushion —turned to look at her. Porthos was impenetrable. He had understood the sigh well, but he pretended to be deaf.

The lady with the red cushion produced a very striking effect, for she was extremely beautiful. She made a great impression on the lady in the black hood, who saw in her a truly formidable rival; a great impression upon Porthos, who thought her both much younger and much prettier than the lady in the black hood; and, lastly, a great impression upon d'Artagnan, who recognised in her the lady of Meung, whom his persecutor, the man with a scar, had addressed by the title of My Lady.

D'Artagnan, without losing sight of this lady with the velvet cushion, continued to watch Porthos's game, which amused him highly. He ventured to guess that this lady in the black hood was the solicitor's wife of the Rue aux Ours; especially as that was not far from the church of St. Leu.

He then, by inference, divined that Porthos wished to revenge his defeat at Chantilly, when the lady had shown herself so refractory in regard to her purse.

But, amidst all this, d'Artagnan thought he could remark

that no sign responded to the gallantries of Porthos. It was all chimera and illusion: but, even for an actual love, and for a well-founded jealousy, what other reality is there than illusions and chimeras?

When the sermon was ended, the solicitor's wife went towards the vessel containing the holy water. Porthos hastened to it before her, and, instead of putting in only one finger, he immersed his whole hand. The lady smiled, in the belief that it was for her that Porthos had taken so much trouble. But she was quickly and cruelly undeceived. Whilst she was only about three paces from him, he turned aside his head, keeping his eyes invariably fixed upon the lady with the red cushion, who had arisen, and followed by her negro boy and waiting-woman, was approaching the place where he stood.

When she had come near to Porthos, he drew his hand, all dripping with holy water, out of the vessel: the beautiful devoted touched with her slender fingers the enormous hand of Porthos, smiled as she made the sign of the cross, and left the church.

This was too much for the solicitor's wife, who no longer doubted that there was an understanding between this lady and Porthos. If she had been a lady of quality, she would have fainted, but, as she was only a solicitor's wife, she contented herself with saying in a concentrated rage.

'So, M. Porthos! you do not offer me any holy water?'

Porthos, at these words, started like a man just awakening from a sleep of a thousand years.

'Ah, madame!' exclaimed he, 'is it indeed you? How is your husband, that dear M. Coquenard? Is he still as miserly as ever? Where could my eyes have been, that I did not once perceive you during the two mortal hours that the sermon lasted?'

'I was only two paces from you, sir,' responded the attorney's wife; 'but you did not perceive me, because you had no eyes except for that beautiful lady, to whom you just now offered the holy water.'

Porthos pretended to be abashed.

'Ah,' said he, 'you observed it, did you?'

'One must have been blind not to have observed it.'

'Yes,' said Porthos negligently, 'it is one of my friends— a duchess—whom I have some difficulty in meeting, on account of the jealousy of her husband, and who apprised me that, for the sole purpose of seeing me, she would come

to-day to this wretched church, in this abominable neighbourhood.'

'M. Porthos,' said the attorney's wife, will you have the
goodness to favour me with your arm for a few minutes? I
should be glad to have some conversation with you.'

'How is that, madame?' said Porthos, winking to himself
like a player, who laughs at the dupe whom he is about to
ensnare.

Just at this moment d'Artagnan passed, in pursuit of the
fair lady. He slily glanced at Porthos, and saw that triumphant wink.

'Ah,' said he to himself, reasoning after the peculiarly
easy morality of that age of gallantry, 'there is one who
might readily be equipped by the proper time.'

Porthos, yielding to the pressure of the lady's arm, as a
vessel yields to her helm reached the cloister of St. Magloire,
a retired spot, which was closed by a turnstile at either end.
In the day-time, nobody was to be seen there, but beggars
at their meals, or children at their play.

'Ah! M. Porthos,' exclaimed the attorney's wife, when
she was assured that none but the habitual population of
the place could see or hear them: 'Ah! M. Porthos, you are
a great conqueror, it appears.'

'I, madame!' said Porthos bridling with his head:
'how so?'

'Witness the signs just now, and the holy water. But she
must be a princess, at the least, that lady, with her negro
boy, and her waiting-woman!'

'You are mistaken. Mon Dieu! no; she is really only a
duchess.'

'And that courier who was waiting at the door, and that
carriage, with the coachman in a magnificent livery?'

Porthos had seen neither courier nor carriage; but
Madame Coquenard, with the glance of a jealous woman
had seen all.

Porthos regretted that he had not made the lady with the
red cushion a princess when he was at it.

'Ah! you are the pet of all the most beautiful women,
M. Porthos,' resumed the attorney's wife, with a sigh.

'But,' replied Porthos, 'with such a figure as nature has
bestowed on me, how should I avoid conquests?'

'Mon Dieu! how quickly you men forget!' exclaimed the
attorney's wife, raising her eyes to heaven.

'Less quickly than women, I think,' replied Porthos.

'For, after all, I may say, madame, that I have been your victim, when, wounded and dying, I saw myself abandoned by the surgeons—I, the offspring of an illustrious family, who had depended on your friendship, was near dying of my wounds first, and of hunger afterwards, in a miserable wine-shop at Chantilly, and that without your deigning even to answer the burning epistles which I wrote to you.'

'But, M. Porthos——' muttered the solicitor's wife, who felt that, if judged by the conduct of the noblest dames of the age, hers was very wrong.

'I,' continued Porthos, 'who for your sake had sacrificed the countess of Penaflor——'

'I know it well.'

'The baroness of——'

'M. Porthos, do not overwhelm me!'

'The countess of——'

'M. Porthos, be generous!'

'You are right, madame; and I will not proceed.'

'But it is my husband, who will not listen to a word about lending.'

'Madame Coquenard,' said Porthos, 'do you remember the first letter which you wrote me, and which I cherish, engraven on my heart?'

The lady groaned.

'But,' said she, 'the sum which you proposed to borrow was, really, rather large.'

'Madame Coquenard, I gave you the preference. I had only to write to the duchess of —— but I will not mention her name, for it has never been mine to compromise a woman; but this I know, that I had but to write to her, and she immediately sent me fifteen hundred.'

The attorney's wife let fall a tear.

'M. Porthos,' said she, 'I swear to you that you have punished me sufficiently; and if, in future, you should ever again be so circumstanced, you have only to apply to me.'

'Fie, madame!' said Porthos, as though disgusted; 'do not let us allude to money: it is too humiliating!'

'Then you no longer esteem me!' said the attorney's wife, slowly and sorrowfully.

Porthos maintained a majestic silence.

'And is it thus you answer me? Alas! I understand.'

'Think of the offence which you have given me, madame: it is indelible, here,' said Porthos, putting his hand over his heart, and pressing it with force.

'But I will repair it, my dear Porthos.'

'Besides, what did I ask of you?' continued Porthos, shrugging his shoulders with an air of the utmost simplicity, 'a loan—nothing more. I know that you are not rich, Madame Coquenard, and that your husband is obliged to fleece his poor clients to gain a few pitiful crowns. Oh! if you had been a countess, a marchioness, or a duchess, it would have been another thing, and you would have been indeed unpardonable.'

The solicitor's wife was piqued.

'Learn, M. Porthos,' said she, 'that my strong-box, although the strong-box of a solicitor's wife, is probably far better furnished than that of all those ruined minxes.'

'Then you have doubly offended me, Madame Coquenard,' said Porthos, disengaging the arm of the attorney's wife from his own; 'for, if you are rich, your refusal is without excuse.'

'When I say rich,' replied the attorney's wife, who saw that she had gone too far, 'you must not take my words literally. I am not precisely rich, but in comfortable circumstances.'

'Come, madame,' said Porthos, 'let us say no more about it: you have misunderstood me, and all sympathy between us is destroyed.'

'Ungrateful man!'

'Ah, I advise you to complain!' said Porthos.

'Go to your beautiful duchess? Let me no longer restrain you.'

'Ah! she is not yet so shabby, I believe.'

'Come, then, M. Porthos,' said Madame Coquenard, 'once more, and it is the last time—do you still love me?'

'Alas, madame,' replied Porthos, in the most melancholy tone that he could assume, 'when one is about to commence a campaign—and in this campaign my presentiments assure me that I shall be killed—'

'Oh, do not say such things!' exclaimed the attorney's wife, bursting out into sobs.

'Something tells me that it will be so,' said Porthos, becoming more and more melancholy.

'Say, rather, that you have formed another love,'

'No, I speak frankly to you. No new object has engaged my thoughts; and, indeed, I feel something at the bottom of my heart which pleads for you. But in a fortnight, as you do or do not know, this fatal campaign will open, and I shall be dreadfully busy about my equipment. Besides, I must go into Brittany, to my own family, to provide the funds necessary for my departure!'

Porthos observed a last struggle between love and avarice.

'And,' continued he, 'as the duchess, whom you saw just now, has an estate close to mine, we shall go down together. A journey, you know, appears much shorter when one travels in company.'

'Have you no friends in Paris, M. Porthos?' asked the attorney's wife.

'I once believed I had,' said Porthos, resuming his melancholy manner; 'but I have clearly seen that I deceived myself.'

'You have! you have! M. Porthos,' exclaimed the attorney's wife, in a transport which inspired even herself. 'Come to our house to-morrow. You are the son of my aunt, consequently my cousin; you come from Noyon, in Picardy, and you have several law-suits on your hands, and no attorney. Can you remember all this?'

'Perfectly, madame.'

'Come at dinner-time.'

'Very well.'

'And be on your guard before my husband, who is a shrewd fellow, in spite of his seventy-six years.'

'Seventy-six years! Plague take it! a fine age,' replied Porthos.

'A great age, you mean to say, M. Porthos. So that the poor dear man might leave me a widow at any moment,' added the lady, casting a significant glance at Porthos. 'Fortunately, however, by our marriage contract, all the property reverts to the survivor.'

'All?' said Porthos.

'Yes, all.'

'You are a most provident woman, I perceive, my charming Madame Coquenard,' said Porthos, tenderly pressing the lady's hand.

'Then we are completely reconciled, my dear M. Porthos?' said she, in a most insinuating tone.

'For life,' replied Porthos, in the same tone.

'Farewell, then, till our next meeting, you traitor!'

'Till our next meeting, you forgetful one!'

'Till to-morrow, my angel!'

'Till to-morrow, light of my life!'

30

'My Lady'

D'ARTAGNAN had followed the other lady from the church without being observed by her. He saw her enter her carriage, and heard the orders given to her coachman to drive to St. Germain. It was useless to attempt to follow, on foot, a carriage which was drawn by two vigorous trotting horses; and d'Artagnan therefore returned to the Rue Ferou. In the Rue de Seine he met Planchet, who had stopped before a pastry cook's shop, and appeared to be in perfect ecstasy at the sight of a cake, of most tempting form. D'Artagnan ordered him to go and saddle two horses at M. de Treville's stable, one for each of them, and to come to him at Athos's lodgings. M. de Treville had given d'Artagnan a general permission to avail himself of his stable. Planchet took his way towards the Rue de Columbier, and d'Artagnan to Rue Ferou. Athos was at home, gloomily emptying one of the bottles of that famous Spanish wine which he had brought with him from Picardy. He gave Grimaud a sign to bring a glass for d'Artagnan, and Grimaud obeyed with his habitual silence.

D'Artagnan related to Athos all that had occurred at the church between the attorney's wife and Porthos, and how their companion was already in a fair way of obtaining his equipments.

'For my part,' said Athos, in answer to this recital, 'I am sure enough that it will not be women who will be at the expense of my outfit.'

'And yet, my dear Athos, handsome, and refined, and noble as you are, neither princesses, nor queens even, are beyond what you might seek to win.'

At this moment Planchet modestly thrust his head through the half-open door, and announced that the horses were there.

'What horses?' asked Athos.

'Two which M. de Treville lends me, with which I am going to St. Germain.'

'And what are you going to do at St. Germain?' inquired Athos.

D'Artagnan then proceeded to inform him of his having seen at the church, that lady, who, in conjunction with the gentleman in the black cloak and with the scar upon his forehead, had been the subject of his thoughts.

'That is to say, that you are in love with this one now, as you were with Madame Bonancieux,' ejaculated Athos, shrugging his shoulders, as if in contempt of human weakness.

'Not at all!' exclaimed d'Artagnan. 'I am only curious to penetrate the mystery with which she surrounds herself. I know not why, but I fancy that this woman, unknown as she is to me, and I am to her, has hitherto exercised some influence on my life.'

'You are right, in fact,' said Athos. 'I am not acquainted with any woman who is worth the trouble of being sought after when she is once lost. Madame Bonancieux is lost: so much the worse for her; let her get herself found again.'

'No, Athos, no; you deceive yourself,' said d'Artagnan. 'I love poor Constance more fondly than ever; and if I only knew the place where she now is, were it even at the extremity of the world, I would set out to drag her from her enemies. But I know it not; and all my efforts to discover it have been in vain. What would you expect? One must seek some diversion.'

'Divert yourself with my lady then, my dear d'Artagnan; I recommend it with all my heart, if that will amuse you.'

'But, Athos,' said d'Artagnan, 'instead of keeping yourself here, secluded like a suspect, get upon a horse, and ride with me to St. Germain.'

'My friend,' said Athos, 'I ride on horseback if I have a horse; if I have not, I walk on foot.'

'Well, for my part,' said d'Artagnan, smiling at that misanthropy in Athos, which, in another, would have offended him, 'I am not so proud as you are: I ride whatever I can find. So farewell, my dear Athos.'

'Farewell,' said the musketeer, as he made a sign to Grimaud to uncork the bottle he had brought.

D'Artagnan and Planchet got into their saddles, and took the road to St. Germain.

As they went along, d'Artagnan could not help thinking of all that Athos had said to him about Madame Bonancieux. Although he was not of a very sentimental nature, yet the pretty seamstress had made a real impression on his heart. In the meantime he tried to find out who this lady was. She had talked to the man in the dark cloak, and, therefore, she was certainly acquainted with him. Now the man with the dark cloak had, in d'Artagnan's opinion, certainly carried off Madame Bonancieux the second time, as well as the first. D'Artagnan, therefore, was only telling half a lie, which is not much of one, when he said that, by his pursuit of this lady, he was in a way to discover Constance. Thus meditating, and touching his horse occasionally with the spur, d'Artagnan had gone over the distance, and reached St. Germain. He went skirting the pavilion, where, ten years afterwards, Louis XIV. was born. He was passing through a very solitary street, looking right and left to see if he could not discover some vestige of his beautiful Englishwoman, when, on the ground-floor of a pretty house, which, according to the custom of the time, had no window towards the street, he recognised a countenance he knew. The person in question was walking on a sort of terrace ornamented with flowers. Planchet was the first to recognise him.

'Eh, sir,' said he, 'do you not remember that face, which is now gaping at yonder plant?'

'No,' said d'Artagnan; 'and yet I am convinced it is not the first time that I have seen it.'

'Vive Dieu! I believe you,' said Planchet; 'it is that poor Lubin, the valet of the Count de Wardes, whom you settled so thoroughly a month ago, at Calais, on the way to the governor's house.'

'Oh! yes,' said d'Artagnan, 'I remember him now. Do you believe that he would recognise you?'

'Faith, sir, he was in such a fright, that I doubt whether he could have a very clear recollection of me.'

'Well, then,' said d'Artagnan, 'go and chat with him, and ascertain whether his master is dead.'

Planchet dismounted, and went up to Lubin, who, in reality, did not recognise him; and the two valets began to converse together with the utmost good fellowship; whilst d'Artagnan backed the horses down a lane, and turning behind a house, returned to assist at the conference, concealed by a hedge of hazel bushes. After a minute's observation from behind the hedge, he heard the sound of wheels, and saw the carriage of the unknown lady stop in front of him. There could be no doubt about it, for the lady was inside. D'Artagnan bent down over his horse's neck, that he might see everything, without being himself seen. The lady put her charming fair head out of the door, and gave some orders to her maid. This latter, a pretty girl, of from twenty to two-and-twenty years of age, alert and animated, the fit abigail of a woman of fashion, jumped down the steps, over which she had been seated, according to the custom of the time, and went towards the terrace where d'Artagnan had seen Lubin. D'Artagnan followed the waiting woman with his eyes and saw her going towards the terrace. But, as it happened, an order from the house had called away Lubin, so that Planchet remained alone, looking to see in what direction his master had concealed himself. The waiting-woman approached Planchet, whom she mistook for Lubin, and handed him a small note.

'For your master,' said she.

'For my master?' said Planchet in astonishment.

'Yes, and in great haste; take it quickly then.'

She then hastened towards the carriage, which had already turned in the direction whence it had come, and jumped on the steps; the vehicle moved away. Planchet turned the note over and over again, and then, accustomed to passive obedience, he went along the lane, and, at twenty paces distance, met his master, who having seen all the proceedings, was hurrying towards him.

'For you, sir,' said Planchet, handing the note to the young man.

'For me?' said d'Artagnan: 'are you quite sure?'

'Vive Dieu! I am quite sure of it; for the maid said, "for your master," and I have no other master than you; so—— A pretty slip of a girl that maid is, too, upon my word.'

D'Artagnan opened the letter, and read:

'A person who interests herself about you more than she can tell, would be glad to know on what day you will be able to walk out in forest. A valet, in black and red, will be waiting to-morrow, at the hotel of the Field of Cloth of Gold, for your reply.'

'Oh, oh!' said d'Artagnan, 'this is somewhat ardent. It seems that my lady and I are anxious about the health of the same person. Well! Planchet, how is this good M. de Wardes? He is not dead then?'

'No, sir; he is as well as a man can be with four sword wounds in his body—for you made four in that dear gentleman—and he is yet weak, having lost almost all his blood. As I told you, sir, Lubin did not recognise me, and he related to me the whole of our adventure.'

'Well done, Planchet! You are the very king of valets;

and now mount your horse again, and let us overtake the carriage.'

This did not take them a long time. In about five minutes they saw the carriage standing in the road, and a richly-dressed cavalier waiting at its door. The conversation between the lady and this cavalier was so animated, that d'Artagnan drew up on the other side of the carriage, without being observed by any one but the pretty waiting-maid. The conversation was in English, which d'Artagnan did not understand; but, by the accent, the young man thought he could perceive that the beautiful Englishwoman was very angry. She concluded by a gesture which left no doubt about the nature of the conversation: it was a blow with her fan, applied with such force that the little feminine toy flew into a thousand pieces. The cavalier burst into a roar of laughter, which appeared to exasperate the lady. D'Artagnan thought that now was the time to interpose: he therefore approached the other door, and taking his hat off respectfully said—

'Madame, will you permit me to offer my services? It appears to me that this gentleman has offended you. Say one word, madame, and I will immediately punish him for his want of courtesy.'

At the first words the lady turned, and looked at the young man with astonishment; and, when he had ended, 'Sir,' said she, in very good French, 'I would put myself under your protection with the greatest pleasure, if the person with whom I have quarrelled were not my brother.'

'Ah, excuse me then,' said d'Artagnan; 'I was not aware of that, madame.'

'What is that presumptuous fellow interfering about?' exclaimed the gentleman whom the lady had claimed as her relation, lowering his head to the top of the door: 'why does he not go on about his business?'

'Presumptuous fellow, yourself!' said d'Artagnan, bending on the neck of his horse, and answering through the other door. 'I do not go, because I choose to remain here.'

The gentleman spoke a few words in English to his sister.

'I speak in French to you, sir,' said d'Artagnan; 'do me the favour then, I beseech you, to answer in the same language. You are the lady's brother; but, happily, you are not mine.'

It might have been imagined that the lady, timid as women generally are, would interpose at the commencement of this quarrel, to prevent its proceeding further: but, on the contrary, she threw herself back in her carriage, and coolly ordered the coachman to drive to the hotel. The pretty waiting-maid threw a glance of anxiety at d'Artagnan, whose good looks seemed not to have been lost upon her. The carriage hurried on, and left the two men face to face. No material obstacle now intervened between them. The cavalier made as if to follow the carriage; but d'Artagnan—whose already boiling anger was still further increased by recognising in him the Englishman, who, at Amiens, had won his horse, and was very near winning his diamond from Athos—seized him by the horse's bridle, and stopped him.

'Ah, sir,' said he, 'you appear to be even a more presumptuous fellow than I am; for you pretend to forget that there is already a little quarrel begun between us.'

'Ah, ah!' cried the Englishman, 'is it you, my master? Then one must always play one game or other with you.'

'Yes; and that reminds me that I have a revenge to take. We will see, my dear sir, whether you are as skilful with the sword as with the dice box.'

'You perceive,' said the Englishman, 'that I have no sword with me. Would you show off your courage against an unarmed man?'

'I hope that you have got one at home,' said d'Artagnan; 'if not, I have two, and will play you for one.'

'Quite unnecessary.' said the Englishman; 'I am sufficiently provided with that kind of tool.'

'Well then, sir,' replied d'Artagnan, 'choose the largest, and come and show it me this evening.'

'Oh, certainly, if you please.'

'Behind the Luxembourg, there is a charming spot for promenades of the sort to which I am inviting you.'

'Very well; I will be there.'

'Your hour?'

'Six o'clock.'

'Apropos, you have probably one or two friends?'

'I have three, who will consider it an honour to play the same game as myself.'

'Three—capital! How well it fits in,' said d'Artagnan; 'it is precisely my number.'

'And now, who are you?' demanded the Englishman.

'I am M. d'Artagnan, a Gascon gentleman, serving in the Guards, in the company of M. des Essarts: and pray, who are you?'

'I am Lord de Winter, Baron of Sheffield.'

'Well, then, I am your humble servant, my lord,' said d'Artagnan, 'although you have names which are rather hard to remember.'

And pricking his horse, he put him to the gallop, and took the road to Paris. As he was accustomed to do under similar circumstances, d'Artagnan went straight to Athos's lodging. He found the musketeer stretched upon a large couch, where he was waiting, as he said, for his equipment to come to him. He told Athos all that had occurred, omitting only the letter to M. de Wardes. Athos was quite enchanted when he heard he was going to fight an Englishman. We have said that to do so was his dream. They sent their servants instantly to look for Aramis and Porthos, and to let them know what was in the wind. Porthos drew his sword from the scabbard, and began to lunge at the wall, drawing back from time to time, and capering about like a dancer. Aramis, who was working hard at his poem, shut himself up in Athos's closet, and begged that he might not be disturbed again until it was time to draw his sword. Athos, by a signal to Grimaud, demanded another bottle. D'Artagnan arranged a little plan in his own mind, of which we shall hereafter see the execution; and which promised him an agreeable adventure, as might be seen by the smiles which, from time to time, passed across his face, and lighted up its thoughtfulness.

31

English and French

AT the appointed time they proceeded, with their four servants, to an enclosure behind the Luxembourg, which was reserved for goats. Athos gave some money to the goat-herd to keep out of the way; and the valets were ordered to do duty as sentinels.

A silent party soon came to the same field, and joined the musketeers; and then, according to the English custom, the introductions took place.

The Englishmen were all persons of the highest rank. The singular names of the three friends of d'Artagnan were, therefore, not only a subject of surprise to them, but also of disquietude.

'After all,' said Lord de Winter, when the three friends had been named, 'we know not who you are, and we will not fight with men bearing such names. These names of yours are shepherd's names!'

'As you guess, my lord, they *are* false names,' said Athos.

'Which makes us the more desirous of knowing your true ones,' said the Englishman.

'You have played against us without knowing them,' said Athos, 'and, as a token of it, you won our two horses.'

'It is true; but then we only hazarded our pistoles. Now we peril our blood. One plays with anybody, but only fights with one's equals.'

'That is fair,' said Athos.

He then took aside the Englishman with whom he was to fight, and told him his name in a low voice. Porthos and Aramis, on their sides, did the same.

'Does that satisfy you?' asked Athos, of his adversary; 'and do you find me sufficiently noble, to do me the favour of crossing swords with me?'

'Yes, sir,' said the Englishman, bowing

'Well, then, now will you allow me to say one thing to you?' coolly resumed Athos.

'What is that?' said the Englishman.

'It is, that you would have done well not to require me to make myself known.'

'Why so?'

'Because I am thought to be dead. I have reasons for desiring that it be not known that I am alive; therefore, I shall be obliged to kill you, that my secret may not be divulged.'

The Englishman looked at Athos, thinking the latter was jesting. But Athos was not jesting at all.

'Gentlemen,' said he, addressing his companions, and their adversaries, 'are we all ready?'

'Yes!' replied, with one voice, both English and French.

'Guard, then!' said Athos.

And, immediately, eight swords were glittering in the rays of the setting sun, and the combat began with a fury which was natural enough between men who were doubly enemies.

Athos fenced with as much calmness and method as if he had been in a fencing-school.

Porthos, no doubt cured of his over-confidence by his adventure at Chantilly, played a game full of dexterity and prudence.

Aramis, who had the third canto of his poem to finish, worked away like a man in a great hurry.

Athos was the first to kill his adversary. He had only given him one wound, but, as he had forewarned him, that one was mortal, for it passed directly through his heart.

Porthos next stretched his opponent on the grass; having pierced his thigh. Then, as the Englishman had given up his sword, Porthos took him in his arms, and carried him to his carriage.

Aramis pressed his so vigorously, that, after having driven him back fifty paces, he ended by disabling him.

As for d'Artagnan, he had simply and purely played a defensive game. Then, when he saw that his adversary was quite weary, he had, by a vigorous thrust, disarmed him. The baron, finding himself without a sword, retreated two or three steps; but, his foot slipping as he stepped away, he fell upon his back.

With one bound d'Artagnan was upon him, and, pointing his sword at his throat, said to the Englishman—

'I could kill you, sir, but I give you your life from love to your sister.'

D'Artagnan was overwhelmed with joy: he had accomplished the plan he had designed, and the development of which illuminated his face, as we have said, with smiles.

The Englishman, enchanted at having to deal with so complete a gentleman, pressed d'Artagnan in his arms, and caressed the three musketeers a thousand times. And then, as Porthos's adversary was already installed in the carriage, and Aramis's had fairly run away, they had only to attend to Athos's victim.

As Porthos and Aramis undressed him, in the hope that his wound was not mortal, a heavy purse fell from his belt.

D'Artagnan picked it up, and presented it to Lord de Winter.

'Ah! and what the deuce am I to do with that?' said the Englishman.

'You will restore it to his family,' said d'Artagnan.

'Much his family will care about this trifle. They will inherit an income of fifteen thousand louis. Keep this purse for your valets.'

During this scene Athos came up to d'Artagnan.

'Yes,' said he, 'let us give this purse, not to our own, but to the English servants.'

Athos took the purse, and threw it to the coachman.

'For you and your comrades,' cried he.

This loftiness of spirit, in a man without a penny, struck even Porthos himself; and this French generosity, being told by Lord de Winter to his friends, had a great effect everywhere, except upon Messrs. Grimaud, Planchet, Mousequeton, and Bazin.

'And now, my young friend—for I hope that you will permit me to call you by that name,' said Lord de Winter, 'I will, if you wish, present you this evening to my sister, for I wish her ladyship to take you into her favour; and, as she is not entirely without influence at court, perhaps a word from her may be useful to you hereafter.

D'Artagnan glowed with delight, and gave an assenting bow.

As Lord de Winter left d'Artagnan, he gave him his sister's address. She lived at No. 6, in the Place Royale, which was at that time the fashionable part of the town. He also engaged to call for him in order to present him, and d'Artagnan made an appointment, for eight o'clock, at Athos's chambers.

This presentation to 'My Lady' occupied all the thoughts of our young Gascon. He recalled the singular manner in which this woman had before now crossed his path; and, although convinced that she was but one of the cardinal's tools, he yet felt himself irresistibly attached towards her by a sentiment that was inexplicable. His only fear was that she might recognise him as the man whom she had seen at Meung. Then she would also know that he was a friend of M. de Treville, and, consequently, was heart and soul devoted to the king; and this would involve a loss of some of his advantages over her, since, as soon as she knew him as well as he knew her, the game between them would be equal. As for her incipient intrigue with M. de Wardes, our self-complacent gentleman thought but little of that, although the count was young, rich, handsome, and high in favour with the cardinal. It is something to be twenty years of age, and, moreover, a native of Tarbes.

D'Artagnan began by dressing himself out in a flaming style at home; and he then went to Athos, and, according to his custom, told him everything. Athos listened to his projects, then shook his head, and recommended prudence in a tone almost of bitterness.

'What!' said he, 'you have just lost a woman whom you

thought good, charming, perfect, and now you are running after another.'

D'Artagnan felt the justice of the reproach.

'I love Madame Bonancieux,' said he, 'with my heart; but I love 'My Lady' with my head; and, by going to her house, I hope to enlighten myself as to the character she plays at court.'

'Vive Dieu! the character she plays is not difficult to guess, after all that you have told me. She is some emissary of the cardinal's, a woman who will draw you into a trap, where you will right easily leave your head.'

'The plague! My dear Athos, you seem to me to look at things on the dark side.'

'My dear fellow, I distrust women—what would you have? I have paid for it—and particularly fair women. This lady is fair, did you not say?'

'She has the finest light hair that was ever seen.'

'Ah! my poor d'Artagnan!' said Athos.

'Listen! I wish to enlighten myself; and then, when I have learned what I want to know, I will leave her.'

'Enlighten yourself, then!' said Athos coldly.

Lord de Winter arrived at the appointed time; but Athos, who was warned beforehand, went into the inner room. His lordship, therefore, found d'Artagnan alone, and, as it was near eight o'clock, they set out at once.

An elegant carriage was in waiting at the door, and, as two excellent horses were harnessed to it, they were almost immediately at the Place Royale.

Her ladyship received d'Artagnan graciously. Her house was furnished with remarkable splendour; and although the English, as a rule, frightened away by the war, were quitting, or were about to quit France, she proved, by the new outlays which she had just made, that the public measure which drove away the English in general had no influence on her.

'You see,' said Lord de Winter, as he presented d'Artagnan to his sister, 'a young gentleman who had my life in his hands, but would not misuse his advantage, although we were doubly enemies, since it was I who insulted him, and since I am, also an Englishman. Thank him, therefore, madame, on my behalf, if you have any good-will for me.'

The lady slightly frowned; an almost imperceptible cloud passed over her brow; and then a smile so singular appeared upon her lips, that the young man, who saw this triple change, almost shuddered.

Her brother observed none of it; for he had turned aside to play with the lady's favourite monkey, which had pulled him by the doublet.

'Welcome, sir,' said the lady, in a voice the singular softness of which contrasted strangely with the symptoms of ill-humour which d'Artagnan had just observed; 'for you have this day acquired an eternal claim upon my gratitude.'

The Englishman then turned towards them, and related all the circumstances of the combat. Her ladyship listened with the greatest attention; yet it was easy to see, in spite of her endeavours to conceal her emotion, that the account was not agreeable to her. The blood mounted to her face, and her little foot trembled beneath her dress.

Lord de Winter perceived nothing of this, for, as soon as he had ended, he went to a table on which there was a salver, with a bottle of Spanish wine upon it, and filling two glasses, he invited d'Artagnan to drink.

D'Artagnan knew that it was displeasing to an Englishman to decline his toast. He went, therefore, to the table, and took the second glass. But he had not lost sight of the lady, and, by the aid of a mirror, he was a witness to a change which took place in her countenance. Now that she thought she was unobserved, her features assumed an expression, which almost amounted to one of ferocity.

She tore her handkerchief to pieces with her teeth.

The pretty waiting-maid, whom d'Artagnan had noticed, then entered. She spoke a few words in English to Lord de Winter, who immediately begged d'Artagnan's permission to withdraw, excusing himself on account of the urgency of the business that called him away, and commissioning his sister to obtain his pardon.

D'Artagnan shook hands with Lord de Winter, and returned towards her ladyship. The countenance of this woman had, with a surprising power of change, resumed its pleasing expression; but some red stains upon her handkerchief proved that she had bitten her lips until they bled. Those lips were magnificent: they looked like coral.

The conversation now became animated. Her ladyship appeared entirely recovered. She explained that Lord de Winter was her brother-in-law, and not her brother. She had married a younger son of the family, and was left a widow, with a son. This child was the sole heir of Lord de

Winter, if his lordship did not marry. All this exhibited to d'Artagnan a veil which concealed something, but he could not yet distinguish anything beneath that veil.

After half an hour's conversation, d'Artagnan was quite convinced that her ladyship was his own countrywoman. She spoke French with a purity and elegance that left no room for doubt in that respect.

D'Artagnan uttered abundant gallantries and protestations of devotion; and, at all these fooleries that escaped from him, the lady smiled most sweetly. The hour for departure came at last, and d'Artagnan took leave of her ladyship, and quitted her drawing-room, the happiest of men.

On the staircase he met the pretty waiting-maid, who, having touched him gently in passing, blushed to the very eyes, and begged his pardon, in a voice so sweet, that the forgiveness was at once conferred.

D'Artagnan returned the next day, and received a still more favourable reception. Lord de Winter was not present; and it was her ladyship herself, on this occasion, who did the honours of the evening. She seemed to take a great interest in him; inquiring who he was, and who his friends were; and whether he had not sometimes thought of attaching himself to the cardinal's service.

D'Artagnan, who, as we know, was very prudent for a youth of twenty, then remembered his suspicions concerning her ladyship. He uttered a fine eulogium on the cardinal, saying that he should not have failed to enter his eminence's guards, had he chanced to know M. de Cavois, instead of knowing M. de Treville.

The lady changed the conversation without the sligthest affectation; and, with the utmost apparent indifference of manner, asked him whether he had ever been in England.

He replied that he had once been sent over by M. de Treville, to negotiate for a supply of horses, and had even brought back four as a sample. In the course of this conversation her ladyship bit her lips three or four times: she had to deal with a youth who played a pretty close game.

D'Artagnan withdrew at the same hour as on the previous visit. In the corridor, he met once more the pretty Kitty, for that was the abigail's name. The latter looked at him with an expression of mysterious interest. But d'Artagnan was so engrossed by the mistress, that he observed nothing but what was connected with her.

He returned to her ladyship's, on the next day, and the

next again; and, on each occasion, my lady gave him a more flattering welcome.

Every evening, too, either in the antechamber, in the corridor, or on the staircase, he was sure to meet the pretty maid.

But, as we have already said, d'Artagnan paid no attention to this strange persistence on the part of poor Kitty.

32

An Attorney's Dinner

THE duel, in which Porthos had played such a brilliant part, had not made him forget the dinner to which the attorney's wife had invited him. The next day, therefore, at about one o'clock, having received the last polish from Mousqueton's brush, he proceeded to the Rue aux Ours.

His heart beat, but it was not, like that of d'Artagnan, with a youthful and impatient sentiment. No; a more material influence conducted him. He was at last about to cross that mysterious threshold, to ascend that unknown staircase, up which the old crowns of Master Coquenard had mounted one by one. He was really about to see a certain strong-box, of which he had so often beheld the image in his dream—a strong-box, long and deep in form; padlocked, barred, and fastened to the floor—a strong-box of which he had so often heard, and which the attorney's hands were now about to open before his admiring eyes.

And then he—the wanderer over the face of the earth—the man without fortune, or family—the soldier, who frequented wine-shops, inns, taverns, and posadas—the glutton, generally obliged to be contented with chance mouthfuls;—he was about to taste a family meal, to enjoy a comfortable home.

To go in his capacity of cousin, and sit daily at a good table—to smooth the yellow wrinkled brow of the old attorney—to pluck the young clerks a little, by teaching them the greatest niceties of basset, hazard, and lansquenet, and by winning of them, by way of recompense for the lesson he should give them in an hour, all that they had saved within a month;—all this accorded well with the singular manners of the times, and prodigiously delighted Porthos.

And yet the musketeer remembered now and then the many bad reports which were current concerning attorneys; their thrifts, their parings, and their fast-days: but as, after all, with the exception of some fits of economy, which Porthos had always found very unseasonable, the attorney's wife had been very liberal—that is, for an attorney's wife, be it understood—he still hoped to meet with an establishment maintained upon a creditable scale.

He began to feel some doubt, however, at the door. Its appearance was not inviting—there was a dark an filthy passage, and a badly lighted staircase, to which a grayish light penetrated, through a grating from a neighbouring courtyard. On the first floor, he found a low door, studded with enormous nails, like the principal gate of the prison of the Grand Chatelet.

Porthos knocked with his knuckles; and a tall clerk, pale, and buried beneath a forest of hair, opened the door, and bowed to him with the manner of a man who is compelled to respect in another, the size which denotes strength, the military costume which denotes station, and the vermilion complexion which denotes a habit of living well.

There was another clerk, rather shorter, behind the first; another clerk, rather taller, behind the second; and a little stump-in-the-gutter, of twelve years old, behind the third.

In all, there were three clerks and a half, which, considering the period, indicated a highly prosperous business.

Although the soldier was not to arrive till one o'clock, yet the attorney's wife had been on the look-out since noon, and reckoned on the heart, and perhaps, on the stomach, of her adorer, making him come a little before the appointed time.

Madame Coquenard, approaching by the door of the apartment, met her guest almost at the moment that he arrived by the staircase-door, and the appearance of the worthy dame relieved Porthos from a great embarrassment: for the clerks were looking on him with envious eyes; and he, not well knowing what to say to this ascending and descending gamut, had remained entirely mute.

'It is my cousin!' exclaimed the attorney's wife. 'Come in, then; come in, M. Porthos.'

The name of Porthos was not without its effect upon the clerks, who began to laugh; but Porthos turned, and all their countenances at once resumed their gravity. They reached the sanctum of the attorney, after having passed through an antechamber in which the clerks were, and an office in which they ought to have been. The latter was a dark room, well furnished with dusty papers. On leaving the office, they passed the kitchen on the right hand, and entered the drawing-room.

All these rooms, opening into one another, did not produce in Porthos very pleasant ideas. Every word could be heard afar off, through all these open doors; and then, in passing, he had cast a quick investigating glance into the kitchen, and he confessed to himself, to the disgrace of his hostess, and his own great regret, that he had not discovered that fire, that animation, that activity, which, on the approach of an abundant meal, generally reigns throughout that sanctuary of gluttony.

The attorney had undoubtedly been informed of this anticipated visit; for he expressed no surprise at the sight of Porthos, who advanced towards him in an easy manner, and saluted him politely.

'We are cousins, it seems, M. Porthos?' said he, raising himself, by means of his arms, from his cane-work easy-chair.

The old man, enveloped in a large black doublet, in which his weakly frame was lost, was yellow and withered; his gray eyes glittered like carbuncles, and appeared, with his grinning mouth, to be the only part of his countenance in which life remained. Unfortunately, the legs had begun to refuse their services to all this bony machine; and for the last five or six months, during which this weakness had been felt, the worthy attorney had almost become a slave to his wife.

The cousin was received with resignation—nothing more. With good legs, Master Coquenard would have declined all relationship with M. Porthos.

'Yes, sir, we are cousins,' replied Porthos, without being at all disconcerted; for, in fact, he had never calculated on being received by the husband with enthusiasm.

'On the distaff side, I believe?' said the attorney maliciously.

Porthos did not understand the sneer, but mistook it for simplicity, and laughed at it beneath his thick moustache. Madame Coquenard, who knew that a simple attorney would be a rare variety of the species, smiled a little, and blushed a great deal.

Master Coquenard had, since Porthos's arrival, cast many a glance of uneasiness at a large press, placed opposite his own oaken escritoire. Porthos comprehended that this press, although it did not respond in form to that which he had seen in his dreams, must be the blessed strong-box, and he congratulated himself on the fact that the reality was at least six feet taller than the dream.

Master Coquenard did not carry his genealogical investigations any further; but, transferring an uneasy glance from the press to Porthos, he contented himself with saying—

'Your cousin will favour us with his company at dinner some time before he departs for the campaign, will he not, Madame Coquenard?'

This time Porthos received the blow full in his stomach, and felt it too; nor did Madame Coquenard appear entirely insensible to it, for she added—

'My cousin will not repeat his visit, if he finds that we do not treat him well; but, on the other hand, he has too short a time to pass in Paris, and, consequently, to see us, for us not to beg of him almost all the moments that he can devote to us before his departure.'

'Oh, my legs—my poor, dear legs!' muttered M. Coquenard, with an attempt to smile.

This assistance, which had reached Porthos at the moment when his gastronomic hopes were assailed, inspired the musketeer with exceeding gratitude towards his attorney's wife.

The hour of dinner shortly sounded. They entered the dining-room, which was a large dark room, situated opposite the kitchen.

The clerks, who, as it seemed, had snuffed up some perfumes unusual in that house, came with military exactness, and held their stools in their hands, in perfect readiness for sitting down. They might be seen moving their jaws beforehand with fearful anticipations.

'Lord bless us!' thought Porthos, casting a look at these three famished beings—for the stump-in-the-gutter was not, as we may suppose, admitted to the honours of the master's table—'Lord bless us! In my cousin's place, I would not keep such gormandisers. One would take them for shipwrecked people, who had eaten nothing for six weeks.'

M. Coquenard entered, pushed forward in his easy-chair by madame, whom Porthos, in his turn, assisted in rolling her husband to the table.

Scarcely had he entered, before he began to move his nose and jaws after the fashion of the clerks.

'Oh, oh!' said he; 'here is soup which is quite alluring.'

'What the plague do they smell so extraordinary in this soup?' thought Porthos, on beholding a tureen of plentiful, but pale and perfectly meagre broth, on the top of which a few straggling crusts floated, like the islands in an archipelago.

Madame Coquenard smiled; and, on a sign from her, they all eagerly seated themselves.

M. Coquenard was served first, and Porthos next. Madame Coquenard then filled her own plate, and distributed the crusts, without soup, to the three impatient clerks.

At this moment the door of the dining-room opened with a creak, and between the gaping panels, Porthos could perceive the poor little clerk, who, unable to participate in the feast itself, was eating his dry bread, betwixt the odour of the kitchen and that of the dining-room.

After the soup, the servant girl brought in a boiled fowl—an extravagance which expanded the eyelids of the revellers until they seemed almost about to melt entirely away.

'It is very perceptible that you love your family, Madame Coquenard,' said the attorney, with a grin that was almost tragic, 'this is indeed a compliment which you have paid to your cousin.'

The poor fowl was awfully thin, and covered with that bristled skin, which the bones can never pierce, in spite of all their efforts: it must have been patiently sought for, before it was detected on the roost to which it had withdrawn to die of old age.

'Faith!' thought Porthos, 'this is but a melancholy prospect; I respect old age; but I do not much relish it, either boiled or roasted.'

He looked around to see if his own opinion were the general one; but, on the contrary, he saw nothing but glaring eyes, devouring by anticipation this venerable bird, which he so much despised.

Madame Coquenard drew the dish towards her, adroitly detached the two great black paws, which she placed on her husband's plate; cut off the neck, which, together with the head, she laid aside for herself; took off a wing for Porthos; and then returned the animal, otherwise untouched, to the servant who had brought it in: so that it had completely disappeared before the musketeer had found time to note the changes which disappointment had wrought upon the various visages, according to the respective characters and dispositions of those who experienced it.

After the hen, a dish of beans made its appearance—an enormous dish, in the midst of which sundry mutton-bones, which might, at first sight, have been supposed to be accompanied by some meat, displayed themselves.

But the clerks were not the dupes of this deception, and their melancholy looks now settled into resignation.

Madame Coquenard, with the moderation of a thrifty housewife, distributed these viands amongst the young men.

The time for wine was come. Master Coquenard poured, from a stone bottle of very slender proportions, the third of a glass for each of the clerks, about an equal quantity for himself, and then passed the bottle to the side of Porthos and madame.

The young men filled up their glasses with water; when they had drank half, they again filled them up with water; and, by repeating this process, they had come, by the end of the feast, to swallow a beverage which had been transmuted from the colour of the ruby to that of a burnt topaz.

Porthos slowly masticated his fowl's wing: he also drank half a glass of this cherished wine, which he recognised as Montreuil; whilst Master Coquenard sighed as he saw him swallow it neat.

'Will you eat any of these beans, cousin Porthos?' inquired Madame Coquenard, in a tone which plainly said — 'take my word for it, you had better not.'

'Thank you, cousin; I am no longer hungry,' replied Porthos.

There was an awful pause. Porthos did not know how to demean himself, for the attorney kept repeating—

'Ah, Madame Coquenard, I compliment you highly: your dinner was a positive banquet!'

Porthos suspected that they were quizzing him, and began to curl his moustache and knit his brow; but a look from Madame Coquenard recommended forbearance.

At this moment, on a glance from the attorney, the clerks slowly arose from the table, folded their napkins more slowly still, and then bowed and departed.

'Go, young men; go, and aid digestion by labour,' said the attorney, with great gravity.

The clerks being gone, Madame Coquenard arose, and

drew from a cupboard a morsel of cheese, some confection of quinces, and a cake which she had herself manufactured with almonds and honey.

Master Coquenard frowned, because he saw this more ample provision.

'A feast! decidedly a feast!' cried he, moving uneasily in his chair. '"*Epulae Epularum*"—Lucullus dines with Lucullus.'

Porthos looked at the bottle, which was near him, and hoped that, with wine, bread, and cheese, he might yet make a dinner; but the wine was soon gone, the bottle being emptied, and neither Master nor Madame Coquenard seemed to observe it.

'Very well,' said Porthos to himself, 'here I am, out-generalled.' He passed his tongue over a small spoonful of the confection, and stuck his teeth together in Madame Coquenard's glutinous cake.

'And now,' thought he, 'the sacrifice is consummated.'

After the delights of such a repast, it was necessary for Master Coquenard to take his siesta. Porthos hoped that the affair would be managed in the very locality where he sat; but the attorney would hear of no such thing: it was necessary to conduct him to his own room, and he would not be easy till he was before his press, on the edge of which, as a greater precaution, he deposited his feet.

The lady led Porthos into an adjoining room.

'You may come and dine here thrice a week,' said Madame Coquenard.

'Thank you,' said Porthos; 'but I do not wish to abuse a luxury. Besides, I must think of my equipment.'

'That's true,' said the lady, with a groan. 'It is those unhappy equipments—is it not?'

'Alas, yes!' said Porthos, 'that's it.'

'But of what does the equipment of your regiment consist, M. Porthos?'

'Oh, of a great many things,' said Porthos; 'the musketeers, as you know, are chosen troops, and they require many things unnecessary for the guards or the Swiss.'

'But, still, you might give me some particulars of them.'

'Why they may amount to about——' commenced Porthos, who preferred the sum total to the detail.

The attorney's wife listened in fearful expectation.

'To how much?' said she. 'I hope that it will not exceed——' She stopped, for words failed her.

'Oh, no,' said Porthos, 'it will not exceed two thousand five hundred francs. I believe, indeed, that, with economy, I could manage with two thousand.'

'Good God! two thousand francs!' exclaimed she. 'Why, it is quite a fortune, and my husband will never be persuaded to lend such a sum!'

Porthos made a most significant grimace, which madame well understood.

'I asked the particulars,' said she, 'because, as I have many relations and connections in trade, I am sure to be able to get the things a hundred per cent cheaper than you would pay yourself.'

'Ah,' said Porthos, 'is that what you meant?'

'Yes, dear M. Porthos. And so you will want, first——'

'A horse.'

'Yes, a horse. Well, I have got the very thing for you.'

'Ah!' said Porthos, cheering up; 'then that is arranged as regards my own horse; but I shall require another for my servant and my portmanteau. As to arms, you need not trouble yourself; I have got them.'

'A horse for your servant?' resumed the attorney's wife, hesitating; 'but that is really being very grand, my friend.'

'Eh, madame!' said Porthos haughtily: 'do you happen to take me for a beggar?'

'Oh, no! I only mean to say, that a handsome mule often looks as well as a horse; and it seems to me, that by procuring a handsome mule for Mousqueton——'

'Well, as to a handsome mule,' said Porthos, 'you are right: I have seen many great Spanish noblemen, all of whose followers were mounted upon mules. But then, you understand, Madame Coquenard, it must be a mule with plumes and bells.'

'Be quite easy on that score,' said the lady.

'There only remains the portmanteau, then,' added Porthos.

'Oh, do not let that disturb you,' replied Madame Coquenard; 'my husband has five or six portmanteaus, and you shall choose the best. There is one, in particular, which he used to prefer on his journeys, and which is large enough to hold half the world.'

'But, is it empty, this portmanteau?' demanded Porthos.

'Yes, certainly, it is empty,' replied the attorney's wife.

344

'Ah, but the portmanteau I want,' exclaimed Porthos, 'is a well-furnished one, my dear.'

Madame Coquenard breathed forth fresh sighs. Moliere had not yet written his *L'Avare*? Madame Coquenard therefore anticipated *Harpagon*.

At length, the remainder of the equipment was haggled over in the same manner; and the result of the settling was, that the attorney's wife should ask her husband for a loan of eight hundred francs in hard cash, and should furnish the horse and mule which were to have the honour of bearing Porthos and Mousqueton upon their way to glory.

These conditions having been arranged, and the interest and time of payment stipulated, Porthos took leave of Madame Coquenard, and returned home, half-famished, and in a very ill-humour.

33

Maid and Mistress

Now, as we have already said—in spite of the cries of conscience, in spite of the sage counsels of Athos, and the tender memories of Madame Bonancieux—d'Artagnan became each hour more deeply enamoured of her ladyship; nor did he ever fail to offer her a daily homage, to which the presumptuous Gascon was convinced that she must sooner or later respond.

As he arrived one evening, scenting the air like a man who expects a shower of gold, he met the waiting-maid at the carriage-gate; but, on this occasion, the pretty Kitty was not contented with giving him a passing smile. She gently took his hand.

'Good!' thought d'Artagnan; 'she is entrusted with some message for me from her mistress—an appointment for some meeting, which my lady wanted courage to announce herself;' and he looked at the charming girl with the most conquering look he could assume.

'I should be glad to say two words to you, sir,' stammered the waiting-maid.

'Speak, child. Speak!' said d'Artagnan. 'I am listening.'

'Not here, sir; it is impossible. What I have to tell you would take up too long a time, and is, besides, too secret.'

'Well! but what is to be done, then?'

'If you would please follow me, sir,' said Kitty timidly.

'Wherever you please, my pretty child!'

'Then, come.'

By the hand which she had continued to hold, Kitty then led d'Artagnan to a small, dark, winding staircase; and, after having made him ascend some fifteen steps, she opened a door.

'Enter, sir; we shall be alone, and may converse here.'

'And whose room is this, then, my pretty child?' inquired d'Artagnan.

'It is mine, sir; it communicates with that of my mistress, through this door. But you may rely upon it that she will not hear whatever we say, for she never goes to bed till midnight.'

D'Artagnan threw a glance around him. The little room was a charming model of cleanliness and taste; but his eyes involuntarily turned towards the door which communicated, as Kitty had told him, with her ladyship's chamber.

Kitty guessed what was passing in the young man's mind, and gave a sigh.

'Then you are very fond of my mistress, sir?' said she.

'I don't know whether I am very fond of her; but what I do know is, that I am mad for her.'

Kitty gave a second sigh.

'Alas! sir, that is a great pity!'

'And what the plague do you see to pity in it?'

'Because, sir, my mistress does not love you at all.'

'What!' exclaimed d'Artagnan; 'did she desire you to tell me so?'

'Oh! no, sir, no! But I, from the interest that I take in you, have resolved to tell you.'

'Thanks, my good Kitty, but only for the intention; for you must own that the communication is not very agreeable.'

'That is to say, you do not believe what I have told you. Is that your meaning?'

'One is always vexed to believe such things, my charming child, if it were only on account of self-love.'

'Then, you do not believe me?'

'I confess that, until you condescend to give me some proof of what you assert——'

'What do you say to this?'

Kitty drew from her bosom a small unaddressed note.

'For me?' exclaimed d'Artagnan, as he hastily seized the

letter, and, by a movement quick as thought, tore off the envelope, in spite of the cry which Kitty uttered when she saw what he was about to do, or rather, what he did.

'Oh, heavens! sir,' said she, 'what have you done?'

'Vive Dieu!' said d'Artagnan, 'must I not make myself acquainted with what is addressed to me?'

He read as follows:

'You have sent no answer to my first note. Are you, then, in too much suffering, or have you indeed forgotten the glances that you gave me at Madame de Guise's ball? Now is the opportunity, count: do not let it escape you.'

D'Artagnan grew pale: he was wounded in his vanity, but he believed it was in his love.

'This note is not for me!' he exclaimed.

'No, it is for somebody else; but you did not give me time to tell you so.'

'For somebody else! His name—his name!' exclaimed the furious d'Artagnan.

'The Count de Wardes.'

The remembrance of the scene at St. Germain presented itself at once to the mind of the presumptuous Gascon, and confirmed what Kitty had that moment told him.

'Poor, dear M. d'Artagnan,' said she, in a voice full of compassion, as she again pressed the young man's hand.

'You pity me, kind child,' said d'Artagnan.

'Oh, yes, with all my heart; for I know well what love is myself.'

'You know well what love is?' said d'Artagnan, looking at her for the first time with some particular attention.

'Alas! yes.'

'Well, instead of pitying me, then, you would be doing better by assisting me to take revenge upon your mistress.'

'And what kind of vengeance would you seek?'

'I would supplant my rival.'

'I will never assist you in that, sir,' said Kitty quickly.

'And why not?' inquired d'Artagnan.

'For two reasons.'

'Which are?'

'The first—that my mistress will never love you.'

'How can you know that?'

'You have offended her too deeply.'

'In what can I have offended her—I who, since I have

been acquainted with her, have lived at her feet like a very slave? Speak, I beseech you!'

'I will never avow that but to the man who can read to the depths of my soul.'

D'Artagnan looked at Kitty for the second time. There was about the young girl a freshness and a beauty which many a duchess would be glad to purchase with her coronet.

'Kitty,' said he, 'I will read even the very depths of your soul; so let not that restrain you, my dear child—do speak!'

'Oh! no,' exclaimed Kitty, 'you do not love me; it is my mistress whom you love; you have this moment told me so.'

'And does that prevent you making known your second reason?'

'The second reason,' said Kitty, encouraged by the expression of the young man's eyes, 'is, that in love we should all help ourselves.'

Then did d'Artagnan first recall the languishing glances, the smiles, and stifled sighs of Kitty, whenever he had chanced to meet her; whilst, in his absorbing wish to please the titled lady, he had neglected the abigail. He who chases the eagle takes no heed of the sparrow.

But our Gascon saw now, at a single glance, all the advantages which he might be able to derive from this passion which Kitty had so unaffectedly avowed:—such as, the interception of all letters to the Count de Wardes, intelligence of everything that occurred, and an entrance at any hour to that chamber which was contiguous to her ladyship's room. In idea, at least, he was already sacrificing the poor young maiden to her noble mistress.

Midnight at length sounded, and, almost at the same instant, a bell was heard from the adjoining chamber.

'Good God!' exclaimed Kitty, 'there is my mistress wanting me: go now—go directly!'

D'Artagnan arose, and took his hat as though he intended to obey; then, quickly opening the door of a large press, instead of that of the staircase, he squeezed himself within, amidst the robes and night-clothes of her ladyship.

'Whatever are you about?' exclaimed Kitty.

D'Artagnan, who had secured the key beforehand, fastened himself in his press without reply.

'Well!' exclaimed my lady, in a sharp voice, 'are you asleep, then, that you do not answer the bell?'

D'Artagnan heard the door of communication opened violently.

'Here I am, my lady, here I am!' exclaimed Kitty, springing forward, that she might meet her mistress.

They returned together to the bed-chamber, and, as the door continued open, d'Artagnan could hear her ladyship complaining, for a time.

At last, however, she became appeased: and, as Kitty waited on her mistress, their conversation turned upon the listener.

'Well,' said my lady, 'I have not seen our Gascon here, this evening.'

'What, madam,' said Kitty, 'has he not been? Can he have proved fickle before he has been favoured?'

'Oh, no! he must have been hindered, either by M. de Treville, or by M. des Essarts. I have some experience, Kitty, and I hold that man securely!'

'What will your ladyship do with him?'

'What will I do with him? Depend upon it, Kitty, there is a something between that man and me of which he little thinks. He very nearly destroyed my credit with his eminence. Oh! I will have vengeance!'

'I thought that your ladyship loved him?'

'Love him! I detest him. The ninny held Lord de Winter's life in his power, and did not kill him! and, by that alone, he made me lose an income of three hundred thousand francs.'

'It is true,' said Kitty, 'your son is the sole heir of his uncle, and, till he came of age, you would have had the enjoyment of his fortune.'

D'Artagnan shuddered to the very marrow of his bones at hearing this sweet creature censuring him, in that voice whose sharpness she had so much trouble to conceal in conversation, for not having slain a man on whom he had seen her heaping indications of affection.

'Yes,' continued her ladyship, 'and I would have taken vengeance on him before now, if, for some reason or other, that I know not, the cardinal had not insisted on forbearance.'

'Oh, yes; but your ladyship had no forbearance with that little woman whom he loved.'

'What! the mercer's wife of the Rue des Fossoyeurs! Why, has he not already forgotten her existence! A fine vengeance that was, truly!'

Cold drops trickled on the brow of d'Artagnan: this woman was a very monster.

He set himself again to listen, but the toilet was, unfortunately, ended.

'That will do,' said her ladyship; 'go to your own room now, and try, to-morrow, to get me an answer at last to that letter which I have given you.'

'For M. de Wardes?' said Kitty.

'Certainly; for M. de Wardes.'

'Ah!' said Kitty, 'he is one that seems to me of a very different sort from that poor M. d'Artagnan.'

'Leave me, girl,' exclaimed her ladyship; 'I do not like remarks.'

'D'Artagnan heard the noise of the closing door, and then of two bolts with which 'my lady' secured herself within.

Kitty on her side, turned the key in the lock as gently as it was possible. D'Artagnan then pushed open the door of the press.

'Oh! my God!' whispered Kitty, 'what ails you? what makes you look so pale?'

'The abominable wretch!' muttered d'Artagnan.

'Silence! silence! Go away,' said Kitty; 'there is only a partition between my room and my lady's; and everything that is said in the one is heard in the other.'

'Fortunately so: but I will not leave till you have told me what is become of Madame Bonancieux.'

The poor girl swore to d'Artagnan, upon the crucifix, that she was completely ignorant about the matter, as her mistress never allowed her to know above half of any of her secrets. But she thought he might rely upon it that Madame Bonancieux was not dead.

Nor did Kitty really know anything more about the circumstances which had nearly made her mistress lose her credit with the cardinal. But in this particular, d'Artagnan was better informed. As he had perceived her ladyship on ship-board, at the very moment that he was quitting England, he did not doubt but the circumstance had some reference to the diamond studs.

But what was most manifest of the whole affair, was the genuine, deep, inveterate hatred, which her ladyship entertained against him, for not having killed her brother-in-law.

D'Artagnan returned to her ladyship's on the next day. He found her in a very ill-humour, and he understood that it was the disappointment of an answer from de Wardes which thus provoked her. Kitty entered, but 'my lady' treated her harshly. A glance which the maid gave at d'Artagnan seemed to say—'see what I suffer upon your account.'

But, as the evening wore on, the lovely lioness grew gentle. She listened with a smile to the tender compliments of d'Artagnan, and condescended even to give him her hand to kiss.

D'Artagnan left her, scarcely knowing what to think. But, as he was a Gascon, who was not easily to be deceived, he had in his mind contrived a little plan.

He found Kitty at the door, and went, as on the evening before, to her room to collect information. Kitty had been sadly scolded, and accused of negligence. Her ladyship could not comprehend the silence of the Count de Wardes, and had commanded her maid to come to her for orders at nine o'clock on the next morning.

D'Artagnan made Kitty promise to come to him in the morning, to tell him what might be the nature of these new commands. The poor girl promised all that d'Artagnan desired: she was driven mad.

At eleven o'clock, he saw Kitty make her appearance. She held in her hand another note from her ladyship. On this occasion, the poor girl did not even endeavour to withhold it from d'Artagnan; she let him do as he chose; in body and in soul, she belonged to her handsome soldier.

D'Artagnan opened this second note, which, like the other, bore neither signature nor address, and read as follows:—

'This is the third time that I have written to tell you that I love you: take care that I do not write a fourth time, to tell you that I hate you.'

D'Artagnan's colour changed several times, as he perused this note.

'Oh! you love her still!' said Kitty, whose eyes had never once been turned away from the young man's face.

'No, Kitty, you deceive yourself. I no longer love her, but I want to avenge myself for her contempt.'

Kitty sighed.

D'Artagnan took up a pen, and wrote:—

'Madame, Until now, I have been in doubt whether your former notes could really have been meant for me, so unworthy did I feel myself of such an honour; but, to-day, I must at last believe in the excess of your kindness, since

351

not only your letter, but your servant also, affirms that I have the happiness to be the object of your love.'

'At eleven to-night, I shall come to implore your forgiveness. To delay another day, at present, would be, in my opinion, to offer you a new affront.'

'He whom you have rendered the happiest of mankind.'

This note was not precisely a forgery, as d'Artagnan did not sign it, but it was an indelicacy: it was, even according to the standard of our present manners, something like an act of infamy; but the people of those times were less scrupulous than we are now. Moreover, d'Artagnan knew, from her ladyship's own avowal, that she had been guilty of treacheries in the most important affairs, and his esteem for her was singularly small. He had, in a word, to revenge both her fickleness toward himself, and her conduct toward Madame Bonancieux.

D'Artagnan's plot was very simple. Through Kitty's chamber he would enter that of her mistress; he would confound the deceiver, threaten to expose her publicly, and perhaps obtain through her fears all the information which he desired concerning the fate of Constance. It might even happen that the liberation of the mercer's pretty wife might be a result of this interview.

'There,' said the young man, handing the sealed note to Kitty, 'give this letter to her ladyship: it is M. de Wardes' reply.'

Poor Kitty became as pale as death: she suspected what the note contained.

'Listen, my dear child,' said d'Artagnan; 'you understand that all this must come to an end in one way or another. Your mistress may discover that you delivered the first note to my servant, instead of to the Count's; and that it was I who unsealed the others, which should have been unsealed by M. de Wardes. Her ladyship will then dismiss you, and you know that she is not the kind of woman to be moderate in her revenge.'

'Alas!' said Kitty, 'why have I exposed myself to all that?'

'For me, I know, my beauty,' said the young man, 'and very grateful am I for it, I swear.'

'But what does your note contain?'

'Her ladyship will tell you.'

'Alas! you do not love me!' exclaimed Kitty, 'and I am very wretched!'

Kitty wept much before she determined to deliver this letter to her mistress; but, from devotedness to the young soldier, she did determine at last, and that was all that d'Artagnan desired.

34

Concerning the Equipments of Aramis and Porthos

WHILST the four friends were all engaged in looking out for their equipment, there had no longer been any regular meetings between them. They dined, without one another, wherever they chanced to be; and assembled when they could. Duty also, on its side, occupied a part of that precious time which was so rapidly passing away. But they had agreed to meet once a week, about one o'clock, at Athos's chambers, as it was known that he, according to his vow, would never cross the threshold of his door.

The very day on which Kitty had visited d'Artagnan at his own home, was one of their days of meeting; and scarcely had the waiting-maid quitted d'Artagnan, before he proceeded to the Rue Ferou.

He found Athos and Aramis philosophising. Aramis had still some secret inclination to return to the cassock; and Athos, according to his custom, neither dissuaded nor encouraged him. Athos liked every one to exercise his own free-will.

He never gave his advise before it was demanded; and, even then, it must be demanded twice.

'In general, people only ask for advice,' he said, 'that they may not follow it; or, if they should follow it, that they may have somebody to blame for having given it.'

Porthos arrived an instant after d'Artagnan; so the four friends were all assembled.

Their four countenances had four different expressions: that of Porthos, tranquillity; of d'Artagnan, hope; of Aramis, anxiety; and that of Athos, perfect indifference.

After a moment's conversation, in which Porthos obscurely intimated that a lady high in rank had kindly taken upon herself to relieve him from his embarrassment, Mousqueton entered.

He came to request Porthos to come to his lodging, where—so he said in a most melancholy tone—his presence was most urgently required.

'Are my equipages come?' demanded Porthos.

'Yes and no,' replied Mousqueton.

'But what do you mean, I ask you?'

'Come and see, sir!'

Porthos arose, bowed to his friends, and followed Mousqueton.

A moment afterwards, Bazin appeared upon the threshold of the door.

'What do you want, my friend?' inquired Aramis, with that softness of tone which was always observable in him when his ideas inclined towards the church.

'A man is awaiting you, sir, at your rooms,' replied Bazin.

'A man? What sort of a man?'

'A beggar.'

'Give him something, Bazin, and tell him to pray for a poor sinner.'

'This beggar-man insists on seeing you, and pretends to say that you will be very glad to see *him*.'

'Has he not anything particular for me?'

'Yes. "If M. Aramis hesitates to come to me," said he, "tell him I have just arrived from Tours!"'

'From Tours! I will go directly!' exclaimed Aramis. 'Gentlemen, a thousand pardons; but undoubtedly this man brings me the intelligence that I expected.'

And getting up at once, he went off at a run.

There now remained only Athos and d'Artagnan.

'I verily believe that those fellows have settled their affairs,' said Athos. 'What think you about it, d'Artagnan?'

'I knew that Porthos was in a fair way for it; and as for Aramis, to tell the truth, I was never very uneasy about him. But you, my dear Athos, who so generously gave away the English pistoles which were your legitimate property—what will you do?'

'I am very glad that I killed the rascal,' said Athos, 'seeing that he had the silly curiosity to know my real name; but if I had pocketed his pistoles, they would have weighed me down with remorse.'

'Well, my dear Athos, you really have an inconceivable delicacy,' said d'Artagnan.

'Let it pass! But what was M. de Treville saying, when he did me the honour to call and see me yesterday—that you frequent the house of these suspicious English people, whom the cardinal protects?'

'That is to say, that I frequent the house of an English-woman—she of whom I spoke to you.'

'Ah, yes, the fair woman, about whom I gave you some advice, which, naturally enough, you took especial care not to follow.'

'I gave you my reasons. But I am now certain that this woman had something to do with the disappearance of Madame Bonancieux.'

'Yes, I comprehend; to find one woman, you make love to another. It is the longest way, but by far the most amusing.'

We will now leave the two friends, who had nothing very important to say to one another, and follow Aramis.

On entering his room, he found a little man, with intelligent eyes, but covered with rags.

'Is it you who want me?' said the musketeer.

'I am in search of M. Aramis: is that the name by which you are called?'

'Yes. Have you anything for me?'

'Yes, if you can show me a certain embroidered handkerchief.'

'Here it is,' said Aramis, taking a key from his bosom, and opening a small ebony casket, inlaid with mother-of-pearl. 'Here it is. Look!'

'That is right,' said the beggar; 'now dismiss your servant.'

For, in fact, Bazin, curious to know what the beggar wanted with his master, had kept pace with the latter, and arrived almost at the same time. But his speed was of little benefit to him. At the suggestion of the beggar, his master made a sign to him to withdraw, and he had no alternative but to obey.

When Bazin was gone, the beggar glanced rapidly around, to be sure that nobody could either see or hear him, and then, opening his ragged vest, which was badly held together by a leathern belt, he began to unrip the top of his doublet, from which he drew a letter.

Aramis uttered a cry of joy at sight of the seal, kissed the writing, and, with a respect almost religious, opened the letter, which contained the following:—

'My Friend, Fate wills that we be separated for a little longer time, but the bright days of youth are not for ever lost. Do your duty in the camp: I will do mine elsewhere. Take what the bearer will give you; make the campaign like a good and graceful gentleman; and still remember me. Farewell, until we meet again.'

The beggar was yet engaged unripping: he drew from his dirty clothes, one by one, a hundred and fifty double Spanish pistoles, which he placed in a row upon the table; then he opened the door, bowed, and was gone before the astonished young man had dared to address a word to him.

Aramis now perused the letter again, and perceived that it had the following postscript:—

'*P.S.*—You may welcome the bearer, who is a count, and a grandee of Spain.'

'Golden dreams!' exclaimed Aramis; 'oh! heavenly life! yes, we are still young! yes, we shall still bask in brighter days! Oh! thou art my love, my life-blood, my being! All in all, art thou, my beautiful beloved!'

And he kissed the letter passionately, without even glancing at the gold which glittered on the table.

Bazin was scratching at the door, and, Aramis, as he had now no reason for keeping him away, permitted him to enter.

Bazin was confounded at the sight of so much gold, and forgot that he ought to announce d'Artagnan, who, curious to know what this beggar-man was, had come on to Aramis's when he left Athos.

But d'Artagnan never stood on ceremony with Aramis; and therefore, seeing that Bazin had forgotten to announce him, he announced himself.

'Ah, the deuce! my dear Aramis,' said he, on entering, 'these are the plums they send you from Tours: you must forward my congratulations on them to the gardener who gathers them.'

'You are mistaken, my dear fellow,' said the ever-discreet Aramis; 'it is my publisher, who has just sent me the price of my poem, in verses of one syllable, which I began down in the country.'

'Ah! really?' said d'Artagnan. 'Well, all I can say, my dear Aramis, is, that your publisher is very generous.'

'What, sir,' said Bazin, 'does a poem sell for such a sum? It is inconceivable! Oh, sir, you may do whatever you desire—you may become equal to M. Voiture, and M. de Benserade. I like that now, myself. A poet! It is almost an abbé. Ah, sir, establish yourself, then, as a poet, I beseech you!'

'Bazin, my friend,' said Aramis, 'I think that you are interposing in the conversation.'

Bazin understood that he was wrong, bowed his head, and left the room.

'Ah!' said d'Artagnan, with a smile, 'you sell your productions for their weight in gold! You are fortunate, my friend! But take care, or you will lose that letter, which is falling out of your coat, and which, without doubt, is also from your publisher.'

Aramis blushed to the very white of his eyes, replaced the letter, and buttoned up his doublet.

'My dear d'Artagnan,' said he, 'we will, if you please, go to our friends; and, as I am now so rich, we will begin to dine together again, till you become, in turn, rich yourselves.'

'Faith, and with great pleasure,' replied d'Artagnan; 'it is a long time since we have had a proper dinner; and as I have myself rather a hazardous expedition this evening, I shall not be sorry, I confess, to have two or three bottles of old Burgundy mounting up into my head.'

'Well, as for old Burgundy, I do not hate it myself, either,' said Aramis, out of whose head the sight of the gold had driven all thoughts of retirement.

And, having put three or four double pistoles into his pocket for present use, he enclosed the remainder in the ebony casket, incrusted with pearl, which already contained the famous handkerchief that had served him as a talisman.

The two friends went first to Athos, who, faithful to his vow not to go from home, undertook to have the dinner brought to his own rooms. As he was marvellously familiar with all gastronomical details, d'Artagnan and Aramis, had no hesitation in confiding to him this important care.

They then went to Porthos; but, at the corner of the Rue du Bac, they met Mousqueton, who, with a most piteous face, was driving a mule and a horse before him.

D'Artagnan uttered an exclamation of surprise, not unmingled with joy.

'Ah! my yellow horse!' cried he. 'Aramis, look at this horse!'

'Oh, what a frightful beast!' exclaimed Aramis.

'Well, my dear boy, it is the horse on which I came to Paris.'

'What, sir, do you know the horse?' inquired Mousqueton.

'He certainly is of a most original colour,' said Aramis. 'I never saw one with a hide like this before.'

'I can well believe it,' replied d'Artagnan; 'and I sold

him for three crowns, which must have been for the hide, for certainly the carcass is not worth eighteen livres. But how do I find this horse in your hands, Mousqueton?'

'Ah,' said the valet, 'do not say anything about it, sir. It is a horrible trick of our duchess's husband.'

'How so?'

'Yes, we are looked upon most favourably, by a woman of quality, the duchess of——. But, excuse me, my master has enjoined me to be discreet. She obliged us to accept a small souvenir—a magnificent Spanish charger, and an Andalusian mule, which were most marvellous to behold. But the husband found it out, kidnapped, on their way, the two magnificent animals, and substituted these frightful beasts for them.'

'And are you taking them back to him?'

'Yes, exactly so, sir,' replied Mousqueton. 'You know it is impossible for us to accept such frights as these, instead of those which had been promised us.'

'No, egad! though I should have enjoyed seeing Porthos on my yellow horse. It would have given me some idea of what I was myself when I came to Paris. But do not let us detain you, Mousqueton. Go and execute your master's commission: go. Is he at home?'

'Yes, sir,' said Mousqueton, 'but in a very bad humour.'

He then continued on his way towards the quay of the Grands-Augustins, whilst the two friends went to ring at the unfortunate Porthos's door. But the latter had seen them crossing the court, and was careful not to admit them. So their ringing was in vain.

In the meantime, Mousqueton proceeded on, and, crossing the Pont-Neuf—still driving the two sorry beasts before him—he reached the Rue aux Ours, where, in accordance with his master's orders, he fastened the horse and the mule to the knocker of the attorney's door; and then, without disturbing himself about their future fate, he returned to find Porthos, and inform him that his commission had been exactly fulfilled.

After some time, the two unhappy beasts, having eaten nothing since the morning, made so great a noise, by lifting up and letting fall the knocker, that the attorney ordered his stump-in-the-gutter to inquire in the neighbourhood to whom this horse and mule belonged.

Madame Coquenard recognised her present, and could not, at first, at all comprehend this restitution. But a visit from Porthos soon enlightened her. The rage which, in spite of the constraint that he imposed upon himself, sparkled in the musketeers' eyes, alarmed his susceptible admirer. In fact, Mousqueton had not concealed from his master that he had met d'Artagnan and Aramis; and that the former had recognised, in the yellow horse, the very Bearnese nag on which he had arrived in Paris, and which he had sold for three crowns.

Porthos left again, as soon as he had made an appointment to meet the attorney's wife in the cloister of St. Magliore. When her husband saw that Porthos was really leaving, he invited him to dinner—an invitation which the musketeer declined with an air of majestic dignity.

Madame Coquenard trembled as she went towards the cloister St. Magloire, for she anticipated the reproaches that awaited her there. But she was fascinated by the lofty manners of Porthos.

All the imprecations and reproaches that a man, whose vanity is wounded, can pour upon a woman's head, were poured by Porthos on the humble head of the attorney's wife.

'Alas!' said she, 'I did it all for the best. One of our clients is a horse-dealer: he owed us money, and was manifestly reluctant to pay; so I took this mule and horse in discharge of his debt. But he had promised me two royal animals.'

'Well, madame,' said Porthos, 'if his debt was more than five crowns, your horse-dealer is a swindler.'

'It is not forbidden one to look out for a good bargain, M. Porthos,' said the attorney's wife, by way of excuse.

'No, madame; but those who look out for good bargains ought to permit others to look out for more generous friends.'

And, turning on his heel, Porthos made a step toward retiring.

'M. Porthos! M. Porthos!' exclaimed the attorney's wife, 'I confess that it was wrong: I ought not to have thought of bargaining about the equipment of a gentleman like you.'

Without replying, Porthos took a second step toward retiring.

The attorney's wife fancied that she saw him in a glittering hemisphere, encompassed by duchesses and marchionesses, who scattered bags of gold before his feet.

'Stay! in Heaven's name, stay, M. Porthos!' exclaimed she; 'stay, and let us talk it over.'

'To talk with you brings me misfortune,' said Porthos.

'But, tell me, what do you require?'

'Nothing; for that amounts to the same thing as though I required something of you.'

The attorney's wife hung on Porthos's arm, and, in the violence of her grief, exclaimed—

'M. Porthos, I am completely ignorant about all these things. What can I know about a horse! What can I know about equipments!'

'You should leave it to me, then, who do know about them, madame. But you wanted to get things cheap, that you might lend at usury.'

'It was wrong, M. Porthos; and I will give you reparation, on my word of honour.'

'And how so?' demanded the musketeer.

'Listen. M. Coquenard is going this evening to the Duke de Chaulnes, who has sent for him. It is to a consultation which will last at least two hours. Come, then; we shall be alone, and can arrange the business.'

'Good. That is something.'

'And you will pardon me?'

'We shall see,' replied Porthos majestically.

They parted from each other, both repeating—'till this evening!'

'I'faith!' thought Porthos, as he went his away, 'I seem now to be making some approaches towards M. Coquenard's strong-box.'

35

All Cats are alike Gray in the Dark

THE evening, so impatiently expected by d'Artagnan, at length arrived.

At about nine o'clock he went, as usual, to her ladyship's, and, as he found her in a charming humour, he was received more graciously than ever. Our Gascon saw, at the first glance, that the pretended note of the Count de Wardes had been delivered by Kitty to her mistress, and that it was producing its effect.

Kitty came in with some confections. Her mistress looked at her kindly, and smiled on her with her most gracious smile; but the poor girl was so concerned that she did not even notice the latter's good-will.

D'Artagnan looked by turns at these two women, and could not but confess that nature had committed a mistake in their formation: to the great lady she had given a venal and perfidious soul; and, to the waiting-maid, a loving and devoted heart.

At ten o'clock her ladyship began to appear uneasy, and d'Artagnan soon guessed the meaning of her trouble. She looked at the timepiece, got up, sat down again, and smiled at d'Artagnan, with a look which seemed to say—'you are very amiable, no doubt, but you would be charming if you would go.'

D'Artagnan arose, and took his hat, and then her ladyship gave him her hand to kiss. The young man was sensible of a gentle pressure, which he attributed, not to coquetry, but to gratitude on account of his departure.

'She loves him madly!' muttered he, as he went out.

On this occasion Kitty was not awaiting him, either in the antechamber, in the corridor, or at the gate; and d'Artagnan had to discover, alone, the staircase and the little chamber.

Kitty was sitting with her face hid between her hands, crying. She heard d'Artagnan enter, but did not lift up her head. The young man went to her, and took her hands, and then she burst out crying.

As d'Artagnan had suspected, her ladyship, on receiving the letter which she regarded as the Count de Warde's reply, had, in the delirium of her joy, made her waiting-maid acquainted with the whole, and then, as a recompense for the manner in which her mission had been executed, given her a purse of gold.

Kitty, on returning to her own room, had thrown the purse into a corner, where it was lying open, disgorging three or four golden coins upon the carpet.

When at last the poor girl, at d'Artagnan's entreaty, raised her head, he was struck with alarm at the expression of her face. She clasped her hands together with a supplicating air, but without venturing to speak a word.

Little sensitive as was d'Artagnan's heart, he was yet affected by this silent grief. But he was too positive in all his projects, and especially in this one, to deviate at all from his ordained arrangement. He would not give to Kitty the least hope of hindering the rash enterprise on which he had resolved; but he represented it to her as what it really was —that is, as an act of simple vengeance against her ladyship's coquetry; and as the only means which he possessed of obtaining, from her dread of the scandal of exposure, the information that he wanted in respect to Madame Bonancieux.

This plan, further, became the more easy in its execution, from her ladyship having, from some inexplicable motive, to which she appeared to attach extreme importance, commanded Kitty to extinguish all the lights in her apartment, as well as in the abigail's own chamber.

An instant afterwards, her ladyship was heard returning to her chamber. D'Artagnan immediately hurried into his press. Scarcely was he blockaded in it, before the bell rang.

Kitty went to her mistress, and did not leave the door open; but the partition was so thin, that the conversation of the two women was almost wholly audible.

Her ladyship seemed to be intoxicated with joy. She made Kitty repeat to her the most triffling details of her pretended interview with de Wardes, and tell her how he had received her letter, and how he answered it; what was the expression of his face, and whether he seemed much enamoured: and, to all these questions, poor Kitty, who was compelled to keep a good countenance, answered in a stifled voice, of which her mistress, so egotistical is felicity, did not even observe the disconsolate tone.

As the hour of her interview with the count approached, her ladyship had all the lights in her own room actually extinguished, and commanded Kitty to return to her chamber, and to introduce de Wardes as soon as he arrived.

Kitty had not long to wait. Hardly had d'Artagnan seen, through the key-hole of his press, that the whole apartment was in darkness, before he sprang from his dungeon, at the very moment that Kitty closed the communicating door.

'What is that noise?' inquired my lady.

'It is I,' whispered d'Artagnan—'I, the Count de Wardes.'

'Oh, my God! my God!' groaned Kitty, 'he could not even wait for the hour he himself had fixed.'

'Well!' said the lady in a trembling voice, 'why does he not come in? Count, count,' she added, 'you know that I am waiting for you.'

At this appeal, d'Artagnan put Kitty gently aside, and sprang into her ladyship's chamber.

If rage and grief can ever torture the soul, it must be those of the lover who receives, under a name that is not his own, protestations of affection which are addressed to his favoured rival.

D'Artagnan was in a situation of which he had not calculated the suffering: jealousy was gnawing at his heart; and he had to endure almost as much as poor Kitty, who was at the same time weeping in the adjoining chamber.

'Yes, count,' said her ladyship, in her sweetest tones, as she tenderly pressed one of his hands between her own; 'yes I am happy in the love which your glances and words have expressed whenever we have met. And I, too, return your love. Ah! to-morrow you must let me have some souvenir, which will prove you think of me; and, as you might forget me, count, keep this.'

And she slipped a ring from her own finger on that of d'Artagnan.

It was a magnificent sapphire, encircled by diamonds.

The first emotion of d'Artagnan prompted him to return it; but her ladyship added—

'No, no; keep this ring for love of me. Besides,' added she in a voice of much emotion, 'you really do me a far greater service by accepting it than you can possibly imagine.'

'This woman is full of mystery,' thought d'Artagnan.

He felt himself at this moment ready to confess everything. He had, in fact, already opened his mouth to tell her ladyship who he was, and with what desire of vengeance he had come, when she added—

'Poor angel! whom that monster of a Gascon just missed killing.'

That monster was he himself.

'Oh!' continued her ladyship, 'do you still suffer from your wounds?'

'Yes, greatly,' answered d'Artagnan, who was somewhat at a loss what to say.

'Depend upon it,' muttered her ladyship, in a tone which gave but little comfort to her hearer, 'that I will take a cruel vengeance on him for your sufferings.'

'Egad!' said d'Artagnan to himself, 'the time for my confession is scarcely come yet.'

It required some little time for d'Artagnan to recover himself from this little dialogue. All the ideas of vengeance which he had brought with him had completely vanished. This woman exercised an inconceivable power over him: he hated and adored her at one and the same time. Never had he believed that two sentiments so inconsistent could exist together in the same heart, or create, by commingling, such a strange, and, in some respects, diabolical love.

But the clock had struck one, and it was time for them to separate. At the moment of quitting her ladyship, d'Artagnan was only sensible of a deep regret at having parted from her; and in the passionate adieu which they reciprocally addressed to one another, a new meeting was agreed upon in the ensuing week.

Poor Kitty hoped to have an opportunity of saying a few words to d'Artagnan as he passed through her chamber, but her mistress led him out herself in the darkness, and only left him when they reached the staircase.

In the morning of the next day, d'Artagnan hastened to Athos; for, being engaged in such a singular adventure, he wished for his advice. He told him everything; and Athos's brow was often knitted during the narration.

'Your lady,' said he, 'appears to me to be an infamous creature; but you are not, on that account, the less wrong in thus deceiving her. You may now be sure that, in one way or another, you will have a bitter enemy with whom to deal.'

Whilst still speaking, Athos looked earnestly at the sapphire, encircled with diamonds, which d'Artagnan now wore in the place of the queen's ring, which was carefully deposited in a case.

'You are looking at this ring?' said the Gascon, proud of displaying before his friends such a splendid gift.

'Yes,' replied Athos; 'it reminds me of a family jewel.'

'It is beautiful, is it not?' said d'Artagnan.

'Magnificent!' rejoined Athos; 'I did not believe that there were two sapphires existent of so fine a water. Did you exchange your diamond for it?'

'No,' replied d'Artagnan; 'it is a present from my beautiful Englishwoman, or, rather, my beautiful Frenchwoman—for, although I have not asked her, I am sure she was born in France.'

'And this ring was given to you by her ladyship,' said Athos, in a voice in which it was easy to perceive extreme emotion.

'Yes, by herself: she gave it to me last night.'

'Let me look at it,' said Athos.

'Here it is,' said d'Artagnan, drawing it from his finger.

Athos examined it, and became very pale; he then tried it on the ring-finger of his left hand, and it fitted as if it had been made for him.

A shade of anger and revenge passed across the generally calm forehead of the gentleman.

'It is impossible that it can be the same,' said he. 'How could this ring come into the hands of that lady? And yet it is very strange that two jewels should be so singularly alike.'

'Do you know that ring?' asked d'Artagnan.

'I thought I recognised it,' said Athos, 'but I dare say I am deceived.'

He then returned the ring to d'Artagnan, without, however, ceasing to fix his gaze upon it.

'Let me entreat you,' said he, an instant afterwards, 'either to take that ring from your finger, or to turn the stone inside: it summons up to me such painful remembrances, that I should not be collected enough for any conversation. Did you not come to ask my advice: did you not say that you were in a difficulty as to what to do? But stop, let me look at that sapphire again? The one I mentioned had one of its surfaces scratched by an accident.'

D'Artagnan again drew off the ring, and handed it to Athos.

Athos trembled. 'Look,' said he, 'look! Is it not strange?' And he pointed out to d'Artagnan the scratch that he remembered should be there.

'But whence came this sapphire, Athos?'

'It was my mother's, who had received it from her mother. As I told you, it is an ancient jewel, which ought never to have gone out of the family.'

'And you—sold it?' demanded d'Artagnan, with some hesitation.

'No,' replied Athos, with a singular smile; 'I gave it away, during a moment of love, even as it was given to you.'

D'Artagnan grew pensive in his turn. He thought that he could discern, in her ladyship's life, abysses which were black and terrible in their depths.

He put the ring, not on his finger, but into his pocket.

'Listen,' said Athos, taking the young man's hand. 'You know how much I love you, d'Artagnan. Had I a son, I could not love him more dearly. Well, take my advice—renounce this woman. I do not know her; but a kind of intuition tells me that she is a lost creature, and that there is something fatal in her.'

'You are right,' said d'Artagnan, 'and I *will* renounce her. I will confess that this woman frightens even me.'

'And will you have the resolution?' asked Athos.

'Yes; and at once, too,' replied d'Artagnan.

'You are quite right, my dear d'Artagnan,' said Athos, pressing his hand with an affection almost paternal; 'and God grant that this woman, who has scarcely been a part of your existence, may leave no pestilential trace upon it!'

And Athos bowed his head, like a man who would rather be left to his own thoughts.

On reaching home, d'Artagnan found Kitty awaiting him.

A month of fever would not have made a greater change in the poor girl than had been produced by an hour of jealousy and grief.

She had been sent by her mistress to the Count de Wardes.

Her mistress was mad with love—intoxicated with joy: she wanted to know when the count would accord her a second interview.

The pale and trembling Kitty waited there for d'Artagnan's reply.

Athos had considerable influence over the young man. The counsels of his friend, co-operating with the sentiments of d'Artagnan's own heart, and with the memory of Madame Bonancieux, which was but rarely absent from him, had made him resolve, now that his pride was saved, to see her ladyship no more. As his only answer, he took a pen and wrote the following letter, which he sent, as he had done the preceding one, unsigned:—

'Do not reckon any more on me, madame. Now that I am becoming convalescent, I have so many interviews of the same kind to grant, that I must put them into some regular order. When your turn comes round, I shall have the honour to inform you. I kiss your hands.'

Not a word was said about the sapphire; the Gascon wished to keep it for the present, as a weapon against her ladyship.

It would be wrong to judge of the actions of one age by the habits of another. The conduct which would now be regarded as a disgrace to a man of honour, was, at that time, quite simple and natural.

D'Artagnan handed the open letter to Kitty, who read it at first without understanding it, and who very nearly went mad, when she read it a second time.

Kitty scarcely could believe in such happiness; and d'Artagnan was obliged to repeat to her, verbally, the assurance which the letter gave in writing. Whatever might be the danger which, on account of the passionate character of her mistress, the poor girl incurred in delivering such a note to her ladyship, she none the less ran back, as fast as her legs could carry her, to the Place Royale.

The heart of the kindest woman is pitiless towards a rival's pains.

Her ladyship opened the letter with an eagerness equal to that with which the abigail had brought it; but at the first words that she read, she became actually livid: then, she crushed the letter in her hand, and turned, with lightning in her eyes, to Kitty.

'What is this letter?' said she.

'It is the answer to your ladyship's,' said the trembling Kitty.

'Impossible!' exclaimed the lady; 'impossible, that a gentleman should have written such a letter to a lady!'

Then, suddenly, she cried—

'My God! could he know——'

She checked herself, shuddering. She ground her teeth—her face was of an ashy colour. She endeavoured to take a step towards the window for air, but she could only stretch out her arms: her strength failed her, and she sank back into an easy-chair.

Kitty, thinking she was fainting, rushed forward to open her corset. But, raising herself up suddenly, she exclaimed—

'What do you want? why do you touch me?'

'I thought your ladyship was ill, and I wished to assist you,' replied the poor damsel, frightened at the terrible expression which the countenance of her mistress had assumed.

'*I* unwell! Do you take me for a weak woman? When I am insulted, I do not feel unwell—I avenge myself! Do you hear?'

And she motioned to leave the room.

The Dream of Vengeance

IN the evening, her ladyship gave orders that M. d'Artagnan should be admitted as usual, as soon as he should come. But he came not.

On the next morning Kitty went again to see d'Artagnan, and told him all that had occurred on the previous day. D'Artagnan smiled. This jealous anger of her ladyship was his revenge.

The patience of the indignant lady had increased by night. She renewed her orders relative to the young Gascon; but, as on the preceding evening, her hopes were in vain.

On the next morning Kitty visited d'Artagnan. She was, however, no longer joyous and alert, as on the previous days, but, on the contrary, overcome with grief.

D'Artagnan inquired of the poor girl what ailed her; but the latter, as her sole reply, drew from her pocket a letter, which she handed to him.

This letter was in her ladyship's handwriting: only, on this occasion, it was really meant for d'Artagnan, and not for M. de Wardes.

He opened it, and read as follows:—

'DEAR M. D'ARTAGNAN,

'It is wrong thus to neglect your friends, especially when about to part for so long a time. I and my brother looked for you in vain, both yesterday and the day before. Will it be the same this evening?

'Your very grateful,
'LADY DE WINTER.'

'This is all very plain,' said d'Artagnan, 'and I expected this letter. My credit rises as that of the Count de Wardes falls.'

'And will you go?' asked Kitty.

'Listen my dear child,' replied the Gascon, who sought to excuse himself in his own eyes for failing in his promise to Athos. 'You must see that it would be imprudent to refuse so imperative an invitation. Her ladyship, on seeing that I kept away, would wonder at the cessation of my visits, and might perhaps suspect something. And who can tell the limits of such a woman's vengeance?'

'Oh, mon Dieu!' exclaimed Kitty, 'you know how to represent things in such a way that you are always right. But you will go and pay your court to her again; and if you should happen to please her now, with your own face and under your true name, it will be far worse than before!' The poor girl guessed, by instinct, something of what was about to occur.

D'Artagnan comforted her as well as he was able, and promised her that he would remain insensible to her ladyship's seductions.

He sent word, by way of answer, that he was as grateful as man could be for her ladyship's kindness, and that he would not fail to wait upon her as she commanded; but he did not venture to write to her, lest, to her experienced eyes, he should be unable to disguise his handwriting sufficiently.

At nine o'clock d'Artagnan was at the Place Royale. It was obvious that the servants, who were waiting in the antechamber, had already received their orders; for, as soon as he had appeared, before he had even inquired if her ladyship was to be seen, one of them hastened to announce him.

'Show him in,' said my lady, in a voice so piercing that he heard it in the antechamber.

He was at once admitted.

'Not at home to anybody,' said her ladyship; 'do you hear? Not to anybody.'

D'Artagnan observed the lady with great curiosity. She was pale, and her eyes were heavy, either from weeping or from want of sleep. The customary lights in the room had been designedly diminished in number; and yet the young woman could not conceal the traces of the fever which had been consuming her for two days. D'Artagnan approached her with his usual gallantry; and she made a mighty effort to receive him, but never did a more agitated face contradict a more enchanting smile.

To d'Artagnan's questions respecting her health, she replied—

'Bad, very bad.'

'Then,' said d'Artagnan, 'I am indiscreet in coming: you

are unquestionably in want of a little peace, and I will immediately retire.'

'No,' said her ladyship, 'remain, M. d'Artagnan. Your pleasing company will, on the contrary, give me great relief.'

'She has never been so charming before,' thought d'Artagnan; 'let me keep upon my guard.'

Her ladyship assumed the most affectionate air possible, and gave the utmost charm to her conversation. At the same time that fever, which had for a moment left her, returned, to restore the lustre to her eyes, the roses to her cheeks, and the carmine to her lips. D'Artagnan again saw the Circé who had already encompassed him with her enchantments. Her ladyship smiled, and he felt that he would dare perdition for that smile.

There was a moment, during which he experienced something like remorse for what he had contrived against her.

Her ladyship became, by degrees, more communicative. She asked d'Artagnan whether his heart were occupied by any love?

'Alas!' said he, assuming the most sentimental manner that he could, 'how can you be so cruel as to ask me such a question—me, who, ever since I first saw you, have only breathed and lived by you and for you?

The lady smiled most strangely.

'And so you love me?' said she.

'Need I tell you so now? And have you never perceived it?'

'Yes, I have; but, you know, the prouder hearts are, the more difficult they are to win.'

'Ah, no difficulties can ever daunt me,' replied d'Artagnan: 'my only fear is, of impossibilities.'

'Nothing is impossible,' said the lady, 'to one who truly loves.'

'Nothing, madame?'

'Nothing,' she replied.

'I'faith,' thought d'Artagnan, 'the time is changed. Will the capricious creature chance to fall in love with me; and will she be disposed to give me another sapphire, equal to that she gave me for de Wardes?'

'Come,' resumed her ladyship, 'let me hear what you would do to prove the love that you profess?'

'Everything that you can ask. Command; and I am ready to obey?'

'Everything?'

'Yes, everything!' exclaimed d'Artagnan, who knew beforehand that he did not risk much by such an engagement.

'Well, then, let us talk a little about it,' said she, drawing her chair nearer d'Artagnan.

'I am all attention, madame,' said the latter.

The lady paused for a moment, thoughtful and undecided; then, appearing to form her resolution, she said—

'I have an enemy.'

'You, madame!' cried d'Artagnan, feigning surprise. 'Mon Dieu! beautiful and good as you are, is it possible!'

'A mortal enemy!'

'Indeed?'

'An enemy who has so cruelly insulted me, that there is war to the death between us. Can I reckon upon you as an ally?'

D'Artagnan instantly perceived at what the vindictive creature was aiming.

'You can, madame,' said he emphatically. 'My arm and my life belong to you, as well as my love.'

'Well, then,' said her ladyship, 'since you are as generous as you are enamoured——' She hesitated.

'Well?' demanded d'Artagnan.

'Well,' resumed her ladyship, after a moment's silence, 'cease, from this day, to speak of impossibilities.'

'Do not overwhelm me with my happiness!' exclaimed d'Artagnan, throwing himself on his knees, and covering with kisses the hands which she abandoned to him.

'Yes!' thought the lady, 'avenge me on that wretch, de Wardes, and I shall easily get rid of you afterwards — double fool! living sword-blade!'

'Yes!' thought d'Artagann also, on his side, 'tell me that you love me, after having so audaciously deceived me; and then, dangerous and hypocritical woman! I will laugh at you, in concert with him whom you wish to punish by my hand.'

Raising his head, d'Artagnan said, 'I am ready.'

'You understand me, then, dear d'Artagnan?' said her ladyship.

'I can read your every look '

'Then you will, for me, employ that arm which has already gained such great renown?'

'Yes, instantly.'

'And how,' said her ladyship, 'shall I ever repay a service so important?'

'Your love is the only recompense that I desire—the only one that would be worthy either of you or me,' replied d'Artagnan.

'Infatuated creature!' said she, smiling.

'Ah!' exclaimed d'Artagnan, carried away for an instant by the passion which this woman had the power of exciting in his heart—'ah! your love appears to me improbable, and, fearful of seeing it vanish like a dream, I am impatient to receive from your own lips the assurance of its reality.'

'Do you already merit such an avowal?'

'I am at your command,' replied d'Artagnan.

'Are you quite determined?' said she, with a lingering doubt.

'Name the wretch who has drawn tears from your beautiful eyes!'

'And who has told you that there have been tears?' exclaimed she.

'I imagined so.'

'Women of my character never weep,' replied her ladyship.

'So much the better. But tell me his name?'

'Remember that his name is all my secret.'

'Yes I must know it.'

'Yes, you must. See what confidence I place in you.'

'You overpower me with joy! What is his name?'

'You know it.'

'Indeed!'

'Yes.'

'It is not one of my friends?' said he, feigning hesitation, as an evidence of his ignorance.

'And if it were one of your friends—would you hesitate?' said her ladyship, whilst a threatening flash was sparkling in her eyes.

'Not if it were my brother!' exclaimed d'Artagnan, as though carried away by enthusiasm.

Our Gascon advanced without danger, for he knew where he was going.

'I love your devotedness,' said the lady.

'Alas! do you love only that in me?' said d'Artagnan.

'I will tell you that another time,' replied she, taking his hand.

And this pressure made d'Artagnan tremble, as though the fever which her ladyship endured had also infected him.

'You will love me some day—you?' exclaimed he. 'Oh! if that should come to pass, the bliss will deprive me of reason!'

D'Artagnan was, in fact, intoxicated with joy; and in his temporary delirium, he almost believed in the tenderness of her ladyship, and in the crime of de Wardes. If the latter had been at that moment near him, he would have slain him.

The lady seized the opportunity.

'He is called——' she uttered, in her turn.

'De Wardes—I know it!' interrupted d'Artagnan.

'And how do you know it?' asked she, seizing his two hands and looking into his eyes, as if striving to read his very soul.

D'Artagnan felt that he had allowed himself to be led into a fault.

'Tell me, tell me, tell me, then,' she exclaimed, 'how do you know it?'

'How do I know it? repeated d'Artagnan.

'Yes!'

'I know it, because yesterday, in a drawing-room where I was, de Wardes displayed a ring, which he said you gave him.'

'The wretch!' exclaimed her ladyship.

It will easily be understood that this epithet resounded in the very depths of d'Artagnan's heart.

'Well?' continued she.

'Well, I will avenge you on this—wretch!' said d'Artagnan, giving himself the airs of Don Japhet of Armenia.

'Thanks, my brave friend!' exclaimed the lady. 'And when shall I be avenged?'

'To-morrow—immediately—whenever you command!'

Her ladyship was about to exclaim—'immediately!' but she reflected that such precipitation would be but little complimentary to d'Artagnan. She had, moreover, a thousand precautions to take, and a thousand counsels to impress on her defender, that he should avoid all explanations with the count in the presence of witnesses.

'To-morrow,' resumed d'Artagnan, 'you shall be revenged, or I shall no more exist.'

'No,' said she, 'you will revenge me, and you will not die. I know something in reference to that.'

'What do you know?'

'Why, it seems to me that, in your former contest with him, you had no reason to complain of fortune.'

'Fortune is a fickle jade: to-day, favourable; she may betray me to-morrow.'

'Does this mean, that you now hesitate?'

'No. I do not hesitate; God forbid! But——'

'Silence!' she interrupted; 'I hear my brother; it is inexpedient that he should find you here.'

She rang the bell, and Kitty entered.

'Go through this door,' said she to d'Artagnan, as she opened a small secret door, 'and return at eleven o'clock, when we can end this conversation. Kitty will conduct you to me.'

As the poor girl heard these few words, she felt as if she would sink into the earth.

'Well! what are you about, mademoiselle, that you stand there as motionless as a statue? Come, show this gentleman out!—Remember, at eleven to-night.'

'It appears that all your appointments are for eleven o'clock,' thought d'Artagnan: 'it is a confirmed habit.'

The lady gave him her hand, which he kissed with tenderness.

'Well,' thought he, as he went away, scarcely replying to the reproaches of Kitty, 'well, I must not make a fool of myself: unquestionably this woman is an abominable wretch: I must be on my guard!'

37

The Lady's Secret

D'ARTAGNAN had gone out of the hotel, instead of at once ascending to Kitty's room, there to wait for the hour of his appointment with her ladyship. He had two reasons for adopting this course: the first was, that, by this means, he avoided the recriminations and entreaties of the girl; and the second was, that he wished coolly to reflect on the secret thought of the lady, and, if possible, to penetrate it.

What seemed to him most certain, was, that he was exposing himself to love her ladyship like a madman; whilst she, on the other hand, did not love him the least in the world, and never would. At one time he considered that the best thing to do would be to return home, and write a long letter to her ladyship, in which he would confess, that, as far as he was concerned, he and de Wardes were the same individual, and, consequently, that it was only by suicide he could kill the de Wardes by whom she thought herself injured; but—with the conviction that she would still detest him, and would regard him only as a vile instrument of vengeance, that she could break when it had served her turn—the yearning to avenge himself returned to his heart. He longed to rule over the woman who had trifled with and insulted him, and wounded him also, in his sincere and pure love, by becoming an accomplice in the abduction of Madame Bonancieux.

He went five or six times round the Place Royale, agitated by all these conflicting emotions, and returning every ten paces to regard the light which was still visible through the blinds of her ladyship's apartment. It was manifest that she was not, on this occasion, in such eager haste to return into her chamber.

At length it struck eleven. This sound drove all irresolution from d'Artagnan's heart. He recalled each detail of the interview which he had just had with her ladyship; and, by one of those revulsions so common in similar cases, he entered the house with his heart palpitating, and his head on fire, and rushed into Kitty's room.

The poor girl, pale as death, and trembling in every limb, would have kept d'Artagnan back; but her mistress, with her ear on the watch, had heard the noise he had made in entering, and opened the door.

'Come,' said she.

D'Artagnan was no longer sane. He felt himself entangled in one of those fantastic intrigues which are ours in dreams. He advanced towards her ladyship, attracted by the magnetic power which the loadstone exercises over the steel.

The door was closed behind them.

Kitty, in her turn, rushed forwards to the door.

Jealousy, and fury, and offended pride—all the passions, in a word, which rule the heart of an enamoured woman— impelled her to a confession. But she would be herself ruined, if she confessed her participation in such a machination; and, above all, d'Artagnan would be for ever lost to her. This last thought of love still urged her to the crowning sacrifice.

D'Artagnan, upon his side, had surrendered himself entirely to the inspiration of vanity. It was not now a rival who was loved in his person: it was himself, apparently, to whom the love was given. A secret voice, from the depths of his own heart, truly told him that he was only a weapon, which was caressed until it had inflicted death; but pride, and self-love, and folly, silenced this voice, and stifled this murmur; and besides, our Gascon, with the degree of confidence which we know him to possess, compared himself with de Wardes, and inquired why, taking one consideration with another, he should not be loved for himself alone.

Thanks to the influence of these thoughts, her ladyship ceased to be a woman of wicked dispositions, who had for a moment terrified him: she became a charming being, who promised to experience herself the love that she excited.

Nevertheless, the lady, who had not the same motives as d'Artagnan for forgetfulness, quickly drew him from his contemplations, and recalled him to the reality of their interview. She inquired whether the measures which were to bring about a meeting with de Wardes, on the next day, were, all definitely determined on, beforehand, in his own mind.

But d'Artagnan, whose ideas had taken quite another course, forgot himself, like a fool, and gallantly answered, that it was not in her presence, when he was occupied with nothing but the happiness of seeing and of hearing her, that he could think of duels with the sword.

This coldness, on the only subject which interested her, alarmed her ladyship, and her questions became more pressing.

Then d'Artagnan, who had never seriously thought of this impossible duel, endeavoured to turn the conversation, but found himself unable. Her ladyship kept the conference within the limits that she had herself traced beforehand, with her irresistible spirit, and her iron will.

D'Artagnan then thought himself very clever in endeavouring to persuade her to renounce, by forgiving de Wardes, the furious projects she had formed.

But, at the first words that he uttered, her countenance assumed a most repulsive expression.

'Are you afraid, dear M. d'Artagnan?' cried she in, a sharp and mocking voice, that sounded strangely in the young man's ears.

You cannot think so, my adored,' replied d'Artagnan; 'but what if this poor Count de Wardes was less culpable than you imagine?'

'In any case,' said her ladyship seriously, 'he has deceived me, and, from that moment, has deserved death.'

'Then he shall die, since you condemn him,' said d'Artagnan, in a tone so firm that it appeared to her ladyship the expression of an unconquerable devotion.

She smiled upon him once more.

'Yes, I am prepared,' continued d'Artagnan, with an involuntary excitement; 'but, first, there is one thing of which I would fain be sure.'

'What?' inquired the lady.

'That you love me!'

'Your presence here is a proof of that, I think,' replied she, feigning some embarrassment.

'Yes! And I am yours, body and soul. Dispose of my arm!'

'Thanks, my brave defender; and, even as I prove my love by admitting you here, you will, in your turn, prove yours—will you not?'

'Certainly. But, if you love me, as you say,' resumed d'Artagnan, 'do you not fear anything on my account?'

'What can I fear?'

'I might be dangerously wounded—killed even.'

'Impossible,' said the lady; 'you are so valiant a man, and so expert a swordsman.'

'Then you would not prefer,' resumed d'Artagnan, 'a method which would equally well revenge you, yet render the combat unnecessary?'

The lady looked at the young man in silence: her clear eyes had an expression singularly malevolent.

'Really,' said she, 'I verily believe that you are now faltering again.'

'No, I have no hesitation; but this poor de Wardes awakens my compassion, now that you no longer love him; and it appears to me that a man must be sufficiently punished by the loss of your love, without meriting further chastisement.'

'And who has told you that I ever loved him?' asked her ladyship.

'At least, I may believe, without any great folly, that you love another,' replied the young man gallantly, 'and I repeat, that I am interested in the count.'

'You?' demanded the lady. 'And why?'

'Because I alone know——'

'What?'

'That he has been far less culpable towards you than you think.'

'Really?' said the lady, with an uneasy look. 'Explain

yourself; for, upon my word, I cannot understand what you mean.'

And she looked at d'Artagnan with eyes which were gradually lighted up by a more baleful flame.

'Yes, I am a man of honour,' said d'Artagnan, determined now to finish what he had begun; 'and, since you have confessed your love for me, since I am quite sure of possessing it—for I possess it, do I not?'

'Entirely! But proceed.'

'Well, then, I find myself quite transformed, and a confession forces itself from me.'

'A confession?'

'If I doubted your love, I would not venture on it; but you do love me—do you not?'

'Undoubtedly!'

'Then, if through excess of love to you I had committed a fault, you would forgive me?'

'Perhaps so. But this confession,' said she, becoming pale—'what is this confession?'

'You had an interview with de Wardes, last Thursday, in this very chamber, had you not?'

'I? No! it is not true,' said the lady, in a tone so firm, and with a countenance so impassive, that, had d'Artagnan not possessed such perfect certainty, he must have doubted.

'Do not lie, my beauteous angel,' said d'Artagnan, endeavouring to smile; 'it is quite useless.'

'What do you mean? Speak, now, for you kill me!'

'Oh! be at ease you are not culpable towards me, and I have already forgiven you.'

'What next—what next?'

'De Wardes has nothing to boast of.'

'How? You told me yourself that this ring——'

'That ring, I myself have! The de Wardes of Thursday, and the d'Artagnan of to-day, are the same person.'

The imprudent young man expected a surprise, mixed with bashfulness—a little storm, which would dissolve in tears; but he strangely deceived himself, and his error was quickly apparent.

Pale and terrible, her ladyship raised herself up, and pushing away d'Artagnan, who was near her, by a violent blow on the chest, sought to hasten from him.

D'Artagnan restrained her by her robe, in order to implore her pardon. But, with a powerful and resolute effort, she endeavoured to escape. In this effort, her robe gave way near the corset; and then, one of her beautiful shoulders being uncovered, d'Artagnan, with inexpressible horror, perceived upon it the fleur-de-lis—that indelible mark impressed by the degrading hand of the executioner.

'Great God!' exclaimed he, letting fall the robe; and he remained mute, motionless, and rooted to his place.

But the lady felt herself denounced, even by d'Artagnan's horror. Doubtless he had seen everything. The young man now knew her secret—that terrible secret, of which the whole world was ignorant, except him!

She turned, no longer like a mere furious woman, but like a wounded panther.

'Ah, wretch!' said she, 'you have betrayed me like a coward; and, moreover, you have learned my secret! You must die!'

And she ran to an inlaid cabinet on her toilet table, opened it with a feverish, trembling hand, drew from it a small dagger, with a golden hilt and a sharp and slender blade, and returned with one bound to the side of d'Artagnan, her vesture in pieces.

Although the young man was, as we know, brave, he was frightened at that convulsed countenance, at those horrible dilated pupils, at those pale cheeks, and bleeding lips: he arose, and recoiled, as from the approach of a serpent that had crawled towards him; and, instinctively putting his perspiring hand to his sword, he drew it from the sheath.

But, without being at all dismayed at the sight of the sword, her ladyship still advanced towards him to strike him, and only stopped when she felt the sharp point upon her bossom.

Then she attempted to seize the sword in her hands; but d'Artagnan always withheld it from her grasp, by pointing it, without touching her, sometimes at her eyes, and sometimes at her breast; whilst he still retreated, endeavouring to find the door which opened into Kitty's room. During all this time, her ladyship was rushing at him in horrible transports of rage, and howling in a fearful manner.

Nevertheless, as this was ending in a strong resemblance to a duel, d'Artagnan gradually recovered his coolness.

'Well done! beautiful lady, well done!' said he; 'but, for God's sake, be calm, or I will draw a second fleur-de-lis on the other shoulder.'

'Wretch! wretch!' vociferated her ladyship.

But d'Artagnan, still seeking the door, maintained himself on the defensive.

At the noise that they made by overturning the furniture —she to get at him, and he to get behind it, out of the way—Kitty opened the door. D'Artagnan, who had never ceased manœuvring to get near this door, was only three paces from it. With one bound, therefore, he sprang out of the lady's chamber into that of her maid, and, as quick as lightning, closed the door again, and leaned against it with his whole weight, whilst Kitty fastened the bolts.

Her ladyship then endeavoured, with a force far beyond the strength of an ordinary woman, to break down the barriers which confined her in her own room; but, finding this impossible, she stabbed the door with her dagger, sometimes penetrating the entire thickness of the panels. Each blow was accompanied by some horrible imprecation.

'Quick, quick! Kitty,' said d'Artagnan in a whisper, when the bolts were fastened. 'Make haste to let me out of the hotel, or she will have me killed by the lackeys. Let us be quick, do you hear? For it is a matter of life and death.'

Kitty too well understood him. She drew him down the stairs in the darkness. And it was time. Her ladyship had already rung, and aroused the whole of her establishment. The porter drew the cord at Kitty's call, at the very instant that his mistress screamed from the window—'Do not open!'

The young man fled, whilst she still menaced him with an impotent gesture. At the same moment that she lost sight of him, she fell senseless in her chamber.

38

How, without disturbing himself, Athos obtained his Equipment

D'ARTAGNAN was so completely confounded, that, without considering what would become of Kitty, he ran through half of Paris, and did not stop till he found himself at Athos's door. The confusion of his mind, the terror which spurred him on, the shouts of some of the watch, who had pursued him, only made him the more expeditious in his progress. He traversed the court, mounted the two flights of stairs, and knocked as if he would break down the door.

Grimaud opened it, with his eyes swollen by sleep; and d'Artagnan rushed into the antechamber with such violence as almost to overthrow him as he passed.

This time, at any rate, in spite of his habitual taciturnity, Grimaud found his tongue, 'Hollo!' he cried, 'what do you want, hussy?' D'Artagnan then rid himself of the woman's hood and cloak given him to escape in, by Kitty. At the sight of d'Artagnan's naked sword, the poor fellow saw that he had to deal with a man—with some assassin, perhaps.

'Help, help! murder!' exclaimed he.

'Be silent, you unlucky dog!' said the young man; 'I am d'Artagnan. Do you not know me? Where is your master?'

'You, M. d'Artagnan!' exclaimed the panic-stricken Grimaud. 'Impossible!'

'Grimaud!' said Athos, as he quietly emerged from his chamber in his dressing-gown; 'Grimaud, I believe that you are permitting yourself to speak!'

'Ah! sir, it is because——'

'Silence!'

Grimaud then contented himself with pointing to d'Artagnan with his finger.

Athos, phlegmatic as he was, burst out into a fit of laughter, which was occasioned by d'Artagnan's wild appearance—hood askew, skirt falling, sleeves tucked up, moustache bristling!

'Do not laugh, my friend,' exclaimed d'Artagnan: 'in the name of Heaven, do not laugh! for, upon my soul, I assure you that there is nothing to laugh at.'

He uttered these words with so much solemnity, and with such undissembled horror, that Athos immediately seized his hands, saying—

'Are you wounded, my friend? You are very pale.'

'No; but something very terrible has just happened to me. Are you alone, Athos?'

'Sang Dieu! who would you expect to be with me at this time of night?'

'Good! good!'

And d'Artagnan hurried into Athos's chamber.

'Well, speak now,' said the latter, bolting the door: 'is the king dead? Have you killed the cardinal? You are altogether upset. Come, speak, for I am dying with anxiety.'

'Athos,' replied d'Artagnan, 'prepare to hear something perfectly incredible—unparalleled.'

'Speak, then, speak,' said Athos.

'Well, then,' continued d'Artagnan, bending towards Athos's ear, and whispering, 'her ladyship is branded with a fleur-de-lis upon her shoulder!'

'Ah!' exclaimed the musketeer, as if he had received a bullet in his heart.

'But are you quite sure,' continued d'Artagnan, 'that *the other* is really dead?'

'*The other!*' murmured Athos, in a voice so faint, as scarcely to be audible.

'Yes; she of whom you told me, one day, at Amiens?'

Athos groaned, and his head fell upon his hands.

'This one,' said d'Artagnan, 'is a woman of from twenty-six to twenty-eight years of age.'

'Blonde?' said Athos.

'Yes.'

'With clear blue eyes, of an uncommon brightness, and with black eyelashes and eyebrows?'

'Yes.'

'Tall, and well made? Has she also lost a tooth, near the eye-tooth, on the left side?'

'Yes.'

'The fleur-de-lis is small, of a red colour, and as if somewhat effaced by layers of paste applied to it?'

'Yes.'

'And yet you say that this woman is English?'

'She is called 'my lady,' but she may yet be a Frenchwoman: Lord de Winter is only her brother-in-law.'

'I must see her, d'Artagnan!'

'Take care, Athos, take care. You wished to kill her: she is a woman who would willingly pay you back, and is not likely to fail.'

'She dare not say a word—it would be denouncing herself.'

'She is equal to anything! Did you ever see her furious?'

'No,' said Athos.

'A tigress! a panther! Ah! my dear Athos, I fear that I have drawn down upon us both a terrible vengeance.'

D'Artagnan then recounted everything— the lady's maddened rage, and her menaces of death.

'You are quite right; and, upon my soul, I would sell my life for a hair,' said Athos. 'Happily, however, we leave Paris the day after to-morrow, and shall probably go to La Rochelle. Once off——'

'She will pursue you to the end of the world, Athos,

should she recognise you. Let her, then, vent her hatred on me alone.'

'Ah, my friend, what does it signify that she should kill me?' said Athos. 'Do you for an instant suppose that I am at all anxious to live?'

'There is some horrible mystery under all this, Athos, I am certain that this woman is one of the cardinal's spies.'

'In that case, take care of yourself. If the cardinal does not greatly admire you for that London affair, he hates you thoroughly; but as he has, all being considered, nothing to bring forward openly against you, and yet must gratify his revenge, take care of yourself. If you go out, do not go alone: if you eat, use every precaution: distrust everything, even your own shadow.'

'Happily,' said d'Artagnan, 'we only need to manage till to-morrow evening without accident; for, when once with the army, I hope that we shall only have men to fear.'

'In the meantime,' said Athos, 'I renounce my plan of seclusion, and shall go everywhere with you. You must return to the Rue des Fossoyeurs, and I will accompany you.'

'Be it so, my dear Athos; but first, let me return to you this ring, which I received from that woman. This sapphire is yours. Did you not tell me that it was a family jewel?'

'Yes; my father gave two thousand crowns for it, as he formerly told me; it was a part of the marriage present that he made my mother. It is magnificent. My mother gave it to me; and, instead of guarding it as a sacred relic—madman that I was!—I gave it to that wretch.'

'Well, take back your ring; for I understand that you must prize it.'

'*I* take it, after it has passed through that wretch's hands? Never! the ring is polluted, d'Artagnan.'

'Then sell it, or pledge it: you can borrow a thousand crowns on it. With that sum you will be well off; and then, with the first money you obtain, you can redeem it, cleansed of its ancient stains, since it will have passed through the hands of usurers.'

Athos smiled.

'You are a charming companion, my dear d'Artagnan,' said he; 'your eternal gaiety revives the souls of the afflicted. Well, then, let us pledge this ring of mine, but on one condition.'

'And what is that?'

'That you will have five hundred crowns, and I shall have five hundred.'

'But think a moment, Athos. I shall not want a quarter of that sum—I, who am only in the guards; and, by selling my saddles, I can easily procure it. What do I really want? A horse for Planchet—nothing more. Besides, you forget that I have a ring also.'

'Which you value even more than I do mine: at least I think that I have so observed.'

'Yes; for, in extremities, it might relieve us, not only from great embarrassment, but even from great danger. It is not only a simple diamond—it is also an enchanted talisman.'

'I do not understand you, yet I believe what you say. But, to return to my ring, or rather ours: you shall take half the sum it may produce, or I will throw it into the Seine; and I much doubt whether, as in the case of Polycrates, a fish would be so obliging as to restore it to us.'

'Well, then, I agree to it,' said d'Artagnan.

At this moment Grimaud came in, accompanied by Planchet, who was uneasy about his master, and anxious to know what had happened to him.

Athos dressed himself; and, when he was ready to go out, made the gesture of a man taking aim to Grimaud. The latter immediately took down his carbine, and prepared to follow his master.

D'Artagnan and Athos, attended by their servants, reached the Rue des Fossoyeurs in safety. M. Bonancieux was at his door, and looked at d'Artagnan with a bantering air.

'Hollo, my dear lodger,' said he, 'make haste. There is a pretty young girl waiting for you; and the women, you know, do not like to be kept waiting.'

'It is Kitty!' exclaimed d'Artagnan to himself, as he rushed towards the stairs.

In fact, on the landing-place before his apartment, and crouching against his door, he found the poor trembling girl. As soon as she saw him, she exclaimed—

'You promised me your protection—you promised to save me from her anger: remember, it is you who have ruined me?'

'Yes, certainly,' said d'Artagnan; 'make yourself easy about that, Kitty. But what happened after I was gone?'

'I can scarcely tell,' replied Kitty. 'At the outcries that she made, the lackeys ran to her. She was furious with passion. Whatever can be uttered in the way of imprecation, she vomited forth against you. Then, I thought she would remember that it was through my room that you had entered hers, and would take me for your accomplice; so I collected the little money that I had, and my most precious clothes, and ran hither for safety.'

'Poor child! But what am I to do with you? I am going off the day after to-morrow.'

'Anything you like, sir. Send me away from Paris— send me out of France.'

'But I cannot take you with me to the siege of La Rochelle,' said d'Artagnan.

'No; but you might place me in the service of some lady of your acquaintance—in your own province, for instance.'

'Ah! my child, in my own province the ladies have no waiting-maids. But wait; I know what I will do. Planchet, go to Aramis, and ask him to come here directly. We have matters of great importance to discuss with him.'

'I understand,' said Athos; 'but why not Porthos? It appears to me, that his marchioness——'

'Porthos's marchioness, sooner than keep a lady's-maid, would have her clothes put on by her husband's clerks,' said d'Artagnan, laughing. 'Besides, Kitty would rather not live in the Rue aux Ours! Would you, Kitty?'

'I will live where you please,' said Kitty, 'provided I am concealed, and that nobody knows where I am.'

'But, Kitty, now that we are going to be separated, and that you are therefore no longer jealous of me——'

'Sir,' interrupted Kitty, 'far or near, I shall never cease to love you.'

'Where the plague does constancy repair to nestle!' muttered Athos.

'And I, also,' said d'Artagnan—'I, also shall always love you, you may be sure. But, now, answer me. This question is one of great importance:—did you never hear anything said about a young woman who was abducted one night?'

'Wait a minute. Oh! Mon Dieu! sir! Do you still love that woman?'

'No. It is one of my friends who loves her. Yes—it is Athos there.'

'I!' exclaimed Athos, in a tone pretty much like that of the man who sees himself about to tread upon an adder.

'Yes, to be sure, you!' said d'Artagnan, pressing Athos's hand. 'You know the interest that we all take in that poor little Madame Bonancieux. Besides, Kitty will not tell—

will you, Kitty? You understand, my child,' exclaimed d'Artagnan, 'that she is the wife of that ugly ape whom you saw upon the doorstep, as you came in.'

'Oh, my God!' exclaimed Kitty, 'you remind me how frightened I was lest he should have recognised me!'

'How, *recognised!* Then you have seen this man before?'

'Yes, he came twice to my lady's.'

'As might be expected. About what time?'

'About a fortnight ago.'

'Just about the time.'

'And yesterday evening he came again.'

'Yesterday evening?'

'Yes, a minute before you came yourself.'

'My dear Athos, we are enveloped in a web of spies! And do you believe that he recognised you, Kitty?'

'I drew down my hood, when I saw him—but perhaps it was too late.'

'Go down, Athos—he suspects you less than me—and see whether he is still at the door.'

Athos went down, and returned immediately.

'He is gone,' said he, 'and the house is closed.'

'He is gone to make his report, and to say that all the pigeons are at this moment in the dovecot.'

'Well, then, let us be off,' said Athos, 'leaving only Planchet here to bring us intelligence.'

'Wait one instant! And what about Aramis, whom we have sent for?'

'True,' said Athos, 'let us wait for Aramis.'

An instant afterwards, Aramis entered. They explained the affair to him, and told him how urgent it was for him to find, amongst some of his high connections, a situation for Kitty.

'And will this really be a service to you, d'Artagnan?'

'I will be grateful for it for ever.'

'Well, then, Madame de Bois Tracy has requested me to find a trustworthy waiting-maid for one of her friends, who lives in the provinces; and if you, my dear d'Artagnan, can answer for the young woman——'

'Oh! sir,' exclaimed Kitty, 'I shall be entirely devoted, be assured, to the lady who will give me the means of leaving Paris.'

'Then,' said Aramis. 'nothing can be better.'

He sat himself down at the table, and wrote a short note, which he sealed with a ring, and gave to Kitty.

'And now, my child,' said d'Artagnan, 'you know that this place is no safer for us than for you. So let us separate. We shall meet again in happier days.'

'And at whatever time or place we may meet again, sir,' said Kitty, 'you will find me loving you still more than now.'

'A gamester's vow!' said Athos, whilst d'Artagnan was accompanying Kitty down the stairs.

A few minutes afterwards, the three friends separated, after making an appointment for four o'clock at Athos's chambers, and leaving Planchet to mind the house.

Aramis returned home, and Athos and d'Artagnan busied themselves about pledging the sapphire.

As our Gascon had foreseen, they easily procured three hundred pistoles on the ring; and the Jew moreover declared, that, if they chose to sell it, as it would make a splendid drop for ear-rings, he would give as much as five hundred pistoles for it.

Athos and d'Artagnan, with the activity of two soldiers, and the science of two connoisseurs, scarcely spent three hours in purchasing the equipment of the musketeer. Besides, Athos had the character and manners of a nobleman, even to his fingers' ends. Directly anything suited him, he paid for it at once, without haggling to reduce the price.

D'Artagnan wished to make some objections to this; but Athos laid his hand on his shoulder, smiling; and d'Artagnan understood that it was very well for a little Gascon gentleman like him to bargain, but not for a man who had the deportment of a prince.

The musketeer saw a superb Andalusian horse, as black as jet, with fiery nostrils, and fine and elegant legs, rising six years. He examined it, and found it faultless. He got it for a thousand francs. Perhaps he might have had it for less; but while d'Artagnan was discussing the price with the dealer, Athos counted down the hundred pistoles on the table.

Grimaud had a cob, from Picardy, which cost three hundred francs.

But when the saddle of this latter horse, and Grimaud's arms, were bought, Athos had not one sou remaining of the hundred and fifty pistoles. D'Artagnan therefore begged his friend to bite a mouthful out of his share, which he could restore to him afterwards, if he chose. But Athos only answered by shrugging his shoulders.

'How much did the Jew say he would give for the sapphire, to buy it out and out?' asked he, at last.

'Five hundred pistoles.'

'That is two hundred pistoles more—a hundred for each of us. Why, that is quite a fortune! Let us go to the Jew again, my friend.'

'But would you really do this?

'Yes; this ring would unquestionably recall memories too melancholy. Besides, we shall never have three hundred pistoles to redeem it with; therefore, we should actually lose two hundred by the bargain. Go and tell him that the ring is his, d'Artagnan, and come back with the two hundred pistoles.'

'Reflect, Athos.'

'Ready money is scarce in these times, and we should learn to make sacrifices. Go, d'Artagnan, go. Grimaud shall bear you company with his carbine.'

Half an hour afterwards, d'Artagnan returned with the two thousand livres; no accident having befallen him on his way.

It was thus that Athos found, without giving himself any trouble, resources which he did not expect.

39

A Charming Vision

At the appointed hour the four friends were re-united at the house of Athos. Their anxiety about equipment had entirely disappeared, and their faces no longer bore the marks of any but their own secret care—for, behind all present happiness, there lurks some fear about the future.

Suddenly Planchet entered, bearing two letters, addressed to d'Artagnan. One was a little note, delicately folded lenghtwise, with a pretty seal of green wax, on which was depicted a dove bearing a green bough. The other was a large square envelope, glittering with the terrible arms of his eminence, the cardinal-duke.

At sight of the little letter, d'Artagnan's heart bounded, for he believed that he recognised the writing; and, though he had only seen that writing once, the memory of it was engraven in his heart's core. So he took the note, and unsealed it hastily.

'Walk out' [it said] 'about six or seven o'clock on Wednesday evening next, on the Chaillot road, and look carefully into the carriages as they pass. But as you value your own life, or that of some who love you, do not speak, do not make one motion which may show that you have recognised her who exposes herself to every ill, only to see you for an instant.'

There was no signature.

'It is a snare,' said Athos; 'do not go, d'Artagnan.'

'And yet,' said d'Artagnan, 'I think that I know the writing well.'

'But it may be feigned,' said Athos. 'At six or seven o'clock, at this season, you would be as solitary on the Chaillot road as if you went to walk in the Forest of Bondy.'

'But what if we should all go?' said d'Artagnan. 'Surely they could not eat us all four, besides the four servants, the horses, and our arms: the act would certainly bring on a fit of indigestion.'

'Besides it will be a fine opportunity to display our equipments,' said Porthos.

'But, if it is a woman who writes,' said Aramis, 'and this woman does not wish to be seen, consider that you compromise her, d'Artagnan, which is not becoming in a gentleman.'

'We will remain behind,' said Porthos, 'and he can advance alone.'

'Yes, but a pistol-shot is easily fired from a carriage going at full speed.'

'Bah!' said d'Artagnan, 'it would miss me. And we would then overtake the carriage, and exterminate whoever might be in it. It would be still so many enemies the fewer.'

'He is right,' said Porthos; 'let us give battle! Besides, we needs must try our arms.'

'Faith! let us give ourselves this treat,' said Aramis, in his soft and careless way.

'Just as you please,' said Athos.

'Gentlemen,' said d'Artagnan, 'it is now half-past four, and we have but just time to get to the Chaillot road by six.'

'Besides, if we go out too late, no one will see us,' said Porthos; 'and that would be a sad pity. Let us get ready, gentlemen.'

'But this second letter,' said Athos; 'you forget that. And yet, I fancy, the seal indicates that it is worth opening. As for me, I confess, my dear d'Artagnan, that I think much more of it than of that little gew-gaw which you so gently bestowed, just now, over your heart.'

D'Artagnan grew crimson.

'Well,' said the young man, 'let us now see what his eminence wants with me.'

D'Artagnan opened the letter, and read:—

'M. d'Artagnan, of the King's guards, of M. des Essarts company, is expected at the cardinal's palace, at eight o'clock this evening. 'LA HOUDINIERE

'Captain of the Guards.'

'The devil!' said Athos, 'here is an appointment, not a whit less disquieting, in other respects, than the first.'

'I will go to the second, on returning from the first,' said d'Artagnan. 'One is at seven, the other at eight. There will be time enough for both.'

'Hum! I would not go,' said Aramis. 'A gallant gentleman cannot decline an appointment made by a lady; but a prudent gentleman may excuse himself from waiting on his eminence, particularly when he has some reason to believe that he is not sent for to listen to compliments.'

'I am of Aramis's opinion,' said Porthos.

'Gentlemen,' replied d'Artagnan, 'I have already received a similar invitation from his eminence, through M. de Cavois. I neglected it; and the next day a great misfortune happened to me—Constance disappeared. Whatever may be the result, I will go.'

'If you are determined,' said Athos, 'do it.'

'But the Bastile,' said Aramis.

'Bah! you will get me out again,' rejoined d'Artagnan.

'Certainly,' replied Aramis and Porthos, with the greatest coolness, and as if it had been the simplest thing in the world—'certainly, we will pull you out again. But, as we must be off the day after to-morrow, you would do better not to run the risk of getting in.'

'Let us do better,' said Athos; 'let us not leave him throughout the evening. Let each of us, accompanied by three musketeers, wait at a gate of the palace. If we see any closed carriage, that looks suspicious, coming out, we will fall upon it. It is a long time since we have had a crow to pluck with the cardinal's guards; and M. de Treville must think us dead.'

'Decidedly, Athos,' said Aramis; 'you were cut out for the general of an army. What do you say to the plan, gentlemen?'

'Splendid!' cried the young men, in chorus.

'I have got no horse,' said d'Artagnan, 'but I can go and take one of M. de Treville's.'

'That is unnecessary,' remarked Aramis; 'you can have one of mine.'

'How many have you, then?' inquired d'Artagnan.

'Three,' replied Aramis, smiling.

'My dear fellow,' said Athos, 'you are certainly the best paid poet in France.'

'Or, in Navarre,' added d'Artagnan.

'But listen my dear Aramis,' said Athos; 'you will not know what to do with three horses, will you? I do not understand, indeed, why you have bought three.'

'Nor did I, in fact, buy more than two,' replied Aramis.

'Did the third come from the clouds, then?'

'No; the third was brought to me this morning, by a servant without livery, who would not tell me from whom he came; and who merely said, that he had been ordered by his master——'

'Or his mistress,' interposed d'Artagnan.

'That makes no difference,' said Aramis, colouring; 'and who merely said, that he had been ordered by his master, or his mistress, to put this horse in my stable, without telling me from whom it came.'

'It is only to poets that such things happen,' gravely remarked Athos.

'Well, then, in that case we can do better,' said d'Artagnan. 'Which of the two horses will you ride, Aramis? that which you bought, or that which was given you?'

'That which was given to me, without doubt. You understand, d'Artagnan, that I could not so affront——'

'The mysterious donor,' added d'Artagnan.

'Or the mysterious donatrix,' said Athos.

'Then that which you bought becomes of no use to you.'

'Almost so.'

'You chose it yourself?'

'And with the greatest care. The safety of the horseman, you know, depends almost always on his horse.'

'Well, then, let me have him at the price you gave?

'I was going to offer you this trifle, my dear d'Artagnan, giving you your own time to repay me.'

'And how much did he cost you?'

'Eight hundred francs.'

'Here are forty double pistoles, my dear friend,' said d'Artagnan, taking that sum from his pocket. 'I know that it is the same piece in which you are paid for your poems.'

'You are in cash, then?'

'Rich—rolling in wealth!' said d'Artagnan, rattling the rest of his pistoles in his pocket.

'Send your saddle, then, to the hotel of the musketeers, and your horse shall be brought here with ours.'

'Very well. But it is almost five o'clock. Let us make haste.'

In about a quarter of an hour afterwards, Porthos appeared at the end of the Rue Ferou, on a magnificent Spanish horse. Mousqueton was following him, on a small but strong horse from Auvergne. Porthos was radiant with joy and pride.

At the same time Aramis was seen, at the other end of the street, mounted on a superb English steed. Bazin followed, on a roan horse, leading a vigorous Mecklenburgian horse, which now belonged to d'Artagnan.

The two musketeers met at the door: Athos and d'Artagnan were looking at them from the window.

'By my faith!' said Aramis, 'you have a grand horse there, my friend.'

'Yes,' replied Porthos, 'it is the one that was to have been sent at first. A foolish joke of the husband's substituted the other: but the husband has been well punished since, and I have obtained reparation.

Grimaud appeared in his turn, leading his master's horse. D'Artagnan and Athos came down; got into their saddles by the side of their companions; and they all four proceeded towards the quay—Athos, on the horse for which he was indebted to his wife; Aramis, on the horse for which he was indebted to his mistress; Porthos, on the horse for which he was indebted to the attorney's wife; and d'Artagnan, on the horse for which he was indebted only to his own good-fortune, which is the best of all mistressses.

The valets followed them.

As Porthos had expected, the cavalcade produced a fine effect; and, if Madame Coquenard had been in Porthos's path, and could have seen how well he looked upon his fine Spanish steed, she would hardly have regretted the bleeding operation that she had performed upon her husband's strong-box.

Near the Louvre, the four friends met M. de Treville, returning from St. Germain's. He stopped them, to compliment them on their equipment, which drew around them, in an instant, a few hundred loafers.

D'Artagnan took advantage of this circumstance to speak to M. de Treville about the great letter, with the great red seal and ducal arms. It will be imagined that, of the other letter, he did not breathe a syllable.

M. de Treville approved of the resolution they had formed, and assured him, that if he should not be seen again on the next day, he would manage to find him out, wherever he might be.

At that moment, the clock of the Samaritan struck six. The four friends excused themselves, on account of an engagement, and set off.

A short gallop took them to the Chaillot road. The day was beginning to decline. Carriages were passing backwards and forward. D'Artagnan, supported by his friends at a little distance, looked eagerly into every carriage, but saw no face he knew.

At length, after about a quarter of an hour's expectation, and as the twilight thickened around, a carriage, advancing at the utmost speed of the horses, was seen upon the Sevres road. A presentiment announced to d'Artagnan that this carriage contained the individual who had made the appointment with him. The young man was himself astonished at the violent beating of his heart. Almost at the same instant, a woman's head was visible at the window, with two fingers on the lips, as if to enjoin silence, or to send a kiss. D'Artagnan uttered a faint cry of joy. This woman, or rather this apparition, for the carriage passed away with the rapidity of a vision, was Madame Bonancieux.

By an involuntary movement, and in spite of the caution he had received, d'Artagnan set his horse to a gallop, and in a few bounds was beside the carriage; but the window was hermetically closed—the vision was no longer there.

D'Artagnan then remembered the warning:—'If you value your own life, and that of those who love you, remain motionless, as if you had seen nothing.'

He stopped, therefore; trembling not for himself, but for the poor woman, who had evidently exposed herself to no trifling peril by the appointment she had made.

The carriage proceeded on its way, and, still advancing rapidly, soon entered Paris, and disappeared.

D'Artagnan had remained speechless on the same spot, knowing not what to think. If it were really Madame Bonancieux, and if she were returning to Paris, why this fugitive meeting, why this passing interchange of glances, why this kiss, committed to the winds? If, on the other hand, it were not really she—which was in fact very possible, for the insufficiency of light made error easy— might not this be the beginning of an attack prepared by the attraction of a woman for whom his love was known?

The three companions gathered around him. They had all distinctly seen a woman's head at the window, but neither of them, except Athos, knew Madame Bonancieux by sight. Athos believed that it was really that lady whom they had seen; but, having been less engrossed than d'Artagnan by that pretty face, he thought that he had seen a second head, and a manly one, at the back of the carriage.

'If that is the case,' said d'Artagnan, 'they are undoubtedly conveying her from one prison to another. But what can they want to do with the poor creature, and how shall I ever rejoin her?'

'My friend,' said Athos gravely, 'remember that the dead are the only ones whom we can never encounter again on earth. You know a story to that effect, as well as I do, do you not? Now, if your mistress is not really dead, if it was actually her whom we saw just now, at one time or another you will meet with her again. And perhaps,' added he, in those tones of misanthropy which were habitual to him, 'perhaps more quickly even than you might have wished!'

It now struck half-past seven; the carriage had been twenty minutes beyond the appointed time. His friends reminded d'Artagnan that there was another visit to pay, which, however, it was yet possible for him to decline.

But d'Artagnan was, at the same time, both obstinate and curious. He had, in his own mind, determined to go to the cardinal's palace, and to know what his eminence had to say to him. Nothing could make him change his resolution. They reached the Rue St. Honoré, and the Place du Palais Cardinal, where they found the twelve musketeers walking about, whilst they awaited their companions. Then, for the first time, was the business they had met for communicated to these brave allies.

D'Artagnan was well known to the honourable company of king's musketeers, amongst whom, it was further understood, he would one day take his place: he was therefore regarded as a comrade, by anticipation. It resulted from this, that every one willingly engaged in the affair to which he had been invited; and they had, moreover, the probability of doing an ill turn to the cardinal or his people; and for such expeditions these worthy gentlemen were always well prepared.

Athos divided them into three parties: of one, he took the command himself; the second, he gave to Aramis; and the third, to Porthos; and then each party placed itself in ambush, opposite an entrance of the palace.

D'Artagnan, on his part, boldly entered by the principal gate.

Although he felt himself strongly supported, the young man did not ascend the grand staircase without uneasiness. His conduct towards her ladyship had some slight resemblance to a treachery, and he suspected that there were political relations between this woman and the cardinal. Moreover, de Wardes, whom he had handled so roughly, was a faithful follower of his eminence; and d'Artagnan well knew, that, while the cardinal was a terror to his enemies, he was also constant in his attachment to his friends.

'If de Wardes has related all our interview to his eminence, of which there can be no doubt, and if he has recognised me, which is probable, I may consider myself almost a condemned man,' thought d'Artagnan, shaking his head. 'But why should he have waited till to-day? It is clear enough her ladyship has made complaints against me, with all that hypocritical sorrow which renders her so interesting; and this last crime has made the vase run over. Fortunately,' added he, 'my good friends are below, and they will not let me be carried off without a conflict. And yet M. de Treville's company of musketeers, alone, cannot carry on a war against the cardinal, who disposes of the forces of all France, and before whom the queen has no power, and the king no will. D'Artagnan, my friend, thou art brave, thou art prudent, thou has excellent qualities, but—women will destroy thee!'

He had come to this sad conclusion, just as he entered the antechamber. He gave his letter to the officer on duty, who showed him into the waiting-room, and himself proceeded into the interior of the palace.

In this room there were five or six of his excellency's guards, who, recognising d'Artagnan, and knowing that it was he who had wounded Jussac, looked at him with a singular smile.

This smile seemed to d'Artagnan a bad omen. But as our Gascon was not easily intimidated, or, rather, thanks to the abundant pride natural to men of his province, did not easily betray what was passing in his mind, when what was passing there resembled fears—he stood boldly before the gentlemen of the guards, and waited, with his hand upon his hip, in an attitude not ungraceful.

The officer returned, and made a sign to d'Artagnan to follow him.

It seemed to the young man, that, as he left the room, the guards began to whisper to each other.

He went along a corridor, passed through a large saloon, entered a library, and found himself before a man, who was seated at a desk, writing.

The officer introduced him, and retired without uttering a word.

D'Artagnan remained standing, and examined this man.

At first, d'Artagnan thought that he was in the presence of a judge, who was examining his papers; but he soon saw that the man at the desk was writing or, rather correcting, lines of an unequal length, and was scanning the words upon his fingers: d'Artagnan found that he was in the presence of a poet. At the expiration of a minute, the poet closed his manuscript, on the back of which was written, '*Mirame;* a Tragedy, in five acts.'

He raised his head; and d'Artagnan recognised the cardinal.

40

A Terrible Vision

RICHELIEU rested his elbow on his manuscript, and his cheek on his hand, and looked at d'Artagnan for an instant. No one had an eye more profoundly penetrating than the cardinal; and the young man felt this gaze running through his veins like a fever.

Nevertheless, he kept a good countenance, holding his hat in his hand, and waiting his eminence's pleasure, without too much pride, but at the same time without too much humility.

'Sir,' said the cardinal, 'are you one d'Artagnan, of Bearn?'

'Yes, my lord.'

'There are several branches of the d'Artagnans in Tarbes, and in its neighbourhood: to which of them do you belong?'

'I am the son of him who fought in the religious wars, with the great King Henry, the father of his gracious majesty.'

'That is it: it is you who set out from your native place, about seven or eight months ago, to come and seek your fortune in the capital?'

'Yes, my lord.'

'You came by Meung, where something happened to you—I do not exactly know what—but something?'

'My lord,' said d'Artagnan, 'this is what happened——'

'Unnecessary, quite unnecessary,' interrupted the cardinal with a smile which indicated that he knew the story quite as well as he who wished to narrate it. 'You were recommended to M. de Treville, were you not?'

'Yes, my lord, but in that unlucky affair at Meung——'

'The letter of introduction was lost,' resumed his eminence. 'Yes, I know that. But M. de Treville is a skilful physiognomist, who knows men at the first sight, and he has placed you in the company of his brother-in-law, M. des Essarts, leaving you to hope, that, some day or other, you will be enrolled in the musketeers.'

'Your lordship is perfectly correct.'

'Since that time, many things have happened to you: you walked behind the Chartreux, one day, when you had much better have been elsewhere; then you made a journey to the waters of Forges, with your friends; they stopped upon the road, but you—you continued your journey. That was natural enough: you had business in England.'

'My lord,' said d'Artagnan, quite confounded, 'I went—'

'To hunt at Windsor, or somewhere else. That is no business of anybody's. I know it, because it is my duty to know everything. On your return, you were received by an august person, and I see with pleasure that you have kept the souvenir which she gave you.'

D'Artagnan put his hand on the diamond which the queen had given him, and quickly turned the stone inwards: but it was too late.

'On the next day, you were waited upon by Cavois,' continued the cardinal: 'he came to beg you to come to the palace. But you did not return that visit; and, in that, you were wrong.'

'My lord, because I feared that I had incurred your eminence's displeasure.'

'And why so, sir? Because you had performed the orders of your superiors, with more intelligence and courage than another could have done? Incur my displeasure, when you merited praise! It is those who do not obey that I punish; and not those who, like you, obey—too well. And to prove it, recall the date of the day on which I sent for you to come to see me, and seek in your memory what happened on that very night.'

It was the evening on which Madame Bonancieux was carried off. D'Artagnan shuddered; and he remembered, that, half an hour before this present moment, the poor woman had passed before him, no doubt again borne away by the same power which had directed that abduction.

'At last,' continued the cardinal, 'as I had heard nothing of you for some time, I wished to know what you were doing. Besides, you certainly owe me some thanks: you have yourself remarked what consideration has been always shown towards you.'

D'Artagnan bowed respectfully.

'That,' continued the cardinal, 'proceeded not only from a sentiment of natural justice, but also from a plan that I had traced respecting you.'

D'Artagnan was more and more astonished.

'It was my desire,' continued the cardinal, 'to explain this plan to you on the day that you received my first invitation; but you did not come. Fortunately, nothing has been lost by the delay; and to-day you shall hear the explanation. Sit down, then, before me, M. d'Artagnan: you are gentleman enough not to be kept standing whilst you listen.'

The cardinal pointed out a chair to the young man, who was so astonished at what was taking place, that he waited, before he obeyed, for a second intimidation from his interlocutor.

'You are brave, M. d'Artagnan,' resumed his eminence; 'and you are prudent, which is far better. I love men of head and heart. Do not be alarmed,' he added, smiling; 'by men of heart, I mean courageous men. But, young as you are, and only on the threshold of the world, your enemies are very powerful. If you do not take care, they will destroy you.'

'Alas! my lord,' replied the young man, 'they will

undoubtedly accomplish it very easily; for they are strong and well-supported, whilst I stand alone.'

'Yes, that is true: but, alone as you are, you have already done much, and will, I doubt not, do still more. Yet you have, I believe, need of a guide in the adventurous career you have undertaken; since, if I am not deceived, you have come to Paris, with the ambitious intention of making a fortune.'

'I am at the age of foolish hopes, my lord,' said d'Artagnan.

'No hopes are foolish, except for blockheads, sir; and you are a man of ability. Come, what would you say to an ensigncy in my guards, and a company at the end of the campaign?'

'Ah, my lord!'

'You accept it—do you not?'

'My lord——' replied d'Artagnan, with an embarrassed air.

'What? Do you decline it?' exclaimed the cardinal, with a look of astonishment.

'I am in his majesty's guards, my lord, and I have no cause to be discontented.'

'But it seems to me,' said his eminence, 'that my guards are also his majesty's guards; and that whosoever serves in a French regiment, serves the king.'

'My lord, your eminence has misunderstood my words.'

'You want a pretext, do you not? I understand. Very well! This pretext, here it is—promotion, the opening of a campaign, the opportunity which I offer you—these will be sufficient for the world: for yourself, the necessity of sure protection. For, it is as well for you to know, M. d'Artagnan, that I have received serious complaints against you. You do not consecrate your nights and days exclusively to the service of the king.'

D'Artagnan blushed.

'Moreover,' added the cardinal, laying his hand on a roll of papers, 'I have here a whole bundle of particulars about you. But, before reading them, I wished to talk with you. I know that you are a man of resolution; and your services, if well directed, instead of leading you to evil, might benefit you greatly. Come, reflect and make up your mind.'

'Your goodness confounds me, my lord,' replied d'Artagnan; 'and I discover in your eminence a greatness of soul, which makes me insignificant as the crawling worm; but, in fact, since your eminence permits me to speak frankly—'

D'Artagnan stopped.

'Yes, speak.'

'Well, then, I must inform your eminence that all my friends are amongst the musketeers and the king's guards; and that all my enemies, by some inconceivable fatality, are in the service of your eminence. On this account, I should be unwelcome here, and despised there, if I accepted what your eminence is good enough to offer.'

'And can you already have the proud idea that I do not offer you as much as you deserve, sir?' inquired the cardinal with a smile of scorn.

'My lord, your eminence is a hundred times too good to me; and, on the contrary, I do not think that I have yet done enough to merit your kindness. The siege of La Rochelle is about to commence, my lord. I shall serve under your eminence's own eyes; and, if I shall have the good fortune to conduct myself in such a manner at the siege, as to merit your approbation, it will be well! After that, I shall at least have to my credit, some action of sufficient brilliancy to justify the protection with which your eminence may condescend to honour me. Everything should be effected at an appropriate time. Perhaps, hereafter, I may have the right to give myself away—at present, I should be supposed to sell myself.'

'That is to say, you refuse to serve me, sir?' said the cardinal, in a tone of anger, through which, however, might be traced a sentiment of esteem. 'Remain in freedom, then, and still preserve your hatreds and your sympathies.'

'My lord——'

'Well, well,' continued the cardinal; 'I am not offended with you; but you must understand—it is quite enough to protect and recompense one's friends: one owes nothing to one's enemies. And yet I will give you one piece of advice. Take care of yourself, M. d'Artagnan; for, from the moment that I shall have withdrawn my hand from you, I would not give one farthing for your life.'

'I will do my best, my lord,' replied the Gascon, with modest confidence.

'And hereafter, at the moment that any misfortune has befallen you, remember'—said Richelieu, with some feeling—' that it is I who have sought you, and that I have done what I could to avert from you that misfortune.'

'Let what may happen,' said d'Artagnan, bowing, with his hand upon his breast, 'I shall retain a sentiment of eternal gratitude to your eminence, for what you are doing for me at the present time.'

'Well, then, M. d'Artagnan, as you say, we shall see each other again after the campaign. I shall keep my eyes upon you, for I shall be there,' continued the cardinal, pointing to a magnificent suit of armour which he was to wear. 'And, on our return, we will decide on our arrangement!'

'Ah! my lord!' exclaimed d'Artagnan, 'spare me the weight of your displeasure: remain neutral, my lord, if you find that I behave gallantly.'

'Young man,' said Richelieu, 'if I can once more say to you what I have said to-day, I promise you that I *will* say it,'

This last expression of Richelieu involved a terrible doubt. It alarmed d'Artagnan more than a threat would have done; for it was a warning: it implied that the cardinal was endeavouring to shield him from some impending evil. He opened his lips to answer; but, with a haughty gesture, the cardinal dismissed him.

D'Artagnan left the room; but, at the door, his heart almost failed him, and he was strongly tempted to return. Yet the serious and severe countenance of Athos arose before his mind. If he agreed to what the cardinal proposed, Athos would no longer offer him his hand—Athos would disown him.

It was this fear that determined him. So powerful is the influence of a truly noble character over all that approaches it.

D'Artagnan went down by the same staircase that he had ascended; and found, before the door, Athos and the four musketeers who were awaiting him, and were beginning to be anxious about him. With one word he reassured them; and Planchet ran to the other posts to announce that any further guard was unnecessary, as his master had returned safe and sound, out of the cardinal's palace.

When they were housed at Athos's, Aramis and Porthos inquired about the object of this singular interview; but d'Artagnan merely told them that Richelieu had sent for him to offer him an ensign's commission in the guards, and that he had refused it.

'And you were right!' exclaimed Aramis and Porthos, with one voice.

Athos fell into a profound reverie, and said nothing. But, when he was alone with d'Artagnan, he said—

'You have done as you ought, although, perhaps, you were imprudent.'

D'Artagnan sighed; for this voice responded to a secret whisper of his own soul, which announced that great misfortunes were preparing for him.

The next day was occupied in preparations for departure.

D'Artagnan went to take leave of M. de Treville. At this time, it was still believed that the separation of the guards and musketeers would be but momentary—the king holding his parliament that very day, and proposing to set out on the next. M. de Treville therefore only asked d'Artagnan whether he wanted anything of him; but d'Artagnan replied, that he had all he should need.

In the evening, all the comrades of M. de Treville's and M. des Essarts's companies, who had become attached to one another, met together. They were about to part, to meet again, when, and if it should please God to let them. The night was, therefore, as may be supposed, a very boisterous one; for, on such occasions, nothing but extreme pleasure can drive away extreme care.

The next day, at the first sound of the trumpets, the friends separated: the musketeers hastened to M. de Treville's hotel, and the guards to that of M. des Essarts. Each captain then led his company to the Louvre, where the king reviewed them.

His majesty was sad, and seemed in ill-health, which detracted somewhat from his usual dignified appearance. In fact, the evening before, a fever had attracted him, even whilst he was holding a court of judicature, amidst the parliament. But he was not the less determined to set out in the evening; and, in spite of all their presentations which had been made to him, he would hold this review, hoping, by the first vigorous opposition, to overpower the malady that had assailed him.

The review being ended, the guards alone began their march—the musketeers being to set out only with the king —a delay which gave Porthos an opportunity of displaying his superb equipage in the Rue aux Ours.

The attorney's wife saw him passing by, in his new uniform, and on his splendid horse. But she loved Porthos too well to let him leave her thus; so she beckoned to him to dismount and enter. Porthos was magnificent: his spurs rattled, his cuirass beamed, and his sword smote dashingly against his legs. The clerks had no disposition to laugh this time: the musketeer looked too much like one who would soon slit their ears.

The visitor was introduced to Maitre Coquenard, whose little gray eyes glistened with rage when he beheld his pretended cousin so showily adorned. Nevertheless, he had one source of inward consolation. It was everywhere reported that the campaign would be a rough one; and he gently hoped, at the bottom of his heart, that Porthos might be one of the slain.

Porthos presented his compliments to Maitre Coquenard, and took his leave. The attorney wished him all sorts of prosperity. As to Madame Coquenard, she was unable to restrain her tears, but no evil thoughts could be suggested by her grief: she was known to be strongly attached to her relations. on whose account she had always had the bitterest contentions with her husband.

Whilst the attorney's wife was able to follow her handsome cousin with her eyes, she waved a handkerchief, and leaned from the window as though she was about to precipitate herself into the street. Porthos received all these indications of tenderness like a man hardened to such demonstrations. But, as he turned the corner of the street, he raised his hat, and waved it in token of adieu.

Aramis, on his part, wrote a long letter. To whom? None knew. In the next room, Kitty, who was to set off that very evening for Tours. was waiting for this mysterious epistle.

Athos drank, sip by sip, the last bottle of his Spanish wine.

In the meantime, d'Artagnan was marching with his company. In passing through the faubourg St. Antoine, he turned, and looked gaily at the Bastile, which he had at least as yet escaped. As he looked only at the Bastile, he did not see my lady, who, mounted on a dun horse, pointed him out with her finger to two ill-looking men, who immediately approached the ranks to reconnoitre him. To an interrogation which they addressed to the lady by a look, she answered by a sign that it was really he. Then, certain that there could be no mistake in the execution of her orders, she spurred her horse, and disappeared.

The two men followed the company; and, at the end of the faubourg St. Antoine, they mounted two horses, which a servant out of livery was holding in readiness for them.

41

The Siege of La Rochelle

THE siege of La Rochelle was one of the greatest events of the reign of Louis XIII.

The political views of the cardinal, when he undertook the siege, were extensive. Of the important cities which had been given by Henry IV. to the Huguenots, as places of safety, La Rochelle alone remained. The cardinal wished to destroy this last bulwark of Calvinism.

La Rochelle, which had derived additional importance from the ruin of the other Calvinistic towns, was, besides, the last port which remained open to the English in the kingdom of France; and, by closing it to England—our eternal enemy—the cardinal would end the work of Joan of Arc, and of the Duke of Guise.

Thus it was, that Bassompierre, who was at the same time both Protestant and Catholic—Protestant, from conviction; and Catholic, as commander of the order of the Saint Esprit—Bassompierre, who was a German by birth, and a Frenchman at heart—Bassompierre, who had a particular command at the siege of La Rochelle—said, on charging at the head of many other Protestant noblemen like himself: 'You will see, gentlemen, that we shall be fools enough to take La Rochelle.'

And Bassompierre was right. The cannonades of the Isle of Rhé were a prelude to the dragonnades of the Cevennes; the taking of La Rochelle was the preface to the edict of Nantes.

But, by the side of these general views of the levelling and simplifying minister, which belong to history, the chronicler is obliged to dwell upon the petty objects of the lover and the jealous rival.

Richelieu, as every one knows, had been enamoured of the queen. Had this love a purely political aim; or was it one of those profound passions, with which Anne of Austria inspired those who were around her? This is what we cannot satisfactorily decide. Yet, at all events, it has been seen, by the circumstances which have been detailed in this history, that Buckingham had gained a superiority over him in two or three points, and that, especially in the affair of the diamond studs—thanks to the devotion of the three musketeers, and the courage of d'Artagnan—he had most cruelly befooled him.

It was Richelieu's object, therefore, not merely to rid France of an enemy, but to revenge himself on a rival. The revenge ought, too, to be great and signal, and completely worthy of the man who held in his hand, as a weapon, the forces of a whole realm.

Richelieu knew, that, in fighting against England, he was fighting against Buckingham; that, in triumphing over England, he should triumph over Buckingham; and, lastly, that in humiliating England in the eyes of Europe, he should humiliate Buckingham in the eyes of the queen.

On his part, Buckingham, whilst he was putting the honour of England prominently forward as his motive, was impelled by interests absolutely similar to those of the cardinal.

Buckingham also pursued a private revenge. Under no pretext had Buckingham been able to enter France as an ambassador; and he wished, therefore, to enter it as a conqueror. It follows from this, that the true stake, in this game which two powerful kingdoms were playing for the pleasure of two amorous men, was nothing more than a glance from the eye of Anne of Austria.

The Duke of Buckingham had gained the first advantage. Arriving unexpectedly before the Isle of Rhé, with ninety vessels and twenty thousand men, he had surprised the Count de Toiras, who was the king's commander in that isle, and, after a bloody contest, had accomplished a disembarkation.

Let us record, by the way, that the Baron de Chantal fell in this combat, leaving an orphan daughter, a little girl, eighteen months old. This little girl was afterwards Madame de Sevigné.

The Count de Toiras retreated into the citadel of St. Martin with his garrison, and threw a hundred men into a small fort, which was called the port of La Prée.

This event had hastened the decision of the cardinal; and, until he and the king could go and take the command of the siege of La Rochelle, which was resolved on, he had sent his majesty's brother forward to direct the first operations, and had made all the troops of which he could dispose march towards the theatre of war.

It was to this detachment of the army, which was sent forward as a vanguard, that our friend d'Artagnan belonged. The king, as we have said, was to follow when his court of justice had been held. On rising from this sitting, on the twenty-eighth of June, he had found himself seized with fever. He had, nevertheless, persisted in setting out; but, getting worse, he had been obliged to stop at Villeroi.

Now, where the king stopped, there also stopped the musketeers. Hence it followed, that d'Artagnan, who was only in the guards, found himself separated, for a time at least, from his good friends, Athos, Porthos, and Aramis. This separation, which was only annoying to him, would certainly have become a source of serious anxiety, had he been able to discern by what unsuspected dangers he was surrounded.

Nevertheless, he arrived without mishap at the camp before La Rochelle.

Everything was at present in the same state. The Duke of Buckingham and the English, in possession of the Isle of Rhé, continued to besiege, but without success, the Fort of La Prée and the citadel of St. Martin; and the hostilities with La Rochelle had commenced two or three days before, about a battery which the Duke d'Angoulême had just constructed near the city.

The guards, under M. des Essarts, were stationed at the Minimes.

But we know that d'Artagnan, engrossed by the ambition of becoming a musketeer, had formed but few intimacies with his comrades, and found himself, therefore, isolated, and abandoned to his own reflections.

And these reflections were not cheerful. During the year that he had been in Paris, he had engaged himself in public affairs, and consequently his own private affairs, either of love or fortune, had made no great advances.

As to love, the only woman for whom he had a sincere affection was Madame Bonancieux; and Madame Bonancieux had disappeared, nor could he yet discover what had become of her.

As to fortune, he—a mere insect—had made an enemy of the cardinal; that is to say, of a man before whom the nobles of the kingdom trembled, and even the king himself.

That man had power to crush him, and yet he abstained.

To a mind as clear-sighted as that of d'Artagnan, this

forbearance was a dawn which gave promise of a happier futurity.

Then, he had made himself another enemy, less to be dreaded as he thought, but one whom he felt instinctively was not to be dispised. That enemy was her ladyship.

In exchange for all this, he had the protection and good-will of the queen; but her majesty's good-will was, in the circumstances of the times, only an additional course of persecution; and her protection, it is known, protected very badly—witness Chalais, and Madame Bonancieux.

So that what he had most manifestly gained, in all this, was the diamond, worth five or six thousand francs, which he wore upon his finger; and even this diamond, supposing that he must preserve it, to remind the queen at some future day of her gratitude, had not, in the meantime, since he could not dispose of it, any greater value than the pebbles that he trampled beneath his feet. We say the pebbles that he trampled beneath his feet, for d'Artagnan made these reflections whilst he was walking alone in a pretty little path which led from the camp to an adjoining village. But these reflections had led him further than he intended, and the day was beginning to decline, when, by the last ray of the setting sun, he seemed to perceive the barrel of a musket glittering behind a hedge.

D'Artagnan had a quick eye, and a ready wit. He comprehended that the musket had not come there of itself, and that he who held it was not concealed behind a hedge with any very amicable intentions. He determined, therefore, to gain the open country; but, on the other side of the road, behind a rock, he perceived the muzzle of a second musket. It was evidently an ambuscade.

The young man gave a glance at the first musket, and beheld with some anxiety that it was aiming in his direction; but, as soon as he saw the orifice of the barrel motionless, he threw himself upon his face. At that instant the shot was fired, and he heard the whistling of a ball, as it passed above his head.

There was no time to lose. D'Artagnan raised himself up with a bound, and, at the same moment, the bullet of the second musket scattered the stones in the very part of the path where he had thrown himself down.

D'Artagnan was not one of those foolishly brave men who seek a ridiculous death in order to have it said of them that they never retreated a step. Besides, courage could do nothing here: he had fallen into an ambuscade.

'If there is a third shot,' said he to himself, 'I am a dead man.'

He immediately scampered towards the camp, with all the swiftness of his countrymen, who are so famous for their activity; but, fast as was his course, the one who had fired first, having had time to reload his gun, made another shot at him, so well directed this time, that the ball passed through his hat, and drove it ten paces before him.

As d'Artagnan had no other hat, he picked it up as he ran; and reaching his lodging, pale and out of breath, he sat down, without speaking to any one, and began to reflect.

This event might have three causes. The first, and most natural, was, that it might be an ambuscade from La Rochelle, whose citizens would not have been sorry to kill one of his majesty's guards, as it would make one enemy the less, and that enemy might have a well-filled purse in his pocket.

D'Artagnan took his hat, examined the hole that the ball had made, and shook his head. The bullet did not belong to a musket, but to an arquebuss; the precision of the aim had already made him think that it was fired by a civilian weapon: so it was not a military ambuscade, since the ball was not of that calibre.

It might be a kind memorial of the cardinal. It may be remembered that, at the very moment when, thanks to the blessed beam of sunshine, he had perceived the gun-barrel, he was marvelling at the leniency his eminence had shown towards him. But d'Artagnan shook his head with an air of doubt. The cardinal seldom had recourse to such means, towards people whom a movement of his hand might crush.

It might be her ladyship's revenge.

This conjecture was more reasonable.

He tried in vain to recall either the features or the dress of the assassins; but he had hurried away too rapidly to have leisure to remark them.

'Ah! my poor friends,' muttered d'Artagnan, 'where are you? Alas! how much I miss you!'

D'Artagnan passed a very bad night. Three or four times he awoke with a start, fancying that a man approached his bed to stab him. Yet the day dawned, without any accident having occurred during the darkness.

But d'Artagnan suspected that what is deferred is not therefore lost.

He remained in his quarters throughout the whole day;

and gave, as an excuse to himself, the dullness of the weather.

At nine o'clock on the next morning, they beat to arms. The Duke of Orleans was visiting the pickets. The guards mustered, and d'Artagnan took his place amidst his comrades.

His royal highness passed in front of the line; and then all the superior officers approached to pay their respects to him. M. des Essarts, the captain of the guards, went with the others.

After a short time, d'Artagnan thought that he perceived M. des Essarts making a sign to him to draw near. He waited for another gesture, fearing that he might have been mistaken; but on its being repeated, he left the ranks, and advanced to receive the order.

'His royal highness is about to ask for volunteers for a dangerous expedition, which will be honourable to those who perform it; and I made you a sign, that you might hold yourself in readiness.'

'Thank you, captain,' replied d'Artagnan, who required nothing better than to distinguish himself before the eyes of the lieutenant-general.

The Rochellois had, in fact, made a sortie during the night, and recaptured a bastion which the royal army had invested two days before. The idea was to push a forlorn hope so forward, as to be able to discover in what manner the enemy guarded this bastion.

After a few minutes, his royal highness raised his voice, and said—

'I want three or four volunteers for this expedition, led by a man who can be depended upon.'

'As for your trustworthy man, here he is,' said M. des Essarts, pointing to d'Artagnan; 'and as for the four or five volunteers, your royal highness has only to make your wishes known, and the men will not be wanting.'

'Four men, who will volunteer to come and be killed with me!' cried d'Artagnan, raising his sword.

Two of his companions in the guards rushed towards him instantaneously; and two other soldiers having joined them, the number was complete. D'Artagnan, therefore, rejected all others, to avoid injustice to those who had the prior claim.

It was not known whether the Rochellois, after having taken the bastion, had evacuated it, or placed a garrison in it. It was therefore necessary to examine the spot from a point sufficiently near to ascertain this point.

D'Artagnan went off with his four companions, in the line of the trench. The two guards marched by his side, and the two soldiers in the rear.

Sheltering themselves in this manner by the rampart, they arrived within a hundred paces of the bastion; and, on turning round at that moment, d'Artagnan perceived that the two soldiers had disappeared. Believing them to have remained behind from fear, he continued to advance.

At the turn of the counterscarp, they found themselves about sixty yards from the bastion; but they saw no one, and the bastion seemed evacuated.

The three volunteers deliberated whether they should advance farther, when suddenly a circle of smoke appeared, and a dozen balls whistled around d'Artagnan and his companions.

They knew now what they had come to learn: the bastion was guarded; a longer delay, therefore, in so dangerous a place, would have been only an unnecessary imprudence. So d'Artagnan and the two guards turned their backs, and began a rapid retreat.

On reaching the angle of the trench, which would serve as a rampart to them, one of the guards fell with a ball through his chest, whilst the other, who was safe and sound, made the best of his way to the camp.

D'Artagnan would not thus abandon a companion, and leaned over him to lift him up, and aid him to regain the lines; but, at that very moment, two shots were fired: one ball shattered the head of the man who was already wounded and the other was flattened against a rock after having passed within two inches of d'Artagnan's body.

The young man turned very quickly; for this attack could not come from the bastion, which was hidden by the angle of the trench. The remembrance of the two soldiers who had abandoned him, occurred to his mind, and suggested to him his assassins of the previous evening. He resolved, on this occasion, to find out what it meant; and fell, therefore, upon the body of his comrade, as though he had been dead. He immediately saw that two heads were raised above an abandoned breastwork, which was about thirty yards from him: they were those of the two soldiers. D'Artagnan was not mistaken: these men had remained behind solely for the purpose of assassinating him, hoping that the death of the young man would be imputed to the attack of the enemy.

But as he might be only wounded, and might denounce their crime, they drew near to complete their work. Happily, deceived by the sight of d'Artagnan's position, they neglected to reload their muskets. When they were about three paces from him, d'Artagnan, who had taken especial care, in falling, not to relinquish his sword, suddenly arose, and sprang upon them.

The assassins were well aware, that, if they fled towards the camp without having killed their man, they should be accused by him; and therefore their first impulse was to pass over to the enemy. One of them took his gun by the barrel, and made use of it as a club: he dealt a terrible blow at d'Artagnan, who avoided it by jumping aside; by this movement, however, d'Artagnan opened a passage to the bandit, who immediately sprang forth towards the bastion. But as the Rochellois who guarded it were ignorant of his intentions in advancing, they fired upon him, and he fell, with his shoulder broken by a ball.

In the meantime, d'Artagnan threw himself on the second soldier with his sword. The struggle was not long. This wretch had only his discharged fusee to defend himself with. The sword of the guardsman glided along the barrel of this useless weapon, and passed through the assassin's thigh. As soon as he had fallen, d'Artagnan applied the point of his weapon to his throat.

'Oh, do not kill me!' exclaimed the bandit. 'Pardon, sir! sir, and I will confess everything!'

'Is it worth my while to grant you your life for your secret?' demanded the young man.

'Yes, if you consider life of any value to a man of twenty-two years of age, who, being as handsome, and as brave as you are, may accomplish anything.'

'Wretch!' cried d'Artagnan, 'come, speak quickly. Who engaged you to assassinate me?'

'A woman whom I do not know, but who was called "my lady." '

'But, if you do not know this woman, how came you to know her name?'

'My comrade knew her, and called her so: it was with him that she arranged the affair—not with me. He has a letter from this person now in his pocket which would be of great importance to you, according to what I heard him say.'

'But how came you to be his partner in this ambuscade?'

'He proposed to me to join him in it, and I agreed.'

'And how much has she paid you for this pretty expedition?'

'A hundred louis.'

'Well, upon my word,' said the young man, laughing, 'she thinks me of some value. A hundred louis! It is quite a fortune for two wretches like you. I can well understand that you would accept it; and so I pardon you, but on one condition.'

'What is that?' said the soldier, uneasy at discovering that all was not yet ended.

'That you go and get me the letter out of your companion's pocket.'

'But,' exclaimed the bandit, 'that is only another way of killing me. How can you ask me to go for the letter, under the very fire of the bastion?'

'But you must make up your mind to go for it, or I swear that you shall directly die by my hand.'

'Mercy! sir, mercy! in the name of that young lady whom you love, and whom, perhaps, you imagine dead, but who is not so,' screamed the bandit, throwing himself upon his knees, and supporting himself on his hand; for he was beginning to lose his strength along with his blood.

'And how do you know that there is a young lady whom I love, and that I have believed her to be dead?' demanded d'Artagnan.

'By that letter in my comrade's pocket.'

'You see, then, that I must have that letter,' said 'dArtagnan. 'So, let us have no longer delay, no more hesitation, or, whatever may be my repugnance to bathe my sword a second time in the blood of such a wretch as you are, I swear to you, on the word of an honourable man——'

At these words, d'Artagnan made such a threatening gesture, that the wounded man arose.

'Stop! stop!' exclaimed he, recovering courage through the very force of fear: 'I will go—I will go.'

D'Artagnan took the soldier's arquebuss, made him walk before him, and urged him at the same time towards his companion, by pricking him in the loins with the point of his sword.

It was a fearful spectacle to witness this unhappy being leaving a long track of blood upon the path he took, growing pale from the approach of death, and yet striving to drag himself, without being seen, to the body of his accomplice, which was stretched out at a distance of twenty paces.

Terror was so depicted on his countenance, which was covered with an icy sweat, that d'Artagnan both pitied and despised him.

'Come!' said he, 'I will show you the difference between a man of courage, and a coward like you! Wait where you are: I will go!' And with an active step, and his eye upon the bastion, observing the proceedings of the enemy, and availing himself of every inequality of ground, he managed to advance as far as the second soldier.

There were two methods of accomplishing his purpose: either to search him where he was; or to carry him away, making a buckler of his body, and then to search him at leisure in the trench.

D'Artagnan preferred the second plan, and had thrown the body of the assassin on his shoulders just at the very moment that the enemy fired.

A slight tremor, a final cry, a shudder of agony, proved to d'Artagnan that he who had sought to assassinate him, had now saved his life.

D'Artagnan reached the trench, and threw the body by the side of the wounded man, who was quite as pale as the dead one.

He then began to take an inventory. There was a leather pocket-book, a purse, which evidently contained a part of the sum which the banditti had received, and a dice-box and dice; and these composed the inheritance of the dead man.

He left the dice-box and dice where they had fallen, threw the purse to the wounded man, and eagerly opened the pocket-book.

Amongst several unimportant papers, he found the following letter: it was that for which he had gone to search at the hazard of his life—

'Since you have lost the track of that woman, and she is now in safety in the convent, which you never ought to have allowed her to reach, take care at any rate not to miss the man; otherwise, you know that I have a long arm, and you shall pay dearly for the hundred louis which you have had of mine.'

There was no signature.

Nevertheless, it was evident that the letter was from her

ladyship. He kept it, therefore, as a testimony against her; and finding himself in safety behind the angle of the trench, he began to question the wounded man. The latter confessed that he had been engaged with his comrade, the same who had now been killed, to carry off a young woman, who was to leave Paris by the barrier of La Villette; but that, having stopped drinking at a wine-shop, they had been ten minutes too late for the carriage.

'But what were you to have done with this woman?' demanded d'Artagnan, in an agony of doubt.

'We were to have taken her to an hotel in the Place Royale,' said the wounded man.

'Yes, yes,' muttered d'Artagnan, 'that is it; to her ladyship herself.'

The young man shuddered as he comprehended with how terrible a thirst for vengeance this woman was impelled to destroy him, and those who loved him; and how well she was acquainted with the secrets of the court, since she had detected even this. For this exact information she was indebted to the cardinal.

But, as some degree of compensation, he ascertained with unfeigned joy that the queen had at last discovered the prison to which Madame Bonancieux had been sent to expiate her devotion, and had already rescued her from it. Thus the letter, which he had received from the young woman, and her appearance in the carriage on the Challiot road, were explained to him.

Thenceforth, as Athos had predicted, it was possible to find Madame Bonancieux again, and a convent was not impregnable.

This idea disposed his heart to clemency. He turned towards the wounded man, who watched all the changes of his countenance with anxiety, and stretching out his arm to him—

'Come,' said he, 'I will not leave you here. Rest on me, and let us return to the camp.'

'Yes,' said the wounded man, who could hardly credit so much magnanimity; 'but is it not to have me hanged?'

'You have my word,' replied he; 'for the second time, I grant you your life.'

The wounded man fell on his knees, and kissed the feet of his preserver; but d'Artagnan, who had no longer any motive for remaining so near the enemy himself, cut short these displays of gratitude.

The guard, who had returned at the first discharge from the bastion, had announced the death of his four companions. There was, therefore, both great astonishment and great joy in the regiment, when they saw the young man returning safe and sound.

D'Artagnan explained the sword-wound of his companion by a sortie, which he invented. He recounted the death of the other soldier, and the perils they had run. This account was the occasion of a veritable triumph to him. For one day the whole army spoke of this expedition; and his royal highness himself sent to compliment him on his conduct.

And, lastly, as every good action brings its recompense with it, that of d'Artagnan had the happy result of restoring to him the tranquillity that he had lost. In fact, the young man thought that he might cease to be disturbed, since, of his two enemies, one was killed, and the other devoted to his interests.

This tranquillity, however, proved one thing—that d'Artagnan did not yet thoroughly estimate her ladyship.

42

The Wine of Anjou

AFTER almost hopeless accounts of the king, the report of his recovery began to spread through the camp; and as he was in great haste to be at the siege in person, it was said that he would set out as soon as he could mount his horse.

In the meantime, his royal highness—who knew that he should soon be superseded, either by the Duc d'Angoulême, or by Bassompierre, or by Schomberg, who were already disputing with one another for the command—did but little, lost his time in petty attacks, and dared not hazard any great enterprise to drive the English from the Isle of Rhé, where they besieged the citadel of St. Martin, and the fort of La Prée; whilst the French, on their side, were besieging La Rochelle.

D'Artagnan, as we have said, had become now easy in his mind, as always happens after a past danger, and when peril seems to have entirely vanished.

Yet one anxiety still remained to him, which was, that he received no tidings of his friends.

But one morning he received an explanation, in the following letter, addressed from Villeroi—

'M. d'Artagnan,

'Messrs. Athos, Porthos, and Aramis, after having had a capital dinner party at my house, and enjoyed themselves very much, made so great a noise, that the provost of the castle, who is a strict disciplinarian, put them in confinement for a few days. I must, nevertheless, execute the orders that they gave me, to send you a dozen bottles of my Anjou wine, which they greatly admired. They hope that you will drink to their healths, in their own favourite wine.

'I have done this; and am, sir, with great respect, your most obedient, humble servant,

'GODEAU.

'The host of Messieurs the Musketeers.'

'Good!' exclaimed d'Artagnan; 'they think of me amidst their pleasures, as I have thought of them in my weariness. Certainly I will drink to them, and with all my heart, too; but not alone.'

And d'Artagnan hastened to the quarters of two guards, with whom he had become more intimate than with any of the others, to invite them to come and drink some of the delicious wine of Anjou, which had just arrived from Villeroi.

One of the two guards was to be on duty in the evening, and the other on the morrow; so the appointment was made for the day after.

D'Artagnan sent his twelve bottles of wine to the mess-room of the guards, desiring to have it kept with care; and on the day of the entertainment, as the dinner was fixed for twelve o'clock, he sent Planchet at nine to get everything prepared.

Planchet, elated at this exaltation to the dignity of butler, determined to perform his duties like an intelligent man. To effect this, he called in the aid of the valet, named Fourneau, of one of his master's guests, and also that of the pretended soldier who had sought to slay our hero, and who, belonging to no regiment, had, since the Gascon spared his life, entered into d'Artagnan's service, or, rather, into Planchet's.

The appointed dinner-hour being come, the two guests

arrived and took their places, and the dishes were arranged upon the table. Planchet waited, with a napkin on his arm; Fourneau uncorked the bottles; and Brisemont, for that was the invalid's name, decanted the wine, which seemed to have been somewhat disturbed by the shaking of the journey. The first bottle being a little thick towards the bottom, Brisemont poured the lees into a wine glass, and d'Artagnan permitted him to drink it, for the poor wretch was still very weak.

The guests, having finished their soup, were just conveying the first glass of wine to their lips, when suddenly the cannon sounded from Fort Louis and Pont-Neuf. The guards, thinking that there was some unexpected attack, either from the garrison, or from the English, immediately seized their swords: d'Artagnan did the same, and the three hastened out towards their posts.

But scarcely were they out of the mess-room, before they found the reason of this great noise. Cries of 'Long live the king!' 'Long live the cardinal!' re-echoed on every side, and drums were beat in all directions.

In fact, the king, in his impatience, had made such forced marches that he had at that moment arrived, with a reinforcement of ten thousand men. His musketeers preceded and followed him. D'Artagnan, placed in line with his company, with an expressive gesture saluted his friends and M. de Treville, whom he at once recognised.

The ceremony of reception being ended, the four friends were soon united.

'Egad!' exclaimed d'Artagnan, 'you could not have arrived in better time; the dinner will not have had even time to get cold. Is it not so, gentlemen?' added the young man, turning to the two guards, whom he presented to his friends.

'Ah! ah!' said Porthos, 'it appears that you were feasting.'

'I hope,' said Aramis, 'that there are no ladies at your dinner.'

'Is there any wine that is drinkable in this paltry place?' said Athos.

'Why, sang Dieu! there is your own, my dear friend,' answered d'Artagnan.

'Our wine?' said Athos, in astonishment.

'Yes, that which you sent me.'

'Wine that we sent you?'

'Yes, you know very well; that wine from the hills of Anjou.'

'Yes, I know what wine you are talking of——'

'Your favourite wine——'

'Ay, when I have neither champagne nor chambertin.'

'Well, in the absence of champagne and chambertin, you must be contented with this.'

'And so we, gluttons as we are, have sent you some wine, have we?' said Porthos.

'No, but it is the wine which was sent by your orders.'

'By our orders?' echoed the musketeers.

'Did you send the wine, Aramis?' inquired Athos.

'No; did you, Porthos?'

'No; did you, Athos?'

'No.'

'If it was not you,' said d'Artagnan, 'then it was your host.'

'Our host?'

'Yes, your host—Godeau, at Villeroi.'

'Faith, let it come from whom it may, no matter!' said Porthos. 'Let us taste it, and, if good, let us drink it.'

'No,' said Athos, 'let us not drink any wine without knowing whence it comes.'

'You are right, Athos,' said d'Artagnan. 'Did none of you direct the host, Godeau, to send me the wine?'

'No; and yet he sent you some in our names?'

'Here is the letter,' said d'Artagnan, and he presented the letter to his companions.

'It is not his writing,' said Athos: 'I know his hand, for it was I who, before we left, settled our joint account.'

'A false letter!' said Porthos indignantly; 'we have not been imprisoned.'

'D'Artagnan,' said Aramis, in a tone of reproach, 'how could you believe that we had become noisy?'

D'Artagnan grew suddenly pale, and a convulsive trembling shook his limbs.

'You frighten me,' said Athos; 'what can have occurred?'

'Let us run, my friends, let us run,' said d'Artagnan: 'a horrible suspicion crosses my mind. Can this, too, be another of that woman's acts of vengeance?'

It was now Athos who, in his turn, grew pale.

D'Artagnan sprang towards the mess-room, followed by the three musketeers and the two guards.

The first object which struck d'Artagnan's sight on entering the room was Brisemont, extended on the floor, writhing in most horrible convulsions. Planchet and

Fourneau, looking as pale as corpses, were endeavouring to assist him; but it was evident that all aid was useless: the features of the dying man were contracted with agony.

'Ah!' cried he, when he perceived d'Artagnan, 'you pretended to forgive me, and you poison me!'

'I, wretch! I!' exclaimed the young man; 'what can you mean?'

'I say that it is you who gave me the wine; and it is you who told me to drink it. You wanted to take your revenge —oh! it is dreadful!'

'Do not think so, Brisemont,' said d'Artagnan, 'for I swear——'

'Oh! but God is there—God will punish you! My God! may you one day suffer what I suffer now!'

'Upon the gospel,' cried d'Artagnan, rushing towards the dying man, 'I swear that I knew not that this wine was poisoned, and also that I was about to drink it as well as yourself.'

'I do not believe you,' exclaimed the soldier; and he expired in exaggerated tortures.

'Horrible! horrible!' muttered Athos; whilst Porthos broke the bottles; and Aramis—rather late, it must be confessed—sent off for a confessor.

'Oh! my friends,' said d'Artagnan, 'you have now again saved my life; and not mine only, but the lives of these gentlemen also. Gentlemen,' continued he, addressing the guards, 'may I request your silence concerning this catastrophe? Persons of high condition may be implicated in what you have now seen, and the misery of it all would fall upon us.'

'Ah! sir,' stammered out Planchet, more dead than alive; 'ah! sir, what a narrow escape I have had!'

'What, you rascal!' cried d'Artagnan, 'were you going to drink my wine?'

'To the king's health, sir: I was going to drink one little glass, if Fourneau had not said that some one called me.'

'Alas!' said Fourneau, whose teeth were chattering with fright, 'I wanted to get rid of him that I might drink some myself.'

'Gentlemen,' said d'Artagnan, addressing the guards, 'you must be aware that our entertainment would be but a melancholy affair after what has passed. I beseech you, therefore, to receive my excuses, and let us postpone it till some other day.'

The two guards courteously accepted these apologies; and, understanding that the four friends wished to be alone, they took their departure.

When the young guard and the three musketeers were without witnesses, they looked at one another for an instant, in a way which proved how well they understood the seriousness of their situation.

'First,' said Athos, 'let us quit this room: a dead man is but sorry company.'

'Planchet,' said d'Artagnan, 'I recommend you to look to the body of this poor devil, and see that it is buried in consecrated ground. He had committed a crime, it is true; but he had repented of it.'

Having entrusted the funeral rites of Brisemont to Planchet and Fourneau, the four friends quitted the room.

The host gave them another chamber, and furnished them with fresh eggs, whilst Athos himself fetched water for them from the well. Aramis and Porthos were, in a few words, informed of all that had occurred.

'Well!' said d'Artagnan to Athos, 'you see, my dear friend, it is war to the death!'

Athos shook his head. 'Yes, yes,' said he, 'I see it well enough; but are you sure that it is she?'

'Perfectly.'

'Nevertheless, I confess that *I* have still some doubts.'

'But that fleur-de-lis upon her shoulder?'

'It is an Englishwoman, who has committed some crime in France, and has been branded in consequence.'

'Athos, it is your wife, I tell you,' repeated d'Artagnan. 'Do you not remember how the two marks agree?'

'And yet I should have thought that the other was dead —I had hanged her so thoroughly!'

It was d'Artagnan who shook his head this time.

'But, after all, what is to be done?' said the young man.

'The fact is, that it is impossible to remain in this manner, with a sword always suspended over one's head,' replied Athos; 'and you must get freed from such a situation.'

'But how?'

'Listen: try to find her, and to come to an understanding with her. Say to her—'peace or war? On the honour of a gentleman, I will never say one word, or take one step, to injure you. On your part, give me a solemn oath to remain neutral with respect to me. If not, I will go to the chancellor, to the king, and to the executioner: I will excite the court against you, and will declare you branded: I will cause you to be tried; and, if you are acquitted, well then, on the word of a gentleman, I will kill you myself, as I would a mad dog.''

'I like this plan well enough,' said d'Artagnan; 'but how am I to find her?'

'Time, my dear friend—time brings opportunity: opportunity is man's martingale: the more one has shipped, the more one gains when he knows how to wait.'

'Yes; but to wait surrounded by assasins and poisoners.'

'Bah!' said Athos, 'God has preserved us hitherto, and God will preserve us still.'

'Yes. Besides, we are men, and, after all, it is our business to risk our lives; but, she?' added d'Artagnan in a low voice.

'And who is she?' asked Athos.

'Constance.'

'Madame Bonancieux? True! I had forgotten, 'said Athos. 'Poor fellow! I forgot that you were in love.'

'Well,' said Aramis. 'but did you not see, by the very letter that you found on the wretch who was killed, that she was in a convent? One is quite safe in a convent, and as soon as the siege of La Rochelle is ended, I promise you, on my own part——'

'Good!' said Athos, 'good! Yes, my dear Aramis, we know that your views all tend towards religion.'

'I am only a musketeer temporarily,' said Aramis meekly.

'It would seem that he has not heard from his mistress for a long while,' said Athos, in a whisper, to d'Artagnan; 'but do not make any remark—we know it.'

'Well,' said Porthos, 'it seems to me that there is a very simple means.'

'And what is that?' demanded d'Artagnan.

'She is in a convent, you say?' continued Porthos.

'Yes.'

'Well, as soon as the siege is raised, we will take her out of this convent.'

'But, first, we must know what convent she is in.'

'Ah, that is true.' said Porthos.

'But, do you not say, my dear d'Artagnan,' said Athos, 'that it is the queen who has chosen this convent for her?'

'Yes. I believe so, at least.'

'Well, then, Porthos will help us in that case.'

'How so, pray?' asked Porthos.

'Why, through your marchioness, or duchess, or princess: she ought to have a long arm.'

'Hush!' said Porthos, putting his fingers on his lips; 'I fancy she is a cardinalist, and she must know nothing about it.'

'Then,' said Aramis, 'I undertake to get some news of Madame Bonancieux.'

'You, Aramis?' exclaimed the three friends; 'you, and how so?'

'Through the queen's almoner, with whom I am very intimate,' answered Aramis, blushing.

On this assurance the four friends, who had ended their simple repast, separated, with the promise of meeting again the same evening. D'Artagnan returned to the Minimes, and the three musketeers went to the king's quarters, where they had to provide themselves with lodgings.

43

The Red Dove-Cot Tavern

ALMOST as soon as he had reached the camp, the king—who was in great haste to find himself before the enemy, and who participated in the cardinal's hatred of Buckingham—wished to complete the preparations, first, for driving the English from the Isle of Rhé, and then for forcing the siege of La Rochelle. But, in spite of all his endeavours, he was retarded by the dissensions which broke out between de Bassompierre and Schomberg against the Duke of Angoulême.

Schomberg and de Bassompierre were marshals of France, and insisted on their right to command the army, under the superintendence of the king; but the cardinal, apprehensive that Bassompierre, who was a Huguenot at heart, might fight feebly against the English and the Rochellois, who were his co-religionists, supported the Duke of Angoulême, whom his majesty had, at his instigation, already made lieutenant-general. The result was, that, with the alternative of seeing Schomberg and de Bassompierre desert the army, they were compelled to give each a separate command. Bassompierre took his station at the north of the city, from Lalen to Dompierre; the Duke of Angoulême took his to the east, from Dompierre to Périgny; and Schomberg, to the south, from Périgny to Angoulin.

His royal highness fixed his quarters at Dompierre; his

majesty was sometimes at Estré, and sometimes at Jarrie; and the cardinal established himself at a simple house, without any entrenchment, at Pont de la Pierre, upon the downs.

Thus, his royal highness overlooked Bassompierre: the king, the Duke of Angoulême; and the cardinal, M. de Schomberg. As soon as this arrangement had been established, they had occupied themselves in driving the English from the isle.

The conjuncture was favourable. The English—who, above all things, require to be well-fed in order to prove good soldiers—eating only salted provisions and bad biscuits, had many invalids in their camp; and, moreover, the sea—which was, at that season of the year, highly dangerous on all the western coasts—was every day disastrous to some small vessel or other, and the shore, from the point of l'Aiguillon to the trenches, was literally strewed at every tide with the wrecks of pinnaces, cutters, and feluccas. The result was, that, should the king's troops even keep within their camp, Buckingham, who remained in the Isle of Rhé only from obstinacy, would sooner or later be obliged to raise the siege.

But, as M. de Toiras announced that everything was preparing in the enemy's camp for a new assault, the king concluded on adopting final measures, and issued the necessary orders for a decisive affair.

Our intention being, not to make a journal of the siege, but merely to record those events in it which bear upon the history we are relating, we shall be contented with stating that the enterprise succeeded to the great satisfaction of the king, and the great glory of the cardinal. The English, beaten back foot by foot, conquered in every encounter, trodden down in their passage from the isle, were compelled to re-embark, leaving, on the field of battle, two thousand men, amongst whom were five colonels, three lieutenant-colonels, two hundred and fifty captains, and twenty gentlemen of quality, as well as four pieces of cannon and sixty flags, which last were conveyed to Paris by Claude de St. Simon, and suspended with great pomp to the arched roof of Notre-Dame.

Te Deums were sung in the camp, and soon spread themselves thence throughout the whole of France.

The cardinal was thus at liberty to carry on the siege, without having, at least for the time, any reason to be apprehensive of the English.

But, as we have just said, the security was only momentary. An envoy of the Duke of Buckingham, one whose name was Montague, having been seized, they found upon him proofs of a league between the Empire, Spain, England, and Lorraine. This league was formed against France.

And in the quarters of Buckingham, which he had been forced to abandon precipitately, there had been found papers confirming—as the cardinal declares in his memoirs —the existence of this league, and compromising greatly Madame de Chevreuse, and, consequently, the queen.

It was upon the cardinal that all the responsibility rested; for a man can never be an absolute minister without being responsible. On this account, all the resources of his vast genius were exerted by night and day, and occupied in listening to the last breath that stirred in any one of the great realms of Europe.

The cardinal was well aware of the activity, and, above all, of the hatred of Buckingham. If the league which threatened France should triumph, all his influence would be lost. The policies of Spain and Austria would have each its representatives in the cabinet at the Louvre, where they had as yet only partisans. He, Richelieu, the French minister, the minister emphatically national, would be ruined; and the king, who, even whilst he was obeying him like a child, hated him as a child hates its masters, would abandon him to the combined vengeance of his royal highness and the queen. He should be ruined himself, and perhaps France with him; and these were disasters the he was bound to prevent.

On this account couriers, becoming more numerous every instant, were seen succeeding each other by night and by day, at that small house, at the Pont de la Pierre, in which the cardinal had fixed his home.

There were monks, who wore the monastic habit so ill that it was easy to recognise them as belonging to the church militant; women, a little awkward in their pages' costumes, the looseness of whose dresses would not entirely conceal their rounded forms; and countrymen, with blackened hands, but fine limbs, who might be known for men of quality at a league's distance.

Other visits, too, there were, more disagreeable; for it had been two or three times reported that the cardinal had narrowly escaped assassination. It is true that the enemies of his eminence declared, that it was he himself who had employed these unskilful assassins, so that he might, on occasion, have the right of retaliation: but we should believe neither what ministers say, nor what their enemies say.

Yet this did not prevent the cardinal, whose most violent detractors never called in question his personal courage, from making many nocturnal expeditions; sometimes to communicate important orders to the Duke of Angoulême, sometimes to enter into council with the king, and somtimes to confer with some messenger, whom he did not choose to have admitted to his own abode.

The musketeers, on their side, not having much to occupy them in the siege, were not very strictly controlled, and led a merry life. This was the more easy to our three companions especially, as, being friends of M. de Treville, they readily obtained from him special permissions to absent themselves, even after the hour at which the camp was closed.

Now, one evening, when d'Artagnan, who was in the trenches, could not accompany them, Athos, Porthos and Aramis, mounted on their chargers, enveloped in their service cloaks, and with their hands on the butt-ends of their pistols, were returning together from a tavern, which Athos had discovered two days before on the La Jarrie road, and which was called the Red Dove-Cot. They were proceeding on the road toward the camp, keeping a good look-out for fear of an ambuscade, when, about a quarter of a league from the village of Boisnau, they thought they heard the sound of horses coming towards them. They all immediately halted, in close rank, and waited, keeping in the middle of the road. After a short time, and just as the moon emerged from behind a cloud, they saw, coming round the corner of the road, two horsemen, who, upon perceiving them, halted also, appearing to deliberate whether they should advance or retreat.

This hesitation excited the suspicion of our three friends; and Athos, advancing a few paces, cried out, in his firm voice—

'Who goes there?'

'Who goes there, yourself?' replied one of the two horsemen.

'That is no reply, that!' said Athos. 'Who goes there? Answer, or we charge!'

'Take care what you are about, gentlemem,' said a sonorous voice, which appeared to be accustomed to command.

'It is some officer of rank who is making his nightly rounds,' said Athos, turning towards his companions. 'What will you do, gentlemen?'

'Who are you?' said the same voice, in the same commanding tone. 'Reply, or you may find yourselves in some trouble for your disobedience.'

'King's musketeers!' answered Athos, more than ever convinced that he who thus questioned him had the right to do so.

'Of what company?'

'Company of Treville.'

'Advance, and give an account of what you are doing here at this hour.'

The three companions advanced, with their ears a little drooping; for they were all now convinced that they had to deal with one more powerful than themselves. They left Athos to be their spokesman.

One of the two horsemen—he who had spoken the second time—was about ten paces before his companion. Athos made a sign to Porthos and Aramis to remain in the same manner in the rear, and advanced alone.

'Excuse us, sir,' said Athos, 'but we did not know who you were, and you may see that we kept a good look-out.'

'Your name?' said the officer, who covered part of his face with his cloak.

'But you, yourself, sir,' said Athos, who began to be indignant at this questioning, 'give me, I beg, some proof that you have the right thus to question me.'

'Your name?' said the cavalier a second time, letting his cloak fall, so that his countenance might be seen.

'The cardinal!' cried the astounded musketeer.

'Your name!' repeated his eminence, a third time.

'Athos,' said he.

The cardinal made a sign to his equerry, who approached him.

'These three musketeers will follow us,' said he in a low voice: 'I do not wish it to be known that I have left the camp; and, by making them follow us, we shall be certain that they will not tell any one.'

'We are gentlemen, my lord,' said Athos: 'ask us for our words, and do not be in doubt about us. Thank God, we know how to keep a secret.'

The cardinal fixed his piercing eyes upon the daring speaker.

'You have a fine ear, M. Athos,' said the cardinal, 'but

now listen to this: it is not through distrust that I request you to follow me: it is for my own security. Undoubtedly your two companions are Messrs. Porthos and Aramis?'

'Yes, your eminence,' said Athos, whilst the two musketeers came forward, hat in hand.

'I know you, gentlemen,' said the cardinal; 'I know you. I am aware that you are not entirely my friends, and I am sorry for it; but I know that you are brave and loyal gentlemen, and that you may safely be trusted. M. Athos, do me the honour, therefore, to accompany me with your two friends, and then I shall have an escort which might excite the envy of his majesty, if we should meet him.'

The three musketeers bowed to the very necks of their horses.

'Well, then, upon my honour,' said Athos, 'your eminence is right to take us with you. We have met some sinister faces on the road, and we have even had a quarrel with four of them at the Red Dove-Cot.'

'A quarrel! And on what account, gentlemen?' said the cardinal. 'I do not like rufflers, you know.'

'That is exactly why I have had the honour to warn your eminence of what has just happened; for you might hear it from others, and, from a false report, be induced to believe that we had been at fault.'

'And what were the consequences of this quarrel?' demanded the cardinal, frowning.

'Why, my friend Aramis there has received a slight wound in the arm, which, however, as your eminence may see, will not hinder him from mounting to the assault to-morrow, if your eminence commands the attack.'

'But you are not the kind of men to take wounds in that way,' said the cardinal. 'Come, be frank, gentlemen; you certainly gave some in return: confess yourselves; you know that I have the right to pronounce absolution.'

'I, my lord,' said Athos, 'did not even draw my sword; but I took him, with whom I was engaged, up in my arms, and threw him out of the window; and,' continued Athos, with some slight hesitation, 'I fancy that, in falling, he broke his thigh.'

'Ah, ah!' said the cardinal; 'and you, M. Porthos?'

'I, my lord, knowing that sword-play is forbidden, seized a bench, and gave one of these brigands a blow which, I think, broke his shoulder.'

'Very well,' said the cardinal: 'and you, M. Aramis?'

'I, my lord, as I am naturally very gentle, and am, besides, as your eminence perhaps does not know, on the point of taking orders, I wanted to lead away my companions, when one of these wretches treacherously stabbed me through the left arm; my patience then failed me, I drew my sword in turn, and as he returned, to the charge, I fancy that I felt, as he threw himself upon me, that the weapon passed through his body. I only know that he fell, and seemed to be carried away with his two companions.'

'The fiend, gentlemen!' said the cardinal: 'three men disabled in a tavern quarrel! You have rather active hands. But, by the way, what was the cause of the quarrel?'

'These wretches were drunk,' said Athos, 'and, knowing that a lady had arrived at the tavern that evening, they wanted to force her door.'

'And was this woman young and pretty?' demanded the cardinal, with some anxiety.

'We did not see her, my lord,' replied Athos.

'You did not see her? Ah! very good!' briskly replied the cardinal; 'you did right to defend the honour of a woman; and as I am myself going down to the Red Dove-Cot, I shall know whether you have told me the truth.'

'My lord,' proudly replied Athos, 'we are gentlemen, and would not tell a lie to save our lives.'

'Nor do I doubt what you have told me, M. Athos—no, not for one moment; but,' added he, to change the conversation, 'was this lady alone?'

'The lady had a cavalier closeted with her; but as he did not show himself, in spite of the noise, it is to be presumed that he is a coward.'

'Judge not rashly, says the Gospel,' replied the cardinal. Aramis bowed.

'And now, gentlemen,' said the cardinal, 'I know what I wanted to learn—follow me.'

The three musketeers fell behind the cardinal, who again covered his face with his cloak, and went forward, keeping himself eight or ten paces before his four companions.

They soon arrived at the silent, solitary tavern. The landlord was unquestionably aware what an illustrious visitor he was to expect, and had dismissed all troublesome persons.

Ten paces before he reached the door, the cardinal made a sign to his equerry, and to the three musketeers, to halt. A ready-saddled horse was fastened to the shutter. The cardinal knocked three times in a peculiar manner.

A man, enveloped in a cloak, came out directly, and quickly exchanged a few words with the cardinal; after which he mounted the horse, and went off towards Surgrèe, which was also the road to Paris.

'Come forward, gentlemen,' said the cardinal. 'I find that you have told me the truth, gentlemen, and it will not be my fault if our meeting this evening should not turn out to your advantage. In the meantime, follow me.'

The cardinal dismounted, and the three musketeers did the same. The cardinal cast his bridle over the arm of his equerry, and the musketeers fastened theirs to the shutters. The landlord stood on the step of his door: to him, the cardinal was only an officer coming to visit a lady.

'Have you any chamber on the ground floor, where these gentlemen may wait for me, by a good fire?' inquired the cardinal.

The landlord opened the door of a large room, where a sorry, closed iron stove had lately been replaced by a large and excellent chimney.

'I have this,' replied he.

'That will do excellently,' said the cardinal. 'Enter, gentlemen, and be pleased to wait for me here: I shall not be more than half an hour.'

And whilst the three musketeers entered the chamber on the ground floor, the cardinal, without requiring any direction, ascended the stairs, like a man who has no need to be told the way.

44

The Utility of Stove Funnels

It was evident, that, unconsciously, and moved solely by their chivalrous and adventurous character, our three friends had rendered a service to some one whom the cardinal honoured with his own especial protection.

But, who was that some one? This was the question which our three musketeers first asked themselves; then, finding that none of the replies which their intelligence suggested were satisfactory, Porthos called the landlord, and asked for some dice.

Porthos and Aramis placed themselves at a table, and

began to play, whilst Athos walked up and down the room, in deep thought.

As he walked and meditated, he passed and repassed before the funnel of the former stove, which had been half broken off, and of which the other end went into the apartment above. Each time that he passed he heard the murmur of speech, which at last attracted his notice. Athos approached, and distinguished some words, which certainly appeared to deserve so much attention, that he made signs to his two companions to be silent, and remained himself with his ear bent down to the level of the lower opening of the funnel.

'Listen, my lady,' said the cardinal. 'The business is important. Sit down, and let us talk about it.'

'My lady!' muttered Athos.

'I am listening to your eminence with the greatest attention,' replied a voice, which made him start.

'A small vessel, with an English crew, whose captain is devoted to me, awaits you at the mouth of the Charente, at the Fort de la Pointe; it will sail to-morrow morning.'

'I must go there to-night, then?'

'Directly; that is to say, as soon as you have received my instructions. Two men, whom you will find at the door when you go out, will escort you. You will let me depart first, and then, half an hour after, you will depart yourself.'

'Yes, my lord. Now, let us return to the commission which you are pleased to charge me; and, as I am anxious to continue to merit your confidence, deign to explain it, in clear and precise terms, so that I may not make any error.'

There was a moment of profound silence between the two interlocutors. It was evident that the cardinal was weighing beforehand the expressions he was about to use, and that the lady was collecting all her intellectual faculties to understand what he was going to say, and to engrave it on her memory when it was said.

Athos took advantage of this moment to tell his two companions to fasten the door inside, and to beckon them to come and listen with him. The two musketeers who loved their ease, brought a chair for each of themselves, and one for Athos. They all three seated themselves, with their heads close together, and their ears wide open.

'You are going to London,' resumed the cardinal; 'on arriving there, you will seek out Buckingham.'

'I would observe to your eminence,' said her ladyship,

'that since the affair of the diamond studs, in which the duke has always suspected me, his grace mistrusts me.'

'But you have no occasion this time,' said the cardinal, 'to gain his confidence: you are to present yourself frankly and loyally, as an ambassadress.'

'Frankly and loyally!' repeated the lady, with an indescribable accent of duplicity.

'Yes, frankly and loyally,' replied the cardinal, in the same tone; 'all this business must be transacted openly.'

'I will follow your eminence's instructions to the very letter, and I wait for you to give them.'

'You will go to Buckingham from me, and you will tell him that I am aware of all the preparations he is making, but that I do not much disturb myself about them, seeing that, at the first step on which he ventures, I will destroy the queen.'

'Will he believe that your eminence is in a condition to execute your threats?'

'Yes, for I am in possession of proofs.'

'It will be necessary for me to be able to submit these proofs to his examination.'

'Certainly; and you will say to him, first, that I shall publish the report of Bois-Robert, and of the Marquis de Beautru, concerning the interview which the duke had with the queen, at the house of the high-constable's lady, on the evening that the latter gave a masked ball; and you will add—in order to leave him no room for doubt—that he came in the costume of the Great Mogul, which was to have been worn by the Duke of Guise, and which he bought of this latter for the sum of three thousand pistoles.'

'Good, my lord!'

'All the details of his entry into the Louvre, where he introduced himself in the character of an Italian fortune-teller, and of his leaving in the night, are known to me; and you will tell him, in order that he may be again assured of the accuracy of my information, that he had, under his cloak, a large white robe, thickly-covered with tears, and death's heads, and cross-bones, in which, in case of surprise, he was to personate the phantom of the white lady, who, as is well known, revisits the Louvre whenever any great event is about to be accomplished.'

'Is that all, my lord?'

'Tell him that I know all the particulars of the adventure at Amiens; and that I shall make a little spiritually-turned romance of it, with a plan of the garden, and the portraits of the principal actors in that nocturnal scene.'

'I will tell him this.'

'Tell him, further, that I have got Montague in the Bastile: it is true we found no letter on him, but the torture may make him tell all he knows—and even a little more.'

'Perfect!'

'And, lastly, add, that his grace, in his hurry to leave the Isle of Rhé, forgot to remove from his quarters a certain letter of Madame de Chevreuse, which strangely compromises the queen, inasmuch as it proves, not only that her majesty can love the enemies of the king, but, also, that she can conspire with the enemies of France. You now thoroughly comprehend all that I have told you, do you not?'

'Your eminence shall judge: the high-constable's lady's ball; the night at the Louvre; the evening at Amiens; the arrest of Montague; and the letter of Madame de Chevreuse.'

'That is right, my lady; that is right; you have an excellent memory.'

'But,' resumed she to whom the cardinal had just addressed this compliment, 'if, in spite of all these reasons, the duke should not surrender, and should continue to menace France?'

'The duke is in love like a madman, or rather like a ninny,' replied Richelieu, with intense bitterness. 'Like the Paladins of old, he has only undertaken this war to obtain a glance from his mistress's eyes. If he knows that the war will cost the lady of his love her honour, and perhaps her liberty, I warrant you that he will look twice at it before he decides.'

'But yet,' said the lady, with a perseverance which proved that she was determined to understand all that was included in the mission that she was about to undertake; 'but yet, if he should persist?'

'If he persists?' said the cardinal. 'But it is not probable!'

'It is possible!' rejoined the lady.

'If he persists?'—His eminence paused, and then continued: 'If he persists—well, I must put my hope in one of those events which change the fortune of nations.'

'If your eminence would cite to me some of those historical events,' said her ladyship, 'I might possibly participate in your confidence concerning the future.'

'Well, look for example,' said Richelieu, 'when, for a cause very similar to that which now actuates the duke, his majesty Henry IV., of glorious memory, went, in 1610, to invade at the same time both Flanders and Italy, in order that he might assail Austria on both sides, did not an event occur which saved Austria? Why should the king of France not have the same good fortune as the emperor?'

'Your eminence alludes to the assassin's knife in the Rue de la Féronniere?'

'Precisely so,' said the cardinal.

'Is your eminence not afraid that the fate of Ravaillac would deter those who might be for an instant tempted to imitate his example?'

'In all times and all countries, especially in those countries which are divided within by religious faith, there are always fanatics who would be well contented to be regarded as martyrs. And here, at this very moment, it occurs to me that the Puritans are furious against the Duke of Buckingham and that their preachers speak of him as the anti-Christ.'

'Well?' inquired her ladyship.

'Well,' continued the cardinal, in a careless tone, 'it would be only necessary, for instance, to find some young, beautiful, and clever woman, who wanted to take revenge upon the duke. Such a woman may be found. The duke has been a favoured lover; and, if he has sown much affection by his promises of eternal constancy, he has also sown much hatred by his continual infidelities.'

Unquestionably,' remarked her ladyship coldly, 'such a woman may be found.'

'Well, such a woman would, by putting the knife of Clément or of Ravaillac into the hands of an assassin, save France.'

'Yes! but she would be an accomplice in assassination!'

'Have the accomplices of Ravaillac, or of Jacques Clément, ever been discovered?'

'No; for they were perhaps too high in station for any one to dare to seek them where they really were. It is not for everybody, my lord, that the Palace of Justice would be burned down.'

'What, do you not believe, then, that the burning of the palace was an accident of chance?' asked Richelieu, in the very tone with which he would have asked the most unimportant question.

'I, my lord,' replied her ladyship, 'I have no belief about it. I cite a fact—nothing more. Only, I would say, that if I were called Mademoiselle de Montpensier, or the queen Marie de Médicis, I should take fewer precautions than I do, now that I am simply named Lady de Winter.'

'That is quite fair,' said Richelieu; 'what is it, then, that you require?'

'I require an order, ratifying beforehand whatever I may think it necessary to do for the prosperity of France.'

'But we must, first, find the woman I alluded to, who craves revenge upon the duke.'

'She is found!' said the lady.

'Then we must find out the wretched fanatic who will serve as the instrument of God's justice.'

'He shall be found!'

'Well,' said the cardinal, 'it will then be time enough to solicit the order that you have just demanded.'

'Your eminence is right,' resumed her ladyship, 'and I was to blame for seeing, in the mission with which you honour me, anything beyond what it in truth embraces: that is—to announce to his grace, in your eminence's name, that you are aware of the different disguises under which he contrived to approach the queen at the entertainment given by the constable's lady; that you have proofs of the interview which the queen granted at the Louvre to a certain Italian astrologer, who was no other than the Duke of Buckingham; that you have given directions for a spiritual little romance concerning the adventure at Amiens, with a plan of the garden in which it occurred, and portraits of the actors who took part in it; that Montague is in the Bastile, and that the torture may make him tell all that he remembers, and even much that he does not remember; and, finally, that you possess a certain letter from Madame de Chevreuse, which was found in his grace's quarters, and which strangely compromises, not only her who wrote it, but also her in whose name it has been written. But, if he persists in spite of these representations, as this is the limit of my commission, it will only remain for me to pray to God to perform a miracle for the salvation of France. This is my precise mission, is it not, my lord; and I have nothing else to do?'

'Exactly so,' said Richelieu coldly.

'And now,' continued her ladyship, without appearing to observe the altered manner of his eminence towards her, 'since I have received your eminence's instructions with regard to your enemies, will your lordship permit me to say a few words concerning mine?'

'You have enemies, then?' said Richelieu.

'Yes, my lord, enemies against whom you are bound to

434

support me, since I made them in the service of your eminence.'

'And who are they?' demanded the cardinal.

'There is, first, a little busybody, of the name of Bonancieux.'

'She is in prison, at Nantes.'

'That is to say, she was there,' replied the lady; 'but the queen has inveigled an order from the king, by the assistance of which she has removed her to a convent.'

'To a convent?' said the cardinal.

'Yes; a convent.'

'And in what convent?'

'I do not know: the secret has been well kept.'

'I will know it, though!'

'And your eminence will let me know in what convent this woman is?'

'I see no objection to that,' replied the cardinal.

'Very well. Now I have another enemy, whom I fear far more than this little Madame Bonancieux.'

'Who is that?'

'Her lover.'

'What is his name?'

'Oh! your eminence knows him well,' exclaimed the lady, carried away by her anger; 'it is the evil genius of both of us: it is he who, in an encounter with your eminence's guards, turned the victory in favour of the king's musketeers; it is he who gave three sword wounds to de Wardes, your eminence's emissary, and who rendered the affair of the diamond studs abortive; and, lastly, it is he who, knowing that it was I who had deprived him of Madame Bonancieux, has sworn my death.'

'Ah, ah!' said the cardinal, 'I know who you mean.'

'Yes, I mean that wretch, d'Artagnan.'

'He is a bold fellow, that,' said the cardinal.

'And it is exactly because he is a bold fellow that he is the more to be feared.'

'We ought first,' said the cardinal, 'to have some proof of his association with the duke.'

'A proof!' exclaimed the lady; 'I will have a dozen.'

'Well, then, let me have the proof, and it is the simplest thing in the world: I will send him to the Bastile.'

'Very well, my lord; but then afterwards?'

'When a man is in the Bastile, there is no *afterwards*,' said the cardinal in a hollow voice. 'Ah, Mort Dieu!'

continued he, 'if it was as easy for me to get rid of my enemy as it is to rid you of yours, and if it was against such people as these that you asked me for impunity——'

'My lord,' said the lady, 'boon for boon, life for life, man for man: give me the one, and I will give you the other.'

'I do not understand what you mean,' replied the cardinal, 'nor do I wish to do so; but I shall be glad to oblige you, and I see no objection to giving you the order you demand, as to such an insignificant creature as this; and the more willingly, as you tell me that this little d'Artagnan is a libertine, a duellist, and a traitor.'

'A wretch, my lord—a wretch.'

'Then give me a pen, ink, and paper,' said the cardinal.

'Here they are, my lord.'

'Perfect.'

There was a moment's silence, which proved that the cardinal was occupied in thinking of the words in which the order should be written, or perhaps in writing it. Athos, who had not lost one word of the conversation, took a hand of each of his companions, and led them to the other end of the room.

'Well,' said Porthos, 'what do you want, and why do you not let us hear the end of the conversation?'

'Hush!' said Athos in a whisper, 'we have heard all that it was necessary for us to hear; besides, I do not hinder you from hearing the rest, but I must go.'

'You must go,' said Porthos: 'but if the cardinal should ask for you, what are we to say?'

'You will not wait for him to ask. You will tell him beforehand, that I am gone in advance to clear the way, since from certain words of our landlord's, I have been led to suppose that the road is not quite safe. I will drop a word or two to the cardinal's equerry. The rest concerns myself— do not be uneasy about it.'

'Be prudent, Athos,' said Aramis.

'Make yourself easy,' replied Athos; 'you know that I am cool enough.'

Porthos and Aramis returned to their places near the funnel.

'As for Athos, he went out without any disguise, took his horse, which was fastened along with those of his two friends to the shutter, convinced the equerry in four words of the necessity of an advance-guard on their return, looked with affected care at the priming of his pistols, put his sword between his teeth, and set off as a forlorn hope, on the road that led towards the camp.

45

A Conjugal Scene

As Athos had foreseen, the cardinal was not long before he descended. He opened the door of the room in which he had left the three musketeers, and found Porthos and Aramis engaged in a most earnest game of dice. With a rapid glance, he examined every corner of the room, and saw that one of his men was missing.

'What has become of M. Athos?' he asked.

'My lord,' replied Porthos, 'he is gone forward on the look out, as some remarks of our landlord's led him to suspect that the road was not safe.'

'And what have you been doing, M. Porthos?'

'I have won five pistoles from Aramis.'

'And can you now return with me?'

'We are at your eminence's command.'

'To horse, then, gentlemen; for it is getting late.'

The equerry was at the door, holding the cardinal's horse. At a little distance two men and three horses were visible in the shade: these men were the individuals who were to conduct her ladyship to the Fort de la Pointe, and to superintend her embarkation.

The equerry confirmed what the two musketeers had already told the cardinal concerning Athos. Richelieu gave a sign of approbation, and resumed his journey, taking the same precautions in his return as he had done in his advance.

Let us leave him on his way to the camp, protected by the equerry and the two musketeers, and return to Athos.

For a hundred yards he had preserved the same pace. But, once out of view, he had pushed his horse to the right, had made a small circuit, and had returned to within twenty paces, where, concealed in the coppice, he awaited the passage of the little troop. Having recognised the laced hats of his companions, and the gold fringe of the cardinal's cloak, he tarried till the party had turned the corner of the road; and having lost sight of them, he galloped up to the tavern, and was admitted without any difficulty.

The landlord recognised him again.

'My officer,' said Athos, 'has forgotten a communication of importance which he should have made to the lady on the first floor, and has sent me to repair his forgetfulness.'

'Go up,' said the landlord; 'the lady is still in her chamber.'

Athos availed himself of this permission, and ascended the stairs with his lightest step; and when he had reached the landing-place, he perceived, through the half-open door, the lady, who was fastening on her hat.

He entered the room, and closed the door behind him.

Enveloped in his cloak, and with his hat drawn down over his eyes, Athos stood upright before the door.

On seeing this figure, mute and motionless as a statue, the lady was alarmed.

'Who are you, and what do you want?' exclaimed she.

'Yes! it is indeed she,' muttered Athos.

Letting his cloak fall, and lifting up his hat, he advanced towards her ladyship.

'Do you recognise me, madame?' said he.

The lady took one step forward, and then recoiled as though she had seen a serpent.

'Come,' said Athos, 'I can see that you recognise me.'

'The Count de la Fére!' muttered her ladyship, growing deadly pale, and drawing back till the wall prevented her retreat.

'Yes, my lady,' replied Athos, 'the Count de la Fére in person, who returns expressly from the other world to have the pleasure of seeing you. Let us sit down then, and converse, to quote the cardinal.'

Impelled by an inexpressible terror, her ladyship sat down, without uttering a word.

'You are a demon let loose upon the earth,' said Athos. 'Your power is great, I know; but you know, also, that, with God's assistance, men have often overcome the most terrible demons. You have once before crossed my path. I thought that I had crushed you, madame; but, either I deceived myself, or hell has given you new life.'

At these words, which recalled most fearful memories, the lady held down her head, and groaned.

'Yes, hell has given you new life,' resumed Athos; 'hell has made you rich, hell has given you another name, hell has almost endowed you with another face; but it has not expunged either the brand from your body or the stains from your soul.'

The lady arose, as if moved by a spring, and her eyes darted lightning. Athos remained seated.

'You thought me dead, did you not?' he continued, 'as I thought you dead; and the name of Athos has concealed the Count de la Fére, even as the name of Lady de Winter has concealed Anne de Breuil? Was that not what you were called, when your honoured brother married us? Our position is truly strange,' continued Athos, laughing: 'we have both of us only lived till now, because each thought the other dead; and remembrance is less burdensome than a reality—although a remembrance, even, is sometimes a voracious thing!'

'But, after all,' said the lady in a hollow voice, 'what brings you here to me, and what want you with me?'

'I want to tell you, that, although I have been invisible to you, I have not lost sight of you.'

'You know what I have done?'

'I can recite your actions, day by day, from your entrance into the cardinal's service, until to-night.'

A smile of incredulity passed across the pale lips of her ladyship.

'Listen. It is you who cut the two diamond studs from Buckingham's shoulder; it is you who stole away Madame Bonancieux; it is you who, enamoured of de Wardes, and thinking to receive him, opened your door to M. d'Artagnan; it is you who, believing that de Wardes deceived you, wished to have him slain by his rival; it is you who, when this rival had discovered your disgraceful secret, sought to have him assassinated in his turn, by two murderers, whom you sent to dog him; it is you who, when you found bullets fail, sent poisoned wine, with a forged letter, to make your victim fancy that it was the present of his friends; and, lastly, it is you who—here in this very room, seated on the very chair where I now sit—have this moment made an engagement with the Cardinal Richelieu to get the Duke of Buckingham assassinated, in exchange for his undertaking to allow you to assassinate M. d'Artagnan.'

Her ladyship was livid.

'You must indeed be Satan!' said she.

'Perhaps so,' replied Athos; 'but, at all events, mark this well: assassinate the Duke of Buckingham, or cause him to be assassinated—it is of no consequence to me: I know him not; and he is, besides, the enemy of France. But, touch not one single hair of the head of d'Artagnan, who is my faithful friend, whom I love and will protect; or I swear to you, by my father's head, that the crime which you have then committed, or attempted to commit, shall be indeed your last.'

'M. d'Artagnan has cruelly insulted me,' said she, 'and he must die.'

'Indeed! And is it possible that you can be insulted, madame?' said Athos, laughing: 'he has insulted you, and he must die!'

'He shall die!' repeated her ladyship: 'She, first; and he, afterwards.'

Athos felt his brain begin to reel. The sight of this creature, who had nothing of the woman in her nature, recalled most fearful recollections. He thought how one day, in a situation less perilous than that in which he now stood, he had already sought to sacrifice her to his honour. His murderous desire came burning back upon him, like an invading fever. He arose in his turn, and put his hand to his belt, from which he drew a pistol, which he cocked.

The lady, pale as a corpse, endeavoured to cry out; but her frozen tongue could only utter a hoarse sound, which had no resemblance to the human voice, but seemed rather the growl of some savage beast. Glued as it were against the sombre tapestry, with her dishevelled hair, she looked like the appalling image of Terror—

Athos slowly raised the pistol, stretched forth his arm until the weapon almost touched the lady's forehead, and then, in a voice the more terrible, as it had all the intense calmness of an inflexible resolution.

'Madame,' said he, 'you must immediately give me the paper which the cardinal wrote just now, or, on my soul, I will blow out your brains.'

With any other man the lady might have had some doubt; but she knew Athos. Nevertheless, she remained motionless.

'You have one second in which to decide,' continued he.

The lady saw, from the contraction of his brow, that the shot was coming: she hastily put her hand to her bossom, and drew forth a paper, which she handed to Athos.

'Take it,' said she, 'and may you be accursed!'

Athos took the paper, replaced the pistol in his belt, went to the lamp to assure himself that it was the right paper, unfolded it, and read—

'It is by my order, and for the good of the state, that the bearer of this did that which he has now done.   'RICHELIEU.'

'And now,' said Athos, resuming his cloak, and replacing his hat upon his head, 'and now, that I have drawn your teeth, bite if you can!'

He left the room without even looking once behind him.

At the door he found the two men with the led horse.

'Gentlemen,' said he, 'his lordship's order is, you know' to conduct this woman, without loss of time, to the Fort de la Pointe. and not to leave her until she is on board.'

As these words exactly accorded with the order which they had received, they bowed their heads in token of assent.

As for Athos, he sprang lightly into his saddle, and went off at a gallop. Only, instead of keeping to the road, he went across the fields, pushing his horse on very fast, and halting from time to time to listen.

In one of these halts, he heard the sound of several horses on the road. He did not doubt that it was the cardinal and his escort. Taking immediately another direction forward, and then rubbing his horse with some sweet broom and leaves, he placed himself in the middle of the road, at not more than two hundred paces from the camp.

'Who goes there?' cried he, when he heard the horsemen.

'It is our brave musketeer, I believe,' said the cardinal.

'Yes, my lord,' replied Athos, 'it is he in person.'

'M. Athos,' said Richelieu, 'accept my best thanks for the care that you have taken. Gentlemen, we have reached our destination. Take the gate to the left hand; the word for the night is—'Roi et Rhé.' '

As he said this, the cardinal bowed to the three friends, and turned to the right, followed by his equerry; for, on that night, he slept in the camp.

'Well,' said Porthos and Aramis, as soon as the cardinal was out of hearing. 'well, he signed the paper that she demanded.'

'I know it,' said Athos quietly, 'for here it is.'

The three friends did not exchange another word before they reached their own quarters, excepting to give the word to the sentinels on guard.

But they sent Mousqueton to tell Planchet that his master was requested, on leaving the trenches, to come immediately to the musketeers' rooms.

On the other hand, as Athos had foreseen, her ladyship, on finding the two men at the door, followed them without hesitation. She had, for an instant, an idea of seeking another interview with the cardinal, and relating to him what had passed; but a revelation on her part would produce one on that of Athos. She might easily say that Athos had ruined her; but he would state that she was branded. So she thought it better to be silent, to depart discreetly, to accomplish with her accustoned ability the difficult commission which had been entrusted to her, and then, when these things were ended to the cardinal's satisfaction, to return and claim her vengeance.

Consequently, having travelled all night, she was at Fort la Pointe by seven in the morning; at eight she had embarked; and at nine the vessel weighed anchor, and made sail for England.

46

The Bastion of St. Gervais

On arriving at his friends' quarters, d'Artagnan found them assembled in one room. Athos was thinking; Porthos was twisting his moustache: and Aramis was reading his prayers in a charming little book, bound in blue velvet.

'By my soul, gentlemen,' said d'Artagnan, 'I hope that what you have to tell me is worth the trouble, otherwise I should not forgive your having made me dismantle a bastion, entirely by myself. Ah! why were you not there, gentlemen? It was hot work!'

'We were in another place, where it was by no means cold either,' said Porthos, giving his moustache a turn peculiar to himself.

'Hush!' said Athos.

'Oh, oh!' said d'Artagnan, understanding the slight frown of the musketeer, 'it seems that there is something fresh astir.'

'Aramis,' said Athos, 'you breakfasted at the Parpaillot tavern, the day before yesterday, I believe?'

'Yes.'

'How are things there?'

'Why, I fared but badly myself; it was a fast-day, and they had nothing but meat.'

'What,' said Athos, 'in a sea-port, and no fish?'

'They say that the mound which the cardinal is building drives the fish out into the open sea,' said Aramis, resuming his pious reading.

'But that is not what I wanted to know, Aramis,' continued Athos. 'Were you free, and did no one disturb you?'

'Why, I think that there were not many idlers,' replied Aramis. 'Yes, in fact, for what you want, Athos, I think we shall do well enough at the Parpaillot.'

'Come, then; let us to the Parpaillot,' said Athos, 'for here the walls are like leaves of paper.'

D'Artagnan, who was accustomed to his friend's manner, and understood by a word, a gesture, or a look from him, that circumstances called for seriousness, took his arm, and went out with him, without uttering a word. Porthos followed them, in conversation with Aramis.

On their way they met Grimaud, and Athos beckoned to him to attend them. Grimaud, according to custom, obeyed in silence: the poor fellow had finished by almost forgetting how to speak.

When they arrived at the Parpaillot, it was seven in the morning, and the day was just beginning to dawn. The three friends ordered breakfast, and entered a room where, the landlord assured them, that they would not be disturbed.

The hour was, unfortunately, ill-chosen for a conference. The morning drum had just been beaten; every one was busy shaking off the sleepiness of night, and, to drive away the dampness of the morning air, coming to take a drop at the tavern. Dragoons, Swiss, guards, musketeers, and light cavalry, succeeded one another with a rapidity very beneficial to the business of mine host, but very unfavourable to the designs of our four friends, who replied, but sullenly, to the salutations, toasts, and jests of their companions.

'Come,' said Athos, 'we shall bring some good quarrel on our hands presently, and we do not want that just now. D'Artagnan, tell us about your night's work: we will tell you about ours afterwards.'

'In fact,' said one of the light-cavalry, who whilst rocking himself, held in his hand a glass of brandy, which he slowly sipped—'in fact, you were in the trenches, you gentlemen of the guards, and it seems to me that you had a squabble with the Rochellois.'

D'Artagnan looked at Athos, to see whether he ought to answer this intruder who intruded on the conversation.

'Well,' said Athos, 'did you not hear M. de Busigny, who did the honour to address you? Tell us what took place in the night, as these gentlemen seem desirous to hear it.'

'Did you not take a bastion?' asked a Swiss, who was drinking rum mixed with a glass of beer.

'Yes, sir,' replied d'Artagnan, bowing, 'we had that honour. And also, as you may have heard, we introduced a barrel of powder under one of the angles, which, on exploding, made a very pretty breach, without reckoning that, as the bastion is very old, all the rest of the building is much shaken.'

'And what bastion is it?' asked a dragoon, who held spitted on his sabre, a goose which he had brought to be cooked.

'The bastion St. Gervais,' replied d'Artagnan, 'from behind which the Rochellois annoyed our sappers.'

'And was it warm work?'

'Yes. We lost five men, and the Rochellois some eight or ten.'

'Balzampleu!' said the Swiss, who, in spite of the admirable collection of oaths which the German language possesses, had got the habit of swearing in French.

'But it is probable,' said the light-horseman, 'that they will send pioneers to repair the bastion this morning.'

'Yes, it is probable,' said d'Artagnan.

'Gentlemen,' said Athos, 'a wager!'

'Ah! a wager,' said the Swiss.

'What is it?' asked the light-horseman.

'Stop,' said the dragoon, laying his sabre like a spit on the two great iron dogs which supported the fire in the chimney, 'I am in it! A dripping-pan here, instantly, you noodle of a landlord, that I may not lose one drop of the fat of this estimable bird.'

'He is right,' said the Swiss; 'the fat of a goose is very good with sweetmeats.'

'There!' said the dragoon; 'and now for the wager. We are listening, M. Athos.'

'Well, M. de Busigny,' said Athos, 'I bet you, that my three comrades, Messieurs Porthos, Aramis, and d'Artagnan, and myself, will go and breakfast in the bastion of St. Gervais, and that we will stay there for one hour by the clock, whatever the enemy may do to dislodge us.'

Porthos and Aramis looked at one another, for they began to understand.

'Why,' said d'Artagnan, stooping to Athos's ear, 'you are going to get us all killed without mercy.'

'We shall be more certainly killed if we do not go,' replied Athos.

'Ah, faith, gentlemen,' said Porthos, throwing himself back in his chair, and twirling his moustache, 'that is a fine wager, I hope.'

'And I accept it,' said M. de Busigny. 'Now we must fix the stakes.'

'You are four, gentlemen,' said Athos, 'and we are four: a dinner for eight—will that suit you?'

'Just the thing!' replied M. de Busigny.

'Exactly,' said the dragoon.

'That will do!' exclaimed the Swiss. The fourth auditor, who had remained silent throughout the conversation, bowed his head, as a sign that he acquiesced in the proposition.

'The dejeuner of these gentlemen is ready,' broke in the landlord.

'Well, then, bring it here,' said Athos.

The landlord obeyed. Athos called Grimaud, showed him a large basket, which was lying in a corner, and made him a sign to wrap up in the napkins all the eatables which had been brought.

Grimaud, comprehending at once that they were going to breakfast on the grass, took the basket, packed up the eatables, put in the bottles, and took the basket up in his arms. 'But where are you going to eat this breakfast?' said the landlord.

'What does it signify to you,' replied Athos, 'provided you are paid for it?' And he threw two pistoles majestically on the table.

'Must I give you the change, sir?' said mine host.

'No; but add a couple of bottles of champagne, and the balance will pay for the napkins.'

The landlord had not made quite such a good thing of it as he at first expected; but he recompensed himself for it by palming off on his four guests two bottles of Anjou wine, instead of the two bottles of champagne.

'M. de Busigny, will you regulate your watch by mine, or permit me to regulate mine by yours?' inquired Athos.

'At your pleasure,' said the light-dragoon, drawing from his fob a very beautiful watch, encircled with diamonds. 'Half-past seven,' added he.

'Five-and-thirty minutes after seven,' said Athos; 'we shall remember that I am five minutes in advance, sir.'

Then, bowing to the astonished party, the four young men took the road towards the bastion of St. Gervais, followed by Grimaud, who carried the basket, not knowing where he was going, and, from the passive obedience that was habitual to him, not even thinking of inquiring.

Whilst they were within the precincts of the camp, the four friends did not exchange a word: they were, besides, followed by the curious, who, having heard of the wager, wished to know how they would extricate themselves from the affair. But when once they had got beyond the lines of circumvallation, and found themselves in the open country, d'Artagnan, who was entirely ignorant of what they were about, thought it high time to demand some explanation.

'And now, my dear Athos,' said he, 'do me the favour to tell me where we are going.'

'You can see well enough,' replied Athos; 'we are going to the bastion.'

'But what are we going to do there?'

'You know very well—we are going to breakfast there.'

'But why do we not breakfast at the Parpaillot?'

'Because we have most important things to tell you, and it was impossible to converse for five minutes in that tavern, with all those troublesome fellows, who come and go, and continually accost us. Here, at least,' continued Athos, pointing to the bastion, 'no one will come to interrupt us.'

'It appears to me,' said d'Artagnan, with that prudence which was so thoroughly and so naturally united with his extreme courage—'it appears to me, that we could have found some retired spot, somewhere among the downs, on the sea-shore.'

'Where we should have been seen all four in council together, so that, in a quarter of an hour, the cardinal would have been informed by his spies that we were holding a consultation.'

'Yes,' said Aramis, 'Athos is right: *animadvertuntur in desertis*.'

'A desert would not have been a bad place,' remarked Porthos; 'but the difficulty is to find one.'

'There is no desert where a bird could not pass over one's head, or a fish jump from the water, or a rabbit run from her burrow; and I believe that bird, fish, and rabbit are all amongst the cardinal's spies. It is much better, therefore, to pursue our enterprise. Besides, we cannot now recede without disgrace. We have made a bet—a bet which could not have been foreseen, and of which I defy any one to guess the true motive. To win it, we must remain an hour in the bastion. Either we shall, or shall not, be attacked. If we are not, we shall have time to talk, and no one will hear us; for I will answer for it that the walls of that bastion have no ears. If we are attacked, we will talk just the same, and shall moreover, by defending ourselves, be covered with glory. So you see that everything is favourable to us.'

'Yes,' said d'Artagnan, 'but we shall indubitably be shot.'

'Well,' rejoined Athos, 'but you know very well that the bullets most to be feared are not those of the enemy.'

'Yet it seems to me,' said Porthos, 'that, for such an expedition, we should at least have brought our muskets.'

'You are a simpleton, friend Porthos; why should we encumber ourselves with a useless burden?'

'I do not find a good regulation musket, with a dozen cartridges and a powder-flask, useless in front of an enemy.'

'Well,' rejoined Athos, 'did you not hear what d'Artagnan said?'

'And what did d'Artagnan say?' asked Porthos.

'D'Artagnan says, that, in last night's attack, as many as eight or ten Frenchmen were killed, and as many of the enemy.'

'Well!'

'There has not been time to strip them, has there, seeing there was something more urgent to which to attend?'

'Well!'

'Well, we shall find their muskets, powder-flasks, and cartridges, and, instead of four muskets and a dozen balls, we shall have about fifteen muskets and a hundred rounds of ammunition to fire.'

'Oh, Athos!' said Aramis, 'you are really a great man!'

Porthos bowed his head in token of acquiescence.

D'Artagnan alone did not appear completely convinced.

Grimaud unquestionably partook of the young man's incredulity; for, seeing that they continued to march towards the bastion, which he suspected before, he plucked his master by the skirt of his coat.

'Where are we going?' he inquired by a sign.

Athos pointed to the bastion.

'But,' said the silent Grimaud, still in the same dialect, 'we shall leave our skins there.'

Athos raised his eyes and his fingers towards heaven.

Grimaud set down his basket on the ground, and seated himself upon it, shaking his head.

Athos took a pistol from his belt, looked at the priming, cocked it, and levelled it at Grimaud's ear.

447

Grimaud found himself raised up, upon his legs, as if by the force of a spring.

Athos then beckoned to him to take up the basket, and to march in front.

Grimaud obeyed: so that all the poor fellow had gained by this momentary pantomine, was, that he had been transformed from the rear guard to the advanced guard.

Having reached the bastion, the four friends looked behind them. More than three hundred soldiers, of every arm, had assembled at the entrance of the camp; and, in a separate group, they saw M. de Busigny, the dragoon, the Swiss, and the fourth wagerer.

Athos took off his hat, raised it on the end of his sword, and waved it in the air.

All the spectators returned his salutation, accompanying this act of politeness with a loud hurrah, which reached the ears of the party.

After this occurrence they all four disappeared in the bastion, where Grimaud had already preceded them.

47

The Council of the Musketeers

As Athos had foreseen, the bastion was only occupied by about a dozen dead bodies, French and Rochellois.

'Gentlemen,' said Athos, who had taken the command of the expedition, 'whilst Grimaud prepares the table, let us begin by gathering together the muskets and ammunition. We can, moreover, converse whilst we are doing it. These gentlemen,' added he, pointing to the dead bodies, 'do not hear us.'

'But we may, nevertheless, throw them into the ditches,' said Porthos, 'having first satisfied ourselves that they have nothing in their pockets.'

'Yes,' replied Athos, 'but that is Grimaud's affair.'

'Well, then,' said d'Artagnan, 'let Grimaud search them, and throw them over the walls.'

'Not upon any account,' said Athos; 'they may be of use to us.'

'These dead be of use to us!' exclaimed Porthos. 'Ah, nonsense! you are going crazy, my dear friend!'

'Do not judge rashly, say both the gospel and the cardinal,' replied Athos, 'How many muskets are there, gentlemen?'

'Twelve.'

'How much ammunition?'

'A hundred rounds.'

'It is quite as many as we need: let us load our muskets.'

The four companions set themselves to work; and just as they had loaded the last musket, Grimaud made a sign to them that breakfast was ready.

Athos indicated by a gesture that he was contented with what was done, and then pointed out to Grimaud a sort of sheltered box, where he was to place himself as sentinel. But, to relieve the tedium of his watch, Athos allowed him to take with him a loaf, two cutlets, and a bottle of wine.

'And now, to breakfast!' said Athos.

The four friends squatted upon the ground, like Turks or tailors.

'And now,' said d'Artagnan, 'as you are no longer afraid of being heard, I hope that you are going to let us know your secret.'

'I hope that I provide you at the same time both with amusement and glory, gentlemen?' said Athos. 'I have induced you to take a charming little excursion: here is a most sustaining breakfast; and below there, are five hundred persons, as you may perceive through the embrasures, who take us for madmen or heroes—two classes of fools who very much resemble each other.'

'But this secret?'

'I saw her ladyship last night,' said Athos.

D'Artagnan was just conveying his glass to his lips; but, at the sound of her ladyship's name, his hand trembled so that he placed his glass upon the ground, in order that he might not spill its contents.——

'You have seen your wi——'

'Hush, then!' interrupted Athos: 'you forget, my dear fellow, that these gentlemen are not, like you, initiated in the privacies of my family affairs. I have seen her ladyship.'

'And where did that happen?' demanded d'Artagnan.

'About two leagues from hence, at the Red Dove-Cot.'

'In that case, I am a lost man,' said d'Artagnan.

'Not just yet,' replied Athos; 'for, by this time, she must have quitted the shores of France.'

D'Artagnan breathed again.

'But, after all,' inquired Porthos, 'who is this lady?'

'A charming woman,' said Athos, sipping a glass of sparkling wine. 'Scamp of a landlord!' exclaimed he, 'who gives us Anjou for champagne, and thinks we shall be deceived by the subterfuge! Yes,' continued he, 'a charming woman, to whom our friend d'Artagnan has done something unpardonable, for which she has been endeavouring to avenge herself—a month ago, by trying to get him shot; a week ago, by sending him some poison; and yesterday, by demanding his head of the cardinal.'

'What! demanding my head of the cardinal?' cried d'Artagnan, pale with terror.

'Yes,' said Porthos, 'it is true as gospel; for I heard her with my own ears.'

'And I also,' said Aramis.

'Then,' said d'Artagnan, letting his arm fall in a despond'-ing manner, 'it is useless to struggle longer: I may as well blow out my brains at once, and have done with it.'

'That is the last folly to be perpetrated,' said Athos, 'seeing it is the only one which will admit of no remedy.'

'But, with such enemies, I shall never escape,' said d'Artagnan. 'First, my unknown antagonist of Meung; then de Wardes, on whom I inflicted four wounds; next, this lady, whose secret I found out; and, lastly, the cardinal, whose revenge I defeated.'

'Well!' said Athos, 'and all this makes only four, and we are four—against one. Vive Dieu! if we may trust to Grimaud's signs, we are now about to be engaged with a far greater number of foes. What's the matter, Grimaud? Considering the seriousness of the circumstances, I permit you to speak, my friend; but be brief, I beseech you. What do you see?'

'A troop.'

'Of how many persons?'

'Twenty men.'

'What sort of men?'

'Sixteen pioneers, and four soldiers.'

'How far off are they?'

'Five hundred paces.'

'Good! we have still time to finish this fowl, and to drink a glass of wine. To your health, d'Artagnan!'

'To your health!' repeated Aramis and Porthos.

'Well, then, to my health; although I do not imagine that your good wishes will be of much benefit to me.'

'Bah!' said Athos, 'God is great, as the Mahometans say, and the future is in His hands.'

Then, having swallowed his wine, and put the glass down, Athos carelessly arose, took the first musket which came to his hand, and went towards an embrasure.

The three others did the same. As for Grimaud, he had orders to place himself behind them, and to reload their muskets.

An instant afterwards, they saw the troop appearing. It came along a kind of branch trench, which formed a communication between the bastion and the town.

'Mort Dieu!' said Athos, 'it was scarcely worth while to disturb ourselves for a score of fellows armed with pick axes, mattocks, and spades. Grimaud ought to have quietly waved to them to go about their business, and I am quite convinced that they would have left us to ourselves.'

'I much doubt it,' said d'Artagnan, 'for they come forward with great resolution. Besides, in addition to the workmen, there are four soldiers, and a brigadier, armed with muskets.'

'That is because they have not seen us,' replied Athos.

'Faith,' said Aramis, 'I confess that I am reluctant to fire upon these poor devils of citizens.'

'He is a bad priest,' said Porthos, 'who pities heretics.'

'Upon my word,' said Athos, 'Aramis is right. I will give them a notice.'

'What the plague are you doing?' cried d'Artagnan; 'you will get yourself shot, my dear fellow.'

But Athos paid no attention to this warning; and mounting on the breach, his fusee in one hand, and his hat in the other—

'Gentlemen,' said he, bowing courteously, and addressing himself to the soldiers and pioneers, who, astonished by this apparition, halted at about fifty paces from the bastion— 'gentlemen, we are, some of my friends and myself, engaged in breakfasting in this bastion. Now you know that nothing is more disagreeable than to be disturbed at breakfast; so we entreat of you, if you really have business here, to wait till we have finished our repast, or to come back in a little while; unless, indeed, you experience the salutary desire of forsaking the ranks of rebellion, and coming to drink with us to the health of the king of France.'

'Take care, Athos,' said d'Artagnan; 'don't you see that they are aiming at you.'

'Yes, yes,' said Athos; 'but these are civilians, who are shocking bad marksmen, and will take care not to hit me.'

In fact, at that moment four shots were fired, and the bullets whistled around Athos, but without one touching him.

Four shots were instantaneously fired in return, but with a far better aim than that of the aggressors: three soldiers fell dead, and one of the pioneers was wounded.

'Grimaud,' said Athos, from the breach, 'another musket.'

Grimaud obeyed immediately.

The three friends had also reloaded their arms. A second discharge soon followed the first, and the brigadier and two pioneers fell dead. The rest of the troop took to flight.

'Come, gentlemen, a sortie!' said Athos.

The four friends rushed out of the fort, reached the field of battle, picked up the muskets of the soldiers, and the half-pike of the brigadier; and, satisfied that the fugitives would never stop till they reached the city, they returned to the bastion, bearing with them the trophies of their victory.

'Reload the muskets, Grimaud,' said Athos; 'and let us, gentlemen, continue our breakfast and conversation. Where were we?'

'I recollect,' said d'Artagnan; 'you were saying, that, after having demanded my head of the cardinal, her ladyship had left the shores of France. And where is she going?' added d'Artagnan, who was painfully anxious about the itinerary of the lady's journey.

'She is going to England,' replied Athos.

'And why?'

'To assassinate the Duke of Buckingham, or to get him assassinated.'

D'Artagnan uttered an exclamation of surprise and horror.

'It is infamous!' exclaimed he.

'Oh! as to that,' said Athos, 'I beg you to believe that I concern myself very little about it. Now that you have finished, Grimaud,' continued he, 'take the half-pike of our brigadier, fasten a napkin to it, and fix it on the end of our bastion, that those rebellious Rochellois may see that they are opposed to brave and loyal subjects of the king.'

Grimaud obeyed without reply; and an instant afterwards the white flag floated over the heads of the four friends.

A cry of joy, a thunder of applause, saluted its appearance. Half the camp was at the barriers.

'What!' said d'Artagnan, 'you concern yourself but little about her assassinating Buckingham, or causing him to be assassinated? The duke is our friend.'

'The duke is an Englishman; the duke fights against us: let her do therefore what she likes with the duke. I care as little about him as about an empty bottle.'

As Athos said this, he threw, some fifteen yards before him, a bottle which he held in his hand, and from wich he had just poured the last drop into his own glass.

'Wait an instant,' said d'Artagnan, 'I do not abandon Buckingham in that manner: he gave us some very fine horses.'

'And especially some beautiful saddles,' added Porthos, who was then wearing the lace of his upon his cloak.

'Besides,' said Aramis, 'God wishes for the conversion, not death, of a sinner.'

'Amen!' said Athos, 'and we will return to that by and by, if such is your pleasure; but that which most engaged my attention at the time, and I am sure you will understand why, d'Artagnan, was how to take from this woman a *carte-blanche*, which she had extorted from the cardinal, and by means of which she might get rid of you, and perhaps the whole of us, with impunity.'

'This creature is a very demon!' said Porthos, holding his plate to Aramis, who was cutting up a fowl.

'And this document,' said d'Artagnan; 'did it remain in her hands?'

'No, it passed into mine. I cannot say that it was without some trouble; for, if I said that, I should tell a lie.'

'My dear Athos,' said d'Artagnan, 'I must no longer count the times I owe my life to you.'

'Then it was to visit her that you quitted us?' said Aramis.

'Exactly so.'

'And you have got the cardinal's letter?' inquired d'Artagnan.

'Here it is,' replied Athos.

He took the precious paper from the pocket of his coat. D'Artagnan unfolded it with a hand, of which he did not attempt to hide the tremor, and read—

'It is by my order, and for the good of the state, that the bearer of this did that which he has now done.

'RICHELIEU.'

'It is, in fact, a regular indulgence,' said Aramis.

'We must destroy this paper,' said d'Artagnan, who seemed to read in it his own sentence of death.

'On the contrary,' replied Athos, 'it must be most scrupulously preserved; and I would not give it up for the gold that would cover it in coin.'

'And what will she do now?' inquired d'Artagnan.

'Why,' said Athos carelessly, 'she will probably write to the cardinal, that a cursed musketeer, named Athos, took her safe-guard from her by force; and she will, at the same time, advise his eminence to get rid of him, and also of his two friends, Porthos and Aramis. The cardinal will recollect that these are the very men that are always in his way. Then, some fine morning, he will have d'Artagnan arrested, and, that he may not be annoyed by solitude, will send us to keep him company in the Bastile.'

'Ah! then,' said Porthos, 'I think that you are cracking somewhat melancholy jokes.'

'I am not joking,' replied Athos.

'Do you know,' said Porthos, 'that I fancy it would be less of a crime to twist this cursed lady's neck, than those of these poor devils of Huguenots, who have never committed any greater crime than singing, in French, the very psalms which we sing in Latin!'

'What does the abbé say to that?' quietly asked Athos.

'I say that I am quite of Porthos's opinion.'

'And I also,' said d'Artagnan.

'Happily, she is far away,' added Porthos, 'for I confess that she would annoy me much here.'

'She annoys me in England, as well as in France,' said Athos.

'She annoys me everywhere,' said d'Artagnan.

'But, when you had her in your power,' said Porthos, 'why did you not drown, strangle, or hang her? It is only the dead who never return.'

'Do you think so, Porthos?' replied Athos, with a dark smile, which d'Artagnan alone could understand.

'I have an idea,' said d'Artagnan.

'Let us hear it,' cried the musketeers.

'To arms!' exclaimed Grimaud.

The young men arose hastily, and ran to their muskets.

This time there was a small band advancing, composed of twenty or of five-and-twenty men, no longer pioneers, but soldiers of the garrison.

'Suppose we now return to the camp,' said Porthos; 'it seems to me that the match is not equal.'

'Impossible, for three reasons,' answered Athos. 'The first is, because we have not finished our breakfast. The second, because we have still some important affairs to talk about; and the third, it wants yet ten minutes before the hour is elapsed.'

'All the same,' said Aramis, 'we must arrange a plan of battle.'

'It is vastly simple,' replied Athos. 'As soon as the enemy is within musket-shot, we must fire; if he continues to advance, we must fire again; in fact, we must blaze away as long as we have guns loaded. If the remnant of the band should then wish to mount to the assault, we must let the besiegers descend as far as the ditch, and then we must heave on their heads a large mass of the wall, which only stays up now by a miracle of equilibrium.'

'Bravo!' exclaimed Porthos. 'Athos, you were undoubtedly born to be a general; and the cardinal, who thinks himself a great warrior, is a mere nothing to you.'

'Gentlemen,' said Athos, 'do not waste your ammunition, I beseech you: let each pick out his man.'

'I have got mine,' said d'Artagnan.

'And I mine,' said Porthos.

'And I the same,' said Aramis.

'Fire!' cried Athos.

The four guns made but one report, and four men fell.

The drum then beat, and the little band advanced to the charge.

The shots of the four friends were then fired without regularity, but invariably with the same deadly effect. Yet, as though they had known the numerical weakness of their opponents, the Rochellois continued to advance at a quick pace.

At three other reports, two men fell; yet the march of those who remained unwounded did not slacken.

Having reached the foot of the bastion, there were still twelve or fifteen of the enemy. A last discharge received, but did not arrest, them. They leaped into the ditch, and prepared to scale the breach.

'Now, my friends,' said Athos, 'let us finish them at one blow. To the wall! to the wall!'

And the four friends, assisted by Grimaud, set themselves to topple over, with the barrels of their muskets, an enormous mass of wall, which bowed as though the wind waved it, and, loosening itself from its foundation, fell with a tremendous crash into the ditch. A fearful cry was then heard; a cloud of dust ascended toward the skies; and—and that was all.

'Can we have crushed them all, from the first to the last?' said Athos.

'Faith, it looks very like it,' replied d'Artagnan.

'No,' said Porthos; 'there are two or three of them escaping, quite crippled.'

In fact, three or four of these unfortunate beings, covered with mire and blood, fled along the hollow way, and regained the town. They were all the survivors of the little band.

Athos looked at his watch.

'Gentlemen,' said he, 'we have been here an hour, and now the wager is gained: but we must be good players; besides, d'Artagnan has not yet told us his idea.'

And the musketeer, with his habitual coolness, seated himself before the remains of the breakfast.

'Would you like to hear my plan?' said d'Artagnan to his three companions, when, after the alarm which had had so fearful a termination for the little troop of Rochellois, the quartette had resumed their places before the remnants of their meal.

'Yes,' replied Athos; 'you said that you had an idea.'

'Ah! I have it,' exclaimed d'Artagnan. 'I will go to England for the second time, will find his grace of Buckingham, and warn him of the plot which has been concocted against his life.'

'You will do no such thing, d'Artagnan,' said Athos coldly.

'Why not? Did I not go before?'

'Yes, but at that time we were not at war; at that time the Duke of Buckingham was an ally, and not an enemy: what you now suggest would amount to treason.'

D'Artagnan understood the force of this reasoning and was silent.

'But,' said Porthos, 'I fancy that I, in my turn, have also got an idea.'

'Silence for M. Porthos's idea,' cried Aramis.

'I will ask leave of absence of M. de Treville, on any pretext whatsoever that you can suggest: I am not very clever at excuses myself. The lady does not know me: I will get near her without exciting her alarm; and, when I have found the beauty, I will strangle her.'

'Ah,' said Athos, 'I am really somewhat disposed to adopt Porthos's idea.'

'Fie, then!' exclaimed Aramis; 'kill a woman! No! Listen, I have the right idea.'

'Let us have your idea, Aramis,' said Athos, who felt much deference for the young musketeer.

'We must announce it to the queen.'

'Ah, faith, yes!' cried d'Artagnan and Porthos together; 'I believe that we have found the true course at last.'

'Announce it to the queen?' said Athos; 'and how can we do that? Have we any friends at court? Can we send any one to Paris, without its being known in the camp? There are a hundred and forty leagues between here and Paris, and our letter will not have reached Angers before we ourselves shall be in a dungeon.'

'As for getting a letter safely delivered to the queen,' said Aramis, blushing, 'I myself will undertake it. I know a very skilful person at Tours——'

Aramis stopped, on seeing Athos smile.

'Well; will you not adopt this plan, Athos?' inquired d'Artagnan.

'I do not entirely reject it,' replied Athos, 'but I would merely observe to Aramis, that he cannot himself leave the camp; and that, with anybody but one of ourselves, there will be no security that, two hours after the messenger has started, all the capuchins, all the alguazils, all the black-bonnets of the cardinal, will not know your letter by heart; and that you and your very skilful person will not be immediately arrested.'

'Without calculating,' added Porthos, 'that the queen would save the Duke of Buckingham, while leaving us to our fate.'

'Gentlemen,' said d'Artagnan, 'Porthos's objection is full of sense!'

'Ah, ah! what is going on in the town?' said Athos. 'They are beating to arms.'

The four friends listened, and the sound of the tattoo reached their ears.

'You will see,' continued Athos, 'that they will send an entire regiment against us.'

'You do not expect to hold your ground against an entire regiment?' said Porthos.

'Why not?' replied the musketeer. 'I feel myself in the humour, and would hold it against an army, if we had only had the precaution to bring a dozen bottles more.'

'Upon my word, the drum comes nearer,' said d'Artagnan.

'Let it come,' replied Athos; 'there is a quarter of an hour's march between the town and this place. It is more time than we shall require to arrange our plans. If we go away from here, we shall never again find such a convenient spot. And listen, gentlemen; the very idea has come into my mind.'

'Let us hear it.'

Athos made a sign for his valet to come to him.

'Grimaud,' said Athos, pointing to the dead bodies, which lay in the bastion, 'you will take these gentlemen, fix them upright against the wall, put their hats on their heads, and place their muskets in their hands.'

'Oh, great man!' cried d'Artagnan, 'I understand you.'

'You understand him?' said Porthos.

'And you, Grimaud, do you understand?' inquired Aramis.

Grimaud gave a sign in the affirmative.

'It is all that is necessary,' said Athos; 'now, let us return to my idea.'

'I should like, however, to understand as well,' said Porthos.

'It is of no use.'

'Yes, yes, the idea of Athos!' said d'Artagnan and Aramis at the same time.

'This lady, this woman, this creature, this demon, has a brother-in-law, I think you told me?'

'Yes; I even know him, and I believe that he has no great sympathy with his sister-in-law.'

'There is no harm there,' replied Athos; 'and if he detested her, even, it would be so much the better.'

'In that case, we are fitted to a nicety.'

'Nevertheless,' said Porthos, 'I should like to understand what Grimaud is about.'

'Silence, Porthos!' cried Aramis.

'What is the name of this brother-in-law?'

'Lord de Winter.'

'Where is he at present?'

'He returned to London on the first report of the war.'

'Well, there is exactly the man we want,' said Athos. 'It is to him that we must give information: we must let him know that his sister-in-law is going to assassinate some one, and entreat him to keep his eye upon her. There must be in London, I should hope, some establishment like the Madelonettes, or the Magdalen: he must place his sister-in-law there, and we shall then be at peace.'

'Yes,' said d'Artagnan, 'until she gets out again.'

'Ah, faith,' said Athos, 'you ask too much, d'Artagnan. I have given you all that I have, and I tell you that my budget is now empty.'

'I think it the best plan we can devise,' observed Aramis; 'we will inform the queen and Lord de Winter at the same time.'

'But by whom shall we convey the one letter to London, and the other to Tours?'

'I answer for Bazin,' replied Aramis.

'And I for Planchet,' added d'Artagnan.

'In fact,' said Porthos, 'if we cannot leave the camp, our lackeys can.'

'Certainly,' added Aramis; 'so we will write the letters this very day, give them some money, and send them on the journey.'

'We will give them some money?' said Athos; 'then you have got money, have you?'

The four friends looked at each other, and a cloud passed over the brows which had been for an instant brightened.

'Attention,' cried d'Artagnan; 'I see black and red points in motion, below there. What were you saying about a regiment, Athos? It is a regular army.'

'Faith, yes,' replied Athos, 'there they are. Do you see the crafty fellows, who are advancing without drum or trumpet? Ah, ah! Have you finished, Grimaud?'

Grimaud gave a sign in the affirmative, and pointed to a dozen dead bodies, which he had placed in the most picturesque attitudes—some carrying arms, others seeming to take aim, others sword in hand.

'Bravo!' cried Athos, 'that does credit to your imagination.'

'That may be,' said Porthos; 'and yet I should like to understand it.'

'Let us decamp first,' said d'Artagnan; 'you will understand afterwards.'

'One moment, gentlemen—wait one moment; let us give Grimaud time to take away the breakfast things.'

'Ah!' said Aramis, 'here are the black and red points becoming visible larger, and I am of d'Artagnan's opinion: I believe that we have no time to lose in regaining the camp.'

'Faith,' said Athos, 'I have nothing more to say against a retreat: we betted for an hour, and we have remained an hour and a half. There is nothing more to communicate; so let us be off, gentlemen, let us be off.'

Grimaud had already commenced his retreat, with the basket and the fragments. The four friends followed behind him, and had taken about a dozen steps, when——

'Ah! What the plague are we about, gentlemen?' exclaimed Athos.

'Have you forgotten anything?' inquired Aramis.

'The flag: zounds! we must not leave a flag in the hands of the enemy, even though it be a napkin.'

And Athos rushed back into the bastion, mounted the platform, and took down the flag. But, as the Rochellois had come within musket-shot, they opened a sharp fire upon this man, who thus exposed himself, as if for amusement, to their discharge. It might have been fancied, however, that Athos bore a charmed life: the bullets whistled around him, yet he stood unharmed.

Athos waved his standard, and bowed towards the camp as he turned his back on the town. Loud shouts resounded on both sides—shouts of anger from the one; and, from the other, of enthusiasm.

A second discharge soon followed the first, and three balls, by passing through the napkin, made a regular standard of it.

They heard the whole camp exclaiming—'Come down! come down!'

Athos slowly descended. His companions, who waited for him with anxiety, welcomed his re-appearance with joy.

'Come along, Athos, come along,' said d'Artagnan; 'let us make haste. Now that we have found everything, except money, it would be absurd to get killed.'

But Athos persisted in his majestic walk; and his companions, finding all remonstrance useless, regulated their pace by his.

Grimaud and his basket had formed the advance guard, and were both soon out of range. After a minute or two the quartette heard the sound of furious firing.

'What is that?' asked Porthos; 'at what are they firing! I do not hear the bullets whistle, nor do I see anybody.'

'They are firing at our dead men!' replied Athos.

'But our dead men will not return their fire.'

'Exactly so. They will then believe that there is an ambuscade: they will deliberate, and will afterwards reconnoitre; and by the time they discover the trick, we shall be beyond the reach of their fire. Thus, you see, it is unnecessary to give ourselves a fit of the pleurisy by over haste.'

'Oh! I understand now!' said the astonished Porthos.

'That's very fortunate,' replied Athos, shrugging his shoulders.

At length, a fresh volley was heard, and this time the bullets were actually flattened on the stones around the four friends, and whistled mournfully about their ears. The Rochellois had at last taken possession of the bastion.

'They are a set of awkward fellows,' remarked Athos; 'how many of them have we shot? A dozen?'

'Or fifteen.'

'How many did we crush?'

'Eight or ten.'

'And in exchange for this, we have not got a scratch. Ah! yes, though! What is the matter with your hand there, d'Artagnan? It bleeds, I think?'

'It is nothing,' replied d'Artagnan.

'Was it a spent ball?'

'No.'

'What then?'

We have said that Athos loved d'Artagnan as his own son; and, though of a gloomy and inflexible character he sometimes manifested towards the young man a solicitude truly paternal.

'Merely a scratch,' replied d'Artagnan. 'I caught my fingers between two stones—that of the wall, and that of my ring—and the skin is broken.'

'See what it is to wear diamonds, my master,' said Athos contemptuously.

'Ah!' exclaimed Porthos, 'there is a diamond, in fact; and why the plague, then, as there is a diamond, do we complain of having no money?'

'See, there, now!' said Aramis.

'Well done, Porthos; this time you really have got an idea.'

'Certainly,' continued Porthos, bridling up at Athos's compliment; 'and since there is a diamond, let us sell it.'

'But,' said d'Artagnan, 'it is the queen's diamond.'

'All the more reason,' said Athos—'the queen saving the Duke of Buckingham, her lover: nothing can be more just— the queen saving us, her friends: nothing can be more moral. Let us sell the diamond. What does the abbé say? I do not ask Porthos's opinion—that is already given.'

'Why, I think,' said Aramis, blushing, 'that as the ring does not come from a mistress, and, consequently, is not a love-token, d'Artagnan may sell it.'

'My dear fellow, you speak like theology personified. So your advice is—'

'To sell the diamond,' replied Aramis.

'Well,' said d'Artagnan gaily, 'let us sell the diamond, and say no more about it.'

The fusillade still continued, but the friends were beyond its range, and the Rochellois seemed to be firing only for the satisfaction of their own consciences.

'Faith,' said Athos, 'it was quite time for this idea of Porthos's to present itself; for here we are at the camp. So now, gentlemen, not another word about this business. We are observed. They are coming to meet us, and we shall be borne home in triumph.'

In fact, as we have already said, the whole camp was in commotion. More than two thousand persons had witnessed as at a theatre, the fortunate bravado of the four friends—a bravado, of which they had been far from suspecting the true motive. Nothing could be heard but cries of 'long live the guards!' 'long live the musketeers!' M. de Busigny was the first who came to press the hand of Athos, and to confess that he had lost his bet. The dragoon and the Swiss had followed him; and all their comrades had followed the dragoon and the Swiss. There was no end to the congratulations, shaking of hands, embraces, and inextinguishable laughter at the Rochellois; and, at last, the tumult was so great, that the cardinal supposed there was a mutiny, and sent La Houdinière, the captain of his guards, to ascertain the cause of the disturbance.

The circumstance was related to his messenger with all the warmth of enthusiasm.

'Well?' demanded the cardinal, when he saw La Houdinière.

'Well, my lord,' replied the latter, 'it is three musketeers and a guardsman, who laid a wager with M. de Busigny to go and breakfast in the bastion of St. Gervais; and who, whilst at breakfast, maintained their ground for two hours against the Rochellois, and killed I know not how many of the enemy.'

'Did you learn the names of these musketeers?'

'Yes, my lord.'

'What are they?'

'Messieurs Athos, Porthos, and Aramis.'

'Always my three brave fellows!' muttered the cardinal. 'And the guardsman?'

'M. d'Artagnan.'

'My young madcap again! Decidedly these four men must be mine.'

On the same evening, the cardinal spoke to M. de Treville of the exploit, which formed the subject of conversation throughout the whole camp. M. de Treville, who had heard the recital of the adventure from the lips of those who were its heroes, recounted it in all its particulars to his eminence, without forgetting the episode of the napkin.

'Very good, M. de Treville,' said the cardinal; 'give me this napkin, I beg of you. I will get three fleurs-de-lis embroidered on it in gold, and will give it to you as a standard for your company.'

'My lord,' said M. de Treville, 'that would be unjust towards the guards. M. d'Artagnan does not belong to me, but to M. des Essarts.'

'Well, then, take him,' said the cardinal; 'it is not fair that these four brave soldiers, who love each other so much, should not serve in the same company.'

On the same evening, M. de Treville announced this good news to the three musketeers and to d'Artagnan, inviting them to breakfast with him on the morrow.

D'Artagnan could not contain himself for joy. We know that the dream of his whole life had been to be a musketeer. The three friends were also much delighted.

'Faith,' said d'Artagnan to Athos, 'yours was a triumphant idea; and, as you said, we have gained glory by it, besides being able to hold a conversation of the greatest importance.'

'Which we may henceforth renew without suspicion; for, with God's help, we shall henceforth be regarded as cardinalists.'

On the same evening d'Artagnan went to pay his respects to M. des Essarts, and to inform him of his promotion.

M. des Essarts, who had great affection for d'Artagnan, offered him any assistance that he might require, as this change of regiment brought with it new expenses of equipment.

D'Artagnan declined this assistance, but, thinking the opportunity a good one, requested him to ascertain the value of the diamond, which he placed in his hands, stating that he wished to turn it into money.

At eight o'clock the next morning, M. des Essarts's valet came to d'Artagnan, and handed to him a bag, containing seven thousand livres in gold. It was the price of the queen's diamond.

48

A Family Affair

ATHOS had found the right expression. It was necessary to call Buckingham's *a family affair!* A family affair was not subject to the investigation of the cardinal. A family affair concerned no one: they might occupy themselves before all the world with a family affair.

Aramis had found the idea—the valets!

Porthos had found the means—the diamond!

D'Artagnan alone, generally the most inventive of the four, had found nothing; but we must also confess that the very name of her ladyship paralysed him. Yet, we are mistaken—he had found a purchaser of the diamond.

The breakfast at M. de Treville's was charmingly gay. D'Artagnan had already got his uniform. As he was about the same size as Aramis, and as Aramis, being so handsomely paid, as may be remembered, by the bookseller who had bought his poem, had furnished himself with everything in duplicate, he had accommodated his friend with a complete equipment.

D'Artagnan would have been completely happy, had he not seen her ladyship like a dark cloud on the horizon.

After the breakfast, they agreed to meet again in the evening at Athos's quarters, in order to terminate their arrangements.

D'Artagnan passed the day in displaying his musketeer's uniform in every avenue throughout the camp.

At the appointed time in the evening, the four friends assembled. There were but three things left to decide: what they should write to the lady's brother-in-law; what they should write to the clever person at Tours; and which of the valets should be the bearer of the letters.

For the latter purpose, each offered his own. Athos

vaunted the discretion of Grimaud, who only spoke when his master permitted him to open his mouth; Porthos boasted of the strength of Mousqueton, who was big enough to drub four men of ordinary dimensions; Aramis, confident in the cunning of Bazin, made a pompous eulogium on his candidate; and, lastly, d'Artagnan had entire dependence in Planchet's bravery, and recalled to their minds how well he had behaved in their most hazardous encounter at Calais.

These four virtues for a long time contended for the mastery, and gave occasion for some magnificent speeches, which we shall not report lest they should be deemed tiresome.

'Unhappily,' said Athos, 'it is necessary that he whom we send, should possess in himself all the four qualities united.'

'But where can we find such a servant?'

'It is impossible, I know,' said Athos; 'so take Grimaud.'

'Take Mousqueton.'

'Take Bazin'.

'Take Planchet: he is frank and skilful: so there are two qualities out of the four.'

'Gentlemen,' said Aramis, 'the chief thing is, not to know which of our four valets is the most discreet, the strongest, the most cunning, or the bravest, but to find out which of them is the most fond of money.'

'What Aramis says is full of sense,' said Athos; 'it is necessary to calculate upon the defects of mankind, and not upon their virtues. M. Abbé, you are a great moralist!'

'Unquestionably so,' said Aramis; 'for we need to be well served, not only to succeed, but not to fail; since, in case of failure, it will endanger the head, not of the valet—'

'Not so loud, Aramis,' said Athos.

'You are right: not of the valet,' resumed Aramis, 'but of the master, or, even, of the masters. Are our valets sufficiently devoted to us to hazard their lives for us? No.'

'Faith!' said d'Artagnan, 'I would almost answer for Planchet.'

'Well, then, my dear friend, add to that devotion a good round sum, which will secure him some independence, and, instead of answering for him once, you may answer twice.'

'Ah, good God! you will be deceived just as much.' said Athos, who was an optimist in reasoning on things, and a pessimist when reasoning on men; 'they will promise everything to get money, and, when the occasion comes, fear will prevent their acting. Once taken, they will be imprisoned;

and, once imprisoned, they will confess everything. What the plague! we are not children! To get to England' (Athos lowered his voice), 'one must pass through the whole of France, which is thickly sown with the spies and creatures of the cardinal. Then, a passport is necessary for embarkation; then, English must be spoken, to find the way to London. Ah, I see that it is a very difficult affair.'

'Not at all,' said d'Artagnan, who was very anxious that the thing should be accomplished; 'I can see that it is easy enough. We know, without being told, vive Dieu! that if we wrote to Lord de Winter, loudly proclaiming all manner of enormities concerning the cardinal——'

'Not so loud,' said Athos.

'Or communicating state secrets and intrigues,' continued d'Artagnan, profiting by his friend's warning, 'we know, without being told, that we should all be broken on the wheel; but, for God's sake, do not forget what you have said yourself, Athos—that we only write about a family affair—that we write with the sole motive of getting this lady, as soon as she arrives in London, placed in such a situation that she cannot injure us. I would therefore write him a letter in something like these terms.'

'Now let us hear,' said Aramis, putting on a critical face beforehand.

' 'Sir, and dear friend——' '

'Ah! yes; 'dear friend' to an Englishman!' broke in Athos; 'that's a good start! Bravo, d'Artagnan! For that word alone you will be quartered, instead of broken on the wheel.'

'Well, then, I would say, 'Sir,'—quite short.

'You might even say, 'My lord,' rejoined Athos, who thought a good deal of the proprieties.

'My lord,—Do you remember the little enclosure for goats, near the Luxembourg?'

'Good! the Luxembourg, indeed! That will be taken for an allusion to the queen-mother. How very ingenious!' said Athos.

'Well, then, we will simply say: 'My lord,—Do you remember a certain little enclosure where your life was spared?'

'My dear d'Artagnan,' said Athos, 'you never will be anything but a vastly bad composer: where your life was spared!—for shame! It is not dignified: no one reminds a gallant man of such services. A benefit cast up is always an insult.'

'Ah! my dear fellow,' said d'Artagnan, 'you are unbearable; and if one must write under your critical eye, I renounce the task.'

'And you do wisely. Handle the sword and the musket, my dear boy—you perform those exercises admirably well; but give up the pen to the abbé—it is his vocation.'

'Yes,' said Porthos, 'give up the pen to Aramis, who writes theses in Latin.'

'Very well! so be it,' answered d'Artagnan. 'Compose this note for us, Aramis; but, by our holy father the Pope, mind what you are about, for I shall pluck you in turn, I warn you.'

'I ask nothing better,' said Aramis, with that natural confidence which every poet has in himself; 'but first make me acquainted with all the circumstances. I have indeed heard, now and then, that his sister-in-law is a minx. I have, in fact, got proof of it, by listening to her conversation with the cardinal.'

'Zounds! Not so loud, then,' cried Athos.

'But, continued Aramis, 'the particulars I do not know.'

'Nor I, either,' said Porthos.

D'Artagnan and Athos looked at one another for some time in silence. At last Athos, having collected himself, and become even paler than usual, gave a sign of assent; and d'Artagnan understood that he might speak.

'Well, then, here is what you must write,' resumed d'Artagnan.

'My lord,—Your sister-in-law is a wicked woman, who wished to have you killed in order to obtain your inheritance. But she could not marry your brother, being already married in France, and having been——' D'Artagnan stopped, as if he was seeking for the right word, and looked at Athos.

'Driven away by her husband,' dictated Athos.

'Because she had been branded,' continued d'Artagnan.

'Bah!' cried Porthos; 'impossible! and did she wish to have her brother-in-law killed?'

'Yes.'

'And she was really married?' demanded Aramis.

'Yes.'

'And her husband found out that she had a fleur-de-lis on her shoulder?' cried Porthos.

'Yes.' Three times had Athos uttered this 'yes,' each time in a more gloomy tone.

'And who saw this fleur-de-lis?' demanded Aramis.

'D'Artagnan and myself; or, rather, to observe the chronological order, I and d'Artagnan.' replied Athos.

'And the husband of this horrible creature is yet alive?' inquired Aramis.

'Yes.'

'You are quite sure of it?'

There was a moment of profound silence, during which each felt himself affected according to his disposition.

'This time,' said Athos, first breaking silence, 'd'Artagnan has given us a good start, and it is that which we must write first.'

'The devil!' said Aramis; 'you are right, Athos, and the composition is difficult. The chancellor himself would be at a loss to compose an epistle of this significancy, and yet the chancellor draws up a criminal process very agreeably. Never mind—be quiet—I will write.'

Aramis took a pen, reflected for a few moments, and then wrote eight or ten lines in a charming little feminine hand; then, in a soft and slow voice, as if every word had been scrupulously weighed, he read what follows:—

'MY LORD,—

'The person who writes these few lines had the honour of crossing swords with you in a little enclosure in the Rue de l'Enfer. As you have been kind enough, since, often to declare yourself the friend of that person, he is bound to reciprocate that friendship by an important warning. You have twice escaped being the victim of a near relation, whom you consider your heiress, because you know not, that, before contracting her marriage in England, she had been already married in France. But the third time, which is now, you might become her victim. Your relation has left La Rochelle for England. Watch for her arrival, for she has great and terrible designs. If you wish really to know of what she is capable, read her past history on her left shoulder.'

'Well, that is admirable,' said Athos; 'and you have the pen of a secretary of state, my dear Aramis. De Winter will keep a good lookout now, provided he receives the letter; and, should it ever fall into the hands of his eminence, we could not be compromised. But, as the valet whom we send might make us believe that he had been to London, whilst he only stopped at Chatellerault, give him only half the sum, promising him the other half on receipt of the answer. Have you the diamond?' continued Athos.

'I have better than that,' replied d'Artagnan. 'I have got the money;' and he threw the bag upon the table.

At the sound of the gold, Aramis lifted up his eyes, Porthos started, and as for Athos, he remained unmoved.

'How much is there in this little bag?' said he.

'Seven thousand livres, in twelve franc-pieces.'

'Seven thousand livres!' exclaimed Porthos. 'Was that paltry little diamond worth seven thousand livres?'

'So it seems,' said Athos, 'since there they are. I presume that our friend d'Artagnan has not put in any on his own account.'

'But, gentlemen,' continued d'Artagnan, 'we forget the queen. Let us take some little care of the health of her dear Buckingham. It is the least that we owe her.'

'That is true,' said Athos; 'but this concerns Aramis.'

'Well,' inquired the latter, colouring, 'what must I do?'

'Why,' replied Athos, 'it is very simple: just compose a second letter to that clever person who lives at Tours.'

Aramis resumed the pen, began to reflect again, and wrote the following lines, which he submitted immediately to the approbation of his friends:

'My dear Cousin—'

'Ah, ha!' said Athos, 'this clever person is your relation!'

'Cousin-german,' replied Aramis.

'Practically cousin.'

Aramis continued—

'My dear Cousin,—

'His eminence the cardinal, whom may God preserve for the happiness of France, and the confusion of the enemies of the realm, is about to exterminate the rebellious heretics of La Rochelle. It is probable that the aid of the English fleet will not even arrive in time within sight of the place: I might almost venture to say, that his grace of Buckingham will even be prevented from leaving England by some great event. His eminence is the most illustrious politician of time past, time present, and, most probably, of time to come. He would extinguish the sun, if the sun were in his way. Give this happy intelligence to your sister, my dear cousin. I dreamed that this cursed

Englishman was dead. I do not remember whether it was by poison, or the sword; only, I am sure that he was dead; and you know that my dreams are always fulfilled. Be assured, therefore, that you will shortly see me return.'

'Wonderfully good!' said Athos; 'you are the king of poets, my dear Aramis; you are eloquent as the Apocalypse, yet are as true as the gospel. There only remains, now, the address to put upon this letter.'

'That is easy enough,' said Aramis.

He folded the letter in a coquettish manner, and wrote—

'Mademoiselle Michon, seamstress, at Tours.'

The three friends looked at each other, and laughed. They were caught.

'Now, gentlemen,' said Aramis, 'you understand that Bazin alone can convey this letter to Tours. My cousin only knows Bazin, and will trust no one else. To send any other messenger would only ensure a failure. Besides, Bazin is ambitious and learned. Bazin has read history, gentlemen: he knows that Sextus the Fifth became pope after having herded swine; and, as he intends to enter the Church at the same time as myself, he does not despair of becoming himself a pope, or at any rate a cardinal. You will understand that a man who has such views will not allow himself to be caught, or, if he should be caught, will rather suffer martyrdom than speak.'

'Very well,' said d'Artagnan, 'I allow you Bazin with all my heart; only allow me Planchet. Her ladyship once sent him away well caned. Now Planchet has a good memory; and I promise you that, if he thought revenge possible, he would allow himself to be broken on the wheel rather than not effect it. If the business at Tours belongs peculiarly to you, that in London is peculiarly mine. So I entreat you to choose Planchet, who has, on his part, already been to London with me, and knows how to say, very correctly—'London, sir, if you please'; and, 'My master, Lord d'Artagnan.' You may be quite sure that, with this knowledge, he will find his way there and back.'

'In that case,' said Athos, 'Planchet must receive seven hundred livres for each half of his journey, and Bazin three hundred. That will reduce the sum to five thousand livres. We will each take a thousand livres, to spend as we please, and we will leave a fund of a thousand, of which the abbé shall take care, for extraordinary expenses and our common wants. What do you say to that?'

'My dear Athos,' said Aramis, 'you speak like Nestor, who was, as everybody knows, the wisest of the Greeks.'

'Then it is settled,' continued Athos; 'Planchet and Bazin will set out. After all, I am not sorry to keep Grimaud: he is accustomed to my ways, and I could depend upon him. Yesterday's expedition must have rather shaken him already; and this voyage would undo him altogether.'

Planchet was sent for to receive his instructions. He had already received some intimation of the journey from his master, who had instanced to him, first, the glory; then, the profit; and lastly, the danger.

'I will carry the letter in the lining of my coat,' said Planchet, 'and will swallow it if I am taken.'

'But then you will be unable to perform your commission,' said d'Artagnan.

'You will give me a copy this evening, which I shall know by heart to-morrow.'

D'Artagnan looked at his friends, as much as to say, 'Well, did I not tell you so.'

'Now,' continued he, addressing Planchet, 'you have eight days to reach Lord de Winter, and eight days to return here; that is, sixteen days in all. If, on the sixteenth day from your departure you have not arrived at eight o'clock in the evening, not a farthing more money shall you have, though you were only later by five minutes.'

'Then, sir,' said Planchet, 'buy me a watch.'

'Here, take this,' said Athos, with heedless generosity, giving him his own, 'and be a brave lad. Consider that, if you talk, if you babble, you will sacrifice the head of your master, who has so much confidence in your fidelity that he has answered for you to us. But remember, also, that if, by any fault of yours, any such calamity should befall d'Artagnan, I will hunt you out wherever you may be, and completely perforate you.'

'Oh, sir!' cried Planchet, humiliated at the suspicion, and particularly alarmed by the calmness of the musketeer.

'And I,' said Porthos, rolling his great eyes, 'remember, that I will skin you alive.'

'Ah, sir!'

'And I,' said Aramis, with his soft and melodious voice, 'remember, that I will roast you at a slow fire, as if you were an untutored savage.'

'Ah, sir!'

And Planchet began to cry; but we cannot venture to say whether it was from terror on account of the threats he had heard, or from being affected at seeing so close a union of hearts between the four friends.

D'Artagnan took his hand. 'You see, Planchet,' said he, 'that these gentlemen speak thus from affection towards me; but, notwithstanding all this, they esteem you.'

'Ah, sir!' said Planchet, 'I shall either succeed, or I shall be quartered; and, were I even quartered, you may rely upon it that not one piece of me will speak.'

It was decided that Planchet should start the next day, at eight in the morning, in order that, as he said, he might, during the night, have time to learn the letter by heart. He gained just twelve hours by this arrangement, as he was to return at eight o'clock on the evening of the sixteenth day.

Just as he was about to mount his horse in the morning, d'Artagnan, who felt his heart incline towards Buckingham, took Planchet aside.

'Listen,' said he; 'when you have delivered your letter to Lord de Winter, and he has read it, say to him, 'Watch over the Duke of Buckingham, for they are seeking to assassinate him.' But this, do you see, Planchet, is a thing of such momentous importance, that I would not even confess to my friends that I have confided the secret to you; and, even for a captain's commission, I would not write it down.'

'Be easy, sir,' said Planchet; 'you shall see whether you can trust me.'

'Mounted on an excellent horse, which he was to leave at twenty leagues from La Rochelle, to take the post, Planchet went off at a gallop; his heart was a little shaken by the threats of the musketeers, but, on the whole, he was in a most favourable state of mind.

Bazin left the next morning for Tours, and had eight days allowed him for his expedition.

The four friends, during the whole time of their absence, had, as may be well supposed, their eyes more than ever on the watch, their noses in the wind, and their ears upon the alert. The days were consumed in trying to catch every report, to watch the movements of the cardinal, and to scent out the couriers who arrived. More than once an unconquerable anxiety seized them, on being sent for on some unexpected service. They had also to be watchful of their own safety: her ladyship was a phantom, who, having once appeared to any one, would never more allow him to sleep in tranquillity.

On the morning of the eighth day, Bazin, fresh as ever, and smiling as usual, entered the room at the Parpaillot, just as the four friends were sitting down to breakfast, saying, according to the agreement they had made—

'M. Aramis, here is the answer from your cousin.'

The four friends exchanged a joyful glance. Half their work was done: it is true that it was the shortest and easiest half.

Aramis took the letter, blushing in spite of himself. The writing was vulgar, and the spelling wretched.

'Good God,' said he, laughing, 'I decidedly despair of her. This poor Michon will never write like M. de Volture!'

'Who does that mean—'this poor Michon?' asked the Swiss, who was commencing a gossip with the four friends when the letter was brought.

'Oh, mon Dieu! less than nothing,' replied Aramis. 'She is a charming little seamstress, whom I was very much in love with, and from whom I have begged a few lines, in her own handwriting, by way of remembrance.'

'Egad!' said the Swiss, 'if she is as ladylike as her own penmanship, you must be a happy fellow, comrade.'

Aramis read the letter, and handed it to Athos.

'Just see what she writes, Athos,' said he.

Athos threw a glance over the letter, and then, to destroy any suspicions which might have been awakened, read it aloud—

'COUSIN,—

'My sister and I understand dreams very well, and we are shocking.frightened at them: but of yours it may be said, I hope—all dreams are false! Adieu! Take care of yourself, and let us hear of you from time to time.

'MARIE MICHON.'

'What dream is she talking about?' asked the dragoon, who had approached whilst they were reading the letter.

'Yes, what dream?' said the Swiss.

'Oh! vive Dieu!' said Aramis, 'it is plain enough: about a dream of mine that I told them.'

'Ah! yes,' said the Swiss, 'it is quite natural to tell one's dreams; but, for my part, I never dream at all.'

'You are very fortunate,' said Athos, rising, 'and I wish I could say the same thing!'

'Never,' repeated the Swiss, delighted that a man like Athos should envy him in anything—'never, never!'

D'Artagnan, seeing Athos rise, did the same, and took his arm and left the room.

Porthos and Aramis remained behind, to face the gossip of the Swiss and the dragoon.

As for Bazin, he went to sleep upon a truss of straw, and, as he had more imagination than the Swiss, dreams that M. Aramis, who had become pope, was placing on his head a cardinal's hat.

But, as we have already said, Bazin had, by his fortunate return, removed only a part of the uneasiness which tormented the four friends. The days of suspense are always long, and d'Artagnan, especially, could have sworn that each of these days was eight-and-forty hours long. He forgot the unavoidable delays of navigation; he exaggerated the power of her ladyship; he gave to this woman, who appeared to him to resemble a demon, auxiliaries as supernatural as herself; and he fancied, at every noise, that they were coming to arrest him, or were bringing Planchet to be confronted with himself and his friends.

And, more than that, his extraordinary confidence in the worthy Picard diminished day by day. This suspense was so powerful, that it infected Porthos and Aramis. Athos alone remained unmoved, as though no danger filled the air around him, and he breathed in his habitual atmosphere.

On the sixteenth day, particularly, these signs of agitation were so perceptible in d'Artagnan and his two friends, that they could not remain in any one place, and wandered about like shadows on the road by which Planchet was expected to return.

'Really,' said Athos, 'you are not men; you are only children, to let a woman frighten you so much. And, after all, what is it that you fear? Imprisonment? Well, we should be released from prison, as Madame Bonancieux has been. Execution? Why, we gladly expose ourselves, every day, in the trenches, to worse than that: for a bullet might break a leg; and I am quite sure that a surgeon puts one to more pain in amputating a thigh, than an executioner in cutting off a head. So, keep yourselves easy: in two, four, six hours, at the latest, Planchet will be here. He has given us his promise; and I, for my part, have great confidence in the promises of Planchet, for he seems to me a very worthy lad.'

'But what if he should not come?' said d'Artagnan.

'Well, and if he should not come, he has been delayed —that's all. He may have fallen from his horse; he may have made a somersault over a bridge; he may have brought on a disease of his chest, by running too quickly. Come, gentlemen, let us allow for accidents. Life is a large chaplet of little miseries, which the philosopher shakes with a laugh. Be philosophers, like me, gentlemen: come around the table and let us drink. Nothing makes the future of so rosy a hue, as to look at it through a glass of chambertin.'

'That is all very well,' replied d'Artagnan; 'but I am weary of imagining, every time I drink, that the wine may have come from her ladyship's cellar.'

'You are very fastidious!' said Athos. 'Such a beautiful woman!'

'A woman with a brand!' said Porthos, with his horse-laugh.

Athos started, passed his hand over his forehead, to wipe off the perspiration, and rose, in his turn, with a nervous agitation that he was unable to restrain.

The day, however, glided on, and the evening came more slowly; but, at last, it arrived. The taverns were full of customers. Athos, who had pocketed his share of the diamond, now scarcely ever left the Parpaillot. He had found in M. de Busigny, who, moreover, had given them a superb dinner, a partner worthy of himself. They were playing together, according to custom, when the clock struck seven; and they heard the patrols passing to change the guard. At half-past seven the drums beat the last post.

'We are lost,' whispered d'Artagnan in Athos's ear.

'You mean to say that we *have* lost,' replied Athos, with great tranquillity, drawing at the same time ten pistoles from his pocket, and throwing them upon the table. 'Come, gentlemen,' continued he, 'that is the last drum; let us go to bed.'

And Athos left the Parpaillot, followed by d'Artagnan. Aramis came behind, giving his arm to Porthos. Aramis was mouthing verses; and Porthos, from time to time, tore a few hairs from his moustache, in token of despair. But behold, suddenly, in the obscurity, a shadow was perceptible, of a form familiar to d'Artagnan, and a wellknown voice said to him—'Sir, I have brought you your cloak, for it is cold this evening.'

'Planchet!' exclaimed d'Artagnan, intoxicated with joy.

'Planchet!' exclaimed Aramis and Porthos.

'Well—yes, Planchet,' said Athos; 'what is there surprising in that? He promised to be back by eight o'clock, and it is now just striking eight. Bravo, Planchet! You are a lad of your word, and, if ever you leave your master, I will keep a place for you in my service.'

'Oh, no, never!' said Planchet; 'I shall never leave M. d'Artagnan.'

And at the same moment d'Artagnan felt Planchet slip a small note into his hand.

D'Artagnan had a great desire to embrace Planchet; but he was afraid such a mark of delight, conferred upon his valet in the public highway, would look rather odd to any passer-by; so he restrained himself. 'I have got the letter,' said he to Athos and his friends.

'Very well,' said Athos, 'let us go to our quarters, and read it.'

The letter burned the hand of d'Artagnan. He wished to hurry on; but Athos kept a firm hold of his arm, and the young man was compelled to regulate his speed by that of his friend.

They reached their tent at last, and lighted a lamp; and, whilst Planchet stood at the door, to see that the four friends were not interrupted, d'Artagnan, with a trembling hand, broke the seal, and opened the long-expected letter.

It contained half a line in a hand truly British, and of a brevity truly Spartan.

'Thank you: be easy.'

Athos took the letter from d'Artagnan's hands, put it to the lamp, lighted it, and did not quit his hold until it was reduced to ashes. Then, calling Planchet—

'Now, my boy,' said he, 'you have a right to the other seven hundred livres; but you did not run much risk with such a letter as that.'

'Nevertheless, I have invented a great many ways of securing it,' replied Planchet.

'Well,' said d'Artagnan, 'tell us all about it.'

'But it is a long story, sir,' answered he.

'You are right, Planchet,' said Athos; 'besides, the last drum has sounded, and we shall be observed if we burn our light longer than other people.'

'Well, then, let us go to bed,' said d'Artagnan; 'sleep well, Planchet.'

'Faith, sir, it will be my first time for sixteen days.'

'And mine also,' said d'Artagnan.

'And mine too!' exclaimed Porthos.

'And mine too!' re-echoed Aramis.

'Well, shall I confess the truth? and mine too!' said Athos.

49

Fatality

IN the meantime, her ladyship—intoxicated with rage, and raging on the vessel's deck like an excited lioness—had been even tempted to cast herself into the sea: for she could not bring herself to brook the thought, that she had been insulted by d'Artagnan, and threatened by Athos, and was now quitting France without having obtained revenge. So insupportable had this idea at last become, that, at the risk of the most terrible consequences to herself, she had entreated the captain to land her on the French coast. But the captain, anxious to escape from his false position—where he was placed between the English and French cruisers, like a bat between the rats and the birds—was in extreme haste to arrive in England. He obstinately refused, therefore, to obey what he regarded as a woman's caprice; he promised, however, to his passenger, who had been particularly recommended to his care by the cardinal, to land her at some port in Brittany, either Brest or Lorient, should the weather and the French permit. But, in the meantime, the wind was contrary, and the sea rough: they tacked about continually; and, nine days after her departure from Charente, her ladyship, pale with grief and rage, saw only the blue shores of Finisterre.

She calculated that, to traverse that angle of France, and return to the cardinal, would take her at least three days; add one day for landing, and that would make four. Add these four to the nine already elapsed, and here were thirteen days lost—thirteen days, during which so many important events might have occurred in London. She considered that the cardinal would undoubtedly be furious at her return, and, consequently, would be disposed to listen more to any accusations which were made against her, than to those which she might make against others. Without solicitation, therefore, she permitted the captain to carry her past Lorient and Brest; and he, on his part, was careful not to remind her of her wishes. She thus continued her voyage; and on the very day that Planchet embarked at Portsmouth, to return to France, the messenger of his eminence entered the port triumphantly.

The whole town was in a state of extraordinary excitement. Four large ships, recently built, had just been launched into the sea. Standing on the jetty, covered with gold, and glittering as usual with diamonds and precious stones, his hat adorned with a white plume which dropped upon his shoulder, Buckingham was visible, surrounded by a staff almost as gorgeous as himself.

It was one of those few and fine summer days, when Englishmen remember that there is a sun. The pale, but still splendid luminary, was just setting on the horizon, empurpling the heavens and the sea with bands of fire, and casting a last golden ray on the towers and the old buildings of the town, which made the windows gleam as with the reflection of a conflagration. Her ladyship—as she inhaled the sea-breeze, which is fresher and more balmy in the vicinity of land, and contemplated all those mighty preparations which she was ordered to destroy, and all the might of that armament against which she had come to contend alone—a woman, with a few bags of gold—mentally compared herself to Judith, the terrible Jewess, when she penetrated into the camp of the Assyrians, and saw the enormous mass of chariots, of horses, of men, and of arms, which one movement of her hand was to dissipate like a cloud of smoke.

They entered the roads, but, just as they were making ready to cast anchor, a small, strongly-armed cutter, presenting itself as a coast-guard, approached the merchant-vessel, and put off its gig which was steered toward them. The gig contained an officer, a lieutenant, and eight men. The officer alone came on board, where he was received with all the respect which his uniform inspired.

The officer conversed for a few minutes with the captain, and inspected some papers which the latter brought with him; and then, on the captain's order, all the crew and passengers of the vessel were mustered upon deck. When this had been done, the officer inquired aloud, as to where the brig had come from, what had been its course, and where it had put in; and to all these questions the captain

478

replied satisfactorily, without hesitation or difficulty. The officer then began to examine all the persons on deck, one after the other, and, stopping before her ladyship, he looked at her very earnestly, but without uttering a single word.

Having returned to the captain, and made some new communication to him, the officer, as if he had now taken command of the vessel, gave an order which the crew immediately executed. By this means the vessel was again in motion; but it was still escorted by the little cutter, which kept beside it, menacing its broadside with the mouths of her cannons; the boat followed in the vessel's wake, an object scarcely visible behind the enormous mass.

Whilst the officer had been examining her ladyship, she as may be well imagined, had, on her side, not failed to scrutinize him most intently. But however much this woman, with her eye of fire, was accustomed to read the hearts of those whose secret she desired to discover, she had found at last a countenance so perfectly impenetrable that no insight followed her investigation.

The officer who stood before her, and silently studied her with so much care, might be about twenty-five or twenty-six years of age. He had a very fair complexion, with blue eyes, rather deeply set. His fine and well-cut mouth continued perfectly motionless in its classic lines. His well-developed chin denoted that strength of will which, in the prevailing English character, is commonly no better than obstinacy; and his slightly receding forehead—such as is accorded to poets, to enthusiasts, and to soldiers—was scantily shaded by short thin hair, which, as well as the beard that covered the lower part of his face, was of a beautiful deep chestnut colour.

When they entered the harbour it was already dark. The fog increased the obscurity, and formed, around the lanterns of the ships and jetties, a circle similar to that which surrounds the moon, when it threatens rainy weather. The atmosphere was melancholy, damp, and cold.

Her ladyship, firm as she was, felt herself shivering, in spite of all her efforts.

The officer had had her ladyship's packages indicated to him, and ordered them to be put into the boat; after which, offering his hand to assist her, he requested her to descend herself.

Her ladyship looked at the man, and hesitated.

'Who are you, sir,' said she, 'who are so good as to trouble yourself so particularly about me?'

'You may see, madam, from my uniform, that I am an officer in the English navy,' replied the young man.

'But is it usual for the officers of the English navy to put themselves at the service of their countrywomen, when they approach a British port, and to display their gallantry so far as to conduct them on shore?'

'Yes, my lady, it is the custom—not from gallantry, but prudence—that, in time of war, strangers may be conducted to a certain appointed hotel, in order that they may, until every information be obtained concerning them, remain under the inspection of the government.'

The words were uttered with the most exact politeness, and the most perfect calmness: and yet they did not satisfy her ladyship.

'But I am not a foreigner, sir,' said she, in an accent as pure as was ever uttered between Portsmouth and Manchester. 'My name is Lady de Winter, and this proceeding——'

'This proceeding is general, my lady, and you will in vain endeavour to escape it.'

'I will follow you, then, sir.'

And, accepting the officer's hand, she began to descend the ladder, at the bottom of which the boat was waiting. The officer followed her. A large cloak was spread in the stern: the officer made her seat herself on it, and placed himself by her side.

'Give way!' said he to the sailors.

The eight oars all fell into the water at the same instant, and the boat seemed to fly along the surface of the harbour. In five minutes they reached the shore. The officer sprang upon the quay, and gave his hand to her ladyship. A carriage was waiting for them.

'Is this carriage for us?' demanded the lady.

'Yes, madam,' replied the officer.

'Then the hotel is at some distance?'

'At the other end of the town.'

'Let us go,' said her ladyship.

She then entered the carriage with a resolute step.

Having superintended the safe consignment of the baggage, the officer took his place beside her ladyship, and closed the carriage door.

Then, without any orders being given to him, or any indication as to where he was to go, the coachman set off at a gallop, and was soon threading the streets of the town.

A reception so strange naturally supplied her ladyship

with abundant matter for reflection. And, seeing that the young officer did not appear at all inclined to enter into conversation, she leant back in one of the corners of the carriage, and passed in review, one after the other, all the suppositions which presented themselves to her mind.

But, in about a quarter of an hour, surprised at the length of their journey, she looked out of the window to observe where they were going. She could no longer see any houses; but trees were visible in the darkness, like vast black phantoms, chasing one another.

Her ladyship shuddered.

'But we have left the town, sir,' she remarked.

The young officer remained silent.

'I positively declare, sir, that I will go no further, if you do not tell me where you are conveying me.'

This threat produced no reply.

'Ah! it is too much!' exclaimed her ladyship. 'Help! help!'

No voice responded to her cries. The carriage continued its rapid course. The officer seemed to be a statue.

Her ladyship gazed on him with one of those terrible glances which were peculiar to her own face, and which so rarely failed of their effect. Passion made her eyes positively sparkle in the gloom; but the young man continued perfectly immovable.

She then attempted to open the door and throw herself out.

'Take care, madam,' coldly observed the officer; 'you will kill yourself if you leap out.'

The lady resumed her seat, foaming with rage. He leant forwards, looked at her in his turn, and seemed surprised to find a countenance, before so beautiful, now so convulsed with rage, as to have become almost hideous. The crafty creature, comprehending that she would sacrifice her own interests by thus betraying her true nature, at once composed her features, and, in a beseeching voice, said—

'For Heaven's sake, sir! tell me if it be to yourself, or to your government, or to an enemy, that I am to impute this violence that is inflicted on me?'

'No violence is inflicted, madam; and that which has befallen you is the result of a very simple measure, which we are forced to pursue towards all those who land in England.'

'Then you do not know me, sir?'

'It is the first time that I have had the honour of seeing you.'

'And, upon your honour, you have no cause of enmity against me?'

'None whatever, I swear.'

There was so much calmness, so much serenity, so much gentleness even, in the young man's voice, that her ladyship was reassured.

At last, after about an hour's drive, the carriage stopped at an iron gate, at the entrance of a narrow road, which led to a gloomy-looking, massive, and isolated castle. And, as the carriage-wheels rolled over a soft gravel, her ladyship heard a mighty roaring, which she recognised as the sound of the sea breaking upon a rocky coast.

The carriage passed under two arches, and stopped at last in a square and gloomy courtyard. The door was almost immediately opened, the young officer leapt lightly out, presented his arm to her ladyship, who leaned upon it, and got out, in her turn, with great calmness.

'So, I am a prisoner,' said she, looking around, and then fixing her eyes on the young man with the most gracious smile imaginable. 'But I shall not be one long, I am certain,' added she. 'My own conscience and your politeness give me that assurance, sir.'

Flattering as the compliment might be, the officer made no reply, but, drawing from his pocket a small silver whistle, like those used by boatswains on board of men-of-war, he sounded it three times, in three different modulations. Several men immediately appeared, who unharnessed the horses, and took the carriage into a coach-house.

The officer, still preserving the same calm politeness, invited his prisoner to enter the castle. The latter, with the same smile upon her countenance, took his arm, and passed with him under a low arched doorway, which led them, through a vault lighted only at the end, to a stone staircase, winding round an angle of the same material. They then stopped before a massive door, which, upon the application of a key that the young man carried, slowly swung upon its hinges, and gave access to the apartment intended for her ladyship.

In one glance, the prisoner grasped the minutest particulars of this room. It was a chamber, of which the furniture was at the same time suitable for a prison, and for the habitation of the free. But the bars to the windows, and the locks outside the doors, decided the question in favour of the prison. For an instant, all the strength of mind of this creature, although hardened from the most vigorous sources, abandoned her. She sank into a seat, folded her arms, drooped her head, and waited in momentary expectation of seeing a judge enter to interrogate her.

But no one came, except two or three marines, who brought in her baggage, and having deposited it in a corner, withdrew without uttering a word.

The officer presided over all these details with the same calmness which her ladyship had invariable observed, not speaking a syllable, and enforcing obedience merely by a gesture of his hand, or a note from his whistle. One would have said that, between this man and his inferiors, verbal language either had never existed, or had become unnecessary.

Her ladyship could at last no longer restrain herself, and she thus broke the silence.

'In Heaven's name, sir,' she exclaimed, 'what does all this mean? Relieve my perplexity: I have courage to face any danger which I can see approaching, any misfortune which I comprehend. Where am I, and why am I here? Am I free? Wherefore these bars and doors? Am I a prisoner? What crime have I committed?'

'You are here, madam, in the apartment destined for you. I was ordered to go and arrest you at sea, and to conduct you to this castle. I have accomplished that order, I think, with the rigid exactitude of an officer, but, at the same time, with the courtesy of a gentleman. There terminates, at least for the present, the charge with which I have been entrusted concerning you. The remainder devolves upon another person.'

'And this other person—who is he?' demanded her ladyship; 'can you not tell me his name?'

As she spoke, the clashing of spurs was heard upon the staircase; some voices passed by, and were lost in the distance, and the sound of a solitary step approached the door.

'That person is now here, madam,' said the officer, standing on one side, and assuming an attitude of submission and respect.

At the same instant the door opened, and a man appeared upon the threshold. He was without a hat, carried a sword at his side, and was crushing a handkerchief between his fingers.

Her ladyship thought that she recognised this shadow in

the gloom; and, supporting herself with one hand on the arm of the chair, she advanced her head, in order, as it were, to meet a certainty.

The stranger slowly approached, and as he advanced and gradually came within range of the rays emitted by the lamp, her ladyship involuntarily recoiled. And then, when she had no longer any doubt—

'What! my brother,' she exclaimed, overwhelmed with astonishment, 'is it you?'

'Yes, fair lady,' replied Lord de Winter, making her a bow, half courteous and half ironical, 'myself.'

'But, then, this castle——'

'Is mine.'

'This apartment——'

'Is yours.'

'Then I am your prisoner?'

'Or something very like it.'

'But it is a frightful abuse of power.'

'No hard words, madam: let us sit down and have some quiet conversation, as is suitable between brother and sister.'

Then, turning towards the door, and perceiving that the young officer awaited his final orders:

'It is all right,' said he, 'I thank you. Now leave us, Mr. Felton.'

50

A Chat between a Brother and Sister

DURING the time which Lord de Winter occupied in shutting and bolting the door, and bringing a seat beside the easy-chair of his sister-in-law, her ladyship was thoughtfully directing her glance into the depths of possibility, and discovering the whole of that plot, of which she could form no conception, so long as she continued ignorant of the person into whose hands she had unhappily fallen. She knew her brother-in-law to be a true gentleman, who was fond of the chase, played freely, and was gallant in regard to women, but of powers below the average in respect to intrigues. How had he been able to know of her arrival, and to have her arrested; and why did he desire to detain her?

Athos had let fall a few words, which proved that her conversation with the cardinal had been heard by other ears; but she could not imagine that he could so promptly and so boldly lay a countermine. She rather feared that her former proceedings in England had been discovered. Buckingham might have guessed that it was she who had cut off his diamond studs, and have sought to avenge himself for that petty treachery. But Buckingham was incapable of any extremities against a woman, especially if that woman were supposed to have been actuated by a sentiment of jealousy.

This supposition appeared the most probable: she thought that they wished to revenge the past, and not to anticipate the future.

But, at any rate, she congratulated herself on having fallen into the hands of her brother-in-law, with whom she contemplated little difficulty, rather than into those of a former enemy.

'Yes, brother, let us have some chat,' she said, with a sort of sprightliness, determined as she was to draw from this conversation, in spite of all the dissimulation which Lord de Winter might bring to it, such information as she needed to guide her future conduct.

'You have made up your mind, then, to return to England,' said Lord de Winter, 'in spite of the determination you so often expressed to me, in Paris, never again to set your foot upon the territory of Great Britain?'

Her ladyship replied to this question by another.

'First, tell me,' said she, 'how you could manage to have me watched so closely, as not only to know beforehand that I was coming, but also the day, the hour, and the port at which I should arrive?'

Lord de Winter adopted the same tactics as her ladyship, thinking that, as his sister-in-law employed them, they were undoubtedly the best.

'But, tell me yourself, my dear sister, for what purpose you are come to England?'

'Why, I have come to see you,' replied the lady, ignorant of how much she aggravated by this answer the suspicions which d'Artagnan's letter had excited in her brother-in-law's mind, and only wishing to captivate the kindness of her auditor by a lie.

'Oh! to see me!' said Lord de Winter sneeringly.

'Assuredly, to see you. What is there surprising in that?'

485

'And you had no other motive in coming to England than to see me?'

'No.'

'Then it is for my sake alone that you have given yourself the trouble to cross the straits?'

'For you alone.'

'I'faith, your tenderness is excessive, my dear sister!'

'But am I not your nearest relation?' demanded the lady, in a tone of the most touching simplicity.

'And you are also my sole heiress, are you not?' said Lord de Winter, in his turn, fixing his eyes upon those of her ladyship—'that is to say, through your son.'

Great as was her power of self-command, her ladyship could not refrain from starting; and as, in uttering these last words, Lord de Winter had laid his hand upon his sister's arm, this start had not escaped him.

In truth, the blow was both direct and deep. The first idea in the lady's mind was, that Kitty had betrayed her, and had disclosed to the baron that interested aversion whose manifestations she had imprudently permitted to escape her before her maid; and she also recollected the furious and impolitic attack which she had made on d'Artagnan, after he had saved her brother-in-law's life.

'I do not understand what you mean, my lord,' said she, wishing to gain time, and to make her adversary talk: 'is there some concealed signification in your words?'

'Oh! no,' said Lord de Winter, with apparent good humour; 'you wish to see me, and you come to England I am informed of this wish, or rather I suspect that you feel it, and, to spare you all the inconvenience consequent on a nocturnal arrival in the harbour, and all the fatigues of landing, I send one of my officers to meet you. I put a carriage at your disposal, and he brings you here to this castle, of which I am the governor, where I come every day, and where, to satisfy our mutual desire of seeing one another I have had an apartment prepared for your reception. What is there in all this more surprising than in what you have told me?'

'No; but what surprises me, is, that you should have received previous intelligence of my arrival.'

'And yet it is the simplest thing in the world, my dear sister. Did you not observe, that, on entering the Roads, the captain of your little vessel sent forward his log-book and the register of his passengers and crew, that he might obtain permission to enter the port? I am the governor of the port: this book was brought to me, and I recognised your name. My heart told me what your speech has just confirmed; that is to say, your motive for thus braving the dangers of a sea so perilous, or, at any rate, so fatiguing, at this season; and I sent out my cutter to convey you. You know what followed.'

Her ladyship was satisfied that his lordship lied, and she was only the more alarmed.

'Brother,' said she, 'was not that the Duke of Buckingham whom I saw on the jetty as I disembarked.'

'Himself,' replied Lord de Winter. 'Oh! I can well imagine that the sight of him would strike you. You come from a country where they must think a good deal about him; and I know that his armaments against France much engage the attention of your friend, the cardinal?'

'My friend, the cardinal!' exclaimed the lady, perceiving that on this point, also, as on the other, Lord de Winter seemed to be equally well-informed.

'Is he not your friend, then?' carelessly inquired the baron. 'Oh! pardon me; I thought he was. But we will discuss his grace hereafter. Let us not abandon the sentimental turn which the conversation had taken. You came, you say, to see me?'

'Yes.'

'Well, I have told you that your wish shall be gratified, and that we shall see one another every day.'

'Must I then remain here for ever?' demanded the lady, with some degree of dread.

'Do you find yourself badly lodged here, my dear sister. Ask for what you want, and I will hasten to provide it.'

'But I have neither my own women, nor my servants, with me here.'

'You shall have everything you want of that kind. Only tell me what kind of establishment your first husband kept for you, and, although I am but your brother-in-law, I will fix your present home upon a similar footing.'

'My first husband?' exclaimed the lady, looking at Lord de Winter, with wildness in her eyes.

'Yes, your French husband—I do not mean my own brother. But, if you have forgotten it, as he is yet alive, I can write to him, and he can send me the necessary information on the subject.'

Cold drops rolled down her ladyship's forehead.

'You are jesting,' said she, in a hoarse voice.

'Do I look like it?' inquired the baron, rising, and retreating a step.

'Or, rather, you mean to insult me,' continued she, convulsively grasping the arms of her chair, and raising herself by that means.

'I insult you!' said Lord de Winter, contemptuously; 'and do you really think that possible, madam?'

'Sir,' said her ladyship, 'you are either drunk or mad. Leave me, and send me my women.'

'Women are very indiscreet, my dear sister. Cannot I serve you as a waiting-maid? And thus all our secrets will remain in the family.'

'Insolent fellow!' exclaimed her ladyship. Then, as if moved by a spring, she bounded towards the baron, who awaited her with composure, yet with a hand upon the hilt of his sword.

'Ah, ah?' said he, 'I know that you have a habit of assassinating people; but I will defend myself, I warn you, even against you.'

'Ah! you are right,' said the lady, 'and you look to me like one who is coward enough to raise his hand against a woman!'

'And, if I did, I should have an excuse. Besides, mine would not be the first man's hand that had been laid upon you, I imagine.'

And the baron, by a slow accusing gesture, pointed to the lady's left shoulder, which he almost touched with his finger.

Her ladyship uttered a hoarse cry, and retreated to the further corner of the room, like a panther drawing back before its spring.

'Oh, roar as much as you please!' exclaimed Lord de Winter, 'only do not try to bite; for, I warn you, that would only prove the worse for you. There are no lawyers here, who regulate successions beforehand; there is no knight-errant, who will pick a quarrel with me for the sake of the fair lady whom I keep imprisoned; but I have at hand, judges, that will dispose of a woman, who, being already married, was shameless enough to intrude herself into our family; and these judges will hand you over to an executioner who will make your two shoulders alike.'

The eyes of her ladyship shot forth such lightning glances, that, although he was an armed man, before an unarmed woman, he felt the chill of fear penetrating his very soul. Nevertheless, he continued, but with increasing fury:—

'Yes, I understand: after having inherited my brother's property you would like to inherit mine also; but, be assured in advance, though you may be able to assassinate me, or to get me assassinated, my precautions are already taken:—not one penny of what I possess shall come either into your hands or into those of your son. Are you not already wealthy enough in the enjoyment of nearly half a million; and can you not arrest yourself in your fatal course, if you do not really do wickedness from a limitless and intense love of it! Oh, doubt not, if my brother's memory had not been still sacred to me, that you should be sent to rot in some dungeon of the state, or to satiate the curiosity of the mob at Tyburn! I shall, however, be silent; but you must learn to endure your confinement with tranquillity. In a fortnight or three weeks I shall set out with the army for La Rochelle; but, on the evening before my departure, you will be sent on board a vessel, which I shall watch set sail, and which will convey you to one of our southern colonies; and you may rely upon it, that I shall associate with you a companion who will blow out your brains on the first attempt that you may make to return to England, or to the continent.'

Her ladyship listened with an attention that expanded the pupils of her burning eyes.

'Yes,' continued Lord de Winter, 'but at present you will continue in this castle: the walls are thick, the doors are strong, the bars are solid; and, besides, your window looks directly down into the sea. My ship's company, who are devoted to me in life and death, keep guard around this chamber, and command every passage that conducts into the courtyard; and, even there, you would find three iron-grated doors, to pass which, the watchword is requisite; hence, therefore, a step, a motion, or a word, which bears the semblance of an intention to escape, will draw their fire upon you. If you should be killed, English justice ought, I think, to be grateful to me for having spared her some trouble. Ah! your features have resumed their composure, and your countenance regains its confidence. "Ten days, or a fortnight," you say to yourself—"Bah! by that time, some idea will suggest itself to my inventive mind; I have an infernal disposition, and shall find some victim. Within a fortnight from this time, I shall have escaped from here."—Well, try your fortune!'

Finding her thoughts thus plainly read, her ladyship dug

her nails into her flesh, that she might deprive her face of every expression but that of agony.

Lord de Winter continued—

'As to the officer who holds the command here in my absence, you have seen him; therefore you already know him. You are aware that he can keep to his instructions; for you did not travel from Portsmouth here without trying to make him talk. What think you of him? Could a marble statue be more impassive or mute? You have already tried the power of your seductions over many men, and, unfortunately, you have always succeeded; but try it now on this man, and, by Jove! if you succeed, I shall believe you to be the very fiend himself.'

He went towards the door, and opened it suddenly.

'Call Mr. Felton,' said he. And again, 'Wait a moment, madam, and I will recommend you to his care.'

During the strange silence which was then maintained between them, the sound of a slow and regular step was heard approaching. In the shadow of the corridor a human form was soon apparent, and the young lieutenant, with whom we have already made acquaintance, stood at the door, in waiting for the baron's orders.

'Come in, my dear John,' said Lord de Winter, 'come in, and shut the door.'

The young officer entered the room.

'Now,' said the baron, 'look at this woman. She is young and beautiful; she has every wordly attraction; but she is a monster, who, at twenty-five years of age, has committed as many crimes as you could read of in a year in the archives of our tribunals. Her voice prepossesses you in her favour; her beauty fascinates her victims. She will attempt to seduce you—perhaps to kill you. I have rescued you from misery, Felton; I have had you made lieutenant; I have once saved your life—you remember on what occasion; I am not only your protector, but your friend—not only your benefactor, but your father. This woman has come to England to plot against my life. I have got the serpent into my power. Well, I call you here, and I say to you—"My dear Felton—John, my son—defend me, and guard yourself especially, from this woman. Swear that you will preserve her for the punishment that she deserves! John Felton, I trust to your word—John Felton, I confide in your honour."'

'My lord,' answered the young officer, exhibiting on his open face all the hatred for the lady, that he could find in his heart, 'I swear to you that everything shall be done as you desire.'

Her ladyship received this look like a resigned victim. It was impossible to see a softer or more submissive expression than that which then reigned upon her beautiful face. Scarcely could Lord de Winter himself recognise the tigress which he had the instant before almost prepared to fight.

'She must never leave this room—do you hear, John?' continued the baron; 'she must have no communication with any one; she must speak to no one but yourself, if, indeed, you will do her the honour to talk with her.'

'It is quite enough, my lord—I have sworn!'

'And now, madam,' said the baron, 'endeavour to make your peace with God, for you have been judged by men.'

Her ladyship let her head droop, as if she felt herself actually crushed by this sentence. Lord de Winter left the room, making a sign to Felton, who followed him, and closed the door.

Directly afterwards was heard in the passage the heavy tread of a marine, who was keeping guard, with his axe at his belt, and his musket in his hand.

Her ladyship remained for a few minutes in the same position, for she fancied that they might be watching her through the keyhole. Then, she slowly raised her head, which had resumed a formidable expression of menace and defiance; ran to the door and listened, looked out of the window, and returned to bury herself in an immense easychair, and abandon herself to anxious consideration.

51

The Officer

In the meantime, the cardinal was expecting news from England; but as no news arrived, excepting such as was vexatious and alarming, La Rochelle was formally invested. However certain success appeared—thanks to the precautions which had been taken, and more especially to the mole, which no longer permitted any vessel to approach the besieged town—the blockade might yet continue a long time; and it was a great affront to the arms of the king, and a great annoyance to the cardinal, who had no longer, it is true, to embroil Louis XIII. with Anne of Austria, for that had been accomplished, but to reconcile M. de Bassompierre, who had quarrelled with the Duke of Angoulême.

The town, in spite of the incredible persistance of its mayor, had attempted a sort of mutiny in order to surrender. But the mayor had sent the mutineers to be hung. This execution subdued the most unruly, who were thereby determined to submit, in preference, to death from starvation, as the latter mode of dying appeared to them less certain and more slow than that of strangulation.

The besiegers, on their side, occasionally captured some of the messengers whom the Rochellois despatched to Buckingham, or the spies whom Buckingham had sent to the Rochellois. In both cases, the captives were subjected to a summary trial. The cardinal pronounced the single word—'Hung!' His majesty was invited to the execution.

The king came languidly, and chose a good place for observing all the details of the operation. This amused him for a time, and gave him a little patience with the siege; but it did not prevent him from becoming heartily weary, or from talking incessantly of returning to Paris; so that, if the messengers or spies had fallen short, his eminence, in spite of all his fertility of imagination, would have found himself in very considerable embarrassment.

Nevertheless, the time passed away, and still the Rochellois did not surrender. The last spy who had been captured was the bearer of a letter, which informed Buckingham that the town was at the last extremity; but instead of adding—'if your assistance should not arrive before a fortnight, we must surrender,' it merely said—'if your assistance should not arrive before a fortnight, we shall be all dead from hunger when it does arrive.'

The Rochellois, therefore, had no hope but in Buckingham—Buckingham was their Messiah! It was manifest that, if they should receive indubitable information that no further dependence was to be placed on Buckingham, their courage would forsake them, along with their hope.

The cardinal, on this account, waited with extreme impatience for intelligence from England, which might announce to him that Buckingham would not arrive.

The question of taking the town by assault, which had been often debated in the king's council, had been always dismissed. In the first instance, La Rochelle appeared to be impregnable; and then the cardinal, whatever he might himself have said about it aloud, was well aware that the horror of the blood which would have been shed in such an encounter—where Frenchmen fought against Frenchmen—would have been a retrogression of sixty years imprinted on his policy; and the cardinal was, at that epoch, what we now call a man of progress. In fact, the sack of La Rochelle, and the slaughter of three or four thousand Huguenots who would have perished, would have had, in 1628, too great a resemblance to the massacre of St. Bartholomew, in 1572. Finally, in addition to all this, this extreme measure, to which his majesty, like a good catholic, had no repugnance, always broke down before this argument of the besieging generals: 'La Rochelle is impregnable, except by famine.'

The cardinal was unable to dismiss from his own mind the fear which he entertained of his terrible emissary; for he also had understood the strange characteristics of that woman, who was half lioness and half serpent. Had she betrayed him? Or, was she dead? He knew her well enough, in any case, to be assured that, whether she was acting for him or against him, whether enemy or friend, she could not remain inactive without very powerful obstructions. But whence could these obstructions arise? This was what he was unable to divine.

After all, however, he had, with good reason, much confidence in her ladyship. He had suspected, in her past career, circumstances so terrible, that his own red mantle was required to conceal them; and he felt that, from some cause or other, this woman was his own, because from him alone could she obtain support more potent than the danger which pursued her.

The cardinal resolved, therefore, to conduct the war alone, and to expect aid foreign to himself only as one may expect the coincidence of a fortunate chance. He continued the construction of that famous embankment, which was to carry famine into La Rochelle; and, in the meantime, he cast his eyes over that unhappy city, which contained so much profound misery, and so many heroic virtues, recalling to his mind the expression of Louis XI., who had been his own political predecessor, as he himself was the predecessor of Robespierre, and adopting this maxim of the companion of Tristran—'Divide, to govern.'

When Henry VI. besieged Paris, he had thrown over the walls bread and other edibles. The cardinal threw over brief addresses, in which he represented to the Rochellois how unjust, and self-willed, and barbarous, had been the conduct of their chiefs, who possessed abundance of wheat, yet did not distribute it; and who adopted as a maxim—for they also had their maxims—that the death of women, of old men, and of children, was a thing of little moment, so that the men who were to defend the walls continued vigorous and well. Until then, either from devotion or from inability to contend against it, this maxim had, without being generally adopted, passed from theory into practice; but these addresses successfully assailed it. They reminded the men, that these women, children, and old men, who were allowed to die of hunger, were their wives, their offspring, and their sires; and that it would be more just if all were alike subjected to the common misery, so that a similarity of position might give occasion for unanimity of resolution.

But, at the very moment that his eminence saw his measure beginning to bear fruit, and was applauding himself for having adopted it, an inhabitant of Rochelle, who had arrived from Portsmouth, managed to pass through the royal lines, God knows how—so complete was the threefold watchfulness of Bassompierre, Schomberg, and the Duke of Angoulême, themselves overlooked by the cardinal—and announced that he had seen a splendid fleet, ready to set sail before another week. Buckingham, moreover, declared to the mayor, that the great league against France was at last about to be proclaimed, and that the kingdom would be speedily invaded, at the same time, by the armies of England, Spain, and the empire. This letter was publicly read in all parts of the town, copies of it were posted at the corners of the streets, and even those who had attempted to commence negotiations, interrupted them, with a resolution to wait for the succour which was so soon to reach them.

This unexpected circumstance renewed all the original anxieties of Richelieu, and compelled him to turn his eyes once more across the sea.

During all this time, the royal army, free from the inquietude of its only true commander, led a most joyous life, for provisions were not scarce in the camp, or money either. The regiments were all at rivalry in gaiety and audacity. To take spies and to hang them, to undertake the daring expeditions on the mole or the sea. to imagine follies and to execute them calmly—such were the pastimes

494

which made those days seem short to the army, while they were long not only for the Rochellois, who were worried by famine and anxieties, but for the cardinal, who blockaded them so vigorously.

Sometimes, when the cardinal, who was always riding about like the humblest soldier of the army, directed his thoughtful eyes over the works which advanced so slowly in comparison to his desires, although constructed by engineers whom he had recruited from the remotest corners of France, if he met with a musketeer of M. de Treville's company, he approached him, and looked at him in a singular way; and then, not recognising him as one of our four companions, he transferred to other objects his penetrating glance and his vast thoughts.

One day, when, consumed by a mortal lassitude of mind, without hopes of treating with the Rochellois, and without intelligence from England, the cardinal went forth, with no other aim but that of going out, and only accompanied by Cahusac and La Houdinière, wandering along the sands, and mingling the immensity of his own dreams with the immensity of the ocean, he came at a gentle pace to a small hill, from the top of which he perceived behind a hedge, reclining on the grass, and protected from the sun by a clump of trees, seven men, surrounded by empty bottles.

Four of these men were our musketeers, getting ready to listen to the reading of a letter which one of them had just received. This letter was so important, that it had made them desert some cards and dice which they had left upon a drum.

The three others were the valets of the gentlemen, and were at the moment engaged in opening an enormous demijohn of Collioure wine.

The cardinal, as we have said, was in a gloomy mood; and, when he was in this state of mind, nothing so much increased his sullenness, as the gaiety of others.

He had, besides, a singular habit of always supposing that the circumstances which caused his sadness, were those which excited the gaiety of strangers. Making a sign to Cahusac and La Houdinière to halt, he got off his horse, and approached these suspicious laughers; hoping, by the aid of the sand, which deadened the sound of his steps, and of the hedge, which concealed his person, to hear some words of a conversation which appeared so interesting. At ten paces from the hedge he recognised the Gascon dialect of d'Artagnan; and, as he had already seen that these men were musketeers, he did not doubt that the three others were those who were called the inseparables—that is to say, Athos, Porthos, and Aramis.

It may be imagined that this discovery increased his desire of hearing the conversation. His eyes assumed a strange expression, and, with the stealthy tread of a tigercat, he approached the hedge; but he had been only able to catch a few vague syllables, having no definite meaning, when a sonorous and brief exclamation made him start, and attracted the attention of the musketeers.

'Officer!' called out Grimaud.

'You are speaking, I think, rascal,' said Athos, raising himself on one elbow, and fascinating Grimaud with his sparkling eye.

Grimaud, therefore, did not add one word, contenting himself with pointing with his finger towards the hedge, and indicating by this gesture the cardinal and his escort.

The four musketeers were on their feet with one bound, and bowed respectfully.

The cardinal appeared furious.

'It seems that the gentlemen of the musketeers have themselves guarded!' said he. 'Is it because the English are expected by land, or do the musketeers regard themselves as superior officers?'

'My lord,' replied Athos—for, in the midst of the general confusion, he alone had preserved that coolness and calmness of the nobleman which never failed him—'my lord, the musketeers, when their duty is ended, or when they are off duty, play and drink, and are very superior officers to their own servants.'

'Their servants!' growled out the cardinal; 'servants who have a watch-word to warn their masters when any one approaches. They are not servants—they are sentinels.'

'Your eminence may, however, perceive, that had we not taken this precaution, we should have run the hazard of permitting you to pass without paying our respects, and without offering our thanks to you for uniting d'Artagnan and ourselves,' continued Athos. 'You, d'Artagnan, who were but now wishing for an opportunity of expressing your gratitude to his eminence, here is one given to you: take advantage of it.'

These words were uttered with that imperturbable coolness which distinguished Athos in times of danger, and with that excessive politeness which made him, on certain occasions, a king more dignified than kings by birth.

D'Artagnan came forward, and stammered out some words of thanks, which quickly died away before the severe gaze of the cardinal.

'It does not signify, gentlemen,' continued the cardinal, without appearing in the slightest degree turned from his first intention by the incident which Athos had suggested; 'it does not signify. I do not like simple soldiers, because they have the advantage of serving in a privileged regiment, to play the great man. Discipline is the same for all.'

Athos allowed the cardinal to finish his sentence, and bowing assent, thus replied:—

'Discipline, my lord, has been, I hope, in no degree forgotten by us. We are not on duty; and we believed that, not being on duty, we might dispose of our time precisely as we pleased. If it should fortunately happen that your eminence has some special orders to give us, we are ready to obey them. Your lordship perceives,' continued Athos, frowning, for this species of interrogatory began to irritate him, 'that, to be ready at the least alarm, we have brought with us all our arms.'

He pointed with his finger to the four muskets, stacked near the drum which bore the cards and dice.

'Your eminence may believe,' added d'Artagnan, 'that we should have come to meet you, if we could have supposed that it was you who approached us with so small a retinue.'

The cardinal bit his moustaches, and even his lips.

'Do you know what you look like—always together as you now are, armed as you now are, and guarded by your valets?' said the cardinal. 'You look like four conspirators.'

'Oh! as to that, my lord,' said Athos, 'it is true; and we do conspire, as your eminence might have seen the other morning—only, it is against the Rochellois.'

'Ah! gentlemen politicians,' replied the cardinal, frowning in his turn, 'the secret of many things might be found in your brains, if one could read in them, as you were reading in that letter which you concealed the moment that you saw me coming.'

The colour flew into the face of Athos, and he made one step towards his eminence.

'It might be thought that you really do suspect us, my lord, and that we are undergoing a real examination. If that be the case, would your eminence deign to explain yourself, and we should at least know what we are to expect.'

'And if it were an examination,' replied the cardinal, 'others besides you have been subjected to one, M. Athos, and have answered.'

'And therefore, my lord, have I said, that your eminence has only to question, and that we are ready to reply.'

'What letter was that which you were reading, M. Aramis, and which you concealed?'

'A letter from a woman, my lord.'

'Oh, I understand,' said the cardinal: 'discretion is necessary as to epistles of that kind; but nevertheless they may be shown to a confessor, and you know I am in orders.'

'My lord,' said Athos, with a calmness the more fearful, that he slightly moved his head whilst making this answer— 'my lord, the letter is from a woman, but it is not signed either by Marion de Lorme, or by Madame de Courbalet, or Madame de Chaulnes.'

The cardinal became as pale as death. A savage flash was emitted from his eyes. He turned about as if to give an order to Cahusac and La Houdinière. Athos saw the movement, and took a step towards the muskets, on which the eyes of his three friends were fixed, like those of men who were not inclined to allow themselves to be arrested. The cardinal was himself only the third man of his party. The musketeers, including their valets, were seven. He judged, also, that the game would be still more unequal, if Athos and his friends were really conspiring; and, by one of those rapid changes which he always had at command, all his anger melted into a smile.

'Come, come,' said he, 'you are brave young men, proud in the sunshine, but faithful in the dark; and there is no great harm in keeping a good watch over yourselves, when you watch so well over others. Gentlemen, I have not forgotten the night when you served as my escort in going to the Red Dove-Cot. If there were any danger to be feared on the road I am about to take, I would beg you to accompany me; but as there is none, remain where you are, and finish your wine, your game, and your letter. Adieu, gentlemen.'

And again mounting his horse, which Cahusac had brought him, he saluted them with his hand, and went his way.

The four young men, erect and motionless, followed him with their eyes, but without uttering a word, until he was out of sight. Then they looked at each other.

The countenance of all of them indicated consternation; for, in spite of the amicable adieu of his eminence, they well knew that the cardinal had gone away with rage in his heart.

Athos alone smiled, with a haughty and disdainful smile.

When the cardinal was out of reach of sound, as well as out of sight—

'That Grimaud called out very late,' said Porthos, who had a great desire to vent his ill-humour on some one.

Grimaud was about to answer by excusing himself, when Athos raised his finger, and Grimaud remained silent.

'Would you have given up the letter, Aramis?' said d'Artagnan.

'I had decided,' said Aramis, in the softest, most melodious voice, 'that if he had persisted in requiring the letter, I would have presented it to him with one hand, and passed my sword through his body with the other.'

'I expected as much,' said Athos, 'and that is the reason that I threw myself between you. Verily, that man is extremely imprudent to talk in such a style to other men. One would imagine that he had never been engaged with any but women and children.'

'My dear Athos,' said d'Artagnan, 'I admire you; but yet we were wrong, after all.'

'How wrong!' said Athos. 'Whose, then, is this air we breathe? Whose this ocean, over which our looks extend? Whose is this land, on which we were reclined? Whose is this letter from your mistress? Do all these belong to the cardinal? Upon my honour, this man fancies that the world belongs to him. There were you, stammering, stupefied, and overwhelmed as though the Bastile stared you in the face, and the gigantic Medusa had transformed you into stone. Is it a conspiracy, I wonder, to be in love? You are in love with a woman whom the cardinal has chosen to confine; you wish to rescue her from his hands: it is a game which you are playing against his eminence. This letter is your hand. Why should you show your card to your adversary? If he can guess it, very good. We shall easily guess his, you may be assured.'

'In fact, Athos, what you now say is full of sense,' replied d'Artagnan.

'In that case, let us not say another word about what has just occurred, and let Aramis resume his cousin's letter where the cardinal interrupted him.'

Aramis re-extracted the letter from his pocket; the three

499

friends drew near him; and the three valets again grouped themselves around the capacious demi-john.

'You had only read one or two lines,' said d'Artagnan: 'begin over again at the very beginning.'

'With pleasure,' replied Aramis.

'MY DEAR COUSIN,

'I really believe that I shall decide on going to Bethune, where my sister has made our little servant enter into a convent of the Carmelites. That poor child is quite resigned: she knows that she cannot live anywhere else, without endangering her salvation. Nevertheless, if our family affairs should be settled as we wish, I think that she will run the danger of perdition, and will return to those whom she regrets; more particularly, as she knows that they are always thinking of her. In the meantime, she is not very unhappy; all that she now desires is a letter from her intended. I know very well that this sort of article has some difficulty in passing through the gratings; but after all, as I have proved to you, my dear cousin, I am not very unskilful, and I will undertake the commission. My sister thanks you for your good and enduring remembrance: she was for a short time in great anxiety, but she is at present more composed, having sent her agent down there, that nothing may happen unexpectedly.

'Adieu, my dear cousin. Let me hear from you as often as you can; that is to say, as often as you can safely.—I embrace you.

'MARIE MICHON.'

'Oh, what do I owe you, Aramis!' exclaimed d'Artagnan. 'Dear Constance! At last I have intelligence of her. She lives—she is in safety in a convent—she is at Bethune! And where is Bethune, Athos?'

'On the frontiers of Artois and Flanders: when once the siege is raised, we may make a tour there.'

'And it will not be long, it is to be hoped,' said Porthos, 'for this morning they hung another spy, who declared that the Rochellois were now reduced to feed upon the uppers of their shoes. Supposing that, after having eaten the uppers, they should consume the sole, I do not exactly see what can remain for them afterwards, unless they should take to eating one another.'

'Poor fools!' said Athos, emptying a glass of excellent

Bordeaux, which, without possessing at that time the reputation that it now enjoys, did not the less deserve it—'poor fools! as if the catholic faith were not the most profitable and the most agreeable of all religions. Yet never mind,' added he, smacking his tongue against his palate, 'they are brave fellows. But what the plague are you doing, Aramis?' continued Athos: 'are you putting that letter into your pocket?'

'True,' said d'Artagnan; 'Athos is right: it must be burned. And who knows, even then, but that the cardinal may have some secret for interrogating ashes?'

'He must have one,' said Athos.

'But what will you do with the letter?' inquired Porthos.

'Come here, Grimaud,' said Athos. 'To punish you for having spoken without leave, my friend, you must eat this piece of paper: then, to reward you for the service which you will have rendered us, you shall afterwards drink this glass of wine. Here is the letter first: chew it hard.'

Grimaud smiled, and with his eyes fixed on the glass, which Athos filled to the very brim, chewed away at the paper, and finally swallowed it.

'Bravo, Master Grimaud!' said Athos; 'and now take this. Good! I will dispense with your saying thank you.'

Grimaud silently swallowed the glass of Bordeaux; but during the whole time that this pleasant operation lasted, his eyes, which were fixed upon the heavens, spoke a language, which, though mute, was not therefore the less expressive.

'And now,' said Athos, 'unless the cardinal should form the ingenious idea of opening Grimaud's stomach, I believe that we may be pretty easy.'

During this time, his eminence pursued his melancholy way, murmuring under his moustaches—

'Decidedly, these four men must belong to me!'

52

The First Day of Imprisonment

LET us now return to her ladyship, of whom, a glance, given to the coast of France, has made us lose sight for an instant.

We shall again find her in the same desperate position in which we left her: digging for herself an abyss of dark reflections—a gloomy hell—at the gate of which she had almost left hope behind her; for, for the first time, she doubts; and, for the first time, she fears.

Twice has her fortune failed her; twice has she seen herself betrayed; and, on both of these occasions, it was against that fatal talent, sent no doubt by Providence on purpose to oppose her, that she had been wrecked. D'Artagnan had conquered her;—her, who had been, until then, invincible in evil.

He had abused her in her love, humiliated her in her pride, checked her in her ambition; and, now, he was ruining her in her fortune, depriving her of her liberty, and menacing even her life. But, more than all, he had raised up a corner of her mask—of that ægis which had covered her, and rendered her so potent.

D'Artagnan had averted from Buckingham, whom she hated—as she did everything that she had once loved—that tempest with which Richelieu threatened him, through the person of the queen. D'Artagnan had personated de Wardes, for whom she had felt the caprice of a tigress irresistible as the caprices of women of that character ever are. D'Artagnan had discovered that terrible secret which she had sworn that none should know, and not die. And, lastly, at the very moment that she had obtained from Richelieu an instrument, by means of which she hoped to avenge herself on her enemy, that instrument is snatched from her hands, and it is d'Artagnan who holds her a prisoner, and who is going to transport her to some infamous Tyburn of the New World.

For all this comes unquestionably from d'Artagnan. By whom, except him, could so many disgraces be accumulated on her head? He alone could have transmitted to Lord de Winter all these frightful secrets, which he had himself discovered one after another by a kind of fatality. He knew her brother-in-law, and must have written to him.

How much of hatred she distils! There, motionless, with fixed and ardent eyes, seated in her solitary chamber, how well do the outbreaks of those stifled howls, which escape at times from the recesses of her heart, accord with the sound of surge which rises, bellows, moans, and breaks, like some eternal, impotent despair, against the rocks on which that dark and haughty edifice is built! How, by the light of those flashes which her furious anger casts across her mind, does she conceive against Madame Bonancieux, against Buckingham, but, most of all, against d'Artagnan, projects of magnificent revenge, which are imperceptible in the remoteness of the future!

Yes, but to avenge herself, she must be free; and for the prisoner to get free, there is a wall to pierce, bars to loosen, boards to break through; and these are enterprises, which the patience and force of a man may accomplish, but before which the febrile irritation of a woman must infallibly be exercised in vain. Besides, for all these labours, time is needed—months, or perhaps years—and she has but ten or twelve days, according to the declaration of Lord de Winter, her fraternal yet most fearful gaoler.

And yet if she were a man, she would attempt all this, and might perchance succeed. Why, then, has Heaven committed the mistake of enshrining a soul so strong within a form so frail and delicate?

Thus were the first moments of her captivity terrible: convulsions of rage, which she was impotent to restrain, paid to nature the tribute of her feminine weakness. But, by degrees, she overcame these ebullitions of distempered anger: the nervous tremblings which had agitated her frame, subsided; and she at length fell back upon her own strength, like a tired serpent taking its repose.

'Come, come, I was a fool to be so violent,' said she, as she looked at the reflection of her burning glances in the glass in which she seemed to interrogate herself. 'No violence! Violence is a proof of weakness. Besides, I have never succeeded by that means. Perhaps if I used my strength against women, I might chance to find them more feeble than myself, and, consequently, might vanquish them; but it is against men that I struggle, and I am only a woman to them. Let me struggle like a woman. My strength is in my weakness.'

Then, as if to satisfy herself of the changes to which she could subject her most flexible and expressive features, she made them successively assume all expressions, from that of anger which contracted every muscle, to that of the softest, most affectionate, and most seductive smile. Then, under her artistic hands, her hair was made to adopt every undulation which might add to the varied attractions of her charming face. At last, in self-complacency, she murmured—

'Well, there is nothing lost! I am still beautiful.'

It was nearly eight o'clock in the evening. Her ladyship perceived a bed, and she thought that a few hours of repose would not only refresh her head, but her complexion also. Yet, before she lay down, a still better idea suggested itself. She had heard something said about supper. She had already been above an hour in the room: they could not tarry long before they brought her meal. The prisoner did not wish to lose any time, and resolved, even this very evening, to make some attempt to feel her way, by studying the characters of those to whom her wardship had been confided.

A light appeared beneath the door, and this announced the return of her gaolers. Her ladyship, who had risen up, threw herself hastily into the chair, with her head thrown back, her beautiful hair loose and dishevelled, her throat half-naked under the ruffled lace, and one hand on her heart, and the other hanging down.

The bolts were drawn; the door grated on its hinges; steps were heard in the chamber, and approached her.

'Place the table there,' said a voice, which the prisoner recognised as that of Felton.

The order was obeyed.

'You will bring lights, and change guard,' continued Felton; and this double order, which the young lieutenant gave to the same individuals, proved to the lady that her attendants and her guards were the same men, that is to say, soldiers.

The commands of Felton were executed with a silent rapidity, which gave a good idea of the flourishing state of discipline that he maintained.

At last Felton, who had not yet looked at her ladyship, turned toward her.

'Ah! ah!' said he, 'she sleeps; very well, when she awakes she will sup.'

And he took a few steps towards the door.

'But, lieutenant,' said a soldier, who was less stoical than his officer, who had approached her ladyship, 'this woman is not asleep.'

'What! not asleep!' said Felton. 'What is she about, then?'

'She has fainted. Her face is very pale, and I can scarcely hear her respiration.'

'You are right,' said Felton, after he had looked at her ladyship from the place where he stood, without taking a single step towards her: 'go and tell Lord de Winter that his prisoner has fainted; for I do not know what to do, the circumstance being unexpected.'

The soldier left the room to execute his officer's commands. Felton seated himself in a chair, which happened to be near the door, and waited, without uttering a word or making the least movement. Her ladyship was mistress of that great art, so studied by women, of seeing everything by means of a mirror, a reflection, or a shadow; and she perceived in the glass Felton, who had turned his back towards her. She continued watching him for about ten minutes, and during these ten minutes he did not once look round.

It then occurred to her that Lord de Winter would soon arrive, and, by his presence, add power to her gaoler. Her first experiment had failed; and she bore it like a woman who had confidence in her own resources. She therefore raised her head, opened her eyes, and sighed feebly.

At this sigh, Felton at length turned round.

'Ah! you are awake at last, madam,' said he, 'so I have nothing more to do here. If you require anything, you will call.'

'Oh, my God! my God! what I have suffered!' murmured her ladyship, in that harmonious tone of voice, which, like the tones of the enchantresses of old, fascinated all whom she desired to destroy.

On raising herself in her chair, she assumed an attitude more graceful and more alluring than that which she had assumed during the time she was reclining.

Felton arose.

'You will be waited upon in this way, madam, three times a day,' said he; 'in the morning, at nine o'clock; in the afternoon, at one o'clock; and in the evening, at eight. If this should be not agreeable to you, you can appoint your own hours, instead of those which I propose, and on this point your wishes shall be attended to.'

'But am I to remain always alone, in this large, melancholy room?' demanded her ladyship.

'A woman from the neighbourhood has received instructions to attend upon you: she will henceforth reside in the castle, and will come whenever you require her presence.'

'I thank you, sir,' replied the prisoner humbly.

Felton bowed slightly, and went towards the door. Just as he was about to cross the threshold, Lord de Winter appeared in the corridor, followed by the soldier who had been sent to inform him that her ladyship had fainted. He held in his hand a bottle of salts.

'Well, what is the matter here?' said he, in a jeering tone, when he saw the lady standing, and Felton just about to leave the room. 'Is this dead person alive again? By Jove, Felton, my boy, did you not see that she took you for a novice, and gave you the first act of a comedy, of which we shall doubtless have the pleasure of seeing all the continuation?'

'I thought so, my lord,' said Felton. 'But as, after all, the prisoner is a woman, I wished to show that consideration for her, which is due from every well-bred man to a woman, if not for her sake, at least for his own.'

Her ladyship shuddered throughout her frame. These words of Felton's penetrated like ice through all her veins.

'So,' continued Lord de Winter, still laughing, 'these beautiful locks, so skilfully displayed, that delicate complexion, and that languishing look, have not yet seduced you, stony heart?'

'No, my lord,' replied the insensible young man; 'and, believe me, it requires more than the petty stratagems and affectations of a woman to corrupt me.'

'As that is the case, my brave lieutenant, let us leave the lady to find something new, and let us go to supper. Oh, you may be quite easy; she has a very fertile imagination, and the second act of this comedy will soon follow the first.'

As he uttered these words, Lord de Winter took Felton by the arm, and led him away, laughing.

'Oh, I will surely be a match for you!' muttered her ladyship, between her teeth. 'Make yourself easy, poor spoiled monk, poor converted soldier, whose uniform has been cut out of a churchman's habit!'

'Apropos, my lady,' said Lord de Winter, stopping on the threshold of the door, 'do not allow this failure to disturb your appetite. Taste this fowl, and that fish, which, I give you my honour, I have not had poisoned. I am on good terms with my cook, and, as he is not to be my heir, I have great confidence in him. Do as I do. Farewell, my dear sister, till your next fainting-fit.'

This was all that her ladyship was able to endure. Her hands grasped the arms of her chair convulsively, she ground her teeth heavily, her eyes followed the movement of the door as it closed behind Lord de Winter and Felton; and then, as soon as she found herself alone, a new paroxysm of despair invaded her—her glance wandered to the table: she saw a knife that glittered on it, and, rushing forward, she snatched it up; but dreadful was her disappointment when she found that the edge was rounded, and the blade of flexible silver.

A shout of laughter resounded from behind the half-closed door, and it was again opened.

'Ah, ah!' exclaimed Lord de Winter, 'do you see, Felton? It is exactly as I told you. That knife was intended for you, my boy: she would have killed you. It is one of her eccentricities, thus to get rid, in one way or another, of those who annoy her. If I had attended to you, the knife would have been of steel, and sharp; and then—farewell, Felton. She would have cut your throat first, and all our throats afterwards. Just look, John, how well she holds her knife?'

Her ladyship, in fact, still held the inoffensive weapon in her convulsive grasp; but these last words, this crowning insult, unnerved her hands, her strength, and even her will, and the knife fell upon the ground.

'You are quite right, my lord,' said Felton, in a tone of deep disgust, which penetrated to the very recesses of her ladyship's heart. 'You are right, and I was in the wrong.'

And they both once more left the room.

But, on this occasion, the lady lent a more attentive ear than before, and she heard their steps becoming more distant, until the sound was lost in the depths of the corridors.

'I am undone!' she muttered: 'I am in the power of people over whom I shall have no greater influence than over statues of bronze or of granite. They know me thoroughly, and bear breastplates proof against my arms. And yet,' she continued, a moment after, 'it is impossible that everything should terminate as they have willed it.'

In fact, as this last remark, and this instinctive return to hope, indicated, fear and all feeble sentiments could not long predominate in that deep-thinking soul. Her ladyship seated herself at table, ate of various viands, drank a small quantity of Spanish wine, and felt that all her resolution was restored.

Before she retired to rest, she had already studied, analysed, commented on, and examined, in every possible way, the words, the steps, the gestures, the signs, and even the silence of her gaolers; and, from this learned, and profound, and skilful examination, it resulted that Felton was, upon the whole, to be held the least invulnerable of the two.

One word, especially, recurred to the prisoner's mind.

'If I had attended to you,' said Lord de Winter to Felton.

Felton, then, had spoken in her favour, since Lord de Winter had refused to listen to him. 'Weak or strong,' reasoned her ladyship, 'this man has a ray of pity in his soul; and of this ray I will make a flame that shall consume him. As to the other one, he knows me, he fears me, and knows what he has to expect from me should I ever escape from his hands: it is, therefore, perfectly useless to attempt anything with regard to him. But, with Felton, it is different. He appears to be a simple, pure, and virtuous young man. There are means of winning him.'

Her ladyship laid down, and slept with a smile upon her lips. Any one who had seen her sleeping, would have taken her for a young girl, dreaming of the garland of flowers which she was to braid around her forehead at an approaching ball.

53

The Second Day of Imprisonment

HER ladyship was dreaming that she had at last defeated d'Artagnan, and was looking on the spectacle of his death; and it was the sight of his abominated blood, flowing beneath the executioner's axe, which aroused the charming smile that hovered on her lips.

She slept like a prisoner lulled by dawning hope.

On the next morning, when they entered the room, she was still in bed. Felton remained in the corridor. He had brought with him the woman of whom he had spoken on the previous evening, and who had just arrived. This woman entered, and approached her ladyship's bed, offering her services.

Her ladyship was naturally pale, and her complexion would, therefore, easily deceive any one who saw her for the first time.

'I am feverish,' she said; 'I have not slept a moment throughout the tedious night. I am in dreadful suffering: will you be more humane than they were yesterday evening? All I ask, is to be permitted to remain in bed.'

'Would you like a physician to be summoned?' asked the woman.

Felton listened to this dialogue, without uttering a word.

Her ladyship reflected, that the more numerous the persons who surrounded her, the more there would be to soften, and the more severe would be the vigilance of Lord de Winter. Besides, the physician might declare that the malady was feigned; and her ladyship, having lost her first throw, did not design to lose her second.

'A physician?' said she—'and for what purpose? Those gentlemen declared, yesterday, that my illness was all a comedy. It will undoubtedly be the same to-day; for, since last night, there has been abundant time to prejudice the doctor.'

'Then,' said Felton, in a tone of impatience, 'say yourself, madam, what you desire to have done.'

'Ah, my God! how can I tell? I feel my sufferings, and that is all. Give me what you please—it is of little consequence to me.'

'Go for Lord de Winter,' said Felton, wearied by these repeated complaints.

'Oh, no, no!' exclaimed the lady: 'no, sir, do not send for him, I beseech you! I am very well—I do not want anything—do not send for him!'

She uttered this exclamation with a vehemence so natural, that Felton was attracted for a few steps into the chamber.

'He is touched,' thought her ladyship.

'And yet, madam,' said Felton, 'if you are *really* suffering, we must send for a physician. If you are deceiving us, so much the worse for yourself; but, at all events, we shall have nothing with which to reproach ourselves.'

Her ladyship made no reply; but, turning her beautiful head on the pillow, she burst into a paroxysm of tears and sobs.

Felton looked at her for a moment with his ordinary insensibility; but, seeing that the crisis threatened to continue, he left the room.

The woman followed him; and Lord de Winter did not make his appearance.

'I think I begin to see a method,' muttered the lady, with savage delight, as she buried herself under the bed-clothes, to hide from those who might be watching her this burst of heartfelt satisfaction.

Two hours passed away.

'It is now time for my malady to end,' thought she. 'Let me get up, and gain some benefit to-day. I have but ten days, and by this evening two of them will have already passed away.'

When the servants entered the lady's chamber in the morning, her breakfast had been brought. She concluded that they would soon return to take it away, and that she should then see Felton again.

Her ladyship was not deceived. Felton reappeared, and, without noticing whether the lady had touched anything or not, he ordered the attendants to remove the table, which was generally brought in with everything laid out upon it. Felton, holding a book in his hand, saw every other person leave the room.

Reclining in an easy-chair near the fire-place, beautiful, pale, and resigned, her ladyship looked like a holy virgin expecting martyrdom.

Felton approached her and said—

'Lord de Winter, who, like yourself, madam, is a catholic, has imagined that the loss of the rites and ceremonies of your religion might be painful to you: he therefore permits you to read the daily office of your mass; and here is a book which contains the ritual.'

From the manner with which Felton laid the book on the little table near her ladyship, from the tone in which he pronounced the words, *your mass*, and from the contemptuous smile with which he accompanied them, her ladyship raised her head, and looked more attentively at the officer.

Then—by that stiff manner of wearing the hair, by that dress of exaggerated simplicity, by that forehead, as polished as marble, but equally hard and impenetrable— she recognised one of those gloomy puritans, whom she had so often met with, both at the court of King James, and at that of the King of France, where, in spite of the recollections of St. Bartholomew, they sometimes came to seek a refuge.

She then experienced one of those sudden inspirations which are reserved for geniuses alone, on those great emergencies, those momentous crises, which decide their fortunes or their lives.

Those two words—*your mass*—and a single glance at Felton, had, in fact, revealed to her all the pregnancy of the answer which she was about to make.

But, with that rapidity of intelligence which was peculiar to her, that answer presented itself, as if ready framed, upon her lips.

'I?' said she, in an accent of contempt, equal to that which she had observed in the voice of the young officer —'I, sir!—*my mass?* Lord de Winter, the corrupted catholic, well knows that I am not of his religion, and it is a snare which he wishes to spread for me.'

'And of what religion are you then, madam?' demanded Felton, with an astonishment, which, in spite of his self-command, he could not perfectly conceal.

'I will tell it,' exclaimed the lady with feigned enthusiasm, 'when I shall have suffered sufficiently for my faith.'

The looks of Felton displayed to her ladyship all the extent of space which she had opened to herself by this single expression.

And yet the young officer remained mute and motionless. His countenance alone had spoken.

'I am in the hands of my enemies,' continued she, in the enthusiastic tone which she knew was popular amongst the puritans. 'Well! either may my God save me, or may I perish for my God! That is the answer which I beg you to convey to Lord de Winter; and as to this book,' continued she, pointing to the ritual with the tip of her finger, but without touching it, as though she would have been contaminated by the contact—'you may carry it away, and make use of it yourself; for you are, undoubtedly, doubly the accomplice of Lord de Winter— an accomplice in his persecution, and an accomplice in his heresy.'

Felton made no reply; but he took the book with the same repugnance that he had before manifested, and, in a pensive mood, withdrew.

Lord de Winter came at about five in the evening. During the day, her ladyship had found time to trace a plan of procedure; and she received him like a woman who had already recovered all her advantages.

'It appears,' said the baron, seating himself on a chair opposite the lady, and stretching his feet carelessly toward the hearth—'it appears that we have made a slight apostacy.'

'What do you mean, sir?'

'I mean, that, since the last time we met, we have changed our religion. Have you by chance married a third husband—a protestant?'

'Explain yourself, my lord,' replied the prisoner, with great dignity; 'for I hear your words, but I do not understand them.'

'Then, the truth must be, that you have no religion at all. Well, I like that the better,' said Lord de Winter, with a sneer.

'It is certainly more in unison with your own principles,' coldly replied the lady.

'Oh, I confess to you, that it is quite a matter of indifference to me.'

'You can avow no religious indifference, my lord, but what your debauchery and crimes sufficiently confirm.'

'What! and do you talk of debauchery, Madame Messalina? Do you talk of crimes, Lady Macbeth? Either I have misunderstood you, or you are, by God, exceedingly impudent.'

'You speak thus, my lord, because we are overheard,' coldly replied her ladyship, 'and you wish to prejudice your gaolers and your executioners against me.'

'My gaolers! my executioners! Why, madam, you speak poetically, and yesterday's comedy is turned to-night to tragedy. But, after all, in eight days you will be where you ought to be, and my task will be accomplished.'

'Infamous task! impious task!' replied the lady, with the feigned enthusiasm of the martyr who provokes her judge

'I verily believe, upon my honour,' said Lord de Winter rising, 'that this singular creature is going mad. Come, come, calm yourself, Madam Puritan, or I will put you into a dungeon. By Jove, it is my Spanish wine that has got into your head, is it not? But be quiet: this sort of intoxication is not dangerous, and will have no bad consequence.'

And Lord de Winter left the room, swearing, which was, at that time, considered a habit perfectly gentlemanly.

Felton was, in fact, behind the door, and had not lost one syllable of this conversation.

Her ladyship had judged correctly.

'Yes, go, go!' said she to her brother. 'The consequences are, on the contrary, fast approaching. But you, fool that you are, will not know them until it is too late to evade them.'

Silence again prevailed; and two more hours elapsed

Supper was served, and her ladyship was found engaged in prayers—prayers which she had picked up from an austere puritan, an old servant of her second husband. She appeared to be in a sort of ecstasy, and not even to observe what was passing around her.

Felton made a sign that she was not to be disturbed; and when everything was arranged, he softly left the room with the soldiers.

The lady knew that she might be watched, and, therefore, she continued at her prayers until the end. She fancied that the sentinel at her door did not maintain his usual step, but seemed to listen to her.

For the present, she desired nothing more. She arose, seated herself at the table, ate a little, and only drank some water.

In an hour afterwards, the table was removed, but her ladyship remarked that, on this occasion, Felton did not accompany the soldiers.

He was afraid, then, of seeing her too often.

She turned her head aside to smile; for there was so much of triumph in that smile, that it alone would have betrayed her.

She allowed half an hour to elapse; and as everything was then entirely silent in the old castle—as no sound was heard but the eternal murmur of the surge, that mighty respiration of the sea—with her pure, thrilling, and harmonious voice, she began the first stanza of the psalm which was then in great favour with the puritans:

> 'Thou leavest us, oh Lord!
>   To prove if we are strong;
>   But then, thou dost afford
> The meed that to exertion should belong.'

These verses were not excellent; they were, indeed, far enough from it; but, as every one knows, the puritans did not pride themselves on poetry.

Even as she sung, her ladyship listened. The sentinel on duty at her door had stopped, as if transformed to stone. Her ladyship judged by that of the effect she had produced.

She then continued her psalm, with a fervour and feeling which are indescribable. It seemed to her as the sound diffused itself afar off beneath the arches, and went like a magic charm to melt the hearts of her oppressors. Nevertheless, it appeared as if the soldier on guard, a zealous

Catholic, no doubt, shook off the charm, for, through the grating which he opened, he exclaimed,—

'Be silent, madam! Your song is as melancholy as a '*De Profundis!*' and if, besides the pleasure of being shut up in this garrison, we must be compelled also to hear these things, it will be perfectly unbearable.'

'Silence there!' cried a severe voice, which the lady recognised as that of Felton. 'What business is it of yours, fellow? Did any one order you to hinder that woman from singing? No. You were told to guard her—to fire upon her if she attempted to escape: guard her, then; shoot her if she tries to escape; but go not beyond your orders.'

An inexpressible gleam of joy illuminated the lady's countenance; but this gleam was transient as the lightning's flash; and, without appearing to have heard the dialogue, of which she had not lost a word, she resumed her singing, giving to her voice all the charm, all the power, all the seduction, with which Satan had endowed it—

'For all my fears and cares,
For exile, and for chains,
I have my youth, my prayers,
And God, who keeps a record of my pains.'

That voice, of uncommon power and of sublime passion, gave to the rude unpolished poetry of these psalms, a magic and an expression that the most exalted puritans rarely detected in the songs of their brethren, which they were compelled to adorn with the aids of imagination. Felton thought that he was listening to the singing of the angel who comforted the three Israelites in the fiery furnace.

The lady continued—

'But God, the just and strong!
Our morn of freedom sends
And should our hopes be wrong,
Still martyrdom, still death, our trials ends!'

This last couplet, into which the terrible enchantress had poured her whole soul, completed the disorder in the young officer's heart. He opened the door suddenly, and her ladyship saw his countenance, as pale as ever, but with flashing and almost delirious eyes.

'Why do you sing in this manner,' said he, 'and in such tones?'

'Pardon me, sir,' said her ladyship softly; 'I forgot that

my songs were not becoming in this house. I have no doubt wounded your religious feelings, but I assure you that it was unintentionally. Pardon, therefore, a fault which may be great, but which was certainly involuntary.'

Her ladyship looked so beautiful at that moment, and the religious enthusiasm which she had assumed had given such an expression to her countenance, that Felton, completely dazzled, fancied that he now saw the angel whom he had before only heard.

'Yes, yes!' replied he, 'yes, you vex, you agitate, the inhabitants of the castle.'

But the poor madman did not perceive the incoherence of his own language, whilst her ladyship plunged her lynx eye into the very depths of his heart.

'I will be silent,' said she, casting down her eyes, with all the softness that she could give to her voice, and with all the resignation which she could impart to her manner.

'No, no, madam,' said Felton; 'only, do not sing so loudly, and especially at night.'

After these words, Felton, feeling that he could no longer preserve his usual severity towards his prisoner, rushed out of the room.

'You are right, lieutenant,' said the soldier; 'those songs disturb the soul; and yet one becomes in time accustomed to them—the voice is so beautiful!'

54

The Third Day of Imprisonment

FELTON was attracted; but more than this must yet be done: it was necessary to retain him; or, rather, it was necessary that he should remain of himself; and her ladyship had only an obscure perception of the means by which this result must be achieved.

But even more was needed. He must be made to speak, that she might answer him; for her ladyship was well aware that her most seductive power was in her voice, which could run skilfully through the whole scale of tones, from mortal speech, upwards to the language of heaven.

And yet, in spite of all this seduction, her ladyship might fail; for Felton had been forewarned against her, even to the minutest chance. From this time she studied all her actions, all her words, and even her slightest glance and gesture, nay even her respiration, which might be interpreted as a sigh. In short, she studied everything, like a skilful actress, who had just accepted a rôle which she had never been accustomed to perform.

Before Lord de Winter, her behaviour was easier to arrange, and she had therefore determined upon that the evening before. To remain silent and dignified in his presence; from time to time to irritate him by affected contempt, or, by a disdainful expression; to urge him to menaces and violence, which contrasted so completely with her own perfect resignation—such was her ladyship's plan. Felton would see this: perhaps he would say nothing; but, at any rate, he would see it.

In the morning, Felton came as usual; but her ladyship allowed him to preside over all the preparations for breakfast, without addressing him. At the very moment that he was about to leave the room, she had a gleam of hope, for she thought that he was really about to speak; but his lips moved, without any sound issuing from them, and, controlling himself by an effort, he suppressed in his own breast the words which he had nearly uttered, and withdrew.

About noon, Lord de Winter entered.

It was rather a fine summer's day, and a beam of that pale English sun, which enlightens, but does not warm, penetrated through the bars of the prison.

Her ladyship looked out of the window, and pretended not to have heard the door open.

'Ah, ah!' said Lord de Winter, 'after having represented comedy and tragedy, we are now doing melodrama.'

The prisoner did not answer.

'Yes, yes,' continued his lordship; 'I understand it very well. You would gladly enough be free upon this beach. You would gladly enough, in some good ship, glide through the waves of that sea, which is as green as an emerald. You would gladly enough, whether on land or on the ocean, concoct against me one of those pretty little plots which you are so dexterous in contriving. Patience, patience! In four days you shall be permitted to approach the beach, and the sea will be open to you—more open, perhaps, than you would wish—for in four days England will be rid of you.'

Her ladyship clasped her hands and raised her eyes to heaven.

'Lord! Lord!' exclaimed she, with an angelic sweetness of gesture and of intonation, 'forgive this man, as I myself forgive him!'

'Yes, pray, accursed creature,' exclaimed the baron. 'Your prayer is the more generous, as you are in the power of a man, who, I swear, will never pardon you.'

And he left the room.

At the moment he went out, a piercing glance through the half-opened door enabled her to perceive Felton, who drew himself quickly back that he might not be seen.

She then threw herself upon her knees and began to pray—

'My God! thou knowest for what sacred cause I suffer: give me, therefore, strength to bear my trials.'

The door opened softly; the beautiful suppliant pretended not to have heard it, and, with a voice almost choked by tears, she continued—

'O God, the avenger! O God of mercy! wilt thou permit the wicked designs of this man to be accomplished?'

Then only did she appear to hear the sound of Felton's footsteps; and rising as quickly as thought, she blushed, as though ashamed at being seen upon her knees.

'I do not like to interrupt those who pray,' gravely observed Felton, 'so do not disturb yourself on my account, I beseech you, madam.'

'How do you know that I was praying, sir?' said her ladyship, in a voice suffocated by sobs: 'you are mistaken, sir; I was not praying.'

'Do you think, then, madam,' replied Felton, in his habitual grave voice, but with a gentler accent, 'that I assume to myself the right of preventing a fellow-creature from throwing herself at the foot of her Creator? God forbid! Besides, repentance is becoming in the guilty, whatever crime they may have committed; and a criminal, prostrate before God, is sacred in my eyes.'

'I, guilty!' replied the lady, with a smile which would have disarmed the angel at the day of judgment. 'Guilty! Oh, my God! thou knowest what I am! Suppose that I am condemned, sir—yet you know that God, who loves martyrs, sometimes permits the innocent to be condemned.'

'Were you condemned, were you innocent, and were you a martyr,' replied Felton, 'you would have still more reason to pray, and I would myself assist you with my prayers.'

'Oh, you are a just man!' exclaimed her ladyship, throwing herself at his feet. 'I can no longer restrain myself, for I fear that my strength will fail me at the moment wherein I must endure the trial, and confess my faith. Listen, then, to the supplication of a woman in despair. They deceive you, sir. But that is not the point: I only ask one favour of you, and, if you grant it, I will bless you both in this world and in that which is to come.'

'Speak to my superior, madam,' said Felton. 'Fortunately, I have no commission either to pardon or to punish: it is to one higher than me that God has given this responsibility.'

'To you—no, to you alone. Listen to me, rather than contribute to my destruction and my shame.'

'If you have deserved this disgrace, madam—if you have incurred this ignominy—you should bear it as a sacrifice to God.'

'What mean your words? Oh! you do not understand me. When I talk of ignominy, you think that I speak of some punishment—of imprisonment, or of execution. Would to God it were so! What care I for death or imprisonment?'

'It is I that do not understand you now, madam,' said Felton.

'Or pretend that you do not understand me,' replied the prisoner, with a smile of doubt.

'No, madam, by the honour of a soldier, by the faith of a Christian!'

'What! do you not know the designs which Lord de Winter has against me?'

'I do not know them.'

'Impossible! You are his confidant.'

'Madam, I never lie!'

'Oh! but he is too unreserved for you to have failed to guess them.'

'Madam, I never attempt to guess anything: I always wait for confidence; and, except what Lord de Winter has said in your presence, he has told me nothing.'

'Then,' exclaimed the lady, with an indescribable accent of truth, 'you are not his accomplice? You do not know that he designs for me a disgrace, which all the punishments on earth could not equal in horror?'

'You are mistaken, madam,' said Felton, colouring; 'Lord de Winter is not capable of such a crime.'

'Good!' said the lady to herself: 'without knowing what it is, he calls it a crime.'

Then, she added, aloud—

'The friend of the wretch is himself capable of anything.'

518

'And whom do you call the wretch?' said Felton.

'Are there, then, two men in England to whom that term can be applied?'

'You mean George Villiers,' said Felton.

'Whom the pagans, the Gentiles, and the infidels, call Duke of Buckingham,' resumed her ladyship. 'I would not have believed that there was a man in all England who would have required so much explanation to recognise the person to whom I alluded.'

'The hand of the Lord is stretched over him: he will not escape the punishment that he deserves.'

Felton only expressed concerning the duke, that sentiment of execration which had been vowed by every Englishman against him, whom Catholics themselves called the tyrant, the extortioner, and the profligate; and whom the puritans simply termed Satan.

'Oh, my God! my God!' exclaimed the lady, 'how I beseech thee to inflict upon that man the punishment which is his due. Thou knowest that I seek not the gratification of my own revenge, but that I implore the deliverance of all the people.'

'Do you know him then, madam?' inquired Felton.

'He questions me at last?' said her ladyship to herself, delighted at having so quickly obtained this great result.

'Oh, yes! I know him! Oh, yes! to my misfortune—to my eternal misfortune!' And her ladyship writhed her arms, as if in a paroxysm of grief.

Felton no doubt felt that his strength was giving way: he made some steps towards the door; but the prisoner, who did not lose sight of him, bounded after him, and stopped his progress.

'Sir,' said she, 'be good—be merciful—hear my prayer! That knife, of which the fatal prudence of the baron deprived me, because he knew the use that I should make of it—oh, hear me to the end!—that knife, return it to me only for one instant, for mercy's sake, for pity's sake! I embrace your knees! See! you may shut the door—I do not want to injure you. O God! How could I have any design against you—you, the only just, and good, and compassionate being that I have met with!—you, perhaps, my preserver! One minute the knife—only one minute!—I will return it to you through the wicket of the door! Only one minute, Mr. Felton, and you will have saved my honour.'

'To kill yourself!' exclaimed Felton, in great terror, and

forgetting to withdraw his hands from the hands of his prisoner—'to kill yourself!'

'I have said it, sir,' murmured the lady, dropping her voice, and sinking exhausted on the floor: 'I have divulged my secret! He knows all, and, O my God! I am lost!'

Felton remained standing, motionless and irresolute.

'He still doubts,' thought the lady. 'I have not been true enough to the character I am acting.'

Some one was heard in the corridor; and her ladyship recognised the slow step of Lord de Winter.

Felton also recognised it, and approached the door.

Her ladyship rushed forwards.

'Oh! not one word,' she cried, in a concentrated voice. 'Tell not to that man one word of what I have said to you, or I am lost; and it is you—you——'

Then, as the steps drew nearer, she was silent, lest her voice should be heard, and merely pressed her beautiful hand on Felton's lips, with a gesture of infinite terror.

Felton gently repulsed her, and she sank upon a couch.

Lord de Winter passed by the door without stopping, and his departing steps were heard in the distance.

Felton, pale as a corpse, stood for some moments intently listening; then, when the sound had entirely ceased, he breathed like a man awakening from a dream, and rushed out of the room.

'Ah!' said her ladyship, as she listened in turn to the sound of Felton's steps, as he retreated in the direction opposite to that of Lord de Winter,' at last, then, you are mine!'

But instantly her countenance grew dark.

'If he should speak to the baron,' said she, 'I am ruined; for the baron, who well knows that I would not destroy myself, will place me before him with a knife in my hands, and he will at once perceive that all this great despair is but a farce.'

She went and stood before a glass, and gazed upon herself. Never had she been more beautiful.

'Oh, yes,' she said, smiling, 'but he will *not* tell him!'

In the evening, Lord de Winter came in, when the supper was served.

'Sir,' said her ladyship to him, 'is your presence to be a compulsory aggravation of my imprisonment, and cannot you spare me that additional torture which your visits cause me.'

'Why, my dear sister,' said the baron, 'did you not

sentimentally announce to me, with that pretty mouth which is to-day so cruel, that you came to England for the sole purpose of seeing me without restraint—a pleasure of which, you told me, you felt the loss so strongly that you had, for it, risked sea-sickness, storms, and captivity. Well, here I am, and you ought to be satisfied. But, besides, I have a particular reason for my visit, this time.'

Her ladyship shuddered, for she thought that Felton had spoken. Never, perhaps, in her whole life, had this woman, who had experienced so many strong and opposite emotions, felt so violent a beating of her heart.

She was sitting down. Lord de Winter took a chair, drew it to her side, and seated himself upon it; and he produced a paper from his pocket, which he slowly unfolded.

'Here,' said he, 'I wished to show you the sort of passport which I have myself drawn up, and which will serve as a kind of warrant, in the life which I permit you to lead.'

Then, directing her ladyship's eyes to the paper, he read—

''Order to convey to——'

'The name is left blank,' said the baron; 'if you have any preference, you will let me know, and, provided it be a thousand leagues from London, your request shall be granted. So I resume— 'Order to convey to——Charlotte Backson, branded by the justice of the kingdom of France, but liberated after punishment. She will reside in that place, without ever going more than three leagues from it. In case of any attempt at escape, she is to be put to death. She will be allowed five shillings a day for her lodging and board!'

'This warrant does not concern me,' said her ladyship coldly, 'since a name is inserted in it which is not mine.'

'A name! And have you one?'

'I have that of your brother.'

'You make a mistake: my brother was only your second husband, and your first is still alive. Tell me his name, and I will insert it instead of Charlotte Backson. No, you will not—you are silent. Very well; you shall be registered under the name of Charlotte Backson.'

Her ladyship remained silent: not now from artifice, but from fear. She believed that the warrant was to be immediately executed; she thought that Lord de Winter had hurried forward her departure; she suspected, even, that she was to go that very evening. For an instant, therefore, she imagined that all hope was gone; when all of a sudden she perceived that the warrant had no signature.

The joy she experienced at this discovery was so great that she was unable to conceal it.

'Yes, yes,' said Lord de Winter, who saw what was passing in her mind; 'yes, you are looking for the signature, and you say to yourself—"all is not lost, since the warrant is not signed! He shows it to me to frighten me, that is all."— But you deceive yourself: this warrant will be sent to-morrow to the Duke of Buckingham; on the day after it will be returned, signed by his hand, and sealed with his seal; and four-and-twenty hours after that, I answer for it that the execution of it shall have been begun. Adieu, madam; this is all that I have to say to you.'

'And I reply to you, sir, that this abuse of power, this banishment under a false name, are infamous!'

'Would your ladyship prefer being hanged under your true name? You know that the English laws are inexorable concerning the abuse of the marriage contract. Explain yourself freely. Although my name, or rather my brother's, is mixed up in all this, I will risk the scandal of a public trial, to be sure of my aim in getting rid of you.'

Her ladyship made no answer; but she became as pale as a lifeless form.

'Oh, I see you would rather travel. Very well, madam: there is a proverb which says that travelling is beneficial to youth. Faith, you are right after all. Life is sweet and that is the reason why I am not very anxious that you should take mine away. There remains, then, only the settlement of the five shillings a day. I am a little too parsimonious, am I not? But it is because I do not wish you to corrupt your keepers. Besides, you will still have your charms with which to seduce them. Try them, if your failure as to Felton has not disgusted you with attempts of that kind.'

'Felton has not spoken,' said her ladyship to herself; 'so nothing is lost after all.'

'And now, madam, farewell; to-morrow I shall come and apprise you of the departure of my messenger.'

Lord de Winter arose, bowed sarcastically to her ladyship, and left the room.

Her ladyship breathed again. She had yet four days before her; and four days would serve her to complete the seduction of Felton.

And yet a terrible idea suggested itself to her mind. Perhaps Lord de Winter might send Felton himself to Buckingham with the warrant; and thus Felton would escape her; for, to ensure her success, it was necessary that the magic charm of her seduction should be undisturbed.

Yet, as we have said, one thing reassured her; Felton had not spoken.

She did not wish to appear disheartened by the threats of Lord de Winter: she therefore placed herself at table, and ate. Then, as she had done the night before, she fell upon her knees, and repeated her prayers aloud. And, as on the previous evening, the soldier ceased his beat, and stood to listen.

But she soon heard steps, lighter than those of the sentinel, approaching from the end of the corridor, and which ceased before her door.

'It is he!' she said. And she began the same religious strains which had so violently excited Felton on the previous evening.

But, although her soft, full, sonorous voice now thrilled more touchingly and more harmoniously than ever, the door continued closed. It did indeed appear to her ladyship, in one of those furtive glances which she directed to the little wicket, that she could perceive, through the close grating, the ardent eyes of the young man; but, whether this were a reality or a vision, he had at least sufficient self-control, on this occasion, to keep himself from coming in.

Yet, a few moments after the conclusion of her religious song, her ladyship fancied that she heard a deep sigh, and then the same steps that she had heard approaching, retired slowly, and, as it were, with reluctance.

55

The Fourth Day of Imprisonment

WHEN Felton entered the room the next day, he found her ladyship mounted on a chair, holding in her grasp a cord made of some cambric handkerchiefs, torn into strips, twisted together, and fastened end to end. At the noise Felton made in opening the door, her ladyship lightly jumped off her chair, and endeavoured to conceal behind her the extemporaneous cord which she held in her hand.

The young man was even more pale than usual, and his eyes, red from want of sleep, proved that he had passed through a feverish night. And yet his forehead bore a serenity more austere than ever.

He slowly advanced towards her ladyship, who had seated herself; he took hold of the end of this murderous woof, which inadvertently, or perhaps intentionally, she had left unconcealed.

'What is this, madam?' he asked coldly.

'That? Nothing!' said her ladyship, smiling with that melancholy expression which she so well knew how to impress upon her smile. 'Weariness, you know, is the mortal enemy of prisoners. I was wearied, and, therefore, I amused myself with twisting this cord.'

Felton cast his eyes up to that part of the wall where he had seen her ladyship standing on the chair which she now was sitting on, and, above her head, he saw a gilded hook, fastened in the wall, which was placed there to support either clothes or arms.

He started, and the prisoner saw him start; for, though her eyes were cast down, nothing escaped her observation.

'And why were you standing on this chair?' he asked.

'What does it signify to you?' replied the lady.

'But,' insisted Felton, 'I desire to know.'

'Do not question me,' said the prisoner; 'you know that to us true Christians it is forbidden to speak falsehood.'

'Well,' said Felton, 'I will tell you what you were doing, or, rather, what you were about to do. You were about to complete the fatal work which you meditated. Remember, madam, if your God has forbidden you to speak falsehood, He has much more emphatically forbidden you to commit suicide.'

'When God sees one of His creatures unjustly persecuted —placed, as it were, between suicide and dishonour— believe me, sir,' replied her ladyship, in a tone of profound conviction, 'God will pardon suicide, for suicide then becomes martyrdom.'

'You either say too much, or too little. Speak, madam; in the name of Heaven, explain yourself!'

'What! shall I relate my misfortunes to you, that you may treat them as fables—shall I tell you my designs, that you may disclose them to my persecutor! No, sir! Besides, of what consequence can the life or the death of an unhappy convict be to you? You are only responsible for my body, are you not? And provided that you produced a dead body, which could be recognised as mine, no more would be required of you, and perhaps you might even receive **a** double recompense.'

'I, madam—I!' exclaimed Felton. 'Then you suppose that I would ever receive a price for your life? Oh! you do not think what you are pleased to say!'

'Leave me to my self, Felton—leave me to myself.' said her ladyship, with some excitement; 'every soldier ought to be ambitious, ought he not? You are a lieutenant: well, you would follow at my funeral with the rank of captain.'

'But what have I done to you, then?' said Felton much alarmed, 'that you should burden me with such a heavy responsibility before God and men? In a few days you will be far from here, madam. Your life will then be no longer under my care; and,' he added with a sigh, 'then—then, you can do with it what you will.'

'So!' exclaimed her ladyship, as if she were unable to restrain her holy indignation. 'You, a pious man—you, who pass for a just man—you only demand one thing, and that is, not to be inculpated, not to be inconvenienced, by my death.'

'It is my duty to watch over your life, madam, and I will do so.'

'But, do you understand the duty you discharge? It is cruel, even if I were guilty; but what name will you give it —with what term will the Almighty brand it—if I am innocent?'

'I am a soldier, madam; and I execute the orders that I have received.'

'And do you believe that, at the day of final judgement, the Almighty will make a distinction between the hoodwinked executioner and the unrighteous ¡udge? You will not allow me to kill my body, and yet you make yourself the instrument of him who wishes to kill my soul!'

'But, I repeat to you,' said Felton, much moved, 'that no danger threatens you: I answer for Lord de Winter, as for myself.'

'Madman!' exclaimed her ladyship, 'poor madman, who presumes to answer for another, when the wisest, those who are the most after God's own heart, are afraid of answering for themselves, and join the party of the strongest and most fortunate, to conquer the weakest and most miserable!'

'Impossible, madam, impossible!' muttered Felton, who yet felt in his heart's core the force of this argument; 'whilst a prisoner, you will not recover your liberty through me; whilst alive, you will not lose your life by my connivance.'

'Yes,' exclaimed her ladyship, 'but I shall lose what is much dearer to me than life—I shall lose my honour, Felton; and it is you whom I will make responsible, before God and man, for my shame and infamy!'

On this occasion, Felton, impassive as he was, or as he pretended to be, could no longer resist the secret influence which had already enthralled him. To see this woman, so beautiful, fair as the brightest vision—to hear her by turns imploring and threatening—to suffer under the combined ascendancy of grief and beauty, was too much for a brain whose strength was sapped by the ardent dreams of an ecstatic faith: it was too much for a heart corroded, at the same time, by the love of heaven, which burns, and by the hatred of mankind, which destroys.

Her ladyship perceived his agitation: she felt, as it were by intuition, the contending passions which burned with the blood in the young fanatic's veins; and, like a skilful general, who sees the enemy preparing to retreat, and then rushes upon him with a shout of victory, she arose—beautiful as a priestess of antiquity—inspired as a Christian virgin— with extended arms, and neck uncovered, and dishevelled hair—and with a hand modestly confining her dress upon her bosom, and with a glance illuminated by that fire which had already carried disorder into the senses of the young puritan, she walked towards him, uttering, to an impetuous air, in that sweet voice to which she gave so terrible an emphasis—

> 'To Baal his victim send;
> To lions cast the martyr:
> Yet vengeance is God's charter!
> To Him, my cries ascend.'

Felton stood like one petrified.

'Who are you? What are you?' exclaimed he, clasping his hands; 'are you an angel or a demon? Are you Eloas or Astarte?'

'Have you not recognised me, Felton? I am neither angel nor demon: I am but a daughter of the earth, a sister of the faith;—nothing more!'

'Yes, yes,' said Felton, 'I suspected it at first, but now I am satisfied.'

'You are convinced! And yet you are the accomplice of that child of Belial, whom men call Lord de Winter. You are convinced, and yet you leave me in the hands of my enemies—of the enemy of England, and of the enemy of God! You are convinced, and yet you deliver me up to him who fills and pollutes the world with his heresies and debaucheries—to that infamous Sardanapalus, whom the blind call Buckingham, and the believers Antichrist!'

'I deliver you up to Buckingham! I! What do you mean?'

"They have eyes," exclaimed the lady, "and they will not see; they have ears, and they will not hear."

'Yes, yes,' said Felton, drawing his hand over his damp forehead, as if to drag away his last remaining doubt; 'yes, I recognise the voice that speaks to me in my dreams; yes, I recognise the features of the angel which visits me each night, crying to my sleepless soul—strike! save England! save thyself! for thou wilt die without having appeased the Lord! Speak,' cried Felton, 'speak! I can understand you now.'

A flash of delight, fearful, but rapid as thought, gleamed from her ladyship's eyes.

Fugitive as was this homicidal glance, Felton perceived it, and started, as if it had thrown light into the dark abysses of that woman's heart.

He suddenly recalled the warnings of Lord de Winter, the seductions of her ladyship, and her first attempts on her arrival: he retreated a step, and drooped his head, but without ceasing to regard her; as if, fascinated by this singular being, he could not avert his eyes.

Her ladyship was not the woman to misunderstand the meaning of this hesitation. In the midst of these apparent emotions, her icy coolness did not leave her. Before she was obliged, by Felton's answer, to resume a conversation which it would be so difficult to maintain in the same exalted tone, she let her hands fall, as if the weakness of the woman resumed its ascendancy over the enthusiasm of the inspired saint.

'But, no,' said she, 'it is not for me to be the Judith who will deliver Bethulia from this Holofernes. The sword of the Eternal One is too heavy for my arm. Let me, then, escape dishonour by death—let me find a refuge in martyrdom. I neither ask for liberty, like a criminal; nor for vengeance, like a pagan. To be allowed to die, is all that I demand. I entreat you, I implore you on my knees—let me die—and my last sigh shall breathe forth a blessing on my preserver!'

Before this voice, so soft and supplicating at this look, so timid and submissive, Felton advanced towards her. By degrees, the enchantress had resumed that magic charm which she took up and laid aside at pleasure; that is to say, beauty, softness, tears, and above all, the irresistible attraction of that mystical voluptuousness which is the most irresistible of all kinds of voluptuousness.

'Alas!' said Felton, 'I can only pity you, if you prove to me that you are a victim. But Lord de Winter makes most serious complaints against you. You are a Christian woman —you are my sister in the faith. I feel myself drawn towards you—I, who have never loved any one but my benefactor —I, who have only found traitors, and infidels, throughout my life. But you, madam—you, so really beautiful—you, apparently so pure, must have committed many crimes for Lord de Winter to pursue you thus.'

' 'They have eyes,' ' repeated the lady, with indescribable softness, ' 'and they will not see; they have ears, and they will not hear.' '

'But then,' exclaimed the young officer, 'speak—oh, speak!'

'What, to confide my shame to you!' exclaimed the lady, with the blush of modesty upon her face; 'for, often, the crime of one is the same of another. To confide my crime to you, a man, and I a woman! Oh!' she continued, modestly placing her hand before her eyes, 'Oh! never, never could I dare!'

'To me, as to a brother!' pled Felton.

The lady regarded him for a long time with an expression which Felton took for doubt, but which was nevertheless, only observation and a desire to fascinate.

A suppliant in his turn, Felton clasped his hands.

'Well, then!' exclaimed the lady, 'I will dare to trust my brother.'

At this moment the step of Lord de Winter was heard. But the dreaded brother-in-law was not contented, this time, with merely passing the door, as he had done the evening before: he stopped, and, after exchanging two words with the sentinel, he opened the door and entered.

Whilst these words were passing, Felton had rapidly moved from the lady's side, and, when Lord de Winter appeared, he was at some paces distance from the prisoner.

The baron entered slowly, and let his searching glance travel from the prisoner to the young officer.

'You have been here a long time, John,' said he. 'Has

this woman related her crimes to you? If so, I can comprehend the duration of the interview.'

Felton started; and her ladyship felt that she was lost if she did not come to the assistance of the disconcerted puritan.

'Ah! you fear that your prisoner will escape you!' said she. 'Well! ask your gaoler what the favour was that I but now solicited of him.'

'And were you asking a favour?' said the baron suspiciously.

'Yes, she was, my lord,' replied the young man, much confused.

'And what favour? Come, let us hear,' added Lord de Winter.

'A knife—which she would return to me, through the wicket, an instant after she received it.' replied Felton.

'Is there any one, then, concealed here, whose throat this gracious person wishes to cut?' inquired Lord de Winter, in a tone of mockery and contempt.

'Yes, I am concealed here!' replied her ladyship.

'I gave you your choice between America and Tyburn,' replied Lord de Winter: 'choose Tyburn, my lady: the rope is, believe me, surer than the knife.'

Felton grew pale, and made one step forward; for he remembered that, when he came in, the lady held a cord in her hand.

'You are right,' said she, 'and I had already thought of it.' Then she added, in a lower voice, 'I will think of it again.'

Felton shuddered, even to the very marrow of his bones. Lord de Winter probably observed this; for he said—

'John, my friend, distrust yourself. I have reposed my confidence in you: be watchful; I have warned you. Besides, be of good cheer, my boy: in three days we shall get rid of this creature, and where I send her, she can never again injure any one.'

'You hear him!' cried her ladyship, with a burst of indignation, which the baron thought was addressed to heaven, but which Felton comprehended was for him.

Felton held down his head and mused.

The baron took the officer by the arm, looking over his own shoulder, so as not to lose sight of the lady whilst he was in the room.

'Come, come,' reasoned the prisoner, when the door was shut, 'I am not so far advanced as I believed myself to

be. De Winter has changed his customary stupidity into unparalleled prudence. This is the desire of vengeance; and thus does that desire form a man! As to Felton, he hesitates. Ah! he is not a man of resolution, like that cursed d'Artagnan.'

Nevertheless, her ladyship remained in anxious expectation. She thought that the day would not pass away without her seeing Felton again. At last, in about an hour after the scene that we have just narrated, she heard some whispering at the door, and soon afterwards it was opened, and she recognised Felton.

The young man came hastily into the room, leaving the door open behind him, and making a sign to her ladyship to be silent. His countenance was fearfully agitated.

'What do you want?' said she.

'Listen!' replied Felton, in a slow voice. 'I have just dismissed the sentinel, that I may remain here without any one knowing that I have come, and speak to you without any one overhearing what I say. The baron has just related to me a terrible tale.'

The lady assumed her smile of a resigned victim, and shook her head.

'Either you are a demon,' continued Felton, 'or the baron—my benefactor, my more than father—is a monster. I have known you four days—I have loved him ten years: therefore I may well hesitate between you two. Be not alarmed at what I say: I want to be convinced. This night, after midnight, I will come to you, and you must convince me.'

'No, Felton—no, my brother.' said she, 'the sacrifice is too great, and I see what it will cost you. No, I am lost—do not destroy yourself with me. My death will be far more eloquent than my life, and the silence of the corpse will convince you better than the living prisoner's words.'

'Hush, madam,' said Felton, 'and do not speak to me thus. I am come that you may promise me upon your honour—that you may swear to me by that which is most sacred to you—that you will make no attempt upon your life.'

'I will not promise,' said her ladyship; 'for no one respects an oath more than I do; and, if I promise, I must keep my word.'

'Well,' said Felton, 'bind yourself only till I have seen you once again. If, after we have met, you still persist, you shall then be free, and I myself will provide you with the weapon you have asked for.'

'So be it!' said her ladyship; 'for your sake, I shall wait.'

'Swear it.'

'I swear it by our God! Are you satisfied?'

'Well,' said Felton, 'this night.'

And he rushed out of the apartment, shut the door again, and waited outside, with the soldier's half-pike in his hand, as if he were mounting guard.

The soldier having returned, Felton gave him back his weapon.

Then, through the wicket, which she had approached, her ladyship saw the young man cross himself with delirious fervour, and hurry along the corridor in a transport of delight.

As for herself, she returned to her seat with a smile of savage scorn upon her lips, and she blasphemously repeated the fearful name of that God by whom she had just sworn, without ever having learned to know Him.

'My God!' said she. 'Fanatical fool!—*My* God is myself; and whoever will assist in my revenge!'

56

The Fifth Day of Imprisonment

Her ladyship had, however, achieved a half triumph, and the success she had obtained renewed her strength.

There was no difficulty in vanquishing, as she had hitherto done, men ready to be led astray, whom the education of a gallant court swiftly drew into her snares. Her ladyship was beautiful enough to fascinate the senses, and skilful enough to prevail over all the obstacles of the mind.

But, on this occasion, she had to strive against an untutored nature, concentrated by austerity. Religion and penitence had made of Felton a man impenetrable of all ordinary seductions. Schemes so vast, projects so tumultuous, were floating in that fervid brain, that there was no room for love—the sentiment that feeds itself on leisure, and thrives and fattens on corruption. Her ladyship had made a breach, by her false virtue, in the opinion of a man prejudiced against her, and, by her beauty, in the heart and senses of a pure and candid man. By this experiment upon the most rebellious subjects that nature and religion could submit to her examination, she had at last taken the measurement of powers hitherto unknown even to herself.

Often, however, during the evening, had she despaired of fate, and of herself. We know that she did not invoke the aid of God: she trusted in the genius of evil—that boundless sovereignty which rules over the details of human life, and through which, as in the Arabian fable, a pomegranate seed suffices to build up again a ruined world.

Her ladyship, being quite prepared to receive Felton, was at liberty to make her batteries ready for the next day. She well knew that only two days remained for her; that, were the warrant once signed by Buckingham—and Buckingham would sign it the more freely, as it bore a false name, and he could not recognise the real woman whom it concerned—this warrant once signed, we say, the baron would immediately embark her; and she knew, also, that women condemned to transportation, use, in their seductions, arms much less powerful than those pretended virtuous women, whose beauty is illumined by the sun of fashion, whose wit is vaunted by the voice of the world, and whom an aristocratic beam gilds with its enchanted light. To be a woman condemned to a wretched and disgraceful punishment, is no impediment to beauty, but it is an insurmountable obstacle to power. Like all persons of real genius, her ladyship well knew what accorded with her nature and her means. Poverty disgusted her—subjection deprived her of two-thirds of her greatness. Her ladyship was only a queen amongst queens: the enjoyment of satisfied pride was essential to her sway. To command beings of an inferior nature, was, to her, rather a humiliation than a pleasure.

She would most assuredly return from her banishment: of that she had not the slightest doubt; but how long would that banishment continue? To an active and ambitious nature, like that of her ladyship, the days which are not spent in self-elevation are unlucky ones. What then can we call the days of bitter descent? To lose one, two, three years, that is an actual eternity; to return, perhaps, after the death or the fall of the cardinal; to return when d'Artagnan and his friends, happy and successful, had received from the queen the recompense that they richly merited for their services to her—these were the desolating thoughts which a woman like her ladyship was altogether unable to endure. Besides, the storm which raged in her breast was increasing in its violence, and she would have burst her prison walls if her body could have enjoyed, for a single instant, the same proportions as her soul.

And then, in the midst of all this, she was goaded by the remembrance of the cardinal. What would be thought, what would be said, of her silence by that cardinal, so distrustful, so anxious, and so suspicious—that cardinal, who was not only her sole support, her sole stay, her sole protector, for the present, but, also, the principal instrument of her future fortunes and revenge? She knew him well: she knew that, on her return after a fruitless expedition, she might talk in vain of her imprisonment—she would in vain exaggerate her sufferings. The cardinal would answer, with the mocking calmness of the sceptic, strong at once in power and in genius:

'You should not have allowed yourself to be entrapped.'

Her ladyship then concentrated all her energy, murmuring forth, in the intricacies of her thought, the name of Felton, the sole gleam of light which visited her, in the depths of that hell into which she had fallen; and, like a serpent coiling and uncoiling its rings, to satisfy itself of its own strength, she, by anticipation, enveloped Felton in the countless folds of her own inventive imagination.

Yet time rolled on. The hours, one after the other, appeared to arouse the clock as they passed, and every stroke vibrated in the prisoner's heart. At nine o'clock, Lord de Winter paid his customary visit; looked at the windows and bars; sounded the flooring and the walls; and examined the chimney and the doors; yet, during this long and minute investigation, not one word was uttered either on her part or on his.

'Come, come,' said the baron, as he left the room, 'you will not escape to-night.'

At ten o'clock Felton came to relieve the sentinel at the door. Her ladyship now recognised his step, as a mistress recognises that of her lover, and yet she both hated and despised this weak fanatic. It was not the appointed time, so Felton did not enter the room.

Two hours after, just on the stroke of twelve, the sentinel was relieved.

And now the time had come, and, from this moment, her ladyship waited with impatience.

The new sentinel began to walk along the corridor.

In ten minutes Felton came. Her ladyship listened.

'Observe,' said the young man to the sentinel; 'on no account whatever are you to leave this door; for you know that a soldier was punished for leaving his post for a moment last night, although it was I who kept guard during his short absence.'

'Yes, I know that,' said the soldier.

'I advise you, therefore, to adopt the strictest vigilance. For my part, I am going to inspect the room again, and to observe this woman, who has, I fear, conceived some violent designs against herself. My orders are to watch her closely.'

'Good!' murmured her ladyship. 'There is the austere puritan, telling a lie.'

The soldier smiled.

'Plague take it, lieutenant,' said he, 'you are not badly off in getting such a commission, especially if your orders are not to go till she is ready for bed.'

Felton blushed. Under any other circumstances he would have rebuked the soldier, who indulged himself in such a joke; but his own conscience was now criminating him too loudly to permit his tongue to speak.

'If I call,' said he, 'come in; and also, if any one comes, call me.'

'Yes, sir,' said the soldier.

Felton entered the room. Her ladyship arose.

'You are come,' said she.

'I promised to come,' replied Felton, 'and I have come.'

'You promised me something else, though,' said she.

'What then, oh, my God!' said the young man, who, in spite of all his self-command, felt his knees tremble, and his brow grow damp.

'You promised to bring me a knife, and to leave it with me after our interview.'

'Do not speak of that, madam,' said Felton; 'there is no situation, however terrible it may be, that can permit one of God's creatures to destroy himself. I have reflected that I never ought to render myself accessory of such a crime.'

'Ah! you have reflected!' said the prisoner, again seating herself in her chair, with a disdainful smile. 'And I, also, have reflected!'

'About what?'

'That I had nothing to say to a man who did not keep his word.'

'Oh, my God!' murmured Felton.

'You may leave the room,' said her ladyship; 'I shall not speak.'

'Here is the knife,' said Felton, taking from his pocket the weapon, which he had, according to his promise, brought, although he hesitated to entrust it to his prisoner.

'Let me look at it,' said the lady.

'For what purpose?' said Felton.

'I will return it immediately, upon my honour. You may lay it upon that table, and stand between it and me.'

Felton gave the weapon to her ladyship, who examined it attentively, and tried its point upon the end of her finger.

'Very well,' said she, returning the knife to the young officer; 'it is a serviceable weapon: you are a faithful friend, Felton.'

Felton took the knife, and laid it upon the table, as had been agreed with the prisoner.

Her ladyship's eyes followed his act, with a satisfied glance.

'Now,' said she, 'listen to me.'

The injunction was unnecessary; for the young man stood before, her, waiting for her words, that he might feast upon them.

'Felton,' said her ladyship, with a melancholy solemnity —'Felton, suppose your sister, the daughter of your father, should say to you—'Whilst still young, and unfortunately beautiful, I was decoyed into a snare, but I resisted—temptations and assaults were multiplied around me, but I resisted—the religion that I serve, and the God whom I adore, were blasphemed, because I called that God and that religion to my aid, and I resisted—then, outrages were heaped upon me, and, as they could not sacrifice my soul they determined for ever to defile my body—at last—' '

Her ladyship stopped, and a bitter smile was visible on her lips.

'At last—' said Felton, 'and what did they do at last?'

'At last, they resolved one night to paralyse that resistance which they could not overcome otherwise; one night they mixed a powerful narcotic with my drink. Scarcely had I finished my repast, before I found myself sinking gradually into an unusual torpor. Although I had no suspicions, yet a nameless dread made me struggle against this drowsiness. I arose; I endeavoured to reach the window, to call for help; but my limbs refused to support me; it seemed to me as if the ceiling lowered itself on my head, and crushed me with its weight. I stretched forth my arms, and endeavoured to speak, but could only utter inarticulate sounds; an irresistible numbness stole upon me, and I clung to my chair, feeling that I was about to fall; but even this support was soon insufficient for my feeble arms; I fell, first on one knee, then on both; I sought to pray, but my tongue was frozen: God neither saw, nor heard me, and I sank upon the floor, subjugated by a sleep resembling death.

'Of all the time which elapsed during this sleep, I had no recollection whatever. The only thing I can remember, is, that I awoke, and found myself transported into a circular chamber, most sumptuously furnished, into which no light penetrated but through an opening in the ceiling. There seemed to be no door to enter by: it looked like a magnificent prison.

'It was a long time before I could observe the place in which I was, or recall the circumstances which I now relate. My mind appeared to struggle in vain against the oppressive darkness of that sleep, from which I was unable to escape. I had some vague perceptions of a space passed over, and of the rolling of a carriage; but all this was so misty, and so indistinct, that these events appeared rather to belong to the life of some other person than to my own, and yet to be incorporated with mine by some fantastical duality.

'For some time, the state in which I found myself appeared so strange, that I supposed it was a dream. By degrees, however, the fearful reality forced itself upon me: I was no longer in the house which I had inhabited. As well as I could judge by the light of the sun, two-thirds of the day were already spent. It was on the evening of the previous day that I had fallen asleep: my slumber had, therefore, lasted nearly four-and-twenty hours. What had happened during this protracted sleep?

'I arose, staggering. All my slow and torpid movements showed that the influence of the narcotic had not yet ceased. I found that my chamber had been furnished for the reception of a woman; and the most complete coquette could not have formed a wish, that, in looking around the apartment, she would not have found satisfied.

'Assuredly I was not the first captive who had been confined within that splendid prison. But you understand, Felton, the more beautiful the prison, the more was I alarmed. Yes, it was a prison; for in vain I endeavoured to escape. I tried all the walls to find a door; but everywhere the walls gave back a dull and heavy sound. I went round this room, perhaps twenty times, seeking some kind of outlet: there was none; and I sank upon a chair, worn out with terror and fatigue.

'In the meantime, the night approached rapidly; and, with the night, my fears increased. I knew not what to do: it seemed as if I were encompassed by unknown dangers, amidst which I must plunge at every step. Although I had eaten nothing since the evening before, my fears prevented me from feeling hunger.

'No external noise, by which I could compute the lapse of time, had reached me, but I presumed that it must be about seven or eight in the evening; for we were in the month of October, and it was quite dark.

'Suddenly the noise of a door turning on its hinges startled me: a ball of fire appeared above the window in the ceiling, casting a brilliant light into the room; and I perceived, with horror, that a man was standing at a few paces from me.

'A table with two covers, with a supper all prepared, was arranged, as if by magic, in the middle of the room.

'And this man was he who had pursued me for a year, who had sworn my dishonour, and who, from the first words which fell from his lips, left me no hope of being at any future time restored to liberty.'

'Infamous!' murmured Felton.

'Oh, yes! the wretch!' exclaimed her ladyship, seeing the interest which the young officer, whose soul seemed hanging on her lips, took in this strange tale. 'Oh, yes! the wretch! He thought that it was quite enough to have abducted me in my sleep: he now came, hoping that I should yield to my shame, since that shame was consummated—he came to offer me his fortune in exchange for my love.

'Everything that a woman's heart can conceive of haughty scorn, and of contemptuous speech, I poured out upon that man. Undoubtedly he was habituated to such reproaches, for he listened to me with a calm and smiling look, and with his arms folded on his breast; and then, when he thought that I had nothing more to say, he approached to take my hand:—I rushed towards the table, seized a knife, and placed it to my bosom. 'Take one step more,' I cried, 'and, besides my dishonour, you shall have to answer for my death!'

'Doubtless there was, in my look, my voice, my whole appearance, that character of truth which carries conviction into the most wicked minds; for he paused.

' 'Your death!' cried he. 'Oh, no! you are much too charming a prisoner for me to consent to lose you so. Adieu, beatiful creature! I will wait until you are in a better temper, before I pay you another visit.'

'At these words, he whistled; and the flaming globe which illuminated my room ascended, and disappeared. I found myself once more in total darkness. The same noise of a door opening and shutting was, an instant afterwards, again audible; the globe of light descended anew, and I was once more alone.

'This moment was frightful. Had I been at all uncertain about my misery, every doubt was now dispelled before this fearful reality. I was in the power of a man whom I not only detested, but despised—of a man who had already given me a fatal proof of what he dared to do.'

'But who was that man?' demanded Felton.

Her ladyship gave no answer to his question, but continued her recital.

'I spent the night upon a chair, starting at the least noise; for, about midnight, the lamp went out, and I was again in darkness. But the night passed away without any reappearance of my persecutor. Daylight came: the table was gone; and I had still the knife in my hand. This knife was my sole hope.

'I was overwhelmed with fatigue: my eyes were burning from sleeplessness: I had not dared to close them for a single instant. Daylight reassured me. I threw myself on my bed, still grasping the protecting knife, which I concealed beneath my pillow.

'When I awoke, another table was arranged. But now, in spite of my terrors, in spite of my agonies, a ravenous hunger made itself be felt. For eight-and-forty hours I had enjoyed no nourishment. I ate some bread and a little fruit. Then, remembering the narcotic mingled with the water I had drunk, I did not touch that which was on the table, but went and filled my glass from a marble reservoir fixed in the wall above my toilet-table.

'And yet, in spite of this precaution, I remained for some time in extreme anguish; though on this occasion my fears were unfounded. I passed the day without experiencing anything that resembled what I feared. I took the precaution, however, to empty the decanter of half the water, that my distrust might not be perceived.

'The evening came; but, profound as was the darkness,

my eyes began to grow accustomed to it. In the midst of this obscurity, I saw the table sink into the floor; a quarter of an hour afterwards, it reappeared bearing my supper: a moment later, thanks to the same lamp, my apartment was again lighted.

'I was resolved only to eat of those things with which it was impossible to mingle anything somniferous. Two eggs and some fruit composed my meal, and then I drew a glass of water from my guardian fountain, and drank it. At the first mouthful, it appeared to me no longer to have the same taste as in the morning. A sudden suspicion seized me. I stopped; but I had already swallowed half a glass. I threw the remainder away with horror, and waited, with the icy dew of terror on my brow. Some invisible witness had unquestionably seen me take the water from the fountain, and had taken advantage of my confidence, the more certainly to accomplish my ruin, so coldly planned, so cruelly pursued.

'Half an hour had not passed over, before the same symptoms began to reappear. Only, as I had now taken no more than half a glass of water, I struggled longer against them, and, instead of sleeping soundly, I fell into that kind of slumber which left me the perception of all that passed around me, whilst it quite deprived me of the power of resistance or defence. I dragged myself towards my bed, to seek the sole bulwark which remained—my guardian knife. But I could not reach the pillow. I fell upon my knees, grasping with my hands one of the posts at the foot of the bed.'

Felton became fearfully pale, and a convulsive shudder pervaded all his frame.

'And what was more horrible,' continued the lady, her voice trembling as if she yet felt the anguish of that terrible moment, was, that, on this occasion, I was conscious of the danger which hung over me. My soul, if I may so express myself, was watching over my sleeping body. I saw—I heard —as in a dream, it is true; but my perceptions were, on that account, only the more terrific. I saw the lamp again ascending, and was gradually left in utter darkness. I then heard the sound of that door, so well recognized, although it had been opened but twice. I felt instinctively some one was approaching me. It is said that the wretched beings who are lost in the deserts of America thus feel the approach of the serpent. I wished to make an effort. I endeavoured to cry out. By an incredible exertion of my will, I even raised myself up; but it was only to fall down again immediately.'

'But tell me, then, who was your persecutor?' exclaimed the young officer.

Her ladyship saw at a glance how deeply she affected Felton, by dwelling on each detail of her narrative; but she did not wish to spare him any torture. The more deeply she wounded his heart, the more surely would he avenge her. So she once more proceeded, as if she had not heard his question, or as if she thought that the time for answering it had not yet come.

'I heard him exclaim, when he perceived me, 'Oh, these miserable puritan women! I knew that they harassed their executioners, but I believed them to be less earnest in resisting their seducers.' '

Felton listened without uttering aught but a sort of roar. The perspiration trickled down his brow; and, with a hand hidden beneath his dress, he tore his flesh.

'My first impulse, on returning to myself,' continued her ladyship, 'was to look under my pillow for the knife, which I had been unable to reach: if it had not served as a defence it might at least be useful for an expiation. But, on taking this knife, Felton, a terrible idea suggested itself to me. I have sworn to tell you everything, and I will do so: I have promised you the truth, and I will tell it, though it should ruin me.'

'The idea suggested itself to you to revenge yourself on this man, did it not?' exclaimed Felton.

'Well! yes,' said her ladyship, 'it was as you have guessed. That idea was not becoming in a Christian, I know. Undoubtedly the eternal enemy of our souls himself breathed it into my mind. In fact—how shall I confess it, Felton?' continued her ladyship, in the tone of a woman accusing herself of a crime—'that idea not only came into my mind, but had never left it since. And, perhaps, my present sufferings are but the punishment of this homicidal thought.'

'Go on—go on,' said Felton; 'I long to hear of the accomplishment of your revenge.'

'Oh! I determined that it should be as short a time as possible delayed. I doubted not that he would return on the following night. During the day I had nothing to fear. On this account, at breakfast time, I did not hesitate to eat and drink. I was resolved to pretend to sup, but to taste nothing. I must, therefore, by the morning's nourishment, prepare myself to sustain the evening fast. I concealed a glass of water from my breakfast, as thirst had been my severest suffering when I remained forty-eight hours without eating or drinking.

'The day passed without producing any other effect upon me than to strengthen the resolution I had taken. But I took care that my face should not betray the thoughts of my heart; for I doubted not that I was watched. Many times, indeed, I even felt a smile upon my lips. Felton, I dare not tell you the idea at which I smiled—you would abominate me for it!'

'Go on—go on,' said Felton; 'you see that I listen to you, and I want to know the end.'

'The evening came,' continued her ladyship, 'and the usual circumstances took place. During the darkness, my supper was served as usual; and then the lamp was lighted, and I placed myself at table. I ate only some fruit, and pretended to pour some water from the decanter, but drank that which I had kept in my own glass: the substitution was, however, so adroitly made, that my spies, if I had any, could have no suspicion of the truth. After supper, I exhibited all the appearances of the drowsiness that I had felt the evening before: but this time, as if overwhelmed with fatigue, or as if I was familiarised with danger, I pretended to fall asleep. I had now found my knife, and, whilst I feigned to sleep. my hand convulsively grasped the handle.

'Two hours glided away, without anything new occuring. On this occasion—oh, my God! who would have predicted that on the previous night!—I actually began to fear that he might fail to come.

'At last I saw the lamp gently rising, and disappearing in the depths of the ceiling. My apartment became dark; but I made an effort with my glances to penetrate the gloom. About ten minutes then elapsed, during which I heard nothing but the beating of my own heart. I implored of heaven that he might come.

'At length I heard the well-known creak of the door opening and shutting; I perceived, in spite of the thickness of the carpet, a step which made the floor groan; I saw, in spite of the darkness, a shadow which approached my couch.'

'Make haste! make haste!' interrupted Felton; 'do you not see that every one of your words burns me like molten lead!'

'Then,' continued her ladyship, 'I collected all my strength. I called to mind that the moment of revenge, or rather of justice, had now arrived. I considered myself a second Judith. I held the knife in my hand; and, when I saw him near me, then, with a last cry of grief and of despair, I struck him in the middle of the breast! The wretch! he had foreseen the blow. His breast was covered by a coat of mail: the knife itself was blunted.

'"Ah! ah!" cried he, seizing me by the arm, and tearing from me the weapon which had so badly served me; "you want to kill me, my pretty puritan: but that is more than hatred—it is ingratitude. Come, come, calm yourself, my charming girl. I thought you had grown gentler. I am not one of those tyrants who keep women in opposition to their wills. You do not love me? I had my doubts about it, with my usual folly; now, I am convinced of it. To-morrow you shall be free."

'I had only one wish, which was that he should kill me.

'"Take care," said I, "for my liberty shall be your disgrace!"

'"What mean you, my beautiful sibyl?"

'"Yes, for as soon as I am free, I will tell everything: I will proclaim your violence towards me—I will proclaim my captivity—I will denounce this palace of infamy. You are greatly exalted, my lord, but tremble! Above you is the king—and above the king, is God."

'Master as he appeared to be of himself, my persecutor allowed a sign of anger to escape him. I could not see the expression of his countenance, but I had felt the trembling of his arm, on which my hand rested.

'"Then you shall never leave this place," said he.

'"Right! right!" I exclaimed: "then the site of my punishment shall be also the site of my tomb. Right! I will die here, and you shall see whether an accusing phantom be not even more terrible than the living enemy who menaces."

'"But you shall have no weapon."

'"There is one, which despair has placed within the reach of every creature who has courage to make use of it—I will die of hunger."

'"Come," said the wretch, "is not peace of more value than such a war? I give you your liberty this instant; I will proclaim your virtue, I will call you the Lucretia of England."

'"And I will proclaim you the Sextus: I will denounce you before men, as I have already denounced you before

God; and if it should be necessary, that, like Lucretia, I should attest the accusation with my blood, I *will* attest it."

'"Ah, ah," said my enemy, in a tone of mockery, "then it is quite another thing. Faith, after all, you are very well off here. You shall want for nothing; and, if you allow yourself to die of hunger, it will be your own fault."

'At these words he left the room. I heard the door open and shut, and remained overwhelmed:—not so much, I confess, with grief, as with the shame of having failed in my revenge.

'He kept his word. The next day and the night passed without my seeing him; but I kept mine, also, and neither ate nor drank anything. I was resolved, as I had told him, to let myself die of hunger. I spent the day and night in prayer; for I hoped that God would forgive my selfmurder. On the second night, the door was opened. I was lying on the floor, for my strength began to fail me. At the noise, I raised myself upon my hand.

' "Well," said a voice which vibrated on my ear too terribly to be mistaken—"Well, have you become a little more compliant, and will you purchase liberty by a mere promise of silence? Come, I am a good noble." added he, "and although I do not love the puritans, I do them justice, as well as to their women—when they are pretty. Come, give me a little oath upon the cross: I ask for nothing more."

' "On the cross!" I exclaimed, raising myself up, for, at that detested word I had recovered all my strength. "Upon the cross I swear, that no promise, no threat, no torture, shall close my lips! Upon the cross I swear to denounce you everywhere, as a murderer, as a violater of honour, as a coward! On the cross I swear, if ever I accomplish my escape, to demand vengeance against you from the whole human race!"

' "Take care!" said the voice in a tone of menace that I had not yet heard; "I have one expedient, which I will only employ at the last extremity, to stop your mouth; or, at least, to prevent any one from believing a syllable of what you say."

'I rallied all my strength to answer by a laugh of scorn.

'He saw that from this time it was war to the death between us.

' "Listen," said he: "I yet give you the remainder of this night, and to-morrow. Reflect! Promise to be silent; and wealth, consideration, honours even, shall surround you. Threaten, to speak, and I condemn you to infamy."

543

' "You?" I exclaimed, "you!"

' "To eternal, ineffaceable infamy!"

' "You!" I repeated. Oh! I assure you, Felton, I believed that he was mad.

' "Yes, I!" he replied.

' "Ah, leave me," I cried, "leave me, if you do not wish me to dash out my brains against the wall, before your very eyes."

' "Well!" said he; "you demand it? I therefore leave you till to-morrow evening."

' "Till to-morrow evening," I replied, sinking on the floor, and biting the carpet in my rage."'

Felton supported himself with a chair; and her ladyship saw, with a demoniacal joy, that the fortitude of the young officer would probably give way before the end of her recital.

57

An Event in Classical Tragedy

AFTER a moment's silence, which her ladyship employed in observing the young officer who was listening to her, she continued her recital.

'For nearly three days, I had neither eaten nor drunk,' said she, 'and I was suffering dreadful tortures, Sometimes, a feeling as of passing clouds, which pressed upon my brow and dimmed my sight, came over me: it was delirium. The evening arrived. I was so weak that I fainted constantly; and each time that I fainted, I thanked God, for I believed that I was dying. During one of these fainting fits, I heard the door open, and terror recalled me to my self. My persecutor entered, followed by a man in a mask. He was himself also masked; but I recognised his step, his voice, and that commanding air which hell has given to his person, for the misfortune of mankind.

' "Well," said he, "have you determined to take the oath which I require of you?"

' "You have yourself said that the puritans are faithful to their word; and you have already heard my resolution—it is, to appeal against you here, on earth, to the tribunal of men, and, in heaven, to the tribunal of God!"

' "So! you persist?"

' "Yes! I swear it before that God who hears me—I will call the whole world to witness to your crime, and will never cease until I have found an avenger."

' "You are an abandoned woman," said he, in a voice of thunder, "and you shall suffer the punishment of prostitutes! Tainted as you are in the eyes of that world which you invoke, try to prove to it that you are neither guilty nor insane."

'Then, addressing the man who accompanied him— "Executioner," said he, "do your duty!" '

'Oh! his name! his name!' cried Felton, in a new burst of rage; 'tell me his name!'

'Then, in spite of my cries, in spite of my resistance— for I began to understand that something worse than death was meditated against me—the executioner seized me, threw me on the floor, and bound me so as to wound and bruise me by his violence; and then—whilst I was suffocated by my sobs, almost senseless, and calling aloud on that God who would not listen to my cries—I uttered suddenly a fearful shriek of agony and shame. A burning instrument— a red-hot iron—the brand of the executioner—had been stamped upon my shoulder!'

Felton groaned.

'Look!' said her ladyship, rising with all the majesty of a queen—'look, Felton, how a new kind of martyrdom has been invented for a pure young girl, the victim of a monster's brutal crime! Learn to know the hearts of men, and, henceforth, be more reluctant to become the instrument of their unjust revenge.'

Her ladyship, with a rapid motion, tore open her robe, tore away the cambric which covered her shoulder, and, crimsoned by pretended rage and simulated shame, exposed to the young man the ineffaceable mark which dishonoured that beautiful shoulder.

'But,' exclaimed Felton, 'it is a fleur-de-lis that I see!'

'And in that consists the greater infamy,' replied her ladyship. 'The brand of England would have made it necessary for him to prove from what court the sentence had been issued; and I should have made a public appeal to all the tribunals of the realm: but the brand of France —oh! by that I was indeed branded!'

It was more than Felton could endure. Pale, motionless, petrified by this frightful revelation—dazzled by the superhuman loveliness of that woman, who unveiled herself before him with an immodesty which appeared to him sublime—he fell upon his knees before her, as did the first Christians before those pure and holy martyrs whom the persecution of the emperors delivered, in the Circus, to the sanguinary violaters of the mob. The mark of infamy disappeared—the beauty alone remained.

'Forgive me, forgive me!' exclaimed Felton; 'Oh, forgive me!'

Her ladyship read in his eyes—'Love! love!'

'Forgive you—for what?' she inquired.

'Forgive me for uniting myself with your oppressors.'

Her ladyship held out her hand.

'So beautiful! so young!' exclaimed Felton, covering that hand with kisses.

Her ladyship cast upon him one of those glances which convert the slave into a monarch. Felton, puritan as he was, relinquished her hand to kiss her feet. He had before violently loved—he now adored her!

When this crisis had passed over—when her ladyship appeared to have resumed the calmness she had never really lost,—

'Ah!' said he, 'I have now only one thing more to ask of you: it is the name of your true executioner—for, in my opinion, there was only one: the other was an instrument —nothing more.'

'Brother!' exclaimed her ladyship, 'can it be necessary for me now to tell his name? Have you not already guessed it?'

'What!' resumed Felton, 'him—again him!—What! the true criminal?'

'The true criminal,' said her ladyship, 'is the plunderer of England, the persecutor of all true believers, the cowardly destroyer of woman's honour—he who, for a caprice of his polluted heart, is about to shed so much of England's blood —who protects the Protestants to-day, and to-morrow will betray them!'

'Buckingham! It is indeed Buckingham, then!' exclaimed the exasperated Felton.

Her ladyship hid her face in her hands, as if she was unable to endure the shame which that name recalled.

'Buckingham! the violator of this angelic creature!' exclaimed Felton. 'And thou, O God! hast not smitten him! Thou hast left him, noble, honoured, powerful, for the destruction of us all!'

'God abandons him who ceases to be constant to himself,' said her ladyship.

'But, surely he must wish to draw down upon himself the chastisement reserved for the accursed!' continued Felton, with increasing excitement. 'Surely he must wish that human vengeance should anticipate the chastisement of heaven!'

'Yet men fear, and spare him!'

'Oh!' exclaimed Felton, 'I fear him not, neither will I spare him!'

Her ladyship felt her heart bathed in a flood of infernal joy.

'But how,' continued Felton, 'does Lord de Winter—my protector, my father—come to be concerned in this?'

'Listen, Felton,' replied her ladyship.—'By the side of the cowardly and contemptible, there are always men of noble, generous natures. I was betrothed to a man whom I loved and who loved me; a heart like yours, Felton—a man like you. I went to him, and told him what had taken place. He knew the duke well, and did not entertain a moment's doubt. He was a nobleman—a man equal in every respect to Buckingham. He spoke not, but he girded on his sword, wrapped his cloak around him, and proceeded to the palace of the duke.'

'Yes, yes,' said Felton, 'I understand: yet, with such men, it is not the sword that should be used, but the dagger.'

'Buckingham had departed on the previous evening, on an embassy to the court of Spain, where he went to demand the hand of the Infanta for King Charles I., then Prince of Wales. My lover returned.

' "Listen," said he: "this man is gone, and, consequently, for the present he escapes my vengeance. But, in the meantime, let us be united, as we ought to be; and, then, depend on Lord de Winter to support his own honour and the honour of his wife." '

'Lord de Winter!' exclaimed Felton.

'Yes,' said her ladyship, 'Lord de Winter. And now you understand it all, do you not? Buckingham remained absent nearly a year: eight days before his return, Lord de Winter died suddenly, leaving me his sole heiress. Whence came this blow? God, who sees everything, doubtless knows: as for me, I accuse nobody.'

'Oh, what an abyss! what an abyss!' exclaimed Felton.

'Lord de Winter had died without confiding in his brother. The terrible secret was to have been concealed from every one, until it burst like thunder on the head of the guilty duke. Your protector had seen, with pain, this marriage of his brother with a young and dowerless girl; and I perceived that I could expect no assistance from a man who was disappointed in his hopes of an inheritance. I went to France, resolved to remain there for the remainder of my life. But my whole fortune was in England; and all communications being stopped by the war, I was in want of everything, and was in fact compelled to return. Six days ago, I arrived at Portsmouth.'

'Well?' said Felton.

'Well! Buckingham had unquestionably been apprised of my return, and announced it to Lord de Winter, who was already prejudiced against me, and at the same time he persuaded him that his sister-in-law was a dissolute and branded woman. The pure and noble voice of my husband was no longer there to defend me. Lord de Winter no doubt believed all that he heard, and the more readily, because it was to his interest to believe it. Hence he caused me to be arrested, conveyed here, and placed under your charge. You know the sequel. The day after to-morrow he sends me forth amongst the infamous. Oh! the woof is well woven, the plot is skilfully planned. and my honour will perish in it. You see, Felton, that I must die! Felton, give me the knife!'

At these words, as if all her strength was exhausted, her ladyship sank, weak and languishing, into the arms of the young officer.

'No, no!' said he; 'no, you shall live—you shall live, honoured and pure—you shall live, to triumph over your enemies!'

Her ladyship gently forced him back with her hand, whilst she attracted him by her look.

'Oh, death! death!' said she, lowering her eyelids and her voice; 'death, rather than disgrace, Felton—my brother, my friend—I implore you!'

'No!' exclaimed Felton, 'no! you shall live, and you shall be avenged.'

'Felton, I bring misfortune upon everything that surrounds me! Felton, desert me—let me die!'

'Well, then, let us die together!' exclaimed he.

Several knocks sounded on the door.

'Listen!' said she; 'we have been overheard. They come, and it is all over. We are undone!'

'No,' said Felton, 'it is the sentinel, who merely lets me know that the guard is about to be changed.'

'Hasten, then, to the door, and open it yourself.'

Felton obeyed her. This woman already wholly engrossed his thoughts—she was already mistress of all his soul.

On opening the door he found himself confronted by a sergeant, who commanded a patrol of the guard.

'Well, what is the matter?' demanded the young lieutenant.

'You told me,' replied the sentinel, 'to open the door if I heard you call for help, but you forgot to leave me the key. I heard you cry out, without knowing what you said: I tried to open the door, but it was fastened inside; and therefore I called the sergeant.'

'And here I am,' said the sergeant.

Felton—wandering, wild, verging upon madness—remained speechless.

Her ladyship saw at once that she must relieve him from this embarrassment. She ran to the table, and seized the knife, which he had placed there.

'And by what right would you prevent my death?' said she.

'Great God!' exclaimed Felton, as he saw the knife glittering in her hand.

At this moment a burst of ironical laughter resounded down the corridor. The baron, attracted by the noise, stood, in his dressing-gown, and with his sword under his arm, upon the threshold of the door.

'Ah, ah!' said he, 'here we are at the last act of the tragedy. You see, Felton, the drama has presented all the phases that I indicated. But don't concern yourself—no blood will be spilled.'

Her ladyship felt that she was ruined, unless she gave to Felton an immediate and terrible proof of her courage.

'You deceive yourself, my lord! Blood will be spilled; and may that blood return on those who cause it to flow!'

Felton uttered a cry, and rushed towards her; but he was too late—she had dealt the blow.

The knife had, however, fortunately—we ought to say skilfully—encountered the steel busk, by which, as by a cuirass, the chests of women were at that period defended, and, glancing aside, had torn the robe, and penetrated diagonally between the flesh and the ribs. The lady's dress was, nevertheless, instantaneously stained with blood, and she fell back, apparently insensible.

Felton snatched away the knife.

'See, my lord,' said he, with a gloomy look; 'this woman, who was under my guard, has slain herself!'

'Make yourself easy, Felton,' replied Lord de Winter; 'she is not dead: demons do not die so simply. Make yourself easy, and go and wait for me in my apartment.'

'But, my lord——'

'Go, I command you!'

This order from his superior, Felton obeyed; but, as he went out, he placed the knife in his bosom.

As for Lord de Winter, he contended himself with summoning the woman who waited upon her ladyship; and when she came, having recommended the prisoner, who was still insensible, to her care, he left them together.

Nevertheless, as the wound might, after all, in spite of his suspicions, be really serious, he immediately despatched a man on horseback for a surgeon.

58

The Escape

As Lord de Winter had suspected, her ladyship was not very dangerously wounded. As soon, therefore, as she found herself alone with the attendant whom the baron had summoned, and who hastened to undress her, she opened her eyes. It was, however, necessary to counterfeit weakness and pain; and, to an actress like her ladyship, this was no difficult matter. So completely, indeed, was the poor woman the dupe of her prisoner, that, against her entreaties, she persisted in watching over her throughout the night.

But the presence of this woman was no impediment to her ladyship's thoughts. There could be no longer any doubt that Felton was converted—that Felton was hers; and that, had an angel appeared to the young man to accuse her, he would certainly have taken him, in his present state of mind, for an envoy of the Evil One. Her ladyship smiled at this idea, for Felton was henceforth her only hope, her sole means of safety.

Yet Lord de Winter might have suspected him, and Felton might now perhaps himself be watched.

About four o'clock in the morning the surgeon arrived, but her ladyship's wound had already closed. He therefore could determine neither its direction nor its depth; but, from the pulse of his patient, he concluded that the case was not very serious.

In the morning, under the pretence that she had not slept during the night, and had need of repose, her ladyship dismissed the woman who had watched beside her bed. She entertained a hope that Felton would visit her at breakfast time. But Felton came not. Had her secret fears, then, been realised? Had Felton become suspected by the baron, and would he fail her, now, at the decisive moment? She had only one day remaining. Lord de Winter had fixed her embarkation for the twenty-third, and this was the morning of the twenty-second. Nevertheless, she still waited in tolerable patience till the hour of dinner.

Athough she had eaten nothing in the morning, her dinner was brought to her at the usual time, and her ladyship then perceived with alarm that the uniform of the soldiers who guarded her was different.

She hazarded a question as to what had become of Felton. The answer was, that Felton had departed, on horseback, an hour before. She inquired whether the baron was still at the castle; and the soldier replied that he was, and had ordered him to let him know if the prisoner should express a wish to speak to him.

Her ladyship said she was too weak at present, and that her only wish was to remain alone.

The soldier then quitted the room, leaving the dinner served on the table.

Felton, then, had been sent away, and the marines who guarded her were changed. It was obvious, therefore, that Felton was suspected. This was the last blow inflicted on the prisoner.

As soon as she was left alone, her ladyship arose. That bed, to which she had confined herself in order that it might be thought her wound was serious, scorched her like a glowing furnace. She cast a glance at the door: a board had been nailed over the wicket. The baron, no doubt, feared that she might, through this opening, still find some diabolical means of seducing her guards. Her ladyship smiled with joy. She could now give way to her emotions without observation. She roamed about her chamber with all the violence of a raving lunatic, or a tigress imprisoned in her iron cage. Had the knife still been there, she would certainly have resolved to kill, not herself, but the baron.

At six o'clock Lord de Winter entered. He was armed to the very teeth. This man, in whom her ladyship had hitherto seen only an elegant and polished gentleman, had now become an inexorable goaler. He seemed to expect everything, to conjecture everything, to anticipate everything. A single glance at her ladyship told him what was passing in her soul.

'So,' said he, 'you will not kill me to-day, for you are without a weapon; and, moreover, I am on my guard. You had begun to corrupt my poor Felton: he has already felt your infernal influence: but I wish to save him, and you shall see him no more. It is all ended now: you may pack your clothes, for, to-morrow, you will set out. I had fixed the embarkation for the 24th, but I have reflected that the sooner it takes place the surer it will be. By twelve o'clock to-morrow, I shall receive the order for your banishment, signed by Buckingham. If you say one single word, to any one whatever, before you are on board the vessel, my sergeant will blow out your brains: he has received his orders to do so. If, when on board, you speak to any one without the captain's permission, the captain will have you cast into the sea. This is all determined on. And now, farewell till our next meeting: I have nothing more to say to you to-day. I shall see you again to-morrow, to take leave of you.'

At these words, the baron left the room.

Her ladyship had listened to this threatening tirade with a smile of scorn upon her lips, but with fury in her heart.

The supper was brought in. Her ladyship felt that she needed strength, for she knew not what might be the events of that night, which was now approaching in gloom. Huge clouds were already careering in the skies, and distant flashes announced a tempest. About ten o'clock the storm burst forth; and her ladyship found some consolation in seeing Nature partake of the commotion in her own breast. The thunder bellowed in the air like the angry passions in her soul; and it seemed to her as if the passing gusts disturbed her brow, as they did the trees of which they bent down the branches and swept off the leaves. She howled like the tempest, but her voice was unheard amidst the vast voice of Nature, which also appeared to be herself groaning in despair.

From time to time she looked at a ring which she wore upon her finger. The bezel of this ring contained a subtle and violent poison—this was her last resource!

Suddenly she heard something strike the window; and,

by the light of the gleaming flash, she saw the countenance of a man appear behind its bars. She ran to the window and opened it.

'Felton!' she exclaimed, 'I am saved!'

'Yes,' said Felton, 'but silence! silence! I must have time to file your bars: only be careful that we are not perceived through the wicket.'

'Oh! it is a token that the Lord is on our side, Felton.' replied her ladyship; 'they have closed up the wicket with a board!'

'Good!' said Felton. 'Our God has deprived them of their senses!'

'But what must I do?' inquired her ladyship.

'Nothing—nothing! only shut your window. Go to bed; or, at least, lie down with your clothes on; and, when I have finished, I will tap upon the glass. But will you be able to accompany me?'

'Oh, yes!'

'But your wound?'

'It pains me, but does not prevent me walking.'

'Be ready, then, at the first signal.'

Her ladyship closed the window, put out her lamp as Felton had advised, and threw herself upon the bed. Amidst the raging of the storm, she heard the grating of the file against the bars, and by the light of every flash she beheld the form of Felton behind the glass.

She passed an hour, in almost breathless suspense; icy drops stood upon her brow; and at every sound that issued from the corridor, her heart was convulsed with frightful agony. There are hours which seem prolonged into years. At the expiration of this time, Felton again tapped. Her ladyship bounded from her bed, and opened the window: the removal of two bars had formed an opening large enough to admit a man.

'Are you ready?' demanded Felton.

'Yes. Must I carry anything away with me?'

'Money—if you have any.'

'Fortunately, they have left me what I had.'

'So much the better; for I have used all mine in chartering a vessel.'

'Here!' said her ladyship, placing in Felton's hand a bag of gold.

Felton took the bag, and threw it to the foot of the wall.

'Now,' said he, 'will you come?'

'Here I am.'

Her ladyship mounted on a chair, and passed the upper part of her body through the window. She saw the young officer suspended over the abyss by a ladder of ropes. For the first time, a sentiment of fear reminded her that she was a woman. The void terrified her.

'I was afraid you would be terrified,' said Felton.

'It is nothing—it is nothing,' exclaimed her ladyship: 'I will descend with my eyes shut.'

'Have you confidence in me?' said Felton.

'Need you ask me!'

'Then put your two hands together, and cross them. That's right.'

Felton fastened the two wrists with his handkerchief, and then bound a cord above the handkerchief.

'What are you doing?' demanded her ladyship, in surprise.

'Place your arms round my neck, and do not be afraid.'

'But I shall make you lose your balance, and we shall both be dashed to pieces.'

'Do not alarm yourself; I am a sailor.'

There was not a moment to be lost. Her ladyship passed her arms around Felton's neck, and allowed herself to glide through the window.

Felton began to descend the ladder, slowly, step by step. In spite of the weight of the two bodies, the blast of the hurricane swung them in the air. Suddenly Felton paused.

'What is the matter?' demanded her ladyship.

'Silence!' said Felton, 'I hear footsteps!'

'We are discovered!'

There was silence for a few moments.

'No,' said Felton, 'it is nothing.'

'But what is that noise?'

'It is the patrol, who are about to pass on their round.'

'And which way do they go?'

'Immediately beneath us.'

'Then we shall be discovered.'

'No—if there should be no lightning.'

'They will strike against the bottom of the ladder.'

'Fortunately, it is too short by six feet.'

'There they are! My God!'

'Silence!'

They both remained suspended—motionless, and scarcely even venturing to breathe—at a height of twenty feet in the air, whilst the soldiers passed beneath them, laughing and talking. It was a fearful moment for the fugitives! the patrol passed by. They heard the sound of their retreating steps, and the murmur of their voices, which became gradually weaker in the distance.

'Now,' said Felton, 'we are saved!'

Her ladyship breathed a sigh, and fainted.

Felton continued to descend. Having reached the bottom of the ladder, and finding no further support for his feet, he now descended by his hands, until he clung to the last step, when, suspending himself by the strength of his wrists, he found that his feet touched the ground. He picked up the bag of gold, which he took between his teeth; and raising her ladyship in his arms, retreated rapidly in a direction opposite to that which the patrol had taken. Leaving the circuit of the guard he plunged down amidst the rocks; and, when he had reached the seashore, he whistled. His signal was replied to in a similar manner; and, in five minutes afterwards, a boat appeared, manned by four men.

The boat approached the shore; but there was too great a depth of water for it to be grounded. Felton waded into the sea up to his waist, not wishing to entrust his precious burden to any other hands. Fortunately the tempest was beginning to abate, although the sea was still violent. The little boat bounded on the waves like a nutshell.

'To the sloop!' said Felton, 'and pull quickly.'

The four men bent themselves to their work; but the sea was too heavy for their oars to make much way. Nevertheless, they began to leave the castle behind them; and that was the principal point. The night was profoundly dark, and it was already almost impossible for them to perceive the shore; much less could any one upon the shore be able to perceive their boat. A black speck was rocking on the sea. It was the sloop.

Whilst the boat was advancing towards it with all the force of its four rowers, Felton unbound the cord and the handkerchief which confined her ladyship's hands. Then, when these were once more at liberty, he took some sea-water and sprinkled it upon her face. Her ladyship heaved a sigh, and opened her eyes.

'Where am I?' said she.

'Saved,' replied the young officer.

'Oh! saved! saved!' exclaimed she. 'Yes, I see the heavens and the ocean! This air which I breathe is that of liberty! Ah!—thanks, Felton, thanks!'

The young man pressed her to his heart.

'But what is the matter with my hands?' asked her ladyship; 'my wrists feel as though they had been crushed in a vice.'

She lifted up her arms: her wrists were indeed horribly lacerated.

'Alas!' said Felton, looking at those beautiful hands, with a melancholy shake of the head.

'Oh! it is nothing—it is nothing!' exclaimed her ladyship. 'I remember now.'

Her ladyship looked around her for something.

'It is there,' said Felton, pointing to the bag of gold.

They neared the sloop. The seamen on watch hailed the boat, from which an answer was returned.

'What vessel is this?' demanded her ladyship.

'That which I have chartered for you.'

'And whither will it take me?'

'Wheresoever you please, after you have landed me at Portsmouth.'

'What have you to do at Portsmouth?' demanded her ladyship.

'To execute the orders of Lord de Winter,' said Felton, with a gloomy smile.

'What orders?' inquired her ladyship.

'Do you not understand, then?' replied Felton.

'No; explain yourself, I beg of you!'

'As he distrusted me, he determined to guard you himself; and has sent me, in his stead, to procure Buckingham's signature to the order for your transportation.'

'But, if he suspected you, how came he to intrust you with this order?'

'He supposed me ignorant of its purport, as he had told me nothing respecting it. I had, however, received my information from you.'

'True! And you are going to Portsmouth?'

'I have no time to lose: to-morrow is the twenty-third, and Buckingham departs on that date with the fleet.'

'Departs to-morrow! Where is he going?'

'To La Rochelle.'

'He must not go!' exclaimed her ladyship, forgetting her habitual presence of mind.

'Make yourself easy,' answered Felton, 'he will not go!'

Her ladyship trembled with delight. She had just penetrated the most secret depths of the young man's heart, and had there seen the death of Buckingham ineffaceably registered.

'Felton,' whispered she, 'you are as great as Judas Maccabeus. Should you die, I shall die with you! I can say no more.'

'Hush,' said Felton, 'we have reached the vessel.'

They were, in fact, beside the sloop. Felton ascended the ladder, and gave his hand to her ladyship, whilst the sailors supported her, for the sea was still agitated. In a moment afterwards, they were upon the deck.

'Captain,' said Felton, 'here is the lady of whom I spoke to you. You must take her, safe and sound, to France.'

'For a thousand pistoles,' replied the captain.

'I have already paid you five hundred of them.'

'Right,' said the captain.

'And here are the other five hundred,' added her ladyship, putting her hand to the bag of gold.

'No,' said the captain, 'I have but one word, and that I gave to this young man. The other five hundred pistoles are not my due until we make Boulogne.'

'And shall we make it?'

'Safe and sound,' replied the captain, 'as sure as my name is Jack Butler.'

'Well!' said her ladyship, 'if you keep your word, instead of five hundred, I will give you a thousand pistoles.'

'Hurrah, for you, then, my pretty lady!' exclaimed the captain, 'and may fortune often send me such passengers as your ladyship.'

'In the meantime,' said Felton, 'run into Chichester Bay, just by Portsmouth. You remember that it was agreed you should take us there first?'

The captain replied by issuing orders for the necessary evolutions, and, towards seven o'clock in the morning, the little vessel hove-to in the appointed bay.

During this passage Felton related everything to her ladyship: how, instead of going to London, he had chartered this little vessel; how he had returned; how he had scaled the wall, by placing, in the interstices of the stones, as he ascended, cramp-irons to support his feet; and how at last, having reached the bars of her window, he had secured the ladder to them. Her ladyship was well aware of the remainder.

On her side, her ladyship endeavoured to encourage Felton in his design; but, at the first words she uttered, she clearly perceived that it was necessary rather to moderate than to excite the young fanatic.

It was agreed that her ladyship should wait for Felton

until ten o'clock; and if he should not have returned by that hour, she was to set sail.

In the latter case, and supposing him to be afterwards at liberty, he was to rejoin her in France, at the Carmelite Convent of Bethune.

59

What Happened at Portsmouth, on the Twenty-third of August, 1628

FELTON took leave of her ladyship, just as a brother who is going out for a mere walk takes leave of his sister, by kissing her hand. His whole manners and appearance indicated a state of ordinary tranquillity; except that a strange gleam, like the brilliancy of fever, beamed from his eyes. His forehead was even more calm than usual; his teeth were firmly closed; and his speech had a short and abrupt tone, which seemed to denote that his thoughts were intent upon some gloomy purpose.

As long as he remained in the boat which took him ashore, he had kept his face turned towards her ladyship, who, standing on the deck, followed him with her eyes. Neither of them now entertained much fear of being pursued. Her ladyship's apartment was never entered before nine o'clock in the morning, and it took some hours to travel from the castle to London.

Felton set his foot on shore, climbed the rising ground which led to the top of the cliff, saluted her ladyship for the last time, and took his way towards the town. After a hundred steps, as the path descended as it proceeded, he could no longer see more than the mast of the vessel.

He hastened as fast as possible in the direction of Portsmouth, which, through the morning mist, he could discern in the distance. Beyond the town, the sea was covered with innumerable ships, whose masts, like a forest of poplars stripped of their leaves by winter, were bending before the breath of the wind.

During this rapid walk, Felton resolved in his mind all the accusations, whether true or false, with which ten years of ascetic meditation, and a long intercourse with the puritans, had furnished him against the royal favourite. When he compared the public crimes of this minister—crimes which were notorious, and, in a manner, European—with those private and unknown vices of which her ladyship had accused him, Felton found that the most culpable of the two beings whom Buckingham united in himself, was the one whose life was hidden from the world. His own love, so singular, and fresh, and ardent, made him see the infamous and imaginary accusations of her ladyship, as one sees, through a microscope, the form of frightful monsters, atoms of insects, otherwise imperceptible. The rapidity of his progress, also inflamed his blood. The idea that he left behind him, exposed to a dreadful vengeance, the woman whom he loved, or, rather, adored as a saint—his past emotions, and his present fatigue—all tended to excite and elevate his soul above the feelings of humanity.

On entering Portsmouth, he found the whole population astir. The drums were beating in the streets and in the harbour, and the troops about to be embarked were descending towards the sea. Felton arrived at the Admiralty-house, covered with dust, and wet with perspiration. His usually pale face was purple with heat and anger. The sentinel wished to stop him; but Felton called for the officer on guard, and drew from his pocket the letter which he carried.

'An express from Lord de Winter,' said he.

At the name of Lord de Winter, who was known to be one of Buckingham's most intimate friends, the officer gave an order for the admission of Felton, who, moreover, wore the uniform of a naval officer himself.

Felton rushed into the house, but, the moment he reached the hall, another man also entered, covered with dust, and out of breath; having left at the door a posthorse, which, on reaching it, had fallen on its knees. Both individuals addressed Patrick, the duke's confidential valet, at the same moment. Felton named the Baron de Winter. The stranger refused to mention any name, and declared that he could make himself known to no one but the duke. Both insisted on being allowed priority of admission. Patrick, who knew that Lord de Winter was connected, both by profession and friendship, with his grace, gave the preference to him who came in his name. The other was obliged to wait, and it was easy enough to see how heartily he cursed the delay.

The valet conducted Felton through a large room, in which were waiting the deputies from La Rochelle, headed by the Prince de Soubise; and introduced him into a cabinet, where Buckingham, having just left the bath, was finishing his toilet, to which, now, as ever, he accorded extreme attention.

'Lieutenant Felton,' said Patrick, 'from Lord de Winter.'

'From Lord de Winter?' repeated Buckingham. 'Show him in.'

Felton entered. At this moment Buckingham threw upon a sofa a rich dressing-gown, brocaded with gold, and put on a doublet of blue velvet, entirely embroidered with pearls.

'Why did the baron not come himself?' demanded Buckingham. 'I expected him this morning.'

'He desired me to inform your grace,' replied Felton, 'that he very much regretted not having that honour; but that he was prevented by the watch which he is obliged to keep at the castle.'

'Oh, yes,' said Buckingham; 'I know about that: he has a lady-prisoner there.'

'It is, in fact, about that prisoner that I wish to speak to your grace,' replied Felton.

'Well, proceed.'

'What I have to say to you, my lord, must be heard by yourself alone.'

'Leave us, Patrick,' said Buckingham, 'but keep within earshot: I will call you presently.'

Patrick left the room.

'We are alone, sir,' said Buckingham. 'Speak.'

'My lord,' replied Felton, 'the Baron de Winter lately wrote to your grace requesting you to sign an order for the transportation of a young woman, named Charlotte Backson.'

'Yes, sir; and I replied, that he should either bring or send me the order, and I would sign it.'

'Here it is, my lord.'

'Give it to me,' said the duke.

Taking the paper from Felton's hands, his grace cast a rapid glance over its contents. Then, perceiving it was really that which had been referred to, he laid it on the table, took a pen, and prepared to sign it.

'Pardon me, my lord,' said Felton, interrupting the duke, 'but, is your grace aware that Charlotte Backson is not the real name of this female?'

'Yes, sir, I know that,' replied the duke, dipping his pen into the ink.

'Then your grace is acquainted with her real name?' demanded Felton, in an abrupt tone.

'I do know it.'

The duke put the pen to the paper. Felton became pale.

'And, knowing this real name,' resumed Felton, 'will your grace still sign the paper?'

'Certainly,' said Buckingham, 'and rather twice than once.'

'I cannot believe,' continued Felton, in a voice which became more and more abrupt and reproachful, 'that your grace is aware that this refers to Lady de Winter.'

'I am perfectly aware of it, although I am astonished that you should be.'

'And your grace will sign this order without remorse?'

Buckingham looked haughtily at the speaker.

'Do you happen to know, sir,' said he, 'that you are asking me some strange questions, and that I am very foolish to answer them!'

'Answer them, my lord!' said Felton; 'your position is perhaps more serious than you suppose.'

Buckingham thought that as the young man came from Lord de Winter, he probably spoke in his name; he therefore restrained himself.

'Without any remorse whatever,' said he; 'and the baron knows, as well as I do, that her ladyship is a great criminal, to whom it is almost a favour to reduce her punishment to transportation.'

The duke again put his pen to the paper.

'You shall not sign that order, my lord,' said Felton, making a step towards the duke.

'I shall not sign this order?' exclaimed Buckingham; 'and why not?'

'Because you will consult your own conscience, and will render justice to the lady.'

'It would be bare justice, if she were sent to Tyburn,' said the duke; 'her ladyship is an infamous creature.'

'My lord, her ladyship is an angel! You know it well, and I demand her liberty.'

'Ah!' said Buckingham, 'are you mad, thus to speak to me!'

'Excuse me, my lord; I speak as I am able—I restrain myself. Yet, my lord, think of what you are about to do: beware lest the cup should overflow——'

'What does he mean?—God forgive me,' exclaimed Buckingham. 'I verily believe he threatens me!'

'No, my lord—I implore you still, and I warn you:— one drop of water is sufficient to make the full vase overflow— a slight fault is sufficient to draw down vengeance, upon the head which has been spared to this day, in spite of so many crimes.'

'Mr. Felton,' said Buckingham, 'you will leave this room, and immediately place yourself under arrest.'

'And you, my lord, will hear me to the end. You have seduced this young girl, you have violated and polluted her!—repair your crimes towards her, let her depart freely, and I will exact nothing more of you.'

'You will *exact* nothing more!' cried Buckingham, looking at Felton with astonishment, and dwelling on each syllable of the words which he had just pronounced.

'My lord,' continued Felton, becoming more excited as he spoke—'my lord, be careful: the whole of England is wearied by your iniquities; my lord, you have abused the royal power, which you have almost usurped; my lord, you are an abomination to God and man. God will punish you in eternity, and I will punish you now.'

'Ah! This is rather too much!' exclaimed Buckingham, making a step towards the door.

Felton opposed his progress.

'I humbly entreat you,' said he, 'to sign an order for the liberation of Lady de Winter. Reflect that it is the woman whom you have dishonoured.'

'Leave the room, sir!' said Buckingham, 'or I will call my servants to eject you!'

'You will not call them,' replied Felton, throwing himself between the duke and the bell, which was placed upon a stand inlaid with silver: 'take care, my lord, for you are now in God's hands!'

'In the devil's hands, you mean!' exclaimed Buckingham, elevating his voice so as to attract the attention of those without, without exactly calling them.

'Sign, my lord—sign the liberation of Lady de Winter!' said Felton, pushing a paper towards the duke.

'Under compulsion? You are making a fool of yourself! Hollo, there! Patrick!'

'Sign, my lord!'

'Never!'

'Never?'

'Help!' cried the duke, at the same time leaping towards his sword.

But Felton did not give him time to draw it: the open knife with which her ladyship had wounded herself was concealed under his doublet, and in one bound he was upon the duke.

At that same moment Patrick entered the room, exclaiming—

'My lord, a letter from France.'

'From France!' cried Buckingham, forgetting everything as he imagined from whom that letter came.

Felton took advantage of the moment, and buried the knife up to its handle in the duke's side.

'Ah, traitor!' exclaimed Buckingham, 'thou hast slain me!'

'Murder!' shouted Patrick.

Felton cast his eyes around, and, seeing the door free, he rushed into the adjoining room, where, as we have said, the deputies from La Rochelle were waiting, passed through it still running, and hurried towards the staircase. But, upon the first step, he met Lord de Winter, who—on seeing him wild-looking, and livid, and with blood upon his hands and face—rushed upon him, and exclaimed—

'I knew it—I foresaw it! One minute too late! Alas, alas! how unfortunate is my lot!'

Felton did not attempt to resist, and Lord de Winter handed him over to the guards, who, in the meantime, conducted him to a little terrace overlooking the sea. His lordship himself hastened into Buckingham's cabinet.

On hearing the duke's cry, and Patrick's shout, the man whom Felton had met in the antechamber rushed into his grace's room. He found the duke reclining on a sofa, pressing the wound with his convulsed hand.

'La Porte,' said the duke, in a dying voice—'La Porte, do you come from her?'

'Yes, your grace,' replied the faithful servant of Anne of Austria, 'but, I fear, I come too late.'

'Hush! La Porte—you might be overheard. Patrick, let no one enter. Oh, I shall not know what she says to me. My God! I am dying!'

The duke fainted.

Nevertheless, Lord de Winter, the deputies, the chiefs of the expedition, and the officers of Buckingham's household, had already forced their way into the room. Cries of despair resounded on every side. The tidings which had filled the house with lamentation and groans, soon spread, and became generally known throughout the town; whilst the report of a cannon announced that something new and unexpected had occurred.

Lord de Winter tore his hair. 'One minute too late!' exclaimed he. 'One minute too late! Oh, my God! my God! what a misfortune!'

He had, in fact, at seven o'clock in the morning, received information that a rope-ladder had been found suspended from one of the windows of the castle; and instantly hastening to her ladyship's chamber, he had found it empty, the window open, and the bars filed through. Remembering, then, the verbal warning which d'Artagnan had sent to him by his messenger, he had trembled for the duke; and, without a moment's delay, he had mounted the first horse available, and galloped at full speed to Portsmouth, dismounted in the courtyard, and hastily ascended the staircase where, as we have already said, he encountered Felton on the topmost step.

But the Duke was not yet dead. He recovered his senses, again unclosed his eyes, and hope revived in all their hearts.

'Gentlemen,' said he, 'leave me alone with Patrick and La Porte. Ah, it is you, de Winter! You sent me a strange madman, this morning! See what he has done to me!'

'Oh, my lord!' exclaimed the baron—'oh, my lord, never shall I forgive myself for it!'

'And there you would be wrong, de Winter,' said Buckingham, giving him his hand. 'I know not any man who is worthy to be regretted by another throughout the whole of his life. But leave us, I beseech you!'

The baron left the room, sobbing.

There remained in the cabinet only the wounded duke, La Porte, and Patrick. A surgeon had been summoned, but could not be found.

'You will live, my lord—you will live!' repeated the messenger of Anne of Austria, kneeling before the duke.

'What has she written to me?' said Buckingham feebly, as the blood gushed from him, and he subdued, in order to speak of her he loved, his enormous pains: 'what has she written to me? Read me her letter.'

'Oh, my lord!' exclaimed La Porte.

'Well, La Porte, do you not see that I have no time to lose?'

La Porte instantly broke the seal, and held the parchment before the duke's eyes; but Buckingham in vain attempted to decipher the writing.

'Read it, then,' said he; 'read it—read quickly; for I can

no longer see! Read it—for I shall soon be no longer able to hear, and shall die without knowing what she has written to me.'

La Porte no longer hesitated. The letter was as follows:—

'MY LORD,

'By all that I have suffered through you, and for you, since I have known you, I conjure you, if you have any regard to my repose, to put an end to those vast preparations which you are making against France, and to relinquish a war, of which, it is openly said, religion is the avowed, and your love of me the secret, cause. That war may not only bring great calamities on France and England, but even upon yourself, my lord—misfortunes for which I could never be consoled. Be careful of your own life, which is threatened, and which will be dear to me, from the moment when I shall no longer be obliged to consider you an enemy. Yours affectionately, 'ANNE.'

Buckingham roused all his fast-failing energies to listen to this letter; and when it was ended, as if he had experienced a bitter disappointment—

'And have you nothing more to tell me—no verbal message, La Porte?' demanded he.

'Yes, my lord; the queen charged me to bid you be upon your guard, for she had been warned that you were to be assassinated!'

'And is that all? Is that all?' resumed Buckingham impatiently.

'She charged me also to tell you that she always loved you.'

'Ah!' said Buckingham. 'God be praised! My death, then, will not be to her as the death of a stranger!'

'Patrick,' continued the duke, 'bring me the casket which contained the diamond studs.'

Patrick brought the object he demanded, which La Porte recognised as having belonged to the queen.

'Now, the white satin bag, on which her initials are embroidered in pearls.'

Patrick again obeyed.

'Here, La Porte,' said Buckingham, 'here are the only tokens which I have received from her—this silver casket, and these two letters. You will restore them to her majesty; and, for a last souvenir'—he looked around him for some precious object—'you will add them——'

He still strove to find some gift; but his eyes, dimmed by

death, encountered nothing but the knife which had fallen from Felton's hand, with the crimson blood still reeking on its blade.

'And you will add to them this knife,' said the Duke, pressing La Porte's hand.

He was still able to place the satin bag in the casket, and to drop the knife upon it, as he made a sign to La Porte, that he could no longer speak. Then, in a last convulsion, against which he was no longer able to contend, he glided from the sofa to the floor.

Patrick uttered a loud cry.

Buckingham endeavoured to smile once more, but death arrested the thought, which remained engraven on his forehead and lips like a last farewell of love.

At this moment the duke's surgeon arrived, completely bewildered. He had already been on board the admiral's ship, whence he had been so hastily summoned. He approached the duke, took his hand, held it for a moment in his own, and then let it fall again.

'It is all in vain,' said he—'he is dead!'

'Dead! dead!' echoed Patrick.

At this cry the whole crowd re-entered the apartment, and there was nothing to be seen but consternation and confusion.

As soon as Lord de Winter knew that Buckingham had expired, he ran to Felton, whom the soldiers still guarded on the terrace.

'Wretch!' said he to the young man, who, since Buckingham's death, had recovered that tranquillity and coolness which were never more to abandon him—'wretch! what have you done?'

'I have avenged myself!' he replied.

'Yourself!' cried the baron; 'say, rather, that you have been the instrument of that cursed woman; but, I swear to you, that it shall be her last crime.'

'I do not know what you mean,' replied Felton calmly, 'and I am quite ignorant of what woman you are speaking, my lord. I have killed the Duke of Buckingham, because he twice refused to make me a captain at your request. I have punished him for his injustice—for no other reason!'

De Winter looked, in his astonishment, at the men who were binding Felton, and knew not what to think of such insensibility.

One single idea, however, still left a cloud upon Felton's brow. At every step that he heard, the simple puritan thought he recognised the step and voice of her ladyship, who had come to throw herself into his arms, to accuse herself, and to perish with him.

Suddenly he started. His glance was fixed upon a point on the sea, which the terrace where he stood completely overlooked. With the eagle eye of a sailor, he had discovered there, where another could only have seen a speck upon the ocean, the sail of a sloop, which was bearing on towards the shores of France. He grew pale, pressed his hand upon his heart, which was bursting, and at once comprehended the whole extent of the treachery.

'Grant me one last favour?' said he to the baron.

'What is it?' demanded the latter.

'What time is it?'

The baron drew out his watch. 'It wants ten minutes to nine,' said he.

Her ladyship, then, had anticipated the time of her departure by an hour and a half. As soon as she heard the cannon which announced the fatal event, she had ordered the anchor to be weighed.

The boat was now visible, under a blue sky, at a great distance from the shore.

'It was God's will!' said Felton, with the resignation of a fatalist, but still unable to tear his eyes from that barque, on board of which he doubtless believed that he could distinguish the fair vision of her for whom he was about to sacrifice his life.

De Winter followed his glances, scrutinised his emotions and comprehended all that had occurred.

'Be punished *alone*, wretch, in the first place!' said his lordship, to Felton, who allowed himself to be dragged away, with his eyes still turned towards the sea; 'but I swear to you, by the memory of my brother, whom I so truly loved, that your accomplice is not saved.'

Felton held down his head without uttering a word.

As for de Winter, he hastily descended the stairs, and betook himself to the harbour.

60

In France

THE first apprehension of the king of England, Charles I, on hearing of the Duke of Buckingham's death, was, lest intelligence so terrible might discourage the Rochellois: hence he endeavoured, says Richelieu in his Memoirs, to conceal it from them as long as possible, closing all the ports of his kingdom, and being scrupulously careful that no vessel should leave until after the departure of the army which Buckingham had been preparing, and whose embarkation he now undertook to superintend in person. He even enforced this order with so much strictness as to detain in England the Danish ambassador, who had already taken leave; and the ambassador from Holland, who was to take back into Flushing those Dutch Indiamen whose restitution Charles had procured.

But, as the king had not thought of issuing this order until five hours after the event, two ships had already left the port: one bearing, as we know, her ladyship, who, already suspecting what had happened, was confirmed in her belief by seeing the black flag unfolding itself from the mast of the admiral's ship.

As for the second vessel, we shall hereafter be told whom it carried, and how it got away.

During this interval, nothing extraordinary had occurred at the camp before La Rochelle; except that the king, who was, as usual, bored, and perhaps more so at the camp than elsewhere, resolved to go *incognito* to enjoy the fetes of Saint-Louis at Saint-Germain, and requested the cardinal to provide for him an escort of twenty musketeers. The cardinal, who sometimes was wearied by the gloominess of the king, willingly gave this leave of absence to his royal lieutenant, who promised to return by the twelfth of September.

When M. de Treville was informed of this journey by his eminence, he prepared his baggage; and as, without knowing the cause, he was fully aware of the earnest desire, or rather the imperious necessity, that the four friends had for visiting Paris, he marked them out as part of the escort. The four young men received the intelligence a quarter of an hour after M. de Treville, as they were the very first persons to whom he communicated it; and then it was that d'Artagnan fully appreciated the favour which the cardinal had conferred upon him in promoting him to the musketeers; since, but for that circumstance, he would have been compelled to remain at the camp, whilst his companions departed.

It will be seen, hereafter, that his anxiety to return to Paris was occasioned by the danger which Madame Bonancieux was likely to incur from encountering her mortal enemy, Lady de Winter, at the convent of Bethune. Thus, as we have said, Aramis had written immediately to Marie Michon—that seamstress of Tours who had such exalted acquaintances—that she might solicit from the queen an order empowering Madame Bonancieux to leave the convent, and to take refuge either in Lorraine or Belgium. The answer was not long delayed, for in eight or ten days Aramis had received this letter:—

'My dear Cousin,

'I send the order empowering our little servant to withdraw from the convent of Bethune, where you think that the air does not agree with her. My sister sends you this order with great pleasure, for she is much attached to this little girl, whom she hopes to benefit in the end. I embrace you.

'MARIE MICHON.'

To this letter was appended an order in these terms:—

'The superior of the convent of Bethune will deliver into the hands of the bearer of this note, the novice who entered her convent under my recommendation and patronage.

'At the Louvre, August 10, 1628.'   ANNE.

It may well be imagined how much this relationship between Aramis and a seamstress at Tours, who called the queen her sister, enlivened the young men; but Aramis, after having two or three times blushed up to the whites of his eyes at the coarse jokes of Porthos, had begged his friends not to revert to the subject, declaring that if another word were said about it, he would not again employ his cousin as an agent in affairs of the kind.

So nothing more about Marie Michon was said between the four musketeers, who had, moreover, obtained what they wanted—the order to withdraw Madame Bonancieux from the convent of Bethune. It is true that this order would be of no great advantage to them, whilst they continued in the camp at La Rochelle, that is to say, at the other extremity of France. D'Artagnan was about to ask leave of absence from M. de Treville, plainly confiding to him how important it was that he should depart; when the intelligence reached him, as well as his three companions, that the king was about to proceed to Paris with an escort of twenty musketeers, of which they were to form a part. Great was their joy. Their servants were sent forward with the baggage, and they themselves set out in the morning of the sixteenth.

The cardinal attended the king from Surgères to Mauzes, where the king and his minister took leave of each other with great professions of friendship. Nevertheless, the king, although he travelled very fast, since he wished to reach Paris by the twenty-third, was so anxious for amusement, that he halted from time to time to hunt the magpie—a pastime for which he had acquired a taste from de Luynes, the first husband of Madame de Chevreuse, and for which he had always preserved a great liking. Sixteen of the twenty musketeers much enjoyed this sport when it occurred; but four of them cursed it most heartily. D'Artagnan more especially had a perpetual humming in his ears; which Porthos thus explained—

'A woman of the highest rank assured me that it is a sign that some one is talking about you, somewhere.'

On the night of the twenty-third, the escort at length passed through Paris. The king thanked M. de Treville, and allowed him to grant four days' leave of absence to his men, on condition that not one of the favoured individuals should appear at any public place, under pain of the Bastile.

The first four leaves were granted, as may be imagined, to our four friends; and, more than that, Athos persuaded M. de Treville to extend it to six days instead of four, and managed to cram two more nights into these six days; for they set off on the twenty-fourth, at five o'clock in the evening, and M. de Treville had the complaisance to post-date the leave to the morning of the twenty-fifth.

'Oh, Mon Dieu!' said d'Artagnan, who, as we are well aware, never foresaw difficulty, 'it appears to me that we are making a great disturbance about a very simple matter. In two days, by foundering two or three horses, which I should not care about, since I have plenty of money, I could be at Bethune. I should then deliver the queen's letter to the abbess, and could bring back the dear treasure which I am seeking—not to Lorraine, not to Belgium, but to Paris, where she might be much more securely concealed, particularly whilst the cardinal remains at La Rochelle. Then, when the campaign is once ended, partly from the protection of her cousin and partly from what we have ourselves personally done for her, we shall obtain from the queen whatever we desire. Remain, therefore, here: do not fatigue yourselves uselessly. I and Planchet shall be quite sufficient for so simple an expedition.'

To this, Athos quietly replied—

'And we, also, have got some money; for I have not yet quite drunk the remains of the diamond, and Porthos and Aramis have not quite eaten them up. So we may as well founder four horses as one. But remember, d'Artagnan,' he added, in a voice so sad that his accent made the young man shudder—'remember that Bethune is a town where the cardinal has made an appointment with a woman, who, wherever she goes, brings misfortune with her. If you had only four men to deal with, d'Artagnan, I should let you go alone. But you have to deal with this woman, so let all four of us go; and God grant that, with our four valets, we may be in sufficient number.'

'You quite terrify me, Athos!' exclaimed d'Artagnan: 'what, then, do you dread?'

'Everything!' replied Athos.

D'Artagnan looked into the countenances of his companions, which like that of Athos, bore the impress of profound anxiety; and they continued their journey at the utmost speed of their horses, but without uttering another word.

On the evening of the twenty-sixth, as they were entering Arras, and just as d'Artagnan had dismounted at the tavern of the Golden Harrow, to drink a glass of wine, a cavalier came out of the yard of the change-house, where he had just changed his horse, and proceeded at full gallop on the road to Paris. At the moment that he issued from the great gate into the street, the wind opened the cloak in which he was wrapped, although it was the month of August, and lifted up his hat, which he caught and pushed violently down upon his forehead.

D'Artagnan, whose looks were fixed upon this man, turned very pale, and let fall his glass.

'What is the matter, sir?' cried Planchet. 'Oh! here, here. Make haste, gentlemen my master is ill!'

The three friends hastened in, and found d'Artagnan, who, instead of being ill, was running to his horse. They stopped him on the threshold of the door.

'Hollo! where the plague are you going in this manner?' cried Athos.

'It is he!' exclaimed d'Artagnan, pale with passion, and with the perspiration in beads on his brow—'it is he! let me get at him.'

'But who do you mean!' demanded Athos.

'He! that man!'

'What man?'

'That cursed man, my evil genius, whom I have always seen when I was threatened with some misfortune—he who accompanied that horrible woman, when I met her the first time—he whom I was seeking when I affronted our friend Athos—he whom I saw the very morning of the day when Madame Bonancieux was abducted—the Man of Meung, in fact! I saw him—it is he! I recognised him when the wind opened his cloak.'

'The devil!' said Athos, musing.

'To horse, gentlemen—to horse! Let us pursue him—we must catch him!'

'My dear fellow,' said Aramis, 'consider that he is going exactly the opposite road to ours; that he has a fresh horse, whilst our horses are done; and that, consequently, we should knock up our horses without even a chance of overtaking him.'

'Hollo, sir!' cried out a stable-boy, running after the stranger—'Hollo, sir! here is a paper which fell out of your hat. Hollo, sir! Hollo!'

'My friend,' said d'Artagnan, 'half a pistole for that paper?'

'Faith, sir, with the greatest pleasure: here it is.'

The stable-boy, delighted with the good day's work he had made of it, returned into the yard of the hotel, and d'Artagnan unfolded the paper.

'Well?' inquired his friends, listening.

'Only one word!' said d'Artagnan.

'Yes,' said Aramis, 'but that word is the name of a town.'

'*Armentières*,' read Porthos—'Armentières? I do not know the place.'

'And this name of a town is written in her hand,' said Athos.

'Come, come, let us take great care of this paper,' said d'Artagnan; 'perhaps I shall not have thrown away my half pistole. To horse, my friends—to horse!'

The four companions went off at a gallop. on the road to Bethune.

61

The Carmelite Convent of Bethune

GREAT criminals are endowed with a kind of predestination which enables them to surmount every obstacle, and to escape every danger, until the moment on which a wearied providence has fixed for the shipwreck of their unhallowed fortunes.

Thus was it with her ladyship. She passed between the cruisers of two nations, and landed at Boulogne without mishap.

When she disembarked at Portsmouth, her ladyship had been an Englishwoman, driven from Rochelle by the persecutions of France. When she came on shore at Boulogne, after a voyage of two days, she represented herself as a Frenchwoman, whom the English annoyed at Portsmouth, on account of the hatred which they entertained for France.

Her ladyship had, moreover, the best of pasports—beauty —aided by the liberality with which she scattered her pistoles. Freed from the customary formalities, by the affable smile and gallant manners of an old governor of the port, who kissed her hands, she only remained at Boulogne a sufficient time to put into the post a letter written in these terms:—

'*To his Eminence the Lord Cardinal Richelieu, at his camp before La Rochelle.*'

'My lord, your eminence may be assured that his grace the Duke of Buckingham will not set out for France.

LADY DE ****

'Boulogne, August 25th—Evening.

'P.S.—According to your eminence's desire, I am proceeding to the Carmelite convent, at Bethune, where I shall await your orders.'

573

In fact, her ladyship began her journey on the same night. Darkness overtook her, and she stopped, and slept at a tavern on the road; at five o'clock the next morning, she resumed her journey, and in three hours reached Bethune. She inquired her way to the convent of the Carmelites, and immediately entered it. The abbess came to meet her, and when her ladyship showed the cardinal's order, a chamber was immediately prepared for her, and breakfast served.

The scenes of the past had all faded from this woman's sight, and, with her eyes fixed upon the future, she only saw the high fortune which was reserved for her by that cardinal whom she had so well served, without his name being at all compromised by the bloody deed. The ever-changing passions which consumed her, gave to her life the appearance of the clouds which ascend into the sky, reflecting sometimes the azure tint, sometimes the lurid, and sometimes the blackness of the storm, yet leaving no traces but those of devastation and of death.

After breakfast, the abbess came to pay her a visit. There are but few amusements in the cloister, and the good superior was in haste to strike up acqaintance with her new boarder.

Her ladyship wished to please the abbess, and this was a very easy task for a woman so truly superior: she endeavoured to be amiable, and became charming; so that her entertainer was seduced by her varied conversation, as well as by the grades which appeared in all her person.

The abbess who was of a noble family, loved more especially that gossip of the court which so rarely reaches the extremities of the kingdom, and which has, especially, so much difficulty in passing through the walls of a convent, on whose threshold all worldly sounds should cease.

Her ladyship, however, was well versed in all the intrigues of the aristocracy, in whose midst she had constantly lived for five or six years; she therefore set about amusing the good abbess with an account of all the worldly practices of the French court, mixed up with the excessive devotions of the king. She gave her also the chronicle of scandals concerning those lords and ladies of the court, with whose names the abbess was familiar, and touched lightly on the amours of the queen and Buckingham—talking, herself, a great deal, that she might thus induce the abbess to talk a little.

But the abbess contented herself with listening, and

smiling, without replying. Nevertheless, as her ladyship perceived that these sort of stories amused her greatly, she continued them; only she diverted the conversation to the cardinal. On this point, however, she was slightly embarrassed, as she knew not whether the abbess was royalist or cardinalist. She therefore kept prudently to a middle path. The abbess, on her part, maintained a still more prudent reserve, contenting herself with making a profound inclination of the head as often as the traveller mentioned the cardinal's name.

Her ladyship soon began to think that she should find this convent very tiresome. She resolved, therefore, to hazard something, in order to know what course to steer. Wishing to ascertain how far the discretion of the abbess would extend, she began to speak unfavourably, at first by hints, and then most circumstantially, of the cardinal: relating the amours of that minister with Madame d'Aiguillon, Marion de Lorme, and some other women of gallantry.

The abbess listened more attentively, gradually became more animated, and smiled.

'Good,' thought her ladyship, 'she begins to relish my conversation. If she is a cardinalist, she is, at any rate, no very fanatical one.'

She then dwelt upon the persecution which the cardinal conducted against his enemies. The abbess merely crossed herself, without approving or blaming. This confirmed her ladyship in the belief that the good superior was more of a royalist than a cardinalist; so she continued her remarks, becoming more and more severe.

'I am very ignorant on all such matters,' said the abbess at last; 'but remote as we are from the court, secluded as we find ourselves from intercourse with the world, we have most melancholy proofs of the truth of what you have been just relating, and one of our boarders has suffered severely from the vengeance and persecutions of the cardinal.'

'One of your boarders?' said her ladyship. 'Oh! poor creature—how I pity her!'

'And you are right, for she is much to be pitied. Imprisonment, threats, ill-treatment—all these she has endured. But, after all,' continued the abbess, 'the cardinal had perhaps plausible reasons for acting thus; and, although she has the aspect of an angel, we must not always judge of people by their aspects.'

'Good!' said her ladyship to herself: 'who knows—I may perhaps make some discovery here. I am just in the humour for it.'

She then set herself to communicate to her countenance an expression of most perfect candour.

'Alas!' said she, 'I know that: they tell us that we must not trust physiognomies. But what can we trust to, if not to the most beautiful of the Lord's works? As for me, I shall probably be deceived throughout my whole life, for I always confide in that person whose face inspires me with sympathy.'

'You would be induced, then, to believe that this young woman was innocent?' said the abbess.

'The cardinal does not merely punish crimes,' replied her ladyship; 'there are certain virtues which he visits more severely than sins.'

'You will allow me, madam, to express my surprise,' said the abbess.

'At what?' asked her ladyship, with apparent simplicity.

'At the language which you use.'

'And what do you find astonishing in that language!' demanded her ladyship, with a smile.

'You are the cardinal's friend, since he has sent you here; and yet——'

'And yet I speak ill of him', replied her ladyship, expressing the abbess's thought.

'At least, you do not speak much good of him.'

'It is because I am not his friend, but his victim,' said her ladyship, sighing.

'And yet that letter, by which he has recommended you to me——'

'Is an order to me to keep myself in a sort of prison, from which he will remove me through some of his satellites.'

'But why did you not escape?'

'Where should I go? Do you believe that there is a spot upon the earth which the cardinal cannot reach, if he pleases to take the trouble to stretch out his hand? If I were a man, it might, perchance, be possible; but being a woman —what would you have a woman do? This young boarder of yours—has she attempted to escape?'

'No, truly: but her case is different. I fancy that she is kept in France by some love affair.'

'Then,' said her ladyship, with a sigh, 'loving, she is not altogether unhappy.'

'So,' said the abbess, looking with increasing interest at

her ladyship, 'it is another poor persecuted creature that I see?'

'Alas! yes,' said her ladyship.

The abbess looked at her ladyship for an instant with some inquietude, as if a new thought were just arising in her mind.

'You are not an enemy of our most holy faith?' said she, stammering.

'I!' cried her ladyship. 'I a Protestant? Oh, no! I call the God who now hears us to witness that I am, indeed, a zealous Catholic.'

'Then, madam,' replied the abbess, smiling, 'be of good cheer: the house in which you are shall not be a very severe prison to you, and we will do all we can to soften your captivity. Moreover, you shall see that young woman, who is, no doubt, persecuted on account of some court intrigue; she is so amiable, and so gracious, that she is sure to please you.'

'What is her name?'

'She has been recommended to me, under the name of Kitty, by a person of the highest rank. I have not endeavoured to find out her second name.'

'Kitty!' exclaimed her ladyship, 'are you quite sure?'

'Yes, madam; at least so she calls herself. Do you suppose you know her?'

Her ladyship smiled as the idea suggested itself to her that this female might possibly be her former attendant. With her recollection of the young woman, there was associated a sentiment of anger, and a desire for revenge, which somewhat disturbed the serenity of her ladyship's features; but they soon resumed that expression of calmness and benevolence which this woman with a hundred faces had for the time adopted.

'But when may I see this young lady, for whom I already feel so great a sympathy?' demanded her ladyship.

'This evening,' replied the abbess; 'nay, even today. But as you say you have been travelling for four days, and arose this morning at five o'clock, you must now be in want of rest: lie down, therefore, and sleep; and we will awake you at dinner-time.'

Although her ladyship could have very well dispensed with sleep supported as she was by the excitement which a new adventure kindled in her heart, so eager after intrigues, she nevertheless accepted the offer of the abbess. During the previous twelve or fourteen days, she had experienced so many different emotions, that though her iron constitution was still able to endure fatigue, her mind required some repose. She therefore took leave of the abbess. and lay down in peace, comforted by the ideas of vengeance to which the name of Kitty had so naturally led her. She remembered the almost unlimited promise which the cardinal had made to her, on condition of the success of her enterprise. She *had* succeeded; and she might, therefore, avenge herself on d'Artagnan.

One thing alone alarmed her ladyship, and that was the recollection of her husband, the Count de la Fère, whom she had believed to be dead, or, at least, expatriated, and whom she now found in Athos, the dearest friend of d'Artagnan. But, if he was d'Artagnan's friend, he must have assisted him in all those plots, by the aid of which the queen hath thwarted the designs of his eminence; if he was d'Artagnan's friend, he must be the cardinal's enemy, and she should undoubtedly be able to envelop him in that vengeance, in the folds of which she hoped to stifle the young musketeer.

All these hopes formed agreeable thoughts to her ladyship, and, lulled by them, she soon slept. She was awakened by a soft voice, which sounded at the foot of her bed. On opening her eyes, she saw the abbess, accompanied by a young woman with fair hair, and a delicate complexion, who fixed on her a look full of kindly curiosity. The countenance of this young woman was entirely unknown to her. As they exchanged the usual courtesies, they examined each other with scrupulous attention. Both were very beautiful, yet quite unlike each other in their kinds of beauty; and her ladyship smiled on observing that she had herself much more of a high-bred air and aristocratic manners. It is true that the dress of a novice, which the young woman wore, was not very favourable to success in a competition of the sort.

The abbess presented them to one another; and then, as her own duties demanded her attendance in the chapel, she left them alone together. The novice, seeing her ladyship in bed, would have followed the abbess; but her ladyship detained her.

'What, madam,' said she, 'I have scarcely seen you, and you already wish to deprive me of your company, which I have hoped to enjoy during the time that I may remain here?'

'No, madam,' replied the novice, 'but as you are fatigued, I feared that my visit had been badly timed.'

'Well!' said her ladyship, 'what should those who sleep

desire! A pleasant awakening. That is just what you have given me; so let me enjoy it at my ease!'

And, taking her hand, she drew her to a chair near the bed.

'Mon Dieu!' said the novice, seating herself, 'how unfortunate I am. Here have I been in this house for six months, without even the shadow of an amusement. You arrive: your presence would provide me with most charming company; and now, according to all probability, I shall immediately leave the convent.'

'What,' said her ladyship, 'are you going away soon?'

'At least I hope so,' replied the novice, with an expression of joy which she did not in the least attempt to disguise.

'I think I heard that you had suffered from the persecutions of the cardinal,' said her ladyship. That is another bond of sympathy between us.'

'What our good mother has told me is true then, and you are also one of the cardinal's victims?'

'Hush!' said her ladyship; 'even here do not let us speak of him. All my misfortunes have arisen from having spoken scarcely more than you have just said, before a woman whom I thought my friend, and who betrayed me. And are you, also, the victim of treachery?'

'No,' said the novice, 'but of my devotion to a woman whom I loved, for whom I would have died and for whom I would die now.'

'And who deserted you in your distress? I know she did!'

'I was unjust enough to believe so; but within the last two or three days I have had proof to the contrary, and I thank God for it: I should have deeply grieved at the conviction that she had forgotten me. But you, madam—you seem to be free, and able to escape, if you should have any inclination to do so.'

'And where could I go, without friends, without money, in a part of France which I do not know, where——'

'Oh! as to friends,' said the novice, 'you will find them wherever you please: you look so good, and you are so beautiful.'

'That is no reason,' said her ladyship, softening her smile so as to give to it an angelical expression, 'why I should not be foresaken and persecuted.'

'Listen,' said the novice; 'you must trust in Heaven: there always comes a moment when the good that we have done pleads for us before God's throne. Besides, it is perhaps a piece of good fortune for you, that—humble and powerless as I am—you should have met me here; for if I should get away, I have some influential friends, who, having exerted themselves for me, may do the same for you.'

'Oh! when I say that I was solitary and forsaken,' said her ladyship, hoping to make the novice speak more plainly by speaking herself: 'it is not that I have not some lofty acquaintances also; but these acquaintances all tremble before the cardinal. The queen herself does not defend me against this terrible minister; and I have proofs that her majesty, in spite of her excellent heart, has been more than once obliged to abandon, to his eminence's rage, persons who had faithfully served her.'

'Believe me, madam, it may have appeared that the queen forsook her friends: but we must not believe the appearance: the more they are persecuted, the more she thinks of them; and, often at the very moment when they suppose her the least mindful of them, they receive an evidence of her kind remembrance.'

'Alas!' said her ladyship, 'I believe it: the queen is so good!'

'Oh! you know her, then—this beautiful and noble queen —since you speak of her thus!' exclaimed the novice enthusiastically.

'That is to say,' replied her ladyship, rather forced back into her intrenchments, 'I have not the honour of knowing her personally, but I do know many of her most intimate friends. I know M. de Putange; I knew M. Dujart in England; and I know M. de Treville.'

'M. de Treville!' exclaimed the novice; 'do you know M. de Treville?'

'Yes, intimately.'

'The captain of the king's musketeers?'

'Yes, the captain of the king's musketeers!'

'Oh! then you will see presently, that we must be acquaintances—almost friends. If you know M. de Treville, you must have been at his house?'

'Often,' said her ladyship, who, having entered on this path, and finding falsehood profitable, determined to pursue it to the end.

'At his house you must have seen some of his musketeers?'

'All of them whom he is in the habit of receiving,' replied her ladyship, who began to take a real interest in the conversation.

'Name some of those that you know,' said the novice, 'and you will see that they are amongst my friends.'

'Why,' said her ladyship, somewhat confused, 'I know M. de Louvigny, M. de Courtivron, M. de Ferusac.'

The novice let her go on, but, seeing her pause, said—'Do you not know a gentleman named Athos?'

Her ladyship became as pale as the sheets on which she was reclining, and, mistress as she was of her emotions, she could not help uttering a cry, as she seized the hand of the novice, and fastened her gaze upon her.

'Ah! what is the matter with you? Oh! Mon Dieu!' said the poor young woman, 'have I said anything to offend you?'

'No, but I was struck by the name; for I have been acquainted with this gentleman, also; and it seemed strange that I should meet with any one who knew him well.'

'Oh, yes, very well; and his friends, also, M. Porthos, and M. Aramis.'

'Really? And I know them, too,' exclaimed her ladyship, who felt a cold shudder penetrating to her heart.

'Well, if you are acquainted with them, you ought to know that they are good and brave companions. Why do you not apply to them, if you want protection?'

'That is to say,' stammered her ladyship, 'I am not very intimate with any one of them. I know them from having heard them spoken of by one of their friends, M.d'Artagnan.'

'You know M. d'Artagnan!' exclaimed the novice, in turn, seizing her ladyship's hand, and devouring her with her looks. Then remarking the strange expression of her ladyship's countenance—'Pardon me, madam: you know him, but in what character?'

'Why,' replied her ladyship, in some embarrassment, 'in the character of a friend.'

'You deceive me, madam,' said the novice; 'you have been his mistress.'

'It is you who have been that,' said her ladyship, in turn.

'I—I!' said the novice.

'Yes, you:—I know you now—you are Madame Bonancieux.'

The young woman drew herself back, overwhelmed with astonishment and terror. 'Oh! do not deny it; but pray answer,' said her ladyship.

'Well! yes, madam, I love him,' said the novice. 'Are we rivals?'

Her ladyship's face was irradiated by a light so wild, that, under any other circumstances, Madame Bonancieux would have fled from her in terror; but she was not entirely absorbed by jealousy.

'Come, tell me, madame,' said Madame Bonancieux, with an energy of which she would have been thought incapable, 'have you been his mistress?'

'Oh, no!' exclaimed her ladyship, in a tone which prohibited any doubt of her honesty; 'never! never!'

'I believe you,' said Madame Bonancieux; 'but why did you cry out so?'

'What, do you not understand?' said her ladyship, who had already recovered from her confusion, and had resumed all her presence of mind.

'How should I understand? I know nothing——'

'Do you not understand that M. d'Artagnan, being my friend, made me his confidante?'

'Really!'

'Do you not understand that I am acquainted with everything that has taken place: your abduction from the little house at St. Germain, his despair, that of his friends, and their researches ever since that time? Is it strange for me to be astonished on finding myself, without being aware of it, by the side of you, of whom we have so often talked together—of you, whom he loves with all the strength of his soul—of you, whom he made me love before I beheld you! Ah, dear Constance, I find you at last—at last I see you!'

Her ladyship held out her arms towards Madame Bonancieux, who, convinced by what she had just heard, now saw in this woman, whom she had an instant before regarded as a rival, only a sincere and a devoted friend.

'Oh, pardon me, pardon me!' said she, allowing herself to sink upon her ladyship's shoulder, 'I love him so much!'

These two women held each other for an instant thus embraced. Certainly, if her ladyship's strength had been but equal to her hatred, Madame Bonancieux would not have left her arms alive. But, not being able to stifle her, she smiled.

'Oh, dear little pretty thing!' said her ladyship, 'how delighted I am to see you! Let me look at you!' And, as she uttered these words, she did in fact devour her with her looks. 'Yes, it is certainly you. Ah! after what he told me of you, I recognise you now—I recognise you perfectly well.'

The poor young woman could not suspect the horrid cruelty that was raging behind the ramparts of that unruffled brow, or behind those eyes in which she only read the interest of compassion.

'Then you know what I have suffered,' said Madame Bonancieux, 'since he has told you what he himself endured. But to suffer for him is a joy.'

Her ladyship replied mechanically—'Yes, it is a joy.' But she was thinking of something else.

'And then,' continued Madame Bonancieux, 'my punishment draws near its end. To-morrow—this very evening, perhaps—I shall see him once more; and then the past will be forgotten.'

'This evening? To-morrow?' exclaimed her ladyship, aroused from her reverie by these words: 'what can you mean? Do you expect to hear anything of him?'

'I expect him—himself.'

'Himself? D'Artagnan here?'

'Yes, himself.'

'But it is impossible! He is at the siege of La Rochelle, with the cardinal; he will not return to Paris until after the town is taken.'

'You think so; but is there anything impossible to my d'Artagnan, the noble and loyal gentleman?'

'Oh, I cannot believe you!'

'Well, then, read!' said this unfortunate young woman in the excess of her pride and joy, showing a letter to her ladyship.

'The writing of Madame de Chevreuse,' said her ladyship to herself. 'Ah! I was quite sure that there were some communications in that quarter.' And she eagerly read these lines:—

'My dear child, be ready. *Our friend* will soon see you, and he will only come to snatch you from the prison where it was necessary for your own safety to conceal you. So prepare for your departure, and never despair of us. Our brave Gascon has just shown himself as brave and as faithful as ever: tell him that there is much gratitude to him in a certain quarter for the warning which he gave.'

'Yes, yes,' said her ladyship, 'the letter is very precise. And do you know what this warning was?'

'No: I only suspect that he must have warned the queen of some new machination of the cardinal.'

'Yes, that is it, beyond a doubt,' said her ladyship, returning the letter, and letting her head fall pensively on her breast.

At that moment the gallop of a horse was heard.

'Oh!' exclaimed Madame Bonancieux, rushing to the window, 'can this be he?'

Her ladyship remained in her bed, petrified by the surprise. So many unexpected things had suddenly happened to her, that, for the first time, her head failed her.

'He! he!' muttered she, 'and if it should be?' And she continued in bed, with her eyes fixed on vacancy.

'Alas! no,' said Madame Bonancieux. 'It is a man whom I do not know. But he seems to be coming here. Yes, he is riding more slowly; he stops at the gate; he rings.'

Her ladyship sprang out of the bed. 'You are quite sure that it is not he?'

'Oh! yes, certain.'

'Perhaps you do not see him distinctly.'

'Oh! should I see only the plume in his hat, or the skirt of his cloak, I should not fail to recognise him!'

Her ladyship was dressing all the time.—'No matter; the man is coming here, you say?'

'Yes, he has come in.'

'It must be either for you or for me.'

'Oh, Mon Dieu! how agitated you are!'

'Yes; I confess that I have not your confidence; I dread everything from the cardinal.'

'Hush!' said Madame Bonancieux; 'someone is coming.' The door opened, and the abbess entered.

'Did you come from Boulogne?' demanded she, of her ladyship.

'Yes, madam,' replied the latter, endeavouring to resume her composure: 'who wants me?'

'A man, who will not give his name, but who comes from the cardinal.'

'And who wants to speaks to me?' demanded her ladyship.

'Who wants to speak with a lady who has just arrived from Boulogne.'

'Then show him in, madam, I beg of you.'

'Oh! my God! my God!' said Madame Bonancieux, 'can it be any bad news?'

'I fear so.'

'I leave you with this stranger; but, as soon as he shall have gone, I will return, if you will allow me.'

'Yes; I beseech you to do so!'

The abbess and Madame Bonancieux left the room. Her

ladyship remained alone, with her eyes fixed upon the door. A moment afterwards, the jingling sound of spurs was heard on the stairs; then, the steps came nearer; then the door was opened, and a man appeared. Her ladyship uttered a cry of joy. This man was the Count de Rochefort, the familiar of his eminence.

62

Two Kinds of Demons

'Ah!' exclaimed both Rochefort and her ladyship at the same instant, 'it is you!'

'Yes, it is I.'

'And you come from——' demanded her ladyship.

'From La Rochelle. And you?'

'From England.'

'And Buckingham——'

'Is dead, or dangerously wounded. As I was leaving, without having obtained anything from him, a fanatic had just assassinated him.'

'Ah!' said Rochefort, smiling, 'that was a very fortunate chance, which will please his eminence much. Have you informed him of it?'

'I wrote to him from Boulogne. But what brings you here?'

'His eminence, being uneasy, has sent me to look for you.'

'I only arrived yesterday.'

'And what have you been doing since?'

'I have not been wasting my time.'

'Oh! I do not doubt you.'

'Do you know whom I have met with here?'

'No.'

'Guess.'

'How can I?'

'That young woman whom the queen took from prison.'

'What! the mistress of young d'Artagnan?'

'Yes, Madame Bonancieux, whose refuge the cardinal could not discover.'

'Well, then,' said Rochefort, 'this is a chance quite fit to pair with the other. Verily, the cardinal is a fortunate man.'

'Fancy my astonishment,' continued her ladyship, 'when I found myself face to face with this woman.'

'Does she know you?'

'No.'

'Then she looks upon you as a stranger?'

Her ladyship smiled. 'I am her dearest friend.'

'Upon my honour,' said Rochefort, 'my dear countess, it is only you who can perform this sort of miracles.'

'And well it is that I can, chevalier,' said her ladyship, 'for do you know what is about to happen?'

'No.'

'They are coming for her to-morrow, or the next day, with an order from the queen.'

'Really! And who do you mean by they?'

'D'Artagnan and his friends.'

'Verily, they will go such a length that we shall be obliged to put them into the Bastile.'

'And why has it not been done already?'

'How can I tell? Because the cardinal evinces a weakness toward these men which I cannot comprehend.'

'Really! Well, then, tell him this, Rochefort: tell him that our conversation at the Red Dove-Cot was overheard by these four men—tell him that, after his departure, one of them came up and took from me by force the passport he had given me—tell him that they gave Lord de Winter notice of my voyage to England—that, this time again, they nearly prevented the success of my undertaking, as they did in the affair of the diamond studs—tell him that amongst these four men, only two are to be feared, d'Artagnan and Athos—tell him that the third, Aramis, is the lover of Madame de Chevreuse: he must be allowed to live, for his secret is known, and he may be made useful; and as for the fourth, Porthos, he is a fool, a fop, a ninny, not worth giving one's self the smallest trouble about.'

'But these four men ought to be, at this moment, at the siege of La Rochelle.'

'I thought so too; but a letter which Madame Bonancieux has received from Madame de Chevreuse, and which she had the imprudence to communicate to me, leads me to believe that these four men are now on their way to abduct her.'

'The devil! What must we do?'

'What did the cardinal say to you about me?'

'That I was to take your despatches, whether verbal or written, and to return by post. When he knows what you have done, he will give you further directions.'

'I must remain here, then?'

'Here, or in the neighbourhood.'

'You cannot take me with you?'

'No, the order is explicit. In the environs of the camp you might be recognised; and you can understand that your presence might compromise his eminence, especially after what has just happened in England. Only tell me beforehand where you will await the cardinal's orders, that I may know where to find you.'

'Listen; it is **very** probable that I cannot remain here.'

'Why?'

'You forget that my enemies may arrive at any moment.'

'True. But then this little woman will escape his eminence.'

'Bah!' said her ladyship, with a smile peculiar to herself, 'you forget that I am her best friend.'

'Ah! there is something in that. Then I may tell the cardinal, with regard to this woman——'

'That he may make himself easy.'

'Is that all? Will he know what that means?'

'He will guess it.'

'And now, let us see, what ought I to do?'

'You must set off this instant. It appears to me that the news you carry is well worth the trouble of a little haste.'

'My carriage broke down on entering Lilliers.'

'Excellent.'

'What do you mean by *excellent?*'

'Why, that I want your carriage.'

'And how am I to travel, then?'

'On post-horses.'

'You talk of it very unconcernedly; a hundred and eighty leagues.'

'What do they signify?'

'Well, it shall be done. What next?'

'On passing through Lilliers you will send your carriage to me, with directions to your lackey to attend to my commands.'

'Very well!'

'You have, no doubt, some order from the cardinal in your possession.'

'Yes, I have my full powers.'

'You will show that to the abbess, and you will tell her that I shall be sent for either to-day or to-morrow, and that I must accompany the person sent in your name.'

'Very well!'

'Do not forget to speak harshly of me, when you talk to the abbess.'

'Why so?'

'I am one of the cardinal's victims. I must inspire some confidence in that poor little Madame Bonancieux.'

'Right. And now will you make me a report of all that has occurred?'

'I have already told you the events, and you have a good memory; so repeat what I have told you. A paper may be lost.'

'You are right; only let me know where you are to be found, that I may not have to run about the country in vain.'

'Ah! there is something in that. Wait.'

'Do you require a map?'

'Oh, I know this country well.'

'You? When did you ever visit it?'

'I was brought up here.'

'Indeed!'

'It is some advantage, you see, to have been brought up somewhere.'

'You will wait for me, then—?'

'Let me consider a moment—ah! yes, at Armentières.'

'And where is Armentières?'

'It is a little village, on the Lys. I shall only have to cross the river, and I shall be in another country.'

'Capital; but you must remember that you are only to cross the river in case of danger.'

'That is understood.'

'And, in that case, how shall I discover where you are?'

'You do not want your servant? Is he one on whom you can depend?'

'Entirely!'

'Give him to me: no one knows him. I will leave him at the place I quit, and he will conduct you to me.'

'And you say that you will wait for me at Armentières?'

'Yes. At Armentières!'

'Write the name for me on a slip of paper, lest I should forget it. The name of a village will not compromise any one, will it?'

'Ah! who knows? But never mind,' said her ladyship, writing the name on a half sheet of paper, 'I will run the hazard.'

'Good,' said Rochefort, taking from her ladyship's hands the paper, which he folded, and stuffed into the lining of his hat. 'And I shall, besides, do like the children, and, as a safeguard against the loss of the paper, I shall repeat the name all the way I go. Now, is that all?'

'I think so.'

'Let us see:—Buckingham dead, or grievously wounded —your conversation with the cardinal, overheard by the musketeers—Lord de Winter warned of your arrival at Portsmouth—d'Artagnan and Athos to the Bastile—Aramis, the lover of Madame de Chevreuse—Porthos a fool— Madame Bonancieux discovered—to send you the carriage as soon as possible— to put my lackey under your orders— to make you out a victim of the cardinal, that the abbess may have no suspicion—Armentières, on the banks of the Lys: is that right?'

'Verily, my dear chevalier, you are a miracle of memory. But, by the way, add one thing.'

'And what is that?'

'I saw some very pretty woods, which must join the gardens of the convent. Say that I may be allowed to walk in these woods. Who knows?—I may perhaps be obliged to escape by some back door.'

'You think of everything.'

'And you forget one thing.'

'What is that?'

'To ask me whether I want any money.'

'Exactly; how much will you have?'

'All the gold you may have about you.'

'I have nearly five hundred pistoles.'

'I have about as many. With a thousand pistoles, one may face anything. Empty your pockets.'

'There.'

'Excellent: And when do you set off?'

'In one hour: just time enough to eat a morsel, whilst I send to fetch a post-horse.'

'Excellent. Adieu, count.'

'Adieu, countess.'

'My compliments to the cardinal.'

'My compliments to Satan!'

Her ladyship and Rochefort exchanged smiles, and separated.

In an hour afterwards, Rochefort set out at full speed; and five hours afterwards, he passed through Arras. Our readers already know how he was recognised by d'Artagnan, and how that recognition, by exciting the fears of our four musketeers, had given a new activity to their journey.

63

A Drop of Water

SCARCELY had Rochefort left, before Madame Bonancieux returned. She found her ladyship with a smiling countenance.

'Well,' said the young woman, 'what you feared has happened. This evening, or to-morrow, the cardinal will send for you.'

'How do you know that?' asked her ladyship.

'I heard it from the lips of the messenger himself.'

'Come and sit down by me,' said her ladyship; 'but first let me be sure that no one overhears us.'

'And why all these precautions?'

'You will soon know.'

Her ladyship arose, went to the door, opened it, looked along the corridor, and then came back, and seated herself again by the side of Madame Bonancieux.

'Then,' said she again, 'he played his part well.'

'Who did?'

'He who introduced himself to the abbess as the envoy of the cardinal.'

'Was it, then, a part that he was playing?'

'Yes, my child.'

'Then that man is not——'

'That man,' said her ladyship, dropping her voice, 'is my brother.'

'Your brother?' exclaimed Madame Bonancieux.

'Nobody but you knows this secret, my child; if you should entrust it to anybody in the world, I should be ruined and you also, perhaps.'

'Oh, mon Dieu!'

'Listen: this is what has taken place. My brother, who was coming to my aid, to take me away from here, by force if necessary, met the cardinal's emissary, who was on his way to fetch me. He followed me. On arriving at a retired and solitary spot, he drew his sword, and commanded the messenger to deliver to him the papers which he carried. The messenger endeavoured to defend himself, and my brother slew him.'

'Oh!' said Madame Bonancieux, shuddering.

'There was no alternative, remember. My brother then determined to make use of craft instead of force. He took the papers, presented himself here as the emissary of the cardinal himself, and, in an hour or two, a carriage will come to take me away in his eminence's name.'

'I understand: it is your brother who will send this carriage.'

'Of course. But that is not all: that letter which you have received, and which you believe to be from Madame de Chevreuse——'

'Well?'

'Is a forgery.'

'What?'

'Yes, a forgery: it is a snare, that you may make no resistance when they come to fetch you.'

'But it is d'Artagnan who will come.'

'Undeceive yourself: d'Artagnan and his friends are at the siege of La Rochelle.'

'How do you know that?'

'My brother met with some of the cardinal's agents, disguised in the uniform of musketeers. They were to call you out to the gate; you would have believed that you were in the company of friends; and they were to carry you off and convey you to Paris.'

'Oh! my God! my head fails in the midst of such a chaos of iniquities. I feel that if it lasts long,' said Madame Bonancieux, putting her hands to her head, 'I shall go mad.'

'Listen: I hear the step of a horse: it is that of my brother, who is going away. I must take a last farewell of him. Come.'

Her ladyship opened the window, and made a sign to Madame Bonancieux to join her. The young woman joined her; and Rochefort passed by at a gallop.

'Good-bye, brother!' said her ladyship.

The chevalier raised his head, saw the two young women, and, as he went rapidly past, made a friendly farewell salute with his hand.

'That kind George!' said she, closing the window, with an expression of countenance full of affection and melancholy.

She then returned, and sat down in her place, as though plunged in reflections of a personal kind.

'Dear lady!' said Madame Bonancieux, 'pardon me for interrupting you; but what do you advise me to do? You have more experience than I have: speak, and I will listen.'

'In the first place,' said her ladyship. 'I might possibly

be deceived, and d'Artagnan and his friends may really be coming to your assistance.'

'Oh! that would be too fortunate,' said Madame Bonancieux, 'and I fear that so much happiness is not reserved for me.'

'Then, do you see, it would be merely a question of time, a kind of race, as to which would arrive first. If it should be your friends who made best haste, why, then, you would be saved; but, if it were the cardinal's satellites, then you would be ruined.'

'Oh! yes, yes! ruined without mercy. But what must I do—what must I do?'

'There is one very simple and very natural plan.'

'And what is that? Tell me?'

'It would be to wait, concealed in the neighbourhood; and so to make yourself sure who the men were who came to seek you.'

'But where can I wait?'

'Oh! that is not a matter of difficulty. I, myself, must wait, and conceal myself at a few leagues' distance from here, until my brother comes to meet me. Well, then, I will take you with me—we will hide and wait together.'

'But I shall not be allowed to leave this place: I am almost regarded as a prisoner here.'

'As it is supposed that I leave on account of an order from the cardinal, it will not be believed that you are very anxious to follow me.'

'Well?'

'Very well. The carriage being at the door, you will bid me adieu, and you will get upon the steps to embrace me for the last time. My brother's servant, who is coming to fetch me, being forewarned, will give a signal to the postillion, and we shall set off at full gallop.'

'But d'Artagnan—if he should come?'

'Shall we not know it?'

'How?'

'Nothing is more easy. We will send this servant of my brother's, in whom I have told you that I have the greatest confidence, back to Bethune; and he shall disguise himself, and find a lodging opposite the convent. If it should be the cardinal's emissaries who come, he will not stir; if it should be M. d'Artagnan and his friends, he will lead them to where we are.'

'He knows them, then?'

'Certainly; has he not seen M. d'Artagnan at my house?'

'Oh! yes, yes, you are right. Thus, all will go on well. But do not let us go too far away from here.'

'Seven or eight leagues at the most. We will keep upon the frontiers, and, upon the first alarm, quit France.'

'What must we do in the meantime?'

'Wait,'

'But if they should come?'

'My brother's carriage will arrive before them.'

'Suppose I should be away from you when it arrives—at dinner, or at supper, for example?'

'Tell our good abbess, that, in order that we may be as little apart as possible, you request her to allow you to take your meals with me.'

'Will she permit it?'

'What objection can there be to it? Go down now to her, and make your request. I feel my head a little heavy, and so I shall take a turn in the garden.'

'And where may I see you again?'

'Here in one hour from this time.'

'Here, in one hour! Oh! you are very kind, and I thank you.'

'How should I avoid being interested in you? Even if you had not been beautiful and charming, are you not the friend of one of my best friends?'

'Dear d'Artagnan! Oh, how he will thank you!'

'I hope so. Come, it is all arranged: let us go down.'

'You are going to the garden? Proceed along this corridor: a little staircase leads you to it.'

'Good. Thank you.'

And the two ladies separated, exchanging charming smiles.

Her ladyship had spoken the truth; her head was heavy, for her projects, badly arranged, clashed against each other as in chaos. She had need to be alone that she might put a little order into her ideas. She saw dimly into the future; but it required some moments of silence and tranquillity to give to this confused assemblage of conceptions a definite form, and a decided plan. What was now most urgent was, to carry off Madame Bonancieux, and put her in a place of security; and then, should her game fail, to use her as a hostage. Her ladyship began to dread the issue of this terrible duel, in which her enemies were quite as persevering as she herself was unrelenting. Besides, she felt, as one feels the approach of a storm, that the issue was near, and would not fail to be fearful.

The principal point for her was, as we have said, to get possession of Madame Bonancieux. By this means she would hold in her hands the life of d'Artagnan; or more even than his life, for she would hold that of the woman he loved. In case of unprosperous fortune, it was a means of opening negotiations, and of securing favourable terms.

Now, it was certain that Madame Bonancieux would follow her without distrust; and let Madame Bonancieux be but once concealed with her at Armentières, it would be easy to make her believe that d'Artagnan had never visited Bethune. In a fortnight, at most, Rochefort would return. During that time she would meditate on what she must do to avenge herself on the four friends. She should not be impatient: for she should have the sweetest occupation that events can ever give to a woman of her character—a hearty vengeance to complete!

Whilst thus meditating, she cast her eyes around her, and mapped out in her mind the topography of the garden. Her ladyship was like a good general, who foresees at the same time both victory and defeat, and who is quite ready, according to the chances of the battle, either to advance or to retire.

At the expiration of an hour, she heard a soft voice calling her. It was that of Madame Bonancieux. The good abbess had concented to everything, and, to begin, they were just about to sup together. On entering the court, they heard the sound of a carriage, which was stopping at the gate. Her ladyship listened.

'Do you hear?' said she.

'Yes; the rolling of a carriage.'

'It is that which my brother sends for us.'

'Oh! mon Dieu!'

'Come, have courage!'

There was a ring at the convent gate. Her ladyship was not mistaken.

'Go up into your room,' said she to Madame Bonancieux; 'you must have some trinkets that you would like to carry with you.'

'I have d'Artagnan's letters,' replied she.

'Well! go for them, and come back to me in my room. We will sup hastily; for, as we shall perhaps have to travel a part of the night, we must recruit our strength.'

'Great God!' said Madame Bonancieux, placing her hands upon her heart; 'I am choking—I cannot walk.'

'Courage—come, take courage! Think that in a quarter of an hour you will be safe, and think that what you are about to do is done for his sake.'

'Oh, yes—all, all for him! You have restored my courage by that single word. Go; I will rejoin you.'

Her ladyship went hastily up to her own room, where she found Rochefort's valet, and gave him his instructions. He was to wait for her at the gate: if, by chance, the musketeers should arrive, he was to go off at a gallop, make the circuit of the convent, and wait for her at a little village, which was situated on the other side of the wood. In that case, her ladyship would walk through the garden, and reach the village on foot: we have already said that she was perfectly well acquainted with this part of France. If the musketeers should not make their appearance, everything would be conducted as had been previously arranged. Madame Bonancieux was to get into the carriage, on the pretext of wishing her, once more, adieu, and she would then escape with her.

Madame Bonancieux came in; and, to remove all suspicion if she had any, her ladyship repeated to the valet, in her presence, the latter part of his instructions. Her ladyship then made some inquiries about the carriage: it was a chaise, drawn by three horses, and driven by a postillion. The valet was to precede it as a courier.

Her ladyship was altogether wrong in fearing that suspicion troubled Madame Bonancieux. The poor young woman was too honest herself to suspect another of so black a perfidy. Besides, the name of Lady de Winter, which she had heard mentioned by the abbess, was entirely unknown to her; and she had not imagined that a woman had performed so large and fatal a part in bringing about the misfortunes of her life.

'You see,' said her ladyship, when the valet had left the room, 'that everything is ready. The abbess has not the slightest suspicion, and fully believes that I am sent for by the cardinal. The man has gone out to give his final orders: eat something, however little; drink a thimbleful of wine; and let us be off.'

'Yes,' said Madame Bonancieux mechanically, 'yes, let us be off.'

Her ladyship made her a sign to sit down—poured out for her a small glass of Spanish wine, and helped her to a part of the breast of a chicken.

-There,' said she, 'everything is propitious: here is the night approaching; at daybreak we shall have reached his retreat, and no one will suspect where we are. Come, have courage, and take something.'

Madame Bonancieux ate two or three mouthfuls, mechanically, and just put her lips to the wine.

'Come, come,' said her ladyship, lifting her own glass towards her mouth, 'do as I do.'

But, at the moment she was about to drink, her hand was suddenly arrested. Her ears caught the distant sound of an approaching gallop on the road; and then, almost at the same instant, she seemed to hear the neighing of horses. This sound destroyed her exultation, as the uproar of a storm awakens us from a delightful dream. She grew pale, and ran to the window; whilst Madame Bonancieux, who had got up, trembled so as to be obliged to support herself with a chair for fear of falling. Nothing had become yet visible, but the galloping was more distinctly heard.

'Oh, my God!' said Madame Bonancieux, 'what can that noise be?'

'That of our friends or our enemies,' said her ladyship, with a terrible composure. 'Remain where you are, and I will go and ascertain.'

Madame Bonancieux remained standing, mute, motionless, and pale as a statue. The sound became more audible. The horses could not be more than a hundred and fifty yards off, but were not yet visible, on account of a turning in the road. Still the noise was now so distinct, that the number of the horses might have been counted by the clattering of their iron hoofs.

Her ladyship gazed with the most intense attention: there was just light enough to recognise those who were approaching.

Suddenly, at the turn of the road, she saw the glitter oi laced hats, and the waving of plumes; she counted two, then five, then eight horsemen. One of them was two lengths in advance of his companions. Her ladyship gave utterance to a howl. In the foremost rider she recognised d'Artagnan.

'Oh, mon Dieu! mon Dieu!' exclaimed Madame Bonancieux, what is the matter?'

'It is the uniform of the cardinal's guards: there is not a moment to be lost,' exclaimed her ladyship. 'Let us fly! let us fly!'

'Yes, yes, let us fly,' repeated Madame Bonancieux, but without the power of moving one step, rooted as she was to her place by terror.

The horsemen were heard passing under the window.

'Come along! come along!' said her ladyship, endeavouring to drag the young woman by the arm. 'Thanks to the garden, we may yet escape, for I have got the key. But let us make haste: in less than five minutes it will be too late!'

Madame Bonancieux attempted to walk, but, after taking two steps, fell upon her knees.

Her ladyship attempted to lift her up and carry her, but she found herself unable. At this moment they heard the wheels of the carriage, which, on the appearance of the musketeers, went off at a gallop; and then three or four shots resounded.

'For the last time, will you come?' exclaimed her ladyship.

'Oh! my God! my God! you see that my strength is all gone: you see that I cannot walk! Fly, and save yourself.'

'Fly alone! Leave you here! No, no—never!' exclaimed her ladyship.

Suddenly a livid lightning flashed from her eyes: she ran to the table, and poured into Madame Bonancieux's glass the contents of the hollow part of a ring, which she opened with singular dexterity. It was a red particle, which was immediately dissolved. Then, taking the glass, with a firm hand—

'Drink,' said she hastily; 'this wine will give you strength —drink!'

She put the glass to the lips of the young woman, who drank mechanically.

'Ah! it was not thus that I wished to avenge myself,' said her ladyship, putting the glass upon the table, with an infernal smile; 'but, faith! we must do the best we can!' and she rushed out of the room.

Madame Bonancieux saw her escape, without being able to follow her. She was like those who dream that they are pursued, yet feel a perfect inability to move. A few minutes elapsed, and then a frightful noise was heard at the gate.

At every instant Madame Bonancieux expected to see the reappearance of her ladyship, but she did not return. Many times—from terror, no doubt—the cold drops stood upon her burning brow.

At length she heard the rattling of the grated doors,

which were being opened; the noise of boots and spurs resounded on the stairs; and there was a loud murmur of many approaching voices, in the midst of which she fancied that she heard her own name mentioned. Suddenly she uttered a loud scream of joy, and rushed towards the door —she had recognised the voice of d'Artagnan.

'D'Artagnan! d'Artagnan!' she exclaimed; 'is it you? Here! here!'

'Constance! Constance!' replied the young man. 'Mon Dieu! where are you?'

At the same moment the door of the cell was burst in, rather than opened. Many men rushed into the room. Madame Bonancieux had fallen on a chair, without the power of motion. D'Artagnan cast away a still smoking pistol, which he held in his hand, and fell upon his knees before his mistress. Athos replaced his pistol in his belt; and Porthos and Aramis returned the swords, which they had drawn, into their sheaths.

'Oh! d'Artagnan, my beloved d'Artagnan! you come at last! You did not deceive me: it is really you!'

'Yes, yes, Constance, we are at last united!'

'Oh! *she* told me, in vain, that you would never come. I always secretly expected it. I did not wish to fly. Oh, how wisely I have chosen! how happy I am!'

At this word *she*, Athos, who had quietly sat down, suddenly arose.

'*She?*' Who is *she?*' demanded d'Artagnan.

'Why, my companion—she who, through affection for me, wished to withdraw me from my persecutors—she who, taking you for the cardinal's guards, has just fled.'

'Your companion!' exclaimed d'Artagnan, becoming paler than the white veil of his mistress; 'of what companion are you talking?'

'Of her whose carriage was at the door—of a woman who called herself your friend, d'Artagnan—of a woman to whom you confided all our secrets.'

'Her name?' exclaimed d'Artagnan; 'do you not know her name?'

'Yes, I do; they mentioned it before me. Wait—but it is very strange—oh, my God! my head becomes confused—I cannot see anything——'

'Come here, my friends! come here!—her hands are icy,' exclaimed d'Artagnan—'she is very ill. Great God! she is becoming unconscious.'

Whilst Porthos was calling for help with all the power of his lungs, Aramis ran for a glass of water; but he stopped on beholding the fearful alteration in the countenance of Athos, who was standing before the table with his hair on end, and his features frozen with terror, looking into one of the glasses, and seeming to be a prey to the most horrible suspicion.

'Oh!' said Athos, 'oh, no! it is impossible! Such a crime would never be permitted by the Almighty!'

'Some water! some water!' cried d'Artagnan, 'some water!'

'Oh! poor woman! poor woman!' murmured Athos in a faltering voice.

Madame Bonancieux opened her eyes once more, at the caresses of d'Artagnan.

'She is recovering her senses!' exclaimed the young man; 'oh, my God, my God! I thank thee.'

'Madam,' said Athos, 'in the name of Heaven, to whom does this empty glass belong?'

'To me, sir,' replied the young woman, in a failing voice.

'But who poured out the wine which it contained?'

'She did.'

'But who is she?'

'Ah, I remember now,' said Madame Bonancieux— 'Lady de Winter.'

The four friends uttered one unanimous cry; but the voice of Athos overpowered all the others. At the same moment Madame Bonancieux became livid; a deadly spasm assailed her; and she fell panting into the arms of Porthos and Aramis.

D'Artagnan grasped the hands of Athos in indescribable anguish. 'Ah!' said he, 'what do you believe——' His voice was choked by sobs.

'I believe the worst,' replied Athos, biting his lips until they bled.

'D'Artagnan!' exclaimed Madame Bonancieux, 'where are you? Don't leave me—you see that I am about to die!'

D'Artagnan let go the hands of Athos, which he had pressed convulsively, and ran to her. Her countenance, before so beautiful, was entirely distorted; her glassy eyes no longer saw, a convulsive shuddering agitated her whole frame; and icy drops were streaming from her brow.

'In the name of Heaven, run—Aramis—Porthos—and obtain some assistance!'

'All is useless!' asid Athos; 'all is useless! To the poison which *she* pours, there is no antidote.'

'Yes, yes—help! help! help!' murmured Madame Bonancieux. Then, collecting all her strength, she took the hand of the young man between her two hands, looked at him for an instant as though her whole soul were in that last look, and, with a sobbing cry, she pressed her lips upon his.

'Constance! Constance!' exclaimed d'Artagnan.

One sigh came from her lips, breathing over those of d'Artagnan; and that sigh was the passage of her loving soul to eternity.

D'Artagnan held only a lifeless body in his arms. He uttered a cry, and fell beside his mistress, as pale and motionless as herself.

Porthos wept; Aramis raised his hand to heaven; Athos crossed himself.

'At that moment a man appeared at the door, almost as pale as those who were in the chamber. He looked around him, and saw Madame Bonancieux dead, and d'Artagnan unconscious. He entered just at the moment of that stupor which succeeds great catastrophes.

'I was not mistaken,' said he; 'that is M. d'Artagnan; and you are his three friends, Messieurs Athos, Porthos, and Aramis.'

They whose names had been pronounced, looked at the stranger with astonishment, and all thought that they recognised him.

'Gentlemen,' said the newcomer, 'you, like myself are seeking a woman, who,' added he, with a terrible smile, 'must have been present here—for I see a dead body.'

The three friends remained speechless; but the voice, as well as the countenance, recalled to their memory some one they had previously seen, although they could not recollect under what circumstances.

'Gentlemen,' continued the stranger, 'since you will not recognise a man whose life you have probably twice saved, I must needs give my name. I am Lord de Winter, the brother-in-law of that woman.'

The three friends uttered an exclamation of surprise. Athos arose, and offered him his hand.

'Welcome, my lord,' said he; 'you are one of us.'

'I left Porthsmouth five hours after her,' said Lord de Winter; 'reached Boulogne three hours after her; I only missed her by twenty minutes at St. Omer; but at St.

Lilliers I lost all trace of her. I wandered about at chance, inquiring of everybody, when I saw you pass at a gallop. I recognised M. d'Artagnan, and called out to you; but you did not answer me. I attempted to keep up with you, but my horse was too tired to go at the same pace as yours did; and yet in spite of all your haste, it seems that you, also, have arrived too late.'

'The proof is before you,' said Athos, pointing to Madame Bonancieux, who was lying dead, and to d'Artagnan, whom Porthos and Aramis were endeavouring to restore to consciousness.

'Are they both dead?' demanded Lord de Winter coldly.

'No, happily,' replied Athos; 'M. d'Artagnan has only fainted.'

'Ah! so much the better,' said Lord de Winter.

In fact, at that moment, d'Artagnan opened his eyes. He tore himself from the arms of Porthos and Aramis, and threw himself like a madman on the body of his mistress.

Athos arose, walked toward his friend with a slow and solemn step, embraced him tenderly, and then, whilst d'Artagnan broke out into sobs, said to him, in his noble and persuasive tones—

'My friend, be a man! Women weep for the dead— men avenge them!'

'Oh, yes, yes!' cried d'Artagnan, 'if it be to avenge her, I am ready to follow you.'

Athos took advantage of this momentary strength, which the hope of vengeance had given to his unfortunate friend, to make a sign to Porthos and Aramis to fetch the abbess.

The two friends met her in the corridor, already much confounded and disturbed by so many events. She called some of the sisters, who, contrary to their conventual habits, found themselves in the presence of five men.

'Madame,' said Athos, putting his arm under that of d'Artagnan, 'we leave to your pious care the body of this unfortunate woman. She was an angel upon earth, before she became a saint in heaven. Treat her as if she had been one of your sisters: we will return some day to pray for her soul.'

D'Artagnan hid his face against Athos's breast, and sobbed violently.

'Weep,' said Athos; 'weep, heart full of love, and youth, and life. Alas! would that I could weep as you do!' And he led his friend away—affectionately as a father, consolingly as a priest, and firmly, as a man who had himself suffered much.

All five, followed by their servants leading their horses, then went towards the town of Bethune, where the suburbs were within sight; and they stopped at the first hotel they found.

'But,' asked d'Artagnan, 'are we not going to follow that woman?'

'By and by,' said Athos; 'but I have some preparations to make.'

'She will escape,' said the young man—'she will escape, Athos, and it will be your fault.'

'I will answer for her,' said Athos.

D'Artagnan had such perfect confidence in his friend's promise, that he bowed his head, and entered the hotel without making the least reply. Porthos and Aramis looked at each other, at a loss to understand the meaning of Athos. Lord de Winter thought that he sought only to soothe the grief of d'Artagnan.

'Now, gentlemen,' said Athos, when he had ascertained that there were five unoccupied chambers in the hotel, 'let each of us retire to his room. D'Artagnan ought to be alone to weep, and you to sleep. I take charge of everything; make yourselves perfectly easy.'

'It appears to me, however,' said Lord de Winter, 'that if any measures are be to taken against the countess, the concern is mine, seeing that she is my sister-in-law.'

'And,' said Athos, 'she is my wife!'

D'Artagnan started, for he was satisfied that Athos was sure of his revenge, to reveal such a secret. Porthos and Aramis looked at one another in consternation; and Lord de Winter thought that Athos had gone mad.

'Retire, then,' said Athos, 'and leave me to act. You see that, in my capacity of husband, this affair belongs to me. Only, d'Artagnan, if you have not lost it, give me that paper which fell from the man's hat, and on which the name of a village is written.'

'Ah!' cried d'Artagnan, 'I understand: that name is written by her hand——'

'You see,' said Athos, 'that there is still a God in heaven.'

64

The Man in the Red Cloak

THE despair of Athos had given place to a concentrated grief, which made the brilliant qualities of the man even more lucid. Entirely engrossed by one thought—that of the promise he had made, and of the responsibility he had undertaken—he was the last to retire into his chamber, where he requested the landlord to bring him a map of the province; and then he bent himself over it, examined the lines traced on it, and, ascertaining that four different roads led from Bethune to Armentières, he ordered the valets to be called.

Planchet, Grimaud, Mousqueton, and Bazin entered, and received the clear, precise, and serious directions of Athos. At break of day, the next morning, they were to set off, and proceed to Armentières, each by a different road. Planchet, the most intelligent of the four, was to follow that which had been taken by the carriage at which the three friends had fired, and which was attended, as may be remembered, by the lackey of Count Rochefort.

Athos intrusted the valets with this duty, first, because since these men had been in his service or in that of his friends, he had perceived in each of them some different and useful quality; and, next, because servants awaken less suspicion than their masters in the minds of the peasants, and excite more sympathy in the minds of those whom they address. And, lastly, her ladyship knew the masters, whilst she did not know the servants, who, on the other hand, knew her ladyship well. They were all four to be at an appointed place at eleven o'clock the next day. If they had discovered her ladyship's retreat, three of the four were to remain to watch her, and the fourth was to return to Bethune, to inform Athos, and to guide the three friends.

These arrangements being made, the valets withdrew.

Athos then arose from his seat, girded on his sword, wrapped himself up in his cloak and left the hotel. It was about ten o'clock; and at ten at night, in the provinces, the streets are but little frequented. Nevertheless, Athos evidently was looking out for some one, of whom he could ask a question. At last, he met a late passenger, went up to him, and spoke a few words. The man he addressed started back in fear; but yet he answered the inquiry of the musketeer by a sign. Athos offered the man half a pistole to accompany him, but he refused it. Athos then proceeded down the street which the man had indicated with his finger; but, reaching a spot where several streets met, he stopped again in visible embarrassment. But, as this was a more likely place than any other for some one to be seen, Athos waited there. In fact, in an instant after, a watchman passed. Athos repeated the question he had already asked of the person he had first met. The watchman showed the same terror, and also refused to accompany him; but he pointed to the road he was to take. Athos walked in the direction indicated, and soon reached the suburbs of the town, in the opposite direction to that from which he and his companions had entered. There, he again appeared uneasy and embarrassed and stopped for the third time. Fortunately, a beggar who was passing by, came up to solicit alms. Athos offered him a crown to accompany him where he was going. The beggar hesitated an instant, but, at the sight of the piece of silver shining in the darkness, assented, and walked before Athos. Having reached the corner of the street, he pointed out, at a distance, a small isolated, melancholy-looking house, to which Athos proceeded; whilst the beggar, who had received his fee, took himself off at his utmost speed.

Athos walked quite around this house before he could distinguish the door amid the red colour with which the hut was painted. No light pierced through the crevices of the shutters; no sound gave reason to suppose it was inhabited; it was sad and silent as a tomb. Athos knocked three times before any answer was returned. At the third knock, however, steps were heard approaching, the door was partially unclosed, and a man of tall stature, and pale complexion, and with black beard and hair, appeared. Athos exchanged a few words with him in a whisper, and then the tall man made a sign to the musketeer that he might enter. Athos immediately availed himself of the permission, and the door closed behind him.

The man whom Athos had come so far to seek, and whom he had found with so much difficulty, took him into a laboratory, where he was engaged in joining together, with iron wires, the clattering bones of a skeleton. All the body was already adjusted, and the head alone was lying on the table. All the furniture indicated that the owner of the room in which they were was engaged in natural science. There were bottles, filled with serpents, labelled according to their kinds; and dried lizards, shining like emeralds, set in large frames of black wood. And, lastly, boxes of wild, sweet-smelling plants, gifted undoubtedly with virtues unknown to mankind in general, were fastened to the ceiling, and hung down the corners of the room. But there was no family, no servant: the tall man inhabited the house alone.

Athos cast a cold and indifferent glance on the objects we have just described, and, on the invitation of the man whom he had come to seek, sat down opposite him. He then explained the cause of his visit, and the service he required of him; but, scarcely had he stated his demand, before the stranger, who had remained standing before the musketeer, started back in affright, and refused. Athos then drew from his pocket a small paper, on which two lines and a signature were written, accompanied by a seal, and presented it to him who had shown these signs of repugnance so prematurely. The tall man had scarcely read the two lines, and seen the signature, and recognised the seal, before he bowed his head as a token that he had no longer any objection to make, and that he was prepared to obey. Athos demanded nothing more: he arose, left the house, returned by the road he had come, and re-entering the hotel, shut himself up in his own chamber.

At daybreak, d'Artagnan entered his room, and asked him what they were to do.

'Wait,' replied Athos.

A few moments after, the superior of the convent sent to inform the musketeers that the funeral would take place at midday. As for the murderess, no tidings of her had been heard. It was, however, clear that she must have fled through the garden, on whose gravel paths the traces of her steps could be discerned, and whose door had been found locked, with the key missing.

At the appointed hour, Lord de Winter and the four friends proceeded to the convent. The bells were sounding, the chapel was open, and the grating of the choir alone was closed. In the midst of the choir the body of the victim, clothed in the dress of a novice, lay exposed. On every side of the choir, and behind the grating leading to the convent, the whole community of the Carmelites was assembled, listening to the sacred service, and mingling their strains with the songs of the priests, without seeing the laity, or being seen by them.

At the door of the chapel d'Artagnan felt his resolution wavering again, and turned to look for Athos; but he had disappeared. Faithful to his mission of vengeance, Athos had been shown into the garden, and there, on the gravel, following the light steps of that woman who had left a track of blood wherever she had passed, he proceeded onwards until he reached the door which opened on the wood. He had this door unclosed, and he plunged into the forest. But, there, all his suspicions were confirmed. The road by which the carriage had disappeared skirted the wood. Athos followed the road for some distance, with his eyes fixed upon the ground. Slight spots of blood, which proceeded from a wound inflicted either on the courier or on one of the horses, were perceptible on the road. About three-quarters of a league off, and fifty paces from Festubert, a large spot of blood was visible, and the ground was trodden by horses. Between the wood and this denunciatory spot, and rather behind the trampled earth, traces of the same small steps as those in the garden were distinguished. The carriage, therefore, had waited here; and here her ladyship had left the wood, and got into it.

Satisfied with this discovery, which confirmed all his conjectures, Athos returned to the hotel, where he found Planchet impatiently awaiting him. Everything had happened exactly as Athos had foreseen. Planchet had followed the path she had taken; had, like Athos, observed the marks of blood; like Athos, he, too, had discerned the spot where the carriage stopped. But he had gone on farther than Athos; so that, in the village of Festubert, whilst drinking in a tavern, he had, without the trouble of inquiry, learned that, at half-past eight yesterday evening, a wounded man, who attended a lady travelling in a post-carriage, had been obliged to stop, from inability to proceed farther. The accident had been imputed to robbers. who had stopped the carriage in the wood. The man had remained in the village but the woman had exchanged horses, and proceeded on her journey.

Planchet hunted out the postillion who had driven the carriage, and found him. He had taken the lady to Fontenelles, and from Fontenelles she had gone on toward Armentières. Planchet had taken a cross-road, and at half-past seven in the morning he was at Armentières. There was only one hotel there, and Planchet presented himself at it as a servant who was looking out for a situation. He had not talked ten minutes with the servants of the inn, before he ascertained that a woman had arrived alone at ten o'clock the night before, had hired a room, had sent for the landlord, and had told him that she wished to remain for some time in the neighbourhood. Planchet wanted to know nothing more. He hastened to the place of appointment, found the three other valets at their posts, placed them as sentinels at all the outlets from the hotel, and returned to Athos, who had just finished receiving this information from Planchet when his friends returned.

All their faces were indicative of gloom—even the gentle countenance of Aramis.

'What must we do?' said d'Artagnan.

'Wait!' replied Athos.

Each retired to his own chamber.

At eight o'clock in the evening, Athos ordered the horses to be saddled, and sent word to Lord de Winter and his friends to prepare for the expedition. In an instant all the five were ready. Each looked at his arms, and put them in order. Athos came down last, and found d'Artagnan already mounted, and impatient.

'Patience,' said Athos; 'there is still some one wanting.'

The four horsemen looked around them in astonishment, for they inquired in vain, in their own minds, who could be the one still wanting.

At this moment Planchet led up Athos's horse. The musketeer leaped lightly into the saddle.

'Wait for me,' said he; 'I shall be back directly.' And he went off at a gallop.

A quarter of an hour afterwards he returned, accompanied by a man who wore a mask, and was wrapped in a red cloak. Lord de Winter and the three musketeers questioned each other by their glances but none of them could give any information to the others, for all were ignorant about this man. And yet they concluded that it was as it ought to be, since it was Athos who had so arranged it.

At nine o'clock, guided by Planchet, the little cavalcade began its march, taking the same road that the carriage had followed. There was something mournful in the sight of these six men, riding in silence, each buried in his own thoughts, melancholy as despair, gloomy as revenge.

IT was a dark and stormy night. Large clouds careered along the heavens, veiling the brightness of the stars. The moon would not arise till midnight. Sometimes, by the light of a flash that shone along the horizon, the road became perceptible, stretching itself, white and solitary, before them; and then, the flash extinguished, everything again was gloom. At every instant Athos was obliged to check d'Artagnan, who was always at the head of the little troop, and to compel him to take his place in the rank, which, a moment afterwards, he quitted again. He had only one thought—to go forward—and he went.

They passed in silence through the village of Festubert, where the wounded servant had been left, and then they skirted the village of Richebourg. Having reached Herlier, Planchet, who guided the party turned to the left.

On several occasions either Lord de Winter, or Porthos, or Aramis, had endeavoured to address some remark to the man in the red cloak; but, at each interrogation, he had bowed his head without reply. The travellers had thus comprehended that there was some reason for the stranger's silence, and they had ceased to address him.

The storm, too, became more violent: flashes rapidly succeeded one another; the thunder began to roll; and the wind, the precursor of the hurricane, whistled through the plumes and hair of the horsemen. The cavalcade broke into a fast trot. A little way beyond Fromelles, the storm burst forth. There were still three leagues to travel; and they rode them amidst torrents of rain.

D'Artagnan had taken off his hat, and did not wear his cloak. He found some pleasure in letting the water flow over his burning brow and over his body, agitated by the heats of fever.

At the moment that the little troop had passed beyond Goskal, and was just arriving at the change-house, a man who, in the darkness, had been confounded with the trunk of a tree under which he had sheltered himself, advanced into the middle of the road, placing his finger on his lips, Athos recognised Grimaud.

'What is the matter now?' exclaimed d'Artagnan. 'Can she have quitted Armentières?'

Grimaud gave an affirmative nod of the head. D'Artagnan ground his teeth.

'Silence, d'Artagnan!' said Athos: 'I have taken charge of everything, and it is my business, therefore, to question Grimaud.'

'Where is she?' demanded Athos.

Grimaud stretched forth his hand in the direction of the Lys.

'Is it far from here?'

Grimaud presented his forefinger bent.

'Alone?' demanded Athos.

Grimaud made a sign that she was.

'Gentlemen,' said Athos, 'she is half a league from this place, in the direction of the river.'

'Good!' said d'Artagnan; 'lead us on, Grimaud.'

Grimaud took a cross-road, and guided the cavalcade. At the end of about five hundred yards they found a stream, which they forded. By the light of a flash, they perceived the village of Equinheim.

'Is it there?' demanded d'Artagnan.

Grimaud shook his head negatively.

'Silence there!' said Athos.

The troop proceeded on its way. Another flash blazed forth; and, by the bluish glare of the serpentine flame, a small solitary house was perceptible on the bank of the river, not far from a ferry. There was a light at one window.

'We are there,' said Athos.

At that moment a man, who was lying down in a ditch, arose. It was Mousqueton. He pointed with his finger to the window with the light. 'She is there,' said he.

'And Bazin?' demanded Athos.

'While I watched the window, he watched the door.'

'Good!' said Athos; 'you are all faithful servants.'

Athos leaped from his horse, of which he gave the bridle into the hands of Grimaud, and advanced in the direction of the window, after having made a sign to the remainder of the troop to proceed towards the door. The small house was surrounded by a quick set hedge of two or three feet in height. Athos sprang over the hedge, and went up to the window, which had no shutters on the outside, but whose short curtains were closely drawn. He climbed upon the ledge of the stone, that his eye might be above the level of the curtains. By the light of a lamp, he could perceive a woman, covered by a dark-coloured cloak, seated on a stool before an expiring fire. Her elbows were placed upon a mean table, and she rested her head on hands which were as white as ivory. Her face was not visible, but an ominous smile arose upon the lips of Athos. He was not mistaken. He had in truth, found the woman that he sought.

At this moment a horse neighed. Her ladyship raised her head, saw the pale face of Athos staring through the window, and screamed aloud.

Perceiving that he had been seen, Athos pushed the window with his hand and knee. It gave way; the panes were broken, and Athos, like a spectre of vengeance, leaped into the room. Her ladyship ran to the door and opened it. Paler, and more threatening than even Athos himself, d'Artagnan was standing on the sill. Her ladyship started back, and screamed. D'Artagnan, imagining that she had some means of flight, and fearing that she might escape them, drew a pistol from his belt. But Athos raised his hand.

'Replace your weapon, d'Artagnan,' said he; 'it is imperative that this woman should be judged, and not assassinated. Wait awhile, d'Artagnan, and you shall be satisfied. Come in, gentlemen.'

D'Artagnan obeyed; for Athos had the solemn voice and the authoritative air of a judge commissioned by the Deity Himself. Behind d'Artagnan there came Porthos, Aramis, Lord de Winter, and the man in the red cloak. The four valets watched at the door and window. Her ladyship had sunk upon her seat, with her hands stretched out, as if to exorcise this terrible apparition. On seeing her brother-in-law, she uttered a fearful scream.

'What do you want?' demanded her ladyship.

'We want,' said Athos, 'Anne de Breuil, who was called, first, the Countess de la Fère, then Lady de Winter, baroness of Sheffield.'

'I am that person,' murmured she, overwhelmed with surprise. 'What do you want with me?'

'We want to judge you according to your crimes.' said Athos. 'You will be free to defend yourself; and to justify your conduct, if you can. M. d'Artagnan, you must be the first accuser.'

D'Artagnan came forward. 'Before God and men,' said

he, 'I accuse this woman of having poisoned Constance Bonancieux, who died last night.'

He turned towards Aramis and Porthos. 'We can bear witness to it,' said the two musketeers together.

D'Artagnan continued—

'Before God and before men, I accuse this woman of having sought to poison me with some wine, which she sent me from Villeroi, with a forged letter, as if the wine had come from my friends. God preserved me; but a man named Brisemont was killed instead of me.'

'We bear witness to this,' said Porthos and Aramis, as with one voice.

'Before God and men,' continued d'Artagnan, 'I accuse this woman of having urged me to the murder of the Baron de Wardes; and, as no one is present to bear witness to it, I myself will attest it. I have done.' And d'Artagnan crossed over the other side of the room, with Porthos and Aramis.

'It is now for you to speak, my lord,' said Athos.

The baron came forward in his turn: 'Before God and before men,' said he, 'I accuse this woman of having caused the Duke of Buckingham to be assassinated.'

'The Duke of Buckingham assassinated!' exclaimed all, with one accord.

'Yes,' said the baron, 'assassinated! From the warning letter which you sent me, I caused this woman to be arrested, and put her under the custody of a faithful dependent. She corrupted that man; she placed the dagger in his hand; she made him kill the duke; and at this moment, perhaps, Felton has paid with his head for the crimes of this fury.'

A shudder ran through the company at the revelation of these hitherto unsuspected crimes.

'This is not all,' resumed Lord de Winter. 'My brother, who had made you his heiress, died in three hours of a strange malady, which left livid spots on his body. Sister, how did your husband die?'

'Oh, horror!' exclaimed Porthos and Aramis.

'Assassin of Buckingham—assassin of Felton—assassin of my brother—I demand justice on you; and declare that, if it be not accorded to me, I will execute it myself!'

Lord de Winter ranged himself by the side of d'Artagnan, leaving his place open to another accuser.

Her ladyship's head sank upon her hands, and she endeavoured to recall her thoughts, which were confounded by a deadly vertigo.

'It is now my turn,' said Athos, trembling as the lion trembles at the aspect of a serpent. 'It is my turn. I married this woman when she was a young girl. I married her against the desire of all my family. I gave her my property; I gave her my name; and one day I discovered that this woman was branded—this woman bore the mark of a fleur-de-lis upon the left shoulder.'

'Oh!' said her ladyship, rising, 'I defy you to find the tribunal which pronounced on me that infamous sentence —I defy you to find the man who executed it!'

'Silence!' exclaimed a voice. 'It is for me to answer that!' And the man in the red cloak came forward.

'Who is that man? What is that man?' cried out her ladyship, suffocated with terror, and with her hair raising itself up on her head, as if it had been endowed with life.

Every eye was turned towards that man, for he was unknown to all except Athos. And even Athos looked at him with as much astonishment as the others, for he knew not how he could be connected with the horrible drama which was at that moment enacting there. After slowly and solemnly approaching her ladyship, till the table alone separated them, the stranger took off his mask.

Her ladyship looked for some time with increasing terror on that pale countenance, fringed with black hair, of which the only expression was that of a stern and frozen insensibility: then suddenly rising, and retreating towards the wall—'Oh! no, no,' exclaimed she, 'no, it is an infernal apparition! it is not he! Help! help! ' she screamed out, in a hoarse voice, still pressing against the wall, as if she could open a passage through it with her hands.

'But who are you?' exclaimed all the witnesses of this scene.

'Ask this woman,' said the man in the red cloak, 'for you see well that she has recognised me.'

'The executioner of Lille! the executioner of Lille! ' cried her ladyship, overcome by wild affright, and clinging to the wall with her hands for support.

All present recoiled, and the tall man stood alone in the middle of the room.

'Oh, mercy! mercy!' cried the miserable woman, falling on her knees.

The stranger paused for silence. 'I told you truly that she recognised me,' said he. 'Yes, I am the executioner of Lille, and here is my history.'

All eyes were fixed upon this man, whose words were listened to with the most anxious avidity.

'This woman was formerly a young girl, as beautiful as she is at present. She was a nun, in a Benedictine convent at Templemar. A young priest, simple and ingenuous in his nature, performed service in the church of the convent: she attempted to seduce him, and succeeded. She would have seduced a saint. The vows which they had both taken were sacred and irrevocable. She persuaded him to quit the country. But, to quit the country, to fly together, to get to some part of France where they might live in peace, because they would be unknown, they required money. Neither of them had any. The priest stole the sacred vessels, and sold them; but just as they were making ready to escape, they were both arrested. In eight days more she had corrupted the gaoler's son, and saved herself. The young priest was condemned to be branded, and to ten years of the galleys. I was the executioner of Lille, as this woman says. I was obliged to brand the criminal, and that criminal was my own brother! I then swore that this woman, who had ruined him—who was more than his accomplice, since she had urged him to the crime—should at any rate partake his punishment. I suspected where she was concealed. I followed, and discovered her. I bound her, and imprinted the same brand on her that I had stamped upon my own brother.

'The next day, on my return to Lille, my brother also managed to escape. I was accused as his accomplice, and was condemned to remain in prison in his place so long as he should continue at large. My poor brother was not aware of this sentence: he rejoined this woman; and they fled together into Berri, where he obtained a small curacy. This woman passed for his sister. The owner of the estate to which the curacy belonged saw this pretended sister, and fell in love with her. His passion led him to propose to marry her. She left the man whom she had destroyed, and became the Countess de la Fère.'

All eyes were turned towards Athos, whose true name this was, and he made a sign that the executioner's tale was true.

'Then,' continued the latter, 'maddened by despair, and resolved to terminate an existence of which the happiness and honour had been thus destroyed, my poor brother returned to Lille; and learning the sentence which had condemned me in his place, he delivered himself up to justice, and hung himself the same night to the grating of his dungeon. After all, to be fair to them, they who had condemned me kept their word. Scarcely was the identity of the dead body proved, before my liberty was restored. These are the crimes of which I accuse her—these are the reasons why I branded her!'

'M. d'Artagnan,' said Athos, 'what is the punishment that you demand for this woman?'

'The punishment of death,' replied d'Artagnan.

'My Lord de Winter,' continued Athos, 'what punishment do you demand for this woman?'

'Death!' replied his lordship.

'Messieurs Porthos and Aramis,' said Athos, 'you who are her judges—what punishment do you pronounce against this woman?'

'The punishment of death!' replied the two musketeers, in a hollow voice.

Her ladyship uttered a fearful cry, and dragged herself a few paces on her knees towards her judges.

Athos stretched out his hand towards her. 'Anne de Breuil,' said he, 'Countess de la Fère, Lady de Winter, your crimes have wearied men on earth and God in heaven. If you know any prayer, repeat it; for you are condemned, and are about to die.'

At these words, which left no hope, her ladyship raised herself to her full height, and attempted to speak. But her voice failed her. She felt a strong and pitiless hand seize her by the hair, and drag her on, as irresistibly as Fate drags on mankind. She did not, therefore, even attempt to make any resistance, but left the cottage.

Lord de Winter and the four friends went out after her. The valets followed their masters, and the chamber was left empty, with its broken window, its open door, and the smoking lamp burning sadly on the table.

66

The Execution

IT was almost midnight. The waning moon, as red as blood from the lingering traces of the storm, was rising behind the little village of Armentières, which exhibited, in that pale light, the gloomy outline of its houses, and the skeleton of its high ornamented steeple. In front, the Lys rolled along its waters like a river of molten fire; whilst, on its other bank, a dark mass of trees was sharply outlined upon a stormy sky, covered by large copper-coloured clouds, which created a sort of twilight in the middle of the night. To the left, arose an old deserted mill, of which the sails were motionless, and from the ruins of which an owl was uttering its sharp, monotonous, recurring screech. Here and there, in the plain, to the right and left of the path which the melancholy train was pursuing, there appeared a few short and stunted trees, which looked like distorted dwarfs crouched down to watch the men in that ill-omened hour.

From time to time, a brilliant flash opened up the horizon in its whole extent; playing above the black mass of trees, and coming, like a frightful scimitar, to divide the sky and water into equal parts. Not a breath of air was stirring in the heavy atmosphere. A silence as of death weighed down all nature. The earth was moist and slippery from the recent rain; and reanimated plants sent forth their perfumes with more vigorous energy.

Two of the servants, each holding an arm, were leading her ladyship along. The executioner walked behind. The four musketeers and Lord de Winter followed him in turn.

Planchet and Bazin brought up the rear.

The two valets led her ladyship toward the bank of the river. Her mouth was mute, but her eyes were inexpressibly eloquent, supplicating by turns each of those on whom she looked. Finding herself a few paces in advance, she said to the valets—

'A thousand pistoles for each of you, if you will assist me to escape; but, if you give me up to your masters, I have some avengers near, who will make you pay dearly for my death.'

Grimaud hesitated, and Mousqueton trembled in every limb.

Athos, who had heard her ladyship's voice, came up immediately, as did also Lord de Winter.

'Send away these valets,' said he; 'she has spoken to them, and they are no longer to be trusted.'

They called Planchet and Bazin, who took the places of Grimaud and Mousqueton.

Having reached the brink of the stream, the executioner came up, and bound her ladyship's hands and feet.

She then broke her silence to exclaim—'You are cowards —you are miserable assassins! You come, ten of you, to murder a poor woman! But beware! Though I am not assisted, I shall be avenged!'

'You are not a woman,' replied Athos coldly; 'you do not belong to the human race: you are a demon, escaped from hell, and to hell we shall send you back.'

'Oh! you stainless gentleman,' said her ladyship, 'remember that he amongst you who touches a hair of my head is himself a murderer.'

'The executioner can kill without being on that account a murderer, madam,' said the man in the cloak, striking his large sword. 'He is the last judge on earth—that is all. *Nachrichter*, as our German neighbours say.'

And, as he was binding her whilst he uttered these words, her ladyship sent forth two or three wild screams, which had a startling, melancholy effect, as they were borne on the night, and lost themselves amidst the depths of the woods, like birds.

'But, if I am guilty—if I have committed the crimes of which you accuse me,' howled out her ladyship, 'take me before a regular tribunal. You are not judges—you have no power to condemn me!'

'I did propose Tyburn,' answered Lord de Winter; 'why did you not accept my offer?'

'Because I do not wish to die!' exclaimed her ladyship, struggling—'because I am too young to die!'

'The woman whom you poisoned at Bethune was still younger than you are, madam—and yet she is dead,' said d'Artagnan.

'I will enter a convent—I will become a nun!' cried her ladyship.

'You were in a convent,' said the executioner, 'and you left it to destroy my brother.'

Her ladyship uttered a cry of terror, and fell upon her knees. The executioner lifted her in his arms, and prepared to carry her to the boat.

'Oh, my God!' exclaimed she, 'my God! are you going to drown me?'

These cries had something so heart-rending in them, that d'Artagnan, who was at first the most unrelenting in his pursuit of her ladyship, sank down upon the stump of a tree, letting his head fall on his bosom, and stopping his ears with the palms of his hands; and yet, in spite of all this, he still heard her menaces and cries. D'Artagnan was the youngest of all these men, and his heart failed him.

'Oh! I cannot bear this frightful spectacle,' said he; 'I cannot consent that this woman should thus die.'

Her ladyship heard these words, and they gave her a new gleam of hope—'D'Artagnan! d'Artagnan!' exclaimed she, 'remember that I have loved you!'

The young man rose, and made a step towards her. But Athos drew his sword, and placed himself in his path.

'If you take one step more, d'Artagnan,' said he, 'we must cross our swords together.'

D'Artagnan fell on his knees, and prayed.

'Come,' continued Athos, 'executioner, do your duty!'

'Willingly, my lord,' replied the executioner; 'for as truly as I am a good Catholic, I firmly believe that I act justly in exercising my office on this woman.'

'That is right.' Athos took one step towards her ladyship. —'I pardon you,' said he, 'the evil you have done me. I forgive you for my future crushed, my honour lost, my love tainted, and my salvation for ever perilled, by the despair into which you have thrown me. Die in peace!'

Lord de Winter next came forward. 'I pardon you,' said he, 'the poisoning of my brother, the assassination of the Duke of Buckingham, and the death of poor Felton. I forgive you your attempts on my own person. Die in peace!'

'As for me,' said d'Artagnan, 'pardon me, madam, for having, by a deceit unworthy of a gentleman, provoked your rage; and, in exchange, I pardon you for the murder of my poor friend, and your cruel vengeance on myself. I pardon and I pity you. Die in peace!'

'*I am lost!*' murmured her ladyship, in English—'*I must die!*'

She then arose unaided, and threw around her one of those clear glances, which seemed to emanate from an eye of fire. But she could see nothing. She listened; but she heard nothing. There were none around her but her enemies.

'Where am I to die?' demanded she.

'On the other bank of the river,' replied the executioner.

He then placed her in the boat; and, as he was stepping in after her, Athos gave him a sum of money.

'Here,' said he, 'here is the price of the execution, that it may be seen that we are really judges.'

'It is well,' said the executioner; 'but let this woman now know that I am not executing my business, but my duty.' And he threw the money from him into the river.

'Mark,' said Athos; 'this woman has a child, and yet she has not said one word about him.'

The boat proceeded towards the left bank of the Lys, carrying away the criminal and the executioner. All the others continued on the right bank, where they had sunk upon their knees. The boat glided slowly along the rope of the ferry, under the reflection of a pale mist, which skimmed the water at that moment.

It arrived at the other bank, and the two figures stood out in blackness on the red horizon.

During the passage, her ladyship had managed to loosen the cord that bound her feet, and, on reaching the bank, she leapt lightly on shore, and took to flight. But the ground was moist; and, at the top of the shelving bank, she slipped, and fell upon her knees. Probably a superstitious idea had struck her. She understood that Heaven refused to aid her, and remained in the attitude in which she had fallen—her head drooping, and her hands clasped together. Then, from the other shore, they could see the executioner slowly raise his two arms, a ray of the moon was reflected on the blade of his large sword, the two arms descended, they heard the whistling of the cimeter and the cry of the victim; and then a mutilated mass sank down beneath the blow. The executioner took off his red cloak, stretched it out on the ground, laid the body on it, and threw in the head, tied it by the four corners, swung it upon his shoulders, and again, entered the boat. Having reached the middle of the Lys, he stopped the boat, and holding his burden over the river—

'Let the justice of God have its course!' he exclaimed, in a loud voice. And, so saying, he dropped the dead body into the deepest part of the waters, which closed above it.

67

A Message from The Cardinal

THREE days afterwards, the four musketeers re-entered Paris. They were within the limit of their furlough, and, the same evening, they went to pay the usual visit to M. de Treville.

'Well, gentlemen,' inquired the brave captain, 'have you found yourselves amused in your excursion?'

'Prodigiously so!' replied Athos, in his own name, and that of his companions.

On the sixth of the following month, the king, according to his promise to the cardinal to return to Rochelle, quitted Paris, still quite stunned by the news which was beginning to circulate in the city, that Buckingham had been assassinated.

Although warned of a danger in the path of a man whom she had so truly loved, yet the queen, when his death was announced to her, would not believe it: she had even the imprudence to exclaim—'It is false! He has just written to me.'

But the next day there was no refusing credence to this fatal news. La Porte, having, like every one else, been detained by the order of Charles I., at length arrived, and brought with him the last dying gift which Buckingham had sent to the queen.

The king's joy had been extreme. He did not take the slightest pains to disguise it, but manifested it affectedly before the queen. Louis XIII., like all men of weak hearts, was wanting in generosity. But the king soon again became melancholy and ill. His brow was not one of those that can continue long unruffled: he felt that, in returning to the camp, he returned to slavery; and yet he did return there. The cardinal was, to him, the fascinating serpent; and he was the bird that flies from bough to bough without a possibility of making his escape.

The return to La Rochelle was, therefore, profoundly melancholy. Our four friends, especially, excited the astonishment of their companions: they travelled side by side, with heavy eyes and heads depressed. Athos alone sometimes raised his broad forehead: a glance shot from his eye, a bitter smile passed across his lips, and then, like his comrades, he sank again into his reveries. As soon as they arrived in any town, when they had conducted the king to his apartments, the four friends withdrew, either to their own lodgings, or to some secluded tavern, where they neither played nor drank but spoke in a low voice together, and looked attentively that none might hear them.

One day that the king had halted to hunt the magpie, and the four friends, according to their custom, instead of joining in the sport, had stopped at a tavern by the road-side, a man, who was coming post-haste from La Rochelle, stopped at the door to drink a glass of wine, and looked into the chamber where the four musketeers were seated at a table.

'Hollo, M. d'Artagnan,' said he, 'is it you that I see there?'

D'Artagnan raised his head, and uttered an exclamation of joy. This man, who now called him, was his phantom: it was the stranger of Meung, of the Rue des Fossoyeurs, and of Arras. D'Artagnan drew his sword, and rushed towards the door. But on this occasion the stranger, instead of hastening away, jumped off his horse, and advanced to meet him.

'Ah! sir,' said the young man, 'I meet you at last. This time you shall not escape me.'

'It is not my intention either, sir; for I am looking for you this time. In the king's name, I arrest you!'

'What do you mean?' exclaimed d'Artagnan.

'I say that you must give up your sword to me, sir, and without resistance too. Your life depends upon it, I assure you.'

'Who are you then?' demanded d'Artagnan, lowering his sword, but not yet giving it up.

'I am the chevalier de Rochefort,' said the stranger, 'the cardinal de Richelieu's master of the horse, and I am commanded to conduct you before his eminence.'

'We are now returning to his eminence, sir,' said Athos, coming forward, 'and you must take M. d'Artagnan's word that he will go direct to La Rochelle.'

'I must place him in the hands of the guards, who will conduct him back to the camp.'

'We will serve as such, sir, on our words as gentlemen!

But, on our words as gentlemen, also,' continued Athos, frowning, 'M. d'Artagnan shall not be taken from us.'

De Rochefort threw a glance behind him, and saw that Porthos and Aramis had placed themselves between him and the door; and he understood that he was entirely at the mercy of these four men. 'Gentlemen,' said he, 'if M. d'Artagnan will deliver up his sword, and add his word to yours, I will be contented with your promise of conducting him to the quarters of his eminence the cardinal.'

'You have my word, sir, and here is my sword,' said d'Artagnan.

'That suits me so much the better,' said Rochefort, 'as I must continue my journey.'

'If it is to rejoin her ladyship,' said Athos coolly, 'it is useless; you will not find her.'

'And what has become of her?' asked Rochefort anxiously.

'Return to the camp, and you will learn!'

Rochefort remained in thought for an instant; and then, as they were only one day's journey from Surgères, where the cardinal was to meet the king, he resolved to follow Athos's advice, and to return with them. Besides, this plan had the further advantage of enabling him, personally, to watch the prisoner. Thus they proceeded on their journey.

The next day, at three in the afternoon, they reached Surgères. The cardinal was waiting there for Louis XIII. The minister and the king exchanged their caresses freely, and congratulated each other on the happy chance which had freed France from the inveterate enemy who was arming Europe against her. After this, the cardinal, who had been informed by Rochefort that d'Artagnan had been placed under arrest, and who was in haste to interrogate him, took leave of the king, inviting his majesty to go the next day to see the works at the embankment, which were at last complete.

On returning in the evening to his quarters, near the Pont de la Pierre, the cardinal found the three musketeers all armed; and d'Artagnan, who was without his sword, standing before the door of the house which he inhabited. On this occasion, as he had all his retinue about him, he looked sternly at them, and made a sign with his eye and hand for d'Artagnan to follow him. D'Artagnan obeyed.

'We will wait for you, d'Artagnan,' said Athos, loud enough for the cardinal to hear.

His eminence knitted his brow, stopped for an instant, and then went on, without uttering a single word.

D'Artagnan entered behind the cardinal, and Rochefort followed d'Artagnan: the door was guarded. His eminence entered the chamber which he made use of as a cabinet, and signed to Rochefort to introduce the young musketeer. Rochefort obeyed, and retired.

D'Artagnan stood alone before the cardinal. It was his second interview with Richelieu; and he afterwards confessed that he felt quite convinced that it was to be his last. Richelieu remained leaning upon the chimney-piece, and there was a table standing between him and d'Artagnan.

'Sir,' said the cardinal, 'you have been arrested by my orders.'

'So I have been informed, my lord.'

'Do you know why?'

'No, my lord; for the only thing for which I ought to be arrested is yet unknown to your eminence.'

Richelieu looked earnestly at the young man.

'Hollo!' said he, 'what does this mean?'

'If your eminence will first tell me the charges against me, I will afterwards tell you what I have done.'

'There are crimes imputed to you which have cost the heads of people higher far than you are,' replied the cardinal.

'And what are they, my lord?' demanded d'Artagnan, with a calmness which surprised even the cardinal himself.

You are accused of corresponding with the enemies of the realm; of having pried into the secrets of the state; and of having attempted to make your general's plans miscarry.'

'And who is my accuser, my lord?' inquired d'Artagnan, who had no doubt that it was her ladyship; 'a woman, branded by the justice of her country—a woman, who was married to one man in France, and to another in England —a woman, who poisoned her second husband, and attempted to poison me!'

'What are you saying, sir?' exclaimed the astonished cardinal; 'and of what woman are you thus speaking?'

'Of Lady de Winter,' replied d'Artagnan: 'yes, of Lady de Winter—of whose crimes your eminence was undoubtedly ignorant, when you honoured her with your confidence.'

'Sir,' said the cardinal, 'if Lady de Winter has been guilty of the crimes you have mentioned, she shall be punished.'

'She has been punished, my lord!'

'And who has punished her?'

'We have.'

'She is in prison, then?'

'She is dead.'

'Dead!' repeated the cardinal, who could not credit what he heard; 'dead! Did you say that she was dead?'

'Three times she had endeavoured to kill me, and three times I forgave her; but she murdered the woman I loved; and then my friends and I seized her, tried her, and condemned her.'

D'Artagnan then related the poisoning of Madame Bonancieux in the Carmelite convent at Bethume, the trial in the solitary house, and the execution on the banks of the Lys.

A shudder ran through the frame of the cardinal, who was not made to shudder easily. But suddenly, as if from the influence of some silent thought, his dark countenance became gradually clearer, and at last attained perfect serenity.

'So,' said he, in a voice, the gentleness of which contrasted strangly with the severity of his words, 'you constituted yourselves the judges, without considering that those who are not legally appointed, and punish without authority, are assassins.'

'My lord, I swear to you that I have not for one instant thought of defending my head against your eminence. I will submit to whatever punishment your eminence may please to inflict. I do not cling to life sufficiently to fear death.'

'Yes, I know it: you are a man of courage, sir,' said the cardinal, in a voice almost affectionate. 'I may therefore tell you beforehand, that you will be tried, and even condemned.'

'Another might reply to your eminence, that he had his pardon in his pocket. I content myself with saying—command, my lord, and I am ready.'

'Your pardon!' said Richelieu, in surprise.

'Yes, my lord,' replied d'Artagnan.

'And signed by whom? By the king?' The cardinal pronounced these words with a singular intonation of contempt.

'No; by your eminence.'

'By me? You are mad, sir!'

'Your eminence will undoubtedly recognise your own

writing?' And d'Artagnan presented to the cardinal the precious paper which Athos had exorted from her ladyship, and which he had given to d'Artagnan to serve him as a safeguard.

The cardinal took the paper, and read in a very slow voice, and lingering over each syllable—

'It is by my order, and for the good of the state, that the bearer of this has done what he has done.   'RICHELIEU.'

The cardinal, after having read these two lines, fell into a profound reverie, but did not return the paper to d'Artagnan.

'He is deciding by what kind of punishment I am to die,' said the Gascon to himself. 'Well, faith! he shall see how a gentleman can die.' The young musketeer was in an excellent frame of mind for ending his career heroically.

Richelieu continued to meditate, rolling and unrolling the paper in his hand. At last he raised his head, and fixed his eagle eye upon that loyal, open, and intelligent countenance, and read upon that face, all furrowed with tears, the sufferings which d'Artagnan had endured within a month; and he then thought, for the third or fourth time what futurity might have in store for such a youth, of barely twenty years of age, and what resources his activity, courage, and intelligence, might offer to a good master. On the other side, the crimes, the power, the almost infernal genius, of her ladyship had more than once alarmed him; and he felt a secret joy at being for ever freed from such a dangerous accomplice. He slowly tore up the paper which d'Artagnan had so generously returned to him.

'I am lost,' said d'Artagnan, in his own heart.

The cardinal approached the table, and, without sitting down, wrote some words on a parchment, of which two-thirds were already filled up, and then affixed his seal.

'That is my condemnation,' thought d'Artagnan; 'he spares me the misery of the Bastile, and the delays of a trial. It is really very kind of him.'

'Here, sir,' said the cardinal to the young man; 'I took one *carte blanche* from you, and I give you another. The name is not inserted in the commission: you will add it yourself.'

D'Artagnan took the paper with hesitation, and cast his eyes upon it. It was the commission of a lieutenant in the musketeers. D'Artagnan fell at the cardinal's feet.

'My lord,' said he, 'my life is yours—make use of it henceforth; but this favour, which you bestow upon me, is beyond my merits. I have three friends who are more worthy of it.'

'You are a brave youth, d'Artagnan,' said the cardinal, tapping him familiarly on the shoulder, in his delight at having conquered that rebellious nature—'do what you like with this commission, as it is blank; only remember that it is to you I give it.'

'Your eminence may rest assured,' said d'Artagnan, 'that I will never forget it.'

The cardinal turned, and said aloud—'Rochefort!'

The chevalier, who had undoubtedly been behind the door, immediately entered.

'Rochefort,' said the cardinal, 'you see M. d'Artagnan: I receive him into the number of my friends. Embrace one another, and be wise if you wish to retain your heads.'

D'Artagnan and Rochefort embraced coldly, but the cardinal was watching them with his vigilant eye. They left the room at the same moment.

'We shall meet again,' they both said, 'shall we not?'

'Whenever you please,' said d'Artagnan.

'The time will come,' replied Rochefort.

'Hum!' said Richelieu, opening the door.

The two men bowed to his eminence, smiled, and pressed each other's hands.

'We began to be impatient,' said Athos.

'Here I am, my friends,' replied d'Artagnan.

'Free?'

'Not only free, but in favour.'

'You must tell us all about it.'

'Yes, this evening. But, for the present, let us separate.'

In fact, in the evening d'Artagnan went to Athos's lodgings, and found him emptying a bottle of Spanish wine, an occupation which he pursued religiously every night. He told him all that had taken place between the cardinal and himself, and drew the commission from his pocket.

'Here, dear Athos,' said he, 'here is something which naturally belongs to you.'

Athos smiled with his soft and gentle smile. 'Friend,' said he, 'for Athos it is too much—for the Count de la Fère, it is too little. Keep this commission: it belongs to you. Alas! you have bought it dearly enough!'

D'Artagnan left Athos's room, and went to Porthos.

He found him clothed in a most magnificent coat covered with splendid embroidery, and admiring himself in a mirror.

'Ah! is it you, my friend?' said Porthos; 'how do you think this dress suits me?'

'Beautifully,' replied d'Artagnan; 'but I am going to offer you one which will suit you still more.'

'What is it?' demanded Porthos.

'That of a lieutenant of the musketeers.' And d'Artagnan, having related to Porthos his interview with the cardinal, drew the commission from his pocket, 'Here,' said he, 'fill in your name, and be a kind officer to me.'

Porthos glanced over the commission, and returned it, to the great astonishment of the young man.

'Yes,' said Porthos, 'that would flatter me very much, but I could not long enjoy the favour. During our expedition to Bethune, the husband of my duchess died; so that, my dear boy, as the strong-box of the defunct is holding out its arms to me, I marry the widow. You see I am fitting on my wedding garments. So keep the lieutenancy, my dear fellow—keep it.' And he returned it to d'Artagnan.

The young man then repaired to Aramis. He found him kneeling before an oratory, with his forehead leaning on an open book of prayers. He told him, also, of his interview with the cardinal, and, taking the commission from his pocket for the third time, said—

'You, our friend, our light, our invisible protector, accept this commission: you have merited it more than anybody by your wisdom and your counsels, always followed by such fortunate results.'

'Alas! dear friend,' said Aramis, 'our last adventures have entirely disgusted me with the military life. My decision is, this time, irrevocable. After the siege, I shall enter the Lazaristes. Keep the commission, d'Artagnan. The profession of arms suits you: you will be a brave and adventurous captain.'

D'Artagnan, with an eye moist with gratitude, and brilliant with joy, returned to Athos, whom he found still seated at table, admiring his last glass of Malage by the light of his lamp.

'Well,' said he, 'they have both refused it.'

'It is, dear friend, because no one is more worthy of it than yourself.' He took a pen, wrote the name of 'dArtagnan upon it, and gave it back to him.

'I shall no longer have my friends, then,' said the young man. 'Alas! nothing, henceforth, but bitter recollections.' And he let his head fall between his hands, whilst two tears rolled along his cheeks.

'You are young,' said Athos, 'and your bitter recollections have time to change themselves to tender remembrances.'

THE EPILOGUE

THE EPILOGUE

LA ROCHELLE, deprived of the assistance of the English fleet, and of the succour which had been promised by Buckingham, surrendered after a year's siege. On the twenty-eighth of October, 1628, the capitulation was signed.

The king entered Paris on the twenty-third of December, the same year. He received a triumph, as though he had conquered an enemy instead of Frenchmen. He entered, under verdant arches, through the suburb of Saint-Jacques.

D'Artagnan took his promotion. Porthos quitted the service, and married Madame Coquenard, in the course of the following year. The strong-box, so much coveted, contained eight hundred thousand livres. Mousqueton had a superb livery, and enjoyed his life-long dream of riding behind a gilded carriage.

Aramis, after a journey to Lorraine, suddenly disappeared, and ceased to write to his friends. They learned afterwards, through Madame de Chevreuse, that he had assumed the cowl in a monastery at Nancy. Bazin became a lay-brother.

Athos remained a musketeer, under d'Artagnan's command, until 1633; at which time, after a journey to Roussillon, he also left the service, under pretext of having succeeded to a small patrimony in the Blaisois. Grimaud followed Athos.

D'Artagnan fought three times with Rochefort; and wounded him three times.

'I shall probably kill you the fourth time,' said he to Rochefort, as he stretched forth a hand to raise him up.

'It would be better for both of us to stop where we are,' replied the wounded man. 'Vive Dieu! I have been more your friend than you think; for, after our first meeting, I could have got your head off by one word to the cardinal.'

They embraced, but this time it was in sincerity, and without malice.

Planchet obtained, through Rochefort, the grade of sergeant in the regiment of Piedmont.

'M. Bonancieux lived in great tranquility, entirely

ignorant of what had become of his wife, and not much disturbing himself about it. One day he had the imprudence to recall himself to the cardinal's recollection. The cardinal told him that he would so provide for him that he should never want for anything in future. In fact, the next day M. Bonancieux, having left home at seven o'clock in the evening, to go the Louvre, was never seen again in the Rue des Fossoyeurs. The opinion of those who thought themselves the best informed was, that he was boarded and lodged in some royal castle, at the expense of his generous eminence.

BIBLIOGRAPHY
OF THE WORKS OF ALEXANDRE DUMAS

BIBLIOGRAPHY

POETRY AND DRAMATIC WORKS

1825   *Élégie sur la Mort du Général Foy.*
       La Chasse et l'Amour (in collaboration).
1826   *Canaris* (dithyramb).
       La Noie et l'Enterrement (in collaboration).
1828   *Christine* (or *Stockholm, Fontainebleau et Rome*).
1829   *Henri III et sa Cour.*
1831   *Antony.*
       Napoléon Bonaparte, ou Trente Ans de l'Historie de France.
       Charles VII chez ses Grands Vassaux.
       Richard Darlington.
1832   *Térésa.*
       Le Mari de la Veuve (in collaboration).
       La Tour de Nesle.
1833   *Angèle* (in collaboration).
1834   *Catharine Howard.*
1836   *Don Juan de Navarra, ou La Chute d'un Ange.*
       Kean.
1837   *Piquillo* (Comic opera. In collaboration).
       Caligula.
1838   *Paul Jones.*
1839   *Mademoiselle de Belle-Isle.*
       L'Alchimiste.
       Bathilde (in collaboration).
1841   *Un Mariage sous Louis XV.*
1842   *Lorenzino* (in collaboration).
       Halifax.
1843   *Les Demoiselles de Saint-Cyr* (in collaboration).
       Louise Bernard (in collaboration).
       Le Laird de Dumbicky (in collaboration).
1845   *Le Garde Forestier* (in collaboration).
1856   *L'Oreste.*
       Le Verrou de la Reine.

NOTE. Dumas also dramatized many of his novels.

NOVELS AND MISCELLANEOUS PROSE

1826   *Nouvelles Contemporaines.*

1833   *Impressions de Voyage: En Suisse.*

1835   *Souvenirs d'Antony* (Tales).

1838   *La Salle d'Armes* (Tales).
        Le Capitaine Paul.

1839   *Monseigneur Gaston Phoebus.*
        Quinze Jours au Sinaï.

1840   *Aventures de John Davy.*
        Le Capitaine Pamphile.
        Maître Adam le Calabrais.
        Othon l'Archer.
        Une Année à Florence.

1841   *Praxède, Don Martin de Freytas, Pierre le Cruel.*
        Excursions sur les Bords du Rhin.
        Nouvelles Impressions de Voyages.

1842   *Le Speronare* (Travels).
        Aventures de Lyderic.

1843   *Georges. Ascanio. Le Chevalier d'Harmental.*
        Le Corricolo. La Ville Palmieri.

1844   *Gabriel Lambert. Chateau d' Eppstein. Cécile.*
        Sylvandire. Les Trois Mousquetaires. Amaury. Fernande.

1844-45   *Le Comte de Monte-Cristo.*

1845   *Vingt Ans Après.*
        Les Frères Corses. Une Fille du Régent. La Reine Margot
           (Marguerite de Valois).

1845-46   *La Guerre des Femmes.*

1846   *Le Chevalier de Maison-Rouge.*
        La Dame de Monsoreau (Chicot the Jester).
        Le Bâtard de Mauléon.

1846-48   *Mémoires d'un Médecin.*

1848   *Les Quarante-cinq* (The Forty-five Guardsmen).

1848-50   *Dix Ans plus tard, ou Le Vicomte de Bragelonne* (Part I
           The Vicomte de Bragelonne; Part II Louise de
           la Valliere; Part III The Man in the Iron Mask).

1848   *De Paris à Cadix.*
        Le Véloce ou Tanger, Alger et Tunis.

1849   *Les Milles et un Fantômes.*

1850   *La Tulipe Noire.*

1851   *La Femme au Collier de Velours.*

1852 *Olympe de Clèves.*
      Un Gil Blas en Californie.
      Isaac Laquedem.
1853-55 *Le Comtesse de Charny.*
1853 *Ange Pitou, le Pasteur d'Ashbourn. El Saltéador.*
      Conscience l'Innocent.
1854 *Cathérine Blum; Ingénue.*
1854-58 *Les Mohicans de Paris.*
1855-59 *Salvator.*
1855 *L'Arabie Heureuse.*
1857 *Les Compagnons de Jéhu. Le Meneur de Loups.*
1859 *Les Louves de Machecoul.*
      Le Caucase.
1860 *De Paris à Astrakan.*

OTHER WORKS

Autobiographical.
1854 *Mes Mémoires.* Translated, 1961
1852-54 *Mémoires, Souvenirs de 1830-42.* by A. C. Bell.
1860 *Causeries.*
1861 *Bric-à-Brac.*
1868 Histoire de mes *Bêtes.*

Children's Tales.
Histoire d'un Casse-Noisette.
La Bouillie de la Comtesse Berthe.
Le Père Gigogne.
Also: Memoirs of Garibaldi. Reminiscences of various
      writers, historical writings, etc.
Théâtre. 1834-6   6 volumes.
           1863-74   3 volumes.

COLLECTED EDITION

Dumas' Complete works were published by Michel Lévy
Frères from 1860-84, 277 volumes in all.

BOOKS ABOUT DUMAS

Life by P. Fitzgerald, 1873
Life by Blaze de Bury, 1883

Life by Glinel, 1885

Life by Parigot, 1901

Life by H. A. Spurr, 1902

Alexandre Dumas Père: his Life and Works by A. F. Davidson. (With Bibliography). 1902.

Life by Lecomte. 1903.

Alexandre Dumas—the fourth Musketeer by J. Lucas Dubreton. New York. 1929

The Incredible Marquis Alexandre Dumas by Herbert Gorman. 1929.

Bibliography of Alxandre Dumas by F. W. Reed.

Dumas: Father and Son by Francis Gribble. 1931.

Alexandre Dumas, a Biography and Study by A. C. Bell. 1950.

Alexandre Dumas, by André Maurois 1955.

The Three Musketeers: A Study of the Dumas Family by André Maurois. 1957.